SELECTED AND CONDENSED
BY READER'S DIGEST

THE READER'S DIGEST ASSOCIATION LIMITED, LONDON

CONTENTS

A new John Grisham novel is always an exciting event and this, his eighteenth, is no exception. The setting is Italy, a country that Grisham loves, and the book is filled with evidence of his passion for Italian cuisine, the people and the language.

The main character is Joel Backman, a one-time Washington power broker who is released from prison and sent into hiding in Bologna. His survival will depend on his ability to blend into Italian society, for he has old enemies with long memories who will do anything to get their hands on secrets that they believe he still holds.

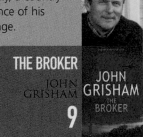

Dan Brown, author of *The Da Vinci Code*, has said of Greg Iles's novels that they 'resonate', and it's certainly true of his latest emotionally charged best seller, set among the lush swamps and forests of Louisiana.

Cat Ferry, a forensic orthodontologist, was eight when her father was murdered in the grounds of her family's mansion. She has no clear recollection of what happened that night, but the chance discovery of a latent blood stain triggers memories that haunt her, setting her on a quest to discover the truth about her family.

Set against a bustling New York backdrop and the exotic splendour of Jordan, *Mosaic* is a thought-provoking novel about a couple whose marriage is beset by a clash of cultures and traditions. Dina and Karim Ahmad have the perfect life: they are rich, successful and have three wonderful children. Then, one terrible day, Dina returns to their apartment to discover that her eight-year-old twins have vanished. To her horror, she discovers that Karim has absconded with them to his family home in Jordan, to start a new life without her.

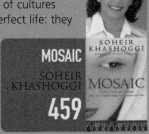

On May 20, 2003, almost fifty years to the day that Sir Edmund Hillary conquered the summit of Everest, another Briton, Pen Hadow, made history by reaching the North Pole completely alone and with only the equipment and supplies that he could haul behind him on a sledge. His story, much of it told through diary extracts, is an inspiration.

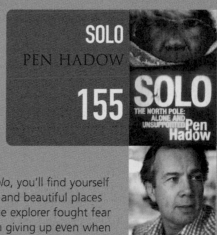

SOLO
PEN HADOW

155 **SOLO**
THE NORTH POLE:
ALONE AND
UNSUPPORTED **Pen Hadow**

When you immerse yourself in *Solo*, you'll find yourself transported to one of the most wild and beautiful places on earth. And you'll discover how the explorer fought fear and loneliness and kept himself from giving up even when his goal seemed unattainable. Among the things that inspired him was a scrap of paper that he keeps pinned to his office wall; on it are the words of a Caribou Eskimo called Igjugarjuk: 'All true wisdom is to be found far from the dwellings of men, in the great solitudes, and it can only be attained through suffering. Suffering and privation are the only things that can open the mind to that which is hidden from his fellows.'

On the day that Pen Hadow reached the North Pole, millions celebrated with him and his family, including readers of *The Times* who'd been following his progress in the newspaper. Why did the explorer's triumph strike such a

universal chord? Perhaps because it was a heartening reminder that even in these highly scientific and techno-logical times, it is possible to find a hero in the true, old-fashioned sense of the word.

Pen Hadow, arriving back in the UK, is reunited with his wife Mary and their children Wilf and Freya—'the people who mean more to me than anything in the world'.

4150

1

2615

2630

2230

The Broker

John Grisham

650.

650.

Joel Backman is six years into a twenty-year jail sentence in America when he is unexpectedly given a presidential pardon and spirited away to Europe by the CIA.

At first Backman is just pleased to be out. But soon the questions start to mount. Why has he been released? And what's the reason behind the full-blown international getaway? Why are the CIA going to so much expense and trouble to protect him?

He has a terrifying feeling he knows the answers.

Chapter 1

In the waning hours of a presidency that was destined to arouse less interest from historians than any since perhaps that of William Henry Harrison (thirty-one days from inauguration to death), Arthur Morgan huddled in the Oval Office with his last remaining friend and pondered his final decisions. At that moment he felt as though he'd botched every decision in the previous four years, and he was not overly confident that he could, so late in the game, get things right. His friend wasn't so sure either, though, as always, he said little and whatever he did say was what the President wanted to hear.

They were about pardons—desperate pleas from thieves and embezzlers and liars, some still in jail and some who'd never served time but who nonetheless wanted their good names cleared. How sad that after four tumultuous years of leading the free world it would all fizzle into one miserable pile of requests from a bunch of crooks.

The last friend was Critz, an old fraternity pal from their student days at Cornell. In the past four years, Critz had served as press secretary, chief of staff, national security adviser, and even secretary of state, though that appointment lasted for only three months and was hastily rescinded when Critz's unique style of diplomacy nearly ignited World War III. Critz's last appointment had taken place the previous October, in the final weeks of the re-election onslaught. With the polls showing President Morgan trailing badly in at least forty states, Critz seized control of the campaign and managed to alienate the rest of the country, except, arguably, Alaska.

It had been a historic election; never before had an incumbent president received so few electoral votes. Three to be exact, all from Alaska, the only state Morgan had not visited, at Critz's advice. Five hundred and thirty-five for the challenger, three for President Morgan. The word 'landslide' did not even begin to capture the enormity of the shellacking.

Critz sat in a thick leather chair and watched his President move from one window to the next, peering into the darkness, dreaming of what might have been. The man was depressed and humiliated. At fifty-eight his life was over, his career a wreck, his marriage crumbling. Mrs Morgan had already moved back to Wilmington and was laughing at the idea of living in a cabin in Alaska. President Morgan had become enamoured of Alaska.

What a campaign! Critz was tempted to write a book. Someone needed to record the disaster.

Their partnership of almost forty years was ending. Critz had lined up a job with a defence contractor for $200,000 a year, and he would hit the lecture circuit at $50,000 a speech. After dedicating his life to public service, he was broke and ageing quickly and anxious to make a buck.

The President had sold his handsome home in Georgetown for a huge profit. He'd bought a small ranch in Alaska and planned to spend the rest of his days there, hunting, fishing, perhaps writing his memoirs. Whatever he did in Alaska, it would have nothing to do with politics and Washington.

'We need to make a decision about Cuccinello,' Critz said.

The President was still standing at a window. 'Who?'

'Figgy Cuccinello, that movie director who was indicted for having sex with a fifteen-year-old starlet. He fled to Argentina, where he's been for ten years. Now he's homesick, says his art is calling him home.'

'Seventeen wouldn't bother me. Fifteen's too young.'

'His offer is up to five million.'

The President looked at Critz. 'He's offering five million for a pardon?'

'Yes, and he needs to move quickly. The money has to be wired out of Switzerland. It's three in the morning over there.'

'Where would it go?'

'We have accounts offshore. It's easy.'

With his right hand, the President began scratching the back of his neck, something he always did when wrestling with a difficult decision. 'No,' he said. 'Fifteen is too young.'

Without a knock, the door opened and Artie Morgan, the President's son, barged in holding a Heineken in one hand and some papers in the other.

'Just talked to the CIA,' he said casually. He wore faded jeans and no socks. 'Maynard's on the way over.'

He dumped the papers on the desk and left the room, slamming the door behind him.

The President sat in his leather rocker and pretended to flip through some useless papers. 'What's the latest on Backman?' he asked.

IN HIS EIGHTEEN YEARS as director of the CIA, Teddy Maynard had been to the White House less than ten times. Back when he could walk, he had occasionally stopped by to confer with whoever happened to be president, and perhaps one or two of his policy makers. Now, since he was in a wheelchair, his conversations with the White House were by phone.

A spy for almost fifty years, Teddy travelled in an unmarked white van—bulletproof glass, lead walls, two heavily armed boys perched behind the heavily armed driver—with his wheelchair clamped to the floor facing back, so that Teddy could see the traffic that could not see him. Two other vans followed at a distance, and any attempt to get near the director would be instantly terminated.

As the van moved along the Beltway at a constant sixty miles an hour, Teddy, wrapped in a grey quilt, sipped green tea poured from a Thermos by Hoby, his faithful aide. Hoby sat next to the wheelchair on a stool.

A sip of tea and Teddy said, 'Where's Backman right now?'

'In his cell,' Hoby answered.

'And our people are with the warden?'

'They're sitting in his office, waiting.'

'How long will it take to get him out of the country?'

'About four hours.'

'And the plan is in place?'

'Everything is ready. We're waiting on the green light.'

'I hope this moron can see it my way.'

CRITZ AND THE MORON were staring at the walls of the Oval Office, their silence broken occasionally by a comment about Joel Backman.

'What will the press do if I pardon Backman?' the President asked.

'Go berserk.'

'That might be fun.'

'You won't be around.'

'No, I won't.' After the transfer of power at noon the next day, he would escape from Washington and go to an old friend's villa on Barbados. At Morgan's instructions, the televisions had been removed from the villa, no newspapers would be delivered, and all phones had been unplugged. He would have no contact with anyone for at least a month. After Barbados, he would sneak up to his cabin in Alaska, and there he would continue to ignore the world and wait for spring.

'Should we pardon him?' the President asked.

'Probably,' Critz said.

The President had shifted to the 'we' mode now, something he invariably did when a potentially unpopular decision was at hand.

Critz said, 'There's a very good chance we wouldn't be here had it not been for Joel Backman.'

'You may be right about that,' the President said.

Six years ago, the Backman scandal had engulfed much of Washington and eventually tainted the White House. A cloud appeared over a popular president, paving the way for Arthur Morgan to stumble his way into the White House. Now that he was stumbling out, he relished the idea of one last slap in the face to the Washington establishment that had shunned him for four years. A reprieve for Joel Backman would rattle the walls of every office building in D.C. and shock the press into a blathering frenzy.

The President smiled into the darkness.

MAYNARD'S WHITE VAN turned off Constitution Avenue onto 18th Street and entered the east gate of the White House. Men with machine guns materialised from the darkness, then Secret Service agents in black trench coats stopped the van. Code words were used, radios squawked, and within minutes Teddy was being lowered from the van.

Once inside, Hoby and a deputy followed the wheelchair into the Oval Office. The President and Critz welcomed their guests and directed them to the sitting area in front of the fireplace.

As they settled in, Teddy glanced around the room, as if looking for bugs and listening devices. He was almost certain there were none; that practice had ended with Watergate. Teddy, however, was wired. Carefully hidden above the axle of his wheelchair was a powerful recorder.

He tried to smile at President Morgan, but he wanted to say something like: You are without a doubt the most limited politician I have ever encountered. Only in America could a moron like you make it to the top.

President Morgan smiled at Teddy Maynard, but he wanted to say something like: I should have fired you four years ago. Your agency has been a constant embarrassment to this country.

Critz said loudly, 'Coffee anyone?'

Teddy said, 'No,' and as soon as that was established, Hoby and the deputy likewise declined. And because the CIA wanted no coffee, President Morgan said, 'Yes, black with two sugars.' Critz nodded at a secretary who was waiting in a half-opened side door.

He turned back to the gathering and said, 'We don't have a lot of time.'

Teddy said quickly, 'I'm here to discuss Joel Backman. As you know, Mr Backman went to prison without saying a word. He still carries some secrets that, frankly, could compromise national security.'

'You can't kill him,' Critz blurted.

'We cannot target American citizens, Mr Critz. It's against the law. We prefer that someone else do it.'

'I don't follow,' the President said.

'Here's the plan. If you pardon Mr Backman, then we will have him out of the country in a matter of hours. He must agree to spend the rest of his life in hiding. This should not be a problem because there are several people who would like to see him dead, and he knows it. We'll relocate him, probably in Europe where he'll be easier to watch. He'll have a new identity. He'll be a free man, and with time people will forget about him.'

'That's not the end of the story,' Critz said.

'No. We'll wait, perhaps a year or so, then we'll leak the word in the right places. They'll find Mr Backman, and they'll kill him, and when they do so, many of our questions will be answered.'

A long pause as Teddy looked at Critz, then the President. 'It's a very simple plan, gentlemen. It's a question of who kills him.'

'Who's after him?' the President asked.

Teddy refolded his veiny hands and recoiled a bit. 'Perhaps the Russians, the Chinese, maybe the Israelis. There could be others.'

Of course there were others, but no one expected Teddy to reveal everything he knew. He never had; never would.

'Why would Backman take such a deal?' Critz asked.

'He may not,' Teddy answered. 'But he's been in solitary confinement for six years. That's twenty-three hours a day in a tiny cell. Bad food—they say he's lost sixty pounds. I hear he's not doing too well.'

Two months ago, after the landslide, when Teddy Maynard conceived this pardon scheme, he had pulled a few of his many strings and Backman's confinement had grown much worse. The temperature in his cell was lowered ten degrees, and for the past month he'd had a terrible cough. The law library that he used twice a week was suddenly off-limits. Backman, a lawyer, knew his rights, and he was threatening all manner of litigation.

'You want me to pardon Joel Backman so you can arrange for him to be murdered?' the President asked.

'Yes,' Teddy said bluntly. 'But we won't actually arrange it.'

'But it'll happen.'

'Yes.'

'And his death will be in the best interests of our national security?'

'I firmly believe that.'

JOEL BACKMAN was trying to sleep when two guards clanged open his door and switched on his light. 'The warden wants you,' one said, and there was no elaboration.

They rode in silence in a prison van across the frigid Oklahoma prairie, until they arrived at Rudley Federal Correctional Facility's administration building. Backman, handcuffed for no apparent reason, was hurried inside, then down a long hall to the big office where lights were on. He saw a clock on a wall; it was almost 11 p.m.

With the warden were three other suits, all earnest-looking men who'd been chatting for some time. With absolutely no introduction, the warden said, 'Sit over there, Mr Backman.'

'A pleasure to meet you,' Backman said, still standing, as he looked at the other men in the room. 'Why, exactly, am I here?'

'We'll discuss that.'

'Could you please remove these handcuffs? I promise not to kill anyone.'

The warden snapped at the nearest guard, who quickly found a key and freed Backman. The warden pointed and said, 'This is Special Agent Adair of the FBI. This is Mr Knabe from the Justice Department. And this is Mr Sizemore, also from Washington.'

Blackman nodded at them, in a halfhearted effort to be polite. His efforts were not returned.

'Please sit,' the warden said, and Backman finally took a chair. 'Thank you. As you know, Mr Backman, President Morgan is on the way out. Right now he is in the Oval Office wrestling with the decision of whether to grant you a pardon.'

Backman was suddenly seized with a violent cough, brought by the shock of the word 'pardon.'

Mr Knabe from Justice handed him a bottle of water, which he gulped at, and he finally managed to stifle the cough. 'A pardon?' he mumbled.

'A full pardon, with some strings attached.'

'But why?'

'I don't know why, Mr Backman. I'm just the messenger.'

Mr Sizemore, introduced simply as 'from Washington', said, 'It's a deal, Mr Backman. In return for a full pardon, you must agree to leave the country, never return, and live with a new identity in a place where no one can find you.'

No problem there, thought Backman. He didn't want to be found. 'But why?' he mumbled again. The bottle of water in his left hand could actually be seen shaking.

As Mr Sizemore from Washington watched it shake, he studied Joel Backman, from his closely cropped hair to his battered dime-store running shoes, and couldn't help but recall the image of the man in his prior life. A magazine cover photo came to mind. Joel Backman in a black Italian suit, impeccably tailored and groomed. The hair was longer and darker, the handsome face was wrinkle free, the waistline was thick and spoke of many power lunches. He loved wine and women and sports cars. He had a jet, a yacht, a place in Vail. The bold caption above his head read: THE BROKER— IS THIS THE SECOND MOST POWERFUL MAN IN WASHINGTON?

The magazine was in Mr Sizemore's briefcase, along with a thick file on Joel Backman. According to the article, the broker's income at the time was reported to be in excess of $10 million a year. The law firm he founded had 200 lawyers, small by Washington standards, but without a doubt the most powerful in political circles. It was a lobbying machine, not a place where real lawyers practised their craft. Oh, how the mighty have fallen, Mr Sizemore thought to himself as he watched the bottle shake.

'I don't understand,' Backman managed to whisper.

'And we don't have time to explain,' Mr Sizemore said. 'It's a quick deal, Mr Backman. 'A snap decision is required. Yes or no. You want to stay here, or you want to live with another name on the other side of the world?'

'Where?'

'We don't know where, but we'll figure it out.'

'Will I be safe?'

'Only you can answer that question, Mr Backman.'

'When will I leave?' Backman asked.

'Immediately,' said Mr Sizemore. 'You will not return to your cell.'

'Oh darn,' Backman said, and the others couldn't help but smile.

'There are some gentlemen waiting in the Oval Office, Mr Backman. Are you going to accept the deal?'

Backman drained the bottle of water, wiped his mouth with a sleeve, then said, 'Is it like a witness protection programme, something like that?'

'It's not an official programme, Mr Backman. But, from time to time, we find it necessary to hide people.'

'How often do you lose one?'

'Nothing is guaranteed. But your odds are good,' Mr Sizemore said.

'Who do you work for?' Backman asked him.

'The President of the United States.'

'Well, tell him I'll take the deal. What fool wouldn't? And tell him I said thanks, OK?'

'Sure.'

Chapter 2

Wearing a well-worn but starched and pressed khaki military uniform, combat boots and a navy parka with a hood that he pulled snugly around his head, Joel Backman strutted out of the Rudley Federal Correctional Facility at five minutes after midnight, fourteen years ahead of schedule.

He was fifty-two years old, divorced, broke, and thoroughly estranged from two of his three children. Not a single friend had bothered to maintain a correspondence beyond the first year of his confinement. An old girlfriend had written for ten months, until it was reported in the *Washington Post* that the FBI had decided it was unlikely that Joel Backman had looted his firm and his clients of the millions that had first been rumoured. Who wants to be pen pals with a broke lawyer in prison?

His mother wrote to him occasionally, but she was ninety-one years old and living in a low-rent nursing home near Oakland. He wrote to her once a week, but doubted if she was able to read anything, and he was almost certain that no one on staff had the time or interest to read to her.

Mr Sizemore and Agent Adair were his escorts. They led him to a dark green, unmarked sport utility vehicle. Joel crawled into the back seat alone, closed his eyes tightly and asked God to please allow the engine to start, the gates to open. Please, God, no cruel jokes. This is not a dream, please!

Twenty minutes later, Mr Backman had ceased praying and had begun crying. The vehicle had been moving steadily, though he had not opened his eyes. He was lying on the rear seat, fighting his emotions and losing badly.

A FEW MINUTES after 4 a.m. they entered the gates of Fort Summit, near Brinkley, Texas. Backman was taken to the base hospital and examined by two physicians. Except for a head cold and the cough, and general gauntness, he wasn't in bad shape. He was then taken to a hangar where he met a Colonel Gantner. Under Gantner's close supervision, Joel changed into a green army jumpsuit with the name Major Herzog stencilled above the right pocket. 'Is that me?' Joel asked, looking at the name.

'It is for the next forty-eight hours,' Gantner said.

At some point during this quick briefing, Mr Sizemore from Washington and Agent Adair slipped away, never to be seen again by Joel Backman.

With the first hint of sunlight, Joel stepped through the rear hatch of a C-130 cargo plane and followed Gantner to the upper level, to a small bunk room where six other soldiers were preparing for a long flight.

'Take that bunk,' Gantner said, pointing to one close to the floor.

'Can I ask where we're going?' Joel whispered.

'You can ask, but I can't answer. I'll brief you before we land.'

'And when might that be?'

'In about fourteen hours.'

With no windows to distract him, Joel situated himself on his bunk, pulled a blanket over his head, and was snoring by takeoff.

JUST AFTER DAWN, long before the inauguration mess began, Critz and his wife were whisked off to London on one of his new employer's many private jets. He was to spend two weeks there, then return to Washington as lobbyist. He hated the idea. He was sick of the political life, but, sadly, he knew nothing else.

President Morgan and Director Maynard had agreed to sit on the Backman story for twenty-four hours, until well after the inauguration. Morgan didn't care; he'd be in Barbados. Critz, however, did not feel bound by any agreement, especially one made with the likes of Teddy Maynard. After a long dinner with lots of wine, some time around 2 a.m. in London, he called a White House correspondent for CBS and whispered the basics of the Backman pardon. Before 8 a.m. the news was roaring around D.C.

Joel Backman had been given a full and unconditional pardon at the eleventh hour! There were no details of his release.

In a very nervous city, the day began with the pardon storming onto centre stage, competing with a new President and his first full day in office.

THE LAW FIRM of Pratt & Bolling was on Massachusetts Avenue, four blocks north of Dupont Circle; not a bad location, but not nearly as classy as the old place on New York Avenue. A few years earlier, when it was Backman, Pratt & Bolling, Joel Backman had paid the highest rent in town so he could stand at the vast windows of his vast office on the seventh floor and look down at the White House. Now there were no power offices with grand vistas; the building had two floors, not seven. And the firm had shrunk from two hundred highly paid lawyers to about thirty struggling ones.

Kim Bolling was currently locked away in alcohol rehab, and from there he would be sent straight to a private mental facility for many years. The unbearable strain of the last six years had driven him over the edge. The task of dealing with the latest Backman nightmare fell into the rather large lap of Carl Pratt. Joel Backman was a free man. The broker was loose. Would he make a comeback? Was he returning to Washington?

It had been Pratt who had uttered the fateful 'I do' twenty-two years earlier when Backman had proposed a marriage of their two small firms. It had been Pratt who had laboured strenuously for sixteen years to clean up behind Backman as the firm expanded and the fees poured in and all ethical boundaries were blurred beyond recognition. And it had been Carl Pratt who had come so close to a federal prosecution himself, just before Joel Backman heroically took the fall for everyone. Backman's plea agreement, and the agreement that exculpated the firm's other partners, required a fine of $10 million, thus leading directly to the firm's bankruptcy.

But bankruptcy was better than jail, Pratt reminded himself almost daily. He lumbered around his sparse office early that morning, mumbling to himself and trying desperately to believe that the news was simply not true. How could a broke, disbarred, disgraced former lawyer/lobbyist convince a lame-duck president to grant a last-minute pardon?

Pratt locked his door and fought the urge to open the office bottle of vodka. He had been forty-nine years old when his partner was sent to prison for twenty years with no parole, and he often wondered what he would do when he was sixty-nine and Backman got out. At that moment, Pratt felt as though he'd been cheated out of fourteen years.

THE COURTROOM had been so crowded that the judge postponed the hearing for two hours until the demand for seating could be organised. Big shots from Justice, the FBI, the Pentagon, the CIA, the NSA, the White House, and Capitol Hill were pressing for seats to watch the lynching of Joel Backman. When the defendant finally appeared in the tense courtroom, the crowd suddenly froze and the only sound was that of the court reporter prepping his steno machine.

Backman was led to the defence table, where his small army of lawyers packed tightly around. In the first row behind the defence table sat Carl Pratt and a dozen or so soon-to-be-former partners of Mr Backman. Though they seethed with hatred for the man, they were also pulling for him. If his plea agreement fell through because of a last-second hitch, then they would be fair game again, with nasty trials just around the corner.

At least they were sitting on the front row, and not at the defence table. At least they were alive. Eight days earlier, Jacy Hubbard, one of their trophy partners, had been found dead in Arlington National Cemetery, in a suicide that few people believed. Hubbard had been a former senator from Texas who had given up his seat after twenty-four years for the sole purpose of offering his significant influence to the highest bidder. Backman, Pratt & Bolling had hired Hubbard for a million bucks a year because good ol' Jacy could get himself into the Oval Office anytime he wanted.

Hubbard's death had worked wonders in helping Joel Backman to see the government's point of view. The logjam that had delayed the plea negotiations was suddenly broken. Not only would Backman accept twenty years, he wanted to do it quickly. He was anxious for protective custody!

There were eighteen counts, alleging crimes ranging from espionage to treason. His lawyer immediately reminded the court that nothing in the indictment had been proven. He explained that his client would be pleading guilty to only four of the eighteen counts—unauthorised possession of military documents.

Hiding on the back row was Neal Backman, Joel's oldest son and an associate with Backman, Pratt & Bolling. He watched the proceedings in a state of shock, unable to believe that his once powerful father was pleading guilty and about to be buried in the federal penal system.

The defendant was eventually herded to the bench, where he faced the judge. He pled guilty to his four counts, then was led back to his seat.

A sentencing date was set for the following month. As Backman was handcuffed and taken away, it became obvious to those present that he would not be forced to divulge his secrets, that he would indeed be incarcerated for a very long time while his conspiracies faded away. The crowd slowly broke up. The reporters got half the story they wanted. The big men from the agencies left without speaking—some were pleased that secrets had been protected, others were furious that crimes were being hidden. Carl Pratt and the other beleaguered partners headed for the nearest bar.

THE FIRST REPORTER called the office just before 9 a.m. Pratt had asked his secretary to tell everyone that he was to be busy in court on some lengthy matter and might not be back in the office for months.

Behind a locked door and alone, Pratt sipped a Bloody Mary and watched the nonstop news on cable. All kinds of experts were brought in to the studio where they prattled on about the man's legendary sins.

Going for the gore, a 'reporter' dug up a piece on Senator Jacy Hubbard, and Pratt reached for the remote. He turned up the volume when a large photo of Hubbard's face was flashed on the screen. The former senator had been found dead with a bullet in the head the week before Backman pled guilty. What appeared at first to be a suicide was later called suspicious, though no suspect had ever been identified. The powder residue on his right hand was suspicious. An autopsy revealed a stout concentration of alcohol and barbiturates in his system. He'd been seen a few hours earlier with an attractive young lady at a Georgetown bar.

The prevailing theory was that the lady slipped him enough drugs to knock him out, then handed him over to his killers. He was hauled to a remote section of the Arlington National Cemetery and shot in the head.

The unspoken theory was that Hubbard was killed by the same people who wanted a shot at Joel Backman. And for years afterwards Carl Pratt and Kim Bolling paid serious money for professional bodyguards just in case their names were on the same list. With time Pratt had loosened the security around himself, though he still carried a Ruger with him everywhere.

BACKMAN WAS FAR AWAY, with the distance growing every minute. Oddly enough, he, too, was thinking of Jacy Hubbard and the people who might have killed him. Whoever did it would want very much to kill Joel Backman, and as he bumped along at 24,000 feet in the rattling cargo plane, he pondered some serious questions. Who had lobbied for his pardon? Where did they plan to hide him? Who, exactly, were 'they'?

Joel closed his eyes, listened to the steady hum of the engines, and tried to tell himself that wherever he was headed he would not live like a man on the run. He would adapt, he would survive, he would not live in fear.

Unwillingly, he dozed off again.

Colonel Gantner was shaking him, whispering loudly, 'Major Herzog, we need to talk.' Backman squeezed out of his bunk, and followed the colonel along the dark cramped aisle between the bunks and into a small room, somewhere closer to the cockpit.

Gantner was holding a file. 'Here's the deal,' he began. 'We land in about an hour. The plan is for you to be sick, so sick that an ambulance will meet the plane at the landing field. The Italian authorities will inspect the paperwork. But we'll be at a US military base, and soldiers come and go all the time. I have a passport for you. I'll do the talking with the Italians, then you'll be taken by ambulance to the base hospital.'

'Italians?'

'Yes. Ever hear of the Aviano Air Base? It's been in US hands since we ran the Germans off in 1945. It's in the northeast of Italy, near the Alps.'

'How long will I be there?'

'That's not my decision. My job is to get you from this aeroplane to the base hospital. There, someone else takes over. Take a look at this bio for Major Herzog, just in case.'

Joel spent a few minutes reading the fictional history of Major Herzog and memorising the details on the fake passport.

'Remember, you're very ill and sedated,' Gantner said. 'Just pretend you're in a coma.'

'I've been in one for six years.'

As THE C-130 rolled to a stop, an air force ambulance backed close to the rear hatch. A stretcher carrying Major Herzog rolled down the gateway and was carefully lifted into the ambulance. The nearest Italian official was sitting inside a US military jeep, watching things halfheartedly and trying to stay warm. The ambulance pulled away, and five minutes later Major Herzog was rolled into the small base hospital and tucked away in a tiny room on the first floor where two military policemen guarded his door.

FORTUNATELY for Backman at the eleventh hour President Morgan also pardoned an ageing billionaire who'd escaped prison by fleeing the country. The billionaire, an immigrant from some Slavic state, used the title of Duke Mongo. The Duke had given trainloads of money to Morgan's presidential campaign. When it was revealed that he'd spent his career evading taxes it was also revealed that over a friendly nightcap, he and the President had discussed pending indictments. The indictment was thirty-eight pages long, but before it rolled off the printer the billionaire took up residence in Uruguay where he thumbed his nose north while living in a palace.

Now he wanted to come home. Critz cut the deal, and minutes after signing the pardon for Joel Backman, President Morgan granted complete clemency to Duke Mongo. It took a day for the news to leak and the press went insane. Here was a man who cheated the federal government out of $600 million over a twenty-year period, and he was about to fly home in his mammoth jet and spend his final days in obscene luxury.

The Backman story now had serious competition. But it was still a hot item. Most of the morning papers along the East Coast ran a picture of 'The Broker' somewhere on the front page. Most ran long stories about his scandal, his guilty plea, and now his pardon.

Carl Pratt read them all online, in a huge messy office he kept above his garage in northwest Washington. The Backman file was in a large storage box, one he kept hidden in a closet. Pratt was going through it for the first time in many years. He'd saved everything—news articles, photos, memos, copies of the indictments, Jacy Hubbard's autopsy report.

What a miserable history.

In JANUARY OF 1996, three young Pakistani computer scientists made an astounding discovery. Working in a hot, cramped flat on the outskirts of Karachi, the three linked together a series of Hewlett-Packard computers they'd purchased online with a government grant. Their new 'supercomputer' was then wired to a sophisticated military satellite telephone, one also provided by the government. The entire operation was secret and funded off the books by the military. Their objective was simple: to locate, and then try to access a new Indian spy satellite hovering 300 miles above Pakistan. A secondary dream was to try to manipulate it.

The stolen intelligence proved to be virtually useless. The new Indian 'eyes' were doing much the same thing the old ones had been doing for ten years—taking thousands of photographs of the same military installations. But another satellite was accidentally discovered, then another and another. They were neither Pakistani nor Indian, and they were not supposed to be where they were found—each about 300 miles above the earth, moving north–northeast at a constant speed of 120 miles per hour, a distance of

400 miles from the other. Over ten days, the hackers monitored the movements of at least six different satellites as they swept through the skies over Afghanistan and Pakistan then headed off for China.

They told no one, and after a month of methodical, twenty-four-hour monitoring, they had pieced together a global web of nine identical satellites, all linked and carefully designed to be invisible to everyone except the men who launched them. They code-named their discovery Neptune.

The three young wizards had been educated in the United States. The leader was Safi Mirza, a Stanford graduate who'd worked briefly at a US defence contractor that specialised in satellite systems. Fazal Sharif had an advanced degree in computer science from Georgia Tech.

The third and youngest member of the Neptune gang was Farooq Khan, who finally wrote the software that penetrated the first Neptune satellite. Once inside its computer system, Farooq began downloading highly sensitive intelligence. There were clear colour pictures of terrorist training camps in Afghanistan, and government limousines in Beijing. Neptune could listen as Chinese pilots bantered back and forth at 20,000 feet. And in a live video feed Arafat himself was clearly seen stepping into an alley in his compound in Gaza, and lighting a cigarette.

The software was in English, and with Neptune's preoccupation with the Middle East, Asia, and China, it was easy to assume Neptune belonged to the United States, with Britain and Israel a distant second and third possibility.

After two days of eavesdropping, the three fled the apartment and reorganised their little cell in a farmhouse ten miles outside of Karachi. The discovery was exciting enough, but they wanted to go one step further. Safi was quite confident he could manipulate the system.

His first success was watching Fazal Sharif read a newspaper. Fazal took a bus into downtown Karachi, bought a newspaper and sat on a park bench. With Farooq feeding commands through a ramped-up sat-phone, a Neptune satellite found Fazal, zoomed down close enough to pick off the headlines of his newspaper, and relayed it all back to the farmhouse.

For weeks and months, the three worked nonstop writing software for their discovery. Eighteen months after they first discovered Neptune, the three had, on four Jaz 2-gigabyte disks, a software program that not only increased the speed at which Neptune communicated with its contacts on Earth but also allowed Neptune to jam many of the navigation, communications, and reconnaissance satellites already in orbit. For lack of a better code name, they called their program JAM.

Though the system they called Neptune belonged to someone else, the three conspirators were able to thoroughly manipulate it, and even to render it useless. A bitter fight erupted. Safi and Fazal got greedy and wanted to sell JAM to the highest bidder. Farooq wanted to give it to the Pakistani military and wash his hands of the entire matter.

In September of 1998, Safi and Fazal travelled to Washington and spent a frustrating month trying to penetrate military intelligence through Pakistani contacts. Then a friend told them about Joel Backman, the man who could open any door in Washington. Their first meeting took place on October 24, 1998, in the offices of Backman, Pratt & Bolling. The meeting would eventually destroy the lives of everyone present.

Backman had called in Jacy Hubbard, his flamboyant million-dollar mouthpiece who still played golf once a week with the President. Hubbard wanted to peddle JAM to the Saudis, who, he was convinced, would pay $1 billion for it. Backman had taken the rather provincial view that such a dangerous product should be kept at home. Hubbard was convinced he could cut a deal with the Saudis in which they would promise that JAM would never be used against the United States, their ostensible ally. Backman was afraid of the Israelis—their powerful friends in the United States, their military, and, most important, their secret spy services.

At that time Backman, Pratt & Bolling represented many foreign companies and governments. In fact, the firm was 'the' address for anyone looking for clout in Washington. The rumour about JAM slowly leaked around their offices. It could potentially be the largest fee the firm had yet seen. As weeks passed, other partners in the firm presented varying scenarios for the marketing of JAM. The firm represented a Dutch company that built avionics for the Chinese air force, and a lucrative deal could be struck with the Beijing government. The South Koreans would rest easier if they knew what was happening to the north. The Syrians would hand over their national treasury for the ability to neutralise Israeli military communications.

Each day Joel Backman and his band of greedy lawyers grew richer. In the firm's largest offices, they talked of little else.

THE DOCTOR at the military hospital was rather brusque. With scarcely a word he checked the pulse, heart, lungs, blood pressure, reflexes, and so on, then, from out of the blue announced, 'I think you're dehydrated. Happens a lot with long flights. We'll start a drip.'

'You mean, like an IV? I don't do IVs.'

'But you're dehydrated.'

'I don't feel dehydrated.'

'I'm the doctor, and I say you're dehydrated.'

'Then give me a glass of water.'

Half an hour later, a nurse entered with a big smile and a handful of med-ications. Joel said no to the sleeping pills, and when she sort of waved a hypodermic he said, 'What's that?'

'Ryax. It's a muscle relaxer.'

'Well, it just so happens that my muscles are very relaxed right now. I haven't complained of unrelaxed muscles. So you can take that Ryax and stick it up your own ass and we'll both be relaxed and happier.'

She almost dropped the needle. After a long pause in which she was completely speechless, she managed to utter, 'I'll check with the doctor.'

On the other side of the base, a Sergeant McAuliffe pecked on his key-board and sent a message to the Pentagon where it was read by Julia Javier, a veteran who'd been selected by Maynard to handle the Backman matter. Ms Javier stared at her monitor, mumbled 'Dammit,' then walked upstairs.

As usual, Teddy Maynard was sitting at the end of a long table, wrapped in a quilt, reading one of the countless summaries that got piled on his desk every hour.

Ms Javier said, 'Just heard from Aviano. Our boy is refusing all medica-tions. Won't take an IV. '

'Can't they put something in his food?' Teddy said at low volume.

'He's not eating.'

'What's he saying?'

'That his stomach is upset.'

'Is he taking liquids?'

'They took him a glass of water, which he refused. Insisted on bottled water. He inspected the cap to make sure the seal had not been broken.'

Teddy rubbed his eyes. The first plan had been to sedate Backman in the hospital, then start the sodium pentothal treatment, the truth serum, which, when used with their veteran interrogators, always produced whatever they were after. This first plan was easy and foolproof. The second one would take months and success was far from guaranteed.

'He's got big secrets, doesn't he?' Teddy said.

'No doubt.'

'But we knew that, didn't we?'

'Yes, we did.'

Chapter 3

Two of Joel Backman's three children had already abandoned him when the scandal broke. Neal, the oldest, had written to his father at least twice a month, though the letters had been quite difficult to write. Neal had been a twenty-five-year-old rookie associate at the Backman firm when his father went to prison. Though he knew little about JAM and Neptune, he was nonetheless harassed by the FBI and indicted by federal prosecutors.

Joel's abrupt decision to plead guilty was aided mightily by what happened to Jacy Hubbard, but it was also pushed along by the mistreatment of his son by the authorities. All charges against Neal were dropped in the deal. When his father left for twenty years, Neal was immediately terminated by Carl Pratt. The Backman name was a curse, and employment was impossible around Washington. After calls here and there Neal landed in the small town of Culpeper, Virginia, working in a five-man firm and thankful for the opportunity.

He craved the anonymity. He did title work, wrote wills and deeds, and settled nicely into the routine of small-town living. He eventually married a local girl and they quickly produced a daughter, Joel's second grandchild.

Neal read about his father's release in the *Post*. He discussed it at length with his wife, and briefly with the partners of his firm. The story might be causing earthquakes in D.C., but the tremors had not reached Culpeper. No one seemed to know or care. He wasn't the broker's son; he was simply Neal Backman, one of many lawyers in a small Southern town. He went about his business and waited on a phone call; somewhere down the road his father would eventually check in.

THOUGH TECHNICALLY a free man, fully pardoned and all that, Backman was still confined to a facility owned by the US government, and still living in a room not much larger than his cell at Rudley. The food there had been dreadful, but at least he could eat it without fear of being sedated. Now he was living on corn chips and sodas. The nurses were only slightly friendlier than the guards who tormented him. The doctors just wanted to dope him, following orders from above, he was certain. Somewhere close by was a little torture chamber where they were waiting to pounce on him after the drugs had worked their miracles. He longed for the outside, for fresh air and sunshine, for plenty of food, for a little human contact with someone not wearing a uniform.

A stone-faced young man named Stennett appeared in his room on the third day and began pleasantly by saying, 'OK, Backman, here's the deal.' He handed Joel a file with Marco Lazzeri written on the front. 'That's you, pal, a full-blown Italian now. That's your birth certificate and national ID card. Memorise all the info as soon as possible.'

'Memorise it? I can't even read it.'

'Then learn. In about three hours, you'll be taken to a nearby city where you'll meet your new best friend who'll hold your hand for a few days.'

Joel laid down the file and stared at Stennett. 'Who do you work for?'

'If I told you, then I'd have to kill you.'

'Very funny. The CIA?'

'The USA, that's all I can say, and that's all you need to know.'

Joel looked at the metal-framed window, complete with a lock, and said, 'I didn't notice a passport in the file.'

'Yes, well, that's because you're not going anywhere, Marco. You're about to live a very quiet life. Your neighbours will think you were born in Milan but raised in Canada, thus the bad Italian you're about to learn. If you get the urge to travel, then things could get very dangerous for you.'

'Dangerous?'

'Come on, Marco. Don't play games with me. There are some really nasty people in this world who'd love to find you. Do what we tell you, and they won't.'

'I don't know a word of Italian.'

'Sure you do—pizza, spaghetti, caffè latte, bravo, *mamma mia*. The quicker you learn, the safer you'll be. You'll have a tutor.' Stennett pulled some bills out of his pocket and laid them on the file. 'There's a hundred euros. One euro is about a dollar. I'll be back in an hour with some clothes. In the file is a small dictionary, two hundred of your first words in Italian. I suggest you get busy.'

An hour later Stennett was back with a shirt, slacks, jacket, shoes, and socks, all of the Italian variety. '*Buon giorno*,' he said.

'Hello to you,' Backman said.

'What's the word for car?'

'*Macchina*.'

'Good, Marco. It's time to get in the *macchina*.'

Another gentleman was behind the wheel of the compact, nondescript Fiat. Joel folded himself into the back seat with a canvas bag that held his net worth. Stennett sat in the front. The air was cold and damp and a thin layer of snow barely covered the ground. When they passed through the gates of the Aviano Air Base, Joel Backman had the first twinge of freedom, heavily layered with apprehension.

He watched the road signs carefully, headed south, he thought. The traffic soon grew heavy as they approached the city of Pordenone.

'This is northern Italy, right?' Joel asked, breaking the thick silence.

'Northeast.'

'How far away are the Alps?'

Stennett nodded in the general direction of his right and said, 'About forty miles that way. On a clear day, you can see them.'

They skirted around the northern edge of Pordenone and were soon on the A28. Joel was very content to ride in silence and gaze at the countryside flying by. It was late January and the fields were empty. Occasionally, above a terraced hillside, an ancient villa could be seen.

He'd actually rented one once. A dozen or so years earlier, wife number two had threatened to walk out if he didn't take her somewhere for a long vacation. They found a fourteenth-century monastery near the medieval village of San Gimignano, complete with housekeepers and cooks, even a chauffeur. But on the fourth day, Joel received the alarming news that the Senate Appropriations Committee was considering deleting a provision that would wipe out $2 billion for one of his defence-contractor clients. He flew home on a chartered jet. Wife number two stayed behind, where, as he would later learn, she began sleeping with the young chauffeur. A month later she filed for divorce, a raucous contest that would eventually cost him over three million bucks. And she was his favourite of the three.

They were all gone now, all scattered for ever. The first, the mother of two of his children, had remarried twice since Joel, and her current husband had gotten rich selling liquid fertiliser in Third-World countries.

Wife number three had jumped ship soon after his indictment.

What a sloppy life. Fifty-two years, and what's to show for a career of bilking clients, chasing secretaries around the office, putting the squeeze on slimy politicians, working seven days a week, ignoring three surprisingly stable children, pursuing money, money, money? Six years in prison. And now a fake name because the old one is so dangerous.

A sign said Venice was sixty kilometres to the south, and Joel decided to break the monotony. 'How much longer?' he asked.

'Not far.'

The A27 led south to Treviso, and when it became apparent they would not bypass the city, Joel began to assume the ride was about to end. The driver slowed, made two exits, and they were soon bouncing through the narrow streets of the city.

'What's the population of Treviso?' Joel asked.

'Eighty-five thousand,' Stennett answered. 'It's a prosperous little city that hasn't changed much in five hundred years. We bombed the hell out of it in World War Two. A nice place, not too many tourists.'

A good place to hide, Joel thought. 'Is this my stop?'

'Could be.'

A tall clock tower beckoned all the traffic into the centre of the city, where it inched along around the Piazza dei Signori. The nameless driver wheeled into a temporary parking place. Stennett pecked numbers on a cellphone, waited, then spoke quickly in Italian. When he was finished, he pointed through the windshield and said, 'You see that café over there, under the red-and-white awning? Caffè Donati?'

Joel strained from the back seat and said, 'Yeah, I got it.'

'Walk in the front door, past the bar to the back where there are eight tables. Have a seat, order a coffee, and wait. A man will approach you after about ten minutes. You will do what he says.'

'Who is this man?'

'Your new best friend, Luigi. Follow him, and you'll probably survive. Try something stupid, and you won't last a month.'

'So it's *adios* for us, huh?' Joel said, gathering his bag.

'*Arrivederci*, Marco, not *adios*.'

Joel got out of the car and began walking away. He tried to look as normal as possible as he strolled down the street, then stopped for a second in front of the *tabaccheria* and scanned the headlines of the Italian newspapers, though he understood not a single word. He stopped because he could stop, because he was a free man with the power and the right to stop wherever he wanted, and to start moving whenever he chose to.

He entered Caffè Donati and was greeted with a soft '*Buon giorno*' from the young man wiping off the bar.

'*Buon giorno*,' Joel managed in reply, his first real words to a real Italian. To prevent further conversation, he kept walking. The back room was dark and cramped and choking under a fog of cigarette smoke. He sat down at one of two empty tables and ignored the glances of the other patrons.

'*Buon giorno*,' a young lady said at his left shoulder.

'*Buon giorno*,' Joel replied. And before she could rattle off anything on the menu, he said, 'Espresso.' When she brought the espresso he said, '*Grazie*,' very softly, and she actually smiled at him. He sipped it slowly, not knowing how long it would have to last.

Italian whirled around him, the soft incessant chatter of friends gossiping at a rapid-fire pace. Did English sound this fast? Probably so. He looked at his paltry little list of 200 words, then for a few minutes tried desperately to hear a single one of them spoken.

And he asked himself for the hundredth time, Why, exactly, was he here? Why had he been whisked away from prison, then out of the country? A pardon is one thing, but why a full-blown international getaway?

He had a hunch. And it terrified him.

Luigi appeared from nowhere. He was in his early thirties, with dark sad eyes and dark hair half covering his ears, and at least four days' worth of stubble on his face. He was bundled in some type of heavy jacket that, along with the unshaven face, gave him a handsome peasant look. He ordered an espresso and smiled a lot.

His perfect English was accented just enough to convince anyone that he was really an Italian. He said he was from Milan. His Italian father was a diplomat who took his American wife and their two children around the world in service to his country. Joel was assuming Luigi knew plenty about him, so he prodded to learn what he could about his new handler.

He didn't learn much. Marriage—none. College—Bologna. Studies in the United States—yes, somewhere in the Midwest. Job—government. He had an easy smile that he used to deflect questions he didn't want to answer. Joel was dealing with a professional, and he knew it.

'I take it you know a thing or two about me,' Joel said.

'I've seen the file. Look, Marco, we're not going to relive the past. We have too much to do now.' Luigi drained what was left of his espresso and placed some euros on the table. 'Let's go for a walk,' he said, standing. Joel lifted his canvas bag and followed his handler out of the café, onto the pavement, and down a side street with less traffic. They had walked only a few steps when Luigi stopped in front of the Albergo Campeol. 'This is your first stop,' he said.

'What is it?' Joel asked. It was a three-storey stucco building wedged between two others. Colourful flags hung above the portico.

'A nice little hotel. "*Albergo*" means hotel. You can also use the word "*hotel*" if you want, but in the smaller cities they like to say *albergo*.'

They entered and walked through the small foyer. Luigi nodded knowingly at the clerk behind the front desk. Joel managed a passable '*Buon giorno*' but kept walking. They climbed three flights of stairs and walked to the end of a narrow hallway. Luigi had the key to room 30, a simple but nicely appointed suite with windows on three sides.

'Nothing fancy, but adequate.' Luigi said.

'You should've seen my last room.' Joel began opening curtains.

Luigi opened the door to the very small closet. 'Look here. You have four shirts, four slacks, two jackets, two pairs of shoes, all in your size. Plus a heavy wool overcoat.' The clothes were hanging perfectly, all pressed and ready to wear. The colours were subdued, and tasteful.

'In the drawer over there you'll find a belt, socks, underwear, everything you'll need. In the bathroom you'll find all the necessary toiletries.'

'What can I say?'

'And here on the desk are two sets of glasses.' Luigi picked up a pair of glasses and held them to the light. The small rectangular lenses were secured by thin black metal, very European frames. 'Armani,' Luigi said. 'I suggest you wear them every moment you're outside this room. Part of the disguise, Marco. Appearance is very important to Italians. Everything must be put together properly or you will get noticed. No shorts, no black socks and white sneakers, no polyester slacks, no golf shirts, and please don't start getting fat.'

'How do you say "Kiss my ass" in Italian?'

'We'll get to that later. Habits and customs are important. For example, never order cappuccino after ten-thirty in the morning. But an espresso can be ordered at any hour of the day. Only tourists order cappuccino after lunch or dinner. A disgrace. All that milk on a full stomach.' For a moment Luigi frowned as if he might just vomit for good measure.

Joel raised his right hand and said, 'I swear I'll never do it.'

'Have a seat,' Luigi said, waving at the small desk and its two chairs. He continued: 'First, the room. It's in my name, but the staff thinks that a Canadian businessman will be staying here for a couple of weeks.'

'A couple of weeks?'

'Yes, then you'll move to another location.' Luigi said this as if squads of assassins were already in Treviso, looking for Joel Backman. 'From this

moment on, you will be leaving a trail. Everything you do, everyone you
meet—they're all part of your trail. The secret of survival is to leave behind
as few tracks as possible. Speak to very few people, including the hotel personnel. Six months from now someone might come to this very hotel and
start asking questions about you. He might have a photograph. He might
offer bribes. And a clerk might suddenly remember you.'

'I have a question. Why here? Why a country where I cannot speak the
language? Why not England or Australia, where I could blend in easier?'

'That decision was made by someone else, Marco. Not me. For the first
few days I will take you to lunch and dinner. We'll move around, always
going to different places. Treviso is a nice city with lots of cafés and we'll
try them all.'

'I have another question.'

'Yes, Marco.'

'It's about money. Are you guys planning to give me an allowance or
something? I'll wash your car and do other chores.'

'Don't worry about money. For now, I take care of the bills.' Luigi
reached into his jacket and pulled out a cellphone. 'This is for you.'

'And who, exactly, am I going to call?'

'Me, if you need something. My number is on the back.'

Joel took the phone and laid it on the desk. 'I'm hungry. I've been
dreaming of a long lunch with pasta and wine and dessert, and of course
espresso, certainly not cappuccino at this hour. What do you say?'

Luigi glanced at his watch. 'I know just the place, but first some more
business. You speak no Italian, right?'

Joel rolled his eyes in frustration. 'I'm an American, OK, Luigi? My
country is larger than all of Europe combined. All you need is English over
there.'

'You're Canadian, remember?'

'OK, whatever, but we're isolated. Just us and the Americans.'

'My job is to keep you safe. To help us do that, you need to learn a lot of
Italian as quickly as possible. You will have a tutor, a student by the name
of Ermanno. You will study with him in the morning and again in the afternoon. The work will be difficult.'

'For how long?'

'That depends on you. If you work hard, then in three or four months you
should be on your own. Ermanno is an excellent teacher. The classroom is
just down the street.'

'Not here, in the hotel?'

'No, no, Marco. You must think about your trail. What would the house-keeper say if a young man spent four hours a day in this room with you? She would listen at the door and hear your lessons. She would whisper to her supervisor. Within a day or two the entire staff would know that the Canadian businessman is studying intensely.'

'Gotcha. Now about lunch.'

They walked to the centre of Treviso, the Piazza dei Signori, the main square lined with arcades and cafés. Joel tried his best to look Italian.

'Inside or outside?' Luigi asked.

'Inside,' Joel said, and they ducked into the Caffè Beltrame. A brick oven was heating the place, and the aroma of the daily feast was steaming from the rear. Luigi and the head waiter both spoke at the same time, then they laughed, then a table was found by a front window.

'We're in luck,' Luigi said as they took off their coats and sat down. 'The special today is *faraona con polenta*, guinea fowl with polenta.'

'What else?'

Luigi was studying one of the blackboards hanging from a rough-hewn crossbeam. '*Panzerotti di funghi al burro*—fried mushroom pastries. *Conchiglie con cavalfiori*—pasta shells with cauliflower. *Spiedino di carne misto alla griglia*—grilled shish kebab of mixed meats.'

'I'll have it all.'

Within minutes a jolly little man with a dirty white apron sped by the table and wrote down nothing as Luigi spat out a long list of what they wanted to eat. A jug of house wine arrived with a bowl of warm olive oil and a platter of sliced focaccia, and Joel began eating. Luigi was busy explaining the customs and traditions and mistakes made by tourists trying to pass themselves off as authentic Italians.

Though Joel sipped the first glass of wine, the alcohol went straight to his brain. A wonderful warmth embraced his body. He was free, and sitting in a rustic little café in an Italian town, drinking a nice local wine, and inhaling the smells of a delicious feast. He smiled at Luigi as the explanations continued, but at some point Joel drifted into another world.

ERMANNO CLAIMED to be twenty-three years old but looked no more than sixteen. He was tall and painfully thin, and with sandy hair and hazel eyes he looked more German than Italian. He was also very shy and quite nervous, and Joel did not like the first impression.

They met Ermanno at his tiny apartment, on the second floor of an ill-kept building six blocks or so from Joel's hotel. There were three small rooms—kitchen, bedroom, living area—all sparsely furnished, but then Ermanno was a student so such surroundings were not unexpected.

They sat around a small desk in the centre of the living room. The room was cold and dimly lit.

Luigi suggested that they study each morning from 9 a.m. to 11 a.m., break for two hours, then resume around 1.30 and study until they were tired. This seemed to suit Ermanno and Joel, who thought about asking the obvious: If my new guy here is a student, how does he have the time to teach me all day long? But he let it pass. He'd pursue it later.

Oh, the questions he was accumulating.

Ermanno eventually relaxed and described the language course. He handed over the first batch of study aids—course book number one, along with a small tape player and two cassettes. 'The tapes follow the book,' he said, very slowly. 'Tonight, you should study chapter one and listen to each tape several times. Tomorrow we'll begin there.'

'Where did you learn English?' Joel asked.

'At the university,' Ermanno said. 'In Bologna.'

'So you haven't studied in the United States?'

'Yes, I have,' he said, shooting a quick nervous glance at Luigi.

Luigi came to the rescue, clearing his throat. 'You will have plenty of time for this small talk later. It is important for you to forget English, Marco. From this day forward, you will live in Italian. Everything you touch has an Italian name for it. Every thought must be translated. It's total, absolute immersion in the language and culture.'

'Can we start at eight in the morning?' Joel asked.

Ermanno glanced and fidgeted, finally said, 'Perhaps eight-thirty.'

'Good, I'll be here at eight-thirty.'

They left the apartment and strolled back to the Piazza dei Signori. Luigi stopped in front of the Trattoria del Monte. He nodded at the door, said, 'I'll meet you here at eight for dinner. You know where your hotel is?'

'Yes, the *albergo*.'

'And you have a map of the city?'

'Yes.'

'Good. You're on your own, Marco.' And with that Luigi ducked into an alley and disappeared.

Joel felt very much alone. Four days after leaving Rudley, he was finally free and unaccompanied, perhaps unobserved, though he doubted it. He decided immediately that he would move around the city, go about his business, as if no one was watching him.

He drifted until he found himself at Piazza San Vito, a small square where the bars weren't closed, just empty. He finally mustered the courage to sneak into one. He pulled up a stool, held his breath, and said the word '*Birra*' when the bartender got close.

The bartender shot something back, and for a split second Joel was tempted to bolt. But he saw the tap, pointed at it as if it was perfectly clear what he wanted, and the bartender reached for an empty mug.

The first beer in six years. It was cool, heavy, and he savoured every drop.

Chapter 4

The Backman affair had been closely chronicled by Dan Sandberg, a veteran of the *Washington Post*. In 1998, he'd broken the story about certain highly classified papers leaving the Pentagon without authorisation. The FBI investigation that soon followed kept him busy for half a year, during which he filed eighteen stories, most of them on the front page. He'd been in the courtroom the day Backman hurriedly pled guilty and disappeared. A year later he'd written one of two books about the scandal. His sold a respectable 24,000 copies in hardback, the other about half of that.

Along the way, Sandberg built some key relationships. A month before Jacy Hubbard's death, Carl Pratt had contacted Sandberg and arranged a meeting. They eventually met more than a dozen times while the scandal ran its course, and in the ensuing years had become drinking buddies.

Three days after the pardon story first broke, Sandberg had called Pratt and arranged a meeting at a college bar near Georgetown University.

Pratt looked awful, as if he'd been drinking for days. He ordered vodka; Sandberg stuck with beer.

'So where's your boy?' Sandberg asked. 'No word from him?'

'None. Not me, not anyone at the firm.'

'Would you be surprised if he called or stopped by?'

'Nothing surprises me with Backman.' A slug of vodka. 'If he never set foot in D.C. again, I wouldn't be surprised. If he showed up tomorrow and announced the opening of a new law firm, I wouldn't be surprised.'

Sandberg sipped his beer and said, 'He can't practise law, can he? I thought they yanked his licence.'

'That wouldn't stop Backman. Lobbying is his specialty, and you don't need a licence for that. But Backman ain't coming back to D.C. Unless you've heard something different?'

'I've heard nothing. He vanished. Nobody at the prison is talking.'

'What's your theory?' Pratt asked.

'I found out today that Teddy Maynard went to the White House late on the nineteenth. Only someone like Teddy could squeeze it out of Morgan. Backman walked away, probably with an escort, and vanished.'

'Witness protection?'

'Something like that. The CIA would love to have a crack at him. They can't do it because it's against the law—they cannot target a US citizen, either here or abroad. So Maynard won't kill him. He'll just set things up so someone else will have the pleasure.'

'So you think Backman's days are numbered?'

'You asked my theory. Let me hear yours.'

A reasonable pull on the vodka, then, 'Same result, but from a slightly different angle. There was an eight-day period between Hubbard's death and Backman's plea. It was a very scary time. Both Kim Bolling and I were under FBI protection around the clock. There were some serious threats by the same people who killed Jacy Hubbard.'

'Who made the threats?'

'The same people who'd love to find Joel Backman. Backman and Hubbard had made a deal to sell their little product to the Saudis for a train-load of money. The deal fell through. Hubbard gets himself killed. Backman hurries off to jail, and the Saudis are not happy at all. Neither are the Israelis, because they wanted to make a deal too. Plus, they were furious that Hubbard and Backman would deal with the Saudis.' Pratt paused and took a drink, as if he needed the fortitude to finish the story. 'Then you have the folks who built the system in the first place.'

'The Russians?'

'Probably not. Jacy Hubbard loved Asian girls. He was last seen leaving a bar with a gorgeous young leggy thing, long black hair, round face, from somewhere on the other side of the world. Red China uses thousands of US students, businessmen, diplomats here to gather information. Plus, their intelligence service has some very effective agents. For a matter like this, they wouldn't hesitate to go after Hubbard and Backman.'

'You're sure it's Red China?' Sandberg asked.

'No one's sure, OK? Maybe Backman knows, but he never told anyone. Keep in mind, the CIA didn't even know about the system. They got caught with their pants down, and ol' Teddy's still trying to catch up.'

'Fun and games for Teddy Maynard, huh?'

'Absolutely. He fed Morgan a line about national security. Morgan, no surprise, falls for it. Backman walks. Teddy sneaks him out of the country, then watches to see who shows up with a gun.'

'And Backman knows this?'

Pratt frowned. 'Backman's not stupid by any measure. But a lot of what we know came to light after he went away. He survived six years in prison, he probably figures he can survive anything.'

CRITZ DUCKED into a pub not far from the Connaught Hotel in London. A light rain grew steadier and he needed a place to stay dry. Mrs Critz was back at the small apartment that was on loan from their new employer, so Critz had the luxury of sitting knocking back a couple of pints in a crowded pub where no one knew him.

He found an empty booth, wedged himself into it and settled in behind his pint. He absorbed the cheery British voices. He didn't even mind the smoke. He was alone and unknown and he quietly revelled in his privacy.

His anonymity was not complete, however. From behind him a small man wearing a battered sailor's cap appeared and fell into the booth across the table, startling Critz.

'Mind if I join you, Mr Critz?' the sailor said.

'Have a seat,' Critz said warily. 'You got a name?'

'Ben.' English was not his native tongue. Ben was about thirty, with dark hair, brown eyes, and a long nose that made him rather Greek-looking.

'No last name, huh?' Critz took a sip from his glass and said, 'How, exactly, do you know my name?'

'I know everything about you, Mr Critz. I'll be brief. I work for some people who desperately want to find Joel Backman. They'll pay serious money. Cash. Cash in a box, or cash in a Swiss bank, doesn't matter. It can be done quickly, within hours. You tell us where he is, you get a million bucks, no one will ever know.'

'How did you find me?'

'It was simple, Mr Critz. We're, let's say, professionals and we're going to find Mr Backman. The question is, do you want the million bucks?'

'I don't know where he is.'

'But you can find out.'

'Maybe.' Critz took a long pull on his pint and contemplated things. 'OK, let's say I'm able to get this information. Then what?'

'Take a Lufthansa flight from Dulles to Amsterdam, first class. Check into the Amstel Hotel on Biddenham Street. We'll find you, just like we found you here.'

Critz paused and committed the details to memory. 'When?' he asked.

'As soon as possible, Mr Critz. There are others looking for him.'

Ben vanished as quickly as he had materialised, leaving Critz to peer through the smoke and wonder if he'd just witnessed a dream. He left the pub an hour later, certain that he was being watched.

THE SIESTA DIDN'T WORK. There was simply too much to think about. He slowly got up from the bed where he'd been lying for an hour, unable to close his eyes, and walked to the small table where he picked up the cellphone Luigi had given him. He took it to the window, punched the numbers taped to its back, and after four rings he heard a familiar voice.

'*Ciao*, Marco. *Come stai?*'

'Just checking to see if this thing works,' Joel said.

'How was your nap?'

'Uh, nice, very nice. I'll see you at dinner.'

'*Ciao.*'

Where was Luigi? Lurking nearby with a phone in his pocket, just waiting for Joel to call? Watching the hotel? If Stennett and the driver were still in Treviso, along with Luigi and Ermanno, that would add up to four 'friends' of some variety assigned to keep tabs on Joel Backman.

He wanted some coffee, but he wasn't ready to pick up the phone and place an order. He could handle the 'Hello' and the 'Coffee,' but there would be a flood of other words he did not yet know. He was afraid to order because he was afraid of the language. Joel Backman had never feared a damn thing, and if he could make one hundred phone calls a day while rarely looking at a Rolodex or a directory, then he could certainly learn enough Italian to order coffee.

He arranged Ermanno's study materials neatly on the table and looked at the synopsis. The first page of lesson one was a rather crude colour drawing of a family living room with Mom and Pop and the kids watching television.

The objects were labelled in both English and Italian—door and *porta*, sofa and *sofà*, window and *finestra*, and so on.

A few pages later was the kitchen, then the bedroom, then the bathroom. After an hour Joel was walking softly around his room whispering the name of everything he saw: bed, *letto*; lamp, *lampada*; clock, *orologio*; soap, *sapone*. He stood before the small mirror (*specchio*) in his bathroom (*bagno*) and tried to convince himself that he was really Marco. Marco Lazzeri. '*Sono Marco, sono Marco,*' he repeated. I am Marco. I am Marco. Silly at first, but that must be put aside. If being Marco would save his neck, then Marco he was. Marco. Marco. Marco.

When it was time for dinner, Marco had memorised all of the first lesson and had listened to the tape of it a dozen times. He stepped into the very cool night and walked happily in the general direction of Trattoria del Monte, where he knew Luigi would be waiting.

Marco greeted Luigi with a flourish. '*Buona sera, signore, come sta?*'

'*Sto bene, grazie, e tu?*' Luigi said with an approving smile. Fine, thanks, and you?

'*Molto bene, grazie,*' Marco said. Very well, thank you.

'So you've been studying?' Luigi said.

'Yes, there's nothing else to do.'

Before Marco could unwrap his napkin, a waiter stopped by with a flask of the house red. He poured two glasses and then disappeared.

'So how often do you bring in someone like me and turn him into an Italian?' Marco asked casually.

Luigi gave a smile and said, 'From time to time.'

'Who do you work for, Luigi?'

'Who do you think?'

'You're part of the alphabet—CIA, FBI, NSA. Maybe some obscure branch of military intelligence.'

'Do you enjoy meeting me in these nice little restaurants?' Luigi asked.

'Do I have a choice?'

'Yes. If you keep asking these questions, then we'll stop meeting. And when we stop meeting, your life will become even more fragile.'

'I thought your job was to keep me alive.'

'It is. So stop asking questions about me.'

With perfect timing the waiter appeared and dropped two large menus between them. Marco frowned at the list of dishes and was reminded of how far his Italian had to go.

'What looks good?' he asked.

'The chef is from Siena, so he likes Tuscan dishes. The risotto with porcini mushrooms is a great first course. The steak florentine is outstanding.'

Marco closed his menu and savoured the aroma from the kitchen. 'I'll take both.'

Luigi closed his too and waved at the waiter. After he ordered, they sipped the wine for a few minutes in silence. The waiter plunked down a basket of mixed breads and a small bowl of olive oil and Luigi began dipping and eating. More food followed, a small tray of ham and salami with olives. Luigi was an operative, or an agent of some strain, but he was first and foremost an Italian. All the training possible could not divert his attention from the challenge at hand when the table was covered.

As he ate, he explained the rigours of a proper Italian dinner. First, the *antipasti*—usually a plate of mixed meats. Then the first course, *primi*, which is usually a serving of pasta, rice, soup or polenta, to sort of limber up the stomach in preparation for the main course, the *secondi*—a hearty dish of meat, fish, pork, chicken or lamb. Be careful with desserts, he warned ominously. He shook his head sadly as he explained that many good restaurants now buy them off premises, and they're loaded with so much sugar or cheap liqueur that they practically rot your teeth out.

Marco managed to appear sufficiently shocked at this national scandal.

'Learn the word, *gelato*,' he said, his eyes glowing.

'Ice cream,' Marco said.

'Bravo. The best in the world. There's a *gelateria* down the street. We'll go there after dinner.'

MARCO KNOCKED on the apartment door ten minutes early for this first session with Ermanno. It was a control thing. Though he tried to resist it, he found himself impulsively reverting to his old ways. He preferred to be the one who decided when the lesson would begin.

Ermanno smiled timidly as he opened the door. '*Buon giorno, Signor Lazzeri.*'

'*Buon giorno, Ermanno. Come stai?*'

'*Molto bene, grazie, e tu?*'

'*Molto bene, grazie.*'

Ermanno opened the door wider, '*Prego.*' Please come in.

Marco stepped inside and placed his books on the small table in the centre of the front room.

'*Vorrebbe un caffè?*' Ermanno asked. Would you like a coffee?

'*Sì, grazie.*'

'You are a student, right?' he asked when Ermanno returned from the kitchen with two small cups.

'*Non inglese, Marco, non inglese.*'

And that was the end of English. Ermanno sat on one side of the table, Marco on the other, and at exactly eight-thirty they turned to page one of lesson one. Marco read the first dialogue in Italian, Ermanno gently made corrections. An hour later, Ermanno began pointing at various objects around the room—rug, book, magazine, chair, quilt, curtains—and Marco responded with ease and with an improving accent. Lesson one was completed after only two hours and they turned to lesson two.

'You've been studying,' Ermanno mumbled in English.

'*Non inglese, Ermanno, non inglese,*' Marco corrected him. By noon, the teacher was exhausted and they were both relieved to hear the voice of Luigi from the hallway. He entered and saw the two of them squared off across the small, littered table, as if they'd been arm wrestling for hours.

'*Come va?*' Luigi asked. How's it going?

Ermanno gave him a weary look and said, '*Molto intenso.*' Very intense.

'*Vorrei pranzare,*' Marco announced, slowly rising to his feet. I'd like some lunch.

Marco was hoping for a nice lunch with some English thrown in but Luigi was inspired to continue the immersion through the meal, or at least the first part of it. The menu contained not a word of English, and after Luigi explained each dish in incomprehensible Italian, Marco threw up his hands and said, 'That's it. I'm not speaking Italian for the next hour.'

'OK then. I suppose we can do English for one hour.'

'*Grazie,*' Marco said before he caught himself.

MIDWAY THROUGH the morning session the following day, Marco abruptly changed direction. In the middle of a particularly tedious piece of dialogue he ditched the Italian and said, 'You're not a student.'

'I am,' Ermanno said, without much conviction.

'No, I don't think so. You're obviously not taking classes, otherwise you wouldn't be able to spend all day teaching me.'

'Maybe I have classes at night. Why does it matter?'

'You're not taking classes anywhere. There are no books here, no student newspaper, none of the usual crap that students leave lying around.'

Ermanno suddenly stood and walked through the tiny kitchen to the rear of the apartment. He returned with some papers, which he slid in front of Marco. It was a registration packet from the University of Bologna, listing the name of Ermanno Rosconi, at the address where they were now sitting.

'I resume classes soon,' Ermanno said. 'Would you like more coffee?'

Marco was scanning the forms, comprehending just enough to get the message. 'Yes, please,' he said. It was just paperwork—easily faked. But if it was a forgery, it was a very good one.

THE ROUTINE CHANGED at dinner. Luigi met him in front of a tobacco shop facing the Piazza dei Signori, and they strolled along a busy alley as shop-keepers were closing up. It was already dark and very cold but Luigi was in no hurry. 'How was your second day of class?'

'Good. Ermanno's OK. No sense of humour, but an adequate teacher.'

'He tells me you have an ear for the language.' Luigi suddenly stopped and looked at what appeared to be a small deli. 'This, Marco, is dinner.'

Marco stared with disapproval. The storefront was no more than fifteen feet across. Three tables were crammed in the window and the place appeared to be packed. 'Are you sure?' Marco asked.

'Yes, it's very good. Lighter food, sandwiches and stuff. You're eating by yourself. I'm not going in.'

Marco looked at him and started to protest, then he caught himself and smiled as if he gladly accepted the challenge.

'The menu is on a chalkboard above the cashier, no English. Order first, pay, then pick up your food at the far end of the counter. Tip is included.'

Marco asked, 'What's the specialty of the house?'

'The ham and artichoke pizza is delicious. So are the panini. I'll meet you over there, by the fountain, in one hour.'

Marco gritted his teeth and entered the café, very alone. He desperately searched the chalkboard for something he could pronounce. Forget taste. What was important was the ordering and paying. The cashier was a smiling middle-aged lady. Marco gave her a friendly '*Buona sera*,' and ordered a '*panino prosciutto e formaggio*'—ham and cheese sandwich—and a Coca-Cola. Good ol' Coca-Cola. The same in any language.

The register rattled and she offered a blur of words that he did not under-stand. But he kept smiling and said, '*Sì*,' then handed over a twenty-euro bill. It worked. With the change was a ticket. '*Numero sessantasette*,' she said. Number sixty-seven.

He held the ticket and moved slowly along the counter towards the kitchen. No one gawked at him, no one seemed to notice. Was he actually passing himself off as an Italian, a real local?

He watched the plates of food as they popped up along the counter near the grill. After about ten minutes, a thick sandwich appeared. A server grabbed it, snatched off a ticket, and yelled, '*Numero sessantasette.*' Marco stepped forward without a word and produced his ticket.

He found a seat at a small corner table and thoroughly enjoyed the solitude of his dinner. The deli was loud and crowded, a neighbourhood place where many of the customers knew each other. Their greetings involved hugs and kisses and long hellos, even longer goodbyes. Marco absorbed the roar of Italian without trying to understand any of it. He caught a word every now and then, and considered this to be progress of some sort.

Almost an hour after he entered the café, he left the warmth of it and walked to the fountain where the water had been turned off so it wouldn't freeze. Luigi strolled up a few minutes later, as if he'd been loitering in the shadows. They walked to the hotel and said good night.

LUIGI'S FIELD SUPERVISOR had diplomatic cover at the US consulate in Milan. His name was Whitaker, and Backman was the least of his priorities. Backman was not involved in intelligence and Whitaker had a full load in that arena without having to worry about an ex-Washington power broker who'd been stashed away in Italy. But he dutifully prepared his daily summaries and sent them to CIA headquarters at Langley to be reviewed by Julia Javier, the veteran with access to Mr Maynard himself.

Teddy wanted a briefing. Ms Javier was summoned to his office on the sixth floor. She entered his station, and once again found him parked at the end of a long wide conference table, sitting high in his wheelchair, bundled in blankets from the chest down, peering over stacks of summaries.

Julia Javier took her customary seat to his right—his right ear caught much more than his left—and he managed a very tired 'Hello, Julia.'

Hoby, as always, sat across from her and prepared to take notes. 'Brief me on Backman,' Teddy said.

Julia looked at her notes. 'He's in place in Treviso, in northern Italy. Been there for three full days, seems to be making the adjustment quite well. Our agent is in complete contact, and the language tutor is a local who's doing a nice job. Backman has no money and no passport, and so far has been quite willing to stick close to the agent. When he's not being tutored or eating, he stays in his room and studies Italian.'

'What does he talk about?'

'Not the past, not old friends and old enemies. Nothing that would inter-est us. He's closed that off, for now anyway. Idle conversation tends to be about his new home, the culture and language.'

'His mood?'

'He just walked out of prison fourteen years early and he's having long meals and good wine. He's quite happy. Never talks about his family.'

'His health?'

'Seems fine. The cough is gone. Appears to be sleeping. No complaints.'

'How much does he drink?'

'He's careful. Enjoys wine at lunch and dinner but nothing excessive.'

'Let's try and crank up the booze, OK? See if he'll talk more.'

'That's our plan.'

'How secure is he?'

'Everything's bugged—phones, room, language lessons, lunches, din-ners. Even his shoes have mikes. Both pairs. His overcoat has a Peak 30 sewn into the lining. We can track him virtually anywhere but as of now, he seems very content to enjoy his freedom and do what he's told.'

'So he feels safe?'

'Under the circumstances, yes.'

'Then let's give him a scare.'

'Now?'

'Yes.' Teddy rubbed his eyes. 'What about his son?'

'Level-three surveillance, not much happening in Culpeper, Virginia. If Backman tries to contact anyone, it will be Neal Backman.'

'His son is the only person he trusts,' Teddy said. After a long pause he said, 'Anything else, Julia?'

'He's writing a letter to his mother in Oakland.'

Teddy opened his eyes and said, 'You think he's stupid enough to mail a letter to his mother?'

'No. But he's been writing her once a week for a long time. It's a habit.'

'Are we still watching her mail?'

'Yes, what little she receives.'

'Very well. Scare the hell out of him, then report back.'

'Yes sir.' Julia gathered her papers and left the office. Teddy picked up a summary and adjusted his reading glasses.

Backman's mother's phone had been tapped in the nursing home in

Oakland, and so far it had revealed nothing. Lydia Backman had survived two strokes and was confined to a wheelchair. When her son was at his pinnacle she lived in relative luxury in a spacious condo with a full-time nurse. His conviction had forced her to give up the good life and live in a nursing home with a hundred others. Surely Backman would not try to contact her.

Chapter 5

After a few days of dreaming about the money, Critz began spending it, at least mentally. With all that cash, he wouldn't be forced to work for the sleazy defence contractor, nor would he be forced onto the lecture circuit.

He made a phone call and took the flat in London for a few more days. He encouraged Mrs Critz to shop more aggressively. She, too, was tired of Washington and deserved an easier life.

Critz blundered badly from the start. First, he used the phone in his borrowed flat, thus making it easy for someone to nail down his exact location. He called Jeb Priddy, the CIA liaison who had been stationed in the White House during the last four years. Priddy seemed slightly irritated by the call. He and Critz had never been close, and Priddy knew immediately that the guy was fishing. Critz eventually said he was trying to find an old pal, a senior CIA analyst he'd once played a lot of golf with. Name was Daly, Addison Daly. Did Priddy perhaps know where he was now?

Priddy knew him well. 'I know the name,' Priddy said. 'Maybe I can find him. Where can I reach you?'

Critz gave him the number at the flat. Priddy called Addison Daly and passed along his suspicions. Daly turned on his recorder and called London on a secure line. Critz answered the phone and went overboard with his delight at hearing from an old friend. He rambled on about how nice it was being a private citizen. He was anxious to get serious about his golf game.

Daly played along well. He offered that he, too, was contemplating retirement and that he caught himself looking forward to an easier life.

How's Teddy these days? Critz wanted to know. What's the mood in Washington with the new administration?

Nothing changes much, Daly mused, just another bunch of fools.

As the conversation was winding down, Critz said with a clumsy laugh, 'Don't guess anybody's seen Joel Backman?'

Daly managed to laugh too. 'No,' he said, 'I think he's well hidden.'

Critz promised to call as soon as he returned to D.C. They'd play eighteen holes then have a drink, just like in the old days.

An hour later, the phone conversation was played for Teddy Maynard.

Since the first two calls had been somewhat encouraging, Critz pressed on. Another old pal was now a well-connected lobbyist who had allegedly maintained close ties to the CIA. They talked politics and golf and eventually, Critz managed to steer the conversation along to Backman. 'What's the gossip on Backman?' he asked. 'Where did Maynard stash him? That's the big question.'

'So it was a CIA job?' his friend asked.

'Of course,' Critz said with the voice of authority. Who else could sneak him out of the country in the middle of the night?

'That's interesting.' His pal then became very quiet. Critz insisted on a lunch the following week, and that's where they left the conversation.

As Critz feverishly worked the phone, he marvelled once again at his endless list of contacts. Power did have its rewards.

JOEL, OR MARCO, said goodbye to Ermanno at five-thirty in the afternoon, completing a nonstop three-hour session. Both were exhausted.

The chilly air helped clear his head as he walked the narrow streets of Treviso, both hands shoved deep into his pockets. When he turned the corner to his hotel, he saw Luigi pacing nervously along the pavement.

'We are leaving, immediately,' Luigi said.

'Why?' Marco asked, glancing around, looking for bad guys.

'I'll explain later. There's a travel bag on your bed. Pack your things as quickly as possible. I'll wait here.'

'What if I don't want to leave?' Marco asked.

Luigi clutched his left wrist then gave a very tight smile. 'Then you might not last twenty-four hours,' he said as ominously. 'Please trust me.'

Marco raced up the stairs and was almost at his room before he realised that the pain in his stomach was not from heavy breathing but from fear. What had happened? What had Luigi seen or been told? And how could anyone have found him this soon? He'd been in Treviso only four days. When everything was packed, Marco sat for a moment, took deep breaths, and told himself that whatever was happening was just part of the game.

When his composure was somewhat restored, he walked slowly down the stairs, through the lobby where he nodded at the gawking clerk, and out of the front door. Luigi snatched his bag and tossed it into a compact Fiat. They were on the outskirts of Treviso before a word was spoken.

'OK, Luigi, what's up?' Marco asked.

'A change of scenery.'

'Got that. Why?'

'Some very good reasons.'

Luigi drove with his left hand, shifted gears frantically with his right, and kept the accelerator as close to the floor as possible while ignoring the brakes. They drove for an hour, generally in a southward direction, clinging to the back roads. Luigi's eyes were narrow, his jaw clenched tightly.

'You're just trying to scare me, aren't you, Luigi? We're playing the spy game—you're the master, I'm the poor schmuck with the secrets. Scare the hell out of me and keep me dependent and loyal. I know what you're doing.'

'Who killed Jacy Hubbard?' Luigi asked, barely moving his lips.

The mere mention of Hubbard made Backman freeze for a second. The name always brought the same flashback: a police photo of Jacy, the left side of his head blown away, blood everywhere.

'You have the file,' Backman said. 'It was a suicide.'

'Oh yes. And if you believed that, then why did you decide to plead guilty and beg for protective custody in prison?'

'So you're saying that the boys who did the Hubbard suicide are after me and somehow they found out I was hiding in Treviso?'

Luigi confirmed it with a shrug.

He would not get the details, if, in fact, there were any. Joel sank a few inches in his seat and closed his eyes. Two of his clients had died first. Safi Mirza had been knifed outside a Georgetown nightclub three months after he hired Backman and handed over the only copy of JAM. A month later Fazal Sharif had disappeared in Karachi, and was presumed dead. JAM was indeed worth a billion dollars, but no one would ever enjoy the money.

IN 1998, Backman, Pratt & Bolling had hired Jacy Hubbard for $1 million a year. The marketing of JAM was his first big challenge. Hubbard bribed his way into the Pentagon in a clumsy effort to confirm the existence of the Neptune satellite system. Some classified documents were smuggled out by a Hubbard mole who was reporting everything to his superiors. The highly sensitive papers purported to show the existence of Gamma Net, a fictitious

Star Wars-like surveillance system with unheard-of capabilities. Once Hubbard 'confirmed' that the three young Pakistanis were indeed correct— their Neptune was a US project—he proudly reported his findings to Joel Backman and they were in business.

Since Gamma Net was supposedly the creation of the US military, JAM was worth even more. The truth was that neither the Pentagon nor the CIA knew about Neptune.

The Pentagon then leaked its own fiction—a fabricated breach of security by a mole working for ex-senator Jacy Hubbard and his powerful new boss, the broker himself. The scandal erupted. The FBI raided the offices of Backman, Pratt & Bolling in the middle of the night, found the Pentagon documents and within forty-eight hours federal prosecutors had issued indictments against every partner in the firm.

The killings soon followed, with no clues as to who was behind them. The Pentagon brilliantly neutralised Hubbard and Backman without tipping its hand as to whether it actually owned and created the satellite system. Gamma Net or Neptune. Neptune, or whatever, was effectively shielded under the impenetrable web of 'military secrets'.

Backman the lawyer wanted a trial, especially if the Pentagon documents were questionable, but Backman the defendant wanted to avoid a fate similar to Hubbard's.

If Luigi's mad dash out of Treviso was designed to frighten him, then the plan suddenly began working. For the first time since his pardon, Joel missed the safety of his little cell in maximum security.

They slept that night in a tiny country inn that had been in the same family since Roman times. The nearest road was narrow, neglected, and virtually free of any vehicle built after 1970. Bologna was not far away.

When Joel Backman/Marco Lazzeri crawled under the blankets and finally got warm, he couldn't see a flicker of light anywhere. Total blackness. And total quiet. It was so quiet he couldn't close his eyes for a long time.

AFTER THE FIFTH REPORT that Critz had called with questions about Joel Backman, Teddy Maynard threw a rare tantrum. The fool was in London, working the phones furiously, for some reason trying to find someone, anyone, who might lead him to information about Backman.

'Someone's offered Critz money,' Teddy barked at Wigline, an assistant deputy director.

'But there's no way Critz can find out where Backman is,' Wigline said.

'He shouldn't be trying. He'll complicate matters. He must be neutralised.'

'What are you saying, Teddy?'

'Neutralise him.'

'He's a US citizen.'

'I know that! He's also compromising an operation. There is precedent. We've done it before.'

Wigline clenched his jaw and said, 'I assume you want it done now.'

'As soon as possible,' Teddy said. 'Show me a plan in two hours.'

THEY WATCHED CRITZ as he left his borrowed apartment and began his late-afternoon walk, one that usually ended with a few pints. Near Leicester Square he entered the Dog and Duck, the same pub as the day before.

He was on his second pint before the stool next to him cleared and an agent named Greenlaw wedged in and yelled for a beer.

'Mind if I smoke?' Greenlaw asked Critz, who shrugged and said, 'This ain't America.'

'A Yank, huh?' Greenlaw said. 'Live here?'

'No, just visiting.' Critz wanted no part of the conversation. He had quickly come to adore the solitude of a crowded pub.

Greenlaw gulped his beer in an effort to catch up with Critz. It was crucial to order the next two at the same time. 'I've been here for a year,' he said.

Critz nodded without looking. Get lost.

'I don't mind driving on the wrong side, or the lousy weather, but what really bugs me here are the sports. It's either soccer or cricket, and these people go nuts over both. I just survived the winter here without the NFL. It was pure misery.'

Critz was a loyal Redskins season-ticket holder and few things in life excited him as much as his beloved team. Greenlaw had spent the day memorising statistics in a CIA safe house north of London. If football didn't work, then politics would be next.

Critz was suddenly homesick. He looked at Greenlaw and said, 'Patriots or Packers?'

'My team didn't make it, but I always pull for the NFC.'

'Me too. Who's your team?'

And that was perhaps the most fatal question Robert Critz would ever ask. When Greenlaw answered, 'Redskins,' Critz actually smiled and wanted to talk. Greenlaw ordered another round and both seemed ready to replay old games for hours.

Halfway through his fourth pint Critz finally needed to pee. He asked directions and disappeared. Greenlaw deftly dropped into Critz's glass one small white tablet of Rohypnol—a strong, tasteless, odourless sedative. When Mr Redskins returned he was refreshed and ready to drink. They talked about the team and thoroughly enjoyed themselves as poor Critz's chin began to drop.

'Wow,' he said, his tongue already thick. 'I'd better be going.'

'Yeah, me too,' Greenlaw said, raising his glass. 'Drink up.'

They drained their pints and stood to leave; Critz in front, Greenlaw waiting to catch him. They made it through the front door and onto the pavement where a cold wind revived Critz, but only for a second. In less than twenty steps he was wobbling on rubbery legs and grasping for a lamppost. Greenlaw grabbed him as he was falling, and for the benefit of a young couple passing by said loudly, 'Dammit, Fred, you're drunk again.'

A car appeared from nowhere and slowed by the pavement. A back door swung open, and Greenlaw shovelled a half-dead Critz into the rear seat. The first stop was a warehouse eight blocks away. There Critz, thoroughly unconscious now, was transferred to a small unmarked lorry. While Critz lay on the floor of the van, an agent injected him with a massive dose of heroin. The presence of heroin always squelched the autopsy results, at the family's insistence of course.

With Critz barely breathing, the van left the warehouse and drove to Whitcomb Street, not far from his apartment. The killing required three vehicles—the van, followed by a large and heavy Mercedes, and a trail car driven by a real Brit who would hang around and chat with the police.

On the third pass, with all three drivers talking to each other, the rear doors of the van were shoved open, Critz fell onto the street, the Mercedes aimed for his head and got it with a sickening thump. The Brit in the trail car slammed on his brakes, jumped out and ran to the poor drunk who'd just stumbled into the street and been run over.

He flagged down a taxi approaching in the other lane, and soon other traffic stopped. Before long, a crowd was gathering and the police arrived. The Brit in the trail car may have been the first on the scene, but he saw very little. He saw the man stumble between those two parked cars over there, into the street, and get hit by a large black car. Or maybe it was dark green. Not sure of the make or model. Never thought about looking at the licence plates. He was too shocked by the sight of the drunk suddenly appearing at the edge of the street.

MARCO WANTED BREAKFAST primarily because he could smell it—sausages on the grill somewhere deep in the main house—but Luigi was anxious to move on. 'Remember, you're leaving a trail, and the signora forgets nothing,' he explained as they hurriedly threw their bags in his car.

They sped down the country lane in search of wider roads.

'Where are we going?' Marco asked.

'We'll see.'

'Stop playing games with me!' Marco growled and Luigi actually flinched. 'Every time I ask a question you give me these vague threats about how I won't last twenty-four hours on my own. I want to know what's going on. Where are we headed? Give me some answers, Luigi, or I'll disappear.'

Luigi turned onto a four-lane and a sign said that Bologna was thirty kilometres ahead. He waited for the tension to ease a bit, then said, 'We're going to Bologna for a few days. Ermanno will meet us there. You will continue your lessons. You'll be placed in a safe house for several months. Then I'll disappear and you'll be on your own.'

'Do you realise how ridiculous this is, Luigi? Someone is spending all this time and money trying to teach me another language and another culture. Why not just stash me in some place like New Zealand?'

'That's a great idea, Marco, but I'm not making those decisions. Do you know Robert Critz?'

Marco paused for a moment. 'I met him a few times over the years.'

'He was killed last night in London. That makes five people who've died because of you—Jacy Hubbard, the three Pakistanis, now Critz. The killing hasn't stopped, Marco, nor will it.'

MARCO'S NEXT HIDING PLACE was a dingy hotel a few blocks from the outer edge of the old city. He followed Luigi through the cramped lobby to the stairs and up to a room on the first floor, a rather small space with a tiny bed and curtains that hadn't been opened in days.

'I like Treviso better,' Marco said, staring at the walls.

Luigi yanked open the curtains. The sunlight helped only slightly. 'Unpack. I'll meet you downstairs in ten minutes. Ermanno is waiting.'

Ermanno appeared as rattled as Marco by the sudden change in location. He was harried and unsettled, as if he'd chased them all night from Treviso. They walked with him a few blocks to a run-down apartment building. They climbed four flights of stairs and entered a tiny, two-room flat that had even less furniture than the apartment in Treviso.

'Your dump's worse than mine,' Marco said, taking it in.

Spread on a narrow table and waiting for action were the study materials they'd used the day before.

'I'll be back for lunch,' Luigi said, and quickly disappeared.

'*Andiamo a studiare,*' Ermanno announced. Let's study.

LUNCH AND DINNER were forgettable, quick snacks in fake trattorias, the Italian version of fast food. Luigi was in a foul mood and insisted that they speak only Italian. At midnight, Marco was in his bed, wrapped tightly in a thin blanket, and memorising list after list of verbs and adjectives.

What could Robert Critz have possibly done to get himself killed by people who might also be looking for Joel Backman? The question itself was too bizarre to ask. But if people were still dying, then it was urgent that he learn the verbs and adjectives scattered on his bed. Language meant survival, and movement. Luigi and Ermanno would soon disappear, and Marco Lazzeri would be left to fend for himself.

MARCO ESCAPED his claustrophobic room, and went for a long walk at daybreak. With a pocket map Luigi had given him he headed west on Via Irnerio along the northern edge of the university section of Bologna. The pavements were centuries old and covered with miles of arching porticoes.

Ahead Marco saw a small green neon sign advertising the Bar Fontana, and as he walked towards it he soon picked up the scent of coffee. The door opened reluctantly, and once inside Marco almost smiled at the aromas—coffee, cigarettes, pastries, breakfast on a grill in the rear. Then the fear hit, the usual apprehension of trying to order in an unknown language.

Marco got a small table near the back. He picked up the wrinkled menu on the table and quickly settled on the first thing he recognised. Just as the waiter stopped and glanced down at him he said, with all the ease he could possibly exude, '*Espresso, e un panino al formaggio.*' A small cheese sandwich.

The waiter nodded his approval. Not a single person glanced over to check out his accented Italian. No newspapers dipped to see who he might be.

Marco removed a vocabulary booklet from his pocket and tried mightily to ignore the people and scenes he wanted to watch. Verbs, verbs, verbs. Ermanno kept saying that to master Italian, you had to know the verbs. The booklet had 1,000 basic verbs. As tedious as rote memorisation was, Marco had conquered 300 verbs when his order arrived. He took a sip, went back to work as if the food was much less important than the vocab.

The chair on the other side of Marco's small round table was vacant, and this caught the attention of a short fat man, dressed entirely in faded black, with wild bunches of grey frizzy hair protruding from all parts of his head. '*Buon giorno. È libera?*' he asked politely, gesturing towards the chair. Marco caught the word 'libera' and assumed it meant 'free' or 'vacant.'

'*Sì,*' Marco managed with no accent, and the man removed a long black cape, draped it over the chair, then manoeuvred himself into position and placed a copy of *L'Unità* on the table. To avoid conversation, Marco buried himself even deeper into Ermanno's verbs.

'American?' his new friend said, in English with no foreign accent.

Marco lowered the booklet. 'Close. Canadian. How'd you know?'

He nodded at the booklet and said, 'English to Italian vocabulary. You don't look British, so I figure you're American.'

Marco was beginning to get nervous. 'And where are you from?' he asked.

'Last stop was Austin, Texas, thirty years ago. Name's Rudolph.'

'Good morning, Rudolph, a pleasure. I'm Marco.'

The waiter leaned in and Rudolph ordered black coffee.

'What brings you to Bologna?' Rudolph asked.

Marco lowered his booklet and said, 'Just travelling around Italy for a year, seeing the sights, trying to pick up some of the language.'

Half of Rudolph's face was covered with an unkempt beard that began fairly high up the cheekbones and sprang in all directions. His eyes were dark green and projected rays that, from under a set of thick sagging eyebrows, took in everything.

'How long in Bologna?' Rudolph asked.

'Got here yesterday. I have no schedule. And you, what brings you here?'

The eyes danced and never blinked. 'I've been here for thirty years. I'm a professor at the university.'

Marco finally took a bite of his cheese sandwich, partly out of hunger, but more importantly to keep Rudolph talking.

'Where's your home?' he asked.

Following the script, Marco said, 'Toronto. Grandparents immigrated there from Milan. I have Italian blood but never learned the language.'

'The language is not hard,' Rudolph said, and his coffee arrived. He grabbed the small cup and leaned forward a bit. 'You don't sound Canadian,' he said, and those eyes appeared to be laughing at him.

Marco was struggling under the labour of acting, and sounding Italian. He'd had no time to even think about putting on Canadian airs.

'Can't help that,' he said. 'How did you get here from Austin?'

'I was once a young professor at the University of Texas law school. When they found out I was a Communist they ran me out of town, so I came here to Bologna, the heart of Italian communism.'

'What do you teach here?'

'Jurisprudence. Law. Radical left-wing legal theories.'

'Still a Communist?' Marco asked.

'Of course. Always. Why would I change?'

Marco nodded at the newspaper and said, 'Ever read papers from home?'

'Home is here, my friend. I became an Italian citizen and haven't been back to the States in twenty years.'

Backman was relieved. He had not seen American newspapers since his release, but he assumed there had been coverage and probably old photos. To quickly shift to another subject, he said, 'This is my first visit to Bologna. Didn't know it was the centre of Italian communism.'

'Bologna is a lot of things, my friend,' Rudolph said. 'It's always been the centre of intellectual activity in Italy, thus its first nickname, *la dotta*, which means the learned. Then it became the home of the political left and received its second nickname, *la rossa*, the red. And the Bolognesi have always been very serious about their food. They believe, and they're probably right, that this is the stomach of Italy.'

A frightening question suddenly hit Marco: Was it possible that Rudolph was part of the static? Was he a teammate of Luigi and Ermanno and Stennett and whoever else was out there in the shadows working so hard to keep Joel Backman alive? The thought passed, but it was not forgotten.

Marco finished his little sandwich and decided he suddenly had a train to catch for another day of sightseeing. He managed to extricate himself from the table and got a fond farewell from Rudolph. 'I'm here every morning,' he said. 'Come back when you can stay longer.'

'*Grazie*,' Marco said. '*Arrivederci.*'

AT MARCO'S INSISTENCE, the morning sessions with Ermanno were beginning at eight, not thirty minutes later. Marco arrived for each lesson with his vocabulary lists thoroughly memorised, his situational dialogues perfected, and his urgent desire to absorb the language barely under control.

The morning he met Rudolph, Marco studied intensely for two hours, then said, '*Vorrei vedere l'università.*' I'd like to see the university.

'*Quando?*' Ermanno asked. When?

'*Adesso. Andiamo a fare una passeggiata.*' Now. Let's go for a walk. Marco was already on his feet, grabbing his coat.

They left the building and headed in the direction of the university.

'*Questa via, come si chiama?*' Ermanno asked. What's the name of this street?

'*È Via Donati,*' Marco answered without looking for a street sign.

They stopped in front of a small crowded shop and Ermanno asked, '*Che tipo di negozio è questo?*' What kind of store is this?

'*Una tabaccheria.*' A tobacco store.

The session became a roving game of name that thing. Ermanno would point and say, '*Cosa è quello?*' What's that? A bike, a policeman, a blue car, a city bus, a bench, a student, a small dog, a café, a pastry shop.

A few minutes after ten, and the university was finally coming to life. The Università degli Studi was found in dozens of handsome old buildings, some 500 years old. Over the centuries the school had grown and now covered an entire section of Bologna. The Italian lesson was forgotten for a block or two as they were swept along in waves of students hustling to and from their classes. Marco caught himself looking for an old man with bright grey hair. He had already made up his mind to see Rudolph again.

At 22 Via Zamboni, Marco stopped and gazed at a sign between the door and a window: FACOLTÀ DI GIURISPRUDENZA.

'Is this the law school?' he asked.

'*Sì.*'

Rudolph was somewhere inside, no doubt spreading left-wing dissent among his impressionable students.

They ambled on, in no hurry as they continued to play name that thing and enjoy the energy of the street.

Chapter 6

The *lezione-a-piedi*—lesson on foot—continued the next day when Marco revolted after an hour of tedious grammar and demanded to go for a walk.

'Let's go. *Andiamo.* I need real conversation, not sentence structure.' When Ermanno hesitated, Marco smiled at him and said, 'Please, my friend. I've been locked in a small cell for six years. There's a vibrant city out there. Let's go explore it.'

Outside the air was clear and brisk, not a cloud anywhere, a gorgeous winter's day that drew every warm-blooded Bolognesi into the streets for errands and long-winded chats with old friends. They drifted along Via San Vitale, one of the main avenues of the university, with porticoes covering the pavements on both sides and thousands of students jostling to early classes. They flowed with the young crowd, picking their way through the foot traffic, and headed generally to *il centro*.

Luigi met them for lunch at a restaurant called Testerino, near the university. The lunch lasted for two hours and not a single word of English was spoken. The Italian was slow, methodical, and often repeated, but it never yielded to English. Marco found it difficult to enjoy a fine meal when his brain was working overtime to hear, grasp, digest, understand, and plot a response to the last phrase thrown at him. He was learning to listen, though, to catch the key words.

The food saved him. Of particular importance was the distinction between tortellini (small pasta stuffed with pork) and tortelloni (larger pasta stuffed with ricotta cheese). As always, Luigi explained that both were exclusively the creations of the great chefs of Bologna.

After two hours, Marco insisted on a break. He finished his second espresso and said goodbye. He left them in front of the restaurant and walked away, alone, his head spinning from the workout.

HE MADE a two-block loop off Via Rizzoli. Then he did it again to make sure no one was following. The long porticoed walkways were ideal for ducking and hiding. When they were thick with students again he crossed Piazza Verdi, stopped at 22 Via Zamboni and once again looked at the massive wooden door that led to the law school. He walked through it and tried his best to appear as if this was his turf. Through the hallway, the building yielded to an open courtyard where students were milling around.

A stairway to his left caught his attention. He climbed to the second floor, where he followed a corridor until he found the faculty offices. Most had names, a few did not. The last belonged to Rudolph Viscovitch, so far the only non-Italian name in the building.

Marco knocked and no one answered. He quickly removed from his coat pocket a sheet of paper he'd taken from the Albergo Campeol in Treviso and scribbled a note:

Dear Rudolph: I was wandering around the campus, stumbled upon your office and wanted to say hello. Maybe I'll catch you again at the Bar Fontana. Enjoyed our chat yesterday. Nice to hear English occasionally. Your Canadian friend, Marco Lazzeri

He slid it under the door and walked down the stairs behind a group of students. Back on Via Zamboni, he drifted along with no particular destination in mind, then slowly made his way back to his hotel.

LUIGI WAITED patiently at Bologna Centrale for the nonstop train from Milano. At 3.35, precisely on schedule, the sleek bullet blew in for a quick stop and Whitaker bounced off.

After a cursory handshake they walked to Luigi's Fiat. 'How's our boy?' Whitaker asked as soon as he slammed the door.

'Doing fine,' Luigi said as he started the engine and drove away. 'He's studying hard. There's not much else for him to do.'

'Is he scared?'

'I think so.'

'He's smart, and he's a manipulator, Luigi, don't forget that.'

'I told him about Critz.'

'Did it scare him?'

'Yes, I think so. He was bewildered. Who got Critz?'

'I'm assuming we did, but you never know. Is the safe house ready?'

'Yes.'

'Good. Let's see Marco's apartment.'

Via Fondazza was a quiet residential street in the southeast section of the old city, a few blocks south of the university. Most of the building had directories on brass plaques next to intercoms, but the one at 112 Via Fondazza was unmarked. It was a safe house, one of three currently under Whitaker's control in northern Italy.

There were two bedrooms, a tiny kitchen, and a living area with a sofa, a desk, two leather chairs, no television. Luigi pointed to the phone and they discussed, in near coded language, the bugging device that had been installed. There were two powerful hidden mikes in each room, that missed no human sound. There were also two microscopic cameras—one hidden in a crack of an old tile that offered a view of the front door. The other was hidden in a cheap light fixture with a clear view of the rear door.

They would not be watching his bedroom. If Marco managed to find a woman willing to visit him, they could catch her coming and going with the camera in the living room, and that was certainly enough for Luigi.

The safe house was bordered to the south by another apartment, with a thick stone wall separating the two. Luigi was staying there in a flat slightly larger than Marco's. His kitchen had been converted into a high-tech snooping room where he could switch on a camera at any time and take a look at what was happening next door.

'I think it's secure enough,' Luigi said. 'Plus I can monitor things.'

Whitaker had seen enough. 'How soon can you move him?'

'This afternoon.'

'Very well. Let's go see him.'

The rendezvous point was a small café called Lestre's. Luigi found a newspaper and sat alone at a table. Whitaker found another newspaper and sat nearby, each man ignoring the other. At four-thirty, Ermanno and his student stopped by for a quick espresso with Luigi.

When the greetings were exchanged and the coats removed, Luigi asked, 'Are you tired of Italian, Marco?'

'I'm sick of it,' Marco replied with a smile.

'Good. Let's talk English.'

'God bless you,' Marco said.

Whitaker had been in Washington a dozen or so years earlier, back when everyone knew the broker. He remembered Joel Backman as the epitome of money and power, the perfect fat cat who could bully and cajole and throw around enough money to get whatever he wanted.

Amazing what six years in prison could do. He was very thin now, and looking quite European behind the Armani eyewear. He had the beginnings of a salt-and-pepper goatee. Whitaker was certain that no one from back home could walk into Lestre's at that moment and identify Joel Backman.

Ermanno excused himself after one espresso. A few minutes later Whitaker left too. He walked a few blocks and found an Internet café. He plugged in his laptop, got online, and typed a message to Julia Javier:

> *Fondazza flat is ready to go, should move in tonight. Laid eyes on our man, having a coffee with our friends. Would not have known him otherwise. All in order here; no problems whatsoever.*

AFTER DARK, the Fiat stopped in the middle of Via Fondazza, and its contents were quickly unloaded—two bags of clothes and some Italian study books. When Marco stepped into his new apartment, the first thing he noticed was that it was sufficiently heated. 'This is more like it,' he said to Luigi.

He looked around, counted four rooms with nice furnishings, nothing extravagant but a huge step up from the last place. Life was improving—ten days ago he'd been in prison.

'Did you see the kitchen?' Luigi asked, flipping on a light switch.

'Yes, it's perfect. How long do I stay here, Luigi?'

'I don't make those decisions. You know that,' Luigi said.

They were back in the living room. 'A couple of things,' Luigi said. 'First, Ermanno will come here each day to study. Eight until eleven, then two until five or whenever you wish to stop. Second, this is a very quiet street, mainly apartments. Come and go quickly, don't chat with your neighbours, don't make any friends. Remember, Marco, you are leaving a trail. Make it wide enough and someone will find you.'

'Relax, Luigi. My neighbours will never see me, I promise. I like it here. It's much nicer than my prison cell.'

THE MEMORIAL SERVICE for Robert Critz was held in a country club-like mausoleum in a ritzy suburb of Philadelphia, the city of his birth. He died without a will, leaving Mrs Critz with the burden of not only getting him home from London but then deciding how to properly dispose of him. A son pressed the idea of cremation and a rather neat interment in a marble vault.

The service was by invitation only, a condition laid down by former president Arthur Morgan, who, after only two weeks on Barbados, was quite unwilling to return and be seen by anyone. If he was saddened by the death of his lifelong friend, he didn't show it. He reluctantly agreed to deliver a eulogy, but only if it could be very brief.

To the small circle of friends and family, it seemed implausible that Robert Critz would get so drunk in a London pub that he would stagger into a busy street and fall in front of a car. When the autopsy revealed a significant level of heroin, Mrs Critz had become distraught. She was absolutely certain her husband had never touched an illicit drug and she was determined to protect his good name.

The London police had readily agreed to lock away the autopsy findings and close the case. They had their questions all right, but they had many other cases to keep them busy, and they also had a widow who couldn't wait to get home and put it all behind her.

Rather than a heart-warming send-off, the service was as cold as the marble walls of the chapel. A Protestant minister of some variety presided.

Morgan attempted to humour the small crowd with some anecdotes about his old pal, but he came off as a man going through the motions.

Hours in the Caribbean sun had convinced Morgan that the blame for his disastrous re-election campaign could be placed squarely at the feet of Robert Critz and he'd already begun to carry a grudge. He didn't linger when the service came to an end. He offered obligatory hugs to Mrs Critz and her children then rushed away with his Secret Service escort. Five hours later he was by the pool watching another Caribbean sunset.

Though the memorial drew only a small crowd, it nonetheless was being keenly observed by others. While it was actually in progress, Teddy Maynard had a list of all fifty-one people in attendance. There was no one suspicious. No name raised an eyebrow.

The killing was clean. The autopsy was buried, thanks to strings pulled at levels much higher than the London police. The body was now ashes and the world would quickly forget about Robert Critz. His idiotic foray into the Backman disappearance had ended with no damage to the plan.

THE DAY BEFORE the death of Robert Critz, the FBI received some startling information. It was completely unsolicited, and delivered by a desperate corporate crook staring at forty years in a federal prison. He'd been the manager of a large mutual fund who had been caught skimming fees. But his mutual fund was owned by an international banking cabal, and over the years the crook had worked his way into the inner core of the organisation. He was voted onto the board of directors and given a luxury condo in Bermuda, the corporate headquarters for his very secretive company.

In his desperation to avoid spending the rest of his life in prison, he became willing to share secrets. Banking secrets. He claimed he could prove that former president Morgan, during his last day in office, had sold at least one pardon for $3 million. The money had been wired from a bank on Grand Cayman to a bank in Singapore, both banks being controlled by the cabal he'd just left. The money was still hiding in Singapore, in an account opened by a shell corporation that was owned by an old crony of Morgan's. The money, according to the snitch, was intended for Morgan's use.

When the wire transfers and the accounts were confirmed by the FBI, a deal was suddenly put on the table. The crook was now facing only two years of light house arrest. Cash for a presidential pardon was such a sensational crime that it became a high priority at the Hoover Building.

The informant was unable to identify whose money had left Grand

Cayman, but it seemed quite obvious to the FBI that only two of the people pardoned by Morgan had the potential of paying such a bribe. The first and likeliest was Duke Mongo, the geriatric billionaire who held the record for the most dollars illegally hidden from the IRS, at least by an individual. The corporate category was still open for debate.

The second suspect was, of course, Joel Backman. While the FBI had believed for many years that he had not hidden a fortune, there had always been doubt. When he was the broker he had relationships with banks in both Switzerland and the Caribbean. He had a web of shadowy friends, contacts in important places. Bribes, payoffs, campaign contributions, lobbying fees—it was all familiar turf for the broker.

The director of the FBI was an embattled soul named Anthony Price. He had been appointed by President Morgan three years earlier but the two had fought constantly. Price had also decided to prove his manhood by crossing swords with Teddy Maynard. Teddy hadn't lost many battles in the CIA's secret war with the FBI, and he certainly wasn't frightened by Price.

But Teddy didn't know about the cash-for-pardon conspiracy that now consumed the director of the FBI. The new President had vowed to get rid of Anthony Price and revamp his agency. He'd also promised to finally put Maynard out to pasture.

Price suddenly had a beautiful opportunity to secure his job, and eliminate Maynard at the same time. He went to the White House and briefed the national security adviser on the suspicious account in Singapore. He strongly implicated former president Morgan. He argued that Joel Backman should be located and hauled back to the United States for questioning. If proven to be true, it would be an earthshaking scandal.

The national security adviser listened intently. After the briefing, he walked directly to the office of the vice president, cleared out the staffers, and unloaded everything he'd just heard. Together, they told the President.

Even after an historic landslide and the thrill of reaching the White House, the new President was unwilling to rise above the mud. He adored the idea of once again humiliating Arthur Morgan. He could see himself, after a sensational trial and conviction, stepping in at the last minute with a pardon of his own to salvage the image of the presidency. What a moment!

At six the following morning, the vice president was driven to the CIA headquarters at Langley. Director Maynard had been summoned to the White House but, suspecting some ploy, had begged off, claiming he was suffering from vertigo and confined to his office by his doctors.

The meeting was brief. Teddy was sitting at the end of his long conference table, in his wheelchair, wrapped tightly in blankets, with Hoby at his side. The vice president entered with only one aide, and after some awkward chitchat about the new administration and such, he said, 'Mr Maynard, I'm here on behalf of the President.'

'Of course you are,' Teddy said with a tight smile. He was expecting to be fired; finally, after eighteen years and numerous threats, this was it.

Instead, the vice president said something completely unexpected.

'Mr Maynard, the President wants to know about Joel Backman.'

'What about him?' Teddy said without hesitation.

'He wants to know where he is and how long it will take to bring him home.'

'Why?'

'I can't say.'

'Then neither can I.'

'It's very important to the President.'

'I appreciate that. But Mr Backman is very important to our operations.'

The vice president blinked first. He inched forward on his elbows and said, 'The President is not going to compromise on this, Mr Maynard. He will have this information, and he'll have it very soon. Otherwise, he will ask for your resignation.'

'He won't get it.'

'Very well. The lines are clear. You come to the White House with the Backman file and discuss it with us or the CIA will have a new director.'

'Such bluntness is rare among your breed, sir, with all due respect.'

'I'll take that as a compliment.'

The meeting was over.

LEAKING LIKE AN OLD DIKE, the Hoover Building practically sprayed gossip onto the streets of Washington. And there to collect it was, among many others, Dan Sandberg of the *Washington Post*. His sources, though, were far better than those of the average investigative journalist, and it wasn't long before he picked up the scent of the pardon scandal. He worked an old mole in the new White House and got a partial confirmation. The outline of the story began to take shape. If it happened to be true—a sitting president selling pardons for cash—Sandberg could not imagine a bigger story.

He was at his landfill of a desk when the call came from London. It was an old friend, another hard-charging reporter who wrote for the *Guardian*.

'Anything on the death of Bob Critz?' his friend asked.

'No, just a funeral yesterday,' Sandberg replied. 'Why?'

'A few questions about how the poor chap went down, you know. That, and we can't get near the autopsy.'

'What kind of questions? I thought it was open-and-shut.'

'Maybe, but it got shut really fast. Nothing concrete, mind you, just fishing to see if there's anything amiss over there.'

'I'll make some calls,' Sandberg said, already very suspicious.

'Do that. Let's talk in a day or so.'

Sandberg hung up and stared at his blank computer monitor. There was a good chance that only Critz was in the Oval Office with Morgan when the last-minute pardons were signed. Perhaps Critz knew too much.

Three hours later, Sandberg left Dulles for London.

Chapter 7

Long before dawn, Marco once again awoke in a strange bed in a strange place. He had dozed for a few fitful hours; it felt like four or five but he couldn't be sure because his rather warm little room was completely dark.

He was thankful for the heat. He slowly placed his feet on the very warm tile floor and again thanked Luigi for the change of residence.

He switched on the light and checked his watch—almost five. In the bathroom he studied himself in the mirror. The growth under his nose and along the sides of his mouth and covering his chin was coming in quite a bit greyer than he had hoped. What the hell. He was fifty-two years old. It was part of the disguise. With the thin face, hollow cheeks, short haircut, and little funky rectangular designer eyeglass frames, he could easily pass for Marco Lazzeri on any street in Bologna.

An hour later he stepped outside and headed towards the university. He refused to use the map tucked away in his pocket. He was determined to learn the city by walking and observing. Thirty minutes later, he emerged onto Via Irnerio on the northern edge of the university section. Two blocks east and he saw the pale green sign for Bar Fontana. Through the front window he saw a shock of grey hair. Rudolph was already there.

Out of habit, Marco glanced down Via Irnerio, from the direction he'd just come. When no one appeared, he went inside.

'My friend Marco,' Rudolph said with a smile. 'Please sit.'

The café was half full, with the same academic types buried in their morning papers. Marco ordered a cappuccino while Rudolph refilled his meerschaum pipe.

'Got your note the other day,' Rudolph said as he shot a cloud of pipe smoke across the table. 'Sorry I missed you. So where have you been?'

As the laid-back Canadian tourist with Italian roots Marco had put together a mock itinerary. 'A few days in Florence,' he said.

'Ah, what a beautiful city.'

They talked about Florence for a while, with Marco rambling on about the sites and art and history of a place he knew only from a cheap guide-book Ermanno had loaned him. They ordered another round and Rudolph repacked his pipe. On the table were three morning newspapers, all Italian.

'Is there a good English newspaper here in Bologna?' Marco asked.

'I'll pick up the *Herald Tribune* occasionally. It makes me so happy that I live here, away from all the crime and traffic and pollution and politicians and scandals. US society is so rotten. And the government is the height of hypocrisy. I hate the US government,' Rudolph grumbled bitterly.

Attaboy, thought Marco. 'What about the Canadian?' he asked.

'I give you higher marks. Slightly higher.'

Marco pretended to be relieved and decided to change the subject. He said he was thinking of going to Venice next. Of course, Rudolph had been there many times and had lots of advice. Marco actually took notes, as if he couldn't wait to hop a train.

When it became apparent that Rudolph was willing to sit and talk through most of the morning, Marco began his exit. They agreed to meet at the same place, same time, the following Monday.

A light snow had begun and as Marco left the warm café behind, he cursed Luigi for his inadequate wardrobe—if it was going to snow then common sense would dictate that a person needed some boots.

The man himself strode alongside him. '*Buon giorno,*' Luigi said.

Marco stopped, smiled, offered a handshake and said, 'Well, *buon giorno*, Luigi. Are you following me again?'

'No. I was out for a walk, saw you pass on the other side of the street. I love the snow, Marco. How about you?'

Marco wanted to believe him but doubted their meeting was an accident.

'It's OK. It's much prettier here in Bologna than in Washington during rush hour traffic.' They were walking again, at a leisurely pace. 'Look, I have two complaints. Actually three.'

'No surprise. Have you had coffee?'

'Yes, but I'll take some more.'

Luigi nodded to a small corner café just ahead. They stepped inside and found all the tables taken, so they stood along the crowded bar and sipped espresso. 'What's the first complaint?' Luigi said in a low voice.

Marco moved closer. 'The first two complaints are closely related. First, it's the money. I would like to have some sort of stipend. No one likes to be broke, Luigi. I'd feel better if I had a little cash in my pocket.'

'How much?'

'Oh, I don't know. What about a hundred euros a week for starters. That way I can buy newspapers, books, magazines, food—you know, just the basics. Uncle Sam's paying my rent and I'm very grateful. Come to think of it, he's been paying my rent for the past six years.'

'You could still be in prison, you know.'

'Oh, thank you, Luigi. I hadn't thought of that.'

'I'm sorry, that was unkind on my—'

'Listen, Luigi, I'm lucky to be here, OK. But, at the same time, I am now a fully pardoned citizen of some country, not sure which one, but I have the right to be treated with dignity. I don't like being broke, and I don't like begging for money. I want the promise of a hundred euros a week.'

'I'll see what I can do.'

'Thank you.'

'The second complaint?'

'I would like some money so I can buy some clothes. Right now my feet are freezing because it's snowing outside and I don't have proper footwear. I'd also like a heavier coat, perhaps a couple of sweaters.'

'I'll get them.'

'No, I want to buy them, Luigi. Get me the cash and I'll do my own shopping. It's not asking too much.'

'The third complaint?' Luigi said.

'It's Ermanno. He's losing interest very fast. We spend six hours a day together and he's getting bored with the whole thing. You teach me. I like you, Luigi, we have good times together.'

'I am not a teacher.'

'Then please find someone else. I'm not making much progress.'

Luigi looked away and watched two elderly gentlemen enter and shuffle by. 'I think he's leaving anyway,' he said. 'He wants to go back to school.'

'I have a fourth complaint.'

'Five, six, seven. Let's hear them all.'

'You've heard it before, Luigi. I really want to be transferred to London where I won't waste ten hours a day trying to learn a language. If you're going to hide me, then stash me someplace where I can survive.'

'I've already passed this along, Marco. I'm not making these decisions.'

'I know, I know. Just keep the pressure on, please.'

'Let's go.'

The snow was heavier as they left the café and resumed their walk under the covered pavement. The street itself was busy as small cars and scooters dodged the city buses and tried to avoid the accumulating slush.

'How often does it snow here?' Marco asked.

'Not much, and we have these lovely porticoes to keep us dry. Some date back a thousand years, did you know that?'

'No. I have very little to read, Luigi. If I had some money then I could buy books, then I could read and learn such things.'

'I'll have the money at lunch.'

'And where is lunch?'

'Ristorante Cesarina, Via San Stefano, one o'clock.'

LUIGI WAS SITTING with a woman at a table near the front of the restaurant when Marco entered, five minutes early. The woman stood, reluctantly, and offered a limp hand and a sombre face as Luigi introduced her as Signora Francesca Ferro. She was attractive, in her mid-forties, and radiated an air of sophisticated irritation.

As they settled into their seats Luigi said to Marco, 'Signora Ferro is a language teacher and a local guide.'

Marco glanced at the signora and smiled, to which she responded with a forced smile of her own. She appeared to be bored with him already.

Luigi continued in Italian. 'She is your new Italian teacher. Ermanno will teach you in the mornings, and Signora Ferro in the afternoons.' Marco managed a smile in her direction and said, 'Va bene.' That's good.

Francesca fired up a cigarette and crunched her full red lips around it. She exhaled a huge cloud of smoke and said, 'So, how is your Italian?' Her English was slow, very refined, and without an accent.

'Terrible,' Marco said.

'He's doing fine,' Luigi said. The waiter handed over the menus. A long silent spell followed as they contemplated food and ignored each other.

Finally she said to Marco, 'I'd like to hear you order in Italian.'

'No problem,' he said. He'd found some things he could pronounce without drawing laughter. The waiter appeared and Marco said, '*Sì, allora, vorrei un'insalata di pomodori, e una mezza porzione di lasagna.*' Yes, OK, I'd like a salad with tomatoes and a half portion of lasagna.

'*Non c'è male,*' she said. Not bad.

She and Luigi stopped smoking when the salads arrived. Eating gave them a break in the awkward conversation. His past and hers were off-limits, so they bobbed and weaved through the meal with light talk about the weather, almost all of it mercifully in English.

When the espressos were finished Luigi grabbed the check and they hurried from the restaurant. In the process, and while Francesca wasn't looking, he slid an envelope to Marco and whispered, 'Here are some euros.'

'*Grazie.*'

The snow was gone, the sun was up and bright. Luigi left them at the Piazza Maggiore. They walked in silence for a while, until she said, '*Che cosa vorrebbe vedere?*' What would you like to see?

Marco had yet to step inside the main cathedral, the Basilica di San Petronio. They walked to its sweeping front steps and stopped. 'It's both beautiful and sad,' she said in English. 'The original design was for it to be even larger than Saint Peter's Cathedral, but the plans fell short. The pope opposed it, and Rome diverted money elsewhere, some of which went to the founding of the university.'

'When was it built?' Marco asked.

'Say that in Italian,' she instructed.

'I can't.'

'Then listen: "*Quando è stata costruita?*" Repeat that for me.'

Marco repeated it four times before she was satisfied.

'I don't believe in books or tapes or such things,' she said. 'To learn to speak the language, then you have to speak it, over and over and over, just like when you were a child.'

'Where did you learn English?' he asked.

'I can't answer that. I've been instructed to say nothing about my past. And yours too.'

For a split second, Marco came very close to turning around and walking away. He was sick of people who couldn't talk to him.

'Would you like to see inside the cathedral?' she asked.

'*Certamente,*' he said.

They climbed the steps and stepped inside. Other than a group of Japanese tourists the cathedral was empty. It was a Friday in February, not exactly peak tourist season.

They saw all twenty-two side chapels and looked at most of the paintings, sculptures, and frescoes. The chapels, built over the centuries by wealthy Bolognesi families, were a history of the city, and Francesca knew every detail. Though sometimes inundated with names and dates, Marco gamely held on as the tour inched around the massive structure. Her voice captivated him, her rich slow delivery, her perfectly refined English.

Long after the Japanese had abandoned the cathedral, they made it back to the front door. They stepped outside and she immediately lit a cigarette.

'How about some coffee?' he said.

'I know just the place.'

He followed her across the street to Via Clavature; a few steps down and they ducked into Rosa Rose. 'It's the best cappuccino around,' she assured him as she ordered two at the bar. He started to ask her about the prohibition of drinking cappuccino after ten-thirty in the morning, but let it pass.

They took a table near the front window. She stirred in two sugars until things were just perfect. She hadn't smiled in the past three hours, and Marco was not expecting one now.

'I have a copy of the materials you're using with the other tutor,' she said, reaching for the cigarettes. 'I suggest that each afternoon we do conversation based on what you have covered that morning.'

'Fine,' he said with a shrug.

She lit a cigarette, then sipped the coffee.

'What did Luigi tell you about me?' Marco asked.

'Not much. You're a Canadian. You're taking a long vacation through Italy and you want to study the language. Is that true?'

'Are you asking personal questions?'

'No, I simply asked if that was true.'

'It's true.'

'It's not my business to worry about such matters.'

'I didn't ask you to worry.'

She had mastered the distracted pouty look so popular among European women. She held the cigarette close to her face, her eyes studying the pavement and seeing nothing. Idle chitchat was not one of her specialities.

'Are you married?' he asked.

A grunt, a fake smile. 'I have my orders, Mr Lazzeri.'

'Please call me Marco. And what should I call you?'

'Signora Ferro will do for now.'

'But you're ten years younger than me.'

'Things are more formal here, Mr Lazzeri.' She stubbed out the cigarette, took another sip, and got down to business. 'We've done English for the last time, Mr Lazzeri. Next lesson, we do nothing but Italian.'

'Fine, but I'd like for you to keep one thing in mind. You're not doing me any favours, OK? You're getting paid. If we don't get along, then I'll find someone else to study with.'

'Have I offended you?'

'You could smile more.'

She nodded slightly and her eyes were instantly moist. She looked away, through the window, and said, 'I have so little to smile about.'

THE SHOPS along Via Rizzoli opened at 10 a.m. on Saturday and Marco was waiting, studying the merchandise in the windows. With the 500 fresh euros in his pocket, he had no choice but to go in and survive his first real shopping experience in Italian. As the door closed behind him he prayed for a nice young clerk who spoke perfect English.

Not a word. It was an older gentleman with a warm smile. In less than fifteen minutes, Marco had pointed and stuttered and, at times, done quite nicely when asking sizes and prices. He left with a pair of hiking boots, a black waterproof parka with a hood and almost 300 euros still in his pocket. Hoarding cash was his newest priority.

He hustled back to his apartment, changed into the boots and the parka, then left again. The thirty-minute walk to Bologna Centrale took almost an hour with the snaking and circuitous route he used. He never looked behind him, but instead would duck into a café and study the foot traffic. If they were following, he didn't want them to know he was suspicious.

There was a moment of anxiety at the train station when he walked inside, saw the crowd, and looked about desperately for the ticket window. He waited in line and when a window was open he stepped up quickly, smiled at the little lady on the other side of the glass, and said, '*Vado a Milano.*' I'm going to Milan. '*Alle tredici e venti.*' At 1.20.

'*Sì, cinquanta euro,*' she said. Fifty euros.

He gave her a 100-euro bill because he wanted the change, then walked away clutching his ticket and patting himself on the back.

The train arrived on schedule, and Marco followed the crowd as it hurried on board. He grabbed the first available window seat. His car was less than half full when the train began moving, at exactly 1.20.

They were soon out of Bologna and the countryside was flying by. After a while he nodded off. An hour later a rush of gibberish over the loudspeaker announced something to do with Milano, and the scenery began to change dramatically. The sprawling city soon engulfed them as the train slowed. Ermanno's guidebook gave the population of Milano at four million; an important city, the country's centre for finance, fashion, publishing and industry.

They entered the rail yards of Milano Centrale and came to a stop under the vast dome of the station. When Marco stepped onto the platform he was startled at the sheer size of the place. He studied the departures: Stuttgart, Rome, Florence, Madrid, Paris, Berlin, Geneva.

All of Europe was within his reach, just a few hours away.

He followed the signs to the front entrance and found the taxi stand, where he hopped in the back seat of a small white Renault. '*Aeroporto Malpensa*,' he said to the driver. They crawled through heavy Milano traffic then twenty minutes later they left the autostrada for the airport. '*Quale compagnia aerea?*' the driver asked over his shoulder. Which airline?

'Lufthansa,' Marco said. At Terminal 2 the cab found a spot at the curb, and Marco turned loose another forty euros. The automatic doors opened to a mass of people. He checked the departures and found what he wanted—a direct flight to Dulles. He found the Lufthansa check-in desk. A long line was waiting, things were moving quickly.

The first prospect was an attractive redhead of about twenty-five who appeared to be travelling alone. She was second in line at the business-class desk. Marco followed her as she left the counter with her boarding card. As she was headed to the gate, and the first security checkpoint, Marco made his move. 'Excuse me, miss.' She couldn't help but turn and look at him.

'Are you by chance going to Dulles?' he asked with a huge smile and the pretence of being out of breath, as if he'd just sprinted to catch her.

'Yes,' she snapped. No smile. American.

'So was I, but my passport has just been stolen. Don't know when I'll get home.' He was pulling an envelope out of his pocket. 'This is a birthday card for my father. Could you please drop it in the box when you get to Dulles? His birthday is next Tuesday, and I'm afraid I won't make it.'

She looked at both him and the envelope suspiciously.

He was yanking something else out of his pocket. 'Sorry, there's no stamp. Here's a euro. Please, if you don't mind.'

The face finally cracked, and she almost smiled. 'Sure,' she said, taking both the envelope and the euro and placing them in her purse.

'Thank you so much,' Marco said. 'It's his ninetieth birthday. Thank you.'

'Sure, no problem,' she said.

Mrs Ruby Ausberry of York, Pennsylvania, was one of the last passengers at check-in. She had taught world history in high school for forty years and was now having a delightful time spending her retirement funds travelling to places she'd only seen in textbooks. The nice gentleman approached her with a desperate smile and explained that his passport had just been stolen. He would miss his father's ninetieth birthday. She gladly took the card and placed it in her bag. She cleared security and walked to the gate.

Behind her, less than fifteen feet away, the redhead reached a decision. It could be one of those letter bombs. It certainly didn't seem thick enough to carry explosives, but what did she know about such things? There was a waste can near the window. She dropped the letter into the bin.

Marco's taxi ride back to Milano Centrale cost forty-five euros and his return ticket to Bologna was fifty euros. He was down to around 100 euros. His little stash of cash was dwindling rapidly.

It was almost dark when the train slowed at the station in Bologna. Marco was just another weary traveller when he stepped onto the platform, but he was silently bursting with pride at the day's accomplishments. He'd purchased clothing, bought rail tickets, survived the madness of both the train station and the airport in Milano, hired two cabs, and delivered his mail, without a hint of anyone knowing who or where he was.

LUIGI HAD TAKEN a different train, the 11.45 express to Milano. But he stepped off at Parma and got lost in the crowd. He found a cab and took a short ride to the meeting place, a favourite café. As usual, Whitaker was in a foul mood. They ordered quickly and as soon as the waiter was gone, Whitaker said, 'I don't like this woman, Francesca. We've never used her before, right?'

'Right. Relax, she's fine. She doesn't have a clue.'

'What does she look like?'

'Reasonably attractive.'

'Reasonably attractive can mean anything, Luigi. How old is she?'

'I never ask that question. Forty-five is a good guess.'

'Is she married?'

'She married an older man who's in very bad health. He's dying.'

As always, Whitaker was scribbling notes. 'Where'd you find her?'

'It wasn't easy. A friend recommended her. She has a good reputation in the city. And she's available. She agreed to work every afternoon for the next month or so. It's the slow season for guides. Relax, she's good.'

'What's her fee?'

'Two hundred euros a week, until spring when tourism picks up.'

Whitaker rolled his eyes. 'Marco's costing too much,' he said.

'He wants a transfer. He wants to go to Australia or New Zealand or someplace where the language won't be a problem.'

'That's not our decision, is it, Luigi?'

'I guess not.'

The salads arrived and they were quiet for a moment. Then Whitaker said, 'I still don't like this woman. Marco has a history with women. There's always the potential for romance. She could complicate things.'

'I've warned her. And she needs the money.'

'She's broke?'

'I get the impression things are very tight. It's the slow season, and her husband is not working.'

Whitaker almost smiled, as if this was good news. 'Let's talk about e-mail. Marco was never much of a hacker. Back in his glory days he lived on the phone. Never used the computer. He rarely sent e-mails, and when he did it was always through a secretary.'

'What about prison?' Luigi asked.

'No evidence of e-mail. He had a laptop that he used only for letters, never e-mail. Langley's concerned that he might try and contact someone on the outside. He can't do it by phone, at least not now. He has no address he can use, so mail is probably out of the question.'

'He'd be stupid to mail a letter. It might divulge his whereabouts.'

'Exactly. Same for the phone, fax, everything but e-mail.'

'We can track e-mail.'

'Most of it, but there are ways around it.'

'He has no computer and no money to buy one.'

'I know, but, hypothetically, he could sneak into an Internet café, send the e-mail, then clean his trail and walk away.'

'Sure, but who's gonna teach him how to do that?'

'He can learn. He can find a book. It's unlikely, but there's a chance.'

'I'm sweeping his apartment every day,' Luigi said. 'Every inch of it. If he buys a book or lays down a receipt, I'll know it.'

'Scope out the Internet cafés in the neighbourhood. There are several of them in Bologna. Where's Marco right now?'

'I don't know. It's Saturday, a day off. He's probably roaming the streets of Bologna, enjoying his freedom.'

'And he's still scared?'

'He's terrified.'

MRS RUBY AUSBERRY slept from Milano to Dulles International. The coffee they served before landing did little to clear the cobwebs, and as the 747 taxied to the gate she dozed off again. She forgot about the birthday card as she waited to claim her baggage and plod through customs. And she forgot about it when she saw her granddaughter waiting for her at the arrival exit.

She forgot about it until she was safely at home in York, Pennsylvania, and shuffling through her bag for a souvenir. 'Oh my,' she said as the card fell onto the kitchen table. 'I was supposed to drop this off at the airport.' Then she told her granddaughter the story of the poor guy in the Milan airport who lost his passport and would miss his father's ninetieth birthday.

Her granddaughter looked at the envelope. 'Doesn't look like a birthday card,' she said. She studied the address: R. N. Backman, Attorney at Law, 412 Main Street, Culpeper, Virginia, 22701.

'I'll mail it first thing in the morning,' Mrs Ausberry said. 'I hope it arrives before the birthday.'

Chapter 8

At ten on Monday morning in Singapore, the mysterious $3 million sitting in the account of Old Stone Group, Ltd, made an electronic exit and began a quiet journey to the other side of the world. Nine hours later, when the doors of the Galleon Bank and Trust opened on the Caribbean island of Saint Christopher, the money was deposited in a numbered account. Normally it would have been an anonymous transaction but Old Stone now had the full attention of the FBI. The bank in Singapore was cooperating fully. The bank on Saint Christopher was not, though it would soon get the opportunity to participate.

When Director Anthony Price arrived in his office at the Hoover Building before dawn on Monday, the hot memo was waiting. He cancelled everything planned for that morning. Then he called the vice president.

It took four hours of undiplomatic arm-breaking to shake the information loose on Saint Christopher. When the vice president threatened the prime minister with economic sanctions he knuckled under and turned on his bankers.

The numbered account could be directly traced to Artie Morgan, the thirty-one-year-old son of the former president. However, there was still no evidence as to the source of the money.

The scandal was ripening by the hour.

His TUTOR was waiting in the back pew of the Basilica di San Francesco. It was snowing again outside, and in the vast, empty sanctuary the temperature was not much warmer. He sat beside her and said, '*Buon giorno.*'

She acknowledged him with just enough of a smile to be considered polite, and said, '*Buon giorno.*'

As usual, her face was sad and her thoughts were somewhere else. Marco was fed up with her attitude. Ermanno was losing interest by the day. Luigi was always lurking back there, but he, too, seemed to be losing interest. Marco was beginning to think that the break was about to happen. Cut the lifeline and set him adrift to sink or swim on his own. So be it. He'd been free for almost a month. He'd learned enough Italian to survive.

She shifted slightly, cleared her throat and asked him in Italian, 'What did you study this morning with Ermanno?'

'*La famiglia.*'

'*La sua famiglia. Mi dica.*' Tell me about your family.

'It's a real mess,' he said in English. Then he caught himself. He was not Joel Backman, with three ex-wives. He was Marco Lazzeri from Toronto, with a wife, four children, and five grandchildren.

'*Mi dica, in Italiano, di sua moglie?*' Tell me about your wife.

Fortunately, Luigi had given him a little biography on Marco Lazzeri. In very slow Italian, Marco described his fictional wife. Her name is Laura. She is fifty-two years old. She lives in Toronto. And so on. Every sentence was repeated at least three times. Over and over, Marco went on and on about a Laura who did not exist.

Francesca prodded him on, urging perfection, cautioning against speaking too fast. She was strict and no fun, but if he could learn to speak Italian half as well as she spoke English, then he would be ahead of the pack.

An elderly gentleman entered the church and sat in the pew directly in front of them. A light snow was still falling and they ventured back onto the covered pavements and began a thorough lesson about snow. She delivered a short sentence in English, and he was supposed to translate it.

They skirted the edge of the main plaza and stayed under the porticoes. At an intersection they stopped and looked at Le Due Torri, Asinelli and Garisenda, the two towers that the Bolognesi were so proud of.

'Asinelli has four hundred and ninety-eight steps to the top,' she said.

'*Andiamo,*' Marco said quickly. Let's go. They entered the thick foundation through a narrow door, followed a tight circular staircase up to the ticket booth where he bought two tickets, and they started the climb. The tower was hollow, with the stairs fixed to the outside walls.

Francesca took off, up the narrow, sturdy oak steps, with Marco keeping his distance behind. 'Pace yourself,' she called over her shoulder, in English, as she slowly pulled away from Marco.

She was soon out of sight. About halfway up, he stopped at a large window so the wind could cool his face. He caught his breath, then took off again, even more slowly now. After 498 steps he finally stepped onto the top of the tower. Francesca was smoking a cigarette, gazing upon her beautiful city, no sign of sweat anywhere on her face.

The view from the top was panoramic. The red tile roofs of the city were covered with two inches of snow. The pale green dome of San Bartolomeo was directly under them. 'On a clear day, you can see the Adriatic Sea to the east, and the Alps to the north,' she said, still in English. Her eyes were alive, her voice radiant. 'It's just beautiful, even in the snow.'

'Just beautiful,' he said, almost panting.

'This always reminds me of why I love my city,' she said with a rare smile. They stepped to the other side and looked in the distance to the southwest. On a hill above the city they could see the outline of Santuario di San Luca, the guardian angel of the city.

'Have you been there?' she asked.

'No.'

'We'll do it one day when the weather is nice, OK?'

If the climb to the top of the Asinelli Tower had buoyed her spirits, the trip down brought back the same old dour demeanour. They had a quick espresso near the towers and said goodbye. As she walked away, no superficial hug, no cheek-pecking, not even a cursory handshake, he decided he would give her one more week. He put her on secret probation. She had seven days to become nice, or he'd stop the lessons. Life was too short.

She was very pretty, though.

THE ENVELOPE had been opened by his secretary, but inside the first envelope was another, this one addressed simply to Neal Backman. In bold print on the front and back were the warnings: personal, confidential. The envelope was postmarked York, Pennsylvania. The printing looked familiar.

With a letter opener, he slowly cut along the top of the envelope, then pulled out a single sheet of folded white paper. It was from his father. It was a shock, but then it was not.

> *Dear Neal:*   *Feb. 21*
>
> *I'm safe for now but I need your help. I have no address, no phone, no fax. I need access to e-mail, something that cannot be traced. I have no idea how to do this, but I know you can figure it out. I have no computer and no money. There is a good chance you are being watched, so whatever you do, you must not leave a trail. Trust no one. Destroy this letter. Send me as much money as possible. You know I'll pay it back. Never use your real name on anything. Use the following address:*
>
> *Sr. Rudolph Viscovitch, Università degli Studi, University of Bologna, Via Zamboni 22, 44041, Bologna, Italy. Use two envelopes—the first for Viscovitch, the second for me. In your note to him ask him to hold the package for Marco Lazzeri.*
>
> *Hurry!*   *Love, Marco*

Neal placed the letter on his desk and walked over to lock his door. He tried to arrange his thoughts. He had already decided his father was out of the country, otherwise he would've made contact weeks earlier. Why was he in Italy? Why was the letter posted from York, Pennsylvania? Joel was not a topic Neal liked to think about. He had been absent for most of his childhood, and his astounding plunge from power had embarrassed everyone close to him. Neal had sent letters during the incarceration, but he could truthfully say that he did not miss his father.

Neal walked to his desk and read the letter again, then again. It was the same method of operation, whether at home or at the office. Do this, this, and this, and everything will work. Do it my way, and do it now! Hurry! Risk everything because I need you.

Life had been much simpler with his father in prison.

Neal's wife, Lisa, had never met her father-in-law. He'd been in prison for two years when they met. They had sent photos of the wedding, and later a photo of their child, Joel's second granddaughter.

What would he tell her? Honey, that $2,000 we have in our savings account has just been spoken for. And you and the baby keep the doors locked at all times because life just became much more dangerous.

With the day shot to hell, Neal buzzed his secretary and asked her to hold his calls. He stretched out on the sofa, kicked off his loafers, closed his eyes, and began massaging his temples.

AS A SMALL-TOWN LAWYER in Culpeper, Virginia, Neal Backman was earning far less than what he had dreamed about in law school. Back then, his father's firm was such a force in D.C. that the greenest associates at Backman, Pratt & Bolling started at $100,000 a year, and a rising junior partner thirty years of age would earn three times as much. However, less than a year after signing on as a green associate, he was sacked by the firm after his father pled guilty, and was literally thrown out of the building.

But Neal had soon stopped dreaming of the big money. He was perfectly content to practise law with a nice little firm on Main Street and hopefully take home $50,000 a year. Lisa stopped working when their daughter was born. She managed the finances and kept their lives on budget.

After a sleepless night, he awoke with a rough idea of how to proceed. The most painful issue had been whether to tell his wife. Once he decided not to, the plan began to take shape. He went to the office at eight, and puttered online for an hour and a half, until he was sure the bank was open.

Richard Koley ran the nearest branch of Piedmont National Bank. Neal's law firm had banked there for ever. Richard was already at his desk with a tall cup of coffee. He was pleasantly surprised to see Neal, and for twenty minutes they talked about college basketball. When they eventually got around to business, Richard said, 'So what can I do for you?'

'Just curious,' Neal said casually. 'How much might I borrow with just my signature? Rates are so low and I've got my eye on a hot stock.'

Richard was grabbing the mouse and already glancing at the monitor, where all the answers were stored. 'Not a bad strategy. With the Dow at ten thousand again you wonder why more folks don't load up with credit and buy stocks.' He managed an awkward banker's chuckle. 'Income range?' he asked, tapping keys.

'It varies,' Neal said. 'Sixty to eighty.'

'Total debts, outside the mortgage?' Richard asked, tapping again.

'Hmmm, let's see.' Neal closed his eyes. His mortgage was almost $200,000 and Lisa was so opposed to debt that their own little balance sheet was remarkably clean. 'Car loan of about twenty grand,' he said. 'Maybe a thousand or so on the credit cards.'

Richard nodded his approval and never took his eyes off the monitor. When his fingers left the keyboard, he shrugged and turned into the generous banker. 'We could do three thousand on a signature. Six per cent interest, for twelve months.'

'Can you go four thousand?' Neal asked.

Another frown, another hard study of the monitor, then it revealed the answer. 'Sure, why not? I know where to find you, don't I?'

Richard was opening a drawer, looking for forms. Neal said, 'Look, Richard, this is just between us boys. Lisa won't be signing the papers.'

'No problem,' the banker said. 'My wife doesn't know half of what I do on the financial end. Women just don't understand.'

'You got it. And would it be possible to get the funds in cash?'

A pause, a puzzled look, but then 'Sure, give me an hour or so.'

'I need to run to the office and sue a guy, OK? I'll be back around noon to sign everything and get the money.'

Neal hustled to his office with a nervous pain in his stomach. Lisa would kill him if she found out, and in a small town secrets were hard to bury. In four years of a very happy marriage they had made all decisions together.

Repaying the money would pose a challenge. His father had always been one to make easy promises. Sometimes he came through, sometimes he didn't. What the hell. It was only $4,000. Neal would worry about the loan later. His primary concern at that moment was the package to be shipped to Rudolph Viscovitch.

WITH THE CASH bulging in his pocket, Neal fled Culpeper during the lunch hour and hurried up to Alexandria, ninety minutes away, where he found the store, Chatter, in a small strip mall. It advertised itself online as the place to go for the latest in telecom gadgetry, and one of the few places in the United States where one could purchase unlocked cellphones that would work in Europe.

He asked a clerk to show him the Ankyo 850 PC Pocket Smartphone, the greatest technological marvel to hit the market in the past ninety days. The clerk removed it from a display case and, with great enthusiasm, said, 'It's slightly larger than the typical business phone but it's packed with goodies— e-mail, multimedia messaging, camera, video player, word processing, Internet browsing—and complete wireless access almost anywhere in the world. Where are you going with it?'

'Italy.'

'It's ready to go. You'll just need to open an account with a service provider.'

Opening an account meant leaving a trail, something Neal was determined not to do. 'What about a prepaid SIM card?' he asked.

'We got 'em. For Italy it's called a TIM—Telecom Italia Mobile. It's the largest provider in Italy, covers about ninety-five percent of the country.'

'I'll take it.'

The price was $925 plus tax, plus another $89 for the TIM card. Neal paid in cash as he simultaneously declined the extended warranty and owner's programme, anything that would create paperwork and leave a trail. The clerk asked for his name and address and Neal declined.

He left and drove half a mile to a large office supply store. He quickly found a Hewlett-Packard Tablet PC with integrated wireless capability. Another $440 got invested in his father's security, though Neal would keep the laptop and hide it in his office. He found the PackagePost in another strip mall nearby. Inside, at a shipping desk, he hurriedly wrote two pages of instructions for his father, then folded them into an envelope containing a letter. He wedged twenty $100 bills in the small black carrying case that came with the Ankyo marvel. Then he placed the letter and the instructions, the smartphone, and the case inside a mailing carton from the store. He sealed it tightly, and on the outside he wrote with a black marker PLEASE HOLD FOR MARCO LAZZERI. The carton was then placed inside another, slightly larger one that was addressed to Rudolph Viscovitch at Via Zamboni 22, Bologna. The clerk weighed the package, added stamps, and finally said, 'Total is eighteen dollars and twenty cents.'

Neal paid him and was assured that it would be mailed that afternoon.

IN THE SEMIDARKNESS of his small apartment, Marco went through his early-morning routine with his usual efficiency. He'd never been one to linger after waking. There was too much to do, too much to see. He'd often arrived at his office before 6 a.m. breathing fire and looking for the day's first brawl.

He showered in less than three minutes. Over the lavatory he shaved and worked carefully around the quite handsome growth he was cultivating on his face. The moustache was almost complete; the chin was solid grey. He looked nothing like Joel Backman.

His quick morning routine included a little espionage. Someone, Luigi he presumed, entered his room every day while he was studying with either Ermanno or Francesca and went through the drawers.

His desk was in the small living room, under the only window. On it he kept an assortment of papers, notepads, books; a guide to Bologna, a few copies of the *Herald Tribune* and his well-used Italian-English dictionary. But amid the rubble was an invisible scheme. In the dead centre of the desk was a small stain of some sort, probably ink. Every morning, as he was leaving, Marco placed the corner of a sheet of paper directly in the centre of the ink stain. Not even the most diligent of spies would have noticed.

And they didn't. Whoever sneaked in for the daily sweep had not once been careful enough to place the paper back in its precise location. Every day, seven days a week, Luigi and his gang entered and did their dirty work.

Marco wanted to know who else was watching him. How large was the net? If their concern was simply to keep him alive, then why would they sift through his apartment every day? What were they afraid of?

They were afraid he would disappear. And why should that frighten them so? He was a free man and his disguise was good. His language skills were rudimentary but improving daily. Why should they care if he simply drifted away? Wouldn't that make their lives easier? And why keep him on such a short leash, with no passport and very little cash?

He turned off the lights and opened the door. It was still dark outside under the arcaded pavements of Via Fondazza. He locked the door behind him and hurried away, off in search of another early-morning café.

Through the thick wall, Luigi was awakened by the same buzzer that awakened him most mornings at such dreadful hours.

'What's that?' she said.

'Nothing,' he said as he flung the covers in her direction and stumbled, naked, out of the room. He hurried across the living room to the kitchen, where he unlocked the door, stepped inside, and looked at the monitors on a folding table. Marco was leaving through his front door, as usual. And at ten minutes after six, again, nothing unusual about that.

He pushed a button and the monitor went silent. Procedures required him to get dressed immediately, hit the streets, find Marco, and watch him until Ermanno made contact. But Luigi was growing tired of procedures. And he had Simona waiting.

She was barely twenty, a student from Naples, an absolute doll he'd met a week earlier at a club he'd discovered. Last night had been their first together, and it would not be their last. She was already sleeping again when he returned and buried himself under the blankets.

IT WAS A CLEAR, sunny day in early March. Marco finished a two-hour session with Ermanno, who signed off a little early, claiming he had studies of his own to pursue. They shook hands and said goodbye in front of Feltrinelli's, one of the many bookstores in the university section. Luigi appeared from around a corner. '*Buon giorno. Pranziamo?*' Are we having lunch?

'*Certamente.*'

The lunches were becoming less frequent, with Marco getting more chances to dine by himself and handle the menu and the service.

'*Ho trovato un nuovo ristorante.*' I have found a new restaurant. They walked through some narrow streets and came to Via dell' Indipendenza. 'Francesca has a tour this afternoon,' Luigi said. 'A group of Australians called her yesterday. Is she a good teacher?'

'Excellent. Her perfect English inspires me to study more.'

'She says you study very hard, and that you are a nice man.'

'She likes me?'

'Yes, as a student. Do you think she's pretty?'

'Most Italian women are pretty, including Francesca.'

They turned onto a small street, Via Goito, and stopped at the door to Franco Rossi's. 'I've never been here,' Luigi said, 'but I hear it's very good.'

Franco himself greeted them with a smile and open arms. He took their coats and chatted with Luigi as if they were old friends. A table near the front window was selected.

'Our best one,' Franco said with a gush. 'The antipasti here are superb,' Franco added modestly. 'My favourite of the day, however, would be the sliced mushroom salad. The chef adds some truffles, some Parmesan, a few sliced apples . . .' At that point Franco's words faded as he kissed the tips of his fingers.

They agreed on the salad and Franco was off to welcome the next guests. A waiter stopped by and asked about wine. 'Certainly,' Luigi said. 'I'd like something red, from the region.'

The waiter stabbed his pen at the wine list and said, 'This one here, a Liano from Imola. It is fantastic.' Luigi had no choice. 'We'll try it.'

'We were talking about Francesca,' Marco said. 'She seems so distracted. Is something wrong with her?'

Luigi dipped some bread in a bowl of olive oil and chewed on a large bite while debating how much to tell Marco. 'Her husband is not well,' he said.

'Does she have children?'

'I don't think so.'

'What's wrong with her husband?'

'He's very sick. I think he's older. I've never met him.'

Il Signore Rossi was back to guide them through the menus. He explained that the tortellini were particularly superb that day. After the tortellini, an excellent choice would be the veal fillet with truffles.

For more than two hours they followed Franco's advice, and when they left they pushed their stomachs back down Via dell' Indipendenza and discussed their siestas.

HE FOUND HER by accident at the Piazza Maggiore. He was having an espresso at an outdoor table, braving the chill in the bright sunshine after a vigorous thirty-minute walk, when he saw a small group of fair-haired seniors coming out of the Palazzo Comunale, the city's town hall. A familiar figure was leading, a thin, slightly built woman, her dark hair falling out from under a burgundy beret.

He left one euro on the table and headed towards them. At the fountain of Neptune, he eased in behind the group and listened to Francesca at work. She was explaining that the gigantic bronze image of the Roman god of the sea was commissioned by a bishop in 1563 under an urban beautification programme aimed at pleasing the pope. Francesca was a bit livelier with the real tourists than she was with Marco. Her voice had more energy, her smile came quicker. She was wearing a pair of very stylish glasses that made her look ten years younger.

She explained that the Fontana del Nettuno is now one of the most famous symbols of the city. Cameras were pulled from every pocket, and at one point, Marco managed to move close enough to make eye contact with Francesca. When she saw him she smiled, then said a soft '*Buon giorno.*'

'*Buon giorno.* Mind if I tag along?' he asked in English.

'No. Sorry I had to cancel.'

'No problem. How about dinner? To study, of course,' he said.

'No, I'm sorry,' she said. She looked beyond him, across the piazza to the Basilica di San Petronio. 'That little café over there,' she said, 'beside the church. Meet me there at five and we'll study for an hour.'

The tour continued a few steps to the west wall of the Palazzo Comunale, where she stopped them in front of three large framed collections of black-and-white photos. The history lesson was that during World War II the Bolognesi hated Mussolini, his fascists and the German occupiers, and worked diligently in the underground. The Nazis retaliated with a vengeance—in a series of fifty-five massacres in and around Bologna they murdered thousands of young Italian fighters. Their names and faces were on the wall, for ever memorialised.

As Francesca moved on with her group, Marco stayed behind, staring at the faces that covered much of the long wall. He was struck by their youth-fulness, by their promise that was for ever lost—slaughtered for their brav-ery. There were hundreds, maybe thousands of them. Peasants willing to die for their country and their beliefs. But not Marco. No sir. When forced to choose between loyalty and money, Marco had done what he always did. He'd gone for the money. He'd turned his back on his country.

All for the glory of cash.

SHE WAS STANDING inside the door of the café, waiting, not drinking anything but, of course, having a smoke.

'Do you feel like walking?' she said before she said hello.

'Of course.' After a month of doing several miles a day he was in shape. 'Where?'

'It's a long one,' she said.

They wound through narrow streets, heading to the southwest, chatting slowly in Italian. Near the edge of the old city they approached the Porta Saragozza and Marco realised where he was, and where he was going.

'Up to San Luca,' he said.

'Yes. The weather is very clear, the night will be beautiful.'

Sitting almost 1,000 feet above the city on the Colle della Guardia, the Santuario di San Luca has, for eight centuries, looked over Bologna as its protector and guardian. To get up to it, without getting wet or sunburned, the Bolognesi decided to build a covered pavement. Beginning in 1674, and continuing without interruption for sixty-five years, they built arches; 666 arches over a walkway that eventually runs for 3.6 kilometres, the longest porticoed pavement in the world.

The hike up was a steady climb, and they paced themselves accordingly. After 100 arches, his calves were screaming for relief. She, on the other hand, glided. He kept waiting for all that cigarette smoking to slow her down.

When they reached the crest and stepped from under the 666th portico, the magnificent basilica was spread before them. Its lights were coming on as darkness surrounded the hills above Bologna, and its dome glowed in shades of gold. 'It's closed now,' she said. 'We'll have to see it another day. This way,' she said, beckoning him over. 'I know a secret path.'

He followed her along a gravel trail behind the church to a ledge where they stopped and took in the city below them. 'This is my favourite spot,' she said, breathing deeply, as if trying to inhale the beauty of Bologna.

'Could we sit somewhere?'

'Yes, there is a small bench hidden over there.' He followed her down a few steps, then along a rocky path to another ledge with views just as spectacular. 'Are your legs tired?' she asked.

'Of course not,' he lied.

She lit a cigarette and they sat in silence for a long time, both resting, both thinking and gazing at the shimmering lights of Bologna.

Marco finally spoke. 'Luigi tells me your husband is very ill. I'm sorry.'

She glanced at him with a look of surprise, then turned away. 'Luigi told me the personal stuff is off-limits.'

'Luigi changes the rules. What has he told you about me?'

'You're from Canada, travelling around, trying to learn Italian.'

'Do you believe that?'

'Not really.'

'Why not?'

'Because you claim to have a wife and a family, yet you leave them for a long trip to Italy. And if you're just a businessman off on a trip, then where does Luigi fit in? And Ermanno? Why do you need those people?'

'Good questions. I have no wife.'

'So it's all a lie.'

'Yes.'

'What's the truth?'

'I can't tell you.'

She lit another cigarette.

'Do you tell Luigi everything we do?' he asked.

'I tell him very little.'

'Good.'

Chapter 9

Teddy's last visit to the White House was scheduled for 10 a.m. Beginning at seven that morning, he met with his team—all four deputy directors and his senior people. In quiet little conferences he informed those he'd trusted for many years that he was on the way out.

At precisely 8.45, while meeting with William Lucat, his deputy director, he summoned Julia Javier for their Backman meeting.

Julia Javier sat next to the ever-vigilant Hoby. She began matter-of-factly. 'He's still in Bologna, so if we had to activate now we could do so.'

'I thought the plan was to move him to a village in the countryside, someplace where we could watch him more closely,' Teddy said.

'That's a few months down the road.'

'We don't have a few months.' Teddy turned to Lucat, 'What happens if we push the button now?'

'They'll get him somewhere in Bologna. It's a nice city with almost no crime, so his death will get some attention if his body is found there. The Italians will quickly realise that he's not—what's his name, Julia?'

'Marco,' Teddy said without looking at notes. 'Marco Lazzeri.'

Julia said, 'There's no clue as to his real identity. They'll have a body, a fake ID, but no family, no friends, no address, no job, nothing. They'll bury him like a pauper and keep the file open for a year. Then they'll close it.'

'That's not our problem,' Teddy said. 'We're not doing the killing.'

'Right,' said Lucat. 'It'll be a bit messier in the city, but the boy likes to wander the streets. They'll get him. Maybe a car will hit him.'

'And what are our chances of knowing when it happens?' Teddy asked.

Lucat scratched his beard and looked across the table at Julia. 'I'd say fifty-fifty. We'll be watching twenty-four/seven, but the people who'll take him out will be the best of the best. There may be no witnesses.'

Julia added, 'Our best chance will be later, a few weeks after they bury him as a pauper. We have good people in place. I think we'll hear it later.'

'We cannot screw this up, understand? It'll be nice to know that Backman is dead—God knows he deserves it—but the goal of the operation is to see who kills him,' Teddy said as he slurped green tea loudly. 'If we leak it now, how long before he's dead?'

'It depends,' Lucat said cautiously. 'If the Israelis move, it could happen in a week. The Chinese are usually slower. The Saudis will probably hire a freelance agent; it could take a month to get one on the ground. The Russians could do it in a week.'

'I won't be here when it happens,' Teddy said sadly. 'And no one on this side of the Atlantic will ever know. Promise me you'll give me a call.'

'This is the green light?' Lucat asked.

'Yes. Careful how you leak it, though. All hunters must be given an equal chance at the prey.'

They gave Teddy their final farewells and left his office. At nine-thirty, Hoby pushed him into the hall and to the elevator. They rode down eight levels to the basement where the bulletproof white vans were waiting for his last trip to the White House.

THE MEETING WAS BRIEF. Dan Sandberg was sitting at his desk at the *Post* when it began in the Oval Office a few minutes after ten. And he hadn't moved twenty minutes later when the call came from Rusty Lowell, Sandberg's most reliable source at the CIA. Sandberg was reasonably confident that anything he got from Lowell was doled out by Teddy himself.

'It's over,' Lowell said.

'What happened?' Sandberg asked, already pecking at his keyboard.

'As scripted. The President wanted to know about Backman. Teddy wouldn't budge. The President said he was entitled to know everything. Teddy said the information would compromise a sensitive operation. They argued briefly. Teddy got himself fired. Just like I told you.'

'Wow.'

'The White House is making an announcement in five minutes.'

The spin began immediately. The sombre-faced press secretary announced that the President had decided to 'pursue a fresher course with our intelligence operations.' He praised Director Maynard for his legendary leadership. The first question, shot from the front row, was whether Maynard resigned or had been fired.

'The President and Director Maynard reached a mutual understanding.'

'What does that mean?'

'Just what I said.'

And so it went for thirty minutes.

Sandberg's front-page story the following morning dropped two bombs. It began with the definite confirmation that Maynard had been fired after he refused to divulge sensitive information for what he deemed to be raw political purposes. The second blast announced to the world that the President's insistence on obtaining intelligence data was directly tied to a new FBI investigation into the selling of pardons. Sandberg's scoop practically stopped traffic on the Arlington Memorial Bridge.

While Sandberg was hanging around the press room, revelling in his coup, his cellphone rang. It was Lowell, who said, 'Call me on a land line.' Sandberg went to an office and dialled Lowell's number at Langley.

'Lucat just got fired,' Lowell said. 'At eight o'clock this morning he met with the President in the Oval Office. The President pushed on Backman. Lucat wouldn't budge. Got himself fired, just like Teddy.'

'Damn, he's been there a hundred years. Who's next?'

'That's a very good question. Ever meet Susan Penn?'

'No. I know who she is, but I never met her.'

'Deputy director for science and technology. She's in the Oval Office right now. If she's offered the interim, she'll take it. And she'll give up Backman to get it.'

'He is the President, Rusty. He's entitled to know everything.'

'Of course. He's new on the job, wants to flex his muscle.'

'So the FBI should know about Backman real soon?'

'Today, I would guess. Not sure what they'll do when they find out where he is. They'll probably just screw up our operation.'

'Where is he?'

'Don't know.'

'Come on, Rusty, things are different now.'

'The answer is no. End of story. I'll keep you posted on the bloodletting.'

An hour later, the White House press secretary met with the press and announced the appointment of Susan Penn as interim director of the CIA.

LUIGI WAS SITTING on the edge of his bed, fully dressed and alone, waiting for the signal from next door. It came at fourteen minutes after 6 a.m.— Marco was becoming such a creature of habit. Luigi walked to his control room and silenced the buzzer that indicated that his friend had exited through the front door. A computer recorded the exact time and within seconds someone at Langley would know that Marco Lazzeri had just left their safe house on Via Fondazza at precisely 6.14.

Luigi waited a few seconds, slipped out of his back door, then peeked through the shadows of the arcades along Via Fondazza. Marco was headed south and walking at his usual brisk pace, which was getting faster the longer he stayed in Bologna. He was twenty years older than Luigi, but with his penchant for walking miles every day he was in better shape.

He wore the new boots every day. Luigi had not been able to get his hands on them. They remained bug-free, leaving no signal behind. Whitaker worried about this, but then he worried about everything.

Marco turned onto Via San Stefano. Luigi crossed over and followed from the other side. As he practically jogged along, he radioed Zellman, a new guy in town, sent by Whitaker to tighten the web. Zellman's arrival was an indication of the plan moving forward. Luigi knew most of the details now, and was somewhat saddened by the fact that Marco's days were numbered. He wasn't sure who would take him out, and he was praying that he would not be called upon to do the deed. He liked Marco.

Before Zellman picked up the trail, Marco vanished. Luigi stopped and listened. He ducked into a doorway, just in case Marco had stopped too.

MARCO HEARD HIM back there, walking a little too heavily, breathing a little too hard. A quick left on Via Castellata, a sprint for fifty yards, then another left onto Via de' Chiari, and a complete change of direction. He knew the old city so well now, the avenues, alleys, the endless maze of crooked little streets. He could lose Luigi any time he wanted, though most days he played along and kept his trails wide and easy to follow. But it was the fact that he was being watched so closely that spoke volumes.

They don't want me to disappear, he kept saying to himself. And why? Because I'm here for a reason.

After almost an hour of zigzagging through dozens of short streets and alleys, he stepped onto Via Irnerio and watched the foot traffic. Bar Fontana was directly across the street. There was no one watching it.

Rudolph was tucked away in the rear, head buried low in the morning paper, pipe smoke rising in a lazy blue spiral. They hadn't seen each other in ten days, and after the usual warm greetings Rudolph's first question was 'Did you make it to Venice?'

Yes, a delightful visit. Marco dropped the names of all the places he'd memorised from the guidebook.

Where to next? Rudolph enquired. Maybe Sicily, the Amalfi coast. Rudolph, of course, adored Sicily and described his visits there. After half an hour of travel talk, Marco finally got around to business.

'I'm travelling so much, I really have no address. A friend is sending me a package. I gave him your address at the law school. Hope you don't mind.'

'It came yesterday,' Rudolph said. 'From some place in Virginia.'

Marco's heart skipped a beat. 'Hope it wasn't a problem.'

'Not at all.'

'I'll swing by later and pick it up.'

'I'm in the office from eleven to twelve-thirty.'

A COLD RAIN started at midmorning. Marco and Ermanno were walking through the university area and found shelter in a quiet little bar. They finished the lesson early. Ermanno was always ready to quit early.

Since Luigi had not booked lunch, Marco was free to roam, presumably without being followed. But he was careful just the same. He did his loops and backtracking manoeuvres, and back on Via Zamboni he drifted behind a group of students strolling aimlessly along. At the door to the law school he ducked inside, bounded up the stairs, and within seconds was knocking on Rudolph's half-opened door.

Rudolph was hammering away at his ancient typewriter. 'Over there,' he said, pointing to a table. 'That brown thing on top.'

Marco picked up the package. 'Thanks again, Rudolph,' he said, but Rudolph was typing again and in no mood for a visit.

'Don't mention it,' he said over his shoulder.

'Is there a restroom nearby?' Marco asked.

'Down the hall, on your left.'

There was a prehistoric urinal and three wooden stalls. Marco went into the far one, locked the door, lowered the lid, and took a seat. He carefully opened his package and unfolded the sheets of paper. When he saw the words 'Dear Marco,' he felt like crying.

Dear Marco:

Needless to say, I was thrilled to hear from you. I thanked God when you were released and as you know, I will do anything to help.

Here is a state of the art Ankyo 850 PC Pocket Smartphone—fully charged battery—6 hours talk time before recharging, recharger included. This should work fine over there. I've written some instructions on another sheet of paper. I know this will sound like Greek, but it's really not that complicated.

Don't try and call—it's too easy to track. E-mail is the way. Find an Internet café with wireless access or get within 200 feet of it.

*By using KwyteMail with encryption, it's impossible to track our
messages. I suggest that you e-mail only me. On this end I have a
new laptop that I keep near me at all times. My e-mail address is
123Grinch@kwytemail.com*

*This will work, Marco. Trust me. As soon as you're online, e-mail
and we can chat. Good luck, Grinch*   *(March 5)*

Grinch? A code or something. He had not used their real names.

Marco studied the sleek device, thoroughly bewildered by it but also
determined to get the damn thing going. He probed its small case, found the
cash, and counted it slowly as if it were gold.

The page of step by step instructions for sending e-mail was handwritten, obviously when Neal didn't have a lot of time. More notes followed on
the other side, but for Marco, the smartphone was growing heavier by the
minute. For a man who'd never been in an Internet café, he could not begin
to understand how one could be used from within 200 feet of it.

There was an instruction booklet that he opened at random. He read a
few lines and didn't understand a single phrase.

You have no choice here, Marco. You have to master this damn thing.

From a Web site called www.AxEss.com Neal had printed a list of free
wireless Internet places in Bologna—three cafés, and one bookstore.

Marco folded his cash, stuck it in his pocket, then slowly put his package
back together and left the restroom. The phone, the papers, the case and the
small recharger were easily buried in the deep pockets of his parka.

The rain had turned to snow when he left the law school. As he drifted
away from the university area, he pondered ways to hide the wonderful little
assets Neal had sent him—where could he stash them? Nothing was protected in his apartment. He saw in a store window an attractive shoulder bag
of some sort. He went and enquired. It was a Silvio brand laptop case, navy
blue, waterproof. It cost sixty euros, and Marco reluctantly placed them on
the counter. Then he carefully placed the smartphone and its related items
into the bag. Outside, he flung it over his shoulder and tucked it snugly
under his right arm. The bag meant freedom for Marco Lazzeri. He would
guard it with his life.

He found the bookstore on Via Ugo Bassi. The Internet hookups were on
the second floor, in a small coffee shop. He bought a pastry and a Coke and
found a booth where he could sit and watch everyone going and coming.

He pulled out his Ankyo 850 with as much confidence as he could
muster and glanced through its manual. He reread Neal's instructions. He

followed them nervously, typing on the tiny keypad with both thumbs. After each step he looked up to check the movements around the café.

The steps worked perfectly. He was online in short order, much to his amazement, and when the codes worked he was looking at a screen that was giving him the OK to write a message. Slowly, he moved his thumbs around and typed and sent his first wireless Internet e-mail:

Grinch: Got the package. You'll never know how much it means to me. Thank you for your help. Are you sure our messages are completely secure? It's about 8.30 a.m. your time. I'll send this message now, and check back in a few hours. Love, Marco

AT AN UNNUMBERED, nondescript building on Pinsker Street in downtown Tel Aviv, an agent named Efraim entered from the pavement and walked past the elevator to a dead-end corridor with one locked door. There was no knob, no handle. He pulled a device that resembled a small television remote from his pocket and aimed it at the door. Thick tumblers fell somewhere inside, a sharp click, and the door opened into one of the many safe houses maintained by the Mossad, the Israeli secret police. It had four rooms—two with bunk beds where Efraim and his three colleagues slept, a small kitchen, and a large cluttered workroom where they spent hours every day planning an operation that had been practically dormant for six years but was suddenly one of the Mossad's highest priorities.

The four were members of *kidon,* a small, tight unit of highly skilled field agents whose primary function was quick, efficient assassination. Their targets were enemies of Israel who could not be brought to trial because its courts could not get jurisdiction. The men and women of *kidon* were fully licensed to kill for their country.

Efraim tossed a bag of pastries onto one of the folding tables where Rafi and Shaul were ploughing through research. Amos was in a corner at the computer, studying maps of Bologna, Italy.

Most of their research was stale; it had been collected years ago when Backman's killing had first been approved. A preliminary plan to kill him in a car accident in Washington had been jettisoned when he suddenly pled guilty and fled to prison. Not even a *kidon* could reach him at Rudley.

The background was important now only because of his son. Since Joel Backman's surprise pardon and disappearance seven weeks earlier, the Mossad had kept two agents close to Neal. They'd bugged his home and office, and from a lab in Tel Aviv, they read every one of his office e-mails and those from home as well. They monitored his bank account and his credit card spending. They knew he'd made a quick trip to Alexandria six days earlier, but they did not know why. They were watching Backman's mother too, in Oakland.

They wanted Backman dead, but they also wanted him to live a few hours before passing on. They needed to ask some questions, and if the answers weren't forthcoming they knew how to make him talk.

'Do we have an address?' Amos asked from the computer.

'No, not yet,' said Efraim. 'And I'm not sure we'll get one. We're supposed to get a photo of Backman. There's one somewhere, taken recently, after prison. Getting a copy is a possibility.'

'That would certainly be helpful,' Rafi said.

In 1998 the Mossad had first heard rumours of the JAM software that was being shopped around by a powerful Washington lobbyist. Working through their ambassador in Washington, the Israelis pursued the purchase of JAM, thought they had a deal, but were stiff-armed when Backman and Jacy Hubbard took their goods elsewhere. The selling price was never made known. Some money changed hands, but Backman, for some reason, did not deliver the product. Where was it now? Had it ever existed in the first place? Only Backman knew.

The six-year hiatus in the hunt for Joel Backman had given the Mossad ample time to fill in some gaps. They believed that the Chinese had spent a hefty chunk of their national treasury in building the so-called Neptune satellite system; that they had stolen technology from the Americans to do so; that they had brilliantly disguised the launching of the system and fooled US, Russian, and Israeli satellites; and that they had been unable to reprogramme the system to override the software JAM had uploaded. Neptune was useless without JAM, and the Chinese would give up their Great Wall to get their hands on it and Backman.

The Mossad also believed that Farooq Khan, the last surviving member of the trio, had been tracked down by the Chinese and murdered eight months ago. They also believed the Americans were still not sure who built Neptune, and this intelligence failure was an ongoing embarrassment. American satellites had dominated the skies for forty years. Now it appeared to the intelligence world that Neptune was more advanced than anything the United States had ever launched.

These were only assumptions; little had been confirmed. The only copy of JAM had been hidden. Its creators were dead.

Time was very short. The Chinese would blow up half of Italy if they thought Backman would end up in the rubble. The Americans might try and get him too. On their soil he was protected by their Constitution. But on the other side of the world he was fair game.

NEAL BACKMAN kept his new laptop in the same old battered briefcase he hauled home every night. He kept it close, always within a step or two.

He changed his morning routine slightly. He'd bought a card from Jerry's Java, a fledgling drive-through coffee and doughnut chain that was trying to lure customers with fancy coffee and free newspapers, magazines and wireless Internet access.

There were three cars in front of him at the drive-through window. His laptop was on his knees, just under the steering wheel. At the curb, he ordered a double mocha, and waited for the cars in front to inch forward. He pecked away with both hands as he waited. Once online, he went to KwyteMail, typed in his user name—Grinch123—then his pass phrase. Seconds later there it was—the first message from his father.

It worked! The old man had figured it out!

Quickly, he typed:

Marco: Our messages cannot be traced. You can say anything you want, but it's always best to say as little as possible. Delighted you're there and out of Rudley. I'll go online each day at this time—at precisely 7.50 a.m. EST. Gotta run. Grinch

He placed the laptop in the passenger seat, lowered his window, and paid almost four bucks for a cup of coffee.

LAST NOVEMBER, after Arthur Morgan's astounding defeat, Teddy Maynard began devising his Backman pardon strategy. With his customary meticulous planning, he prepared for the day when moles would leak the word of Backman's whereabouts. To tip the Chinese, and do so in a manner that would not arouse suspicion, Teddy began looking for the perfect snitch.

Her name was Helen Wang, a Chinese American who'd worked for eight years at Langley as an analyst on Asian issues. She was very smart, very attractive, and spoke Mandarin Chinese. Teddy got her an assignment at the State Department, and there she began cultivating contacts with diplomats from Red China, some of whom were spies themselves and most of whom were constantly on the prowl for new agents.

When Helen Wang 'accidentally' let it slip that her background included a few years at the CIA, and that she hoped to return soon, she quickly had the attention of intelligence chiefs in Beijing. She accepted an invitation from a new friend to have lunch at a swanky D.C. restaurant, then dinner. She played her role beautifully, always reticent about their overtures but always reluctantly saying yes. Her detailed memos were hand delivered to Teddy after every encounter.

When Backman was suddenly freed from prison, and it became apparent he'd been stashed away, her friends undercover at the Chinese embassy put tremendous pressure on Helen Wang. They offered her $100,000 for information about his location. She appeared to be frightened by the offer, and for two weeks she broke off contact.

Then she called them and demanded $1 million, claiming that she was risking her career and her freedom. The Chinese agreed.

The day after Teddy was fired, she called her handler and requested a secret meeting. She gave him a sheet of paper with wiring instructions to a bank account in Panama, one that was secretly owned by the CIA. When the money was received, she said, they would meet again and she would have the location and a recent photo of Joel Backman.

The drop was a 'brush by', an actual physical meeting between mole and handler. After work, Helen Wang stopped at a Kroger store in Bethesda. She walked to the aisle where the magazines and paperbacks were displayed. Her handler was loitering at the rack with a copy of *Lacrosse Magazine*. Helen picked up another copy of the same magazine, quickly slid an envelope into it, and put the magazine back on the rack. Then she wandered away, but only after she saw her handler take her copy of *Lacrosse Magazine*.

The envelope contained one sheet of paper—a colour photo of Joel Backman as he was apparently walking down the street. He was much thinner, had the beginnings of a greyish goatee, European-style glasses, and was dressed like a local. Handwritten at the bottom of the page was: Joel Backman, Via Fondazza, Bologna, Italy. The handler gawked at it as he sat in his car, then he sped away to the embassy of the People's Republic of China on Wisconsin Avenue NW in Washington.

AT FIRST the Russians seemed to have no interest in the whereabouts of Joel Backman. Much to the surprise of the intelligence world, Russia was managing to keep aloft a robust 160 reconnaissance satellites a year, roughly the same number as the former Soviet Union. For years the Russians had secretly maintained that the so-called Neptune system was one of their own, and this had contributed mightily to the confusion at the CIA.

In 1999, a defector from the GRU, the Russian military's intelligence arm and successor to the KGB, informed the CIA that Neptune was not the property of the Russians. They had been caught off guard as badly as the Americans. Suspicion was focused on the Red Chinese.

The Russians wanted to know about Neptune, but they were not willing to pay for information about Backman. When the overtures from Langley were largely ignored, the same colour photo sold to the Chinese was anonymously e-mailed to four Russian intelligence chiefs.

THE LEAK to the Saudis was handled through an American oil executive stationed in Riyadh. His name was Taggett and he'd lived there for more than twenty years. He was fluent in Arabic and was especially close to a mid-level bureaucrat in the Saudi Foreign Ministry office. Over late-afternoon tea he told him that his company had once been represented by Backman. Further, Taggett claimed to know where Backman was hiding.

Five hours later, Taggett was awakened by a buzzing doorbell. Three young gentlemen in business suits pushed their way into his apartment, explaining that they were with some branch of the Saudi police, and really needed to talk. When pressed, Taggett reluctantly passed on the information he had been coached to disclose. Joel Backman was hiding in Bologna, Italy, under a different name. That was all he knew.

Could he find out more? they asked. Would he leave the next morning for his company's headquarters in New York, and dig for more information. It was very important to the Saudi government and the royal family.

Taggett agreed to do so. Anything for the king.

Chapter 10

E very year in May, just before Ascension Day, the people of Bologna march up the Colle della Guardia, along the longest continuous arcade in the world, to the summit, to the Santuario di San Luca. In the sanctuary they remove their Madonna and proceed back down to the city, where they parade her through the crowded streets and finally place her in the Cathedral of San Pietro, where she stays for eight days. It's a festival unique to Bologna, and has gone on uninterrupted since 1476.

As Francesca and Marco sat in the Santuario di San Luca, Francesca was describing the ritual and how much it meant to the people of Bologna. They had taken the bus this time, thus avoiding the hike up the hill. Marco's calves still hurt from the last visit to San Luca, three days ago.

They left the sanctuary and sneaked around behind the church, to her secret pathway that led down a few steps to the best view of the city. The last snow was melting quickly. It was the eighteenth of March.

She lit a cigarette and seemed content to loiter in silence and admire Bologna. 'Do you like my city?' she asked, finally.

'Yes, very much.'

'What do you like about it?'

After six years in prison, any city would do. He thought for a moment, then said, 'It's a real city, with people living where they work. It's safe and clean, timeless. The people are proud of their history.'

She nodded, approving of his analysis. 'I'm baffled by Americans,' she said. 'When I guide them through Bologna they're always in a hurry, always anxious to see one sight so they can cross it off the list and move on to the next. I've never seen so many people racing around, going nowhere. I don't understand. Everything has to be so fast—work, food, sex.'

'I haven't had sex in six years.'

She puffed on the cigarette. 'Why haven't you had sex in six years?'

'Because I was in prison, in solitary confinement.'

She flinched slightly. 'Did you kill someone?'

'No, nothing like that. I'm pretty harmless.'

Another pause, another puff. 'Why are you here?'

'I really don't know.'

'How long will you stay?'

'Maybe Luigi can answer that.'

'Luigi,' she said as if she wanted to spit. She turned and began walking. He followed. 'What are you hiding from?' she asked.

'It's a very, very long story, and you really don't want to know.'

'Are you in danger?'

'I think so. I'm not sure how much, but let's just say that I'm afraid to use my real name and I'm afraid to go home.'

'Sounds like danger to me. Where does Luigi fit in?'

'He's protecting me, I think.'

'For how long?'

'I really don't know.'

'Why don't you simply disappear?'

'That's what I'm doing now. I'm in the middle of my disappearance. And from here, where would I go? I have no money, no passport, no identification. I don't officially exist.'

'This is very confusing.'

'Yes. Why don't we drop it.'

He glanced away for a second and did not see her fall. She was wearing black leather boots with low heels, and the left one twisted violently on a rock in the narrow pathway. She gasped, fell hard onto the walkway, and shrieked something in Italian. Marco quickly knelt down to grab her.

'It's my ankle,' she said, her pretty face twisted in pain.

He gently lifted her from the wet pathway and carried her to a nearby bench. 'I'm sorry,' she kept saying. She fought the tears but soon gave up.

'It's OK, it's OK,' Marco said, kneeling in front of her and touching it with great care.

'I think it's broken,' she said. She pulled a tissue from her purse and wiped her eyes. She was breathing heavily and gritting her teeth. 'I'm sorry.'

'It's OK.' Marco looked around; they were very much alone. 'Don't move. I'll, uh, go inside and find help.'

He hustled away, almost falling himself. He ran to the rear of the church and saw no one. Outside, he circled San Luca twice before he saw a custodian emerge from a partially hidden door by the gardens.

'*La mia amica si é fatta male.*' My lady friend is hurt, he called out.

'*Dov'è?*' the man grunted. Where?

Marco pointed, '*Lì, dietro alla chiesa.*' Over there, behind the church.

'*Aspetti.*' Wait. He turned and walked back to the door and opened it.

A minute or two dragged by, before a gentleman in a suit came rushing out with the custodian behind him.

'*La mia amica è caduta,*' Marco said. My friend fell.

'Where is she?' asked the gentleman in excellent English.

'Around back, by the lower ledge. It's her ankle; she thinks she broke it.'

The gentleman snapped something at the custodian, who disappeared.

Francesca was sitting on the edge of the bench with as much dignity as possible. She held the tissue at her mouth; the crying had stopped. She and the gentleman chatted in Italian, and Marco missed most of it.

Her left boot was still on, and it was agreed that it should remain so, to prevent swelling. 'It's just a bad sprain,' she said. 'I don't think it's broken.'

'An ambulance will take for ever,' the gentleman, a Mr Coletta, said. 'I'll drive you to the hospital.'

A horn honked nearby. The custodian had fetched a car and pulled up as close as possible.

'I think I can walk,' Francesca said gamely, trying to stand. Marco and Mr Coletta each grabbed an elbow and slowly raised her to her feet. She grimaced when she put pressure on the foot, but insisted on walking. They half carried her towards the car.

Mr Coletta arranged them in the back seat so that her feet were in Marco's lap, elevated, and her back was resting against the left rear door. He jumped behind the wheel and they crawled onto a narrow paved road. Soon, they were moving down the hill, headed for Bologna.

Marco noticed a trickle of blood on Francesca's left knee. He took the tissue from her hand and began to dab it. 'Thank you,' she whispered. 'I'm sorry I've ruined your day.'

'Please stop that,' he said with a smile.

It was actually the best day with Francesca. The fall was making her seem human. It was evoking, however unwilling, honest emotions. It was allowing sincere physical contact, one person genuinely trying to help another. As he held her feet and stared out of the window, Marco realised how desperately he craved a relationship of any kind, with any person.

At the bottom of the hill, she said to Mr Coletta, 'I would like to go to my apartment.'

He looked in the rearview mirror and said, 'But you should see a doctor.'

'Maybe later. I'll rest for a bit and see how it feels.'

'Very well,' said Mr Coletta.

'It's Via Minzoni, near the train station.'

Marco held her feet, her stylish but well-used black boots slightly soiling his wool slacks. At that moment, he couldn't have cared less. When they turned onto Via Minzoni, she said, 'Down two blocks, on the right.' A moment later she said, 'Just ahead. There's a spot behind that green BMW.'

They gently got her to the pavement, where she tried to walk. The ankle gave way; they caught her. 'I'm on the first floor,' she said, gritting her teeth. There were eight apartments. Marco watched carefully as she pushed the button next to the name of Giovanni Ferro. A female voice answered.

'Francesca,' she said, and the door clicked. They stepped into a foyer that was dark and shabby. To the right was an elevator with its door open, waiting. The three of them filled it tightly. 'I'm really fine now,' she said, obviously trying to lose both Marco and Mr Coletta.

'We need to get ice on it,' Marco said as they began a slow ride up.

The elevator made a noisy stop and they shuffled out, both men still holding Francesca by the elbows. Her apartment was only a few steps away, and when they arrived at the door Mr Coletta said, 'I'm very sorry about this. If there are medical bills, would you please call me?'

'No, you're very kind. Thank you so much.'

'Thank you,' Marco said. He rang the doorbell and waited as Mr Coletta ducked back in the elevator. She pulled away and said, 'This is fine, Marco. I can manage from here. My mother is house-sitting today.'

He was hoping for an invitation inside, but he smiled, released her arm, and was about to say goodbye when a lock clicked loudly from inside. She turned towards the door, and her wounded ankle buckled again, causing her to gasp and reach for him.

The door opened just as Francesca fainted.

HER MOTHER was Signora Altonelli, a seventyish lady who spoke no English. Marco carried Francesca to the sofa, raised her feet, and conveyed the concept of '*Ghiaccio, ghiaccio.*' Ice, get some ice. She reluctantly backed away, then disappeared into the kitchen.

Francesca was stirring by the time her mother returned with a wet washcloth and a small plastic bag of ice.

'You fainted,' Marco said, hovering over her.

'*Chi è?*' her mother said suspiciously. Who's he?

'*Un amico.*' A friend. He patted her face with the washcloth and she rallied quickly. She explained to her mother what had happened. Signora Altonelli smiled and patted him on the shoulder with approval. Good boy.

When she disappeared, Francesca said, 'She's gone to make coffee.'

'Great.' He pulled a stool next to the sofa. 'We need to get some ice on this thing,' he said. He unzipped the right boot and removed it as though that foot had been injured too. He went even slower with the left one. Every little movement caused pain. After a few long minutes of delicate wiggling, while the patient suffered with clenched teeth, the boot was off.

Her mother was back, with a glass of water, two pills and some ice. Signora Altonelli arranged the ice around the left ankle.

'She says it's not broken,' Francesca said to him. 'She worked in a hospital for many years.'

Francesca gulped the pills down and propped her head up on some pillows. She exchanged short sentences with her mother then said, 'She has a chocolate torta in the refrigerator. Would you like some?'

'Yes, thank you.'

And her mother was off again, pleased that she had someone to care for and someone to feed. Marco resumed his place on the stool. 'Does it hurt?'

'Yes, it does,' she said, smiling. 'I cannot lie. It hurts.' She closed her eyes and appeared to be napping. Marco crossed his arms over his chest and stared at a huge, very odd painting that covered almost an entire wall.

The building was ancient, but from the inside Francesca and her husband had fought back as determined modernists. The furniture was low, sleek black leather with bright steel frames, very minimalist. The walls were covered with baffling contemporary art.

'We can't tell Luigi about this,' she whispered.

'Why not?'

'He is paying me two hundred euros a week to tutor you, Marco, and he's complaining about the price. He has threatened to find someone else. Frankly, I need the money. Things will pick up in a month when the tourists come south, but right now I'm not earning much.'

He couldn't believe that she was allowing herself to be so vulnerable. The lady was frightened, and he would break his neck to help her.

'I'm sure he will terminate my services if I skip a few days.'

'Well, you're about to skip a few days,' he said.

'Can we keep it quiet? I should be able to move around soon.'

'We can try to keep it quiet, but Luigi has a way of knowing things. He follows me closely. I'll call in sick tomorrow, then we'll figure out something the next day. Maybe we could study here.'

'No. My husband is here.'

Marco couldn't help but glance over his shoulder. 'Here?'

'He's in the bedroom, very ill.'

'What's—'

'Cancer. The last stages. My mother sits with him when I'm working. A hospice nurse comes in each afternoon to medicate him.'

'I'm sorry.'

'So am I.'

'Don't worry about Luigi. I'll tell him I'm thrilled with your teaching style, and that I will refuse to work with anyone else.'

'That would be a lie, wouldn't it?'

'Sort of.'

Signora Altonelli was back with a tray of torta and espresso. She placed it on a coffee table in the middle of the room and began slicing. Francesca took the coffee but didn't feel like eating. Marco ate as slowly as humanly possible and when Signora Altonelli insisted on another slice, he accepted.

Marco stayed about an hour. Riding down in the elevator, he realised that Giovanni Ferro had not made a sound.

RED CHINA'S principal intelligence agency, the Ministry of State Security, or MSS, used small, highly trained units to carry out assassinations around the world, in much the same manner as the Russians, Israelis, British and Americans. One notable difference, though, was that instead of spreading the dirty work around, the Chinese had come to rely on a young man the CIA and Mossad had been watching with great admiration for several years. His name was Sammy Tin, the product of two Red Chinese diplomats. Born in New York City, he'd been educated by private tutors who bombarded him with foreign languages from the time he left diapers. He entered the University of Maryland at the age of sixteen, left it with two degrees at twenty-one. Somewhere along the way he picked up bomb-making as a hobby, with an emphasis on controlled explosions from odd packages—envelopes, paper cups, ballpoint pens. He was an expert marksman, but guns bored him. The Tin Man loved his bombs.

He then studied chemistry under an assumed name in Tokyo, and there he mastered the art of killing with poisons. By the time he was twenty-four he had a dozen different names and crossed borders with a vast array of passports and disguises. To round out his education, he spent a gruelling year in training with an elite Chinese army unit. When he was twenty-six, the MSS decided the boy had studied enough. It was time to start killing.

As far as Langley could tell, he began notching his astounding body count with the murders of three Red Chinese scientists who'd gotten too cosy with the Russians. He got them over dinner at a restaurant in Moscow. While their bodyguards waited outside, one got his throat slit in the men's room while he finished up at the urinal. The second made the mistake of worrying about the first. He went to the men's room, where the Tin Man was waiting. They found him with his head stuffed down the toilet. The third died seconds later at the table. A man in a waiter's jacket hurried by, and without slowing thrust a poison dart into the back of his neck.

As killings go, it was quite sloppy. Too much blood, too many witnesses.

Escape was dicey, but the next day the Tin Man was in Beijing, quietly celebrating his first success.

The audacity of the attack shocked the intelligence world. When it happened again a few months later in Berlin, the Tin Man's legend was born. In London, the Tin Man blew a man's head off with a cellphone. A defector in New York's Chinatown lost most of his face when a cigarette exploded. Sammy Tin was soon getting credit for most of the more dramatic intelligence killings in that underworld. The legend grew rapidly.

As he matured, the hits became less dramatic, and much easier to conceal. He was now thirty-three, and without a doubt the most feared agent in the world. The CIA spent a fortune trying to track his movements. They knew he was in Beijing and when he left, they tracked him to Hong Kong. He boarded a nonstop flight to London, where he changed passports and at the last moment boarded an Alitalia flight to Milan. A car was waiting for him at Milan's Malpensa airport, and he vanished into the city.

MR ELYA certainly looked the part of a wealthy Saudi businessman, though his heavy wool suit was almost black, a little too dark for Bologna, and its pinstripes were much too thick for anything designed in Italy. Stefano had time to analyse his client while they rode in virtual silence from the airport, where Mr Elya and his assistant had arrived by private jet, to the centre of Bologna. They were in the rear of a black Mercedes, with a driver who was silent in the front seat along with the assistant, who evidently spoke only Arabic. After ten minutes in the car with them, Stefano was already hoping they would finish well before lunch.

The first apartment he showed them was close to the university, where Mr Elya's son would soon arrive to study medicine. Four rooms on the first floor, nicely furnished, luxurious for any student—1,800 euros a month. Mr Elya did nothing but frown, as if his spoiled son would require something much nicer. The second stop was on Via Remorsella, one block west of Via Fondazza. The flat had a kitchen the size of a broom closet, was badly furnished, was twenty minutes away from the university and cost 2,600 euros a month. 'This will be fine,' Mr Elya said, and Stefano breathed a sigh of relief. He wouldn't have to entertain them over lunch and he'd just earned a nice commission.

They hurried over to the office of Stefano's company, where paperwork was produced at a record pace. Mr Elya was a busy man with an urgent meeting in Rome. Then the black Mercedes sped them back to the airport, where a rattled and exhausted Stefano said thanks and hurried away as quickly as possible. Mr Elya and his assistant walked across the tarmac to his jet and disappeared inside.

The jet didn't move. Inside, Mr Elya and his assistant ditched their business garb for casual dress. They huddled with three other members of their team. After waiting for an hour, they left the jet, hauled their substantial baggage to the private terminal, then into waiting vans.

LUIGI HAD BECOME suspicious of the navy-blue Silvio bag. Marco never left it in his apartment. It was never out of his sight. He carried it everywhere, tucked tightly under his right arm as if it contained gold.

Whitaker in Milano was suspicious too, especially since Marco had been spotted in an Internet café near the university. He sent an agent named Krater to Bologna to help Zellman and Luigi keep a closer eye on Marco.

It was Krater who got the radio message from Luigi that Marco was drifting towards Piazza Maggiore. Krater spotted him as he strode across the square, dark blue bag under his right arm, looking very much like a local.

Marco passed the cafés and shops, then suddenly, after a furtive glance, stepped into Albergo Nettuno, a boutique hotel just off the piazza. Krater radioed Zellman and Luigi, who was puzzled because Marco had no reason whatsoever to be entering a hotel. Krater waited five minutes, then walked into the lobby. To his right were some chairs and a few magazines strewn over a wide coffee table. To his left was a small empty phone room with its door open, then another room that was not empty. Marco sat there, alone, hunched over the small table under the wall-mounted phone, his bag open.

'May I help you, sir?' the clerk said from the front desk.

'Yes, thanks, I wanted to enquire about a room,' Krater said in Italian.

'I'm sorry, but we have no vacancies. Perhaps another time.'

'Do you by chance have Internet access?'

'Of course.'

'Wireless?'

'Yes, the first hotel in the city.'

'Thanks,' said Krater. 'I'll try again another time.'

He passed the phone room on the way out. Marco had not looked up.

With both thumbs he was typing his text and hoping he would not be asked to leave by the clerk at the front desk. The wireless access was something the Nettuno advertised, but only for its guests.

His e-mail read:

Grinch: I once dealt with a banker in Zurich, name of Mikel Van Thiessen, at
Rhineland Bank, on Bahnhofstrasse, downtown Zurich. See if you can determine
if he's still there. If not, who took his place? Do not leave a trail! Marco

He pushed Send, and once again prayed that he'd done things right. He
quickly turned off the Ankyo 850 and tucked it away in his bag. As he left,
he nodded at the clerk, who was on the phone.

Two minutes after Krater came out of the hotel, Marco made his exit.
Zellman, Krater and Luigi watched him, then followed him as he mixed
with the late-afternoon rush of people leaving work. An hour later, they met
in a bar and retraced his movements. The conclusion was obvious: Marco
was freeloading on the hotel's wireless Internet access. There was no other
reason to enter the hotel lobby, sit in a phone room for less than ten minutes, then abruptly leave. But how could he do it? He had no laptop, no cellphone other than the outdated one Luigi had loaned him. Had he obtained
some high-tech gadget? He had no money. They kicked around various scenarios. Zellman left to e-mail the disturbing news to Whitaker. Krater was
dispatched to begin window-shopping for an identical Silvio bag.

Luigi was left to contemplate dinner. His thoughts were interrupted by a
call from Marco. He was in his apartment, not feeling too well. He'd cancelled his lesson with Francesca, and now he was begging off dinner.

DAN SANDBERG'S phone rang before 6 a.m. It was a colleague at the *Post*.
'You got scooped, buddy,' he announced gravely. 'The *Times* just wiped
your nose for you.'

'Who?'

'Backman. Go see for yourself.'

Sandberg ran to the living room of his messy apartment and attacked his
desk computer. He found the story, written by Heath Frick, a hated rival at
the *New York Times*. The front-page headline read FBI PARDON PROBE
SEARCHES FOR JOEL BACKMAN.

Citing a host of unnamed sources, Frick reported that the FBI's cash-for-
pardon investigation was focusing its attention on Joel Backman. His mysterious disappearance had only fuelled the speculation that he'd bought
himself a pardon and fled to avoid the obvious questions.

'What garbage!' Sandberg snarled as he scrolled down the screen.

Frick wrapped it all up with two paragraphs about Backman, historical
rehash that the paper had run before.

'Just filler!' Sandberg fumed.

SUSAN PENN was driven in an armoured car from her Georgetown home to the White House, where she arrived each morning at 7.15. Along the way she read the ten-page summary of CIA intelligence matters that was placed on the President's desk precisely at 7 a.m. On page four that morning was an item about Joel Backman. He was attracting the attention of some very dangerous people.

The President greeted her warmly and had coffee waiting by the sofa. They were alone, as always, and they went right to work.

'You've seen the *New York Times* this morning?' he asked.

'Yes.'

'What are the chances that Backman paid for a pardon?'

'Very slim. As I've explained before, he had no idea one was in the works. Plus, we're quite confident he didn't have the money.'

'Then why was Backman pardoned?'

'Frankly, Teddy wanted him dead.'

'Why?'

She took a deep breath. 'Backman and Jacy Hubbard got in way over their heads. They had this software, JAM, that their clients had stupidly brought to their office, looking for a fortune.'

'These clients were the young Pakistanis, right?'

'Yes, and they're all dead.'

'Do you know who killed them?'

'No.'

'Do you know who killed Jacy Hubbard?'

'No.'

The President glared at her. 'I find it hard to believe that we don't know these things.'

'Frankly, so do I. And it's not because we haven't tried. It's one reason Teddy worked so hard to get Backman pardoned. He felt that Backman's murder might tell us something. If the Russians kill him, then we can believe the satellite system belonged to the Russians. Same for the Chinese. If the Israelis do it, then there's a good chance Backman and Hubbard tried to sell their product to the Saudis. If the Saudis get to him, then we can believe that Backman double-crossed them. We're almost certain that the Saudis thought they had a deal.'

'But Backman screwed them?'

'Maybe not. We think Hubbard's death changed everything. Backman packed his bags and ran away to prison. All deals were off.'

The President walked back to the coffee table and refilled his cup. He sat across from her and shook his head. 'You expect me to believe that three young Pakistani hackers tapped into a satellite system so sophisticated that we didn't even know about it?'

'Yes. They were brilliant, but they also got lucky. Then they hacked their way in, and wrote some amazing programs that manipulated it.'

'And that's JAM?'

'That's what they called it.'

'Has anybody ever seen the software?'

'The Saudis. That's how we know that it not only exists but probably works as well as advertised.'

'Where is the software now?'

'No one knows, except, maybe, Backman himself.'

A long pause as the President sipped his lukewarm coffee. Then he rested his elbows on his knees and said, 'What's best for us, Susan? What's in our best interests?'

She didn't hesitate. 'To follow Teddy's plan. Backman will be eliminated. The software hasn't been seen in six years, so it's probably gone too. The satellite system is up there, but whoever owns it can't play with it.'

Another sip, another pause. The President shook his head and said, 'So be it.'

THE TIMES STORY was read by Efraim as he rode the train from Florence to Bologna. Rafi and Shaul would arrive early the next morning, Rafi on a flight from Milan, Shaul on a train from Rome. The four Italian-speaking members of the *kidon* were already in Bologna, hurriedly putting together the two safe houses they would need for the project.

The preliminary plan was to grab Backman under the darkened porticoes along Via Fondazza or another suitable side street, preferably early in the morning or after dark. They would sedate him, shove him in a van, take him to a safe house, and wait for the drugs to wear off. They would interrogate him, eventually kill him with poison, and drive his body two hours north to Lake Garda where he'd be fed to the fish.

The plan was fraught with pitfalls, but the green light had been given. There was no turning back. Now that Backman was getting so much attention, they had to strike quickly.

The race was also fuelled by the fact that the Mossad had good reason to believe that Sammy Tin was either in Bologna, or somewhere close.

Chapter 11

The nearest restaurant to her apartment was a lovely old trattoria called Nino's. She knew the place well and had known the two sons of old Nino for many years. She explained her predicament, and when she arrived both of them were waiting and practically carried her inside. They walked her slowly to their favourite table, which they'd moved closer to the fireplace. They brought her coffee and water.

When Marco arrived a few minutes later, the two brothers greeted him like family. It was midafternoon, the lunch crowd was gone. Francesca and her student had Nino's to themselves.

The fall on the gravel at San Luca and the sprained ankle had transformed her. Gone was the frosty indifference. She smiled when she saw him, even reached up and pulled him close so they could blow air kisses at both cheeks. She waved him to the chair directly across from her.

'How's your foot?' Marco asked in English. She put her finger to her lips and said, '*Non inglese, Marco. Solamente Italiano.*'

He frowned and said, 'I was afraid of that.'

Her foot was very sore. She had kept it on ice while she was reading or watching television, and the swelling had gone down. At her mother's insistence, she was using a cane. She found it embarrassing.

'How is your mother?' he asked in Italian.

Very well, very tired. She has been sitting with Giovanni for a month now, and it's taking a toll.

So, thought Marco, Giovanni is now available for discussion. How is he?

Inoperable brain cancer, she said, and it took a few tries to get the translation right. The end is quite close. He is unconscious.

What was his profession, what did he do?

He taught medieval history at the university for many years. They met there—she was a student, he was her professor. At the time he was married. She and her professor fell in love and began an affair that lasted almost ten years before he divorced his wife and married Francesca.

Children? No, she said with sadness. She had regrets, many regrets.

'Tell me all about you,' she said. 'Speak slowly. I want the accent to be as good as possible. What's your real name?'

'For now it's Marco. I have a long history, Francesca, and I can't talk about it.'

'Very well, do you have children?'

Ah, yes. For a long time he talked about his three children—their names, ages, occupations, children. Francesca listened intently, waiting to pounce on any improperly conjugated verb.

She began to fidget after an hour and Marco could tell she was uncomfortable. He finally convinced her to leave, and walked her back down Via Minzoni, her right hand fixed to his left elbow. They walked as slowly as possible. She dreaded the return to her apartment, to the deathwatch. He wanted to walk for miles, to feel the hand of someone who needed him.

At her apartment they traded farewell kisses and made arrangements to meet at Nino's tomorrow, same time, same table.

WHEN SEX WAS NEEDED to set up a kill, Sammy Tin preferred Mae Szun. She was a fine MSS agent in her own right, but the legs and perfect features added a dimension that had proved deadly on at least three occasions. She had no trouble at all getting Jacy Hubbard out of a bar and into a car. She had delivered him to Sammy Tin, who finished him off. Tin summoned her to Bologna, not to seduce but to pretend to be happily married tourists with another agent.

Mae spotted Marco as he moved in a crowd down Strada Maggiore, headed in the general direction of Via Fondazza. She picked up her pace, pulled out a cellphone, and managed to gain ground on him. Then he was gone. He suddenly took a left, turned down a narrow alley, Via Begatto, and headed north, away from Via Fondazza. By the time she made the turn, he was out of sight.

SPRING WAS FINALLY arriving in Bologna. The temperature had approached fifty degrees the day before, and when Marco stepped outside before dawn he thought about swapping his parka for one of the other jackets. He took a few steps under the dark portico, then decided it was still chilly enough to keep the parka. He took off on the morning hike.

He could think of nothing but the *Times* story. To see his name plastered across the front page was unsettling enough but to be accused of bribing the President was actionable at law. In another life he would have started the day by shotgunning lawsuits at everyone involved.

But what would the attention mean for him now? Would Luigi snatch him again and run away? Was he in more danger today than yesterday?

He was surviving nicely, tucked away in a lovely city where no one knew his real name. Not even he recognised himself. Each morning when he finished shaving and put on his glasses, he stood at the mirror and said hello to Marco. Long gone were the fleshy jowls and puffy dark eyes, the thicker, longer hair. Long gone was the smirk and the arrogance. Now he was just Marco, living one day at a time, and the days were piling up.

He passed a man in a dark suit and instantly knew he was in trouble. The suit was out of place. It was something bought off the rack in a low-end store, one he'd seen every day in another life. It was not the type of suit you'd ever see under the porticoes along Via Fondazza. He took a few steps, glanced over his shoulder, and saw that the suit was now following him. White guy, thirty years old, thick, athletic, the clear winner in a footrace or a fistfight. So Marco used another strategy. He suddenly stopped, turned around, and said, 'You want something?'

To which someone else said, 'Over here, Backman.'

His name stopped him cold. For a second his knees were rubbery, his shoulders sagged, and he told himself that no, he was not dreaming.

There were two of them. The one with the voice arrived from the other side of Via Fondazza. He had basically the same suit, but he was older, shorter, and much thinner. Mutt and Jeff. Thick 'n' Thin.

'What do you want?' Marco said.

They were slowly reaching for their pockets. 'We're with the FBI,' the thick one said. They went through the required ritual of flashing their badges, but under the darkness of the portico Marco could read nothing.

'Let's take a walk,' said the thin one. Boston, Irish.

'You got a warrant?' Marco said without moving.

'We don't need one.'

The thick one made the mistake of touching Marco's left elbow, as if he would help him move along to where they wanted to go. Marco jerked away. 'Don't touch me! You boys get lost. You can't make an arrest here.'

'Fine, let's go have a chat,' said the thin one.

'I don't have to talk.' Marco wasn't moving; not that he felt very safe where he was, but he could almost see a dark car waiting around the corner. Where the hell is Luigi right now? he asked himself.

The thin one decided to take control of the encounter. 'We can meet right here. We're investigating the pardon you bought.'

'Then you're wasting a helluva lot of time and money.'

'We have some questions about the transaction.'

'What a stupid investigation,' Marco said, spitting the words at the thin one. 'The FBI spends good money sending two clowns like you all the way to Bologna, Italy, to ask me questions that no fool in his right mind would answer. You're a couple of dumbasses, you know that? Go back home and tell your boss that he's wasting a lot of time and money if he thinks I paid for a pardon.'

'So you deny—'

'I deny nothing. I admit nothing. I say nothing, except that this is the FBI at its absolute worst. You boys are in deep water and you can't swim.'

Back home they'd slap him around a little, but on foreign soil they weren't sure how to behave. Their orders were to find him, to scare him, hit him with some questions about wire transfers and offshore accounts. They had it all mapped out but Mr Lazzeri was annihilating their plans.

'We're not leaving Bologna until we talk,' said the thick one.

'Congratulations, you're in for a long vacation.'

'Just a few questions, please,' said the thin one.

'Go see my lawyer,' Marco said, and began to walk away. They weren't following, and Marco picked up his pace. If they wanted to follow, they waited too long. By the time he darted onto Via del Piombo, he knew they could never find him. These were his streets now, his alleys, his darkened doorways to shops that wouldn't open for three more hours.

They found him on Via Fondazza only because they knew his address.

AT THE SOUTHWESTERN EDGE of old Bologna, near the Porto San Stefano, he caught a city bus and rode it for half an hour, until he stopped near the train station at the northern perimeter. There he caught another bus and rode into the centre of the city. A third bus took him across the city again to the Porta Saragozza, where he began the 3.6-kilometre hike up to San Luca. At the four-hundredth arch he stopped to catch his breath, looked down and waited for someone to come up behind him. There was no one back there.

He slowed his pace and finished the climb in fifty-five minutes. Behind the Santuario di San Luca he followed the narrow pathway where Francesca had fallen, and finally parked himself on the bench where she had waited. From there, his early-morning view of Bologna was magnificent. The sun was up, the air was light and clear, and for a long time Marco sat and watched the city come to life.

He treasured the solitude of the moment. Why couldn't he make the climb every morning, and sit high above Bologna with nothing to do but think? Perhaps call a friend on the phone and catch up on the gossip? He'd have to find the friends first. It was a dream that would not come true.

With Luigi's cellphone he called Ermanno and cancelled their session. Then he called Luigi and explained that he didn't feel like studying.

'Is something wrong?'

'No. I just need a break. It's springtime in Bologna, and I'm going for a long walk.'

'Where?'

'No thanks, Luigi. I don't want company.'

'What about lunch?'

Hunger pains shot through Marco's stomach. Lunch with Luigi was always delicious. 'Sure, Luigi. I'll call you back.'

They met at twelve-thirty at Caffè Atene, an ancient dive with small square tables. The cramped dining room was smoky, loud, and packed with hungry people who enjoyed talking at full volume as they ate.

After a morning of arguing with himself up at San Luca, Marco had decided not to tell Luigi about his encounter with the FBI. His principal reason for holding back was that he did not want to pack up and run again, not on Luigi's terms. If he ran, he would be alone.

He was assuming Luigi knew nothing of the FBI's presence. He certainly seemed to be much more concerned with the menu and the wine list.

The lights went out. Suddenly, Caffè Atene was completely dark, and in the next instant a waiter with a tray of someone's lunch came crashing across their table, yelling and cursing. The legs of the antique table buckled and its edge crashed hard onto Marco's lap. At about the same time, something hit him hard on the left shoulder. Glass was breaking. Bodies were getting shoved, then from the kitchen someone screamed, 'Fire!'

The scramble outside and onto the street was completed without serious injury. The last person out was Marco, who ducked low to avoid the stampede while searching for his navy-blue Silvio bag. As always, he had hung its strap over the back of his chair, with the bag resting so close to his body he could usually feel it. It had disappeared in the melee.

The Italians stood in the street and stared in disbelief at the café. Their lunch was in there, half eaten.

'I lost my bag,' Marco said to Luigi as they watched and waited.

'The blue one?'

'How many bags do I carry around, Luigi?' he answered. 'Yes, the blue one.' He already had suspicions that the bag had been snatched.

A small fire engine with an enormous siren arrived and kept wailing as the firemen raced inside. After an hour of discussion and very little fire-fighting, the situation was under control. 'Something in the restroom,' a waiter yelled to one of the few remaining patrons. The lights were back on.

They allowed them back inside to get their coats. Luigi became very helpful in the hunt for Marco's bag. He discussed the situation with the head waiter, and before long half the staff was scouring the restaurant.

The bag was gone, and Marco knew it.

In a hotel room a few blocks away, Zellman and Krater had the bag on the bed, its contents neatly arranged. Other than the Ankyo smartphone, there were two maps of Bologna, four $100 bills, the cellphone Luigi had loaned him, a bottle of aspirin, and the owner's manual for the Ankyo.

Zellman, the more agile computer whiz of the two, plugged the smart-phone into an Internet access jack and was soon fiddling with the menu. 'This is good stuff,' he was saying. 'The absolute latest toy on the market.'

Not surprisingly, he was stopped by the password. They would have to dissect it at Langley. With his laptop, he e-mailed a message to Julia Javier, passing along the serial number and other information.

Within two hours of the theft, a CIA agent was sitting in the parking lot outside Chatter in suburban Alexandria, waiting for the store to open.

AT 4 P.M., five of the *kidon* were on Via Fondazza, at various points—one drinking coffee at a pavement café, two strolling aimlessly a block apart, one cruising back and forth on a scooter, and one looking out a window from the second floor.

Half a mile away, outside the central city, on the first floor above a flower shop owned by an elderly Jew, the four other members of the *kidon* were playing cards and waiting nervously. They played with little conversation. The night ahead would be long and unpleasant.

THROUGHOUT THE DAY, Marco had struggled with the question of whether to return to Via Fondazza. The FBI boys could still be there, ready for another ugly confrontation. They had superiors back home who demanded results.

Though far from certain, he had a strong hunch that Luigi was behind the theft of his Silvio bag. The fire had not really been a fire; it was more of a diversion. He didn't trust Luigi because he trusted no one.

He'd just lost $400 in cash and his only lifeline to the outside world.

They had his cute little smartphone. Neal's codes were in there somewhere. Could they be broken? Could the trail lead to his son? Marco had not the slightest idea how those things worked.

The urge to leave Bologna was overwhelming. People who weren't supposed to know his whereabouts now knew his exact address. Where to go and how to get there were questions he had not sorted out. He was rambling now, and he felt vulnerable, almost helpless. At a crowded bus stop he cut the line and climbed on, not sure where he was going.

At the last second he jumped off, then walked a few blocks along Via San Vitale until he saw another bus. He rode in circles for almost an hour, then finally stepped off near the train station. He drifted with the crowd, then darted across Via dell' Indipendenza to the bus station. Inside he found one was leaving in ten minutes for Piacenza, an hour and a half away with five stops in between. He bought a ticket for thirty euros and hid in the restroom until the last minute. The bus was almost full. The seats were wide, with high headrests, and as the bus moved slowly through heavy traffic, Marco almost nodded off. Then he caught himself.

This was it—the escape he'd been contemplating since the first day in Bologna. He'd become convinced that to survive he would be forced to disappear, to leave Luigi behind and make it on his own. There was no turning back now.

The first stop was the small village of Bazzano, fifteen kilometres west of Bologna. Marco got off the bus, hid in the restroom of the station until the bus was gone, then crossed the street to a bar where he ordered a beer and asked the bartender about the nearest hotel.

Albergo Cantino was near the centre of the village, five or six blocks away. It was dark when he arrived at the front desk, with no bags, something that did not go unnoticed by the signora who handled things.

'I'd like a room,' he said in Italian.

'The rate is fifty-five euros.'

'Fine.'

'Your passport, please.'

'Sorry, but I lost it.'

Her plucked and painted eyebrows arched in great suspicion, then she began shaking her head. 'Sorry.'

Marco laid two 100-euro bills on the counter in front of her. The bribe was obvious—just take the cash, no paperwork, and give me a key.

'You must have a passport,' she said. Then she folded her arms across her chest, braced for the next exchange. There was no way she was going to lose.

Outside, Marco walked the streets of the strange town. He found a bar and ordered coffee; no more alcohol, he had to keep his wits.

'Where can I find a taxi?' he asked the bartender.

'At the bus station.'

BY 9 P.M. Luigi was walking the floors of his apartment, waiting for Marco to return next door. His disappearance was part of the plan, but Whitaker and Langley thought it would take a few more days. Had they lost him already? That quickly? There were now five agents very close by—Luigi, Zellman, Krater, and two others sent from Milano.

At 9.12, a buzzer quietly went off in the kitchen. Luigi hurried to the monitors in the kitchen. Marco was home. Luigi stared at the digital image from the hidden camera in the ceiling of the living room next door.

Two strangers—not Marco. Two men in their thirties, dressed like regular guys. They closed the door quickly, quietly, professionally, then began looking around. One carried a small black bag. They were good, very good. To pick the lock of the safe house they had to be very good.

Luigi smiled with excitement. With a little luck, his cameras were about to record Marco getting nabbed. Maybe they would kill him right there in the living room, captured on film. He flipped the audio switches and increased the volume. Language was crucial. Where were they from? There were no sounds, though, as they moved about silently. They whispered once or twice, but he could barely hear it.

THE TAXI made an abrupt stop on Via Gramsci. From the back seat, Marco handed over enough cash, then ducked between two parked cars and was soon lost in the darkness. His escape from Bologna had been very brief indeed. He zigzagged out of habit, looping back, watching his own trail.

On Via Minzoni he moved quickly under the porticoes and stopped at her apartment building. He rang twice, desperately hoping that Francesca, and not Signora Altonelli, would answer.

'Who is it?' came that lovely voice.

'Francesca, it's me, Marco. I need some help.'

A very slight pause, then, 'Yes, of course.'

She met him at her door on the first floor and invited him in. Much to his dismay, Signora Altonelli was still there, standing in the kitchen door with a hand towel, watching his entrance very closely.

'Are you all right?' Francesca asked in Italian.

'English, please,' he said, smiling at her mother. 'I need a place to stay tonight. Because I have no passport, I can't even bribe my way into a hotel.'

'That's the law in Europe, you know.'

'Yes, I'm learning.'

She waved at the sofa, then turned to her mother and asked her to make some coffee. He noticed she was barefoot and moving about without the cane. She wore tight jeans and a baggy sweater.

'Why don't you tell me what's going on?' she said.

'It's a complicated story and I can't tell you most of it. Let's just say that I don't feel very safe right now, that I really need to leave Bologna.'

'Where are you going?'

'I'm not sure. Somewhere out of Italy, out of Europe, to a place where I'll hide again.'

She stared at him coldly, without blinking. He stared back because even when cold, the eyes were beautiful. 'Who are you?' she asked.

'Well, I'm certainly not Marco Lazzeri.'

'What are you running from?'

'My past, and it's rapidly catching up with me. I'm not a criminal, Francesca. I was once a lawyer. I got in some trouble, a business deal six years ago. Some very nasty people are not happy with how the deal was finished. They would like to find me.'

'To kill you?'

'Yes. That's what they'd like to do.'

'This is very confusing. Why did you come here? Why did Luigi help you? Why did he hire me and Ermanno? I don't understand.'

'And I can't answer those questions. Two months ago I was in prison, and I thought I would be there for another fourteen years. Suddenly, I'm free. I was fully pardoned and I was given a new identity, brought here, hidden first in Treviso, now Bologna. I think they want to kill me here.'

Signora Altonelli appeared with a tray of coffee, and also a pear torte. As she placed it on a plate for him, he realised that he had not eaten since lunch.

Lunch with Luigi. Lunch with the fake fire and the stolen smartphone. He thought of Neal again and worried about his safety.

'It's delicious,' he said to Francesca's mother in Italian. Francesca watched every move he made, every bite, every sip of coffee. When her mother went back to the kitchen, she said, 'Who does Luigi work for?'

'I'm not sure. Probably the CIA. You know the CIA?'

'Yes. I read spy novels. The CIA put you here?'

'I think the CIA got me out of prison, and here to Bologna where they've hidden me while they try and figure out what to do with me.'

'Will they kill you?'

'Maybe.'

She placed her cup on the table and got to her feet. 'I need to move a little,' she said as she carefully placed weight on her left foot. She walked slowly into the kitchen, where things were quiet for a moment before a heated argument broke out in loud, tense whispers. Then Francesca came limping back with a small bottle of water and took her place on the sofa.

'What was that all about?' he asked.

'I told her you wanted to sleep here tonight. She misunderstood. She's very old-fashioned.'

'Just give me a pillow. I'll sleep on the kitchen table.'

When Signora Altonelli returned to remove the coffee tray, she glared at Marco as if he'd already molested her daughter. She huffed around the kitchen for a few minutes, then retired somewhere back in the apartment.

'Let's talk,' Francesca said. 'Tell me everything.'

HE SLEPT for a few hours on the sofa, and was awakened by Francesca tapping on his shoulder. 'I have an idea,' she said. 'Follow me.'

He followed her to the kitchen, where a clock read 4.15. By the sink was a disposable razor, a can of shaving cream, a pair of glasses, and a bottle of hair something or other—he couldn't translate it. She handed him a small leather case and said, 'This is a passport. Giovanni's.'

He almost dropped it. 'No, I can't—'

'Yes, you can. He won't be needing it. I insist.'

Marco slowly opened it and looked at the distinguished face of a man he'd never meet. The expiration date was seven months away, so the photo was almost five years old. He found the birthday—Giovanni was now sixty-eight years old, a good twenty years older than his wife.

'Are you sure?' he asked. The passport could implicate her, and he would never do that.

'Please, Marco, I want to help. Giovanni would insist. There's a bus for Parma that leaves in two hours. It would be a safe way out of town.'

'I want to get to Milano,' he said.

'Good idea.'

She took the passport and opened it. They studied the photo of her husband. 'Let's start with that thing around your mouth,' she said.

Ten minutes later the moustache and goatee were gone, his face completely shaven. She held a mirror for him as he hovered over the kitchen sink. Giovanni at sixty-three had less grey hair than Marco at fifty-two. Marco sat in a chair facing the table with a towel draped over his shoulders while she gently worked the hair colouring through his hair. Very little was said. Her mother was asleep.

Not long ago Giovanni the professor had worn round tortoiseshell glasses, and when Marco put them on and studied his new look he hardly recognised himself. His hair was much darker, his eyes very different.

'Not bad,' was her assessment of her own work. 'It will do for now.'

She brought in a navy corduroy sports coat, with well-worn patches on the elbows, and he slipped it on.

'He's about two inches shorter than you,' she said. 'What's your real name?' she added, as she tugged on the sleeves and adjusted the collar.

'Joel.'

'I think you should travel with a briefcase. It will look normal.' She left, then came back with a beautiful old briefcase, tan leather with a silver buckle. 'It's Giovanni's favourite, a gift from me twenty years ago. Italian leather.'

'Of course.'

'If you get caught with the passport, what will you say?' she asked.

'I stole it. You're my tutor. I was in your home as a guest. I managed to find the drawer with your documents, and I stole your husband's passport.'

'Do you need money? I have a thousand euros here.'

'No, Francesca, but thanks.'

'You'd better hurry.'

He followed her to the front door where they stopped and looked at each other. 'Do you spend much time online?' he asked.

'A little each day.'

'Check out Joel Backman, start with the *Washington Post*. But don't believe everything you read. I'm not the monster they've created.'

'You're not a monster at all, Joel.'

'I don't know how to thank you.'

She took his right hand and squeezed it with both of hers. 'Will you ever return to Bologna?' she asked. It was more of an invitation than a question.

'I don't know. Can I knock on your door if I make it back?'

'Please do. Be careful out there.'

He stood in the shadows of Via Minzoni for a few minutes, not wanting to leave her, not ready to begin the long journey.

Then there was a cough from under the darkened porticoes across the street, and Giovanni Ferro was on the run.

Chapter 12

As the hours passed with excruciating slowness, Luigi moved from worry to panic. One of two things had happened: either the hit had already occurred, or Marco had gotten wind of something and was trying to flee.

The expensive smartphone had shaken everyone. Their boy had been planning, and communicating. The smartphone was in a lab in the basement of the American embassy in Milan, where, according to the latest from Whitaker, the technicians had been unable to crack its codes.

A few minutes after midnight, the two intruders next door got tired of waiting. As they were making their exit, they spoke a few words loud enough to be recorded. It was English with a trace of an accent. Luigi called Whitaker and reported that they were probably Israeli.

He was correct. The two agents were instructed by Efraim to leave the apartment and take up other positions.

When they left, Luigi decided to send Krater to the bus station and Zellman to the train station. With no passport, Marco could not buy a plane ticket. Luigi decided to ignore the airport.

HE SAT WITH A WINO on a bench in a small park, not far down Via dell' Indipendenza from the bus station. Around five-thirty Marco entered the station behind a young couple and followed them to the ticket counter where he listened as they bought tickets to Parma. He did the same, then hurried to the restroom and hid in a stall.

Krater was sitting in the station's all-night diner, drinking bad coffee behind a newspaper while he watched the passengers come and go. He watched Marco walk by. He noted his height, build, age. The walk was familiar, though much slower. The Marco Lazzeri he'd been following for weeks could walk as fast as most men could jog. But the face was very different. The hair was much darker. The tortoiseshell glasses caught Krater's attention. Marco's stylish Armani frames had fit him perfectly, but the round glasses on this guy begged for attention.

The facial hair was gone; a five-minute job, something anyone would do. The shirt was not one Krater had seen before, and he'd been in Marco's apartment with Luigi during sweeps when they looked at every item of clothing. The blue sports coat with worn elbow patches, along with the handsome attaché, kept Krater in his chair. Marco might somehow find and spend some cash on a smartphone, but why waste it on an expensive briefcase?

Krater watched him until he rounded a corner and was out of sight. A possibility, nothing more. He sipped his coffee and for a few minutes contemplated the gentleman he'd just seen.

Marco stood in the stall with his jeans bunched around his ankles, feeling quite silly but much more concerned with a good cover at this point. The door opened. Marco listened carefully.

Nothing. There was no noise from the lavatories, no one washing their hands. Maybe it was the custodian quietly making his rounds.

In front of the lavatories, Krater bent low and saw the jeans around the ankles in the last stall. Next to the jeans was the fine briefcase. The gentleman was taking care of his business and in no hurry about it.

The next bus left at 6 a.m. for Parma; after that there was a 6.20 departure for Florence. Krater hurried to the booth and bought tickets for both. The clerk looked at him oddly, but Krater couldn't have cared less.

He went back to the restroom. The man in the last stall was still there. Krater stepped outside and called Luigi. He gave a description of the man, and explained that he appeared to be in no hurry to leave the men's room.

'The best place to hide,' Luigi said. 'Do you think it's Marco?'

'I don't know. If it is, it's a very good disguise.'

Rattled by the smartphone, the $400 in American cash, and the disappearance, Luigi was not taking chances. 'Follow him,' he said.

At 5.55, Marco pulled up his jeans, flushed, grabbed his briefcase, and took off for the bus. Waiting on the platform was Krater, nonchalantly eating an apple. When Marco headed for the bus to Parma, so did Krater.

A third of the seats were empty. Marco took one on the left-hand side, halfway back, by a window. Krater was looking away when he passed by, then found a seat four rows behind him.

The first stop was Modena, thirty minutes into the trip. As they entered the city, Marco decided to take stock of the faces behind him. He stood and made his way to the rear, to the restroom, and along the way gave a casual glance to each male.

When he locked himself in the restroom, he closed his eyes and said to himself, 'Yes, I've seen that face before.' Less than twenty-four hours earlier, in Caffè Atene, just a few minutes before the lights went out.

Marco returned to his seat as the bus slowed and approached the station. Think quickly, man, he kept telling himself, don't panic. They've followed you out of Bologna; you can't let them follow you out of the country.

As the bus stopped in Modena the driver announced a brief stop. Four passengers waddled down the aisle and got off. The others were dozing in their seats. Marco closed his eyes and allowed his head to drift against the window. When the driver returned, Marco suddenly eased from his seat, slid quickly along the aisle, and hopped off the bus just as the door was closing. He walked quickly into the station, then turned around and watched the bus back away. His pursuer was still on board.

Krater's first move was to sprint off the bus. He caught himself, though, because Marco obviously knew he was being followed. His last-second exit only confirmed what Krater had suspected. It was Marco all right, running like a wounded animal.

The bus turned onto another street, then stopped for a traffic light. Krater rushed to the driver, holding his stomach, begging to get off before he vomited. The door flew open, Krater jumped off and ran back towards the station.

Marco wasted no time. When the bus was out of sight, he hurried to the front of the station where three taxis were lined up. He jumped into the back seat of the first one and said, 'Can you take me to Milano?'

AFTER AN HOUR of scouring the Modena bus station, Krater called Luigi with the news that was not all bad. He'd lost his man, but the mad dash for freedom confirmed that it was indeed Marco.

Luigi's reaction was mixed. He was frustrated that Krater had been outfoxed by an amateur. He was impressed that Marco could elude a small army of assassins. And he was angry at Whitaker and the fools in D.C. who kept changing the plans and had now created an impending disaster for which he, Luigi, would no doubt get the blame.

He called Whitaker, yelled and cursed some more, then headed for the train station with Zellman and the two others. They'd meet up with Krater in Milano, where Whitaker was promising a full-court press with all the muscle he could pull in.

THE CAB STOPPED a block away from the Milano central train station. Marco paid the driver, then walked into the station. He drifted with the crowd, up the escalators, onto the platform. He found the departure board and studied his options. A train left for Stuttgart four times a day, and its seventh stop was Zurich. He picked up a schedule and bought a city guide with a map.

He took a walk to the centre of the city. The fresh air always helped, and after four blocks his blood was pumping again. Somewhere along the way he would find an inexpensive clothing store and change everything—jacket, shirt, pants, shoes. They had spotted him in Bologna. He couldn't risk it again.

Surely, somewhere in the centre of the city there was an Internet café where he could rent a computer for fifteen minutes. He had little confidence in his ability to sit in front of a strange machine, turn the damn thing on, and get a message to Neal. It was 10.15 a.m. in Milan, 4.15 a.m. in Culpeper, Virginia. Neal would be checking in live at 7.50.

The shop was called Roberto's, a small haberdashery wedged between a jewellery store and a bakery. A shop assistant from the Middle East spoke worse Italian than Marco, but he was determined to transform his customer. The blue jacket was replaced with a dark brown one. The new shirt was a white pullover with short sleeves. The slacks were dark navy. The shoes Marco tried on would have crippled him, so he stayed with his hiking boots for the moment. The best purchase was a tan straw hat that Marco bought because he'd seen one just before entering the store. The new get-up cost him almost 400 euros, money he hated to part with, but he had no choice. Marco left with the blue jacket, faded jeans, and the old shirt folded up in a red shopping bag; again, something different to carry around.

He walked a few minutes and saw a shoe store. He bought a pair of what appeared to be modified bowling shoes. They were black with burgundy striping, built for comfort and not attractiveness. He paid 150 euros for them. It took two blocks before he could muster the courage to look down at them.

LUIGI GOT HIMSELF followed out of Bologna. The kid on the scooter saw him leave the apartment next to Backman's. The kid on the scooter hung back until Luigi quickly crawled into a red Fiat. He drove a few blocks, then slowed down long enough for another man to jump into the car. They took off at breakneck speed, but in city traffic the scooter had no trouble keeping up. When they wheeled into the train station and parked illegally, the kid on the scooter saw it all and radioed Efraim again.

Within fifteen minutes, two Mossad agents dressed as traffic policemen entered Luigi's apartment, setting off alarms—some silent, some barely audible. They kicked open the kitchen door and found the astounding collection of electronic surveillance equipment.

When Luigi, Zellman and a third agent stepped onto the train to Milano, the kid on the scooter had a ticket too. His name was Paul, the youngest member of the *kidon*, at twenty-six, a veteran of half a dozen killings. He radioed that he was on the train and it was moving.

After ten minutes, Efraim called a halt to the break-in. The agents regrouped in one of their safe houses. They had not been able to determine who Luigi was, but it was obvious he'd been spying on Backman around the clock. Could Luigi lead them to him?

IN CENTRAL MILANO Marco strolled along the Galleria Vittorio Emanuele, the magnificent glass-domed gallery that Milano is famous for. Lined with cafés and bookshops, the gallery is the centre of the city's life. With the temperature approaching sixty degrees, Marco had a sandwich outdoors.

Should he leave immediately, or should he lay low for a day or two? In a crowded city of four million people, he could vanish for as long as he wanted. But the bloodhounds behind him would have time to regroup. Shouldn't he leave now, while they were back there still scrambling?

Yes he should, he decided. On a city bus he saw an ad for an Internet café on Via Verri. Ten minutes later he entered the place, ordered an orange juice and paid for half an hour. The clerk nodded in the general direction of a table where a bunch of computers were waiting. Three of the eight were being used by people who obviously knew what they were doing. Marco was already lost.

But he faked it well. He sat down, grabbed a keyboard, stared at the monitor and ploughed ahead as if he'd been hacking for years. It was surprisingly easy; he went to KwyteMail, typed his user name, 'Grinch456', then his password, waited ten seconds, and there was the message from Neal:

Marco: Mikel Van Thiessen is still with Rhineland Bank, now the vice president of client services. Anything else? Grinch.

At exactly 7.50 Eastern Standard Time, Marco typed a message:

Grinch: Marco here—live and in person. Are you there?

He sipped his juice and stared at the screen. Come on, baby, make this thing work. Another sip. Then the message:

I'm here, loud and clear. What's up?

Marco typed: They stole my Ankyo 850. There's a good chance the bad guys are picking it to pieces. Any chance they can discover you?

Only if they have the user name and pass phrase. Do they?

No, I destroyed them. There's no way they can get around a password?

Not with KwyteMail. It's totally secure and encrypted.

And we're completely safe now?

Yes, absolutely. But what are you using now?

I'm in an Internet café, renting a computer, like a real hacker. Here's the deal. Go see Carl Pratt. He was very close to former senator Ira Clayburn from North Carolina. Clayburn ruled the Senate Intelligence Commlttee for many years. I need Clayburn now. Pratt can find him.

Sure, I'll do it as soon as I can sneak away. Are you OK?

I'm on the run. I left Bologna early this morning. I'll try to check in the same time tomorrow.

Marco signed off with a smug look. Mission accomplished. Nothing to it. He made sure his exit was clean from KwyteMail, then finished his orange juice and left the café. He headed in the direction of the train station, stopping first at a leather shop where he managed an even swap of Giovanni's fine briefcase for a black one of patently inferior quality. At a used-book shop he spent two euros on a well-worn hardback containing the poetry of Czeslaw Milosz, all in Polish of course, anything to confuse the bloodhounds; and, finally, at a secondhand accessory store he bought a pair of sunglasses and a wooden cane.

The cane reminded him of Francesca. It also slowed him down, changed his gait. With time to spare he shuffled into Milano Centrale and bought a first-class ticket for Stuttgart for sixty euros, in hopes that he could avoid the exposure of travelling by coach.

Marco climbed aboard at five-thirty, forty-five minutes before departure. He settled into his seat, hid his face as much as possible behind the sun-glasses and the tan straw hat, opened the book of Polish poetry, and gazed out at the platform where passengers walked by his train, all in a hurry.

Except one. The guy on the bus was back; the face from Caffè Atene; probably the sticky-fingered thug who'd grabbed his blue Silvio bag; the same bloodhound who'd been a step too slow off the bus in Modena. He was walking but not going anywhere. His eyes were squinted, his forehead wrinkled in a deep frown. For a professional, he was much too obvious, thought Marco, who, unfortunately, now knew much more than he wanted to know about hiding and covering tracks.

KRATER HAD BEEN TOLD that Marco would probably head either south to Rome, or north to Switzerland, Germany or France. For five hours Krater had been strolling along the twelve platforms, watching the trains, mixing with the crowds, paying close attention to who was getting on. Every blue jacket of any shade or style got his attention, but he had yet to see one with the worn elbow patches.

Marco watched Krater amble along the platform. He was holding what appeared to be a ticket, and as he walked out of sight Marco could swear that he got on the train. Marco fought the urge to get off. The door to his cabin opened, and Madame entered.

ONCE IT WAS DETERMINED that Backman had disappeared, and was not finally dead at the hands of someone else, a frenetic five hours passed before Julia Javier found the file that had been locked away in the director's office, and once guarded by Teddy Maynard himself.

The information had come, reluctantly, from the FBI years earlier when Backman's financial dealings were being investigated. The FBI had been piecing together his travel history when he abruptly pled guilty and was sent away. The guilty plea removed the pressure and with time, the travel research was completed, and eventually sent over to Langley.

In the month before Backman was indicted, he had made two quick trips to Europe. For the first one, he'd flown Air France with his favourite secretary to Paris. She later told investigators that Backman had spent one long day dashing off to Berlin for some quick business, but there were no records of Backman travelling by a commercial airliner to Berlin. A passport would've been required, and the FBI was positive he had not used his. A passport would not have been required for a train ride. Geneva, Bern, Lausanne and Zurich are all within four hours of Paris by train.

The second trip was a seventy-two-hour sprint from Dulles, first class on

Lufthansa to Frankfurt, again for business, though no business contacts had been discovered there. As with Paris, the banking centres of Switzerland are within a few hours' train ride from Frankfurt.

When Julia Javier finally found the file and read the report, she immediately called Whitaker and said, 'He's headed for Switzerland.'

MADAME HAD ENOUGH luggage for a family of five. A harried porter helped her haul the heavy suitcases on board and into the first-class car, which she consumed with herself, her belongings, and her perfume. The cabin had six seats, at least four of which she laid claim to. She sat in one across from Marco, glanced at him, and gushed over a sultry '*Bonsoir*'. Since it didn't seem right to respond in Italian, he relied on old faithful. 'Hello.'

'Ah, American.'

'No, Canadian.'

'Ah, yes,' she said, still arranging bags and settling in. Madame was a robust woman of sixty, with a tight red dress and thick calves. Her heavily decorated eyes were puffy, and the reason was soon evident. Long before the train moved, she pulled out a large flask, unscrewed its top which became a cup, and knocked back a shot of something strong. She swallowed hard, then smiled at Marco and said, 'Would you like a brandy?'

'No thanks.'

'Very well.' She poured another one, drained it, then put away the flask.

Marco pretended to nod off. She ignored him for a few minutes, then said loudly, 'You speak Polish?' She was looking at his book of poetry.

He jerked his head as if he'd just been awakened. 'No, not exactly. I'm trying to learn it, though. My family is Polish.' He held his breath, half expecting her to unleash a torrent of Polish.

'I see,' she said, not really approving.

At exactly 6.15, the train started to move. Fortunately, there were no other passengers assigned to Madame's car. Marco watched the platform as they began moving. The man from the bus was nowhere to be seen.

Their first stop was Como/San Giovanni, then five minutes later they stopped at Chiasso. It was almost dark now, and Marco was pondering a quick exit. There were four more stops before Zurich, one in Italy and three in Switzerland. Which country would work best?

He couldn't risk being followed now. If they were on the train, then they had stuck to him from Bologna, through Modena and Milano, through various disguises. They were professionals, and he was no match for them.

Fatigue finally set in, and Marco fell asleep. He was awakened when the train jerked as it slowed for the stop at Arth-Goldau station. Marco's head jerked too, and his hat fell off. Madame was watching him closely. When he opened his eyes, she said, 'A strange man has been looking at you. He's been by at least three times. He stops at the door, looks closely at you, then sneaks away.'

Marco rubbed his eyes and tried to act as though it happened all the time. 'What does he look like?'

'Blond hair, about thirty-five, cute, brown jacket. Do you know him?'

'No, I have no idea.' The man on the bus at Modena had neither blond hair nor a brown jacket, but Marco was frightened enough to switch plans.

Zug was twenty-five minutes away, the last stop before Zurich. He could not run the risk of leading them to Zurich. Ten minutes out, he announced he needed to use the restroom.

He walked past four cabins to the restroom, locked the door, and waited until the train began to slow. Then it stopped. Zug was a two-minute stop-over, and the train so far had been ridiculously on time. He waited one minute, then walked quickly to the rear of the train where he jumped onto the platform.

It was a small station, elevated with a street below. Marco flew down the steps to the pavement where a taxi sat. 'Hotel, please,' he said, startling the driver, who grabbed the ignition key. He asked something in German and Marco tried Italian. 'I need a small hotel. I don't have a reservation.'

'No problem,' the driver said. As they pulled away, Marco looked up and saw the train moving. He looked behind him, and saw no one chasing.

The ride took four blocks, and when they stopped in front of an A-frame building on a quiet side street the driver said, 'This hotel is very good.'

'Looks fine. Thanks. How far away is Zurich by car?'

'Two hours, more or less. Depends on the traffic.'

'Tomorrow morning, I need to be in downtown Zurich at nine o'clock. How much will it cost to drive me there?'

The driver rubbed his chin, then said, 'Two hundred euros.'

'Good. Let's leave here at six.'

'Six, yes, I'll be here.'

Marco thanked him again and watched as he drove away. A bell rang when he entered the front door of the hotel. The small counter was deserted, but a television was chattering away somewhere close by. A sleepy-eyed teenager finally appeared and offered a smile.

'*Parla Italiano?*' Marco asked.

'A little.'

'I speak a little too,' Marco said in Italian. 'I'd like a room for one night.'

The clerk pushed over a registration form, and from memory Marco filled in the name on his passport, Giovanni Ferro, and its number. The passport was in his coat pocket, and he was prepared to reluctantly pull it out. But the clerk was missing his television show. With atypical Swiss inefficiency, he said, 'Forty-two euros,' and didn't mention the passport.

Giovanni laid the cash on the counter, and the clerk gave him a key to room number 26. Almost as an afterthought, he said, 'I lost my toothbrush. Would you have an extra?'

The clerk reached into a drawer and pulled out a box full of assorted necessities—toothbrushes, toothpaste, disposable razors, shaving cream. Giovanni selected a few items and handed over ten euros.

A luxury suite at the Ritz could not have been more welcome than room 26. Small, clean, warm, with a firm mattress, and a door that bolted twice to keep away the faces that had been haunting him since early morning. He took a long, hot shower, then shaved and brushed his teeth forever,

Chapter 13

In the depths of prison he'd dreamed of Zurich, with its blue rivers and clean shaded streets and modern shops and handsome people, all proud to be Swiss, all going about their business with a pleasant seriousness.

He was on a tram, one he'd caught near the train station, and was now moving steadily along Bahnhofstrasse, the main avenue of downtown Zurich. It was almost 9 a.m. He was among the last wave of the sharply dressed young bankers headed for UBS and Credit Suisse and a thousand lesser-known but equally rich institutions.

Marco pretended to be engrossed in a copy of *Newsweek*, but he was really watching everyone else. No one was watching him. At Paradeplatz the trams wheeled in from east and west and stopped. They emptied quickly as the young bankers scattered in droves. Marco moved with the crowd, his hat left behind under the seat in the tram.

Nothing had changed in seven years. The Paradeplatz was still the same—an open plaza lined with small shops and cafés. He stuck close to three young men with gym bags slung over their shoulders. They appeared to be headed for Rhineland Bank, on the east side. He followed them inside, into the lobby, where the fun began.

The information desk hadn't moved in seven years; in fact, the well-groomed lady sitting behind it looked vaguely familiar. 'I'd like to see Mr Mikel Van Thiessen,' he said as softly as possible.

'And your name?'

'Marco Lazzeri.' He would use Joel Backman later, upstairs, but he was hesitant to use it here. Hopefully, Neal's e-mails to Van Thiessen had alerted him to the alias.

She was on the phone and also pecking at a keyboard. 'It will be just a moment, Mr Lazzeri,' she said. 'Would you mind waiting?'

'No,' he said. Mind waiting? He'd been dreaming of this for years. He took a chair.

Five minutes later, a security man approached him and said, 'Mr Lazzeri, would you follow me?' They rode an elevator up to the second floor where Marco was led into a small room. Two other security agents were waiting. They asked him to place both hands on a biometric fingerprint scanner. It would compare his fingerprints to the ones he left behind almost seven years ago, at this same place. When the perfect match was made there would be a nicer room, the offer of coffee or juice. Anything, Mr Backman.

He asked for orange juice. Mr Backman was now being served by Elke, one of Mr Van Thiessen's shapely assistants. 'He'll be out in just a minute,' she explained. 'He wasn't expecting you this morning.'

Joel smiled at her. Ol' Marco was history now, laid to rest after a good two-month run. Marco had served him well, kept him alive, taught him basic Italian, and introduced him to Francesca, a woman he would not soon forget. But Marco would also get him killed, so he ditched him there on the second floor of the Rhineland Bank. Marco was gone, never to return.

Mikel Van Thiessen met Joel at the door of his office and they shook hands. They had met exactly once before.

If Joel had lost sixty pounds since their last visit, Van Thiessen had found most of it. He was much greyer too. Van Thiessen directed his client to the leather chairs while Elke scurried around to fetch coffee and pastries.

When they were alone, with the door shut, Van Thiessen said, 'I've been reading about you.'

'Oh really. And what have you read?'

'Bribing a president for a pardon. Is it really that easy over there?'

Joel couldn't tell if he was joking or not. 'I didn't bribe anyone, if that's what you're suggesting.'

'Yes, well, the newspapers are certainly filled with speculation.' His tone was more accusatory than jovial, and Joel decided not to waste time.

'Do you believe everything you read in the newspapers?'

'Of course not, Mr Backman.'

'I'm here for three reasons. I want access to my security box. I want to review my account. And I want to withdraw ten thousand dollars in cash.'

Van Thiessen shoved a small cookie in his mouth and chewed rapidly. 'Yes, of course. I don't think we'll have a problem with any of that. I'll just need a few minutes.'

'For what?'

'I'll need to consult with a colleague.'

'Can you do so quickly?'

Van Thiessen practically bolted from the room and slammed the door behind him. The pain in Joel's stomach was not from hunger. If the wheels came off now, he had no plan B. He'd walk out of the bank with no place to go. The escape would be over. Marco would be back, and Marco would eventually get him killed.

Elke retrieved him and asked if he would follow her downstairs.

He'd been to the vault during his prior visit. It was in the basement. Every door was a foot thick, every wall appeared to be made of lead, every ceiling had surveillance cameras. Elke handed him off to Van Thiessen.

Both thumbs were scanned for matching prints. An optical scanner took his photo. 'Number seven,' Van Thiessen said, pointing. 'I'll meet you there,' he said, and left through a door.

Joel walked down a short hallway, passing six steel doors until he came to the seventh. He pushed a button, all sorts of things clicked inside, and the door opened. He stepped inside, where Van Thiessen was waiting.

The room was twelve-foot square, with three walls lined with individual vaults, most about the size of a large shoe box.

'Your vault number?' he asked.

'L2270.'

'Correct.' Van Thiessen stepped to his right, bent slightly to face L2270. On the vault's small keypad he punched some numbers, then straightened himself and said, 'If you wish.'

Under Van Thiessen's watchful eyes, Joel stepped up to his vault and entered the code. As he did so, he softly whispered the numbers, seared in his memory. A green light began blinking on the keypad. Van Thiessen said, 'I'll be waiting at the front. Just ring when you're finished.'

When he was alone, Joel removed the steel box from his vault and pulled open the top. He picked up the padded envelope and opened it. There were the four two-gigabyte Jaz disks that had once been worth $1 billion.

He thought of Safi Mirza, Fazal Sharif and Farooq Khan, the brilliant boys who'd discovered Neptune, then wrote reams of software to manipulate the system. They were all dead now, killed by their naïve greed. He thought of Jacy Hubbard, the charismatic crook who had finally got much too greedy. He thought of Carl Pratt and Kim Bolling and dozens of other partners whose lives had been wrecked by what he was now holding in his hand. He thought of Neal and the humiliation he'd caused his son when the scandal engulfed Washington and prison became a sanctuary.

And he thought of himself. What a miserable mess of a life he'd lived, so far anyway. You've only got a few years left, Joel, or Marco, or Giovanni, or whatever the hell your name is. For the first time in your rotten life, why don't you do what's right, as opposed to what's profitable?

He put the disks in the envelope, the envelope in his briefcase, then replaced the steel box in the vault. He rang for Van Thiessen.

BACK IN the power office, Van Thiessen handed him a file with one sheet of paper in it. 'This is a summary of your account,' he was saying. 'It's very straightforward. As you know, there's been no activity.'

'You guys are paying one percent interest,' Joel said.

'You were aware of our rates when you opened the account, Mr Backman. We protect your money in other ways.'

'Of course.' Joel closed the file and handed it back. 'I don't want to keep this. Do you have the cash?'

'Yes, it's on the way up.'

'Good. I need a few things.'

Van Thiessen pulled over his writing pad. 'Yes,' he said.

'I want to wire a hundred thousand to a bank in Washington, D.C. Can you recommend one?'

'Certainly. We work closely with Maryland Trust.'

'Good, wire the money there, and with the wire open a generic savings account. I will not be writing checks, just making withdrawals.'

'In what name?'

'Joel Backman and Neal Backman.' He was getting used to his name again, not ducking when he said it.

'Very well,' Van Thiessen said. Anything was possible.

'I need some help in getting back to the US Could your girl check the Lufthansa flights to Philadelphia and New York and make a reservation?'

'Of course. When, and from where?'

'Today, as soon as possible. I'd like to avoid the airport here. How far away is Munich by car?'

'By car, three to four hours.'

'Can you provide a car?'

'I'm sure we can arrange that.'

'I prefer to leave from the basement here, in a car driven by someone not dressed like a chauffeur.'

Van Thiessen stopped writing. 'Are you in danger, Mr Backman?'

'Perhaps. I'm not sure, and I'm not taking chances.'

Van Thiessen pondered this for a few seconds, then said, 'You want us to make the airline reservations?'

'Yes.'

'Then I need to see your passport.'

Joel pulled out Giovanni's borrowed passport. Van Thiessen studied it for a long time, his face betraying him. He was confused and worried.

'Mr Backman, you will be travelling with someone else's passport.'

'That's correct.'

'And this is a valid passport?'

'It is.'

'I assume you do not have one of your own.'

'They took it a long time ago.'

'This bank cannot take part in a crime. If this is stolen, then—'

'I assure you it's not stolen. Let's just say it's borrowed, OK?'

'But using someone else's passport is a violation of the law.'

'Let's not get hung up on US immigration policy, Mr Van Thiessen. Just get the schedules. I'll pick the flights. Your girl makes the reservations using the bank's account. Deduct it from my balance. Get me a car and a driver. Deduct that from my balance, if you wish. It's all very simple.'

It was just a passport. Hell, other clients had three or four of them. Van Thiessen handed it back to Joel and said, 'Very well. Anything else?'

'Yes, I need to go online. I'm sure your computers are secure.'

'Absolutely.'

HIS E-MAIL to Neal read:

> Grinch—With a bit of luck, I should arrive in US tonight. Get a new cellphone today. Tomorrow morning call the Hilton, Marriott, and Sheraton, in downtown Washington. Ask for Giovanni Ferro. That's me. Call Carl Pratt first thing this morning. Push hard to get Senator Clayburn in D.C. We will cover his expenses. Tell him it's urgent. Don't take no for an answer. No more e-mails until I get home. Marco

After a quick sandwich in Van Thiessen's office, Joel Backman left the bank building riding shotgun in a shiny green BMW four-door sedan. The driver was Franz. Franz fancied himself a Formula One hopeful, and when Joel let it be known that he was in somewhat of a hurry, Franz slipped into the left lane on the autobahn and hit 150 kilometres per hour.

AT 1.55 P.M., Joel Backman was sitting in a lavishly large seat in the first-class section of a Lufthansa 747 as it began its push back from the gate at the Munich airport. Only when it started to move did he dare pick up the glass of champagne he'd been staring at for ten minutes. The glass was empty by the time the plane stopped at the end of the runway for its final check. When the wheels lifted off the pavement, Joel closed his eyes and allowed himself the luxury of a few hours of relief.

HIS SON, on the other hand, and at exactly the same moment, 7.55 Eastern Standard Time, was stressed to the point of throwing things. How the hell was he supposed to go buy a new cellphone immediately, call Carl Pratt again and solicit old favours, and somehow cajole a cantankerous old senator from Ocracoke, North Carolina, to drop what he was doing and return immediately to a city he evidently disliked immensely? Not to mention the obvious: he, Neal Backman, had a rather full day at the office.

He left Jerry's Java, but instead of going to the office he went home. Lisa was bathing their daughter and was surprised to see him. 'What's wrong?' she said.

'We have to talk. Now.'

He began with the letter postmarked from York, Pennsylvania, and went through the $4,000 loan, as painful as it was, then the smartphone, the encrypted e-mails, pretty much the entire story. She took it calmly, much to his relief. 'You should've told me,' she said.

'Yes, and I'm sorry.'

There was no fight, no arguing. Loyalty was one of her strongest traits, and when she said, 'We have to help him,' Neal hugged her.

'He'll pay back the money,' he assured her.

'We'll worry about the money later. Is he in danger?'

'I think so.'

'OK, what's the first step?'

'Call the office and tell them I'm in bed with the flu.'

THEIR ENTIRE conversation was captured in perfect detail by a tiny mike planted by the Mossad in the light fixture above where they were sitting. It was wired to a transmitter hidden in their attic, and from there it was relayed to a field agent in the Israeli embassy in Washington.

Since Backman's disappearance in Bologna twenty-four hours ago, the bugs planted around his son had been monitored even more closely.

Fortunately, Neal did not mention the name 'Giovanni Ferro' during the conversation with Lisa. Unfortunately, he did mention two of the three hotels—the Marriott and the Sheraton.

Backman's return was given the highest priority possible. Eleven Mossad agents, all located on the East Coast, were ordered to D.C. immediately.

LISA DROPPED their daughter off at her mother's, then she and Neal sped south to Charlottesville, thirty minutes away. In a shopping centre north of town they found the office for US Cellular. They opened an account, bought a phone, and within thirty minutes were back on the road. Lisa drove while Neal tried to find Carl Pratt.

AIDED BY generous helpings of champagne and wine, Joel managed to sleep for several hours over the Atlantic. But when the plane landed at JFK at 4.30 p.m., the relaxation was gone.

At immigration, he at first stepped into the short line with the returning Americans. The mob waiting across the way for non-US was embarrassing. Then he caught himself, glanced around, and hustled over to the foreigners. How stupid can you be?

The passport officer frowned at Giovanni's passport, but then he'd frowned at all the others too.

'Could you remove your sunglasses, please?' the officer said.

'*Certamente,*' Joel said loudly. He took off the sunglasses, squinted as if blinded, then rubbed his eyes while the officer tried to study his face.

Reluctantly, he stamped the passport and handed it over without a word. Joel hustled through the terminal and found the taxi stand. 'Penn Station,' he said.

He was at Penn Station in forty-five minutes. He bought an Amtrak ticket to D.C., and at seven left New York for Washington.

THE TAXI PARKED on Brandywine Street in northwest Washington. It was almost eleven, and most of the fine homes were dark.

Mrs Pratt was in bed when she heard the doorbell. She grabbed her robe and hurried down the stairs. 'Who is it?' she asked through the intercom.

'Joel Backman,' came the answer, and she thought it was a prank.

'Who?'

'Donna, it's me, Joel. I swear. Open the door.'

She peeped through the hole in the door and did not recognise the stranger. 'Just a minute,' she said, then ran to the basement where Carl was watching the news. A minute later he was at the door, holding a pistol.

'Carl, it's me, Joel. Open the door.'

The voice was unmistakable. He opened the door and Joel Backman walked into his life, an old nightmare back for more. There were no hugs, no handshakes, hardly a smile. The Pratts quietly examined him because he looked so different. 'Will you put that gun down?' Joel said coolly.

Pratt put the gun on a side table.

'Have you talked to Neal?' Backman asked.

'All day long.'

'What's going on, Carl?' Donna asked.

Carl had been rubbing his chin, assessing things. 'Donna, we need to talk in private. Old law firm stuff. I'll give you the rundown later.'

She shot them both a look that clearly said, Go straight to hell, then stomped back up the stairs. They stepped into the living room. Carl said, 'Would you like something to drink?'

'Yes, something strong.'

He went to a small bar in a corner and poured single malts—doubles. He handed Joel a drink and without a smile said, 'Cheers.'

'Cheers. It's good to see you, Carl.'

'I bet it is. You weren't supposed to see anyone for another fourteen years.'

'Counting the days, huh?'

'We're still cleaning up after you, Joel. A bunch of good folks got hurt. I'm sorry if Donna and I aren't exactly thrilled to see you.'

'I'd like to go back and change some things,' Backman said. 'But I don't have that luxury. I'm running for my life, Carl, and I need a big favour. Help me now, and I promise I'll never show up on your doorstep again.'

'I'll shoot the next time.'

'Where's Senator Clayburn? Tell me he's still alive.'

'Yes, very much so. And you caught some luck. He's here, in D.C.'

'Why?'

'Hollis Maples is retiring, after a hundred years in the Senate. They had a bash for him tonight. All the old boys are in town.'

'Have you talked to Clayburn?'

'Yes. He didn't like the sound of your name, Joel. Something about being shot for treason.'

'Tell him he can broker a deal that will make him feel like a real patriot.'

'What's the deal?'

'I have the software, Carl. The whole package. Picked it up this morning from a vault in a bank in Zurich. You and Clayburn come to my room in the morning, and I'll show it to you.'

Pratt sucked down two ounces of scotch. He walked back to the bar and refilled his glass, took another toxic dose, then said, 'When and where?'

'The Marriott on Twenty-second Street. Room five-twenty. Nine in the morning.'

'Why, Joel? Why should I get involved?'

'Please, Carl. Bring in Clayburn, and you'll be out of the picture by noon tomorrow. I promise you'll never see me again.'

'That is very tempting.'

NEAL MADE the first pot of coffee, then stepped outside onto the cool bricks of the patio. If his father had indeed arrived back in D.C., he would not be asleep at six-thirty in the morning. The night before, Neal had coded his new phone with the numbers of the Washington hotels, and as the sun came up he started with the Sheraton. No Giovanni Ferro. Then the Marriott.

'One moment, please,' the operator said, then the phone to the room began ringing. 'Hello,' came a familiar voice.

'Marco, please,' Neal said.

'Marco here. Is this the Grinch?'

'It is.'

'Where are you right now?'

'Standing on my patio, waiting for the sun.'

'And what type of phone are you using?'

'It's a brand-new Motorola that I've kept in my pocket since I bought it yesterday.'

'You're sure it's secure.'

'Yes.'

A pause as Joel breathed deeply. 'It's good to hear your voice, son.'

'And yours as well. How was your trip?'

'Very eventful. Can you come to Washington, this morning?'

'Sure. I'm covered at the office. When and where?'

'Come to the Marriott on Twenty-second Street. Take the elevator to the sixth floor, then the stairs down to the fifth. Room five-twenty.'

'Is all this necessary?'

'Trust me. Borrow Lisa's mother's car, make sure no one is following you. When you get to the city, park it at the garage on Sixteenth then walk to the Marriott. Watch your rear at all times.'

Neal glanced around his backyard, half expecting to see agents dressed in black moving in on him.

'Are you with me?' Joel snapped.

'Yeah, sure. I'm on my way.'

IRA CLAYBURN looked like a man who'd spent his life on a fishing boat, as opposed to one who'd served thirty-four years in the US Senate. He was happily teaching economics at Davidson when a compromise appointment sent him to the Senate to fill an unexpired term. He reluctantly ran for a full term, and for the next three decades tried his best to leave Washington. At the age of seventy-one when he finally left the Senate, he took with him a mastery of US intelligence that no politician could equal.

He agreed to go to the Marriott with Carl Pratt, an old friend from a tennis club, only out of curiosity. The Neptune mystery had never been solved, as far as he knew. During the twilight of his Senate career, he had watched Joel Backman perfect the art of twisting arms for huge fees. He was leaving Washington when Jacy Hubbard, another cobra who got what he deserved, was found dead. He had no use for their ilk.

When the door to room 520 opened, he stepped inside behind Carl Pratt and came face-to-face with the devil himself.

Joel introduced himself and his son Neal to Senator Clayburn. All hands were properly shaken, all thanks duly given. Four chairs had been pulled around in a loose circle, and they sat down.

'This shouldn't take long,' Joel said. 'Senator, I need your help. I don't know how much you know about the rather messy affair that sent me away for a few years . . .'

'I know the basics, but there have always been questions.'

'I'm pretty sure I know the answers.'

'Whose satellite system is it?'

Joel took a deep breath. 'It was built by Red China, at an astronomical cost. They stole some of our technology, and they successfully launched the system—nicknamed Neptune—without the knowledge of the CIA.'

'How did they do that?'

'Something as low-tech as forest fires. They torched twenty thousand acres one night in a northern province. It created an enormous cloud and in the middle of it they launched three rockets, each with three satellites. No one in the world knew Neptune existed until my clients stumbled across it.'

'Those Pakistani students. Who killed them?'

'I suspect agents of Red China.'

'Who killed Jacy Hubbard?'

'Same.'

'And how close are these people to you?'

'Closer than I would like.'

Clayburn reached for a doughnut and Pratt drained a glass of orange juice. Joel continued, 'I have the software—JAM as they called it. There was only one copy.'

'The one you tried to sell?' Clayburn said.

'Yes. It's proving to be quite deadly, and I'm desperate to hand it over. I'm just not sure who should get it. I can't trust the CIA. Teddy Maynard got me pardoned so he could sit back and watch someone else kill me.'

'The CIA is a mess right now.' Clayburn said. 'I wouldn't go near it.'

'Who do I talk to?' Joel asked. 'Who can I trust?'

'DIA, the Defence Intelligence Agency,' Clayburn said without hesitation. 'The head guy there is Major Wes Roland, an old friend. He has a ton of experience, smart as hell. And an honourable man.'

'Doesn't he report to the director of the CIA?' Pratt asked.

'Yes, everyone does. There are now at least fifteen different intelligence agencies and by law they all report to the CIA.'

'So Wes Roland will take what I give him and tell the CIA?' Joel asked.

'He has no choice. But he knows how to play the politics. That's how he's survived this long.'

'Can you arrange a meeting?'

'Yes, but what will happen at the meeting?'

'I'll throw JAM at him and run out of the building.'

'And in return?'

'I don't want money, Senator. Just a little help.'

'What?'

'I prefer to discuss it with him. With you in the room, of course.'

There was a gap in the conversation as Clayburn weighed the issues. Finally, he sat back in his chair and said, 'I assume this is urgent.'

'Worse than urgent. If Major Roland is available, I would meet with him right now. Anywhere.'

'I'm sure he'll drop whatever he's doing.'

'The phone's over there.'

Clayburn stood and stepped towards the desk. Pratt cleared his throat and said, 'Look, fellas, at this point, I'd like to check out. I don't want to hear any more. Don't want to be a witness, or another casualty. So if you'll just excuse me, I'll be heading back to the office.'

He was gone in an instant, with the door closing hard behind him.

'Poor Carl,' Clayburn said. 'Always afraid of his shadow.' He picked up the phone and went to work.

In the middle of the call, Clayburn placed his hand over the receiver and said to Joel, 'The software, what's it on?'

'Four disks,' Joel said.

'They have to verify it, you understand?'

'OK, I'll take two disks with me into the Pentagon. That's about half of it.'

Clayburn huddled over the receiver and repeated Joel's condition. Again, he listened for a long time then asked Joel, 'Will you show me the disks?'

'Yes.'

He placed the call on hold while Joel removed the envelope from his briefcase, then the four disks, and placed them on the bed. Clayburn went back to the phone and said, 'I'm looking at four disks. Mr Backman assures me it is what it is.' He listened then punched the hold button again.

'They want us at the Pentagon right now,' he said.

'I'll meet you in the lobby in five minutes,' Joel said.

When the door closed behind Clayburn, Joel stuck two of the disks into his coat pocket, and handed the other two to Neal.

'After we leave, get another room and leave these there. Then stay here till you hear from me.'

THE TAXI DROPPED them at the south lot of the Pentagon, near the Metro stop. Two uniformed members of Major Roland's staff were waiting with credentials and instructions. They walked them through the security clearances and got their photos made for their temporary ID cards.

They took the stairs to the second floor, C wing, and were led into a suite of offices where they were obviously expected. Major Roland himself was standing by, waiting. He was about sixty, still looking trim and fit in his khaki uniform. Introductions were made, and he invited them into his conference room. At one end of the table, three technicians were busy checking out a large computer that had evidently just been rolled in.

Major Roland asked the computer technicians if their equipment was ready. It was, and he asked them to step outside the room.

Joel and Clayburn sat on one side of the conference table. Major Roland was flanked by his two deputies on the opposite side. All three had pens and notepads ready to go. Joel and Clayburn had nothing.

'Let's start and finish a conversation about the CIA,' Backman began, determined to be in charge of the proceedings. 'As I understand the law, the director of the CIA is in charge of all intelligence activities.'

'That's correct,' Roland said.

'What will you do with the information I am about to give you?'

The look that passed between the major and the deputy conveyed uncertainty. 'As you said, sir, the director is entitled to know everything.'

Backman smiled and cleared his throat. 'Major, the CIA tried to get me killed, OK? And, as far as I know, they're still after me.'

'Mr Maynard's gone, Mr Backman.'

'And someone took his place. I don't want money, Major. I want protection. First, I want my own government to leave me alone.'

'That can be arranged,' Roland said with authority.

'And I'll need some help with a few others.'

'Why don't you tell us everything, Mr Backman? The more we know, the more we can help you.'

With the exception of Neal, Joel Backman didn't trust another person on the face of the Earth. But the chase was over; there was no place else to run.

He began with Neptune itself, and described how it was built by Red China, how the technology was stolen from two different US defence contractors, how it was launched under cover and fooled not only the US but also the Russians, the British and the Israelis. He narrated the lengthy story of the three Pakistanis—their ill-fated discovery, their brilliance in writing software that could manipulate and neutralise the system. He spoke harshly of his own giddy greed and the recklessness of Jacy Hubbard in shopping JAM to various governments. Without hesitation, he admitted his mistakes and took full responsibility for the havoc he'd caused. Then he pressed on.

No, the Russians had no interest in what he was selling. They had their own satellites and couldn't afford to negotiate for more.

No, the Israelis never had a deal but they were on the fringes, close enough to know that a deal with the Saudis was looming. The Saudis were desperate to purchase JAM. They had a few satellites of their own, but nothing to match Neptune. In a tightly controlled experiment, two agents from the Saudi secret police were given a demonstration of the software by the three Pakistanis. It had been a dazzling, very convincing display. Backman had watched it, as had Hubbard.

The Saudis offered $100 million for JAM. Hubbard was the point man during the negotiations. A 'transaction fee' of $1 million was wired to an account in Zurich. Hubbard and Backman countered with half a billion.

Then all hell broke loose. The feds attacked with warrants, indictments, investigations, and the Saudis got spooked. Hubbard got murdered. Joel fled to the safety of prison, leaving a wide path of destruction behind and some angry people with serious grudges.

The forty-five-minute summary ended without a single interruption. When Joel finished, none of the three on the other side of the table was taking notes. They were too busy listening.

'I'm sure we can talk to the Israelis,' Major Roland said. 'If they're convinced the Saudis will never get their hands on JAM, I'm quite sure they can be placated.'

'What about the Saudis?'

'We have a lot of common interests these days. I'm confident they'll relax if they know that we have it and no one else will get it. I think they'll write it off as a bad deal. There is the small matter of the transaction fee.'

'A million bucks is chump change to them. It's not negotiable.'

'Very well. I guess that leaves the Chinese.'

Clayburn had yet to speak. He leaned forward on his elbows and said, 'Your clients basically hijacked a zillion-dollar system and rendered it useless without their homemade software. The Chinese have nine of the best satellites ever built floating around up there and they can't use them. They are not going to forgive and forget, and unfortunately, we have little leverage with Beijing on delicate intelligence matters.'

Major Roland was nodding. 'I'm afraid I must agree with the senator. We can let them know that we have the software, but they'll never forget. We'll do what we can with the Chinese, but it may not be much.'

'Here's the deal, gentlemen,' Joel said. 'You give me your word that you'll get the CIA out of my life, and that you'll act quickly to appease the Israelis and the Saudis. Do whatever is possible with the Chinese, which I understand may be very little. And you give me two passports—one Australian and one Canadian. You bring them to me this afternoon and I'll hand over the other two disks.'

'It's a deal,' Roland said. 'But, we need to have a look at the software.'

Joel reached into his pocket and removed disks one and two. Roland called the computer technicians back in, and the entire group huddled around the large monitor.

Chapter 14

A Mossad agent with the code name of Albert thought he saw Neal Backman enter the lobby of the Marriott on 22nd Street. He called his supervisor, and within thirty minutes two other agents were inside the hotel. The knowledge that Joel Backman was probably staying at the Marriott on 22nd Street was extremely important. But first, the killing of an American on American soil was an operation so delicate that the prime minister would have to be consulted.

JOEL CAME CLOSER to a bullet in the head than he would ever know. He and Neal had lunch with the senator in the rear of a Vietnamese deli near Dupont Circle. When they strolled along Connecticut Avenue after lunch, they were closely watched by the Mossad. A sharpshooter was ready in the rear of a rented lorry. Final approval, though, was still hung up in Tel Aviv.

At exactly four o'clock., while sitting in a Starbucks coffee shop on Massachusetts Avenue, Neal took his cellphone and dialled the number given by Major Roland. He handed the phone to his father.

Roland himself answered. 'We're on our way,' he said.

'Room five-twenty,' Joel said. 'How many are coming?'

'It's a nice group,' Roland said.

'I don't care how many you bring, just leave everybody else in the lobby.'

They walked ten blocks back to the Marriott, with every step watched closely by well-armed Mossad agents. Still no action in Tel Aviv.

The Backmans were in the room for a few minutes when there was a knock on the door.

Joel shot a nervous glance at his son, who froze. This could be it, Joel said to himself. This could be the end of the epic journey and road.

'Who is it?' Joel asked as he stepped to the door.

'Wes Roland.'

Joel looked through the peephole, took a deep breath and opened the door. The major was all alone and empty-handed. At least he appeared to be alone. Joel glanced down the hall and saw people trying to hide. He quickly closed the door and introduced Roland to Neal.

'Here are the passports,' Roland said, reaching into his coat pocket and pulling out two broken-in passports. The first had a dark blue cover with AUSTRALIA in gold letters. Joel opened it and looked at the photo first. The technicians had taken the Pentagon security photo, lightened the hair considerably, removed the glasses and a few of the wrinkles, and produced a pretty good image. His name was Simon Wilson McAvoy.

The second was bound in navy blue, with CANADA in gold letters on the outside. Same photo, and the Canadian name of Ian Rex Hatteboro. Joel nodded his approval and handed both to Neal for his inspection.

'There is some concern about the grand jury investigation into the pardon scandal,' Roland said. 'We didn't discuss it earlier.'

'Major, you and I both know that affair is not my scandal. I had no idea a pardon was in the works.'

'You may be called to appear before a grand jury.'

'Fine. I'll volunteer. It'll be a very short appearance.'

Roland seemed satisfied. 'Now, about that software,' he said.

'It's not here,' Joel said, with unnecessary drama. He nodded at Neal, who left the room. 'The package is in another room. Sorry, but I've been acting like a spy for too long.'

'Not a bad practice for a man in your position.'

'I guess it's now a way of life.'

'Our technicians are still playing with the first two disks. It's really an impressive piece of work.'

'My clients were smart boys. Just got greedy, like a few others.'

There was a knock on the door, and Neal was back in the room. He handed

THE BROKER | 143

the envelope to Joel, who removed the two disks, then gave them to Roland.

'Thanks,' Roland said. 'It took guts.'

'Some people have more guts than brains, I guess.'

There was nothing left to say. Roland made his way to the door. He grabbed the doorknob, then thought of something else. 'Just so you know,' he said gravely, 'the CIA is reasonably certain that a Chinese assassin called Sammy Tin landed in New York from Milan this afternoon.'

'Thanks, I guess,' Joel said.

When Roland left the hotel room with the envelope, Joel stretched out on the bed and closed his eyes. Neal found two beers in the minibar and fell into a nearby chair. He waited a few minutes, sipped his beer, then finally said, 'Dad, I want to know everything. And you're going to tell me.'

AT 6 P.M., Lisa's mother's car stopped outside a hair salon on Wisconsin Avenue in Georgetown. Joel got out and said goodbye. Neal sped away, anxious to get home.

Neal had made the appointment by phone, bribing the receptionist with the promise of $500 in cash. A lady named Maureen was waiting, anxious to see who would drop that kind of money on a quick colouring job.

Joel paid first, then sat in front of a mirror.

Maureen put her fingers in his hair and said, 'Who did this?'

'A lady in Italy.'

'What colour do you have in mind?'

'Solid grey. Let's get it almost white.'

She rolled her eyes and went to work. A few minutes into the project, Joel asked, 'Are you working tomorrow?'

'Nope, it's my day off. Why?'

'Because I need to come in around noon for another session. I'll need something darker tomorrow to hide the grey you're doing now.'

Her hands stopped. 'What's with you?'

'Meet me here at noon, and I'll pay a thousand bucks in cash.'

DAN SANDBERG had been loafing at his desk at the *Post* late in the afternoon when the call came. The gentleman on the other end identified himself as Joel Backman, said he wanted to talk.

'The real Joel Backman?' Sandberg said, scrambling for his laptop. 'Last time I saw you, you were in court, pleading guilty to all sorts of bad stuff.'

'All of which was wiped clean with a presidential pardon.'

'I thought you were tucked away on the other side of the world.'

'Yeah, I got tired of Europe. I'm back now, ready to do business again.'

'What kind of business?'

'My specialty, of course. That's what I wanted to talk about.'

'I'd be delighted. But I'll have to ask questions about the pardon.'

'That's the first thing we'll cover, Mr Sandberg. How about tomorrow morning at nine?'

'I wouldn't miss it. Where do we meet?'

'I'll have the presidential suite at the Hay-Adams. Bring a photographer if you like. The broker is back in town.'

WHITAKER SAT in the first-class section of the Alitalia flight from Milano to Dulles. Up front, the booze was free and free-flowing, and Whitaker tried his best to get hammered. The call from Julia Javier had been a shock.

She had begun pleasantly enough.

'The director is very anxious right now, Whitaker. She wants to know if you're going to find Marco.'

'Tell her yes, we'll find him!'

'And where are you looking, Whitaker?'

'Between here, in Milano, and Zurich.'

'Well, you're wasting your time, Whitaker, because ol' Marco has popped up here in Washington. Met with the Pentagon this afternoon. Slipped right through your fingers, Whitaker, made us look stupid.'

'What!'

'Come home, Whitaker, and get here quickly.'

AT 6.02 P.M., Eastern Standard Time, the call came from Tel Aviv to halt the Backman killing. Stand down. Abort. Pack up and withdraw.

For the agents it was welcome news. They were trained to move in with great stealth, do their deed, disappear with no evidence, no trail. Bologna was a far better place than the crowded streets of Washington, D.C.

An hour later, Joel checked out of the Marriott and enjoyed a long walk through the cool air to the Hay-Adams. He stayed on the busy streets, though, and didn't waste any time. This city was different from Bologna after hours. Once the commuters were gone and the traffic died down, things got dangerous.

The reservation had been confirmed, and with a proper smile the clerk handed over a key and welcomed Mr Ferro to their hotel.

THE PRESIDENTIAL SUITE at the Hay-Adams was on the seventh floor, with three large windows overlooking H Street, then Lafayette Park, then the White House. It had a king-size bedroom, a bathroom well appointed with brass and marble, and a sitting room with period antiques. It went for $3,000 a night, but then what did the broker care about such things?

When Sandberg knocked on the door at nine it was yanked open and a hearty 'Morning, Dan!' greeted him. Backman lunged for his right hand and as he pumped it furiously he dragged Sandberg into his domain.

'Glad you could make it,' he said. 'Would you like some coffee?'

'Yeah, sure, black.'

Sandberg dropped his satchel onto a chair and watched Backman pour from a silver coffeepot. Much thinner, with hair that was shorter and almost white, gaunt through the face.

'Make yourself at home,' Backman was saying. 'I've ordered some breakfast. Should be up in a minute.'

He carefully set two cups with saucers on the coffee table in front of the sofa, and said, 'Let's work here. You plan to use a recorder?'

'If that's all right.'

'I prefer it that way. Eliminates misunderstandings.' They took their positions. Sandberg placed a small recorder on the table, then got his pad and pen ready. Backman was all smiles as he sat low in his chair, legs casually crossed, the confident air of a man who wasn't afraid of any question.

'Well, the first question is, where have you been?'

'Europe, knocking about, seeing the Continent. I spent a lot of time on the trains over there, a marvellous way to travel. You can see so much.'

'Why have you returned?'

'This is home. Bumming around Europe sounds like great fun, and it was, but you can't make a career out of it. I've got work to do.'

'What kind of work?'

'The usual. Government relations, consulting.'

'That means lobbying, right?'

'My firm will have a lobbying arm, yes.'

'And what firm is that?'

'The new one.'

'Help me out here, Mr Backman.'

'I'm opening a new firm, the Backman Group, offices here, New York, and San Francisco. We'll have six partners initially, should be up to twenty in a year or so. We plan to cut the ribbon on the first of May.'

'This will not be a law firm?'

'No, but we plan to add a legal section later.'

'I thought you lost your licence when . . .'

'I did, yes. But with the pardon, I'm now eligible to sit for the bar exam again. If I get a hankering to start suing people, then I'll brush up on the books and get a licence.'

'Could you give me the names of some clients?'

'Of course not, but just hang on for a few weeks and that information will be available.'

The phone on the desk rang, and Backman walked over and picked it up. Sandberg heard, 'Backman, yes, hello, Bob. Yes, I'll be in New York tomorrow. Look, I'll call you back in an hour, OK? I'm in the middle of something.' He hung up and said, 'Sorry about that.'

It was Neal, calling as planned, at exactly 9.15, and he would call every ten minutes for the next hour.

'No problem,' said Sandberg. 'Let's talk about your pardon. Have you seen the stories about the alleged buying of presidential pardons?'

'Have I seen the stories? I have a defence team in place, Dan. If and when the feds manage to put together a grand jury I've informed them that I want to be the first witness. I have absolutely nothing to hide, and the suggestion that I paid for a pardon is actionable at law.'

'You plan to sue?'

'Absolutely. My lawyers are preparing a massive libel action now against the *New York Times* and that hatchet man, Heath Frick. It'll be ugly. It'll be a nasty trial, and they're gonna pay me a bunch of money.'

'You're sure you want me to print that?'

'Hell yes! And while we're at it, I commend you and your newspaper for the restraint you've shown so far.'

Sandberg's story of this visit to the presidential suite was big enough. Now, it had just been thrust onto the front page, tomorrow morning.

'Just for the record, you deny paying for the pardon?'

'Categorically, vehemently denied. And I'll sue anybody who says I did.'

'So why were you pardoned?'

Backman was about to launch into a long one when the door buzzer erupted. 'Ah, breakfast,' he said, jumping to his feet. He opened the door and a waiter pushed in a cart holding caviar and all the trimmings, scrambled eggs with truffles, and a bottle of Krug champagne in a bucket of ice. While Backman signed the receipt the waiter opened the bottle.

'A glass of champagne, Dan?'

Sandberg glanced at his watch. Seemed a bit early to start with the booze, but then why not? How often would he be sitting in the presidential suite sipping on bubbly that cost $300 a bottle? 'Sure, but just a little.'

The waiter filled two glasses, put the Krug back in the ice, and left the room just as the phone rang again. This time it was Randall from Boston.

After Backman slammed down the receiver he said, 'Eat a bite, Dan, I ordered enough for the both us.'

'No, thanks, I had a bagel earlier.'

Backman dipped a wafer into a $500 pile of caviar and stuck it in his mouth, like a teenager with a corn chip and salsa while he paced.

'My pardon?' he said. 'I asked President Morgan to review my case. He's a very astute person.'

'Arthur Morgan?'

'Yes, very underrated as a president, Dan. He will be missed. Anyway, the more Morgan studied the case, the more he saw through the government's smoke screen. As an old defence lawyer himself, he understood the power of the feds when they want to nail an innocent person.'

'But you pled guilty.'

'I had no choice. First, they indicted me and Jacy Hubbard on bogus charges. "Bring on the trial," we said. "Give us a jury." We scared the feds so bad that they did what they always do. They went after our friends and families. Those idiots indicted my son, Dan, a kid fresh out of law school who knew nothing about my files. It became a badge of honour for me to take the fall. I pled guilty so all charges would be dropped against my son and my partners. President Morgan figured this out. That's why I was pardoned.'

Backman was pacing back and forth, now, a man with many burdens to unload. Then he suddenly stopped and said, 'Enough about the past, Dan. Let's talk about tomorrow. Look at that White House over there. Have you ever been there for a state dinner, black tie, marine colour guard, slinky ladies in beautiful gowns?'

'No.'

Backman was standing at the window, gazing at the White House. 'Twice I've done that,' he said with a trace of sadness. 'Give me two, maybe three years, and one day they'll hand deliver a thick invitation, gold embossed lettering: The President and First Lady request the honour of your presence . . . That's power, Dan. That's what I live for.'

Sandberg jolted the broker back to reality. 'Who killed Jacy Hubbard?'

Backman's shoulders dropped and he walked to the ice bucket for another round. 'It was a suicide, Dan, plain and simple. Jacy was humiliated beyond belief. The feds destroyed him. He just couldn't handle it.'

'Well, you're the only person in town who believes it was a suicide.'

'And I'm the only person who knows the truth. Print that, would you.'

'I will. Frankly, Mr Backman, your past is much more interesting than your future. I have a pretty good source that tells me that you were pardoned because the CIA wanted you released, that Morgan caved under pressure from Teddy Maynard, and that they hid you somewhere so they could watch and see who nailed you first.'

'You need new sources.' Backman spread his arms so Sandberg could see everything. 'I'm alive! If the CIA wanted me dead, then I'd be dead.' He swallowed some champagne, and said, 'Find a better source.'

Sandberg was flipping back through his notes when the phone rang again. It was Ollie this time, and Backman would have to call him back.

'I have a photographer downstairs,' Sandberg said. 'My editor would like some photos.'

'Of course.'

Joel put on his jacket, checked his tie, hair, and teeth in a mirror, while the photographer arrived, unloaded some gear and fiddled with the lighting.

The best shot, according to the photographer, was a wide one of Joel on the burgundy leather sofa, with a portrait on the wall behind him. He posed for a few by the window, trying to get the White House in the distance.

The phone kept ringing, and Joel ignored it. Neal was supposed to call back every five minutes in the event a call went unanswered, ten if Joel picked up. After twenty minutes of shooting, the phone was driving them crazy. The broker was a busy man.

The photographer finished, collected his gear and left. Sandberg hung around for a few minutes, then finally headed for the door. As he was leaving he said, 'Look, Mr Backman, this will be a big story tomorrow. But just so you know, I don't buy half the crap you've told me today.'

'Which half?'

'You were guilty as hell. So was Hubbard. He didn't kill himself, and you ran to prison to save your ass. Maynard got you pardoned. Arthur Morgan didn't have a clue.'

'Good. That half is not important.'

'What is?'

'The broker is back. Make sure that's on the front page.'

HIS LAST GUESTS in the suite made him cry. Neal, the son he hardly knew, and Lisa, the daughter-in-law he'd never met, handed him Carrie, the two-year-old granddaughter he'd only dreamed about. She cried too, at first, but then settled down as her grandfather walked her around and showed her the White House just over there. He walked her from window to window, from room to room, bouncing her and chatting away as if he'd had experience with a dozen grandkids. Neal took more photos, but these were of a different man. Gone were the bluster and arrogance; he was a simple grandfather clinging to a beautiful little girl.

Room service delivered a late lunch of soups and salads. They enjoyed a quiet family meal, Joel's first in many, many years. He ate with only one hand because the other balanced Carrie on his knee, which never stopped its steady bounce.

He warned them of tomorrow's story in the *Post*, and explained the motives behind it. It was important for him to be seen in Washington, and buy some time, confuse everyone who might still be looking for him. It would be talked about for days, long after he was gone.

Lisa wanted answers as to how much danger he was in, and Joel confessed that he wasn't sure. He would drop out for a while, move around, always being careful. He'd learned a lot in the past two months.

'I'll be back in a few weeks,' he said. 'And I'll drop in from time to time. Hopefully, after a few years things will be safer.'

'Where are you going now?' Neal asked.

'I'm taking the train to Philly, then I'll catch a flight to Oakland. I would like to visit my mother. Eventually I'll end up somewhere in Europe.'

'Which passport will you use?'

'Not the ones I got yesterday. I'm not about to allow the CIA to monitor my movements. Barring an emergency, I'll never use them.'

'So how do you travel?'

'I have another passport. A friend loaned it to me.'

Neal gave him a look of suspicion, as if he knew what 'friend' meant.

While Lisa was in the bathroom changing Carrie's diaper, Joel lowered his voice and said, 'Three things. First, get a security firm to sweep your home, office and cars. It'll cost about ten grand, and it must be done. Second, I'd like you to locate an assisted-living place somewhere close to here. My mother, your grandmother, is stuck out there in Oakland with no one to check on her. A good place will cost three to four thousand a month.'

'I take it you have the money.'

'Third, yes, I have the money. It's in an account here at Maryland Trust. You're listed as one of the owners. Withdraw twenty-five thousand to cover the expenses you've incurred so far, and keep the rest close by. And spend some, OK? Loosen up a little. Take the girl to Disney World.'

'How will we correspond?'

'For now, e-mail, the Grinch routine. I'm quite the hacker, you know.'

'How safe are you, Dad?'

'The worst is over.'

Lisa was back with Carrie, who wanted to return to the bouncing knee. Joel held her for as long as he could.

FATHER AND SON entered Union Station together while Lisa and Carrie waited in the car. The bustle of activity made Joel anxious again; old habits would be hard to break.

He bought a ticket to Philadelphia, and as they slowly made their way to the platform area Neal said, 'I really want to know where you're going.'

Joel stopped and looked at him. 'I'm going back to Bologna.'

'There's a friend there, right?'

'Yes.'

'Of the female variety?'

'Oh yes.'

'She's Italian?'

'Very much so. She's really special.'

'They were all special.'

'This one saved my life.'

'Does she know you're coming back?'

'I think so.'

'Please be careful, Dad.'

'I'll see you in a month or so.'

They hugged and said goodbye.

JOHN GRISHAM

Born: February 8, 1955, Arkansas
Homes: Virginia and Mississippi
Current interest: learning Italian

When it came to finding a setting for *The Broker*, the first novel John Grisham has located outside the United States, the author couldn't resist indulging his love of Italy and all things Italian. 'I had the great luxury of finding anywhere in the world to hide this guy,' he explains, 'and chose Italy by throwing a dart at a map. I have to confess that I was not blindfolded when I threw the dart.'

Grisham's central character, Joel Backman, gets to know Bologna by visiting the city's restaurants—which required arduous research on the author's part. 'My friend Luca Patuelli showed me around. He knows all the chefs in Bologna—no small feat—and, in the course of our tedious work, I put on about ten pounds!' And what does he particularly like about Italy? 'The people. They have got things figured out. They enjoy life.'

Grisham was a lawyer in a small town in Mississippi when he witnessed the trial that was to change his life. After hearing the harrowing testimony of a twelve-year-old rape victim, he was moved to write a novel loosely based on the crime. Called *A Time to Kill*, it achieved modest sales when it was published. It was his second book, *The Firm*, which brought him fame and fortune as it shot into the best-seller lists in 1991 and then became a successful movie. For Grisham it was like winning the lottery. 'I stopped practising law. I stopped practising politics. And so, for fifteen years I've had the luxury of staying at home, being here with my kids, coaching Little League baseball. I didn't miss a school play. I didn't miss anything.' His children, eighteen-year-old Shea and twenty-one-year-old Ty, are now both at college.

John Grisham, who once described himself as 'the luckiest guy in the world', has earned financial rewards beyond his wildest dreams from the success of his books, but he and his wife Renee have always been determined to keep their family life as normal as possible. 'When it's all over I hope I can say it was a whole lot of fun, but I kept my feet on the ground and I didn't change.'

SOLO

THE NORTH POLE: ALONE AND UNSUPPORTED

PEN HADOW

'All men dream; but not all equally. Pen Hadow dreamt of making a 478-mile journey to the North Pole that had never been achieved—alone and using only the supplies he could carry with him. He showed that the Edwardian spirit of adventure displayed by Shackleton and Scott is still very much alive . . .

'This extraordinary triumph of physical and mental endurance should serve as a reminder to us all that our limits are often far beyond where we may assume them to be.

The Times

PROLOGUE

I flew into Resolute Bay on February 26, 2003—the point of no return, the last staging post on the way to the North Pole. I was already deep in the tundra, further north than most citizens of the world, past or present, have ever been, but my destination still lay over a thousand miles to the north.

Resolute Bay, also known as Qausuittuq—'place with no dawn'—in the Inuktitut language, is a sheltered bay on the southern shores of Cornwallis Island, overlooking the ice-choked waters of the Northwest Passage—the grail so many seamen lost their lives seeking. Dependent for supplies on an annual 'sea lift' by a supply vessel escorted by two icebreakers, Resolute Bay is so remote an outpost that no mainland Canadian I have ever met has heard of it. It did not even exist as a settlement until the late 1940s, when the Canadian government laid formal claim to the islands north of the mainland and set up military installations, airfields, exploratory oil and gas rigs, weather stations and civilian settlements in previously uninhabited areas. Resolute Bay was one of these settlements and Canadian Inuit living well to the south were encouraged to resettle there with the dubious promise of rich hunting grounds. It now has about 200 permanent inhabitants, but the only significant employers are the Polar Continental Shelf Project—an international scientific study centre—and the airport complex, with its air-charter operators serving remote outlying communities and ferrying travellers and adventurers to the far north.

The permanent population at Resolute mostly live at the Hamlet, a mile from the airfield, in the shadow of the rocky outcrop rearing 500 feet above the town. As I drove down the dirt road in a battered Ford pick-up, the lights of this forlorn village shimmered through the cold, dark haze of the late winter afternoon. Prominent among them was the steeple light of the tiny church. Constructed of wood, painted pea-green and reminiscent of a chapel high in the Alps, the church lies at the heart of the village—a beacon of hope in a dark, cold place. I pulled up at the side of the dirt road, wheels crunching on the wind-packed snow, and hurried into the church. Its wooden interior seemed barely larger than a doll's house, and I had the strong feeling that I had intruded into a place of childlike faith. But I stayed a while in this oasis of warmth and calm, a refuge both from the frenzy of the final preparations ahead of me and the wildness of the weather outside.

As I left the church, the ferocious cold made me gasp for breath, but nonetheless I went for a walk through the village to retune into life up here. At once I bumped into three old friends: Toni and Mavis Manik, and Diane Guy, wife of Gary, my Canadian base manager at Resolute. Toni has been hired by an endless succession of TV and film crews to demonstrate his traditional Inuit hunting skills. He is one of the two people responsible for maintaining Resolute's power plant and telephone system, and is also the community's lay vicar, christening, marrying and burying his kinsfolk. As if that were not enough to keep him occupied, he has become one of Gary Guy's business partners, providing base camp facilities for polar expeditions in the spring and for wilderness travellers in the summer.

His daughter, Mavis, had been a schoolgirl when I'd first met her in 1994, with dreams of breaking the mould that left the majority of her peers dependent on state handouts. When I returned to Resolute in 1998 she was working as an office assistant for one of the local air charter operators, and was hoping to win a scholarship to flight school down south. I was delighted to see her again and intrigued to know whether her dream had been realised. Sadly the scholarship had never materialised, and she had had to shelve her ambitions. However, she was still working for the charter operation, and in a more senior position. As we talked, I noticed a mop of black hair and two dark eyes peering over her shoulder at me from the safety of a papoose. Oh yes, she had a son and was looking forward to having more children.

After a few minutes standing still, the cold was penetrating my bones. I left my friends and hurried on through the snow-lined streets, walking fast to generate a little body heat. Surrounding the church was a scattering of squat, single-storey houses, raised clear of the permafrost on stilts and constructed of wood, aluminium siding or sheet metal, and painted in muted colours. For eight months of the year, snow is banked against their walls up to roof height. Dogs are chained outside almost every house, but the teams of huskies that pull the hunters' sleds are kept about a quarter of a mile from the settlement. When their incessant barking reaches a particularly frenzied peak, it is a signal that a polar bear has entered the bay.

The surplus Arctic char that the Inuit catch in the lakes and the ptarmigan they shoot are stored on the house roofs or on hanging lines—nature's deep-freezes—until needed, and the one and only store in Resolute Bay also sells convenience foods like pizza, burgers and even ice cream, alongside rifles and computer software. The Inuit clothing and equipment is a similarly eclectic mixture of ancient and modern, like homemade sealskin coats and the traditionally embroidered double-hooded *armanti* coats—often containing a sleeping infant—set off by luridly coloured shell-suit bottoms. As I hurried on through the settlement, I could see the skins of polar bears and seals, stretched on wooden frames to cure in the Arctic wind, hanging next to the pyjamas and underwear from the weekly wash. The huge wooden *komatik* sleds, pulled by dog teams and held together by string and skill alone, were drawn up next to petrol-engined snowmobiles, and kayaks were lashed against the outbuildings alongside upturned boats with outboard motors.

Driving back from the settlement, I hunched over the wheel, my body stiff with cold, my sole focus to get back to the warmth and home comforts of my base. I was going to be operating in these extreme temperatures and worse for months, and at the moment I could hardly cope inside a heated car. But I knew that I would quickly adapt and it occurred to me then, as it has done at the start of every polar season, how remarkable the human body is in being able to adjust to almost any environment.

The sea is normally icebound from the autumn right through to the summer breakup of the ice the following July, but in recent years, perhaps in response to global warming, the floe edge—the interface between the immobile sea ice locked between the islands and the shifting ice pans covering the open sea—has formed closer and closer to Resolute. This year, almost unprecedentedly, it ran south from Resolute Bay. A lead—strictly a navigable channel, but polar travellers use the term for any expanse of open water—had opened in the sea ice and, once established, the tides, currents and winds kept the ice moving enough to prevent it refreezing completely. The presence of open water so near to the settlement had positive implications both for the local hunters and for me, though for different reasons.

Simon Murray, a friend whom I was to partner on an unsupported expedition to the South Pole later in the year, had also flown in to spend a week

camping out on the ice with me. It was a way of building our sledging partnership in an environment similar to Antarctica. Simon and I were doing
our training between Resolute Bay and Griffith Island, just five miles west
of the floe edge, even though sledging and camping that close to a lead is
less than ideal, for where there is open water, seals can come up for air, and
wherever you have seals, polar bears will inevitably gather. We were easier
prey than any seal and we were always on the lookout for bears.

As we sledged, we paused every fifteen minutes to carry out a 360-degree
visual sweep, Simon covering to our left and me to the right, with each of us
overlapping by twenty degrees to be sure of missing nothing. It was not that
easy to do on skis, pulling a heavy sledge, with a huge, fur-trimmed hood
drawn close round the face and wearing goggles and a full-face mask, but
vigilance was essential. At night in our tent—the most vulnerable time—I
kept a loaded double-barrelled shotgun by my sleeping-bag, but once asleep
we took our chances; even the use of huskies as guard dogs or tripwire
alarm systems are no guarantee of waking up alive in the morning. In the
end, we finished our training programme having seen nothing more alarming than bear tracks, and Simon then headed back to warmer climes.

I was elated by the nearby open water and the accompanying thin ice,
because it provided a great opportunity to test my polar 'lilo'—a flotation
and stabilisation device we'd designed that effectively converted my sledge
into a boat—and my immersion suit, in similar conditions to those I would
soon be encountering on my way to the Pole. The immersion suit was an
ultra-lightweight dry suit with integral boots, mitts and hood. Made of
orange Hypalon fabric, it weighed only 1.5 kilos and was designed to be
worn over all my Arctic clothing, including my ski boots. As a result of its
size, however, a lot of air could get trapped inside it. That was great for
buoyancy, but if I slipped and fell headfirst into the water, or became
inverted for any reason while in the water, the trapped air would form a
bubble round my feet, making it almost impossible for me to right myself.

I was anxious about how this suit and I were going to get on, and I
jumped at the chance to test it under semi-controlled conditions, with my
English base team of Ian Wesley and Martin Hartley ready to come to my
aid if needed. My only previous test of the suit had been in the rather less
icy waters of the West Dart River near my Dartmoor home. One February
afternoon my wife, Mary, was driving back from a children's birthday party
with our daughter, Freya, when she spotted our dilapidated Range Rover
parked by the river. She pulled over and found our son, Wilf, larking about

in the shallows. She was about to ask him where I was when what appeared to be a large orange fertiliser bag drifted into view, occasionally spinning in the eddies as it headed downstream towards the rapids. 'Hi, darling. All well?' I shouted over the roar of the water, before turning onto my front and swimming against the current to the bank. As a result, I knew that the immersion suit fitted me, and that it seemed to be waterproof, but I had to test it in true Arctic conditions before I could feel genuine confidence in it.

With my base team around me and snowmobiles standing ready to whisk me back to base if required, I was able to test the suit to its limits. I did so at the floe edge running across Resolute Passage, a stretch of ice and open water with such a fierce current that I tied a rope round my waist so that, if I was swept under the ice, Ian could pull me back. I soon developed a technique for breaking a channel through ice up to two inches thick, using my flailing arms or my body weight to smash through it. Then I eased myself up onto some slightly thicker ice and crawled on all fours, wondering how much abrasion the material covering my knees would take.

Finally I began walking, first on thicker ice, but with increasing confidence on thinner and thinner ice until at last the inevitable happened: I broke through the ice and fell into the water, the most dreaded sensation for any sea-ice traveller. But with all that air in my suit, I seemed to sink in slow motion; it was almost fun. Now I knew that it didn't matter any more if I fell in. As long as I was wearing my immersion suit, I wasn't even going to get wet, let alone suffer hypothermia. The ice, or lack of it, was no longer the threat to success it had always been to me in the past.

I returned to Resolute to make my final preparations for the Pole and to make sure that my chartered aircraft was ready and waiting. I called in at the offices of Kenn Borek Air, my regular charter company in Resolute Bay, to renew acquaintances and make sure they'd received my banker's draft for Can$100,000—the price of two flights, one to drop me off at Ward Hunt Island and the other, with luck, to collect me from the Pole around ten weeks later. I also finalised the dates and timings with the company's duty manager, Bill Gawletz, and the duty pilot, Troy McKerral. We agreed that I would be dropped off at Ward Hunt Island from March 13 onwards, subject to weather. Given that I expected to take sixty-five days to reach the Pole, I should be arriving there around May 16. Adverse weather conditions could easily make a nonsense of even the most carefully estimated timings, but provided I arrived there between May 15 and 25, they both declared themselves satisfied with the proposed schedule.

EARLY on the morning of March 14, Bill Gawletz phoned to confirm that weather conditions over Ward Hunt Island and the midway refuelling stop at the Eureka High Arctic Weather Station were satisfactory and we were 'Go' to depart. I made a last phone call home to Mary—it was the middle of the night in England, but I'd promised to ring before I set out—and discovered that, the day before, Freya had taken her first steps. Then, accompanied by Ian, Martin and Ginny Dougary, a British journalist, I boarded the aircraft—one of Kenn Borek Air's De Havilland DHC-6 Twin Otters: 'the workhorses of the North'. On a good strip with a head wind, a pilot can land and take off in as little as 100 metres, using either wheels or skis.

We took off at 7.30 a.m. and flew due north for almost three hours. Here, even the stunted, scrub Arctic willows and birches, growing no more than a couple of inches above the ground, could not maintain a hold, and we flew on over a landscape as grey and apparently lifeless as a desert. The comparison is apt: there is no more rainfall in the Arctic than the most arid of southern deserts, and only for a few short summer weeks does the heat of the sun melt the ice bound into the frozen surface of the land.

I spent the first part of the flight in conversation with Ian about my mileage plan, my estimate of the distance I aimed to cover in each phase of the expedition. The first part of the plan was a psychological trick: to break the 416 nautical mile distance (1 nautical mile is equivalent to 1.151 statute miles) into manageable portions—of time as well as distance. I knew that sixty days' travelling should pretty much crack it, so I split the journey down, like the minutes of a clock face, into multiples of five days.

My aim was to average three nautical miles a day over the first twenty days—the hardest in terms of ice and weather conditions, and made even more gruelling because the sledge would then be at its heaviest. I would be travelling for no more than six hours a day, reflecting the exhausting battle to drag the sledge over jumbled compressed ice and through deep snowfields in particularly cold temperatures. I would have to stay positive in the daunting early stages, when the day's progress—perhaps as little as a single nautical mile—would seem pitiful. I would have to focus on the fact that the passing days would see the conditions improve in step with the reduction of the sledge weight, allowing me to increase the pace and the hours of travelling to cover up to ten nautical miles a day.

Ian and I also discussed contingency plans if the early targets were not met. There is always a tradeoff: the fewer supplies you drag behind you the faster you can travel, but if you pare the weight down too far you jeopardise the success of the expedition. Life and the expedition would go on without food, but if I ran out of fuel I would have to abandon the expedition, because I needed heat from the stove—not to keep warm but to melt snow for drinking water. It takes a huge amount of snow to produce a small amount of water, and if an emergency forces you to try to eat snow in sub-zero temperatures you're likely to die of hypothermia due to the heat loss as you use your body warmth to melt the snow. In addition, any serious delays would mean that I would still be trying to cross the ice cap as the summer thaw broke it up, making travel increasingly difficult and dangerous. The fogs and overcast skies that always accompany the thaw would also hinder both my progress to the Pole and the final pick-up by aircraft.

I gazed down at the familiar landscape as we flew north. It is undulating country at first, blanketed with snow, but further north the landscape becomes much more dramatic: pyramidal peaks and frost-shattered screes, huge glaciated valleys, and densely crevassed glaciers with broad tongues of vivid, azure-blue ice spilling into the frozen sea. Some people talk about the Arctic as a monotonous wilderness of white, but if you open your eyes and really look at the landscape, especially at this time of year, you realise that there are no whites to be seen. Everything is in pastel shades—cream, grey, blue, green, yellow, orange, pink—and only in the stark bright light at the height of the polar summer, when the sun is high in the sky, do you begin to see true whites among the other colours.

We landed to refuel at Canada's northernmost civilian outpost, the Eureka High Arctic Weather Station, on the west coast of Ellesmere Island, 601 nautical miles from the Pole. A three-kilometre gravel road links the airstrip to the weather station. We could have twenty minutes of jaw-locking cold for free by walking down the road to the station, but the officer-in-charge's warning—'If you want to walk, don't touch the wolves if they get close to you; they may look friendly but they ain't!'—had given the red-coated Ginny cause to remember Little Red Riding Hood's fate. The alternative was to accept a lift in the snug cabin of the OIC's pick-up at a price—£100 each way—that took the breath away almost as fast as the cold. To be fair, the cost of delivering, maintaining and fuelling anything, people or plant, this far north is so great that even the taxi fares, and the other surreally priced services at Eureka, do not even begin to cover the cost of providing them.

As we were only on the ground for forty-five minutes, we all squeezed into the pick-up for the world's most expensive taxi ride. The weather station was a haven of warmth and normality. We walked along a corridor past a labyrinth of bedrooms, a quiet room, a bar, a TV lounge, a fitness room, a dining area with a huge kitchen, and the reason for the station's existence: a small room lined with weather-monitoring instruments. The station's heyday, when fifty scientists and support staff called this home, was long past. The hard-core team of the OIC, three meteorologists, three maintenance personnel and a chef, who work on a three-month rotation with their counterparts, now had the place to themselves, like astronauts in a partially decommissioned space station. We had a cup of tea and a cake with the duty officer and the meteorologists, whom I had got to know well over the years as I passed through on my various Arctic expeditions. It was a bittersweet moment, the last taste of civilisation for many weeks to come.

We returned to the Twin Otter and climbed back aboard for the final leg to Ward Hunt Island, a further 185 miles north. I'd been reasonably relaxed on the flight up to Eureka, but now I withdrew into myself, trying to brace myself for the pressures of the journey ahead. The scene beneath my frosted window was as grainy as an old silent movie. A forest of jagged peaks clawed upwards out of the ice and snow. Between them, glaciers speckled with frost-shattered rock slithered down to bury themselves in the sea. The high Arctic landscape is desolate, of course, but has its own subtle and haunting beauty. Much of the exposed brown rock is overlaid with a delicate filigree of ice and snow, tracing the contours of even the narrowest fault line, rock ledge or gully. The steeper slopes have a herringbone pattern caused by the constant action of the wind on the ice and snow, revealing the texture of the underlying rock like a brass rubbing.

Ward Hunt Island, three miles off the northern shore of Ellesmere Island at roughly 83°5′N, is no more than a couple of miles long and a mile or so wide. It is dominated by Walker Hill, a conical peak like an extinct volcano rising 1,360 feet from the frozen sea, with a narrow apron of ice-covered rock to the east, enclosing a shallow frozen lake. The island marks the frontier between two worlds. From the summit of Walker Hill you can look south towards a vast landmass extending for 10,000 miles, encompassing mountains and plains, forests and deserts, villages and cities. To the north lies no land at all, only ice and black, frigid water.

There are no shades of grey in people's reactions to this ice world. Some polar expeditioners see the Arctic as an enemy to be fought and forced into submission. But a few others revel in this strange and beautiful world and are compelled to return again and again for the love of solitude, simplicity and contemplation that it engenders.

My own relationship with the Arctic has evolved over fifteen years. I was initially fearful of it, keeping a safe distance between 'me' in here and 'it' out there, but as I grew more competent in the strategies and skills of surviving and travelling, I found myself drawn to it. I tolerate the cold, the hardship, the dangers and the backbreaking effort as a fair price to be paid for the privilege of experiencing life on the frozen ocean and seeing sights that no other human has ever seen or ever will see, for one of the wonders of the polar ice cap is that it is ever the same but ever different. It is in a state of constant flux, as the perpetual motion, compression and distortion of the ice opens up fresh leads or crumples the ice caps like paper. Sometimes imperceptibly, sometimes dramatically, the whole sweep of the frozen landscape changes from hour to hour and day to day, leaving an onlooker doubting the evidence of his own eyes.

My route from Ward Hunt Island lay due north, to the north geographic pole. There were certain givens. On a straight-line course, I knew that I would be encountering open water, rubble-fields and pressure ridges of ice, flat ice pans and floes, and areas of recently refrozen water. But unlike a mountaineering expedition, where there are photographs, satellite images, sketches and written accounts of the routes and almost every metre of the way is recorded and can be studied and rehearsed, the chart for the North Pole is essentially a blank piece of paper, but for a point in the middle, the Pole, with a series of concentric circles round it, marking the degrees of latitude, and 360 lines radiating out from it, marking the degrees of longitude. But there is nothing else to record—no rocky outcrops to be avoided or used as landmarks, no mountains or hills, no permanent features of any sort. I would just step off a beach, almost the northernmost beach in the world, and simply keep heading out to sea until I reached the north geographic pole—a pinprick of nothingness in the middle of nowhere.

The location of the Pole is the one constant in this morass of instability and change. In addition to the changing surface features, the whole ice cap is continually drifting, driven by ocean currents, tides and winds in an inexorable and sometimes unpredictable pattern. This imperceptible movement of the ice was the despair of early Arctic explorers. Many trudged northwards through a long polar day only to discover, when they woke the next morning and took a reading of their position, that the ice drift had carried them away further from the Pole than they had been the previous morning.

The wind is as great if not an even greater influence on this ice movement than the unseen currents and tides of the Arctic Ocean. Arctic gales of up to fifty knots seize on every ice ridge, boulder and surface projection, driving the ice sheet before them, ripping it apart into ice islands separated by leads of black, fathomless Arctic waters, or pushing it together with unimaginable force, grinding it into ice rubble, boulder-fields and ridges.

Those features are particularly severe north of Ward Hunt Island, where the prevailing northwesterlies bring the irresistible force of the wind-driven ice cap into collision with the immovable shores of the first land this side of the Pole. As a result, the ice is crumpled like a vast sheet of corrugated iron for miles to the north of the island. The resultant forest of pressure ridges makes for a far harder journey to the Pole than the crossing from Siberia, where the prevailing southeasterlies tend to drive the ice sheet away from the land. No one had ever travelled solo and unresupplied to the Pole from the North American side, whereas the Norwegian explorer, Borge Ousland, had from Siberia, so Ward Hunt Island had to be my starting point. It isn't quite the northernmost point of the North American landmass—Cape Columbia is about ten miles closer to the Pole, but it's too near to the east coast of Greenland, where the East Greenland Current swirling past it produces a powerful ice drift. To start from there would be like trying to climb up a down escalator—two steps forward and one step back, if you're lucky. It's better to start a few miles further from the Pole at Ward Hunt Island, in the middle of a more neutral area in terms of ice drift.

The Twin Otter forged on to meet its deadline. At this latitude the sun had only peeped over the horizon for the first time this year ten days earlier, and daylight was limited to the two hours either side of noon. Troy had to use the shadow, contrast, perspective and definition offered by that brief period of sunlight to select a suitable landing strip on the ice. There is no runway on the island, and each time they fly there, pilots have to identify a new landing strip. There are two potential sites: an area of roughly level ground and a shallow, frozen lake, but both are covered with wind-packed snowdrifts. If a pilot tried to land 'cross-grained' to these, he would hammer the aircraft to pieces within the first few yards, because those steep-faced drifts are up to a metre high and the snow is as hard as concrete.

I had asked Troy to fly ten miles north of Ward Hunt before landing, to give me an idea of ice conditions along my route. We had barely crossed the Ward Hunt Ice Shelf separating the island from the pack ice of the Arctic Ocean when things started to go wrong. In contrast to the forecast clear weather, there was a partial overcast with stinging snow showers, and thirty-knot winds, gusting to forty knots, were scouring over the ice, stripping it bare of snow cover and dumping it in vast drifts on the downwind side of each pressure ridge and boulder-field. That was routine for the Arctic, but what horrified me was the effect the winds had had on the ice cap itself.

Three vast leads had been opened up by the winds that were now battering the plane. Each was half a mile to a mile across, with the water showing black as ink against the surrounding ice. The first was perhaps five miles north of Ward Hunt, the others at roughly three-mile intervals beyond it. They ran parallel to each other, aligned SSW–NNE across the course I had to follow to reach the Pole, and looking down from 5,000 feet I could see that they extended out of sight in both directions. On the open water between the pans of ice, the gale was ripping the crests from the waves and hurling them downwind in long white streamers of spume and spray. Even supposing I could make progress north in temperatures that, including the wind-chill factor, would be the equivalent of –60 or –70°C, there was no possibility of circumventing those leads and, despite having my immersion suit and my 'lilo' for the sledge, there was no way of crossing the choppy black waters in such a wind. I would have drowned in seconds.

It was a devastating blow. I had been sure that I would cross the open water using the equipment and techniques I had developed, confident that only huge expanses of ice too thin to ski across and yet too thick to swim through would delay me. Now that conceit had been blown out of the water.

As Troy turned back for the island and began searching for a landing strip, I knew that I could not set off in these conditions and would have to wait out the storm. When the winds fell and the ice technically referred to as 'light *nilas*' had formed (its opacity indicates that it's safe to walk on; 'dark *nilas*', through which the dark water of the ocean can still be seen, tends to be too fragile to bear a person's weight), I would be able to cross the leads, but until then I would have to mark time at Ward Hunt Island.

Although it is uninhabited, there is a building there, a stout wooden hut, recently renovated by the Canadian National Park Service as a refuge for icebound mariners, scientists, travellers and anyone else in need of shelter in this impossibly remote region. That hut would have to serve as my forward base until the weather relented.

As Troy began his final approach, I could feel the aircraft being thrown around by the wind. Snow was swirling and gusting around us as he came in to land, and visibility near ground level was no more than 200 metres. Troy taxied to a halt, and as the copilot pushed the door ajar it was all he could do to hang on to it with both hands to stop it being torn from his grasp and smashed into the side of the fuselage. Over the previous fifteen years I had made a score of expeditions to the Arctic Ocean, both guiding parties of clients and undertaking two unsuccessful solo attempts on the Pole, but in all that time I had never had such an inauspicious beginning.

It took four of us to transfer the fully loaded sledge from the fuselage floor, at shoulder height, down to the ground. Although the sledge was built to withstand impacts on the ice, one careless movement while working it out of the confined space of the fuselage could easily have ripped off a runner or punctured the Kevlar and fibreglass body. Everyone wanted to be helpful, but a split second's inattention could have jeopardised the expedition, so it's fair to say that I micromanaged its short journey to the ground.

Ian and Martin immediately offered to drag the sledge the 100 metres to the doorway of the hut. Martin grabbed the trace rope, Ian slung the harness over his shoulder and they took up the weight of the sledge and pulled. It did not move an inch. They both lunged forward again, straining every sinew, and it grudgingly moved about six inches, then stopped again. This was the first time they had ever had the chance to feel what it was like to pull a sledge weighing 275 pounds—more than 19 stone—over hard-frozen, flat snow and ice. They coordinated their next lunge, and before the sledge's momentum was lost they were hauling hard towards the hut.

I didn't offer to help them. I made it a policy never to pull a fully laden sledge in front of any members of my base team, let alone a journalist. I knew if they saw me struggling they'd think: He's never going to do it. I chose to exude an air of confidence, as if the sledge would be no more troublesome to me than a trolley full of groceries in a supermarket car park.

A team can travel with a lighter load per person because they can share some of the items between them; you only need one gun, one radio and one tent whether you're one man or three. Being part of a team also helps if someone is injured or in poor health, because his sledge-load can then be shared among the others; if there is a technical problem or strategic issue to be resolved, there is a bigger pool of brains to solve the problem and more pairs of hands to fix it; and they can also share the routine work. When you're on your own, you have to multitask, and it would be hard to overstate the physical and psychological impact of the additional workload and all the extra kilos you have to carry.

I was, however, hauling less weight towards the Pole than any solo expedition had ever done before. I had used the experience and knowledge I had built up over fifteen years to trim even the basic necessities to the bone.

Ian and Martin gratefully laid down the harness and traces outside the hut and I dragged open the part-frozen door and peered into the gloomy interior. I had landed on Ward Hunt Island on previous expeditions, but each time I had set off for the north at once. This was the first time I had ever entered the hut. The temperature inside its single room was almost the same as outside (–33°C) and the ceiling was thick with hoarfrost, but the hut was a refuge from the wind chill and for that alone I was grateful. Ian, Martin and Ginny, together with the two pilots, shuffled in behind me and we pulled up chairs round the Formica-topped table. I found myself switching into host mode, lighting a couple of candles for the table, offering tea from my flask and some biscuits I'd trousered at Eureka. The team seemed in shock. I suspected that they simply could not believe the desolation of this hut, the severity of the weather and the horrors that lay ahead for me on the Arctic Ocean. It's fair to say that the conversation was stilted.

Troy kept casting an eye towards the fading light outside and at last he said, 'Well, Pen, I guess we may as well head off and leave you to it.' There were muffled grunts of agreement, the chairs were pushed back and they rose to leave. I shook hands with the two pilots first and, as they made their way back to the plane, I kissed Ginny, whose eyes were now brimming with tears. Martin made a gallant attempt at humour and then turned for the door. Ian simply said: 'I know I couldn't do this, Pen, but if anyone can, knowing you as I do, it will be you. Good luck, mate.' Then he too was gone.

The plane was only partially visible between gusts of swirling snow. I stood in the hut doorway, catching glimpses of the misted figures behind the aircraft's tiny windows. I heard the engines start up and a few seconds later it lurched forward, wing tips rocking violently in the wind as it taxied back to the downwind end of the strip. Now the plane was invisible in the whiteout, but I waited to see it one last time. Suddenly and silently, the noise of the engines snatched away in the wind, it swept upwards, thrown around by the gale as it banked to begin the journey south. I knew they would be looking down at me and thinking that I cut a forlorn figure, alone at the heart of this maelstrom of wind and snow. I raised a hand in farewell, but almost at once the clouds obscured the plane from view.

I was now the only human being on Ward Hunt Island, and on the whole of the western polar ice cap as well, for no other expeditions were being mounted from the North American side that year. I had thousands of square miles—ten per cent of the earth's surface—entirely to myself. I turned and went inside the hut. As I shut the door, ice shards fell from the eaves with a noise like shattering glass. The first thing I did was to lay my shotgun, fully loaded, on the table. I was only a handful of miles from open water and, as at Resolute Bay, where there was open water, there would be seals, polar bears preying on them and arctic foxes scavenging on the seal carcasses. From now until the moment I was airlifted off the ice cap, the shotgun would always remain loaded and within easy reach.

The hut was your basic model, a single small window at the back and a reinforced glass panel in the door allowing in a modicum of natural light. The bare wooden floor was scuffed and scarred by the boots of countless polar travellers. A couple of chain-sprung beds with thick foam mattresses stood against one wall; there was a table and six chairs, and a kitchen area lined with wooden shelves on which stood a collection of tinned foods and dehydrated rations left by previous visitors, some dating back years. They would probably still have been perfectly edible, but I left them for some more needy future visitor and confined myself to the spare rations I had brought with me: sandwiches, an orange and an apple, and a carton of fruit juice. A visitors' book lay on the table, signed by every traveller who had paused at this hut, but I decided to save the pleasure of reading it until I had eaten and had a night's sleep.

There was a cast-iron pot-bellied stove at one end of the room, but as I was not in an emergency situation I did not waste the fuel stored in a drum behind the hut, and left the stove unlit. I went outside and rummaged in the sledge for my sleeping-bag. I filled a couple of plastic builders' rubble sacks with fresh snow to melt for drinking water and cooking, found my camping stove and some more food supplies and took them inside. Then I closed and barred the door. I wasn't expecting visitors.

The light was fading fast now and the temperature falling. I lit my camping stove, and even though it only took the edge off the bitter cold in its immediate vicinity, the flickering glow of its red and blue flames transformed the hut from abandoned building to friendly refuge. I let the stove roar away as I ate my rehydrated chicken curry supper and drank a cup of tea. As soon as I had finished eating, I extinguished the stove, stripped down to my thermal base layer, and climbed into my sleeping-bag on one of the beds. There was nothing I could do until the weather broke, but I tried to make a positive out of a negative: after the months of preparation and the inevitable last-minute crises, what I needed most of all at this moment was rest.

I woke twenty-two hours later. It was four in the afternoon. My frosted sleeping-bag crackled as I turned over, stretched and yawned. My nose was numb, and the air felt very cold around my face—the only unprotected part of my body. I drifted back to sleep to the sound of the walls of the hut flexing in the rhythmic pounding of the gale-force blasts, and woke up again at six. It was pitch-dark—outside and inside. I had a short-range torch for intent use but its stark blue light only added to the feeling of deep cold, and instead I reached for the head-torch, which gave a softer, warmer, yellow-tinged light that was more likely to entice me out of my sleeping-bag.

As soon as I got up, I cooked my breakfast porridge on the stove, made a cup of tea, then sat down at the table and began to read the visitors' book, my breath fogging in the freezing air. The first entry dated from over twenty years earlier; the last was as recent as the previous summer. Not every traveller who had passed through Ward Hunt had stopped to record his thoughts—like myself in previous years, many set straight off over the ice without even entering the hut—and, frustratingly, virtually none of those who had outlined their hopes, dreams and fears on those pages had ever returned to record their triumphs or disappointments. Lifted out by air, they had flown over the top of Ward Hunt Island with no more than a passing glance. And some had never come back from the ice cap at all; the Arctic is a graveyard for more than men's dreams.

THE BRITON Wally Herbert was the first man to reach the north geographic pole on foot while crossing the entire Arctic Ocean. With three teammates and using dog teams and a series of planned resupplies by aircraft, he set off in February 1968 from Point Barrow on the north coast of Alaska. He and his companions duly reached the Pole on April 5, 1969, then continued the incredible journey to reach the far side of the Arctic Ocean on May 29, before being picked up by a ship off northern Spitsbergen. Yet this incredible expedition was virtually ignored by the media, because Wally had the misfortune to reunite with his support vessel and return home while the world's attention was focused on man's first landing on the moon.

I'm very aware of those who have gone before me and in whose footsteps I tread—giants like Sir Wally Herbert and Sir Ranulph Fiennes, Britain's foremost polar traveller. Fiennes was one of the instigators of the concept of an unsupported journey to the North Pole and it was his repeated attempts to prove its viability that helped to inspire me and a generation of other unsupported expeditioners from the 1990s to the present day. Sir Ranulph's example sparked the thought in my head: Could it actually be done on foot, pulling everything you needed behind you—a 'purer', more challenging version of what had already been achieved? And could I do it?

The next achievement I became aware of was that of Naomi Uemura, a Japanese mountaineer and polar explorer who made a wonderful journey with his dog team in 1978 from Ward Hunt Island to the north geographic pole, with seven resupplies on the way. The next solo success was by the Frenchman Dr Jean-Louis Etienne in 1986. He also started from Ward Hunt Island, this time without dogs and pulling the sledge himself, and he had five resupplies. In 1994, Borge Ousland made the first unsupported expedition to the Pole, travelling solo from the Siberian side of the Arctic Ocean. But despite many other attempts, including two by myself, at least one challenge remained: a solo, unsupported trek from the Canadian coast to the North Pole.

Within the polar community, the terms 'unsupported' or 'unaided', 'without resupply' and 'without aircraft support' all have slightly different connotations. The most all encompassing is 'without aircraft support'—the style of expedition that I was undertaking. You are put down by an aircraft at your starting point and picked up by one from the Pole, but you do not have aircraft support for any reason between those two points.

If you are going to be resupplied, you eat as much as you need and your body is not going to take the pummelling it suffers when you're carrying all your food for the entire expedition. If you do that, you inevitably take less food than you would in other circumstances and suffer as a result, and you have to take greater care of yourself and your kit if you have no recourse to any back-up. Those things both lead to slower progress, but the main difference is the weight of your sledge. People often have a very light sledge for the first fifteen to twenty days so they can rattle over those big pressure ridges north of Ward Hunt Island and then get a resupply, and that makes the whole scale of the undertaking dramatically different.

AS I TURNED the frost-stiffened, brittle and yellowing pages of the visitors' book at Ward Hunt, I read and reread the entries. Some said they were doing it for their country, others for themselves alone. Some of the entries were dispassionate or utterly prosaic—a brief note of date, time, weather and ice conditions—and others were emotional, even lyrical, as the men, and a handful of women, struggled to convey what had brought them to this place and what was driving them on into the void beyond.

I began to wonder what I should write, how I would explain the chain of events that had also led me to this lonely, icebound island at the edge of a frozen sea.

PART ONE
1

Why? That's the question everyone always asks me.

Perhaps it all goes back to Enid Wigley. In 1912 Captain Robert Falcon Scott—Scott of the Antarctic—froze to death in his tent along with his companions on their trek back across the ice, having been beaten to the South Pole by Roald Amundsen. Scott left a wife, Kathleen, and a son, Peter, who was two years old when his father set out on his final journey. Kathleen, tormented by the belief that tales of his father's exploits would inspire her son to follow in Scott's footsteps, was determined that, if so, he was going to be tough enough to survive the exposure to extreme cold that had claimed her husband's life. As a result, she hired a young nanny, Enid Wigley, and gave her strict instructions: Peter was to be inured to the cold by exposing him to the elements, summer and winter, for progressively longer and longer periods, wearing less and less clothing. As a result, he rarely wore shoes throughout his childhood and was encouraged, even compelled, to play outside, even in the snows and frosts of winter. This harsh conditioning regime was followed for five years, between the ages of two and seven, and though it may have shocked onlookers, it certainly appears to have had the desired effect.

Rather than a polar explorer, Peter (later Sir Peter) Scott became a conservationist, wildfowl expert and a founder of the World Wildlife Fund. His passion was for the wildfowl of the Arctic tundra and he went to the Antarctic only once in his life, but my father showed me pictures of Peter Scott: on the deck of a ship ploughing through the Barents Sea, binoculars raised to watch a skein of migrating whooper swans, at his easel sketching red-breasted geese on the Siberian tundra, and bracing a camera to his body by the foot of a cliff to film nesting barnacle geese in Greenland. In every case he was wearing only a short-sleeved Aertex shirt, while those around him were huddled in layers of warm clothing.

When her charge had grown up, Nanny Wigley was, in time, hired to look after a young boy named Nigel Hadow—my father. She never had to apply her hardship regime to him but she did fill his head with Scott and Amundsen's race to the South Pole and tales of other great explorers. When he grew up, my father in turn decided that when he had a son he was going to toughen him up by the same process. As my father's first-born, I had the dubious fortune to be the beneficiary of that decision.

I was born on February 26, 1962. My dad was a pig farmer at the time at a place called Bog Hall in the Scottish Highlands. The family retainer, Nanny Wigley, by then well into her seventies, was recruited to supervise my early upbringing and, under her critical eye, my father applied her spartan programme for the first few years of my life. I had the added misfortune of being born in an area where the winters were ferocious and even the summers often cold enough to send southern visitors scurrying for cover, but it made no difference to the conditioning regime. I was out in all weathers, barefoot and dressed as if it were a balmy summer's day.

I was entered in a bonny baby competition at the local Highland Games and won first prize simply because, thanks to my regular exposure to the elements, I had rosy-red apple cheeks that any greengrocer would have been proud to display. However, the Wigley experiment came to an abrupt end not long afterwards, when a friend of Mum's pointed out that my cheeks were actually frost-nipped. My mother was so mortified that she called a halt to the programme, leaving me only half-conditioned, or half-baked, as Nanny Wigley insisted on pointing out.

Not long afterwards the bottom fell out of the pig market and Dad moved us to the gentler climes of East Sussex. Nanny Wigley remained a friend of the family. She stayed with us regularly and later Dad brought her to live with us until the last days of her life. She was always immaculate, her snow-white hair scraped into a neat bun, and if her methods were strict, she was also a warm and kindly soul, always willing to stop and lay aside her work to inspire her young charge with tales of the polar world and the feats of Scott and his peers. Some of my earliest memories are of those enthralling stories of snow- and icebound lands that alternated between everlasting daylight and eternal night, and of men strong enough in mind and body to venture into those fearsome regions and wrest knowledge and glory from the unyielding ice. They fired my imagination in a way that tales of jungle or desert adventures, or soldiers or mountaineers, never did.

My father also played a big part in stirring my imagination, holding me spellbound with tales of our ancestors on both sides of the family. My mother's family, the Pendrills—my middle name—could trace their descent back to Stuart times. During the English Civil War, five Pendrill brothers saved the future King Charles II's life during his flight from the Battle of Worcester in 1651, by hiding him in an oak tree on their land while

Cromwell's Roundheads scoured the area for him—an incident still commemorated in the scores of English pubs named the Royal Oak. The Hadows were similarly proud of their heritage, and a strong streak of adventure ran through them. Among the ranks of prosperous landowners and businessmen were footloose travellers, sportsmen and soldiers of the Empire travelling to the furthest reaches of the globe.

My father would often talk about his great-grandfather, who for forty years was chairman of one of the Empire's great corporations, P&O. I still have a photograph of one of his eight sons, P. Frank Hadow, a stern Victorian who stares out of the picture frame with a gaze of imperious certainty. On the back of the picture, my father had noted that P. F. Hadow had played cricket for Harrow, Cambridge University and Middlesex, and that he had been a tea planter and big game hunter in Ceylon and India. Two of his brothers also played county cricket, and two others went to India and set up what is still one of the largest carpet manufacturers in the subcontinent.

At the age of just nineteen, the eldest brother, Douglas Hadow, joined Edward Whymper's attempt to make the first ascent of the Matterhorn in 1865. Whymper was in such a hurry to scale the mountain before a rival party that, despite Douglas's non-existent mountaineering experience, he actually recruited him and his travelling companion, a clergyman and accomplished climber, at the foot of the Matterhorn just before he began the ascent. The mountain had been described as 'unclimbable', but Douglas reached the summit with Whymper and the others. However, he was one of the four who fell to their deaths on the descent, when the rope holding them broke.

No one knows what really happened, but the accounts of Whymper and two of his guides implied that Douglas had probably caused the accident by losing his footing. It still frustrates me that so many commentators have been blind to the fact that this British school-leaver made the greatest ascent in mountaineering history at that time through sheer physical aptitude and mental attitude. He had given his best in the most extreme circumstances. What more can you ask of someone?

As well as being a family historian, my father was a tremendous character, good company for adults and children alike, endlessly inventive, patient, tolerant and kind, and a great innovator and organiser. When we lived in Scotland he was one of the driving forces behind setting up the first Highland Games in Auchterader, and he also organised a long-distance road race—something of a rarity in the early 1960s.

As I grew up, I was well aware of the achievements and sporting prowess of my ancestors, and my father was particularly keen that I and my younger brother Henry should fulfil the family tradition by going to Harrow School. Hadow sons had been educated there since the 1800s. We are listed in a tome in Harrow's Vaughan Library and I was told that very few families had had more Harrovian family members. I was about number twenty-one on the Hadow list. The one omission was my father, Nigel.

My grandmother, Sylvia, was widowed in the Second World War, when my father was thirteen, and with limited finances available she decided that her son Nigel would not go to Harrow. It wasn't just a financial issue; the Second World War was raging, and Harrow, high on its hill, was being hit by the occasional bomb. School numbers had dropped from over 700 boys to fewer than 300, and its reputation was at rock bottom. For all those reasons, it made no sense for Dad to go there, but he was devastated when he was sent to another school. He decided he was at the wrong place; he didn't want to be there and behaved accordingly. He had been head boy at his prep school but was then expelled from his public school before ending up at Millfield School in Somerset.

The headmaster and founder of the school, Jack 'Boss' Meyer, was a great character who was passionate about sport. He tended to charge a premium rate to those who could pay it, which went some way to subsidising impecunious boys with sporting talent, and he struck a bizarre deal with my grandmother, which included her undertaking to keep the Millfield lakes supplied with ornamental wildfowl in return for a reduction in the school fees. Dad was happy at Millfield and finished his school career without further incident, but the disruption of his earlier wild years cost him dear, and he left school with the minimum of academic qualifications. It was a handicap that affected him throughout his working life.

As an adult, my dad tried a succession of different businesses, but nothing ever really paid off for him. My mum came from a wealthy family and had a private income from trust funds. When the stock market was high or rising, there was enough money for us to live in style; when the markets fell, the belt had to be tightened. Mum and Dad were determined that our education should never be affected by such downturns and, unaware of the backstage dramas, we blithely went through the happiest of childhoods. I know it hurt my father to find himself having to depend so heavily on invested funds. He had so much to give and was brilliant in so many ways, but neither he nor anyone else seemed to be able to harness his untrained talents to a reliable career path. It was awful to watch as I got older and realised what it was doing to the man I adored, but throughout my time at school he was the most supportive and fun father of them all—by a long way. The grown-up world's loss was my gain and he gave me the things that matter in life, and which no amount of money can buy.

My mother, Anne, was quieter and more reserved than my father—the perfect foil for him for that reason—and a supportive and loving wife, helping him through some grim times. Outside her time with family and close friends, she was rarely happier than when she was with the horses, ponies, donkeys, goats and various dogs and fowl that she bred, tended and showed.

My brother Henry is an entirely different character from me, exuding a relaxed, assured and laid-back air I can only dream of, and, though a fine sportsman and local hero in his home town, notably in the Uckfield Rugby Club, he never seemed to exhibit my burning need to prove myself, to my father or anyone else. We were great friends as youngsters, and would play outside together in all weathers: fishing, animal tracking, building dams on the stream, riding our bikes, and playing cricket and table tennis or our own version of catch, involving throwing eggs over the roof of the house to each other and trying to catch them without breaking them. Although we went to the same schools, we were two years apart and saw much less of each other during term-time. But each holiday we would pick up exactly where we left off and we forged a bond that remains as strong today as it was then.

JUST BEFORE I began prep school—Temple Grove near Uckfield—my dad, who had been the British Army's Middle East heavyweight boxing champion, took me aside and told me I needed to learn how to fight. 'I want you to be able to defend yourself, son. There may come a time when you need to stand up for yourself and give someone a bit of a thumping.' As part of my crash course in the noble art, he got me to punch him repeatedly in the stomach—he had quite a paunch on him by then, so it was a well-padded target. I made a feeble attempt and he wasn't impressed. 'No, no, no, no! Punch me as hard as you can. Hit me like you really mean it.' He made me do it over and over, until I was belting him with everything I'd got. Finally he was happy and let me go. He came into my room the next day with a huge grin on his face, lifted up his shirt and showed me his stomach. It was covered with bruises, but he pronounced himself delighted with it.

I didn't have long to wait before putting his training into effect. Within the first couple of weeks at prep school, I had a fight with the head of the school, even though I was only seven and a half and he was thirteen. We were in the changing rooms getting ready for games. He wanted more room, there was some pushing and jostling and it developed into a fight. All the other boys were standing on the benches shouting and yelling, like a scene from the film *If.* I wasn't particularly strong for my age but I was completely focused on beating this boy who'd tried to bully me. I got on top of him, pinned him down and was pummelling him when, alerted by the noise, a master came bursting in and pulled us apart.

I never had any problems with bullies after that, but I was a tubby little boy, not athletic at all, and my first school sports day was a nightmare. All those, including me, who hadn't qualified for a single event—high jump, long jump, sprints, hurdles, shot putt, discus, et cetera—had to enter the dreaded obstacle race. One of the obstacles was set of three bars. You had to wriggle under the first one, set about a foot off the ground, then clamber over a high one and then crawl under another low one. We'd all been shown the course the day before but we weren't allowed to practise, and I got it into my head that I was too fat to squeeze under the low bars.

I imagined the humiliation of getting stuck and was dreading it so much that I scarcely slept the night before. In the event, I managed to get under it, but the fact that the memory is still so strong—over thirty years later I can still feel my toes curling with embarrassment—suggests that it may well have been the moment when I decided to get serious about sport. By the time I left prep school I had grown almost as big as I am now and had overtaken virtually all my peers in speed and strength. I was playing football, rugby and cricket, and was captain or vice captain of all of them.

It was at prep school that I met my first mentor, Andrew Keith, a dynamic new master there. He picked me out as someone with sporting potential and took me and a few other boys under his wing. He introduced us to the Amateur Athletic Association's star system and pinned a chart to the notice board. It listed about fifteen different disciplines with the points you would acquire for any particular time or distance. Even at that early stage I was becoming aware that competition was not only about whether you could beat the opposition, because that wasn't the best you could do. What was relevant was how well and to what level you could perform, irrespective of the quality of the opposition.

Andrew Keith also introduced me to the concept of training. It was my choice—I didn't have to do it—but he could see I was receptive to the idea. It didn't matter to him if, as was often the case, I was the only one; he'd still come out with me, supervising the session. But often I would train alone, and the longer the distance, the happier I was. I focused my efforts on the 800 metres and trained with repetitions of 100, 200 and 400 metres.

During my last year at prep school I developed a strengthening belief that I should be looking to do something, or be something, out of the ordinary. It is a difficult thing to describe, but it became such an obsession that it affected the quality of my life for many years. It wasn't that I felt bigger or better or cleverer than anyone else, but I did feel a need, almost an obligation, to fulfil my destiny, whatever that might be. I was relentless in pursuit of the goals I set myself, and that single-minded focus on achieving a goal was perhaps the strongest hint of the direction my later life would take.

That year, I passed the entrance exam for Harrow. My dad would have done almost anything and endured almost any hardship to ensure that I went there, and I can only imagine his pride when I succeeded. But the family finances were strained to the limit and my parents were to scrape the barrel to keep me and, in time, my brother Henry there. When I eventually realised the extent of the sacrifices my parents were making, it made me aware of what a debt I owed them and I took on much more responsibility as a result. I felt that I should be getting the maximum out of my time at Harrow, and I pushed myself harder and harder. If my dad was sometimes disappointed by the course that his own career had taken, I was determined that he would be able to take pride in the achievements of his son.

In my first year at Harrow, my running coach gave me a tough training programme for the Easter holidays, including sets of ten 100, 200 and 400 metres, alternating with distance runs. The 400s were killer sessions and I'd be in a pretty bad way by the end of the last one, especially as I had to average one second faster over the ten timed 400-metre runs each week. Dad had paced out the distance down the dead-end lane to the village church— the only reasonably level and quiet 'track' we could find in the area. Dad would always come to help with the stopwatch and give some moral support. By the last week I was really up against it. With three 400s still to go, I was already getting wobbly legs when suddenly a busload of American tourists turned up to look round the church. Within five minutes Dad had them strung along the grass verge to cheer me through those last three 400s and, with their vocal encouragement, I beat my target.

One of the many traditions at Harrow was a run called the Long Ducker, named after an open-air swimming pool at the edge of the school grounds that had originally been a duck pond. The shorter version, Short Ducker, started from the door of your school house on top of Harrow-on-the-Hill, and went down and round the hill, past Ducker at the bottom and then back up. It was a three-mile run and some school and house monitors used it as a punishment for various misdemeanours, but I required no compulsion to do it; I was using it as training for the Long Ducker. That began and ended the same way, but instead of turning round at the bottom of the hill you ran on down to the Grand Union Canal three or four miles away, then along the towpath to Little Venice and up onto the Edgware Road to Marble Arch at the western end of London's Oxford Street, where you turned and retraced your steps, in all covering a marathon distance—twenty-six miles.

In the 1970s, marathons were not a mass public participation sport; there was nothing like the London Marathon or the Great North Run and hardly anyone even went jogging. No one at school had done the Long Ducker while I was there but, in my first or second year, two senior boys in my house started telling everyone that they would do it. They then left school without attempting it, which I thought was pretty poor. I didn't really know what the Long Ducker was at the time, just that it was some sort of long run, but inside I was already burning with curiosity—could I do it?

When I was fifteen I began training for it. I played rugby on Saturdays but I trained on my own every Sunday doing Short Duckers, building my strength and stamina. I didn't even tell people what I was training for, though word soon got around. It was 1977, the year of the Queen's Silver Jubilee, and I decided to raise money for the Jubilee Appeal by getting my school friends and anyone else I could find to sponsor me to run the Long Ducker. When my housemaster heard about it, he was concerned about whether a fifteen-year-old should be running a marathon and insisted I see the school doctor. His opinion boiled down to: 'Well, I don't know, so do it, if that's what you want to do,' and armed with this lukewarm endorsement I felt I was ready to try. I told my Mum and Dad, who came up to Harrow at the first opportunity to check the route with me and find points for 'feeding stations' where they could supply me with water and glucose drinks.

I set off early on a Sunday morning in December, accompanied by a friend, Myles Thompson, on his bicycle, and cheered on my way by the other boys in my house. I ran down the hill, and through the deserted streets to the Grand Union Canal. After what seemed like hours pounding the towpath, I emerged into the noise and bustle of the Edgware Road, drawing curious looks from people taking a Sunday stroll or sipping coffee in the street cafés. As I ran towards the bottom of the Edgware Road, I saw the massive iron gates of the Marble Arch standing wide open. Knowing that I was running to raise money for the Jubilee Appeal, John Reece, a supportive master at the school and a part-time speechwriter for a member of the Royal Household, had used his influence to arrange for the gates to be opened for me. Two friends, Simon Marsh and Alex Budworth, joined me at Marble Arch to run the thirteen miles back with me, and it was just as well because they and Myles really helped to keep me going.

With just over three hours' running behind me, I was absolutely shot by the time we reached the bottom of Harrow Hill. Myles stayed with me but the other two pulled ahead to tell the boys in my house that I'd nearly made it. They all came pouring down the hill in their standard Sunday attire of top hats and tails, ready to run the last few hundred yards with me. The adrenaline surge as I saw them was like a jolt of electricity. One minute I was staggering up the hill, the next I seemed to be cruising effortlessly towards the finish. I almost collapsed after I crossed the line, but I didn't care; I'd run Long Ducker. When I had time to reflect about it later, I began to realise how much of an endurance event is won or lost in the mind rather than the body.

The next morning the headmaster made an announcement in assembly. 'Some of you will know that Pen Hadow ran Long Ducker yesterday. What he doesn't know is that he was the first boy to do this for fifty years.' The standing ovation I received must have started a few other boys thinking, because within a few weeks several were labouring up Harrow Hill in training for their own attempts at Long Ducker, and it is now an annual fixture in the Harrow calendar.

After the run, the psychology of endurance events started to intrigue me and, aged sixteen, I entered and won the school's annual Churchill Essay Prize with an exploration of the mindset of record-breaking runners. It opened: 'Races produce winners. However a winner is not necessarily the first person to pass the tape. There is an alternative, and more realistic definition; a winner is a person who works to exploit his potential. Even if he loses every race, if he has done the best he possibly can, he has won.'

I also quoted Sir Arthur Conan Doyle's description of one of the most enduring images in sport, that of Dorando Pietri entering the home straight to complete the first marathon of the modern Olympic Games in 1908: 'It is a horrible yet fascinating sight, this strange struggle between a set purpose and an exhausted frame. He was practically delirious, staggering along the cinder path like a man in a dream.' I found that level of performance utterly fascinating and, if I knew one thing about the destiny I had long believed in, it was that I would be going through that struggle myself one day.

2

As the time for leaving Harrow approached, I applied to read Geography at University College, London, and was offered a place. I decided to take a gap year before going there, to give myself a chance to see a little of the real world, and I applied for a Short Service Limited Commission with the Scots Guards.

I went through the motions of academic and IQ tests, fitness and physical courses, social skills and confidence assessments, as set by the Regular Commissions Board, and then came the command and leaderless tasks. The scenarios we were set were so artificial—'the yellow oil drums are man-eating crocodiles'—or so ludicrously complicated—'all circular objects are mines, all green-painted wood can only be touched twice by any two of your team in your allotted ten minutes'—that it drained the last vestiges of enthusiasm from me.

Potential officers receive one of four notifications after the RCB course: 'Delighted to have you aboard'; 'If you stick out a few weeks on a toughening-up course we'll take you'; 'Come back in a year or more's time when you've matured . . .'; and the one that I received: 'It's been awfully nice meeting you, but we have no need of your services here.'

Instead I took a job cleaning cars in a showroom to earn some money for a trip to Australia, and returned just in time for my first term at University College. I had expected to carry on playing rugby but I was dubious about whether I was good enough. I could run for ever—I was described as 'perpetual motion Hadow' in a school report—and I could tackle till the cows came home, but I didn't have the explosive speed and powerful physique that really good flankers need. As I was wandering round the Freshers' Fair, I saw the rowing club stand and signed up for that instead. I ended up in the UCL first eight, but there was not the culture of high performance I craved and I soon began to think of rowing as another dead end.

My feelings about university as a whole were much the same. For many people their time at college is one of the happiest periods of their life, but despite a hectic social life I was miserable and became depressed. I read voraciously, but did the minimum amount of academic work to get by. The one exception was an expedition I organised to the desert shores at the head of the Gulf of Aqaba in Jordan. I spent six weeks collecting samples of long-dead coral from raised beaches in the cliffs. By radiocarbon-dating the corals and recording the heights above sea level of the beaches they came from, it was possible to ascertain the rates of uplift of the land over the last 8,000 years. It was a privilege to work alone and unsupervised in a challenging region, with interested scientists back home, and I now see it as my first glimpse into the working world I would later inhabit.

Sadly, when I returned to London I drifted back into my depressed and apathetic routine and finished university with only a 2:2 degree. I had a huge sense of frustration and unhappiness and felt that I was wasting my life, but was unable to get out of the black hole I'd dug for myself. After leaving UCL I continued to drift and, for want of anything better to do, I joined a landscape gardening company with contracts round central London. I was still thinking endlessly about what I might want to do. I knew I didn't want to be an accountant or any of the other standard professional jobs, nor did I want to be a City slicker or a corporate animal. I was so desperate for ideas that I even ploughed through Yellow Pages from 'Abattoirs' to 'Zoos', hoping that something would strike a spark.

One summer's day, with ingrained dirt in my hands and my hair stiff with the debris the mower had thrown up around me, I was flicking through the pages of a newspaper when an article about Mark McCormack's sports agency, International Management Group, caught my eye. IMG had a vast stable of the world's highest-profile sportsmen and women on their books as well as the representation of big events, including the Olympics. I had never thought of acting as a business agent on behalf of sports events and personalities, but it had instant appeal.

I phoned for the company's promotional brochure, analysed which department I thought I might work best in, and then gleaned every scrap of information I could. When I'd completed my research I sent a professionally prepared CV and a short covering letter. I was offered an immediate interview and, despite my lack of relevant experience, I was hired on the spot as their youngest-ever executive. My brief was to take responsibility for the equestrian management rights that the agency had acquired, pulling them together to create a European equestrian division. My sole qualification for that appeared to be that I was one of the few people in the entire organisation who knew which end of a horse to feed a sugar lump to.

The problem was that I didn't actually know how this international operation worked. I was out of my depth and struggling to get up to speed, and in my heart I knew that it wasn't what I wanted to do with my life. I felt that I was supporting people who were doing what they loved—playing golf or tennis, driving fast cars, riding horses—and I actually wanted to be on the other side of the fence myself. That triggered the thought that the real question in life is not what you want to be, but what you want to do. If you can identify what really does it for you, then you'll do it with a natural enthusiasm and ability and put in the extra effort all the time.

So that was the trigger to sort myself out. Apart from pushing my physical limits since the age of eight, the one constant in my life was the distant echoing in my head of Nanny Wigley's tales of great explorers and my dad's stories about my adventurous ancestors. I remained fascinated by them. My shelves groaned with books about the 'gods' of polar exploration—Nansen, Amundsen, Scott and Shackleton—and their modern all-terrain equivalents: John Ridgway, Chay Blythe, Francis Chichester, Ranulph Fiennes, Robin Hanbury-Tennison, Robin Knox-Johnston and Chris Bonnington.

I'd been a Fellow of the Royal Geographical Society since university and I often went into the RGS reading room and leafed through the dusty volumes on the shelves. I was doing this one day when I came across the translated diaries of Bernhard Hantzsch, an obscure nineteenth-century German ornithologist who set off on an Arctic expedition that was compromised before he had even begun, when his boat sank off Baffin Island. He lost nearly all his equipment but managed to reach a remote settlement near Black Rock Island. The missionary there took in Hantzsch and his crewmen, even though their own food supplies for the winter had also gone down with his boat. They eked out the settlement's pitiful rations until the following spring when, undeterred, Hantzsch set off north with hired Inuit companions. His original plan was to cross Baffin Island and then head up the west coast to the northern tip, from where he hoped to sail home on a passing resupply ship, but he got no more than halfway before starvation took its toll. In the end, only two Inuit remained with him. Starving, they killed and ate a polar bear, but shortly afterwards Hantzsch died of exhaustion and malnutrition. It was a testament to their admiration for him that the surviving Inuit brought his diaries and all his meticulous observations of the natural environment back to their settlement, from where they were returned to his family.

As I read his book I realised that I was one of at most a handful of people who had ever done so. But now I'd chanced upon it, I was prepared to believe that fate had guided me to it. He wasn't a Scott or a Shackleton but his efforts and achievements were deserving of a better commemoration than this dusty, forgotten volume. As I stood in that deserted reading room, I decided that I would retrace the steps of Bernhard Hantzsch and finish the journey he never completed.

I began researching and planning the expedition in every spare moment, even squeezing in visits to the library during my lunch breaks. Then one autumn morning in that same year, 1988, I walked into the IMG offices and announced to my bosses, colleagues and clients that I had decided to resign in order to retrace Hantzsch's steps and complete his expedition.

As a complete novice at Arctic exploration, I knew I needed an experienced partner to accompany me and I placed an advertisement in a now defunct magazine, *The Adventurer*. 'Wanted: Arctic experienced HF radio operator for Baffin Island expedition.' It was answered by a man called Vaughan Purvis, who appeared ideal—an experienced polar traveller and a highly qualified radio operator. However, he couldn't help but observe that I had no experience whatsoever of polar expeditions. He suggested that I join his own seventy-day sledge-hauling journey across the archipelago of Svalbard on the edge of the Arctic Ocean, to study and photograph polar bears. He promised to train and teach me in the ways of the Arctic and we could then consider the Baffin Island expedition on our return. I agreed at once. We met regularly that winter to make our preparations, then set out on our two-man trek in the early spring of the following year, 1989.

My first sight of the polar ice cap, the frozen world that had consumed my imagination since childhood, was an overpowering experience. It seemed so vast, so intimidating, so featureless and monochrome, and so utterly alien, that I was as much in fear as in awe of it. But within a short time, I began to see that frozen ice-scape in all its wondrous beauty and variety. It was the start of a lifelong love of the Arctic.

Over the course of our two months' sledging together, I learned a lot from Vaughan about strategy, tactics, procedures and techniques for operating in extreme environments for long periods of time, and how to move around safely on sea ice and glaciers, and near polar bears—we encountered about a dozen during the expedition.

During the flight home, it dawned on me that Vaughan and I had been out on the ice for seventy days. It was one of the longer unsupported sledge-hauling journeys of the time. I had taken part in exactly the sort of expedition that would be needed to have a crack at the Pole. I thought, That's it. I'm ready to go. I've short-circuited the system by doing one huge expedition with a very experienced mentor. I think I can give it a shot.

It was to be some time, however, before that idea became a reality. Meanwhile, Vaughan and I set off on another demanding expedition, piloting an open, rigid-hulled inflatable boat, with no protection from the elements and two enormous 200 horse-power outboard motors on the back, on a voyage from London to Greenland. I secured a substantial cash sponsorship from Shell Unleaded fuel, but it wasn't enough to cover our costs and so I also invested the £30,000 that I'd just inherited from my grandmother. Had I told them, my parents would have been aghast, but it was that or face the prospect of returning to office life within six months of leaving IMG. It kept me actively engaged in the Arctic, but I was fast learning that you cannot operate in the Arctic without cash, and plenty of it, because everything you need—flights, boats, freight, specialist equipment and supplies—comes with a heavy price tag attached.

Within six weeks of landing back at Heathrow, we had organised the new expedition and were bucketing our way downstream from Tower Bridge in London. There were three of us this time, Vaughan and I, and a boat engineer who was travelling with us to Iceland. We were planning to go from London to New York via the Arctic, but it was a wild scheme and not very well thought out. You can only navigate the coast of Greenland in a small boat in August or early September. The rest of the year it's completely locked in by sea ice, so we had to leave at once or wait another year.

We hammered our way north, and even the relatively sheltered first leg from London to Whitby on the Yorkshire coast gave us a taste of the problems that were to dog the voyage. Water was seeping into the hull of the boat through rotten deck fittings. We carried out emergency repairs, then headed on, via the Shetlands and the Faroe Islands, to Hofn on the southeast coast of Iceland. There, driven by a perceived need to get back on schedule for the media following us at home, we had two near-death experiences as we tried to exit the harbour in a Storm Force 10 into a swell the like of which I hope never to see again; thirty-foot monster waves were breaking over the harbour walls. We battered our way on to the volcanic Vestmann Islands and then Reykjavik, where we sheered a drive shaft in one engine and, unknown to us at the time, also ruptured the power head of the other engine as we hit a submerged offshore reef.

After another repairs stop we headed out across the Denmark Straits towards the remote village of Tasiilaq on east Greenland. One of the most powerful memories I have of the Arctic was to see, coming up over the horizon, a forest of jagged snow-covered peaks glistening in the orange light of the setting sun. We were so nearly there, just twenty miles or so left of the 350-mile crossing, when the damaged power head packed up, leaving us with only one engine in an increasingly heavy following sea. The waves began to break over the low-level transom, and soon we were swamped, with our second engine's air intake disappearing below the water line. We were now adrift, with five miles of fragmented sea ice separating us from the village. We spent a night secured by ratchet straps to the deck to avoid being washed overboard, but were eventually towed to the sanctuary of the harbour.

It was an unceremonious end. We had made it to Greenland, but failed to carry on to New York. I'm not proud of failing to achieve our objective but it was a hell of an experience and I learned a lot from it. From a standing start, by the end of 1989, I had already completed two big Arctic expeditions, and could begin to think of myself as a tried and tested Arctic traveller. My only problem was that I was now flat broke and my polar ambitions had to be put on hold while I set about raising some money.

I decided to set up an adventure travel company offering guided tours to the Arctic. My client list could be counted on the fingers of one hand, but one, Robert Owen, was to prove central to my future in the polar regions. Robert wanted a tough four-week expedition in the jungle, the mountains or the polar regions, and the best proposal put to him would get the contract. He visited my spartan home/office, a converted wooden summerhouse in Wiltshire, and instantly felt he was dealing with someone who was more about gnarly expeditions than wasting money on deluxe office space. I duly won the contract with a proposal for a crossing of Spitsbergen—a standard route except that I proposed to do it during the polar night.

We headed to Spitsbergen with our sledges in early February 1991, when there was a little light on the horizon during the middle of the day but it was inky black for well over twenty hours out of the twenty-four, though it grew progressively lighter over the course of the month we were on the ice. During the long hours of darkness, we navigated by compass and used the light of the moon, the stars and the occasional sighting of the Northern Lights to illuminate our way across the ice.

The Northern Lights are not often seen at the highest latitudes and, like most polar travellers, I'm more usually in the Arctic during the periods of twenty-four-hour daylight when they're not visible at all, and it was an experience that I'll never forget. No matter how many times you have seen them in photographs or on television, I guarantee that, like the first time you stand on the edge of the Grand Canyon or scuba-dive off the Great

Barrier Reef, the first sight of those shimmering veils of light cascading across the night sky will leave you speechless. Depending on their altitude, they are sometimes red, sometimes green, sometimes white and sometimes blue, and sometimes accompanied by ethereal *whooshing* sounds. Filling a quadrant of the northern sky at one moment, they can then fade and disappear within seconds, only to reappear in a completely different part of the heavens moments later. I would defy even the most rampant egomaniac not to feel reduced to the insignificance of a flake of snow in the face of something so vast, unknowable and otherworldly.

3

In 1992 my father began to complain of severe headaches. Not long afterwards, he was diagnosed with a cancer of the brain. There were no options for treatment, the disease was inoperable. His headaches grew steadily worse and his speech began to falter. Then his balance started to go and, all too soon, his bed became his world. As often as I could, I drove from Wiltshire, where I was living and working at the time, to my parents' home to support my mother and to spend as much time as possible with Dad.

Finally, after months of suffering in silence, he reached the end of his endurance. On Good Friday, 1993, with my arms supporting his frail body and Mum and Henry at his side, he gave his last breath.

That evening, I went back to the familiar room to pay my last respects and found myself making a vow over his dead body. It was not one he would have wished me to make, but nothing could have stopped me from uttering those words. 'Before I die I'm going to reach the North Pole— alone. No resupplies. If I do nothing else with my life, I will do that.' Then I said goodbye to my father for the last time and closed the door to his room.

I took the first opportunity to fulfil my pledge to my father in the spring of the following year, 1994. If my ambition had been to get to the Pole by any means, I could have done so with relative ease, starting from Siberia and operating as part of a team using airdropped resupplies, but I saw no merit in simply replicating what other men had done before me. It wasn't that I wanted to break records for their own sake, but I did want to break new ground and, in however small a way, push back the frontiers of knowledge of what man can endure—mentally and physically—and achieve.

I conceived it as a solo expedition almost from the start, because I wanted to be accepted as a professional operator in the polar environment and to do that I felt I had to set myself the absolute test of my abilities. I wanted a simple test of everything one has: strength, intelligence, endurance, courage, mental toughness and technical skills, the whole nine yards. But if that was a prime motivation, there was something else that had been driving me forward. When I returned home from the Arctic the first time, I found that every fibre of my body was aching to be back there, and I've never lost that feeling. The New Zealand Maori have an expression for that sense of identification with a place; they would describe it as being 'one of the standing places of my heart', and that's exactly how I feel about the Arctic.

In the longer term I wanted to be associated with a new way of travelling in the polar regions. In mountaineering there is a siege approach and an alpine approach—travel slow and heavy or fast and light—but few polar travellers have got beyond the siege approach: pile up a sledge with all the supplies you need and slog your way there with the aid of a back-up team or air resupplies. I thought I could foresee a time when people who were fit, strong and experienced in the conditions might reach the Pole in twenty days, carrying all they needed in a backpack or on a lightweight sledge.

It's only 470 miles, after all, like walking from Edinburgh to London or from Detroit to New York. Even allowing for the fact that there are no ice fields, pressure ridges and open leads between Detroit and New York, it shouldn't take four times as long to reach the Pole, and the only reason it does is because you're dragging a ruddy great sledge behind you, loaded down with everything but the kitchen sink.

However, for my first expedition to the Pole, I adopted what I thought was a conservative, safety-first approach and made sure I was carrying every conceivable item I might need. In doing so I was already giving myself a severe handicap. At the time I didn't really see the significance of a thirty-pound difference; I thought that hauling a 330-pound sledge would be little if any harder than a 300-pound one, but there is a profound difference and a strength-sapping, cumulative effect. The weight of that sledge showed my lack of polar experience. I was fit and had trained hard but, partly for financial reasons, I had given nothing like the same care and attention to the equipment I was using. My sledge was too heavy in itself and poorly designed for gliding across ice and snow, and I had not even ensured that its runners were spaced to match the width of my ski tracks. I was also carrying too many spares, too many off-the-shelf products and too many items built with strength rather than lightness in mind.

Raising the necessary finance for the expedition proved hard. Sponsorship was essential; I had no hope of covering the costs, which I estimated would be about £60,000. The budget was pared to the absolute minimum, but you cannot mount any sort of expedition to the Pole without serious money. Going into the polar regions involves chartering aircraft to drop you off and pick you up, and to be on standby in case of a serious incident during the expedition. The flight companies want money and plenty of it.

I started the hunt for a sponsor in spring 1993, about twelve months before my intended departure, greatly helped by my girlfriend, Mary Nicholson. We trawled through radio and TV advertisements, magazines and newspapers, billboards and Yellow Pages, and noted the names of potential sponsors on little cards. We approached around 1,200 of them.

We'd rarely get through to a decision-maker, but we'd try them again and again, until the rejection came, as it invariably did. It was a pretty soul-destroying experience and I was just about in despair when I suddenly had a stroke of luck. I was wandering around a shopping centre when I saw a tray of Sector Sport watches. The point-of-sale publicity had some very striking images of people kayaking off waterfalls and jumping out of planes—all sorts of adrenaline-fuelled extreme sports. I made a note of the name and we discovered that the company was based in Italy, in Milan.

They had no one involved in polar exploration and were very interested in adding me to their stable, but though their interest in sponsoring me never waned, the negotiations were protracted. In the end, with a month to go, I flew out to see them in Milan and they finally said, 'OK, we'll sponsor you.' They offered £48,000, well short of what we had originally discussed, but I was in no position to negotiate. I had to take the offer or call the whole thing off. I came out of the meeting full of excitement and happiness that the last obstacle had been removed. But the contract then did not arrive until ten days before my departure, and by the time the money was paid into the expedition account I had just four days to purchase the bulk of the supplies, confirm the charter flights and complete a thousand and one other administrative tasks that could have been sorted out weeks and months before if the sponsors had not been so fond of corporate brinkmanship.

I had chosen Ward Hunt Island as my point of departure, and on March 10, 1994, I set out alone, dragging my fully laden sledge behind me. From the moment I set foot on the ice, I did not look back. I didn't want to see the island dwindle slowly into nothingness behind me.

The ice conditions were daunting. Before I even reached the true sea ice, I had to cross a moonscape of old ice, permanently frozen to the coast, and then the seemingly endless terrain of pressure ridges rising from the pale grey surface of the sea ice. Seen from the air, they look rather like paddocks on Dartmoor or in the Yorkshire Dales: a quilted pattern of stone walls enclosing small fields. But the walls are jumbled blocks of ice, towering as much as twenty or thirty feet above the surface of the ice.

Just as you would make your way through those English fields by taking a meandering course using gates and stiles, so I had to try to find 'gateways' through the pressure ridges, gaps or lower sections in the wall of ice. Sometimes there were none and then I had to scramble up and over the wall of jumbled blocks of ice, crossing where I could, dragging my monstrously heavy sledge over each vertiginous wall of ice, and trying to slow its breakneck descent on the other side, knowing that a moment's ill luck or inattention might see it crashing down on top of me.

At the end of each day, after six to eight hours of gruelling, unremitting effort that left me bone-weary with fatigue, I read my position on the GPS—the global positioning system, a handheld navigational unit that can compute your position to within a handful of metres by tracking the position of satellites moving overhead—and found that I had made no more than one or two miles' progress towards my goal. I was forced to reduce the weight of the sledge. To make a useful difference I had to throw away some of my most crucial supplies, and I left a pile of fuel bottles and some ration packs on the ice. Having done that, I could not afford any further delays.

By the twentieth day, I had travelled just thirty miles north of my starting point. However, I was beginning to encounter better ice and had high hopes of increasing the pace. Then I came to the first really big lead I had encountered. It lay at right angles to my track, a stretch of open water, black as jet against the blue-whiteness of the ice, up to 200 yards wide and stretching away into the distance as far as I could see. I didn't have an immersion suit and my sledge wasn't watertight, so I couldn't swim across it. Either I had to find a way round or wait for it to freeze over.

At the point where I hit the lead, there were terrific fields of ice blocks and rubble to either side of me, and I decided that, rather than spend days battling to the west or east in search of a place where the lead closed up, I'd simply pitch my tent and wait for it to freeze over, allowing me to cross.

I woke up the next morning to find that the lead had indeed frozen over, but the ice pans had also been torn further apart by the wind and tides, exposing a fresh stretch of open water in the middle. For the next five days I woke every morning to make the same disheartening discovery. The lead never closed completely, because each time it froze it also pulled further apart. By this time I was burning up with frustration and I felt enormous pressure to get across somehow and continue northwards. Every day I was consuming more scarce rations and fuel and wasting those precious days of the Arctic spring and early summer when a journey to the Pole is possible.

I was now camped on a platform of solid ice, an old pan or floe culminating in an almost sheer cliff. The platform was around two and a half metres thick, protruding perhaps sixty centimetres above the water level. Beyond it was a forty-metre expanse of progressively thinner ice layers, with a zigzagging line of open water in the middle, in places as little as one or two metres wide. It was narrow enough to jump across, providing that the ice didn't give way beneath me.

Whatever the risks, I had waited immobile long enough. I left my sledge on the ice platform and took off my skis—first mistake. Holding the sledge-traces in one hand, paid out to their fullest extent—second mistake—I began inching my way out across the newer ice. I could feel it flexing beneath me. The movement grew more and more pronounced as I neared the open water, and I could also see the colour of the ice becoming darker beneath my feet—the ice was so thin that the water beneath it was clearly visible.

I was almost on the edge of the ice sheet, and looking down, fascinated, into the inky-black depths of the open water. I had just thought, Maybe I can step over this, when the ice simply crumbled beneath me and I found myself floundering in the frigid waters of the Arctic.

To my surprise I didn't feel instant cold. I was wearing boots, gloves, mitts and layer upon layer of clothing, trapping a lot of air, and at first the layers acted like a rather primitive and leaky wet suit, slowing the rate at which the water came into contact with my body, but within a very short time, probably no more than thirty seconds, my clothes were saturated. As the blood retreated towards the core of my body, my limbs grew leaden and the performance of my muscles began to deteriorate.

I'd taken an involuntary breath as I went into the water. I came up coughing and spluttering and facing an immediate decision: should I go forwards or backwards? That was easy; I had to make for the side where my sledge, tent and supplies were, otherwise I would haul myself out onto the ice only to die from hypothermia. I reached up onto the ice sheet, but each time it either broke as I put my weight on it, or my hands just slipped off the edge, plunging me back into the water.

It began to dawn on me that my only hope of survival was to smash my way like an icebreaker back to the edge of the thick ice, but it was a long way, perhaps ten metres, and I was unsure whether I could make it. I was feeling colder and colder and more and more tired, and my muscles were now barely responding to the commands of my brain. I was starting to suffer from hypothermia and my life systems were beginning to shut down.

In my mind's eye I was seeing front-page headlines: ARCTIC EXPLORER DROWNS IN ARCTIC OCEAN, and I suddenly thought, They won't even know that. No one will ever know what happened, whether I drowned, shot myself by accident, died of starvation or hypothermia or was eaten by a polar bear. That was the call to action—not because people had to know what had happened to me, but because the idea of disappearing without trace into the Arctic Ocean was simply not acceptable. From then on, I was totally focused on doing whatever was necessary to save my life. While I was wondering if I would last long enough to make it, I was also breaking my way through the ice, bringing my numbed arms down in front of me with all the force I could muster, my only forward propulsion coming from feeble kicks of my legs in my huge, waterlogged boots.

Eventually I reached some thicker ice that would not break under my weight. Somehow, like a half-drowned seal emerging from the water, I managed to drag myself out onto the surface. I was drowsy and incredibly weary, and felt that I needed to rest for a minute, but that thought once more set alarm bells clanging in my head: hypothermia was becoming advanced.

I forced myself to get up, shambled to the sledge and began putting up my tent, my hands and fingers so numb that I could barely grasp anything with them. Once the tent was up, I crawled inside, zipped up the flap and tried to light my little portable stove. I had to try over and over again, fumbling with the controls and dropping the matches from my numbed fingers, but at last, almost weeping with relief, I saw it roar into flame. I scraped a few handfuls of snow from outside the tent and put it on to boil for hot food and a cup of tea, then tore off my wet clothing, put on some dry clothes and tried to massage warmth back into my extremities. I used up many precious litres of fuel warming myself and trying to dry my kit, but this was a life-or-death moment. Over an hour passed before I was certain that I had avoided frostbite and that I would survive the threat of hypothermia.

I spent five more days on the edge of that lead, but every day it had widened a little more. A more seasoned polar expeditioner would have just gritted his teeth and tried to go east or west to find a way round it. But knowing whether to go east or west, and how long it's likely to take to circumvent a lead, only comes with experience.

For the first time I faced the probability that I would fail to reach my goal, because I just didn't have enough fuel left to reach the Pole. After agonising for ten days on the edge of that ever-expanding lead, I finally made the call for an airlift off the ice. The sense of failure, as I watched the plane that was to lift me out circle and land, was one of the bleakest feelings I had endured in my life to that point, but I really didn't think there was anything else I could do. I even managed to convince myself that it was just one of those years when there was too much open water, but the hard truth was that I'd blown it. I'd pulled out not so much through any lack of will but from sheer lack of knowledge.

I'd done a few Arctic expeditions, but sea-ice work is totally different from crossing terra firma in Greenland or Svalbard, and I was unfamiliar with the special features of the Arctic Ocean; I hadn't done enough research and preparation, nor gained enough experience. But the greatest lesson I learned from the fiasco of my first polar expedition was that the attitude of 'Whatever it takes, I'll do', which I'd thought was all I needed, is not enough on its own. It's a very useful attribute, but to give yourself a realistic chance of reaching the Pole, you need more than luck and determination; you also have to learn the ways of the Arctic Ocean. The one positive thing I could take from my failure the first time was the knowledge I'd gained on what it would take to succeed the next time.

I HAD BEEN going out with Mary Nicholson since 1992 and she'd been with me through the roller coaster of my father's death, planning the expedition, raising the money and then staying in Britain trying to keep us afloat financially while I was failing to reach the Pole. We'd originally met at a party held in the crypt of a church. The relationship could easily have been stillborn—she was the daughter of an Eton housemaster and I was a product of Eton's hated rival, Harrow—but we hit it off from the start.

When I came back from the Pole, I took her to the Caribbean on holiday. I later discovered that she thought I was finally going to ask her to marry me, so every evening at dinner there was an air of suppressed tension and expectation—was this going to be the big moment? I was unaware of all this emotional turmoil across the table from me and I didn't pop the question until a few weeks later, when we were back in England. So her intuition was perfect but her timing was a bit off. She accepted, and I was delighted, but also anxious because I felt that marriage would be a hard enough adjustment to make without the added stress of having no money coming in. But in the end we took the plunge and decided that, money or no money, we'd get married the following June.

I can't have been great company for the rest of that year. I'd come back from the Pole feeling very low, and knowing that I was going to have to go back. However, the first priority for now was to find a job. I was acutely sensitive that my life could be history repeating itself. I might be my father's son in more ways than one, drifting from one failed career to another.

I was still desperate to get to the Pole solo and unsupported, but I had to sort myself out financially before I could even contemplate another attempt. My only asset was my house, an old workman's cottage in a hamlet called Honeystreet, on the Kennet and Avon Canal in Wiltshire. It was a gorgeous location, but not exactly handy either for potential places of employment or for seeing Mary, and I spent most of my time in London staying at her house. A real grafter, Mary was a very successful PR professional in high-powered media relations, but she had just gone freelance, setting up not only her own PR company but also a designer wedding-dress agency and a graphology consultancy offering personality assessment through the analysis of the subject's handwriting.

Mary suggested that I should make use of the contacts I'd acquired in exploration and adventure travel by setting up my own PR company to service the outdoor clothing and equipment industry. As if she didn't have enough work on her own plate, she helped me set up the Summit Consultancy, and I ran it from the spare room of her house, without notable success. I struggled along, hand-to-mouth, for the rest of that year but then, out of the blue, came a life-changing phone call.

In March 1995, Robert Owen, the client I'd taken on a crossing of Spitsbergen five years before, got in touch. He wondered whether I'd like to do another Arctic expedition with him. We decided on a ten-day expedition to the north magnetic pole, which has traced an erratic NNW path deep into the Canadian high Arctic in recent centuries. At that time it was off the coast of Ellef Ringnes Island, north of Canada's Northwest Passage. He gave me just four weeks' notice, but I abandoned my faltering PR firm without a backward glance. I got us outfitted and equipped and booked flights, and we had fine weather and a great ten days, trekking about ten nautical miles a day.

When I flew back into Heathrow with Robert, Mary was waiting to greet us. She looked me over. I was tanned, fit and radiating an aura of happiness and satisfaction at a job well done. Before we'd even got out of the airport, she sat me down with a coffee and said, 'Well, it's obvious what you should be doing, Pen. You've got to become a polar guide. Everyone knows you're passionate about the polar regions, you're good with people and a great leader. You're not destined for a desk job; get out there and do your stuff.'

I didn't need much convincing she was right. This was the way to fulfil the destiny of which I'd been aware for most of my life. Just like my former clients at IMG, I'd now be earning my living doing the thing I loved most. The Polar Travel Company was born there and then. Robert had been the catalyst, the first spark, but Mary was the one who instilled in me the confidence to do it, and she worked as hard as I did to make it happen.

We spent many hours firing ideas to and fro across the kitchen table. One thing we both agreed was that the Polar Travel Company had to be radically inclusive. Men and women, young and old, of all races, shapes and sizes, experienced or inexperienced, able-bodied or disabled, should all have the opportunity to accept the challenge of a polar expedition at one level of difficulty or another, and experience something of the beauty and allure of the pristine wilderness areas of the Arctic and Antarctic.

In between compiling guest lists and writing invitations for our wedding, I planned a series of Arctic and Antarctic expeditions of varying degrees of difficulty, ranging from a chance to gauge a client's entry level on a Polar Preparation Course for less than £400 on Dartmoor, right up to an 'All the Way' expedition to the North Pole at over £35,000. Once I'd sorted those, I designed and typed a brochure and had it printed. All we had to do then was let the world know that we existed.

Mary and I were married in June 1995, and after an idyllic honeymoon, we buckled down to preparing for the August launch of the Polar Travel Company. We had no money for advertising, so we had to rely entirely on our wits, promoting the company through coverage in newspapers, magazines, radio and TV. Fortunately, my in-house PR person was one of the best in the business. She hired the Explorers' Room in the Carlton Towers Hotel in Knightsbridge, rounded up the media and laid on a splendid stunt for a baking hot day in August: we borrowed the only snowmobile in Britain and parked it in the road outside. An ITN camera crew and battalions of national press photographers turned out for the photocall, and I was just about to do my big launch speech when a report came through that Alison Hargreaves, one of Britain's leading mountaineers, was missing, presumed dead, on K2. With a genuine tragedy involving a British adventurer to cover, the media instantly lost its appetite for self-serving publicity stunts by another one. Instead of the blanket coverage we'd been hoping for, all we got was a paragraph on an inside page of the *Daily Mail*, and even that was wasted because the *Mail* didn't print our phone number and, owing to a great British cock-up, when people phoned Directory Enquiries they were told that there was no number listed for the Polar Travel Company.

By the time she'd sorted that one out, Mary was sobbing in the back garden. The company was sunk before it had even been launched. We couldn't relaunch it with another story because there wasn't another one to do. 'Actually, there is another story,' I said.

One of the first polar projects I'd become involved in was an expedition to the North Pole for someone who has since become one of our greatest friends, Caroline Hamilton. I met her at a drinks party and we had a conversation about how she had been to the Arctic Circle on Midsummer's Day to see the sun go all the way round the horizon. Now Caroline wanted to go further, to the North Pole itself, and I said 'Fine, I can organise whatever style of trip you like.' There were a couple of minor problems: she wouldn't be able to devote months to training because of work commitments; she would have to limit her expedition to three weeks' holiday leave; and she only had £1,500 available. With the best will in the world, you're not going to go all the way to the North Pole in three weeks on £1,500, but I really wanted to make it happen for her because here was my first real client and I felt that I shouldn't be turning any customers away.

I was talking to Mary about the problem when I hit on the solution: an all-women relay format. We would have five teams of four women and Caroline, the leader of the expedition, would be in the last team that would do the final leg to the Pole. She and her teammates would be part of the first all-women North Pole expedition, but no individual would have to put in too much time, effort or money. In order for it to be a truly all-women expedition, I couldn't be the one to act as guide. In the whole world there were only five women qualified to act as Arctic guides at the time and, as only two were available, they pretty much chose themselves.

The point of an all-women expedition was partly to showcase the inclusive nature of the Polar Travel Company; these were ordinary women, with normal jobs, working together to achieve something extraordinary. It was also a concept sure to appeal to the media and, in turn, that would help to attract the sponsors needed to underwrite the cost of mounting the expedition. I asked Caroline if she would mind if we did another press conference to launch both the company and her expedition. She said that was fine, so we hired a room at the Institute of Directors and invited the press to another launch. This time we had a good spread of coverage and a shot in the *Daily Telegraph* of Mary, Caroline and assorted girlfriends, all kitted out in full Arctic gear and sitting in line on a huge sledge like birds on a branch. The theme was that these women were going to the Pole and, if you wanted to join the fun, get in touch. Within a week we had 300 enquiries.

Mary and I had been looking for a house deep in the country since we got married. I couldn't be happy for long living in a town or city and Mary wanted somewhere with stabling for her horse and open country in which to ride it. In December of that year we found our dream home: Wydemeet, a wreck of a house in a valley surrounded by the moors and tors of Dartmoor. A fast-flowing salmon river, the Swincombe, ran through the valley. The house was a large stone fishing lodge with wisteria-clad walls and honeysuckle twining round the door, reached by a twisting drive through gardens full of ash, beech and rowan trees and rich with spring flowers. The wood-panelled rooms didn't seem to have been decorated or cleaned since the year it was built—1914—and even to my inexpert eye there were signs of woodworm and dry rot in the timbers, and a number of slates missing from the roof, but the beauty, peace and isolation of the surroundings must have blinded us to these blemishes, because we made up our minds to buy it.

We moved into Wydemeet on December 21, 1995, and three weeks later we held the first selection and introductory weekend for the seventy-five women on the long list for the expedition to the Pole. The final selection course was in September 1996, when we reduced the list to the final twenty, plus one reserve. They then had six months to prepare themselves and raise their contribution to the expedition. The actual cost of the expedition was going to be £325,000; divided between the twenty women, it worked out at about £16,000 each. Since the aim was to enable women to take part no matter what their personal circumstances, we set the individual contributions at £1,500: enough to demonstrate a commitment to the project but not enough to break the bank. The participants would have to raise the rest of the money through sponsorship.

Unfortunately, even the most successful fundraisers among the chosen twenty women—a mother and daughter who raised £10,000 each—were well short of the target figure, and the rest, except for Caroline and two or three others, raised nothing like that amount. To cover the £250,000 shortfall, Mary and I had to become immersed in working with the team to raise the money ourselves. The company was so strapped for cash that I couldn't even draw any wages. The women thought I was doing it all for the publicity, and of course that was my prime commercial purpose, but by far the biggest motivation was a personal one in wanting to make it happen, and I was taking an enormous financial risk to do so. It was Mary who eventually clinched the sponsorship deal, bringing the biscuit manufacturer McVitie's aboard. The fact that no penguins had yet reached the North Pole inspired them to link the expedition with their Penguin brand and the cash they contributed to purchase the title rights tipped the balance.

By March 1997, when the first team of six women began moving north from Ward Hunt Island on the first leg of the McVitie's Penguin Polar Relay, the Polar Travel Company was also up and running. At the same time I was taking a party to the north magnetic pole using snowmobiles and sledges. And within what seemed like five minutes of coming back from that expedition, I was off with another, leading a group—all of whom, apart from one rock musician, were ex-military men and now chief executives of substantial companies—on the first of what became our most popular expeditions: 'The Last Degree', flying in to 89°N and then sledge-hauling the last sixty miles to the north geographic pole.

In that year alone, we organised three expeditions to the North Pole in the ninety-day window in spring and early summer, when it is possible to trek in the high Arctic, and had set up one to the South Pole earlier in the year. The logistics and fundraising placed huge demands on my time and energy, and I had started recruiting people ahead of the season to spread the load. Even with four of us working flat out, plus Mary handling the PR side, we were still overloaded with work. But because we put so much into the McVitie's Penguin Polar Relay, which reached the Pole successfully on May 27, and all the other expeditions we were running in 1997, we rather took our eye off the ball as far as marketing for the next year was concerned. As 1998 was about to dawn, I found that we had only a handful of clients booked, and none at all in the spring months.

I was already feeling that, despite all my Arctic knowledge and experience, a gap was opening up between what I had actually achieved and what I thought I could do, and I was uncomfortable with the esteem in which I was being held by my clients, when I didn't feel I'd really achieved enough to earn their respect. I was enabling people to do things that they wanted to do, but part of me was thinking, 'If only you could have applied all the effort to your own expedition.' So the opportunity afforded by the lack of clients was too good to miss.

I took a deep breath and then announced to Mary that I was planning to seize the chance to make another solo, unsupported expedition to the Pole, which, if successful, would also act as a PR and marketing flagship for the Polar Travel Company. It turned out that Mary had an announcement of her own to make: she had just discovered that she was pregnant with our first child. That fantastic news could have changed everything, but Mary was insistent that I would be back a good four months before the birth and that I should go ahead with the expedition.

4

I had taken a conservative approach to my first solo polar expedition, reasoning that it was the occasion not to take big risks but to make small improvements on previous expeditions. However, I'd learned that the largest cause of slow progress across the ice was the weight in the sledge. On my next attempt I wanted to take an alpine approach, to use the mountaineering terminology. If I was going to move faster over the ice I'd need less food and fuel—the two biggest weight components—and therefore I could put all my supplies in a rucksack and on a small sledge.

My first problem was the shortage of time; it was now the end of December and I would have to be ready to go in four months. I needed sponsorship money fast. The first person I spoke to was Julian Hanson-Smith, a client who had become a good friend of the Polar Travel Company, and who ran a PR company called Financial Dynamics. He put me in touch with Phil White, the chief executive of the coach company National Express. In late February, just over a month before I was due to leave for the Arctic, I met Phil at his company's headquarters.

As I showed him a map of the Arctic, I gave him my background and Arctic experience and explained my belief in an alpine, lightning-strike approach. My passion must have communicated itself to him, because he said, 'Stay here a moment; I'm going to have a chat with some colleagues.'

He came back a few moments later and told me they'd pay £50,000 in return for my titling the expedition 'The National Polar Express'.

My target was to reach the Pole in forty days instead of the normal sixty to seventy, but I was hoping to do it in thirty-five, and I had deliberately set an unusually late departure date of April 14. As the temperatures then were much higher than in March, I would need fewer calories per day—I took 25 per cent less food per day by weight than on my first expedition—a lighter sleeping-bag, less fuel, less clothing—less everything. Instead of a 330-pound sledge, I would set off with a sledge-load of 140 pounds and a ruck-sack weighing 60 pounds. The warmer ice also offered less friction and resistance to my sledge, so I should travel much faster.

I completed my preparations in some haste and set off from Wydemeet at the start of April 1998. I had guilt pangs about leaving Mary in the throes of pregnancy, with a half-finished house and a business to run, but she brushed my worries aside; she and the baby would be fine without me and she was looking forward to some peace and quiet.

My chartered aircraft dropped me off at Ward Hunt Island on April 14, 1998, exactly as planned. I barely glanced at the wooden hut there, as I began heading north straight away. I'd been apprehensive about the extent of open water I would encounter setting out this late in the season, but in the event it didn't give me any real problems, because the weather proved to be kind.

However, perhaps as a result of the weight of the rucksack and the speed at which I was travelling, I was beset by a series of incidents. Within a couple of days the bindings began to pull away from my skis. I knew the brand of skis well and had used them on previous expeditions, but I didn't know that, although these skis appeared to be the same, the manufacturer had recently changed the method of construction. I had always drilled through the upper surface of the ski to fix the bindings with five substantial screws, but instead of the traditional bonded layers—like a piece of plywood—the ski now had a cellular structure, like a honeycomb sandwiched between the upper and lower surfaces, which meant that some of the screws were not biting into solid wood. The bindings had seemed well secured but, as always, they were subject to extreme shear and lifting forces as I skied across the rough ice, and these continuous stresses gradually worked the screws loose.

I didn't have any spare skis or bindings, so I had to improvise a field repair using the emergency Swan Vesta non-safety matches I carry with me on expeditions. I filled each hole with bits of match, ramming them home with the butt of the handle of my Leatherman multi-tool penknife until they formed an immovable plug. I then shaved off the projecting match stubs with a sharp blade, and screwed the binding into these filled holes. It was the best I could do, but it was demoralising to know that, however well I mended the ski, it was not going to last more than a few days and, on occasion, only a few hours, before it had to be repaired again.

The next incident was more serious. On the tenth day, I was climbing over a pressure ridge when I slipped and fell. My right knee got trapped between two ice blocks under a loose covering of snow and, as I continued to fall sideways, the knee took the full combined weight of myself and the rucksack. I felt a stab of blinding pain and stars flashed in front of my eyes. Then I passed out. When I came to, snow had started to settle on me. I took a look at the damage straight away, unzipping and rolling up the trouser leg. When I saw the grotesque swelling around my knee, the sight and the delayed shock caused me to pass out again. When I came round I was seriously cold, and my first thought was that I could die there if I didn't get down off the ridge and put the tent up.

Fighting waves of pain, I dragged my leg out from between the ice blocks, and crawled down the pressure ridge with the rucksack on my back. I pitched the tent on a patch of roughly level ice about ten metres from the ridge. It took about two hours instead of the usual fifteen minutes. I didn't dare take the strongest painkillers I was carrying—Pethidine, usually given to women during childbirth—because I was nervous that if I took them I might drift off into some drug-fuelled fantasy world and die of exposure out on the ice. The ones I did take barely took the edge off the excruciating pain in my knee. When I had at last managed to erect the tent, I dragged my sleeping-bag and supplies inside and got the stove going.

I made a snow pack in a nylon bag, strapped that round my knee and elevated my leg to help reduce the swelling. I stayed resting it in my tent for thirty-six hours. Then, though my knee was still swollen like a balloon, I set off again. I went on for another thirty days, and had reached 86°15´N when I was hit by a triple whammy: my skis were on the point of disintegration and I had been travelling so slowly because of that and the handicap of my injured knee that, even on the most optimistic projection, I was going to run out of food and fuel well before I could reach the Pole. I had also run out of painkillers. I was faced with the choice of either pulling out completely or radioing for a resupply—if my sponsors, National Express, were willing to meet the £25,000 cost. I asked my Canadian base manager at Resolute Bay, Gary Guy, to contact them and see what their thoughts were, and they very generously agreed to fund the flight. I was airdropped more food, fuel, a fresh pair of skis and painkillers two days later.

I had already gone further than any previous solo expedition on the North American side, but it was a feeble consolation for the bitter knowledge that my hopes of an unsupported trek all the way to the Pole had now evaporated. To be the first Briton to have achieved this or that was of zero interest to me; it had to be something that pushed back the boundaries. But I also understood that my responsibilities went beyond my own personal goals. I was representing National Express and carried the hopes of others for whom reaching the Pole would be a great result.

So I kept plodding north and by the thirty-eighth day on the ice I had reached 87°20′N—as little as twelve days' journey from the Pole—and was skiing over a flat ice pan when the final incident occurred. I had no warning of it. One minute I was skiing along, the next my right ski dropped into a broad, straight crack. These pans often have cracks running across them, ranging upwards from a few centimetres in width. This was just such a one, hidden beneath a layer of frozen snow. Once more I toppled over to the right, and my full body weight was transferred through my knee as my leg became trapped. I felt another blinding flash of pain.

I lay motionless on the ice for ten minutes or so, not even attempting to extricate my leg from the crack. By the time I had hauled myself upright, I realised that this fall had knocked the last bit of stuffing out of me. I had the supplies to reach the Pole, and my body might have been able to make it, but at what cost? If pushing my injured knee beyond yet another pain barrier meant that I could never run again, or even walk comfortably, was that a price worth paying? I realised that the prize, already tarnished by the forced resupply, was simply not worth the risk. My attempt on the Pole was over. I made the radio call asking for a flight out.

WITHIN FIVE WEEKS of returning from my second failed attempt on the Pole, our first child, Wilf, was born. Though I did review my polar ambitions thoroughly in the context of my new responsibilities in our new-found family status, I have to admit—rather uncomfortably—this did not affect my commitment to a further solo polar expedition. Above all other things, even the birth of my son, the vow I had made to my father seemed to be absolutely central to my being.

In the year 2000, I guided one Last Degree team from Resolute Bay up to the North Pole at the spring equinox, to see the dawn of the new millennium as the sun rose above the horizon for the first time that year—the last place on earth to experience the millennial sunrise, eighty days after the first. I had five days back home and then led another Last Degree expedition to the Pole from the Siberian side, immediately followed by a 'Last Half Degree' with a client who was desperate to reach the Pole at the end of that season.

In 2001, I dedicated my whole Arctic Ocean season to guiding a single unsupported polar expedition from Cape Arkticheskiy, the northernmost land on the Siberian side of the ocean, leading a young private client with no previous polar experience. Predictably, the strain of hauling a fully laden sledge in such extreme conditions took its toll on my young charge and, despite his best efforts, it proved to be too much, too soon. The early end to the expedition allowed me to take a few weeks off, relaxing with Mary . . . which may explain why we discovered shortly afterwards that she was expecting our second child.

I organised and led two Arctic survival courses in Spitsbergen in late February and early March 2002, giving me a four-week leeway before the birth of our daughter, Freya, on April 12, so that I was back at home to look after Mary if there were any problems. It was the first time that I had spent Easter in England for five years, and I revelled in all the things that I'd been missing out on: spring sunrises over the moor, the succession of wild flowers in our garden—snowdrops, crocuses, wild daffodils, bluebells, wild geraniums, poppies and foxgloves—the trees coming into leaf, and Easter egg hunts and long walks with Wilf. The Nanny Wigley formula was not being applied to Wilf, but with Dartmoor as his adventure playground he was already showing the spirit of an explorer. There's no greater pleasure for me than walking over the moors or along the riverbank with him, sharing his excitement about the world around him.

It was a brief, wonderful interlude for me, before resuming the relentless round of preparations and expeditions, but the next one was something very special. The previous year I had been approached by a client who was planning to raise awareness and funds for muscular dystrophy through a Last Degree expedition. Word of this plan soon reached the ears of a remarkable man, Michael McGrath, who had the condition, and he asked me if I could set up a separate expedition for him and his support team, arriving at the Pole on the same day as our Last Degree expedition to create a powerful message to the public back home. Michael required the support of his professional guide and friends for much of his journey, but he reached his Pole, on his knees but triumphant.

IN THE EARLY summer of 2002, I had a moment of pure serendipity. It came in the form of a phone call from Robert Elias. I'd first met him in 1999, in Punta Arenas in Chile. I had been on my way to Antarctica to act as a forward base manager and technical consultant to the British all-women M&G ISA expedition; having successfully reached the North Pole, Caroline Hamilton and the team she'd selected from our relay squad were now switching their attentions to the opposite Pole. However, we were stuck at Punta Arenas for twenty-three days while we endured daily briefings from the flight operators, giving the latest reason—aircraft problems, bad weather, surface conditions, etc—why we were unable to fly into Antarctica.

While spending yet another day hanging around the hotel, I had a chance meeting with an imposing, athletic figure, wearing a white T-shirt, blue jeans and a baseball cap. He introduced himself as Robert Elias, and it turned out that he was the president of the Omega Foundation, a Nevada-based organisation with a remit to support work of special cultural, environmental or scientific significance in high altitudes and high latitudes. He was also held up on his way into Antarctica, following one of his supported expeditions.

In the course of conversation, I mentioned that Caroline Hamilton's team now had a budget overrun as a result of the long delay. He came to meet the five women, and subsequently offered to contribute towards the costs of the expedition on the proviso that the Omega Foundation would be a recipient of the scientific data, reports and findings coming out of the expedition.

I'd kept in touch with him since then—we spoke regularly by phone—and I always enjoyed our conversations. Now, after chatting for a few minutes, he told me the purpose of his call was to ask for my help in developing a new aspect of the Foundation's work in Antarctica. I agreed with alacrity.

We talked a while longer and, because we were talking about what gave us the energy to go on in life, I told him about my burning passion to make a solo, unsupported journey from the North American continent to the North Pole. Knowing my interest in undertaking scientific work on polar expeditions, he asked what I had in mind. I replied that I had already been developing separate pilot studies for the oceanographical and psychological raw data I could collect en route with British scientists. 'How much would that cost?' he asked. I told him that at this stage I could only give bracketed figures. 'OK,' he said, 'the Foundation will contribute the midpoint figure.'

I ended the conversation in a stunned state. I hadn't even been looking for sponsorship, we'd just been catching up over the phone, and now the Omega Foundation was underwriting the bulk of the costs of an expedition.

I kept this overwhelming information to myself for the rest of the day, then sat Mary down at the kitchen table before supper and told her that, while I had not committed myself on the phone to Robert, I now had the money to do another solo expedition; I asked her what she thought.

I was not expecting her to jump for joy, mainly because I thought she felt that the Polar Travel Company needed me to be there to make the most of the business that we had spent so long developing. But when we had talked it through, she agreed that it was an opportunity that could not be allowed to pass. It was not pure selfishness on my part, a blind determination to fulfil my pledge to my father whatever the cost to those around me . . . or at least I don't think it was. The Polar Travel Company still had no advertising budget and, if successful, a solo expedition to the Pole offered the prospect of media coverage that would propel the company into the public consciousness in a way that no amount of paid advertising could achieve. But there was another factor. I felt that I had found my métier—polar travelling and guiding—and that I had the capacity to be in the upper branches of that particular tree. This was my showcase, and my peers in the polar community would understand what a huge task I had set myself. No solo expedition had succeeded unsupported from North America.

So I went ahead, and for the first time—on my third attempt—I had most of the funding in place well before I was due to depart. I could now plan, train, obtain the supplies and source and/or design the specialist equipment so that, when I finally got to the starting line, I would have the best kit and the best preparation possible to maximise the likelihood of success.

I hoped to make the journey in sixty days, but planned to take rations for sixty-nine days and fuel for seventy-five, giving me a reasonable contingency to cope with accidents or unusually bad weather or ice conditions. But I was determined to pare down to the absolute minimum the weight of the other equipment and supplies I was hauling.

I would be using a state-of-the-art sledge originally designed by Alex Bierwald in association with Borge Ousland, and another piece of equipment, again developed by Borge with Helly Hansen Spesialprodukter: a lightweight immersion suit that would enable me to swim the kind of leads that had sabotaged my first expedition.

Pretty well every other part of the expedition kit had to be modified or prepared to a greater or lesser extent. It isn't like yachting, where the market is so large that it is worthwhile for suppliers to make and sell every possible piece of kit in all sorts of variations. Whether it's a special sail, rope, deck fittings or navigation software, you can buy it off the shelf. In polar exploration there are only a few of us knocking around, no more than a score of professional guides. We don't constitute a worthwhile market for manufacturers, and so we either have to custom-build our own things from first principles or buy an off-the-shelf product and modify it.

There are always several factors to consider. Everything has to be as light as possible but must also be robust enough to keep working for the duration of the trip. Everything must be easy to operate while wearing mitts or gloves and have minimal heat conductivity. You can take metal items or tools, but anything that you might touch—even with gloves or mitts, let alone your bare hands—is best insulated with foam to reduce the risk of frostnip or worse. And everything has to endure temperatures down to –55°C.

One of my operating principles was to maximise the likelihood of success by getting the last percentage point of performance out of every piece of equipment. This required an unbelievable amount of research, time and effort. I wasted hours trying to source a one-litre titanium vacuum flask—titanium is lighter than the usual stainless-steel ones—but every one I found was only 650 ml. I made do with a one-litre stainless-steel one, but it then had to be modified for polar use. The surface of the flask was smooth metal, and from previous experience I knew that when wearing gloves or mitts I would not be able to get enough traction on the metal to undo the screw-on lid, particularly when, as often happened, a tiny drop of moisture on the thread froze solid in the sledging sessions between breaks. So my base manager, Ian Wesley, wound duct tape round the outside of the flask to attach insulating foam to the body of the flask and, every inch or so, taped a match stick round the lid. He smoothed the tape down round each stick and then used a hair dryer to make the tape adhere to the metal as tightly as possible. I now had a vacuum flask that not only had no exposed metal but also allowed me enough purchase to get it open without a struggle, even if it was frozen shut.

We modified just about every other piece of kit that I was taking. My skis were specially made for me by Arthur Åsnes, of Åsnes Ski in Norway, and Helge Hoflandsdal. They looked like standard Sondre skis but had been reinforced with an additional 200 grams of fibreglass and resin, giving 65 per cent extra strength for a minimal increase in weight. My ski boots, too, were light for the protection they offered. I weighed smaller-size pairs and decided to take a size down from normal. It was a slight risk, in that a boot's warmth is partly a function of the volume of air—the great insulator—that it can hold around the foot, and a smaller size might result in dangerously

cold feet, but I'd worn the boots enough to be confident of avoiding problems. I also swapped the thick wool insulating insoles for lighter foam ones.
Why all this concern for the weight of a boot? Because weight on the body,
and particularly at the end of the limbs, has a disproportionate effect. In the
military, every pound saved on your feet is reckoned to equate to four
pounds on your back. I was going to be taking 16 million footsteps and I
wanted them to be as light as possible.

Similarly, I chose the lightest ski poles that were strong enough for the
task and I made sure they were shorter than standard poles for downhill and
cross-country skiing, which leave a sledge-hauler's hands higher than his
heart, increasing the risk of frostbite because the circulation to them is
impaired by the effects of gravity. I then reduced the weight of the poles a
fraction more by stripping off the paintwork. The tungsten tips were
replaced with larger stainless-steel spikes, ideal for testing the strength and
thickness of the sea ice; the plastic ski-pole baskets were replaced by a
leather crosspiece and aluminium hoop fashioned at our local saddlery; and
the handles had abrasion-resistant, high-density foam tape wrapped round
them to prevent heat transfer between hand and handle.

I'd chosen a sleeping-bag only rated to temperatures of −25°C, even
though I knew I'd be encountering temperatures much lower than this in the
early stages of the expedition—from −35°C right down to −50°C. That left a
temperature deficit but a big saving in weight.

To counter the extreme cold I also had an outer sleeping-bag, which we
trademarked as the 'Mammoth Smock', tailor-made by Andy Woodward of
Antarctica in Llandrindod Wells, who also modified my tent, designed my
clothing, and manufactured an array of gear, including all my mitts and
headwear. The smock was like an ankle-length monk's robe, with three-
quarter-length arms and a generously proportioned lined hood. Made of
very light but warm synthetic fibre-pile enclosed in an outer windproof but
'breathing' fabric, it could be worn when I needed extra warmth outside the
tent but would also pull over the sleeping-bag at night.

By the time I left for the Pole I'd not only invested a lot of time and money
in sourcing and modifying supplies and equipment, I'd also done a vast
amount of training. I needed to be super-fit for a solo, coast-to-Pole expedition, and that required two or three hours training a day, six days a week,
over a period of nine months. Long-range sledge-hauling is specific in its
physical demands, but fortunately there was nothing to be gained by replicating the duration of a sledging day during training. I had adopted several

important training rules over the years. The first was to build up the number, duration and intensity of the training sessions gradually, allowing the first six weeks to create a basic fitness platform. The second was to do a variety of exercises throughout the programme to reduce the likelihood of injury.

Most of my training was aimed at increasing the energy output at which my body could work, so that I would be able to drag the heavy sledge as far as possible while ensuring that my glycogen—the carbohydrate stored in the muscles and liver—was burnt up slowly enough to last the full sledging day of ten to twelve hours. To do this, I had to increase the volume of oxygen I could draw into my lungs, and the efficiency of my body's use of that oxygen, as well as its ability to exploit my body fat.

My standard rotation involved cycling and dragging car tyres attached to a sledging harness on the hilly lanes, hill-walking with a weighted pack, cross-country running on the moors, and indoor rowing on my machine. These longer sessions of forty-five minutes to two hours were supplemented by two to three strength workouts a week in the local fitness centre, and a couple of shorter, harder sessions on the rowing machine or running.

I tended to run on the moor, because my knee has never fully recovered from the damage I did to it on the second solo expedition and the shock-loading on it is not brilliant on the roads. I also did mountain biking, hill walking with a very heavy rucksack—up to ninety pounds—and used walking poles to develop the ski-poling muscles. Working on the rowing machine gets very dull after a couple of hours, but I rowed like a mad thing, because it exercised all sorts of body parts and was particularly good training for pulling a sledge. Tyre-pulling was the most sport-specific but also the most unappealing exercise. Progress is so slow and the friction so unrelentingly great. I drag a chain of tyres behind me along a road, simulating the friction you get hauling a heavy sledge across the ice. The type of surface dictated the number of tyres I needed to pull, but at the start I was usually hauling two car tyres linked by a rope in a line snaking out behind me, and that increased to five tyres in the last three months of my training programme.

The other priority before the expedition was to build up my fat reserves, like a polar bear preparing for winter. When I was in the Arctic I would be consuming about 5,300 calories a day, but my work rate combined with the cold temperatures would be demanding about 7,500 calories, and those extra calories had to come from the fat I carried on my body. My usual weight is twelve and a half stone, but by the time I left for the Arctic I was up to fourteen and a half stone.

AS THE DEPARTURE date approached, as on my previous solo expeditions, I found myself taking mental photographs: little scenes like Mary asleep in our bed with her hair spilling in a halo around her; Freya crawling around on the grass, holding up her finds for us to see and admire; or kissing Wilf good night in his bed. I was trying to concentrate those images, scanning them into my brain so that I could summon them up when I needed them out on the polar ice cap.

I had a few conversations with Wilf in the last few days. He knew I was going away and I didn't think there was any point in lying to him and pretending that it wasn't going to be for a long time. I told him, 'Now you'll be the man of the house, and you've got to try and look after Mum and Freya, like Daddy does. Try to keep Mummy happy, look after your sister, and just do the best you can and I'll come back as fast as I can.' I told him that I would be away a very long time, but that I would come back, of course I would. Over the preceding weeks I had shown him how to find Polaris—a yellowish star positioned almost directly over the North Pole, one hundred times the size of the sun and the only apparently motionless star in the heavens. Now I told him that he would always be able to look at Polaris, the Pole Star, and think, 'That's where Daddy is.'

As I packed my bags, I hesitated over a book of Winnie-the-Pooh stories. I'd grown up near Ashdown Forest in Sussex—the original Winnie-the-Pooh country—and I was brought up on the stories. As an adult, I came across a miniature edition with the original paintings in colour, and I took it on my 1994 expedition because it was the smallest, lightest book I could find, and the simple truths, evocative language and familiar characters of *Winnie-the-Pooh* were just the thing to soothe you and send you to sleep happy. It became a habit to read Pooh stories to my clients on Polar Travel Company expeditions. We would all be there in the tent after supper, dog-tired from our day's sledge-hauling. I'd start reading a Pooh story and before I had got to page four they would all be asleep.

However, when it came to this expedition, I decided that Pooh had to be jettisoned. I felt that I had moved on and didn't need that kind of security blanket, and perhaps I was even a bit weary of those overfamiliar stories—I could probably have recited them word for word from memory. But it might also have been because they were just too personal, a reminder of the family I was leaving behind. I'd read all the Pooh stories to Wilf, and played Pooh sticks with him from the bridge just downriver from our home. Instead, I took one of the James Herriot books. Similarly lightweight, in both senses, it was good-humoured, and evocative of simpler, happier times.

I left Wydemeet in February, when the ground beneath the trees was carpeted with snowdrops and crocuses. I kissed Freya, Wilf and Mary in turn, then hurried away before the emotions of the moment overcame me. I don't talk to Mary at all while I'm away on an expedition; it just doesn't work for either of us. She's got her world in Wydemeet and I've got my world in the Arctic. She can't help with my problems on the ice and I just can't cope with worries about what's happening back at home. I have to be absolutely clear and focused on the task in hand or I won't succeed.

As I drove away from my home and my family, I thought of the comment that the great European explorer Fridtjof Nansen had recorded in his journal on his departure, in 1893, for his epic journey across the polar ice cap:

It was the day of leave-taking, the immutable day. The door closed. Alone one walked for the last time from the house down through the garden . . . Behind lay everything that was dear in life, but what lay ahead and how many years would pass before one might see it all again?

PART TWO
5

I came out of my reverie with a start. I had been sitting still too long in that frozen hut on Ward Hunt Island and I was seriously cold. My chest felt as if it were in the tightening grip of a vice. My booted legs were frozen, wooden and lifeless, from the knee down. The visitors' book still lay open on the table in front of me. I wrote a brief, hasty note:

This is Pen Hadow writing my last words before setting out on a solo expedition to the Pole, without resupply. Who knows what's going to happen? But I feel I've prepared myself as well as I can.

I signed and dated it, then closed the book. Perhaps tomorrow I could begin my journey.

When I woke the next morning, March 16, a dim light was seeping through the windows, and the wind, though still shaking the hut, had lost its bullying gusts. I wriggled free of the sleeping-bag and rushed outside wearing only my bed bootees and thermals. The wind had definitely quietened down. All the same, I knew that the gaping leads to the north were so broad that, even at a temperature of –30°C, it would take a further twenty-four hours of light or no winds for them to freeze enough to bear my weight. I decided to spend one more day in the hut and then set off the following morning. Stiff-limbed, I tottered back inside, headed for my sleeping-bag and nodded off for a couple of hours.

After breakfast, I dressed in my full outdoor gear and went outside. On my two previous solo expeditions, I'd headed north within minutes of landing; now my delayed start offered me an unexpected opportunity to explore.

As I scanned the rising ground behind the hut to pick out my best route up Walker Hill, I saw a flurry of snow, like a dust devil, whirling across the ice towards me. I was thinking, How strange, when it came to a halt on the skyline, and the snow flurry resolved itself into an Arctic hare. A moment later a second hare revealed itself. I wasn't completely alone; even in this icebound wilderness, at least two other creatures were eking out an existence, nibbling on the stunted wisps of vegetation beneath the crust of ice and snow. I stood and watched as they scratched at the snow before lolloping away out of sight, their snow-white fur camouflaging them so perfectly against the ice and snow that only their movement betrayed their presence.

Before I climbed the hill, I walked in a wide circle round the hut and was glad to find no tracks or traces of any larger creatures—polar wolves or polar bears. To my knowledge, only the Japanese explorer Naomi Uemura has actually encountered a bear on Ward Hunt Island, but anywhere that the polar pack ice (the floating sea ice) abuts ice that is permanently frozen to the land, like the ice shelf surrounding Ward Hunt Island, you tend to find them, because the movement of the pack ice against the permanent ice opens shore leads where seals emerge to breathe and, if unwary, become prey. Polar wolves have also been seen on Ward Hunt, but their reputation is worse than their intent. They are curious about humans and their food, but acts of aggression are almost unheard of in unpopulated areas like this.

The attitude of polar bears to humans is much more complex. Not a year goes by without reports of a death somewhere in the Arctic, and whenever I've come across a bear or fresh tracks, my heart rate has gone through the roof. I had been at maximum alert from the moment I stepped off the plane but, so far, there appeared to be none in the immediate area, though on each journey to the far north it always takes a few days to 'get your eye in'. Your mind starts to accept that you are not going to see trees, television, lights and people, and suddenly you reacquire the ability to see the ice cap not as a featureless frozen mass but as a place of endless subtle differences. The ice has a myriad hues of blue, green, aquamarine and grey, and the sunlight refracting through it produces every colour in the spectrum.

Visual experiences are particularly dramatic because some of the other senses almost shut down in the Arctic. There are virtually no smells because the cold suppresses them. You can taste only hot food; the cold stuff—even chocolate—tastes like lumps of wood. Your sense of touch is also diminished because you're almost always wearing gloves and mitts, and in any case your finger ends are permanently numb. And though your hearing is only slightly impaired by your hats, neckovers and hoods, the only sounds are the repetitive *ssst, ssst*, of your skis, the keening of the wind and the creaking and groaning from the ice as it flexes and distorts.

So you are thrown back on your sight and your inner eye. Some, like me, find it rewarding and almost therapeutic, but it can be disturbing for others, who feel the isolation and the lack of stimuli acutely. As I've grown older and have become more confident in that environment, I have come to appreciate the aesthetic experiences even more—in what I now call 'Freya moments', after my beautiful daughter, who bears the name of the Norse goddess of merriment, love and beauty. My 'Wilf moments' are like my son, more physical and vocal. They revolve round phrases we use together: 'Easy, Tiger', if I'm overdoing it and becoming too aggressive with my sledge, and 'Only joking, or no?' in a thick Devon accent, if towards the end of the day, I half think that I might stop. A quick 'Only joking, or no?' would keep me going for another session at least.

My Freya moments included taking in the dazzling variety of colours and the bewildering complexity of sculptural forms carved in the ice. I used to resent anything that was stopping me from going north—even the two minutes it took to stop and take a photograph of some breathtaking ice formation—but I've come to appreciate it as a reward for good progress, or compensation for poor progress, capturing something of lasting value from the day. Those subtle changes in texture, shape and colour are not just of aesthetic interest; they are of operational value. They can mean the difference between life and death, like spotting the almost invisible outline of a polar bear against the ice, or knowing the differing look and texture of 'marginal good', 'marginal' and 'marginal bad' ice. The seasoned polar traveller can identify many different kinds of snow and ice, knows which is the best to use for melting into water or for building a shelter, and will often be able to tell, from the lie of the ice around a lead, which way to head in order to circumvent it. He will learn to gauge the strength of the bending, shifting ice beneath his feet; what will bear his weight and what will not. He will spot a seal's breathing hole, or the tracks of an arctic fox or polar bear, and will also develop an instinct for danger, the thing out of place or the faintest unusual movement in a wind-scoured 'landscape' that is rarely completely still. Such faint clues may save his life.

There are certain precautions you can take to minimise the risks of an attack. Rule One is that, if you are confronted by a bear, do all you can to disabuse the bear of the notion that you're a seal. So never retreat towards a lead or open water, because then you're doing exactly what a seal does. Make as much noise as possible: singing, banging ski poles or whatever you have to hand—all have a deterrent effect. Rule Two is don't try to run away—you'll never win the race and there's nowhere to hide anyway on the sea ice, so get organised, get wrapped up, and prepare for a blisteringly cold showdown with a firearm at the ready. Rule Three is that there is one situation where you can effectively guarantee being attacked and that is if you come between a polar bear and her cubs. It can occur all too easily; you might approach from downwind over a pressure ridge and find the mother on one side of you and the cubs on the other. If that happens, you have to get the hell out of there without hesitation.

Those basic rules apart, polar bear behaviour is essentially unpredictable. They may attack in complete silence and without warning but, particularly if aggravated by humans, they will sometimes make hissing noises, growl or grind their teeth before launching an attack. On a number of occasions I've seen a bear out on the ice make a series of wide but ever decreasing circles round me. None of these bears ever turns its head towards me; it's as if they're saying, 'I hadn't noticed you really; I just happened to be walking in a circle round you', but the circles get tighter and tighter. All the time the bear is circling, it is gathering information and gaining confidence, and eventually it will reach the point where it will either attack or turn away.

If the bear is coming upwind towards you, it is still gathering information about you through its nose and may not be sure what to do. Even if it rears up on its hind legs in what may appear to be an aggressive posture, it still may not be planning an immediate attack. If there is little or no wind, it may be standing up to scent different levels of the air for information. But if the bear is coming towards you with the wind at its back, it is not scenting you at all, and that is a big danger signal, because it means the bear has made up its mind that you're toast.

However, another bear, another time, may simply decide to charge straight at you at top speed without any preliminaries whatsoever. You can't prepare for that sort of attack, least of all if you're lying in your sleeping-bag when a polar bear decides that your tent is a big seal or a walrus. You're just going to have to deal with it the best way you can.

Polar bears can weigh as much as 1,000 kilos. When charging they can attain a speed of 25mph and they are powerful enough to stun a seal or even a small whale with one blow from a forepaw, or toss a 200-kilo seal into the air. Yet they are also subtle enough to mimic a drifting ice floe by floating motionless in the water as they close in on a target seal. They can dive to the seabed for kelp and shellfish, travel overland in summer for up to 100 miles to feed on berries, and roam the dark and icy vastness of the ice cap throughout the long polar winter, never hibernating, and pausing only from the relentless hunt for food when 'denning' cubs.

The risk of attack by polar bears on the Arctic Ocean is growing, simply because global warming is making more and more of the ice cap an attractive proposition to them. In April 2001, shortly after I set off from Siberia to take a client to the north geographic pole, I heard over the satphone that a mother polar bear and her cub had been spotted three miles from the Pole. It used to be a freak occurrence if a bear was spotted 500 miles from the nearest land—a male bear doing a massive transport trek in the breeding season or a marginalised bear, old, diseased or immature, perhaps. But a mother and cub are a different matter. They could only have been there because there was open water near the Pole. Seals could come to the surface there to breathe, and polar bears and arctic foxes inevitably followed to prey on them.

Over the last quarter of a century, the average thickness of the Arctic ice has reportedly shrunk by 25 per cent. What was once thin ice is now open water and large areas of once relatively thick ice are now dangerously thin, and the thinner the ice the more mobile it is and the more prone to breaking up. At present rates I would be surprised if my son Wilf is able to make the Arctic journeys that I have made, simply because by the time he grows up there's going to be too much thin ice and too much open water.

I CLIMBED Walker Hill, picking my way over the ice and the iron-hard drifts of wind-packed snow and scaling the pinnacle of black, frost-shattered rock. It took forty minutes to reach the summit, but it was worth the effort. As I looked down, I transposed the familiar features of my office chart onto the topography of the island below me: the lake, drained in summer by a small river flowing south, that separated Walker Hill from the apron of low-lying land—larger than I had imagined it—at the eastern end of the island. The ice sheet extended north as far as the eye could see, but beyond the west–east corrugations of the Ward Hunt Ice Shelf there was a distinct break in the surface texture—the beginning of the polar pack ice. To my relief, when I looked further to the north I could see no giveaway black strips indicating the presence of open water. The refreezing of the leads was under way.

Raising my eyes still further towards the horizon around me, I felt as if I were standing at the edge of the known world. To the south, past the dazzlingly lit peaks of the Queen Elizabeth Islands, lay a vast landmass extending 10,000 miles, populated by billions of creatures. To the north lay a frozen ocean covering 5 million square miles, populated by no more than a handful of highly adapted mammals: the occasional surfacing ringed seal, a few polar bears making forays beyond the coastal margins, and an odd arctic fox hoovering up the remains of some unwary seal. And tomorrow, one human being would be taking his chances out there too.

It was not the hardest ascent I'd ever done, but I knew that no future climb would ever be able to match this moment. I now felt ready for life on the frozen ocean. Tomorrow I would be on my way. I scrambled down the hill, and went back to the hut for the last time.

The next morning, March 17, 2003, I woke in bright daylight. When I went outside, the temperature was cold, −33°C, but the sun was shining, though its low, flat arc above the horizon would keep it hidden behind Walker Hill for the next few days. The sky was mid-blue overhead, fading to an off-white on the northern horizon. And there was something else . . . or rather an absence of something. There was total silence. The lack of wind gave me confidence that no further new leads would open and that the existing ones would not widen any further.

I ate my breakfast, packed away my gear and reloaded it onto the sledge, leaving the shotgun on top for easy access if needed. I put my 'sledger's nosebags'—the nuts, salami, shortbread and chocolate that I ate in the breaks between sledging sessions—into my rucksack and hitched it onto my back, then took a last look around the hut and closed the door.

I put on my harness and attached the traces of the sledge, then put on my skis and picked up my ski poles. This was the moment, the first step on the long haul to the Pole. There was a slight feeling of dread as I took the strain; I knew how heavy the sledge would be, like trying to drag a twenty-stone comatose man behind me, and the Arctic ice is rough, cracked, pitted and pocketed with holes, lumps, bumps, projections and cracks where your burden can become wedged or threaten to topple over. The low temperature is not just uncomfortable, it also makes the sledge travel more slowly.

However, the first short stretch from the hut was slightly downhill and that, and the adrenaline surge from the knowledge that I was finally on my way, helped to get the sledge moving. I had soon passed the last physical sign of man's presence, a metal pole buried deep in the ice, presumably left by some scientist to measure the movement of the ice shelf. Although there was no visible sign of the transition, within a few minutes I knew that I had left the last land behind and was now dragging the sledge across the ice shelf extending out over the sea. I didn't even glance behind me. The only direction I was interested in lay ahead to the north.

Each movement of my ski poles in, through and out of the ice was accompanied by a squeaking, wrenching, mechanical sound, while the skis made a repetitive rasping *whoosh, whoosh*, as they slid over the snow. On that first day out on the ice, the noise seemed so loud that I found myself cringing and trying to go more quietly, but within a few hours I had tuned out the sound so much that I was barely aware of it. I would listen closely each morning as I set off, however, because the noise was a sure indicator of the air temperature. As any child making snowballs knows, as snow warms up it becomes more pliable and mushy, and as a result the noise of ski poles working through it becomes much softer. I could tell to within a few degrees how cold it was, just by putting a ski pole in and skiing a few paces.

The permanent ice shelf is not flat but gently undulating, and the uniform colour of the ice and the brightness of the light made it difficult to discern the contours. Heading north on Day 1, I just knew I was travelling on a gentle down-slope for a while, and then the horizon began to rise and the effort of hauling the sledge increased as I started to climb towards the next crest. This continued for a few miles until I reached the junction between the permanent ice shelf and the ridge of fresh ice blocks that marked the transition to the polar pack ice. There would be no more gently rolling curves; this was a fractured, fissured, vertiginous and boulder-strewn icescape that had to be climbed as much as crossed. I entered this forbidding region and found a site to make my first camp.

I pitched my tent, filled my plastic rubble sack with snow to melt for drinking water for the night and the next day, piled my in-tent kit and rations onto my sleeping-bag and dragged it through the tunnel entrance into the tent. I closed the drawstring and busied myself with the nightly tasks, arranging everything within reach of my sleeping-bag and then lighting the stove, heating water and preparing supper. As I worked, 'snow' continued to fall even inside my sealed tent as my exhaled breath froze to the canvas and then drifted back down as the fabric was shaken by the wind.

I followed my housekeeping rituals with fanatical care, using the small plastic brush that I had already christened 'Mavis' to sweep the ice, snow, frost and condensation from my headgear, clothes and boot-liners, careful to leave not the smallest scrap behind. I regarded some of the inanimate objects I used as neutral; I thought some were malevolent and didn't trust them at all, but I grew very fond of others. It had become my habit on expeditions to anthropomorphise these favoured objects, assigning names and personalities to them—even the humble sweeping brush—and holding regular conferences with them on the nature of the terrain, the right route to follow and the speed of our progress over the ice. Anyone seeing me in earnest conversation with a small plastic brush would have harboured fears for my sanity, but as well as allowing me to hear the sound of a human voice (even if only my own) in the midst of that great Arctic void, these one-sided 'discussions' also helped me clarify my thoughts and ensured that the decisions I took had been thought through first.

While sledging outside, my ski poles were my companions and advisers, testing ice strength, keeping me balanced on awkward traverses and so on, but inside the tent, Mavis was queen. She made her customary excellent job of sweeping the loose snow from my sleeping-bag, but I knew that, even with this precaution, my exuded body vapours would freeze onto the fibres inside the filling of the bag during the night, forming uncomfortable blocks of ice that would increase in size and weight with each passing night, adding to the load I was hauling, and reducing the thermal efficiency of the sleeping-bag. Only when the sun rose high enough above the horizon to radiate appreciable heat could I start draping the sleeping-bag over my sledge during the day and begin to reduce the ice in it by evaporation.

The first five days were 'the survival phase'. The mission was simply to keep moving the sledge north and establish a pattern both during the sledging day and in the camp at night, to get the systems up and running. Over the next five days I would aim to fine-tune everything, ensuring that I was doing each task in the quickest and most efficient way possible and spending the minimum time on the 'domestic duties' in my tent.

I was aiming to do no more than five to six hours sledge-hauling a day, determined to take a measured approach, and not throw myself into it madly as I used to do on my early expeditions. On the next five days I would pick that up to between six and seven hours; on Days 11 to 15 it would be eight to nine hours, and from Day 16 onwards I'd be aiming for a minimum of nine hours, equating to six full sledging sessions including breaks.

It always seemed to take a few days to get into my routine, and on this first night the tent seemed cluttered and the things I needed weren't always to hand. As a result, every job took a little longer than necessary. As I boiled the water for my food and my cup of tea, I checked my position on the GPS, which recorded my latitude and longitude in degrees, minutes and seconds. (A degree of latitude equates to sixty nautical miles, a minute is one mile and a second is under thirty yards.) I also completed the first of my daily logs of distance travelled—exactly three miles north of Ward Hunt Island— and ice and weather conditions. I was too tired to add much personal detail, and within a few minutes of finishing my meal I had given up the struggle and extinguished my head-torch. Despite my fatigue, I slept poorly.

The next morning and every subsequent morning, I checked my GPS before setting out (though I did not expect any significant overnight drift until two degrees or so further north), and updated the magnetic bearing to the Pole, offset over 80° to the west from the true North bearing because the north magnetic pole was located not far away in the Arctic Ocean. Most of the time I was using solar navigation to keep me on track, by computing my local noon using my longitude and Greenwich Mean Time, but if the sun disappeared behind the clouds I could use the compass to keep my bearings. I preferred solar navigation only because it was quicker.

The highlight of my day was to check my progress on my GPS. It showed not only my position but also the distance I'd travelled that day, and it was such a treat that I always saved it for when I pitched my tent and did my evening jobs. Only when I'd got my outer clothes off and was settled in my sleeping-bag for the night did I allow myself to turn on the GPS. The figures I read would elicit either a groan or a cheer, depending on my progress.

On the following two days—Day 2 and Day 3 on the ice—I crossed the first and second of the three leads, which, as expected, had frozen over to produce 'light *nilas*'—strong enough for my purposes. I'd again slept badly, not helped by the zip on my sleeping-bag having broken already. I improvised a repair with a drawstring. I was also starting to daydream about food, especially butter, a sure sign that the workload was having its effect. They were gruelling days, with a number of rubble-fields to traverse as well as the leads.

Every sense was on maximum alert as I approached each lead. There were other, subtler hazards to beware of, as well as the possibility of black, open water. Some cracks in the ice and edges of leads are covered with a layer of snow and are very hard to distinguish from the snow-covered ice surrounding them. Fortunately, the only hazard from the first lead was that it was still marginal ice—grey *nilas*—with traces of the dark colour of the water below showing through. I tested it thoroughly, then inched my way onto it, feeling it flexing beneath me as I moved. There were a few unsettling creaks and one unnerving cracking sound from the ice, but I made it across. After another night's savage frost, the second lead had frozen solid.

I was now in a region of ice scarred and littered with obstructions, and navigating north through the pressure ridges and boulder-fields was a constant drain on my mental resources as well as my physical strength. The icefields were like a giant's maze, and a good deal of moving west and east was required to circumvent obstacles or to search for an easier way.

If the route was too awkward for the sledge or the gradient so severe that I couldn't move it fully laden, I had to break the load into two or three parts. I'd unhitch the sledge, take off my skis, then move ahead on foot to reconnoitre the best route. Each time I left the sledge, I made myself unstrap the shotgun from the top and take it with me, repeating a mantra: 'Think of your family. Don't take unnecessary risks. Take the gun with you.'

I found that mantras were necessary to keep me focused on important things. It was all too easy to be tempted into an unnecessary risk, through inattention or even just sheer cold-induced laziness. From studies at the South Pole, the US National Science Foundation has found that thought and reaction times are almost three times as slow in extremely cold environments.

Having found the best route, I'd dump my thirty-five-pound rucksack, come back to the sledge for the much heavier webbing bag (eighty-five pounds or more) containing more food supplies, and stagger with that to where I'd left the rucksack. As I walked, I'd prepare the route, stamping down or kicking away any projections from the ice that might snag the sledge. Finally, I'd pick up the traces and pull the sledge through. Sometimes I'd have to repeat that three-stage shuttle a few times, but I never had to make more than five shuttles in sequence to traverse a difficult stretch. Then I'd reload the sledge, put my skis back on and plod on to the north.

The furthest one can usually see from the top of a pressure ridge is perhaps two kilometres, and I was continually keeping in mind the big picture—the optimum overall direction I wanted to take—while also constantly scanning the ice closer in front of me, looking not just for ways through the pressure ridges but also for all the minor imperfections on the surface. It became almost intuitive after a while. I found a high point, scanned the ice ahead, then chose a route that I could navigate by using the distinctive colours and shapes among the jumbles of ice. They were often geometric or architectural shapes—pyramids, cubes, cathedrals, blocks of flats, houses, thatched cottages—and sometimes animals—dolphins and sharks, camels and hippopotamuses. I then rehearsed my route by going over it with my 'team'— the collection of crucial pieces of equipment like my sledge and ski poles upon which, like Mavis the sweeping brush, I had already bestowed names.

The sledge was 'Baskers', because in its inertia and reluctance to move it reminded me of my collie dog, Baskerville, or Baskers for short. He loves going on long runs with Mary's horse, but doesn't like training runs with me. When it dawns on him that the horse will not be joining us, I'm always having to turn round and shout for him, and I invariably find him hiding behind rocks and tufts of grass, hoping to slope off home. My sledge often didn't want to come with me either, and was always getting caught between blocks of ice, out of which it had to be coaxed, threatened or manhandled.

My ski poles were named 'Curves' and 'Swerves'. The former had acquired her eponymous shape after taking my full weight when I slipped, almost fell, and bent my left ski pole over a block of ice. Luckily I let go of it at the critical moment and it didn't snap, but two minutes later I did the same thing again, and as I slipped in different directions my weight sent the other ski pole swerving between three blocks of ice. Somehow she emerged unscathed, so she became Swerves. I'd return from each reconnaissance and then announce, 'Right, Team, it's looking hard, easy, hard, easy. We're going left of the large blue diamond, heading for the white ball, on to the three-humped camel and then left of the cathedral spire.' There was some method in this apparent madness, because the repetition of my planned route, as I rehitched to the sledge, was a way of fixing it in my mind, and breaking down the difficult section into manageable challenges.

I WAS NOW feeling that I was 'in the zone', as unswervingly focused on my goal as any medieval pilgrim, and one of the wonderful things about the North Pole for me is that, like a pilgrimage, there's no correct route, there's no map, and when you arrive it's a completely conceptual experience. It never mattered to me that there was nothing at the Pole; in fact I loved the idea. When I first began travelling and exploring in the polar regions, I had the clichéd idea that it was 'me against the Arctic' and thought of it primarily in terms of the 'challenge'. But though the physical rigour and difficulty is still what generates the sponsorship and media interest, to me the inner mental journey is now equally, if not even more, important.

I trust my competence in looking after myself in Arctic environments. I know that things are going to go wrong, and I'll often have to think on my feet, but it's a real bonus for me that I have to sort it all out myself. I want to operate in a vacuum, cut off from the outside world. If I fail, it's my fault. If I succeed, that's down to me being able to deal with everything—physical and mental—that the journey throws at me. On a pilgrimage, you live a simple life on the road, wearing functional clothing, staying in basic accommodation and eating plain food. A polar journey is similar. You have a hood like a monk's cowl, closing out the wider world and forcing you to focus on the path you must follow. You move at a steady, measured, metro-nomic pace; I try to keep my heart rate at around 130 beats per minute, and I can keep moving for twelve hours a day at that rate. That hypnotic rhythm, plodding north on automatic pilot, frees your mind to think and reflect, and towards the end of the day I get to an almost transcendental stage, where I find I've travelled two or three hours without being aware of it at all.

When you finally reach your destination, you stand in a world turned upside-down. There is no east or west or north at the Pole; whichever way you face, the only direction you can take is south. There is no time—you stand in all twenty-four of the earth's time zones simultaneously—and no familiar, reassuring succession of day and night. The world seems as frozen as the ice beneath your feet: perpetual day, perpetual twilight, or perpetual night.

If the earth's axis is extended into space from the north geographic pole to infinity, it meets an imaginary celestial sphere at an imaginary point: the north celestial pole. This speaks volumes to me about the inner journey and the process of journeying rather than the purely physical experience. If you stand at the Pole on the winter solstice, the stars circle above you all night and not one of them sets. From Polaris, the hub, almost directly overhead, to the last visible star scraping the southern horizon, all travel in perfect con-centric circles across the sky. For the only time in your life, the earth and the heavens really do seem to revolve around you.

I SLEPT for fourteen hours that third night on the ice, and was glad to catch up on the lost sleep, even at the price of a late start the next day, Day 4, when I crossed the last of the three leads during the afternoon. The fierce temperatures of the previous days had done their work and the lead was now completely frozen with a thick layer of opaque ice, but as a result of my late start I managed only 1.9 nautical miles northwards through endless pressure ridges and boulder-fields.

The next day, even though the temperature remained around −40°C and the sun barely climbed above the horizon, there was just enough heat in it to evaporate the rime from my sledge-top for the first time. It was a great psychological boost. I was also starting to find a few larger ice pans among the ridges and boulder-fields. Each ice pan was like a little enclosed field, surrounded by a wall of ice, but there was always a point where the ice wall was lower or easier to cross, making a gateway into the pan beyond.

The Arctic winter was almost at an end, but the endless daylight of the polar summer had not yet begun, and for those first few days I had had a full day and a full night. Even when there was no moon, the nights weren't inky black but more of a dark grey twilight born of the dim phosphorescence of the sunlight leaking from below the horizon. And even in the depths of the Arctic winter, starlight is gathered and reflected by the ice, diminishing the polar darkness, and moonrise brings an opalescent, milky-blue light. Reflected and refracted by the ice, it creates an eerie, softly glowing landscape, devoid of form or shadow, as if seen through water. At a full moon, there is enough light to cross the ice almost as well as by daylight.

When the disc of the sun at last appears above the horizon, another reassuring pillar of the familiar world has been removed. This far north, the sun does not rise in the east and set in the west; at first it rises and sets in the south, and then, for weeks on end, it does not set at all.

I have seen nothing on this earth to equal the beauty of the March polar sunrises and sunsets, when the sun is still low on the horizon. After months of unbroken polar night, to be there for the first sunrise of a new year is a life-affirming experience. There is a long period of false dawn, with the sky gradually lightening but the sun still hidden by the curve of the earth, and then at last the first ray of sunlight reaches across the ice, setting it sparkling like a vast veil sprinkled with diamonds. The air is so cold, arid and clear that the colours of the sky shine with a depth and radiance seen nowhere else on earth. Crimsons, violets, golds, azures and aquamarines wash the morning sky, fading only slowly into the familiar deep blue of the Arctic sky as the sun climbs higher above the horizon. The sunsets are, if anything, even more magnificent, and even when the sun has gone down below the horizon it leaves a halo of light behind, refracted into an arc of jewelled colour through the prism of the ice particles suspended in the air.

At the latitude of Ward Hunt Island, the first sunrise of the year occurs in early March, but at the North Pole the sun doesn't appear above the horizon until the spring equinox—March 21. It makes a complete circuit round the horizon without ever dipping below it, and at the end of that day it has risen a fraction higher in the sky. It spirals ever higher until Midsummer's Day, when it describes its tightest circle, then unwinds the spiral until it disappears below the horizon on September 21—the autumn equinox.

Seen from a few miles north of Ward Hunt, the sun's trajectory included an element of dip—it rose in the mornings and described a low arc through the sky before setting again in the late afternoon, but it neither rose high above the horizon nor sank much below it, and there was soon some dim daylight even at midnight. Late in the afternoon, as the sun began to set, the light cast cream, gold, orange and russet tints over the ice, and then, as it disappeared below the horizon, the colours shifted towards cold, lunar tones of blues and greys, deepening and darkening as the evening advanced. The lower the light, the more it seemed to bring the frozen world around me into relief, sculpting the ice and snow—almost featureless in hard daylight— into scarps, cliffs and screes, mounds and monoliths, and shapes that mimicked every conceivable natural form.

WHEN I WOKE on Day 7, I heard the wind blasting over the ice cap and battering the tent fabric. A gale had blown up during the night and with the temperature at −40°C and dropping, the wind chill of around −90°C made it well-nigh impossible to move north. I did not want to be taking a rest day at this stage, after the enforced idleness at Ward Hunt Island, but I had to stifle my impatience and wait out the storm once more.

It did at least give me time for some running repairs to my smock. The zip had broken the previous day, leaving my right side more exposed to the wind than was comfortable. I couldn't fix the zip, so I had to sew the smock closed and wriggle in and out of it like a snake shedding its skin.

When I awoke on the morning of Day 8, I lay with my eyes closed, listening to the sounds of the Arctic: the brittle rattle of the frozen tent fabric in the breeze, the hiss of loose snow as it surged past or was deposited round the base of the tent, and the occasional booms and pulsations of the ice cap as it flexed and twisted under the pressure of the wind. The wind had died during the night, and through my closed eyelids I could tell that a soft, diffuse light was permeating the tent. It would, I knew, be illuminating the thick layer of ice rime covering the walls and the roof above my head and the intricate feathers and fans of ice crystals that had formed as my exhaled breath froze on contact with the hood of my sleeping-bag during the night. I knew that my first movements would cause those delicate crystal structures to collapse and tumble down into the opening of my sleeping-bag.

I didn't feel well rested, but that was scarcely surprising. I knew that my sleeping-bag was not rated for the temperatures I was enduring and I was paying the price for it in lost sleep. I did what I could to supplement the bag, pulling my smock over it and wearing not only my thermal 'pyjamas', but my 'neckover'—a thick tube of fibre pile that covered my neck, blocking out the draughts at the top of my pyjamas, and pulled up over my chin. The fibre-pile hat, which I kept pulled down to my eyebrows, left only my nose exposed to the cold through a tiny opening in the drawstringed hood of the bag. I also wore some specially made down bootees, and filled my one-litre plastic drink bottle with hot water, using it as a hot-water bottle for my feet.

Getting out of the bag was one of the lowest points of every twenty-four-hour cycle. In the temperatures I was enduring, my nose was vulnerable to frostnip, and I needed to get some warmth onto it straight away. That required movement, however, which would inevitably bring the ice shower down on me. But I had a second, even more pressing reason for getting up: the desperate need for a pee caused by the incompletely understood condition known as cold-induced diuresis. I often had to get up and have a pee during the night and also woke every morning with my bladder at bursting point.

I swung myself up and fumbled with the drawstrings, cursing as the inevitable ice found its way down my neck. I was working by touch, because my eyes were still firmly shut, my eyelashes welded together by my frozen breath. As soon as I could work my hands out of the bag, I gave my eyes a gentle rub, warming them and breaking up the ice. After a few moments I was able to ease them open. Then I dragged myself into a kneeling position in the bag and grabbed the packaging from the previous night's freeze-dried supper. Each night's food packaging became the next morning's pee bottle. Having filled it, I drew back the floor sheet of the tent and poured the urine into the snow—if you poured it gently, the heat of the urine drilled a small hole down through the snow to the ice below.

Next, I picked up the saucepan, which I left upturned on the stove element to stop ice and snow falling into it from the roof of the tent, and causing problems in lighting it. I poured the still slightly warm water from my 'hot-water bottle' flask into the saucepan, took my book of matches from their perch against the outer edge of the fuel preservation unit, and lit the stove.

The stove was such a vital piece of equipment that I carried two stove units and a maintenance kit, including three extra fuel pumps—the most problematic and delicate part. It was just as well, for now, only a week into the expedition, the fuel pump of the first stove was leaking. I set it aside, got the first spare and discovered that the pump on that one did not allow the fuel to flow. The same thing happened with the third one, and I was beginning to sweat. The problem had occurred on previous expeditions when the temperature dropped to around –40°C. The small 'O' ring sealing the fuel pipe to the pump would contract in the cold so much that when the fuel was pumped up to operating pressure it would seep past the seal and pool on the tent floor—a huge fire risk. I held my breath as I tried the fourth and last fuel pump; to my relief I saw the fuel at once begin to flow.

When I applied a light, the naphtha fuel—also known as white gas—ignited with a *whoosh*. Then, as soon as the stove had settled to a steady blue flame and a comforting roar, I increased the ventilation. My tunnel-type tent had air vents near the top at either end, and whenever I was using the stove I had those open, covered with a fine mesh if it was windy or a more open weave if it was still. I also had the zip at the downwind entrance to the tent open a few inches to create an airflow. I made sure I stayed awake while the stove was on because there was a significant risk of carbon monoxide poisoning. There are two easy tests for CO, which builds up gradually, from the groundsheet upwards. If your stove is showing little interest in burning fiercely, that's a big indication that there isn't enough oxygen at the lower levels inside the tent. The other test is to light a match and hold it at the top of the tent and then gradually move it down towards the floor. If the match starts to gutter and even die about two feet from the floor, that's an unmistakable sign that there's a layer of carbon monoxide.

While the water was coming up to a decent temperature, I packed snow blocks from my plastic rubble sack into the saucepan. My breakfast bowl was also my spare saucepan. If you lose or damage your saucepan you have no way of melting snow and creating water, so I always had a spare. I fished out the tea bag, sugar lumps, and sachet of dried full-fat milk to mix with my tea and add to the porridge. Breakfast was always Readybrek, mainly because it's quick to cook and gives a long, slow release of energy throughout the day. You just pour in hot water and stir, but I'd also added clusters of oats, bran, honey and dried fruit. Each day's ration was premeasured into a breakfast pack, along with my tea bags and dried milk. I also took two effervescent vitamin C tablets and seven sugar lumps a day. One lump went into my first cup of tea in the morning, two into my second cup, three into my tea flask for the day's sledging and the final lump into my first cup of tea in the evening. I drank all my hot drinks from a lidded, insulated mug.

After breakfast, I prepared my two vacuum flasks with everything I needed for that day: a litre of hot water in the stainless-steel flask with sugar, milk powder and a fresh tea bag, and another litre in the plastic flask, mixed with a sachet of energy powder and one of the vitamin C tablets. My breakfast, supper and drinks for my flasks were all prepacked in the day's ration bag, but my sledging rations for the day were taken from a central store and placed in the front of the sledge each morning. When I stopped for one of my scheduled breaks, I fished out a flask and delved into the 'sledger's nose-bag', which contained a mixture of chocolate drops, pine nuts, macadamia nuts and cashews, ten slices of salami and a shortbread finger.

For supper I always had a cereal bar as a starter, with a cup of tea. I had three main dishes in rotation: beef and potato stew, cod in a white sauce with potato, and chicken curry with rice. All were precooked and freeze-dried, but after a long day's sledge-hauling they tasted like a gourmet dinner in a Michelin-starred restaurant. I also had a daily ration of a quarter of a pound of butter—a health nightmare in temperate England but a near-essential in the Arctic because it gives more calories per unit weight than almost anything else. I usually mixed part of it into my morning porridge and the rest into my evening meal. After supper I had a hot chocolate drink.

When my food and drink for the day was prepared, I packed my gear away. I always tried to do things quickly and efficiently, but when it's very cold your brain simply doesn't function as effectively, and though I was desperate to get out and start pulling the sledge I had to force myself to think ahead to the various sequences of actions that I was about to perform.

Ian Wesley, my English base manager, later told me that when I spoke to him on the satphone he was staggered by how slow and jumbled my speech was, particularly in the expedition's early stages. With my brain working so slowly, there was a strong inclination to simplify everything into single steps—I would find myself walking backwards and forwards carrying single items between the tent doorway and the sledge. I therefore had to do much of my 'problem-solving' in the tent when I had warmed up a bit, and the solution to that particular problem was to pile everything onto the sleeping-bag and then drag it out alongside the sledge.

When I stepped out of the tent that morning the cold hit me like a fist. It was −45°C, the coldest day so far and 10° lower than it should have been at that time of year, but fortunately there was no wind chill. The early going was difficult, with blocks of ice stacked up in a series of walls that seemed to go on for ever. By halfway through the day I had covered little over half a mile, and I could feel my confidence ebbing away. But soon after I found myself on the biggest, flattest ice pans of the expedition so far, and by the end of my first eight-hour day I had completed 3.5 nautical miles.

My hopes of more flat ice the following day were dashed when I hit a series of exceptionally old pans. The ridges had been filled with snow and weathered down, leaving mounds twenty or thirty feet high, like ocean swells frozen in motion. I had to drag the sledge up at an angle to the wave to reduce the gradient, then plunge down the far side, only to repeat the performance within ten strides.

Before setting off on Day 10, I emptied the sledge and repacked it, taking advantage of the space already created by eating ten kilos of food and using four litres of fuel. Towards the end of the day I came into some second-year rubble-ice that had been partially filled in with snow and carved by the wind into striking shapes. It was like walking through a garden centre full of animal sculptures, hippos and crocs being the most popular models.

When I stopped for the night, I again had problems with my fuel pumps. I hoped that rising temperatures would solve them, but there was no sign of those at the moment; they remained stubbornly the wrong side of −30°C and as low as −40° to −45°C at night.

However, there was one strong positive on which I could focus: I had reached the end of my first ten-day block. I visualised the sixty days of the expedition as a clock face and I had now reached ten past the hour. It was a useful distraction from the minimal mileage I had achieved.

On Day 11, I was grateful for relatively flat pans, because I was suffering from backache. Hauling the sledge was bad enough, but I also had the rucksack on my back to reduce the weight of the sledge. Now I tried putting my rucksack on the sledge, and while it definitely made the sledge feel heavier, it instantly relieved my back, so I left it on the sledge over the flatter pans and put it on for the rough stuff. When I called Ian on the satphone that night, he read me a backlog of funny emails that Mary had sent, about her action-packed social life in my absence and what the children had been getting up to. She was very good at describing little scenes that I could picture and carry with me through the next day, and it was a great morale boost. My only problem was my back, now bad enough to force me to start using some of my precious stock of painkillers.

On Day 12, the temperature had risen a little, from –40° to –35°C, giving hope of warmer times to come. I set out that morning feeling better rested than I had since I left Ward Hunt Island, and was rewarded with a record day of 5.5 miles. I was in such a positive frame of mind that I was singing songs out loud to myself as I crossed the flatter ice pans. I was starting to enjoy my journey at last.

6

Day 14 began badly when I knocked over some hot water in the tent. My sleeping-bag was wet, I'd wasted fuel to melt that water and I'd also wasted time. I had to collect more snow, relight the stove and heat water again. It took forty minutes to turn snow into drinkable water.

A mountain of ice boulders and rubble forced me into a three-hour detour due west, and in eight hours' sledge-hauling I managed to make only three nautical miles northwards. I also lost an hour when the skin of my left ski ripped clear of the screws holding it. I had to stop to repair it, and within twenty minutes of setting off again the skin on the other ski did the same thing. To add a further layer to my frustrations, visibility was poor, and the low light levels and lack of shadow, contrast, perspective and definition made navigation through the jumble of ice very difficult. I just had to hope for better visibility and easier going the next day.

In part, I got my wish. It was the last day of March, and for the first time I was now operating in twenty-four-hour daylight, since the sun was high enough in the sky to remain above the horizon right through the night. Day 15 dawned with brighter, clearing skies, but I felt very weary all day. It was much too early in the expedition to be losing my edge and after I'd eaten my normal supper of a 300-gram pack of cod and potato, I allowed myself another half-pack and an extra mug of sweet tea to see if the additional fluid and calories would give me a boost.

Burning out before I reached my goal was one of the fears that haunted me throughout the expedition. I also had a terror of having to carry out self-dentistry. The risk was far from insignificant. I'm one of those people who has lots of metal fillings, and they're starting to disintegrate. I'd been for a thorough checkup with my dentist before departure, but no checkup can prevent the sort of damage that can be inflicted during an Arctic expedition. I was constantly stressing my teeth and, more particularly, my fillings, which expand and contract at different rates to the teeth. One minute I was drawing in air at temperatures down to −40°C as I hauled my sledge along, and the next I'd be sipping a cup of tea at +70°C as I took my break. I was also biting on sledging rations that were deep-frozen and as hard as rock. Obviously I was trying to protect my teeth, but I only had to forget for an instant or catch one bit of food wrong and there would go a tooth. Inevitably it happened—during my first break on Day 15. I bit down on something, heard a crack and felt a huge new cavity with my enquiring tongue—half a filling and part of a tooth had fallen out.

I waited for the first waves of what dentists like to call 'exquisite pain' as the Arctic air hit an exposed nerve, but miraculously they didn't arrive; either the nerve was already dead, or enough filling and tooth remained in place to protect it. For the rest of the expedition, every time I ate anything, I ate only on the right-hand side of my mouth. It became an instinct to try to minimise the likelihood of either pain or further damage.

As I prepared to halt for the night, I had one solid achievement behind me: I was now a quarter of the way to the Pole—in days if not yet in miles. I'd done 25 per cent of the sixty days I expected to take. In a way, I was fooling myself. I'd only covered 46.5 nautical miles at this point and still had another 369.5 to go. But focusing on the days rather than the mileage wasn't a totally false perspective. In the early stages the sledge was at its heaviest and the ice conditions, temperature and weather were at their worst; every mile then was worth two or three further down the track.

The clear skies brought one other bonus; the temperature remained very low, −40°C at night, and any leads opening up would refreeze enough within a few hours for me to walk across them. The cold meant I was using more fuel, but that was more than outweighed by the speed I could maintain while I wasn't being held up by open water. That night I had crossed a lead of 400 metres of thin ice and pitched camp on the far side.

Before I went to sleep I read two chapters of my Herriot book; it was the first time I'd looked at it. On previous nights it had been too cold in the tent to read, but it felt warm enough to do so now that direct sunlight was heating the tent throughout the night as the dark-coloured walls absorbed much of the sun's energy and re-radiated it into the tent. I was woken by a rumbling and juddering during the night and discovered the next morning that ice movements had driven the northern side of the thin ice right underneath the southern side. It was now half the width and twice the thickness, but it could just as easily have pulled apart and I'd then have woken to find 200 metres of open water on my doorstep.

Even though my sleeping-bag was full of ice, I managed to get a lie-in on Day 16, April 1, 2003. I'd slept for twelve hours and felt well rested. As I packed my sledge that morning, I noticed that for the first time the sledge-load looked flat from end to end, visual confirmation that the load to haul was getting lighter.

I had a gentle start to the day, but I soon hit a huge area of very old ice pans, majestic and almost prehistoric-looking, perhaps decades old. They had the form of giant sand dunes whipped and carved by winter storms. There were steep crests, rough crags, long bleak ridges and sinuous, snow-filled curves. I tried to keep contouring while crossing each ridge, reluctant to lose height. In doing so, I was detouring big distances to each side, and barely going forward at all, but to go up the ridges was such an exhausting manoeuvre that even the longest detour round them seemed preferable.

I had grounds for muted celebrations when I took my GPS reading that night. I discovered that I had crossed the eighty-fourth parallel during the course of the day –84°N—the first line of latitude I had reached since leaving Ward Hunt Island. I opened my first of seven special cards I had brought with me that Mary and the children had made for each latitude reached. A vibrantly yellow handmade silk daffodil dropped out of the envelope and I pinned it to my smock. Every time I looked at it I thought of them all getting on with life on the moor, and it put a smile on my face.

The morning of Day 17 was glorious, with skies of the deepest blue, almost shading into black, and a genuine warmth in the sun. I covered the miles at a steady pace, troubled only by an occasional twinge from the knee I had injured on my last solo attempt on the Pole. I always stopped within a stride and a half of any niggle of any sort anywhere in the body, just to relax, give it a shake-out and then set off again thirty seconds later. I did not want to pull a muscle or tear a tendon through carelessness.

By the time I halted that night, I had covered 5.7 nautical miles, my best daily distance to date. I had 'budgeted' for an average of three miles a day for the first twenty days, and to have done almost double that in a single day was a significant morale boost. I was beginning to feel that reaching the Pole in less than sixty days was now a real possibility.

The bright sunshine that day hadn't been an unmixed blessing because, with the sun getting higher in the sky every day, it brought on the possibility of snow blindness. Sunglasses are the obvious solution, but in temperatures below −35°C they bring their own problems. Warm, damp air rising through your clothing and from your breath instantly converts to ice as it comes in contact with the cold surfaces of the lenses, and you are soon rendered partially blind. So while the sun's daytime elevation was relatively low, I had opted to do without sunglasses in the interests of better navigation through the sea ice. But now I'd reached the difficult time when it was still too cold to keep the lenses clear but the sun's rays were too high and strong to ignore. If you're snow-blind, you cannot open your eyes because they are supersensitive to any light. You get such extreme pain that you simply can't do anything. You just have to lie in your tent and wait for it to pass. That day I felt my eyes starting to feel unusually warm. I stopped at once and checked them; when I closed my eyes I saw a bright orange and red glow behind my lids—a danger sign—and thought at once, Watch out! I pulled out my sunglasses and wore them continuously from that moment on.

I spent some time on the satellite phone that evening, which was an unplanned development. I'd scheduled phone calls to Ian Wesley every day for the first ten days, while we ironed out any bugs in the systems, but the plan was then to phase it down to around once a week. I was looking forward to that, because it helped me to focus on my task.

However, Ginny Dougary's articles for *The Times* were starting to generate so much interest that the expedition website was besieged by people logging on every day from their homes and offices. None of us had been expecting to run daily progress reports on the website but, with all this unexpected interest, it made the expedition appear poorly organised if we did not do daily updates. I therefore had to talk to Ian every day in addition to my scheduled interviews down the phone with Ginny. It was great that there was such interest in what life was like on the Arctic Ocean, but it entailed spending up to half an hour on the satphone every night, instead of just finishing my meal and going straight to sleep. That may not sound much, but over the sixty days of the expedition it came to thirty hours—the equivalent of three whole sledging days.

When I talked to Ian, I gave him a summary of the day's events and conditions: the number of pressure ridges, rubble-fields and leads encountered; the wind speed and direction; the atmospheric pressure and cloud cover; the navigational techniques I was using—solar or compass—and any equipment and health issues. From the data that was transmitted to him by my Argos tracking beacon, Ian then added the temperature readings; my position in the morning and evening; how many miles I had done so far and how many miles were left to the Pole; the ice drift if any; and the daily average necessary from this point onwards to reach the Pole. I wanted to generate quantifiable information that would give children in schools data they could play with, to make maps and graphs, and generally get a feel for the operating environment of the expedition.

My conversations with Ginny were more concerned with personal, human-interest angles. She came alive at the least mention of unusual thoughts, psychological developments or actual incidents, and she loved the anthropomorphic treatment of my equipment, so much so that Mavis the sweeping brush became a personality in her own right. Ginny obviously knew her readership much better than I did, but it was a minor though growing frustration for me that she seemed so uninterested in the physical process of getting to the Pole, but so fascinated by what seemed in my head to be irrelevant trivia. These chats with Ginny and Ian were using battery power much faster than I had planned, and that might have a significant impact by the end of the expedition.

I had one other chore to perform before I could sleep at the end of Day 17: de-icing my boots. I made myself do this not less than every other day, because the encrustations of ice that built up inside them in Arctic conditions, both from sweat icing to the frozen surfaces and external moisture from the snow that would leach its way in through the seams, are at best uncomfortable and at worse dangerous. If the ice inside your boots is occupying space designed for insulating air, your feet will be affected; you could easily lose your toes to frostbite.

Removing the ice from my boots was therefore essential, but it was a time-consuming and surprisingly gruelling task, which left me with aching hands and arms and bleeding fingers. The deep-frozen ice was as sharp as razors and I had to do all the work with bare hands; if I got my gloves wet with melting ice, they'd lose their insulation value and I might end up with frostbitten fingers the next day. By the time I had finished, there was blood everywhere, and my thumbs and forefingers were skinned.

I slept badly and woke the next morning feeling very tired. Nevertheless, despite my weariness, I managed another 5.4 miles that day. Whenever the going allowed, I let my mind drift off to one of a number of pet projects. I ran through a typical day for Mary, Wilf and Freya in the finest detail and tried to guess what each was doing at exactly this time of day back in the UK. I compiled guest lists for dinner parties, and landscaped and planted up swathes of our garden in a variety of styles and colour schemes. I was also mentally designing a yacht that had so many additional features and gadgets that it would assuredly have sunk without trace, but it all helped to distract me from the endless drudgery of putting one foot in front of the other, as the sledge dragged behind me like a sea anchor.

For the first time, the sun was now high and hot enough to burn some of the ice out of my sleeping-bag, which I spread on top of the sledge during the day. It was noticeably lighter and less lumpy when I took it into the tent that night, but I didn't sleep well. I felt so washed out, weak, wobbly and listless that I decided to take the next day off, regardless of the weather. Day 19 was therefore a day of rest, recuperation and repairs, though thanks to a northward ice drift—the first I had encountered—I did end the day 0.12 nautical miles nearer to the Pole than at the start.

Whether because of the rest or the rising air temperatures, I slept better that night, and set off refreshed the following morning, Day 20. It was another sunny day and there was the first sign that the summer thaw was beginning: a lead stretching across my track, the first open water I had seen since setting off. It ran broadly east–west as far as I could see in either direction. I tracked it westwards for around twenty minutes and then said to myself: 'Come on. It's the first water you've seen, the air temperature feels warm, it's not windy; this'll be good practice. Get the immersion suit out.'

I stood on the brink and studied the lead carefully. There was about twelve metres of open water, and the division between it and the ice banks on each side was clearly defined. There was a short apron of thin ice that might or might not bear my weight. I wasn't unduly nervous, more intrigued by what it would feel like. But this would be the first time I had used the immersion suit on my own, with no one to dive in and rescue me if things went wrong.

I ate a little chocolate, both for energy and as a reward to myself for agreeing to do this, then hauled the sledge onto its 'lilo'—the inflatable raft that would keep it higher and better stabilised in the water as I towed it behind me. I could even straddle the sledge and hand-paddle it along like a surfboard or use my shovel as an oar, but it was very cumbersome and, in practice at Resolute Bay, I'd found it easier to tow it behind me while I swam. When I'd secured the sledge, I put on the immersion suit over my sledging gear. All I had to take off were my skis, though I also removed one mitt so that I could work the zips and do some fiddly adjustments with the hood. All my other clothes and gear, even my sledging harness, stayed on.

At the last minute I took off my sledging hat—my head was seriously cold without it, but if I kept it on while swimming it had a habit of working itself down over my eyes so that I couldn't see where I was going; I stuffed it down inside the suit and then used the long drawstring to help me pull the hood over my head. When I'd finished, I crouched down into a tight ball to squeeze the excess air out of the suit, so that when I stood up again it was vacuum-formed against my body. I didn't want to go into the water with air trapped all over the place. I then put the sledging-trace round my waist. I had loops every metre of the trace, so I hooked two together round my waist and clipped them with a climber's metal clip to make a crude belt-harness for the sledge. I took a few deep breaths to relax myself and, as I did so, I took a long, hard look around. If a polar bear came along while I was in the water, I would be exhibiting classic food-source behaviour—swimming around like a seal—and I would be unable to reach the rifle on the sledge. I scanned the foreground, middle distance and horizon in every direction, looking for the least movement or unusual shape or colour. As far as I could tell, there was nothing out there but ice and snow.

It still took a few moments to steel myself to get into the water. The contrast between the snow and ice and the menacing, black water was almost panic-inducing, but after a brief exchange of views with Swerves, Curves, Baskers and the rest of the team I was ready. I sat down on the ice and worked my way out towards the lead on my bottom, keeping the sledge right up behind me so that it would only need a gentle tug to get it into the water; I didn't want to be yanking on the trace to move it and have it come flying into the water and crashing into me. I inched further and further, until I could feel the ice bending beneath me. I paused at the brink, feeling very self-conscious, had one last look around, then took a deep breath, pushed my feet down through the thin ice and dropped into the water.

Even though I knew that my immersion suit would protect me from the cold, I'd been holding my breath in the tension of the first few moments. I let it out with a gasp of relief. I could feel the pressure of the water compressing everything, as if I were being shrink-wrapped. Despite that, and all the air I'd been squeezing out of the suit, there was still a lot of trapped air and I felt unnaturally buoyant, riding unnervingly high in the water like a swimmer in the Dead Sea. I turned round to face the sledge and put both feet up against the ice to brace myself as I pulled it in after me. It was a bit scary, because I was almost pulling the sledge in on top of me, but I couldn't just swim off towing it behind me because, until it was in the water, there was too much inertia and friction to overcome. As I pulled, the sledge slid to the edge of the ice. It caught on a projection and teetered for a moment, then slid into the water with a soft splash. A few icy drops hit my face and the bow wave set me rocking in the water as if in the wash of a passing boat. I turned over and began to breast-stroke my way towards the other side of the lead. The sledge skimmed along behind me, putting no drag on me at all. Just the same, I was glad that the lead was no wider, because the exertion of swimming wearing this giant bin liner would soon make me pour with sweat.

In what seemed like no time, I was breaking through the small apron of thin ice on the far side. Although not strong enough to walk on, the marginal ice at the edge of open leads was often too strong to be easily broken with my arms. Instead, I had to pull myself up onto the ice and load it with my body weight until it broke. When it did, often quite suddenly, I would drop back into the water, and each time there was a niggling fear that the air trapped inside the immersion suit would suddenly shift, tipping me head-first under the water like a dabbling duck. If that happened, the trapped air would make it impossible for me to right myself, and I would drown.

I pushed those unhelpful thoughts away and broke through to some thicker ice, then, kicking with my legs and hauling on the ice as much as the slippery integral mitts of the suit allowed, I launched myself upwards onto the surface of the ice. Streaming water, and still lying flat to spread the load, I worked my way across the thin ice and onto the more solid platform beyond, then stood up and hauled on the trace to bring the sledge out of the water after me. It took another twenty minutes or so to take the suit off, rub it in the snow to soak up the moisture and shake it dry. I then rolled it up from the feet and secured it in a neat bundle, tying it with the drawstring of the hood. It might have taken three hours to walk round the lead; it had taken no more than an hour to swim across it. But I was never entirely comfortable about using what I christened 'Mr Orange'—the colour of the suit. Deliberately immersing myself in the forbiddingly black waters with no one around for hundreds of miles always seemed to be an unnatural act.

As I sledged over the ice, I felt warmer than on the previous days. In fact the ambient air temperature was actually two to five degrees colder than on the previous five days, but my all-black suit was paying dividends as it soaked up the heat of the warming rays of the sun. I rarely clock-watched during the sledging sessions—only twice in the entire expedition can I remember thinking that the time was dragging and wishing that it was time for the next break. My standard day was six seventy-five-minute sessions with a break of eight to ten minutes between each. If there were jobs to do or problems to sort out—checking the screws on my ski bindings, changing the film in my camera or tightening my bootstraps—I tried to save them until the next break, otherwise I was continually stopping and starting. And if I had jobs to do, I hurried my food and drink in that break so as to minimise the time lost before I was moving again.

In midafternoon on Day 20 I came across another recently active lead, where an ice pan had pulled apart and then refrozen. The surface was thin ice, just about walkable, but there were signs of activity to the west where the two halves of the pan were crunching together, with plates of still dripping ice freshly lifted above the water line. In the course of a single day I had now come across a stretch of open water that I'd had to swim and a currently closed but obviously still active lead—confirmation that the spring thaw was under way, and also that I was entering an area of more active sea ice.

DAY 21, April 6: the noises and ice movements that accompanied me all day indicated that the spring breakup of the ice had begun in earnest. There were continual rumblings and rending noises and, every now and then, a crack like a pistol shot as the ice, stressed beyond endurance, fissured and split apart. There was such a big jolt as the ice moved during one tea break that I slopped some precious tea over the side of my mug.

Towards evening, I entered a zone of very active ice movements. After ten hours' hard walking and with no sign of any imminent change in the ice surface, I decided that the risks of continuing were greater than those of staying put. I picked the best area I could find: a flattish slab with a number of straight-line cracks running across it. One or two might have been a metre or more in width, most were no more than a few centimetres, but all were moving and 'breathing'—pulling apart and coming together again with an impact that sent ice fragments tumbling into the cracks. I had the strong sense that I was not in a good place to camp, and as a result I packed everything away after supper so that I was ready for a quick smash and grab to get everything into the sledge and pull away fast if things turned ugly during the night. I slept fully clothed, with my boots at the ready, not wrapped up in a plastic bag as I would normally do to keep them dry.

The night brought very little sleep because I was kept awake by the deafening noise of the pressure ridges erupting around me. It was like trying to sleep near a forge or a metalworks. There were screeching, rending and grinding noises, underpinned by a rhythmic *boom, boom, boom*, as if a giant hammer was pounding some massive lump of iron. When it came to an abrupt stop, the ensuing silence was in some ways even more menacing; then it would begin again in a different, faster tempo. The banshee screams and metallic hammerings and crashings grew so loud and seemed so close that twice during the night I dragged myself out of my sleeping-bag to check that I wasn't about to find myself in an impossibly smashed-up area, unable to retreat or go forwards or sideways to get onto better ice. But, as if the ice had achieved its aim by forcing me out of bed, it began to settle down soon afterwards and all was quiet again by morning. I took the chance to make up for some of the lost sleep and had a lie-in.

Once outside the tent, I could see that the ice pan was now riddled with hairline cracks, extending round and even beneath the tent, and a new pressure ridge had appeared about forty metres away, rising four metres above the surface of the ice pan. It was an unwelcome obstacle to clear at the start of Day 22, but my situation could have been worse. Had the ice been pulling apart rather than grinding together, I could have been plunged into the Arctic Ocean, this time without my immersion suit.

I set off at 2.50 in the afternoon and covered 5.8 nautical miles in eight hours' sledge-hauling. I was pleased to have covered so much ground because there were several other pressure ridges to clear, the worst a huge quadruple ridge. They were no more than a few yards apart and each was composed of large, jumbled blocks that made navigation through them difficult, while the physical effort of dragging the sledge over them left me trembling on the verge of hypoglycaemia. My consolation was that the weight of the sledge was now sufficiently reduced to be manageable in even the most difficult terrain. I could even start to think about transferring the contents of my rucksack to the sledge; unencumbered, I could really start to motor. I was also convinced that carrying the rucksack was damaging my back—I was suffering a lot of pain in the lower back and between the shoulder blades—and I could not afford to let that get any worse.

I enjoyed sledging into the night but it got quite cold after nine o'clock as the sun dipped low towards the horizon, and I stopped at eleven o'clock. Fortunately, there was no repeat of the previous night's scrap-yard symphony and I slept well.

Two days later I met another lead of thin ice and open water. It was progressively thinner towards the middle, following the usual pattern of a lead that had repeatedly frozen, pulled apart and frozen again, and just by looking at the dark colour of the ice I could tell that it was too thin to bear my weight. I'd have to swim, smashing the ice ahead of me as I went.

I put on the immersion suit, lowered myself into the water and set off, pulling the sledge along behind me, but this time the lead was a good seventy-five metres across and I underestimated how long it would take me to break through all that ice. Battering it with my arms was very tiring. I couldn't just go smash, smash, smash, at anything like the speed of normal swimming because the ice wasn't brittle like freshwater ice; it had more of the resilience and plasticity of thick Perspex. Each time I loaded it with my weight, it would bend down and down and down into the water before it finally gave and a plate a foot or more wide broke off.

I also struggled with the sledge. Even kicking my legs and thrashing with my arms, I couldn't generate enough forward momentum to pull the sledge along at the same time as I was breaking through the ice. Instead I had to move forward a few feet through the ice and then pause, get my breath and strength back, and then drag the sledge after me. In theory it should have pulled along the narrow channel I was making easily enough, but all the plates of loose ice that I'd broken were floating to the surface and piling up in front of it, blocking the channel. So every few feet I had to turn on my back, brace my feet against the underside of the unbroken ice on either side of the narrow channel, and then heave at the sledge to pull it through or over the floating ice plates.

It took me about an hour just to get through those seventy-five metres of ice. I was so exhausted at the end of it that I barely had enough strength to haul myself out of the water. I made myself strip off the immersion suit at once and repack the sledge ready to move on, but I then gave myself a double break to allow a bit more recovery time, and an extra portion of sledging rations to rebuild my strength.

Although the muscles under my arms, never normally used, were aching, I was pleased to find that I was soon feeling strong and eager for more work. But at the end of the day I encountered another lead. This one was enormous, between 800 and 1,000 metres from bank to bank. Wraiths of gunmetal-blue frost-smoke were hanging in the air above the surface, as molecules of relatively warm water vapour fogged as they rose from the lead and met the supercooled air at $-30°C$. I climbed up onto a block of ice and looked east and west, searching for a way round or a point where the lead narrowed, but it was like a giant motorway running across the ice. The trail of frost-smoke stretched away to the horizon.

Open water was not such an issue; it would have been hard work but I could have paddled across it on my sledge, but the ice covering the lead was a real killer: too thin to cross on skis but too thick for me to break with my arms. I had struggled to swim seventy-five metres through similar ice that morning; I certainly wasn't going to be able to get through 800 metres. I couldn't put the sledge on its 'lilo' and then paddle across on it like a raft, because once I was up on the sledge I couldn't get enough purchase to smash the ice. It had to be done with my body weight. Hammering at it with a ski pole or even a shovel simply wouldn't break through; it was just too strong.

I could have spent hours tracking left or right and still had no guarantee of getting round the lead. It was better to stop for the night and see how things looked in the light of a new day. I was very frustrated though, because I had thought that with the equipment I'd brought there would be no obstacle I couldn't cross. I now knew that I was wrong.

7

I broke camp on Day 25, April 10, pulled the sledge east for about two hours along the edge of the lead, and achieved nothing beyond sighting a seal that popped its head out of the water just by me. It was the first living creature I had seen since the Arctic hares at Ward Hunt Island, but it wasn't a particularly welcome sight. Seals meant more water about, and polar bears. The lead was even wider than the day before because the ice had pulled apart in the middle, leaving a stretch of black, open water, and the ice flanking it was still not strong enough to support my weight. The sensible course of action was to take the day as a rest day.

Even though I felt I'd made the logical and correct decision, I could not stem the frustration inside me. This was my third rest day in twenty-five days; I could not afford many more unscheduled holdups.

Before I went to sleep that night, I did a thorough 'inventory' of my physical state, and it was obvious that the expedition was already taking its toll. When I tested my resting heart rate I found that it had dropped from its normal rate of about forty-five to thirty-five, and I suspected that it would fall even lower by the end. I was getting a bit bony on the hips—I'd lost a lot of weight, perhaps a stone and a half so far—and I'd also lost the sensation in my fingertips and toes. It wasn't frostbite but nerve tissue damage, and I knew from previous experience that I would not recover from it until about six months after my return to warmer climes.

I was woken by the rumbles, screeches and groans of ice movement during the night and I felt great trepidation the next morning, afraid that I would see a fresh cloud of frost-smoke hanging over an even wider expanse of open water. But far from opening further, one side of the thin new ice covering the lead had simply slid straight under the other during the night. It was a well-known process called 'rafting', but I had never seen such an epic example of it—800 metres of open water and thin ice had now been converted into 400 metres of ice, ten centimetres thick. I was able to walk straight across it. The worst-case scenario had been converted into the best.

Day 26 was the eve of my daughter Freya's first birthday, and I set out determined to give her a personal best that day, so that when she woke up the following morning back at Wydemeet, Mary could show her the mileage achieved, my birthday present to her. I pushed myself so hard that I found myself dropping off to sleep while leaning into my ski poles towards the end of the day, but I just couldn't achieve that personal best.

Once in the tent, I found I had done 7.5 nautical miles, within 325 metres of my previous best daily distance, and the reason I wasn't able to do better was probably because I'd encountered my first negative ice drift—the ice was now moving southwards as I tried to go north. I was walking up the down escalator and in reality had probably travelled around nine miles in the course of the day. I also had reason to be very pleased because during the later stages of the day I encountered my first 'first-year ice'. It would have been open water the previous summer, freezing during the autumn and then being driven by the prevailing winds and currents over the ocean to its position here. Such new ice was invariably pretty flat, and it was encouraging that I was now leaving the pressure ridges and rubble-fields behind and moving into an area of flatter, smoother ice. When I checked my log that night I also discovered that I had now covered 100 nautical miles—100 down, 'only' 316 to go . . .

On Day 27, April 12, Freya's birthday, I faced southwest to Britain and shouted 'Happy birthday, Freya!' before setting out. I imagined her with her friends at her birthday tea party, all sitting round the table near the chart on the wall where Wilf was marking my progress every day. Often, as I plodded northwards, I wandered round the house and the garden in my imagination, picking daffodils with Wilf or watching Mary groom her horse, Philbo, or Freya smilingly smearing jam into her white-blonde tresses.

I covered another seven nautical miles in nine hours, but once more I was feeling pretty wobbly and faint by the end of the day. I camped on a small islet of thicker ice on a huge refrozen lead—a giant ice lake four miles across. The islet was not much bigger than the tent's footprint, but it was the only place within a mile that I could have pitched the tent and there was just enough snow there for me to fill my sack with it for drinking water.

I hadn't eaten my chocolate drops and the shortbread finger that usually went in my nosebag for the day. Instead I'd saved them for a special dessert. When I'd put up the tent and fired up the stove, I brought some water to the boil, and then put my insulated mug in the saucepan as a *bain marie* to melt the chocolate drops. While it was heating, I fashioned a little dish from a piece of aluminium foil, put my shortbread finger inside it and poured the melted chocolate over the top. I put it on the floor of the tent to let it set—at –30ºC, it only took two or three minutes—and, just as it was firming up, I pushed a wooden match into the middle of it with the pink head uppermost. By now I was salivating and really looking forward to my special cake, but I made myself wait until I'd eaten my supper. Then I struck a match, lit the improvised candle on top of the cake and blew it out again, and, in three of the most delicious mouthfuls I've ever had on the Arctic Ocean, I ate this rich, homemade birthday cake. As I did so, I thought fondly of little Freya.

After the celebration I had to carry out some repairs on my mitts. The constant friction from the handles of the ski poles had worn out the palms of both mitts, but they had been designed to be reversible, so I merely had to sew up the holes and then switch the mitts over so that the back of the left mitt was now the palm of the right one and vice versa. Of course, if they wore out again, repairs would be trickier, but by then the temperature should have risen enough to allow me to wear my thinner spare pair.

The next day I crossed the eighty-fifth parallel and travelled 9.2 nautical miles in ten hours—over two nautical miles further than I'd managed on any previous day. To celebrate reaching 85ºN, I opened another of my treasured cards from Mary, exhorting her husband to 'keep at it' and not worry about her and the children.

On Day 32 there was a constant backdrop of crashing, splashing, groaning and grinding from the ice, punctuated by booms like distant cannon fire as the tortured ice tore apart. The wind was usually the big mover of ice, but there hadn't been any wind to speak of for the last few days. I had to assume that the tides were driving the ice movement, or gales occurring far away on the ocean. Whatever the cause, the effect was massive.

· As I skied along, I heard a huge disturbance somewhere ahead of me, a rumbling and crashing, like great ice blocks rolling downhill or smashing into the water. I paused at once, and another crash as I looked towards the northwest gave me a fix on it. I spotted a pressure ridge in that direction. One of the tricks in this situation was to aim for the point where the ridges petered out downwards into the horizon, because when two plates were moving in relation to each other there was often a metre or two of ice at the axis of the movement that was neither being thrown up into a ridge nor pushed apart to reveal water, and thus simple to walk across. The snow was about fifteen centimetres deep and as viscous as treacle, and dragging my sledge through it was a strength-sapping burden. I managed to cover just six nautical miles in the course of the day and the effort exhausted me. Maybe tomorrow would be better.

In fact, it was worse. It was a special day for me, Good Friday, the anniversary of my father's death, and I wanted to put in a big effort for him, but once more the ice conditions were terrible and it was a struggle even to achieve the modest total of five nautical miles. I was now privately conceding to myself that sixty-five days might be a more realistic target than the sixty I had been hoping for, but even on that revised schedule, Day 33 saw me beyond the halfway mark, in time, if not in mileage. I made a concerted effort to regroup and refocus.

Day 34 was Easter Saturday, when my whole family was due to gather at the house of my ever supportive mother-in-law, Esther Nicholson. Knowing that my family and all my in-laws, nephews and nieces were monitoring my progress every day, I wanted to give them an Easter present of a really big mileage. Breaking my normal habit, I kept the GPS in my pocket and checked my mileage at the end of my normal six sledge-hauling sessions. I then discovered that I had covered only 5.6 miles, which was absolutely unacceptable—what kind of a present was that? So I made myself carry on and, helped by some better ice and my decision to start dipping into my extra sledging rations (originally planned for Days 66 to 69), to maintain my blood-sugar levels, I did a further three miles in just two hours.

I felt much happier as I made camp that night. The conditions had been horrendous again, but I felt I'd got the measure of it. It had been another hard day, but those last three miles were a boost, a signal that when conditions improved—as they were bound to—I would really fly over the ice.

The next day, Easter Sunday, I thought of my family and remembered the previous Easter morning when we'd all been together, going to church at

St Raphael's in Huccaby on Dartmoor and having an Easter egg hunt in the garden. I pledged to myself that I'd put in another big day today, both for Mary, Wilf and Freya, and for all the rest of my supporters—my back-up team, family, friends and all those who were tracking the expedition on the website and leaving messages of support.

In lieu of an Easter egg, I gave myself an extra portion of porridge as a treat and some extra nosebag rations for the long day ahead, and then set off. I had done 7.4 nautical miles by the end of the normal sledging day but then put in another four hours, completing a twelve-hour day and adding another 2.6 miles, taking me to 10 for the day—a new personal best.

I rewarded myself with a superb Easter supper. I gave myself an extra serving of cod and potato with my main meal and put some of the milk powder I'd saved from the early days of the expedition into my hot chocolate, along with an effervescent vitamin C pill. It sounds disgusting, but tasted delicious—a rich, creamy, orangey chocolate drink. I put off opening my Easter presents until after supper. Knowing my addiction to chocolate, Mary had put in a Cadbury's creme Egg (frozen solid but soon warmed through enough to eat). Wilf had given me an iridescent green clothes peg from which to suspend my drying socks in the tent, and Freya's present was a 'must-have' micro four-wheel buggy, measuring all of an inch by an inch and a half square, with two moving mechanical brushes to sweep up any crumbs from the floor.

Even though I knew that anything could happen to throw my calculations off track, I was confident that sixty-five days to the Pole would be a worst-case scenario. So I told myself it would be OK to eat the rations for Days 66 to 69 that I'd begun yesterday. It would allow me to give myself 30 per cent extra porridge in the morning, 30 per cent extra nosebag snacks during the day and 30 per cent extra supper at night. That would not only do wonders for my morale, it would also propel me faster and further over the ice.

When I checked my GPS on the evening of Day 36, I discovered that I had crossed the eighty-sixth parallel during the day. Another treasured card from the family marked the latitude and served to remind me how much Mary continued to support my endeavour.

I spoke later to my UK base manager, Ian. He was in the garden of his home on Dartmoor, bathed in spring sunshine. Ian informed me that, by his calculations, the weight of the sledge was now around 220 pounds. Even though he was thousands of miles away and hadn't laid eyes on the sledge since my departure, I had no reason to doubt his maths. Everything I had with me had been weighed and logged before I set off, and every time I emptied a fuel bottle or discarded something, I told Ian and he deducted its weight from the total. However, one part of that weight loss was giving me increasing concern. With about thirty days to go, I had only 7.5 litres of fuel left. I kept my fingers crossed that rising temperatures would reduce my fuel consumption, but, just in case, I began fuel rationing.

The following day, Day 37, I decided to take as a rest day. In one way it was a quixotic decision, to rest so soon after chafing at the delays in my progress and with shortage of fuel a growing concern, but my exertions over the previous few days had left me very tired, I had a backlog of repairs and maintenance and I had grown out of synch with the calendar day. I was going to bed and getting up later and later every day, partly because of the extra sessions I was doing but partly because of the time I was having to spend talking to Ian and Ginny on the satellite phone each night. I had set off at 3.50 on the afternoon of Day 36, and ten hours' sledge-hauling had taken me to 1.50 in the morning of Day 37 before I even began my evening work and satphone calls. It was four in the morning before I finally got to sleep. The only thing to do was to take a day off.

The sun was shining when I woke, so I had thrown away a good weather day, but if I put the day to good use and got up early and well rested on the morning of Day 38, I'd make up the lost time in short order. Meanwhile, I hung out a lot of my gear to dry, spreading my sleeping-bag and my mammoth smock over the sledge to let the sun burn off more ice, and draping my gloves and socks over the skis anchoring each end of the tent. Everything I had was black or very dark blue so that it absorbed the maximum amount of energy from the sun, and things dried or de-iced surprisingly quickly.

I next had the tricky task of changing my contact lenses. I was wearing lenses that could be left in for a month, but these had now been in for about forty days and were getting a bit dirty and smudgy, so it was time to change them. After over five weeks without a proper wash, I was filthy, and my tent was not the most sterile of environments. I was paranoid about getting conjunctivitis, so I cleaned my hands thoroughly with some sterilising wipes before I even touched the packets, let alone the lenses. The saline solution in which the lenses were stored was of course frozen solid, so before I could insert the lenses I had to slide the packets inside my thermal sleeves and let them thaw with my body heat. Meanwhile I faced a protracted struggle to extract the old lenses, which seemed to have become part of the eyeball. In comparison to that, slipping the new lenses in was child's play.

I'd taken a leaf out of the book of the women I had worked with on polar expeditions and begun applying antiseptic cream to my face to start the repair process for the windburn and frostnip on my cheeks and the sides of my nose. It was impossible to avoid minor tissue damage of this kind in temperatures as low as –45°C, but that was no reason not to minimise it and reduce the risk of infection using the limited amount of cream I carried— like my toothpaste—defrosted, up my sleeves morning and night.

I next set to work repairing one of the lilo straps. It had ripped off during the crossing, so I sewed it back on with a huge needle and some thick thread. The watertight seal round the support bar at the front of the sledge had pulled apart under the stresses and strains of crossing the ice, and I had to fix it with Jubilee clips so that I would have a dry sledge even if it nose-dived into the water. Lastly, I glued back the base of my vacuum flask, which had come off, and mended the torn covers of my diary and my data log.

Having completed all my running repairs, I went through my equipment and had a ruthless sort-out. I bagged up four useless fuel pumps, a spare wire stand for the stove, some spare black rubber hosing and the tent bag. My duct tape and spinnaker tape were both on circular card stands which seemed to be unnecessarily weighty, so I threw those out, together with two spare toe-strap leathers and two extra cables for my ski bindings. That left me with no spares but, having assessed the damage to the existing cables, I felt that as they were under much less strain from the lighter sledge they would last the remainder of the expedition. Some of my clothing was also surplus to requirements now that the temperatures were rising. I didn't need a spare hood or a second hat any more, and I also threw out two spare pairs of gloves. These items didn't make a vast difference to the weight of the sledge, but it was a psychological benefit to know that I was only carrying stuff that was actually going to help me get to the Pole.

I was up early as planned the next morning, Day 38, and, within half an hour of setting off, entered a region that had seen considerable ice activity. The ice was making all sorts of noises—groaning, grinding, juddering, squeaking—and it sounded to me as if my sledge had taken to copying the noises. I got so irritated by this that I turned round and snapped, 'For God's sake, Baskers, stop making those noises,' when I suddenly realised that a pressure ridge was forming and the ice was splitting under my feet.

I crossed that one without trouble, but I was soon hauling and manhandling the sledge up the first of a succession of pressure ridges that were steeper and larger than any I had seen since the early days of the expedition.

Around noon I witnessed an extraordinary sight. In front of me, running in from the west and tapering out ahead, was a vast ridge of huge blocks of sea ice. The largest block was almost twice the size of a London double-decker bus, its facing side a vivid blue and showing its layered growth over the years. Despite its prodigious weight—hundreds of tons—it had been jacked up high above the water line by the pressures in the ice cap. There was a steep-sided, canal-sized lead in front of the ridge, but it appeared to come to an abrupt end a little to the east, and I was hoping to walk round it, crossing along the axis of the relative movements of the two ice floes. I was about thirty metres from the crossing point when I heard, fractionally before I saw, this gigantic block of ice begin to move. Gathering speed at a frightening rate, it hurtled down into the water. The next moment I saw a huge wave rearing up. Accelerating and growing as it surged between the narrowing walls of the canal, it blasted into the air like a breaking storm wave smashing against a harbour wall. It had exploded across my path and the wash reached to within a metre of my skis before it subsided, gurgling back into the canal and soaking into the snow around it like a spent wave sinking into a sandy beach. For over a minute, the air was full of spray that turned instantly into ice crystals, creating a miniature frozen rainbow, but I had little appetite for the beauty of the scene. If I had been thirty seconds earlier I might have been swept to my death.

My one consolation for the horrendous ridging I had encountered was that this was also the warmest day I had yet seen—a positively balmy −26°C. I was so warm that, for the first time, I wasn't wearing a hat of any sort and I was only wearing gloves, not mitts. That was not to last, however. I sensed a change was coming before any visible sign of it. The sun was still shining brightly but the air began to feel damper and the temperature started to drop. A few minutes later I saw that a low fog bank was building up across part of the horizon. Within fifteen minutes I was enveloped in thick fog. The temperature had gone down five or ten degrees as the damp air rolled in. The hat and mitts went back on and I began to plod through a grey, formless and silent world. The terrain had also changed again to an eerie ice-scape, a flat plain broken by small plates of ice, perhaps a metre high, rising at all angles from the surface. They looked like tombstones in some lost and long-forgotten graveyard. The fog bank took around ninety minutes to pass and, after a brief interlude of sunshine, there was another and then another.

It wasn't just the cold, the damp and the poor visibility; the fog was also a warning of dangerous conditions ahead. Fog tells you that there are large areas of open water around. That open water generates its own weather; frost-smoke and fog come off the relatively warm water as it meets the frigid air, and are then driven along on the breeze. The fog banks were moving in from the northeast, so I had to assume there were large areas of open water in that direction. They might be tens of miles away—several days' travel—and they might pinch out to the east of my track north, but it was another sign of the times: the spring thaw was accelerating.

To my great relief, when I woke the next morning, Day 39, the sun was once again shining through the tent wall and I was really grateful for it. There had been twenty-four-hour continuous daylight for a few days now, and after eight in the evening the angle of the sunlight was directly in my face, making route selection more challenging. But the sun made such a difference to my mood that I even found myself talking to it every now and again, exhorting it to burn its way through any obscuring clouds and thanking it when it finally won through.

I spoke by satphone to my Canadian base team, Gary and Diane Guy, that night. Gary is a great character with a terrific sense of humour, but some of his advice and anecdotes, delivered absolutely deadpan, had a habit of unsettling me. I don't think he realised how fragile my mental state could be when I was out on the ice. I was telling him about using the immersion suit when he suddenly said, 'You've got to watch out for those Greenland sharks, you know. Once they see you, they just go for you. You don't get any warning, you don't even see the fins above the water.'

I said, 'I don't want to hear this.'

'Oh yes you do. It's all for your own good. Forewarned is forearmed!'

He was roaring with laughter as he told me this, and I was laughing too . . . in a rather nervous way. Of course it was rot, but like all good scare stories it contained enough elements of truth to make it both memorable and believable. The Greenland shark, *Somniosus microcephalus*, also known as the sleeper shark, does live in polar waters. One of the largest of all sharks, it can be as much as seven metres long, and though it does have a dorsal fin, it is small. It is omnivorous, and its reputation for sluggishness is belied by the salmon and other fast-swimming fish that it catches. It also eats seals and carrion, including whale flesh. It suffers from a parasite called a copepod, which infests its eyes and makes them glow an eerie whitish-yellow in the dark Arctic waters. With the seed planted in my mind, courtesy of Gary's little joke, every time I went in the water from now on, I was imagining those sharks in the depths below me.

I slept relatively well that night, without too many dreams of sharks severing my body parts, and woke to another fine morning. It was April 25, Day 40 of the expedition, two-thirds of the way in time, though less than half that in mileage. Even so I'd passed another milestone during the day—the 200-mile mark. I had now covered 203 miles.

Almost every day there was a reason for having another milestone, if not in days or weeks, then in miles or degrees of latitude or even days of the month. And if those failed, there were always special occasions of family and friends, national holidays or anniversaries of expeditions on the Arctic Ocean that I'd noted in advance in my diary. That way, I always had a reason to be positive and to look forward to the day ahead. I also found that it helped to discuss things with my anthropomorphic 'team'—Mavis, Swerves, Curves and Baskers. I'd been doing so for a couple of weeks by this stage, and at every break I'd have a chat with them. During the first day or two I'd felt a bit self-conscious about holding a conversation with a couple of ski poles, a sledge and a de-icing brush, but since there was no one to overhear me it quickly became a non-issue. My daily briefings to the team covered everything from route plans, warnings about potential problems or hazards and appeals not to lose vital bits of kit through carelessness and inattention, to generalised appeals for ever greater efforts—'We're just going to have to take it up a gear today, everyone. Come on, we've got to raise our game'—that sort of thing. I found that verbalising things made an enormous difference to my mood. If I needed to be more positive, just saying it out loud seemed to do the trick, whereas trying to change my mood by the power of thought was markedly less effective.

It wasn't hard to find positives at the end of this particular day. I'd travelled eleven miles in ten hours—my best day so far. Today the surface conditions were very good and the weather near-perfect. The Big Four—ice, weather, health, kit—were all good now, and it was all systems go as everything came together: the sledge was lighter, I was getting more of the newer, flatter Siberian ice; temperatures were now in the low minus twenties.

This otherwise perfect day was marred by a bitter personal tragedy in the shape of the sad demise of the lovely Mavis, the de-icing brush who had been through so much with me. While cleaning ice and snow out of my sleeping-bag that morning, she had suffered a terrible spinal injury—her metal body broke. She had been looking very tired and dishevelled for several days—her hair was falling out in clumps and that once proud, bottle-blonde Afro was a threadbare shadow of her former glorious self, but she was a special bit of kit to me. She had worn herself to a frazzle and beyond, and was still making herself available for duty, broken in body but not in spirit. I continued to use her, holding her torso, and I kept all her body parts so that, in a sense, she would still be seeing it through to the end with me.

A good night's sleep helped me overcome my grief, and Day 41 was another storming day with exceptionally good ice and weather, and another personal best of 11.2 nautical miles. I now realised that, after fifteen years, it really was going to happen—I was going to reach the Pole solo and without resupply . . . providing I could keep it together for another twenty days or so. I'd seen off the worst of the weather and the worst of the ice conditions. I had plenty of food and, with the timely warmer temperatures, it looked as if the fuel was going to be enough after all. Although I was mentally weary, I had no injuries and felt as physically fit as when I'd set out.

There was one cautionary sign: I'd seen fox tracks for the first time. It was another indicator of the changing season and another reason to maintain vigilance at all times. I had already seen a seal in the huge lead that had held me up. Now I'd seen the tracks of the second member of the polar trinity: the arctic fox. All that was now missing was the third.

The next day, Day 42, saw yet another personal best: 12.5 miles. The day's mileage would have been even more impressive but for the loss of forty-five minutes when I had to retrace my steps to retrieve the basket that had become detached from one of my ski poles—Swerves. I had been going for almost an hour when I realised the basket was missing. I couldn't believe that I hadn't noticed it straight away because, as a rule, I was instantly aware of anything even the least bit unusual or awry. I can only think that tiredness had dulled my senses. It wasn't a disaster but it did mean that every now and again the ski pole could just plunge straight through the snow, throwing me off-balance and risking a fall that could be critical on bad ice. So I unhitched the sledge, slung the rifle on my back and skied back the way I had come. It was easy enough to follow the tracks I had made but, inevitably, I had to ski virtually the whole way back before discovering the basket within ten yards of where I had set off from that morning. I fixed it back on to Swerves with some spare wire and hurried back to my sledge to resume the northward journey.

As if to compensate, I had a magic moment as I took my regular break at the end of that sledge-hauling session. I was sitting on the back of my sledge, keeping my back to the breeze as I warmed my face in the sun, when I sensed as much as saw the faintest disturbance, a fluttering in the air. I looked round and could not believe my eyes. A snow bunting, a bird no bigger than a sparrow but with more white plumage, had landed on top of the sledge. It must have got lost on migration and strayed hundreds of miles off course before spotting this unusual surface feature. Now it was taking in the scene, showing no fear whatsoever, its bright eyes fixed on me. It was a beautiful, almost spiritual moment: a brief encounter between two lonely, stressed-out travellers in the middle of this vast empty ocean of ice. It stayed there for only a minute or so, and then took off. It circled overhead as if getting its bearings and then flew southwards, disappearing almost at once into the glare of the sun. I wished it well on its own long journey, as I stood up and prepared to resume mine.

The sun was now relatively high in the sky both by day and by night, giving a stark light that wiped out the pastel tones of the ice-scape, replacing them with a harsh, unyielding white glare. If I took off my sunglasses I simply couldn't look at the snow—its brilliance was too dazzling.

On Day 43 I encountered some of the worst pressure ridging of the whole journey, but I still covered ten miles in ten hours, and I crossed the eighty-seventh parallel just before I stopped for the night. There were now only 180 miles to go. I checked my main meal stocks that evening, and discovered that, at current rates of consumption, I still had twenty-three days supply of food—2.5 servings of cod in sour cream and potato, 6.5 of beef stew and potato and 14 of chicken curry and rice (my favourite, which I tended to save till last).

I had recently been planning for a worst-case scenario of reaching the Pole on Day 65, but aiming for Day 57, and so had just the right amount for that, but there was the possibility of increasing my food intake, extending the duration of the sledging day and getting there faster. I now estimated my fastest time to the Pole as fourteen days. Part of me wanted to go for broke, capitalising on the good ice and good weather, but I'd spent enough time in the Arctic to know that ice and weather could change with bewildering rapidity and that a conservative strategy was always the safest if not the quickest way to achieve my goals. In the end I arrived at a typically British compromise, 'borrowing' a proportion of the potentially spare rations to fuel a charge to the Pole while the weather and ice remained in my favour.

During a call to Ian back at base that morning, he had told me that Wilf wanted a word with me. It would have been a lot better to have waited a few minutes and thought about all the things that I wanted to say, but I didn't and the conversation did not go very well.

Finally, I told him, 'I'm missing you so much, Wilf, but I'm trying not to be too sad, because I know that there's only another three or four weeks, then I'll be coming home to give you the biggest hug in the world. That isn't too long to wait, is it?'

I heard his brave little voice saying, 'No, Daddy,' but I knew that he was thinking it was an eternity. He had tried to be so self-controlled, sensible and mature about everything, but he was only a little boy. The call ended with both of us sad and upset.

8

When I came out of my tent in the morning, I saw that the tides had torn the ice sheet behind me apart, leaving a broad lead, with steep, sheer banks of ice on either side. On almost every previous day the sun had been visible. Day 45 was the first completely cloudy day since I'd left Ward Hunt Island, and the dense overcast made it quite dark. Perhaps that affected my mood; I quickened my pace, as if fearing that some dark force might be overhauling me.

I was also becoming increasingly concerned about the nature of the media coverage that the expedition was being given. It was absurd; I obviously wasn't getting the papers delivered to my tent every morning, so I had no real idea of what was being written. But I'd got it into my head that no one was really able to understand what I was thinking, feeling or doing, and that through my own tiredness and inattention I was making the situation worse rather than better. Was I, through my ill-chosen words, bringing down the monument I was trying so hard to erect in my father's memory? I felt like a ladybird scuttling across a huge white tablecloth, being peered at through a magnifying glass by someone who was trying to count the spots on my back, while all I was concerned about was if I could make it to the other side of the table before events overtook me.

Late that afternoon I came across a series of refrozen leads, each about 100 metres across and stretching out of sight to the east and the west. All had probably opened on the same day, and refrozen to the same degree in the relatively warm temperature of about –15°C to –20°C. The overcast skies meant that the coloration of the ice was different from previous days, conveying a meaning that I had to be careful to interpret correctly. On a bright day, an expanse of freshly set ice might look pale brown, suggesting it could be crossed in safety. In lower light levels, the same ice might look dark brown, suggesting danger. I had to readjust my senses to accommodate the changed situation but, tired and preoccupied by my obsession with the way the expedition was being reported, I was heading for a fall.

I always divided thin ice into three categories: marginal-good, marginal and marginal-bad, and I had decided at the start of the expedition that, for safety reasons, I wasn't going to be crossing any marginal or marginal-bad ice. On previous expeditions, I'd undo the leather toe straps on my skis before crossing marginal ice, so that if I fell through the ice I could kick off my skis and swim to safety. To start undoing my toe straps on this expedition would therefore be a clear indication that I was ignoring my previous resolution.

Up to now, every single time I had been about to cross thin ice, I had only to think of a three-second mental video clip of Wilf in his shorts on a sunny spring evening, picking wild daffodils from the garden to give to his mother, and I would instantly stop, shocked by the awfulness of never reliving that scene. That technique had prompted me to reroute scores of times when otherwise I might have taken an unnecessary and potentially fatal risk.

I crossed a succession of four leads in the space of a few hours, without having to undo my toe straps, and I was into my sixth seventy-five-minute session of sledge-hauling of the day when I came across yet another lead. This lead was wider—about 125 metres—but otherwise it looked no different from the previous four. Before I even set foot on it, I studied it carefully, assessing the general surface texture and colour. The obvious questions were: Is this identical to the leads earlier today? If it's fractionally more marginal, is is still crossable?

These leads were giant slashes across the Arctic Ocean, like fault lines in a rock formation. They sometimes run for fifty to a hundred miles, but I suspect I could have walked round this particular one in no more than three to four hours. As I moved out onto the refrozen ice, I studied the area directly in front of my skis with great care, scanning the 'ice flowers'—salt crystals—and the other minute surface features that offer a big clue to the age of the ice, and therefore its thickness and strength. This lead still looked exactly the same as the previous four I'd crossed, but as I approached the middle I could see there had been some sort of disturbance there.

Judging by its increased opacity and the density of ice flowers on the surface, the ice on the far side actually looked to be fractionally stronger, but the few metres around the fault line seemed to be thinner. There were noticeably fewer ice flowers there and it was darker in colour, always a major clue. Even wearing skis, which spread the load of your body weight, young dark *nilas* isn't safe to cross, but medium to thick light *nilas* is usually passable. I gave it the classic ski-pole test: three hard, well-aimed blows into exactly the same spot. If I could puncture the ice through to the water below on blows one or two, it was too young to bear my weight. If it went through on the third, it was my call, but by any count it was marginal ice. I judged there were perhaps two metres of dodgy, marginal and marginal-bad ice, but it then seemed to be stronger on the other side.

The problem was the fault line that ran through the middle of this weaker area. It had a slightly crinkled edge, three or four centimetres proud of the ice surface, suggesting that there had been a little bit of movement and friction between the two sides of the lead as the surrounding ice pans rocked to and fro. If you have a continuous surface of marginal ice, you can usually get across it, but if there is a crack down the middle of it—even if it's only a few centimetres of water or very thin ice separating the two ice pans—the surface tension is broken. If you then stand near the edge, it can just cave in, dropping you into the water.

Whether through tiredness, inattention or impatience, on this one occasion, for the first time in the whole expedition, the little clip of Wilf picking daffodils didn't pop into my mind. I should have just walked away, saying 'Well, I'm not doing that, I'm off to find a better route. There's always a better way, so stop being idle and keep concentrating.' But I didn't do it and I still can't explain why. Even worse, I actually undid my toe straps.

As I prepared to cross the danger area, I noticed that there was a little platform of thicker ice less than a metre from the edge of the crack. It was about a metre by two metres across, and had obviously been floating around in the open water and then got locked in to the ice when it refroze. I wanted to be unencumbered and not worried about the sledge snagging behind me at a critical moment, so I parked it on the ice platform and put my traces on the maximum extension so I could cross the marginal ice without having to pull the sledge at all. I had to be clear of the bad ice before I hauled the sledge after me.

I tested the ice by putting a bit of my weight on it, releasing it and applying it again, then, completely absorbed in the fine detail of this crossing, I moved my right ski tip up and over the crack, keeping my left one back so that most of my weight was on it. So far so good. I pushed my right ski a little further forward, until it was straddling the crack and moving onto the better ice beyond it. I could feel the ice going downwards, bending slightly, flexing where the surface tension was broken at the two edges.

My right ski was fully on the marginal ice, and I now slid my left ski forward. I was committed, but I knew at once that I'd made a big mistake. My first instinct was: 'Right, ski on. Don't wait around. Go, go, go!' If I could keep moving, continually shifting the load onto new ice, I might be all right, but within a split second of having crossed onto the marginal ice I could feel my rear ski sinking inexorably downwards. I veered hard left, trying to get the ski back onto the more solid ice, but I was sinking further. The ice just bent down, down and down; then finally it broke. I sank up to my knees, up to my waist, and then the ice gave way underneath me completely and I was plunged up to my neck in the icy water.

The first thing I felt was shock, not at the cold—my multiple layers of clothing gave me enough temporary insulation to prevent that—but that I could have let myself get into this situation. The next thought, following hard on its heels, was to leave the inquests for later and channel everything into getting back onto firm ice. Over the next ten or fifteen seconds, the water seeped through my clothing to my skin, but even then it didn't feel heart-stoppingly cold, partly perhaps because I was so focused on saving my life that the sensation of cold didn't register as a priority. Submerged to my armpits, I went into front crawl motion, thrashing my arms down ahead of me to break through the thinner ice, while I kicked with my legs as hard as I could—no easy feat wearing skis—trying to create some propulsion. It's almost impossible to find enough purchase on the ice to haul yourself out when you're hanging vertically in the water, so you've got to get your body horizontal, then generate some forward momentum to help reduce the load on the surface of the ice as you drag yourself out.

I made a few attempts to haul myself up onto the ice, but each time it crumbled beneath me. Then a curiously detached but helpful thought burst into my head, a lesson I'd drawn from previous near-drownings: keep aware of your surroundings, look for options, don't focus on just one route, it may not be the one that can get you out. Slowing down and taking stock was the last thing I felt like doing, but I managed to whip my head round each way to see if I could take in any useful information. And for the first time I saw my sledge where I had positioned it on that little platform of thicker ice.

I changed direction, swimming towards the platform, smashing the thinner ice before me like an icebreaker. But my waterlogged boots and salopettes, and the layers of saturated clothing, made the effort of kicking my legs so draining that I was forced to slow down. My muscles just could not continue at that pace.

It was a frightening feeling, but I took a breather, a little rest just hanging off the edge of the ice for a few seconds, and then had another go. I didn't allow myself to accept even as a possibility that I wouldn't be able to get onto the ice, that what I was doing wasn't going to work. As I drove myself forward again, everything seemed to go into slow motion. I was hyper-aware of every tiny detail and sensation, scanning the ice in front of me for crenellations, lumps or bumps on the ice that might give my clumsy, frozen hands enough purchase to haul myself out. I worked my way left, towards the platform, its upper surface pocked with lumps and small hollows in the ice, and powered myself up onto it, kicking with all the remaining strength in my legs while my hands groped at the ice, searching for grip. One hand caught at a projection, then the other, and the next moment I was inching my way up onto the ice next to my sledge.

For a moment I lay prone across the ice with my feet still dangling in the water. I felt a huge wave of relief, tinged with the continued shock that I'd got myself into this dire situation. Then I noticed that I was only wearing one ski. The left one had fallen off as I struggled in the water. If I couldn't find it, I had a major problem on my hands.

I knelt on the ice and scanned the jumble of broken ice and mushy, part-frozen sea water around me. The ski was nowhere to be seen but I assumed that it would be floating just under the surface somewhere. I knew I was going to have to go back into the water to search for it. So within a minute of getting myself out of the water, I was rummaging around in the sledge for my immersion suit. I got straight into it, still wearing my saturated clothes, because I knew that it was vital to begin the search at once. I lowered myself back into the water and began a search.

It was no easy task. I was searching as much by touch as by sight among pieces of broken ice suspended in a morass of semifrozen mush the colour and opacity of wallpaper paste. I tried to work in a systematic way, moving backwards and forwards in the area of broken ice, a few metres square, but I could find no trace of the ski and, after twenty minutes in the water, my hands and fingers were getting really cold. Despite my exertions, I wasn't generating enough body heat to stave off the risk of frostbite. If I developed frostbite, my worries about the fate of the ski and the expedition would be trivial in comparison. I had to start looking after myself.

I dragged myself out of the water and, still wearing the immersion suit, tied the single rope trace round my waist and hauled the sledge back in the direction I had come from less than an hour before. I moved quickly so that I wasn't standing on the same piece of ice for any length of time, and shuffled rather than walked, like a decrepit old man.

I remembered an area of firm, level snow where I'd come down from the ice pan onto the frozen lead, and as I approached it I rehearsed in my mind the sequence of actions I had to take. I pulled the sledge up over the bank onto the thick ice, then took off the immersion suit because I couldn't work wearing it, and exchanged my wet mitts for dry ones. Then I began erecting the tent as fast as I could, without even bothering to fill the snow valances. I kept focused on the immediate task, deliberately pushing aside worries about my situation and whether my fingers were going to get frostbitten.

As soon as the tent was up, I unrolled my sleeping-bag onto the snow next to the sledge and loaded it with the routine night-time kit—stove, fuel, food—plus the additional things I needed in this situation: dry clothes. I didn't carry many spares but I had some thermal trousers that I'd been using as pyjamas and my much cut-down mammoth smock. I added them to the pile of things on my sleeping-bag, then dragged it into the tent. I folded the sleeping-bag over so that it was sandwiched inside the waterproof sleeping-mat. I could then kneel on that without any moisture seeping into the bag. I sorted out my kit, put snow in the saucepan to melt for drinks and even took my clothes off before lighting the stove. I was fuel-conscious and, though I was cold, I didn't think I was in a critical condition.

I fumbled with my matches, my numbed fingers struggling to hold them firmly enough to strike a light, and eventually managed to light the stove. Then I changed into my dry clothes and got into my sleeping-bag, made myself a cup of tea and some hot food. I had time to gather my thoughts while I was having my brew, and I then called my UK base manager, Ian Wesley, on the satellite phone and gave him the full story.

His first reaction was that it was very important that I made a second search for the ski, if only so that I would know, as I footslogged my way north, that I had done my best to find it. He pointed out how awful it would be to have the nagging thought in my mind that I was having to walk the whole way to the Pole simply because I'd not bothered to make the extra effort to find the ski. I could see at once that he was right.

Before I settled down to sleep, I wrung as much water as I could out of my sodden salopettes, smock, socks and boot-liners, and put them into a spare plastic sack. They would freeze overnight and I wasn't looking forward to getting back into them in the morning, but it would have to be done. I had some spare dry socks and boot-liners. There were giant holes in the heels of the socks, but they'd have to do; I had no others.

As I closed my eyes, I thought through the impact that the loss of the ski might have on my progress, if I couldn't find it. Even without a new snowfall, I was very unlikely to get a firm, hard-packed surface all the way to the Pole. The snow and ice had started to decay as the temperature rose and its structure was weakening. With no skis to spread the load of my weight, I might just break through an inch or I might sink up to my knees at every step, greatly increasing the effort levels and decreasing my speed.

Despite my troubled thoughts, I slept pretty well and woke on Day 46, May 1, full of resolve to get the expedition back on track. I ate breakfast, then gave myself a bit of extra chocolate as I often did before I used the immersion suit, partly to sugar the pill of having to do so, but it also served a practical purpose in putting a bit of sugar into me for all the hard work I'd have to do swimming around in the suit for anything up to an hour. I turned the frozen suit inside-out and hung it up to dry in the sunlight. Even though it was –20°C or so, the thin covering of ice dispersed quite quickly and I was able to brush out the remaining ice.

I climbed into the suit wearing my pyjamas—my thermal trousers and my mammoth smock—my newly darned dry socks, and my dry gloves and mitts. I positioned my sledge at the edge of the lead as a sort of emergency life raft, then lowered myself into the water. I didn't have to break up much ice; it was only semifrozen because the overcast conditions during the night had kept the temperature no lower than –15°C. I completed a search of the open water without finding the ski, then decided to break up the thinner ice on the edge to increase the diameter of the search area. I succeeded in moving the edge back by about four metres in all directions but there was still no sign of the ski. Next I hung from the edge of the ice sheet with my hands and slid most of my body under the ice, until I was right up to my armpits with the water line just below my mouth. I stretched my feet out against the underside of the ice, reaching as far as I could—about a metre and a half from the edge—and raked my feet back towards me, trying to drag out anything lodged under the ice, but though I worked my way right around the edge of the open area, I still didn't find the ski. The writing on the wall could no longer be ignored: I wasn't going to find it.

I decided to keep my other ski, even though it broke the rule I'd set: if something was no longer going to help me get to the Pole, it had to be jetti-soned. I just couldn't bring myself to part with my ski. We'd been through a lot together and I felt it was a memento I'd want to have. It was dead weight—around two kilos—but I did find a use for it as a stake for the upwind guy rope on my tent, maybe the heaviest tent peg in history.

I trudged back to the tent, steeled myself to get into my frozen salopettes and smock, put my dry clothes away and broke camp as fast as possible, keen to get moving north again to generate some heat to dry my clothes. However, first I had to cross that wretched lead. I sledged east for around twenty minutes but there was no evidence of the ice improving, and I decided to cross the lead there and then. I put my immersion suit on again and very cautiously shuffled out across the ice, testing its strength by my weight. Now I wasn't wearing skis, the load I was exerting per square foot had greatly increased. But even at the crack in the middle it didn't give beneath my weight. Either all it had taken was another night's subzero tem-peratures to freeze the ice a little more, or I had picked an area where the ice was already fractionally thicker and more opaque. I hauled the sledge across after me, then took off my immersion suit and headed on north.

I SET OFF at about five o'clock in the afternoon and kept a close watch on my progress, taking a reading from the GPS at each break. I did 1.3 nautical miles in the first session, 1.9 in the second and 1.7 in the third. It was an even better average speed than I had been doing on skis over the previous few days, and it was a great relief. Just as I was starting to relax, I came to a rent in the ice, exposing swirling, dangerous waters below, and instantly I was back on full alert. It looked narrow enough for me to jump over, but the banks of ice on either side were sheer and steep. If I fell in, I wouldn't be able to get out again, because I wouldn't be able to reach up high enough from the water level to pull myself out. It was too wide and deep to use my sledge as a bridge, so the choice was either to jump it or try to find a way round it—and I suspected I'd face a long detour before I found a narrowing or closure. I decided to go for it, but this time I would check every facet before committing myself.

I first measured the gap. It was exactly the length of my ski pole, so I laid that on the ice nearby and did a test jump over it. I cleared it with a good half-metre to spare. I checked that the ice was not going to break as I jumped, and spent some time preparing my takeoff point, packing the snow down with my feet. I also tried to build in some capability for self-rescue. I adjusted my sledge trace to its maximum length and pushed the sledge to the edge of the ice, so that if I fell in I could pull it in after me and clamber onto it. Then I walked back to the end of my run-up, psyched myself up, took a deep breath, sprinted down the runway and took off, clearing it with ease. I hauled the sledge across after me and was on my way north again within five minutes of first sighting the lead.

There were fresh cracks and water all over the place during the course of that day, like crazy paving, but I cleared each one in the same manner and by the end of that first day on foot—a short one because of the late start after the fruitless search for the ski—I had covered 5.4 miles.

The next day, Day 47, was extremely taxing. The ice was rumbling all day—the usual sign of the spring breakup—and, though I set off in sunshine, within an hour or two it clouded over and began to snow. It carried on all day, producing a near-total whiteout and, without my skis, I struggled to make headway. There was much stumbling into snowdrifts and falling into small fissures. Even worse, I was now well into the region of negative drift—the escalator was moving steadily southwards as I attempted to go north.

I slept badly that night and woke feeling weary on Day 48. It was still snowing, and once more it carried on doing so all day. Visibility was barely fifty metres, and forty-eight hours of continuous snowfall, albeit fairly light, had left a mantle of snow averaging about ten centimetres thick but three times that in hollows, holes and fissures. The snow shrouded every surface feature: thin ice, cracks, even sheltered water. It will settle on open water because it's below zero, so you can be walking along thinking you're on snow and find yourself on open water. It made heading north a hesitant process, as I was probing in front of me with a ski pole as I walked. The sledge had to be dragged through snow as cloying and glutinous as my breakfast porridge, and the snow stuck to my boots and then melted, soaking them and adding greatly to their weight. Every footstep I took, I sank into the snow to a different depth, sometimes only an inch or two but sometimes floundering deep in drifts of snow as fine and soft as talc.

On Day 49 the sun was shining first thing, but during my morning call to Ian he warned me of a developing depression, with gale-force winds and ground storms forecast. He'd looked at the weather maps and seen densely compressed isobars slowly tracking in my direction. Sure enough, it soon clouded over and the winds began building—the beginning of the wild weather that Ian had promised. I fell asleep that night to the sound of the tent fabric drumming as the gale shook it.

9

As soon as I opened my eyes the next morning, I knew I would not be going anywhere that day. The wind was shrieking round the tent, blowing at forty knots with stronger gusts. If I had any remaining doubts, they were literally blown away when I went outside to check the sledge. An unexpected gust was so strong that I was blown off my feet and had to crawl back to the tent on my hands and knees with drifting snow, like sand in a desert storm, forcing its way into every crack and crevice, filling the cuffs of my unsecured mitts and penetrating my smock and the back of my hood. The exposed flesh on my face was stung viciously by the wind-whipped snow particles, and such was the intensity of the ground storm that it was impossible to keep my eyes open and even breathing was uncomfortable.

I was forced to lie in the tent all day listening to the storm, while all sorts of thoughts and worries preyed on me. I had just fifteen days of full rations left and was still 125 nautical miles from the Pole. To complete my black mood, the storm coming out of the east-northeast was pushing me west-southwest; by the day's end I was two nautical miles further from the Pole than I had been twenty-four hours earlier.

Day 51 was worse. Once more the storm kept me pinned in my tent and the drift cost me another four nautical miles of hard-won progress. I had mended all there was to mend, written all there was to write, checked all there was to check, and now there was nothing to do but twiddle my thumbs, brood on things and wait to see what tomorrow would bring.

Day 52 was another total write-off, the third in a row. The storm continued, and ice drift saw me another 2.3 miles further from the Pole. Late in the day, the winds moderated, giving hope that I would be able to resume my journey the next morning. I cleaned out the sledge and repacked it so that the heaviest items were in the centre of the sledge and as near the bottom as possible, making it more stable and easier to haul.

I didn't sleep well that night. My worries about the ice conditions when I finally got moving north again were now being reflected in a vivid, recurring nightmare. In the year leading up to my departure for the Pole, I had been having a nightmare about drowning in the Arctic Ocean. Even in my waking hours I had a growing sense that this was going to be how I would die. Now, for the first time on the expedition, the nightmare had returned, and my sleep was constantly disrupted by images of myself trapped under the ice or floundering helpless as black, icy water closed over my head.

I was still tired when I woke—Day 53, May 8—but I lay still for a moment listening, and then I started to smile. After three days of booming and snapping as the winds tore at it, the tent fabric hung limp and still. Though the overcast skies and snow flurries made it a less than perfect day, I was not going to let that spoil my mood—Freedom!—I was back on the road again. My legs were understandably wobbly to start with, but within a couple of hours I began to hit my stride. I crossed the eighty-eighth parallel just before camping for the night; just two degrees of latitude to go.

On Day 54, the sun at last began to show itself between the clouds and not even a couple of fog banks rolling in from the west, suggesting substantial leads of open water in that direction, could dampen my spirits. I covered eleven miles in twelve hours and was delighted with my progress, because in the course of the day I'd had to swim two substantial leads, so wide that I could barely make out the bank on the far side. I was getting a bit less apprehensive about swimming in the immersion suit by now, though I was well aware that it was the single most dangerous thing I did.

I crossed a narrow peninsula of ice onto an area of saturated, rotten ice about half a mile wide, with an upper surface that was flush with the level of the sea water, and had gone no more than a hundred metres when I saw a myriad glints of water to either side of me. I pressed on ahead and reached the edge to find a broad stretch of open water beyond. I then went right, working my way slowly round the edge of the ice pan, completely focused on how I would get across. Then suddenly I came across some sledge tracks and a line of boot prints in the soft, mushy surface of the ice. I stopped dead, shocked. No one could have been here; I knew I was the only person in the whole of the western Arctic Ocean this year. As a Winnie-the-Pooh fan, I should have recognised the situation at once, for the same thing had happened to that Bear of Very Little Brain during a walk round a spinney near the Hundred Acre Wood. I had crossed my own tracks, working my way in a complete circle round the ice pan.

After a rueful pause for reflection, I retraced my steps to the peninsula of ice that had led me onto this time-wasting ice pan, crossed back onto the solid ice and found another way north. There were many more cracks and minor leads and patches of thin ice on my route north, and I had to use all sorts of techniques to get across. Sometimes I used the sledge as a bridge, sometimes bracing the ski and two ski poles to the back of it to extend its length; sometimes I used Mr Orange, and sometimes I even belly-crawled across thin ice.

The time I was now having to spend near open water was adding to my anxieties, and I made a discovery that evening that increased my paranoia. When I checked my rifle I discovered that the barrel and breech mechanism had rusted so badly that it was questionable whether it would fire at all, and even if it did, there was no way that the cartridge would eject—it had rusted to the ejection clamp. I'd been congratulating myself on remembering to bring absolutely everything I needed for the expedition, but it now turned out that I had made one small but potentially life-threatening omission—a tiny tube of low-temperature gun oil. Having cleaned it as well as I could, I melted some butter and rubbed it all over the inside and outside of the rifle.

WITH A FEW more miles under my belt, I began to plan for my arrival at the Pole. I had now reset my goals. The three storm days meant that to reach the Pole in sixty days was no longer possible without pushing to the limit. As a result, I was planning to arrive at the Pole at lunchtime on Sunday, May 18, Day 63, just nine days from now. Despite that level of planning there was no complacency on my part. There were still 109 miles to go, and I knew that ice and weather might have a few more surprises in store for me.

Day 55 was a good day. The omens weren't good when I set off; light snow with mid-level cloud, but as the banks of cloud rolled overhead they seemed to lighten and the snowfall got no worse. Even better, I passed another significant milestone in the course of the day: the Pole was now less than 100 nautical miles away. Best of all, the snow that had fallen over the previous days had settled and compacted, and instead of sinking into it I was walking on top of it. I was scarcely noticing the loss of my skis. I managed eleven nautical miles in less than ten hours. The ice was quite active but quite a lot of the leads were running north to south—my direction of travel—making them easier to avoid. When I did have to cross them, I'd find places narrow enough to jump across, or bridge with my sledge.

I could once again hear the wind howling around the tent and lashing it with particles of drifting snow when I woke on Day 56. It was already blowing at twenty knots, and over the course of the day it picked up to over thirty knots. These were big winds, but the air temperature was only −14°C and even with the wind chill it still felt quite mild, so I decided to press on. For once the escalator was moving my way and at an accelerating speed—I'd even gained 5.6 nautical miles during the night while I was asleep.

In the late afternoon I came to a lead, perhaps 150 metres across. I couldn't see the state of the ice because the surface was obscured by snow, and as a precaution I put on my immersion suit before starting to cross it. The first half was reasonably solid, but near the middle, where it had recently opened and refrozen, it began to thin and I could feel it flexing and bending beneath me. Once it broke, the surface tension would disappear and it would keep on breaking all the way to the bank fifty metres away. There was no point in backtracking; having come this far I might as well keep going. I went into a fast shuffle, sliding my feet gently and quickly forwards over the ice.

I sensed as much as heard the ice give way beneath me. I didn't want to have to swim the rest of the lead, doing my icebreaker routine with my arms, because it was so exhausting, so I kept shuffling forward faster and faster, trying to keep ahead of the breaking ice even as I was starting to sink through it. By now I'd sunk to my waist but, half crawling and half swimming, I broke through the ice for a few metres and then managed to crawl back out by spreading my body horizontally over the unbroken ice in front of me. I cat-crawled forward gingerly for a few metres, then got to my hands and knees, using my ski poles to spread the load of my hands on the ice, and covered the last twenty metres that way, moving flat-out, the ice still breaking behind me and the sledge actually in the water. My hood kept falling forward over my eyes and I couldn't see where I was heading, but I just kept going until my head smacked into the ice bank on the far side.

I crawled out and lay there, sick and dizzy, my chest heaving and blood pounding in my ears. That short burst of intense effort had probably taken no more than a minute, but my body was attuned to the marathon effort of long-distance sledge-hauling, not a 100-metre dash, and the swelteringly hot, heavy and clumsy immersion suit made it even worse. I stripped it off and packed it away and, to my relief, I encountered no more major leads that day. I stopped after only eight hours of sledge-hauling, but I had covered 9.6 miles in that time. Just eighty-eight to go, and that night the southerly winds continued to push me towards my goal.

The wind was still shrieking the next morning, Day 57, beating out a relentless rhythm on the taut fabric of the tent. It sounded terrible but it was sweet music to my ears because the deep anticyclone to the west was still keeping the winds southerly. After casting an eye over the leaden, snow-filled skies, I decided to take a rest day and let the wind do the work for me. I could make some running repairs and gather my strength ready for the 'final push' to the Pole. As I stayed warm in my sleeping-bag, every hour that passed saw the winds push me another two-thirds of a mile nearer to my goal. It was an unexpected bonus, because the Transpolar Drift Stream and the northwesterly winds that usually prevailed would normally have generated a southeasterly drift.

I checked the forecast with Ian Wesley on the satellite phone that evening and discovered that the winds, though diminishing, would stay southerly for at least another day. My sense of contentment was shattered when I checked my satphone batteries after breaking the connection. My two main lithium batteries—each capable of powering the satphone or recharging its two spare batteries—were dead. I'd run through the first battery by Day 35 in the coldest temperatures, and had therefore taken the view that the second battery, in much warmer climes, would last significantly longer—well past Day 70—but I had not been monitoring my use of the phone. It was miles above plan, and as a result the batteries were now even more drained than I was. If my phone failed, I would be reliant only on a prepared roster of numeric codes sent out by my Argos satellite transmitter. All I had left were two small rechargeable lithium power packs, specific to the satphone, with an as yet unknown amount of charge remaining in them.

I slept very badly that night and woke feeling tired. I'd decided to switch from local time, based on my current longitude, over to Greenwich Mean Time, so that I could synchronise my body clock with England and time my arrival at the Pole to fit in with family and all the other interested parties back home, but in so doing I'd given myself very few hours' sleep. Worse, my stomach had been upset, probably because the salami in my sledging rations had gone off. Even though I needed every calorie I could get, I had to take no chances and threw it away.

Despite my fatigue, I made good progress, sailing past the eighty-ninth parallel as I covered thirteen miles in nine hours. I was looking for a camping place when I hit the big lead. My normal rule was to cross any such obstacle before stopping for the night, ensuring a flying start in the morning, but I felt too weak, so I stopped short of the lead and pitched my tent.

I woke on Day 59, May 14, feeling less queasy and a little stronger. It was just as well; I had to swim this lead. Fortunately the sun was shining and there was no wind to speak of as I donned my immersion suit and set out across the lead. As I did my customary sweep for bears before lowering myself into the sea, I noticed a dark smudge of the far bank. I looked at it for some time, trying to force a recognisable shape to emerge, but nothing came. For the first few metres I was moving over and then through very mushy ice, then there was a long stretch of open water, then more rotten ice and finally a broad expanse of very thin ice that I had to crawl across. I was exhausted and trembling with the effort by the time I reached the far side and scrambled up the two-metre, crumbling bank.

In an instant I was on red alert, for about five metres ahead of me was the dark patch that had attracted my attention—the scene of a brutal murder. Dry, blackened blood was spattered across the snow, centring on the cadaver of a seal. The seal must have emerged from the water, just as I had done, and at once been ambushed and killed by a bear. Much of the seal was still intact, as if the bear had known exactly which parts it was interested in feeding on. I dragged my sledge up the bank in double-quick time and slung my gun over my shoulder, where it would remain for the rest of the day. Here I was, approaching 89°N, and I now knew with absolute certainly that there was a polar bear in the vicinity, and until I was lifted off the sea ice I had better remember that fact—operable gun or not.

I'd be lying if I didn't admit to being on tenterhooks for the rest of the day, but I picked up the pace until I hit another enormous lead. This one was well over a kilometre across. There was no way I could sensibly commit to swimming a lead of that size, knowing that a polar bear, technically classified as a marine mammal, *Ursus maritimus*, was in the vicinity. Instead, I walked west and northwest for an hour and a half, trying to find a way round it. Finally I reached a place where it had shrunk to no more than forty metres wide, covered with a thin layer of new ice. I decided that there was little to be gained by looking further west, put on the immersion suit and got ready to cross it. I swam the first twenty-five metres, breaking the ice in front of me with my arms, and I then found that the ice over the last fifteen metres was solid enough to bear my weight, providing I leopard-crawled, spreading the load over as large an area of ice as possible.

I felt exposed and vulnerable while making the crossing; the usual paranoia about Greenland sharks and polar bears being augmented by the belief that my immersion suit was leaking at the ankles and wrists and filling slowly with icy water. In fact my feet and hands were indeed sopping wet, but only because I was sweating buckets through my exertions.

Having got across, I ran out of steam completely and stopped for the night with fourteen miles on the clock for the day, leaving just fifty-four more to go to the Pole. I made a two-minute call to Ian that night and told him that, because of my failing batteries, I was going to cease using the satphone and save the remaining power for vital communications at the Pole and during the airlift out. From now on we would rely instead on the Argos satellite transmitter. When I'd completed the call, I turned off the phone and switched my Argos beacon to Code 3, confirming that there was a problem with the phone. It was one of a series of ten prearranged codes that could convey the most important messages.

0 All OK
1 Poor ice and/or weather conditions
2 Medical problem—manageable
3 Satellite phone problem—manageable
4 Satellite phone—permanent failure
5 Contemplating resupply
6 Resupply requested here. Weather conditions OK for plane
7 Contemplating pick-up
8 Non-urgent pick-up requested here. Conditions OK for plane
9 Looking for suitable ice or waiting for suitable weather for plane

The unit had been operating twenty-four hours a day since I set off from Ward Hunt Island, sending an hourly transmission, including my position and selected code, via Toulouse to my base team. I could also set it to transmit an eleventh emergency code, activating an alarm in the Argos office in Toulouse. They would then contact my base team, day or night, to alert them to my emergency, and in turn they would then contact our air charter operator to effect a rescue.

Day 60 was a terrible day. There was rotten ice and water everywhere: huge leads, lakes and mazes of steep-walled, interlinking canals. In ten hours of gruelling footslogging through mushy ice, and swimming a succession of leads in the immersion suit, I made no more than seven and a half miles. I had only five days' rations left and at this rate it could take me a week to get to the Pole. I was so exhausted that I fell asleep while waiting for my first cup of tea of the evening to cool down.

If I'd thought things could not possibly get any worse, then Day 61, May 16, had a surprise in store. The day dawned with a heavy overcast and thick snow falling, and within thirty minutes of setting out through this partial whiteout I was deep inside the worst area of pressure-ridging, interspersed with mazes of rotten ice, and small, medium and giant leads, that I had ever encountered. I wasted an hour trying to find a way round the whole area and instead just got deeper into it. Even worse, I got my boot drenched while crossing yet another giant rubble ridge—a freak occurrence, because the rubble is normally under compression and not associated with water. All I had to show for the first eight hours of the day was just over two nautical miles of northerly progress. If it continued like this for the last forty nautical miles, I would run out of rations and be unable to reach the Pole.

Suddenly, all the stresses and strains that had been building up came to a head with the realisation that, after fifteen years of unremitting effort, having got this close to my goal, I was still being presented with ever greater challenges and obstacles. I could feel the tears welling in my eyes. I hated the fact that I was cracking, but my desperation to succeed seemed to have met an insurmountable obstacle, and something had to give. I leaned forward, rested my hands on my knees, lowered my head and burst into tears. After a minute or so I found myself speaking out loud. It didn't start as a prayer, but as I said the words I knew it was becoming one: 'I am really struggling here, please help me . . .' There was a long pause before I finished the sentence ' . . . God.'

In that bleak moment I also drew strength from a quotation from a Caribou Inuit, Igjugarjuk. I keep it pinned over my desk in my office at Wydemeet, and I've read and pondered it so often that I can recite it from memory: 'All true wisdom is to be found far from the dwellings of men in the great solitudes and it can only be attained through suffering. Suffering and privation are the only things that can open the mind to that which is hidden from his fellows.'

A few minutes passed. I remained leaning forward, head bowed and my hands on my knees, as my sobs slowed and stopped and my tears began to turn to ice on my cheeks. Finally, I straightened up and took a few deep breaths. I looked around me, telling myself that these conditions were purely a local problem. I just needed to push through them to the better weather and ice that would inevitably await me ahead. I set off once more, and as I plodded onwards I was startled to discover that, having plumbed the depths only a few minutes before, not only did I now feel much calmer, I was also completely relaxed and confident. In fact, I felt invincible. I practically laughed out loud. I now knew, beyond any doubt, that I would reach the Pole. Nothing, not rotten ice, open water, bad visibility, nor wind, snow or storm, was going to stop me now.

If Day 61 had seen me at my lowest ebb, Day 62, May 17, pushed me close to euphoria. The sun was shining from a cloudless sky and the air temperature of –9°C felt positively springlike. There was a bit of movement and noise from ice activity but, unlike the day before, the ice conditions didn't seem to slow me down at all. In thirteen hours' walking I covered 16.5 nautical miles—a record day. As if that wasn't enough, ice drift from the southeast presented me with a bonus of another three miles. I now had just twenty-one miles to go and by trimming my daily rations, I still had four days' supplies.

I was pretty much running on automatic pilot. I couldn't hold a thought in my head for more than a few seconds. Even the simplest mental arithmetic took an age as I tapped and retapped out the numbers with my fingers on the ski poles. As I walked, I chatted away with my 'team' of Baskers, Swerves and Curves, which seemed to do the job of keeping me on track. I was pushing really hard when it suddenly occurred to me that there was no point in thrashing myself to death. My grail was within my grasp.

To celebrate this realisation, for the first time ever, I stopped bang in the middle of a seventy-five-minute sledge-hauling session, got out all my cooking gear in the open air and made myself two mugs of orange-flavoured water and a flask of tea for later on, then set off to complete my longest day yet.

Day 63, May 18, dawned bright and sunny, and in the course of the day, for the first time since I had left Ward Hunt Island, the temperature briefly registered a fraction of a degree above freezing point. I ate an extra half-bag of porridge for breakfast from my dwindling ration packs, because I was aiming to cover fifteen to eighteen nautical miles so as to leave no more than a short burst over the last few miles for the following day. I could then enjoy the moment to the full. Because of the previous day's late finish, I started late as well, around noon, and by the time I got to the fourth session I was already feeling leg-weary. I was dreading the thought of another twelve to twenty hours to cover the necessary miles, so I decided to play a psychological trick on myself. I would do a normal-length day of nine sessions, then stop as if I was getting ready to camp for the night. I'd put up the tent, rehydrate myself fully and have supper, but instead of going to bed I'd fill my flasks, make myself breakfast, and set off again to do the final four hours, or whatever it took to reach the Pole.

The ploy seemed to work, because although I was whacked I was in a good rhythm and just kept pushing on. I kept myself going by belting out snatches of a few songs over and over again: KC and the Sunshine Band's 'Please Don't Go', Rod Stewart's 'Sailing' and 'You're in My Heart', Peter Sarstedt's 'Where Do You Go to My Lovely?' and Elton John's 'Candle in the Wind'. I could remember only snippets and phrases, so there was lots of humming to fill the gaps, and what I lacked in tunefulness I more than made up for in volume and enthusiasm. In the end I didn't make camp until about four thirty in the morning, so in all I had walked for over fifteen hours and covered seventeen nautical miles, a record day in both duration and distance. When I looked at my GPS, it read 89°56′53″N—89 degrees 56 minutes and 53 seconds north. There was less than four miles to go.

Once the tent was up, I wolfed down three full mugs of orange drink, a chicken curry, a portion of porridge and half a bag of sledging nuts and chocolate. I had planned to rest for three or four hours, but I was too excited, and I was concerned that, after fifteen years of effort, some last-minute problem could still prevent me from reaching the North Pole. I knew I might grow careless in my haste, but this was the time to go for it as fast as I could. Once my life's mission was completed, I could rest.

It was 6 a.m. on Day 64, Monday, May 19, 2003. Within twenty minutes of setting off, I'd bent Curves, my left ski pole, even more out of shape and lost the basket again, so, while every instinct was urging me on, I had to force myself to stop, sit down and tie it back on again. Then a horrid, small, winding lead in the middle of a much larger, recently refrozen lead refused to let me head north. I detoured west along its bank, constantly seduced by its hints that, in just a few more metres, it would pinch out. Instead I found myself at an even larger lead and had to join forces with Mr O one last time within three kilometres of the Pole. I had now switched to thinking in metric units instead of nautical miles, so that I could picture the distance to go in the familiar terms of a running track: 3,000 metres was only seven and a half laps of the track—so nearly there.

I swam the lead, folded Mr O, hoping it was for the last time, then pressed on over an area of huge, kilometre-wide ice floes pocked with the remnants of old pressure ridges and ice nodules. The thin snow cover was granular and crunched underfoot as I walked, my boots making a rhythmic, almost hypnotic sound. I was getting very close now, less than 1,000 metres from my goal—in fact I realised I was on the floe that was actually floating over the north geographic pole. I was wholly absorbed in my preparations to navigate my way to the exact point round which our planet rotates, moving slowly forward, holding both ski poles in one hand and my GPS in the other, pulling the sledge, walking relatively upright.

I had closed to within 100 metres of the Pole. I was concentrating so hard on my navigation, that I didn't have time to take in my surroundings or enjoy the anticipation of the moment I'd waited so many years to achieve. The sun and compass were now useless and the GPS was all over the place as I sought the vital reading that would show I had reached the Pole. Before the introduction of GPS in the 1980s, polar travellers had to use sextants to calculate their position. It must have been torture because, even if they were actually standing at the North Pole as they began to take their readings, by the time they'd waited for a clear sun sight and then done their calculations, they would have drifted away from it again. Under those conditions, if you got a reading within a mile of the actual Pole, you'd be doing pretty well. Now, with GPS, it is possible to know your position to within three metres.

All my attention was on that tiny screen, because, even with a GPS, trying to nail down the actual location of the Pole can be fiendishly difficult if there's much drift going on. My longitude was constantly changing with the motion of the polar ice; since the lines of longitude converge at the Pole, they were now no more than a few metres apart. On top of this, precise as the GPS is, it can't actually compute 90°N—the Pole itself. The closest latitude reading it will give is 89°59′59.9″N.

Since each tenth of a second is equal to about three metres, that was as close as the GPS could get me to the Pole—close enough to reach out and touch it, if only I knew in which direction it lay. I had to navigate the last few metres by trial and error, walking backwards and forwards until I achieved the magic reading on my GPS. But the one constant—the north geographic pole—was proving elusive. Finally, I just stood stock still for a few seconds, watching my GPS to see what was happening with the ice.

As I stood there, to my amazement, I saw the display show my latitude start to climb. I was heading directly for the Pole. It read 89°59′59.6″N . . . 59.7 . . . 59.8 . . . 59.9 . . . and *I was there*. By clicking a button, I could make a permanent record of the reading at that particular time and date— 09.54 Greenwich Mean Time on May 19, sixty-four days after setting out from Ward Hunt Island. I pressed the button over and over again, making absolutely sure that I marked the waypoint with the date and time code burnt in. This far north, my Argos tracking beacon was also transmitting a signal of my position by satellite to my base camp every twenty minutes. It had been doing so ever since I left Ward Hunt and now, by an extraordinary coincidence, it sent another of its automatic transmissions as I was actually standing at the Pole. By the time it transmitted again, twenty minutes later, the ice drift had already carried me some distance away, but it was wonderful to discover, when I later spoke to my base, that they had received that instant verification that, at 09.54, my Argos beacon had sent a signal from precisely 90°00′00″N. I had arrived.

10

When I realised that I had really reached the Pole, I didn't plant any flags, I just stood motionless. All was perfectly quiet. The sun was blazing and it was very warm. I stood there numb, not fully understanding what I had done. The incessant drive to head north had suddenly gone. I could feel myself shaking. I had no feeling that I'd conquered or triumphed over something. I was simply there.

I put the GPS, the Argos beacon and my mitts on top of my sledge. Next to them I placed the embroidered family motto that I had carried with me all the way. Then I took off my hat and sank to my knees on the ice, kneeling before my sledge as if it were an altar. My first thought was of my dad, and I murmured, 'I've done it, Dad. I've done it for you.' As I spoke, big tears trickled down my cheeks.

When the moment had passed, I looked up into the brilliant blue sky and another powerful emotion swept over me: relief, utter, utter relief. I had done it. It was over at last. This huge challenge I had set myself was now a part of my past. And as that thought disappeared, a third, totally unexpected realisation starbursted in my head—I was free. I knew that I had fulfilled my destiny, and I was never again going to have to think about how I was going to achieve it. I no longer had to plan for this moment; it was here, it was now, and from this day on I would be entirely unencumbered by its demands. This moment of liberation was so heady that I almost felt I could fly.

I got back to my feet and looked around me for the first time. This ice floe was the scene of my North Pole. I could have found it amid a rubble-field during a blizzard or in the middle of open water in thick fog. But it had finally revealed itself in the centre of a large pan of first-year ice, on a near-perfect day. There was no wind, and the freshly created ice ridges and weathered old pinnacles were gleaming a dazzling white as they were struck by the light of the sun, now high in the sky. I etched every detail into my mind, but I knew that I had probably been at the exact Pole for no more than a few seconds before the inexorable ice drift began to carry me away from it. The Pole was already in the past; it was time to prepare for the future.

I used up a little of the remaining life in my precious satphone batteries to make three calls. The first was to Mary; without her love, help and support, there would have been no expedition. It was the briefest of calls. 'It's me. I'm here. I've made it. I'm on my way home. I love you.' The second call was to Robert Elias of the Omega Foundation, who had also played a critical part in the success of the expedition. The third call was to Ian and was even briefer and more businesslike: 'I've made it, when's the pick-up?'

'Brilliant, Pen, well done. I'll call all the people that I know you planned to call. Now, there's no plane available to pick you up today, the earliest they can get to you is tomorrow, Tuesday, afternoon. Let's speak again, GMT 09.00. Well done again. Bye for now.'

I was in shock as I broke the connection. I couldn't believe my ears. Weather permitting, it was imperative that a pick-up was made as soon as possible after reaching the Pole, but, in the absence of satphone contact, a summit meeting at Resolute between my base team and the aircraft operators had decided that Tuesday would be my most likely arrival date. I had made better-than-expected progress over the last forty-eight hours, but the weather was perfect, I was on an excellent ice floe offering several airstrip orientations, and yet there was not going to be a plane for at least twenty-four hours. This was not good news. The weather had been fine for several days, but how much longer would it stay that way?

With that thought in mind, I began to search for an airstrip. I always regarded it as a point of honour at the end of an expedition to do my best to find a realistic airstrip for the pick-up plane. I looked around for a couple of hours, but although I could see that there were possibilities for three orientations for a runway—so that they could land in different wind directions—I didn't mark them out, because I was stumbling with tiredness and my heart wasn't in it. There was no prospect of the plane arriving that day.

Stifling the frustration I felt, I put up the tent on the ice pan. I was in desperate need of rest, so I lay down and closed my eyes. I thought of Mary, Wilf and Freya: Mary frantically busy in her attic office, fielding enquiries from family and friends, supporters and journalists; Freya chomping her way through her biscuits at elevenses; and Wilf sitting in class at school in Widecombe-in-the-Moor. How excited he'd be today to find out I'd made it. Then he could pin the flag in its proper place on his wall chart at home and know that at last I was on my way back. Friends and relatives would soon be descending on the house for a celebration party, and letting off the giant firework that had been stored against the day when I finally reached the Pole. With those happy thoughts, I drifted off to sleep.

I slept for about eight hours, woke up that evening and had some food, then went back to sleep again for another five or six hours. Over the next three days, while I was recovering from the physical effort during the final dash to the Pole, I probably slept for about twelve to fourteen hours in every twenty-four; after that, I managed no more than six extremely sporadic hours a night, kept awake by a restlessness born of extreme boredom and haunted by the desire to be reunited with Mary, with no idea how long it might be before the plane would come.

By Tuesday afternoon, when the aircraft could have reached me, thick cloud was obscuring the sun and stinging snow flurries were scudding over the ice. The wind was strong enough to whip the pools of meltwater from the surface and drive it over the ice as wraiths and tendrils of mist. There was no point in even trying to identify an airstrip in such conditions. The monochromatic grey light made it impossible to discern the ridges, mounds and ice boulders, large or small, projecting from the surface of the ice pan. They would be fatal for an aircraft attempting to land, and no pilot would ever attempt to do so in such weather.

My GPS showed that I had now drifted four miles from the Pole—I was to drift about thirty-five nautical miles before I was picked up. My Argos beacon was automatically sending out my position every twenty minutes as my ice pan moved away from the Pole. As I'd planned with Ian before the start of the expedition, the meaning of my ten numeric Argos codes had changed as soon as I reached the Pole. Codes 6 'Food finished, fuel only' and 7 'Estimate can hold out for 15 days with remaining fuel, living off water alone', related to my personal state, but the remainder were designed to give the pilots a running commentary on the weather conditions. For example, Code 1 now meant 'Weather marginal for flying and deteriorating'; Code 3 'Weather marginal for flying and improving'. Having checked the weather, I reset the Argos beacon to Code 9—'Weather conditions bad for flying/no airstrip at present'—and then lay back down in my sleeping-bag to continue the long wait. Once, twice or sometimes even more times a day, I drained a little more of my battery power to make the briefest of reports on the conditions. The LED battery indicator display went from three bars to two and then one, and every time I used it I thought it would be the last one, but somehow it held out until almost the last act.

While I was waiting for the weather to lift, the pilots were working from satellite images of the Pole taken every six hours, trying to identify areas of open sky up to 100 miles away from my position and observe their direction and speed of travel, so they could predict when one of those areas would be passing over my ice pan and how long it would take to traverse it. At a minimum, they needed a break in the clouds large enough to give thirty minutes of blue skies over my ice pan. And it had to be predictable a minimum of four and a half hours in advance, because that was the flight time to the Pole from Eureka on Ellesmere Island at 80°N. My role was purely to keep them informed of any changes in my local weather so that they could try to match that to the cloud-cover images on the computer screen at Eureka.

Over the succeeding nine days, the flight to lift me out still failed to materialise. For five of those days there were strong winds, poor visibility, snowfall and thick cloud, and for three of them there were gale-force winds. Even when the wind died away, I was still in partial whiteout conditions.

Before the two Twin Otter planes could take off, the weather had to be viable at three different points: at the Eureka weather station, where the pick-up team was waiting, at the refuelling point between 85° and 86°N, where one of the planes would wait with the necessary aviation fuel to refill the other plane on its return, and at the point on the ice cap where I was waiting for them to land. As each day passed, the three never coincided. By the afternoon of Day 67, I had to switch my beacon back to Code 9, effectively barring them from taking off. By now I was on half-rations, eking out the last of my food for a couple more days.

As day succeeded day and I remained in my tent, waiting in vain for the aircraft to lift me out, I had no interest at any level in reviewing the events of the last ten weeks in my mind, nor revisiting them emotionally, nor going through my expedition diary, adding observations and recollections to it while they were still fresh. I couldn't even bear to look at it.

When I arrived at the Pole, I was exhausted from lack of sleep because I had pushed myself so hard for the last few days, but that sleep deficit was soon recovered and my physical strength regained. However, I was utterly drained mentally, and recuperation from that proved to be much slower. Just as a long-distance athlete times his run to the finishing post so that he is completely spent when he crosses the line, putting everything he's got into achieving the best time or the best position, I had timed my run to the tape and there was nothing left. At the start of the expedition I was doing distance calculations in my head. By the end I could barely add three and five.

So I lay in my tent in a state of total mental lassitude. I had a line running from one end of the tent roof to the other, threaded through two safety pins. As the tent fabric tautened, slackened and flapped in the wind, the line would swing to and fro and the safety pins would revolve around the line, going round and round, sometimes in perfect synchronicity, one way and then the other; then they would start moving apart doing the same thing, and then they would come back together, like some complex dance routine. I watched this performance for hours on end.

I also stared at the green roof of the tent for hours, watching the movement of the ripples of material in the wind, and, like a surfer trying to spot the next big wave, I would try to predict the size of the ripples in the material from the noise of the next gust of wind when it came. It was all completely pointless, self-absorbed nonsense. The only useful task I performed in all that time was to sweep the fresh snowfall from my Argos transmitter.

By Monday, Day 71, I had run out of nosebag rations and porridge, and was down to one cup of water in the morning and one at tea-time, drunk cold to save fuel, and two cups of hot water, one to replace breakfast and the other in the evening, into which I sprinkled a few grains of freeze-dried supper rations—just enough to give the water a little flavour. As I was not trying to establish a record for the number of days spent without food in a tent in the Arctic, I cannot say I enjoyed the pangs of hunger that gnawed at my stomach all day and all night, but I was quite intrigued to discover what it would be like to live on water alone for two or three weeks.

I had been able to make a few brief calls on my satphone to Gary Guy in Resolute. During one of these calls, I had learned a little of the full-blown global media madness that had erupted around the expedition. Unfortunately the coverage was giving the impression that I was starving and at the point of death and needed 'rescuing' from the Pole, and there had been an avalanche of emotional stuff about the family waiting at home whom I might never see again. I heard this with mounting horror, worried about the effect it would have on Mary and the children, and my mother, family and friends, and also furious at the lurid, overblown treatment. It was nothing more than a weather delay to a prearranged, precontracted and fully paid-for flight, not 'a life or death mercy dash', as the tabloids were apparently describing it. There were even networks of churches around Britain, and maybe around the world, all praying for me, which, though I was touched and grateful, I found excruciatingly embarrassing.

Ian, Martin and Ginny had all flown up with the planes from Resolute to Eureka in the expectation of coming on the pick-up flight, but Gary now told me that the pilots were switching to Plan B, and would fly with minimum payload to give them maximum flexibility in choosing if and how to make a landing at my position. Even if they could not land to lift me out, they could always overfly me and drop supplies, and in that way I could remain on the ice cap almost indefinitely. On the morning of May 27, Day 72 of the expedition, the pilots took the decision on their own initiative to try to pick me up, taking advantage of a brief spell of clear weather that they estimated would drift over my position later that day. The battery of my satphone had lasted up to now, but the moment Gary at Resolute confirmed that the planes had taken off from Eureka and would be over my position in four and a half hours, it finally gave up the ghost.

Four hours later, about half an hour before they were due to land, I could see that the sky was definitely lightening from the northeast, but when I at last heard the engine note, faint at first then swelling into a throaty roar as they passed low overhead, the blue skies had not arrived on schedule. In poor visibility they could not risk a landing, but the plane circled a couple of times as they dropped a bundle of food supplies in a vivid fluorescent orange container and two five-litre cans of fuel in case they were forced to fly back without me. Even better, they also dropped a high-frequency radio, allowing me to communicate with them. As I set up the antenna, they were flying on for another forty miles into an area where the skies had cleared, and they put the plane down there to save fuel while they waited.

The chief pilot, Stephen King, called me on the radio to say they could wait for no more than two hours. After that, they would have to fly home. The weather remained stubbornly cloudy. With just half an hour to go Stephen said, 'Look, Pen, it's not looking good; the blue sky should be over your position now and it's stalled, and in fact the weather is starting to close out where we are. So our only hope is for you to find and mark a strip. We'll check it out as we overfly your position and, if it's good enough, we might be able to try and pick you up.'

As he was speaking, I was doing some lightning calculations in my head. It was going to take me five minutes to get from the tent to the most likely of my three potential runways, another ten minutes to walk to the far end of it and ten minutes to walk back, and another five to get back to the tent to report in. That was the full thirty minutes, without allowing any time to do something about any potentially hazardous surface features or to fill sacks with snow to act as markers. The absolute minimum was four—one at each corner of my runway—but several others at intervals down the sides was much better. So I said to him, 'I'm very grateful to you, but can you give me forty-five minutes? I just can't do it in thirty.' There was a long pause, then a single word, 'OK.'

I stumbled out of the tent, and within five minutes, heart pounding, I was at the area where the ice looked generally smooth. I could just make out the pressure ridges all round the perimeter of my floe—the visibility wasn't that good, but at least it wasn't snowing or foggy. I had just one chance, and nowhere near enough time to survey the whole pan, which had low ridges and dome-shaped mounds of buckled ice scattered across the surface, so I dropped to the ground and began doing press-ups every five degrees through a complete circle. I got my eyes right down to the snow level, so low that my nose was actually buried in the snow, and if I could still see the pressure ridge at the end of the ice pan when my nose was in the snow, the chances were that there were no meaningful humps or bumps between me and it.

One of the three strips seemed better than the other two. It was slightly broader, giving a bit more latitude if I found a deformation on one side or another. The minimum size for the runway was 400 metres long and twenty across. I knew that, if the circumstances allowed, the pilots could land in shorter distances, but those were the ground rules I had to follow. I immediately set off along one edge of my proposed strip, pulling my sledge behind me. Every fifty metres I stopped, shovelled snow into one of the blue nylon bags I had been using for storing food and clothing and placed it on the edge of the landing strip. I needed the bags not only to mark the edges so they were visible from the air, but also to create objects of sufficient height to be still visible to me right the way down the strip so I could create straight sides to the runway.

In the same way, still working at top speed, I marked the quarter, halfway, three-quarter points, and the far end. I swung left through ninety degrees and marked out the base line, then turned again and began working my way back down the other side. I stole a glance at my watch—twenty-five minutes gone. After nine days of doing nothing, I was gasping from the effort and my body was clammy with sweat, but there was no time to worry about anything other than filling the next bag and covering the next stretch. All the time I was pacing it out, I was also looking across to the far side, straining my eyes to detect any crack or mound in the ice that might pose a danger to the plane. The runway was only twenty metres from side to side, but it was like being inside a ping-pong ball—a soft, unfocused, white light with very little definition or contrast and no shadows. Although I could see the bags on the other side, it was almost impossible to detect any change in the ice surface, and I was constantly tripping and falling.

As I neared the middle of the strip, I was aghast to find a mound of ice

directly ahead of me and had to detour inwards to avoid it, narrowing the
centre portion of the strip. It was too late to worry about that; I just had to
mark it with a bag and realign the rest of the strip to this new, thinner
dimension. But as I again glanced across towards the other side, I was mortified to glimpse another low, conical mound of ice right in the middle of
the runway. It was about seventy-five centimetres high and a metre across at
its base. There was a crust of snow covering it, but beneath that it was solid,
rock-hard ice. If the aircraft hit that, it would be a wreck.

I grabbed my shovel and started to attack this thing, wielding the shovel
like an ice axe, ramming and smashing it down on the concrete-hard ice
block, sending showers of crystals and jagged shards of ice flying through
the air in every direction. I was going at it like a madman, not pausing for a
second even though I was feeling sick and faint with the effort. I don't
know how long it took, but I managed to reduce the mound until it was
almost level with the surrounding ice, then I wheeled round, stumbled back
to the side of the strip and hurried down to the far end.

I turned and looked back. There were several blocks and mounds to
either side, but the runway itself appeared clear, though it narrowed to an
hourglass shape in the middle, and it was much shorter than the ideal
length, perhaps 280 metres instead of 400. It would have to do; there was no
time left. I stumbled back through the snow to the tent, my legs leaden. I
was shaking and trembling, with cold sweat on my brow, and my fingers
fumbled agonisingly slowly with the keypad of the hf radio.

My chest still heaving and gasping for air, I had to compose myself to
deliver the information he needed. I was very aware that how I spoke to him
was as important as what I said. If I'd given him a garbled account in a desperate tone of voice, and had been excessively positive about the strip,
those things would have combined to make him think twice. He had a marginal situation and the poor visibility meant he couldn't use his own eyes to
verify what I was saying, so he had to decide whether to trust the information I was giving him. If he damaged the plane and couldn't take off again,
he was in serious trouble, not to mention the danger to the lives and limbs
of himself and his copilot.

I took a couple of deep breaths, trying to slow myself down from the
frenzy of effort I had just put in, and gave him the basic details of the strip.
'I've got a strip. It's not great, but I've looked at it as best I can and I have
measured it out. It's on a pan of first-year ice with an eight-foot pressure
ridge thirty metres back from the northern end. The ice is firm underneath a

slightly soft crust. It's not a full-length strip; it's about one hundred and twenty metres short, and narrow at the centre, but it's maybe two metres wider than the plane's skis and it's marked with bagged snow.'

'We're about to come over your position now,' he said. And as he said it, I heard the engine note on the wind and rushed outside the tent. The orange and white plane was just visible, a tiny dot in the distance that suddenly swelled into a huge shape as it came overhead. The pilot circled round my ice pan and then did two laps of the neighbouring one to see if there was anything better, but the visibility was so poor that there wasn't any other option to take; the choice was to use my strip or not to land at all.

Stephen came back to me on the radio and I knew he was wondering if I was trying to sell the strip to him. I kept my voice flat and unemotional as I repeated the information. 'Like I said, the strip has this waisting in the middle and a significant hump of ice to either side if you don't stay between those two markers. But it is my belief, from what I can see, that it is otherwise sound.' That was all I could say. It was now up to him.

He made two low passes first. The plane came down until it was no more than fifteen feet above the surface of the ice and I could see the pilots' faces framed in the cockpit as they checked the strip visually. The third time they came in, they went lower and lower until suddenly I saw twin flurries of snow as the skids touched down. At once, Stephen put the props into full reverse thrust and the blast sent snow clouds billowing upwards. The plane braked from almost 90 mph to a dead stop within 150 metres. I saw it pause for a split second, rocking on its skids as the engine note died down, and then there was a roar as the props began to accelerate again and it swung round and began to taxi back to the start of the runway, ready for takeoff into the wind. It swung round once more and then the engine died away.

The two pilots got out. They were both wearing dark clothing—the first dark objects I had seen in months. They wore big 'moon boots' with their trousers stuffed into the top of them, so their legs looked stumpy, and thick padded jackets; from a distance they looked like two Russian dolls tottering comically towards me. We walked towards each other. They both congratulated me and offered to help me pack my stuff and take the sledge to the plane, but after pulling it over 400 nautical miles I wanted to do the last 400 metres as well. It took ten or fifteen minutes to clear up and load my stuff into the plane, and by then there were inky clouds massing and a sudden haste to be airborne. We scrambled aboard and I strapped myself in.

On the seat next to me were things that the pilots had brought up from

Resolute for me. There was a package of treats and a letter from Mary, cards from Wilf and Freya, pressed flowers from the garden, a cake iced with the words 'Cool Dude', a couple of paintings of Daddy at the North Pole and a lurid purple badge proclaiming 'I've done it and I've done it good', which I put on and wore with pride all the way home. There was also a telegram from Her Majesty the Queen:

> We were pleased to learn of your success in completing your remarkable, unaided journey to the North Pole. You have defied great odds and extreme conditions in your endeavour. Your courage, perseverance and determination have been an inspiration to us all. We offer you our warm congratulations.

As I read those words, the engine whined and fired and the props began to revolve, disappearing into a blur of motion. A few seconds later we were bumping and rattling over the ice, accelerating and then lifting off with a final thud as the skids rose. Looking down from the plane as we banked to head south, I could just make out the line of blue bags marking the strip. Then it disappeared from view, swallowed up in an ocean of ice.

As I took in the fact that I was finally airborne, the biggest smile I have ever had spread across my face. The job hadn't been finished when I'd reached the Pole, huge relief though that was. I had completed the main mission, but I couldn't allow myself to relax until I was in the aircraft and off the ground. Now, for the first time in seventy-five days, my destiny was in someone else's hands. I felt my whole body relax as the realisation sank in; it was finally all over. I was on my way home.

EPILOGUE

I flew back into England on the morning of Thursday, May 29, 2003, but it was not until late that night that we returned to Dartmoor. As we turned off into the narrow, winding valley that leads to our house, the headlights caught the ghostly shape of a barn owl hunting over the fields by the river. I got out to open the gate at the bottom of the drive, then walked up to the house, re-attuning myself to those familiar but half-forgotten sounds: the river tumbling over the rocks in the bottom of the valley and the wind soughing through the trees. A soft summer rain had been falling during the evening and the smell of damp earth mingled with the warm, comforting stables smell from the barn where Mary kept her horse. I felt a cold nose press into my hand and there was Baskers, wagging his tail. Even PC, our semiferal pest-control cat, put in an appearance.

Wilf had fallen asleep in the back of the car on the journey, and I picked him up and carried him into the house, his face nestled into my shoulder. As I laid him down in his bed, he stirred, murmuring in his sleep, and grasped my fingers in his chubby hand. I tried to ease away, but though he was still fast asleep he clung tight to my hand, and I stayed crouching by his bed for a few more minutes, comparing his sleeping features with the mental snapshot of him that I had imprinted on my mind before I set off for the Pole.

The next morning, I woke just before dawn and found that Wilf was already dressed and standing silent at my bedside. As soon as he saw my eyes flicker open, he put his arms round my neck and whispered in my ear, 'Can we go up on the tors, Daddy?' We tiptoed out of the house, leaving Mary and Freya asleep, and set off up the moor with Wilf riding on my shoulders, his strong legs gripping my sides. Baskers's enthusiasm at my return did not extend to coming with us. As soon as he realised that Mary's horse, Philbo, would not be accompanying us, he ducked behind some rocks and sneaked back to the house to resume his interrupted sleep.

It was cool and damp in the grey light of predawn and my boots left dark prints in the dew-sodden grass. There was not a breath of wind, the air so still that tendrils of mist still clung to the surface of the river. A heron stood motionless in the shallows, keeping its lonely vigil. As I looked up, the tors above us were haloed with the first golden light of dawn. We didn't speak much as we climbed up out of the valley, just happy to be together again. I was revelling in the sights, sounds and smells filling my senses, so long starved by the sterile Arctic sea ice. The turf was springy under my feet, the air full of the heady scent of bluebells and flooded with the sound of the dawn chorus of birdsong from the woods flanking the river.

Every hundred yards or so we entered a different microlandscape—from pasture, to woodland, to marsh, to open moorland—and saw fresh vistas of rolling hills open up before us, with the tors standing sentinel above. We followed the rough track down to the ford, pausing to watch a couple of Dartmoor ponies running over the grass, full of exuberance at the breaking day, then climbed the other side of the valley. At the top we reached a cluster of granite crags, as old and timeless as the moor itself.

We'd often been up there before, scrambling over the rocks, looking for shelters and hiding places, and spotting features in the landscape from our favoured cliff-top places in the rock formations. If Wilf was struggling to climb one of the crags, I'd encourage him—just as my dad used to do, standing with his stopwatch in the lane by the church while I ran my sets of 400 metres—'Come on, son. You can do it.' Wilf went on ahead of me this morning, determined to show me how well he could climb, and I stood and watched him. As he pulled himself up and over the rocks, I heard him muttering to himself, 'Come on, son.' He reached the top and turned to look down on me, beaming with pride at what he had achieved. As I followed him up, I missed my footing for a second and my boot slipped off a ledge. I heard him say, half to himself and half to me, 'Come on, son, you can do it!'

At the top of one of the rock stacks, we found our favourite granite 'seats' and sat there watching the line of the sunrise inching down into the valley. That tranquil scene was, in every sense, a world away from the place I had left only a few days before, though already it seemed an eternity. Indeed, it was as if the whole endeavour had been a dream. There were no monochromatic vistas here, no confusing perspectives, no ice and snow, no black, frigid waters, no harsh, blinding light. Everything was softer and gentler, and the moors and valleys around us were coloured a thousand shades of green and bursting with life.

After a while I put Wilf up on my shoulders again and we walked back down the lane towards Wydemeet. The cries of a circling buzzard pierced the silence of the morning, and when we reached the valley bottom the sun was already dappling the river and swallows were skimming the surface. I was back on Dartmoor in the home I loved, with the people—Mary, Wilf and Freya—who meant more to me than anything in the world, and, for now, this small world was all I wanted or needed.

I had half-thought and half-hoped that in completing my solo journey to the Pole, after fifteen long years of unrelenting effort, I would have fulfilled my destiny, but in the same instant that I at last stood at 90°N and felt the profoundest sense of relief, I also realised that the Pole had never really been the finishing post. But one thing had changed for ever: for the first time in my life, I was free.

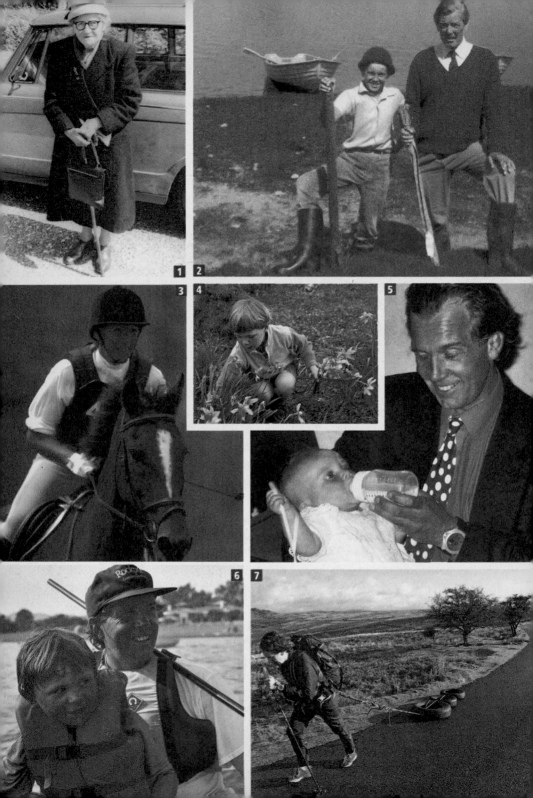

PEN HADOW

Born: February 26, 1962, near Gleneagles
Home: Dartmoor
Former jobs: landscape gardening, PR

Left page: 1 Enid Wigley, the nanny who looked after not only Pen but Sir Peter Scott (Scott of the Antarctic's son) as well as Pen's own father. **2** Pen with his father on one of their countless fish-free fishing forays! **3** Pen's wife, Mary, competing on her beloved horse, Philbo. **4** Thoughts of his son, Wilf, changed Pen's attitude to thin ice. **5** Topping up Freya, the Hadows' second child, just before her christening at St Raphael Church on Dartmoor. **6** Father and son enjoying a sail. **7** The dreaded sport-specific training of tyre-pulling on Dartmoor.

Right page: 8 'Mr Orange', Pen's immersion suit in all its glory. **9** 'Pressure ridges', chaotic jumbles of ice, which come in all shapes and sizes. There were hundreds of them on the route to the north. **10** Hauling the sledge, which weighed over nineteen stone, over an obstacle. **11** At the North Pole, finally. 'First came thoughts of my dad, then, suddenly, the realisation: "At last, I am free."'

GREG ILES

BLOOD
MEMORY

Sometimes families conspire
in a lie in order to protect
each other from the truth.

Sometimes it can take just a
small piece of evidence to
blow that conspiracy apart . . .

CHAPTER 1

W hen does murder begin? With the pull of a trigger? With the formation of a motive? Or does it begin long before, when a child swallows more pain than love and is forever changed?

We judge and punish based on facts, but facts are not truth. Facts are like a buried skeleton uncovered long after death. Truth is fluid. Truth is alive. To know the truth requires understanding. It requires seeing all things at once, forward and backward, the way God sees.

Forward and backward . . .

So we begin in the middle, with a telephone ringing in a dark bedroom on the shore of Lake Pontchartrain in New Orleans, Louisiana. There's a woman lying on the bed, mouth open in the mindless gape of sleep. She seems not to hear the phone. Then suddenly the harsh ring breaks through, and the woman's hand shoots from beneath the covers, and picks up the receiver from the bedside table. The woman is me.

'Dr Ferry,' I croak.

'Are you sleeping?' The voice is male, taut with anger.

'No.' My denial is automatic, but my mouth is dry as a cotton ball, and my alarm clock reads 8.20 p.m. I've been out for nine hours. The first decent sleep I've had in days.

'He hit another one. Garden District. Male Caucasian. Age sixty-nine.'

I blink and try to orient myself in the darkness. 'Bite marks?'

'Worse than the others.'

I'm already getting out of bed. 'This makes no sense. Sexual predators kill women, Sean. Or children. Not old men.'

'We've had this conversation. How fast can you get here?'

I lift yesterday's jeans off the chair and slip them on. 'I'm on my way.'

'Are you sober?'

I haven't had a sip of vodka for nearly forty-eight hours, but I'm not going to give Sean the satisfaction of answering his interrogation. The craving is already awake in my blood, like little teeth gnawing at my veins. I need the anaesthetic burn of a shot of Grey Goose. Only I can't have that any more. I've been using Valium to fight the withdrawal symptoms, but nothing can truly replace the alcohol that has kept me together for so long.

I shift the phone from shoulder to shoulder and pull a silk blouse from my closet. 'What's the victim's name?'

'Arthur LeGendre.' His voice drops. 'Have you taken your meds?'

Sean knows me too well. No one else in New Orleans is even aware that I take anything. Lexapro for depression, Depakote for impulse control. I stopped taking both drugs three days ago, but I don't want to get into that with Sean. 'Stop worrying about me. Is the FBI there?'

'Half the task force is here, and they want to know what you think about these bite marks.'

'What's the address?'

'Twenty-seven twenty-seven Prytania.'

'Sounds like an address with a security system.'

'Switched off.'

'Just like the first one. Moreland.' Our first victim—one month ago—was a retired army colonel, highly decorated in Vietnam.

'Just like that.' Sean's voice drops to a whisper. 'Get your lovely ass down here, OK?'

Today his intimacy makes me want to jab him. 'No "I love you"?' I ask with feigned sweetness.

His reply is barely audible. 'You know I'm surrounded.'

As usual. 'Yeah. I'll see you in fifteen minutes.'

NIGHT FALLS FAST as I drive my Audi to the Garden District, the fragrant heart of New Orleans. I spent two minutes in the bathroom trying to make myself presentable, but my face is still swollen from sleep. I need caffeine. In five minutes I'll be surrounded by cops, FBI agents, forensic techs, the chief of robbery homicide, and possibly the chief of the NOPD. I'm accustomed to that, but seven days ago—the last time this predator hit—I had a panic attack at the crime scene. And panic attacks don't exactly inspire confidence in the hard men and women who work serial murder cases. Word got round about my little episode, and nobody could really believe it. Why did the woman that some call 'the ice queen' suddenly lose her composure? I'd like to know that myself. I have a theory, but analysing one's own mental condition is a notoriously unreliable business.

Four victims now, I remind myself, focusing on the case. Four men between the ages of forty-two and sixty-nine, all murdered within a thirty-day period. If the victims were women, the city would be gripped by terror. But because the victims are middle-aged or older men, a sort of fascinated curiosity has taken hold of New Orleans.

I'm a forensic odontologist, an expert on human teeth, and one of the world's leading experts in the field. If people ask me what I do for a living, I tell them I'm a dentist, which is true enough and all they need to know.

The task force wants my expertise on bite marks tonight, but Sean Regan wants more. When he sought my help on a murder case two years ago, he soon learned that I knew about a lot more than teeth. I completed two years of medical school before I transferred to dental school, and that gave me a strong foundation for a self-education in forensics. Anatomy, haematology, histology, biochemistry . . . I can glean twice as much information from an autopsy report as any detective, and twice as fast.

After Sean and I became closer than the rules allowed, he began using me unofficially to help with difficult cases. By allowing me access—unethical and probably illegal access—to crime scenes, witnesses and evidence, he has put me in a position to solve four major murder cases. Sean took the credit every time—and I let him. Why? Partly because telling the truth would have exposed our love affair, got Sean fired and freed the killers. But also because I didn't care about the credit. I'd tasted the pulse-pounding rush of hunting predators, and I was addicted to it as surely as I am to the vodka I need so terribly at this moment.

For this reason, I've let our relationship run for eighteen months, long past the point where I would usually have sabotaged it. Long enough, in fact, for me to have forgotten one of my hardest-won lessons: *the husband doesn't leave*. Not the husbands I pick, anyway. Sean has gone a long way towards convincing me that this time it's different. And I'm very close to believing him. Close enough to find myself hoping desperately for it in the most vulnerable hours of the night.

Without warning, a wave of nausea rolls through my stomach. I try to tell myself it's alcohol withdrawal, but deep down I know better. It's panic. Pure terror at the idea of giving up Sean and being alone. Don't think about it, says a shaky voice inside me as I decelerate down the interstate ramp to St Charles Avenue. Think about the case . . .

The facts are simple enough. In the past thirty days, three men have been shot by the same gun, bitten by the same set of teeth, and—in two cases—marked by the same saliva, which should provide the strongest evidence against any suspect. The NOPD crime lab did the ballistics that matched the bullets, the state police crime lab did the mitochondrial DNA match, which shows the saliva 87 per cent likely to be from a Caucasian male, and, by using reflective ultraviolet photography and scanning electron microscopy on the bite marks, I concluded that the same killer had murdered all three victims. New Orleans had another predator on the hunt.

My official responsibility ended with matching the bite marks, but I began to analyse other aspects of the case. The NOMURS killings—so dubbed by the FBI for 'New Orleans murders'—are, like all serial murders, at root sexual homicides. And, in such cases, the murderer's selection criteria for his victims hold the key; something always links them, even if it's nothing more than geographic location. But the NOMURS victims have ranged widely in age, physical type, occupation, social status and place of residence. Moreover, none of them is known to have had habits that might attract a predator. None of them was gay, ever arrested for a sexual crime, reported for child abuse or known to frequent strip clubs. The only similarities are that they're white, male, over forty and have families. For this reason the task force has made no progress in finding a suspect.

As I slow the Audi to read a house number on Prytania Street, my skin itches with fear and anticipation. The killer may be watching the progress of the investigation, as serial murderers often do. Watching *me*. And therein lies the thrill. When you hunt a predator, you place yourself in a position to be hunted yourself. If you follow a lion into a thicket, you step within reach of his claws. And my adversary is the deadliest creature in the world: a human male driven by anger and lust, yet governed—at least temporarily—by logic. He stalks these streets confident in his prowess, meticulous in his planning, arrogant in his execution. The only thing I know about him is this: he will kill again and again, until someone unravels the riddle of his psyche or he self-destructs from the intensity of conflict in his own mind.

Sean is standing on the sidewalk, waiting. I park, get out and start to unload my cases. Sean gives me a quick hug, then helps me. He's forty-six years old but looks forty, with the easy, confident grace of a natural athlete. His hair is mostly black, his eyes green with a bit of a twinkle.

'You doin' OK?' he asks in his New Orleans drawl. 'You look rough, Cat.'

'Thanks for the vote of confidence.'

'Sorry. Are you drunk?'

Anger tightens my jaw muscles. 'I'm stone sober for the first time in more years than I can count. Come on. Let's do this.'

'I still need to go in ahead of you.' He looks embarrassed.

'How long? Five minutes?'

'Not that long.'

I wave him off and get back into my car. He walks down the block. I grip the steering wheel and force myself to breathe deeply. As my pulse steadies and my heart finds its rhythm, I pull down the vanity mirror and check my face. I'm not usually compulsive about my appearance, but Sean has made me nervous. And when I get nervous, crazy thoughts flood into my head. Old nightmares, ancient slights, things therapists have said . . .

I consider putting on some eyeliner to strengthen my gaze in case I have to stare somebody down. I don't really need it. Men often tell me I'm beautiful, but men will tell any woman that. My face is actually masculine in structure, a vertical series of V's. The V of my chin slants up into a strong jaw. My mouth, too, curves upwards. Then come my prominent, upward-slanting cheekbones; my tilted brown eyes and sloping eyebrows; and finally the dark widow's peak of my hairline. I see my father in all of this, twenty years dead now but alive in every angle of my face.

Sean has told me I look like a predator myself, a hawk or an eagle. Tonight I'm glad for that hardness in my face. Because as I get out of the Audi and shoulder my cases and tripod, something tells me that maybe Sean is right to be worried about me. Without the familiar chemical barrier that shields me from the sharp edges of reality, I feel more vulnerable to whatever it was that panicked me last time I did this.

Walking down the dusky street lined with wrought-iron fences, I sense a human gaze on my skin. I stop and turn but see no one.

You've done this a hundred times, I tell myself as I climb the steps to the entrance of the large Victorian house. You're fine.

Ten feet inside, I know I'm in trouble.

A BRITTLE AIR of expectancy fills the broad central hallway, and curious eyes track my movements. Before I have to ask the patrolman standing inside the door where the body is, Sean steps into the hall and beckons.

'Body's in the kitchen.' He takes the heavy case from my right hand.

'The Bureau forensic team has done its thing, all but the bite marks. Kaiser says those are your show. That ought to make you feel pretty good.'

'Kaiser' is John Kaiser, a former FBI profiler and the Bureau's representative on the NOMURS task force.

'I'm ready. Let's do it,' I say.

Sean opens the door to a gleaming world of granite, travertine, shining enamel and wood. I sweep my eyes over a blur of faces and nod a greeting. Captain Carmen Piazza nods back. She's a tough, fifty-something Italian-American who came up through the ranks of the Homicide Division and is now the commander. If anyone ever fires Sean for his involvement with me, it will be Piazza. She likes Sean's record of arrests, but she thinks he's a cowboy. And she's right. He is a tough, devilish Irish cowboy.

Someone has set up a floodlight. When I round the island at the centre of the kitchen, I see a corpse; livid bite marks on the chest and face, one bullet hole in the centre of the abdomen, a contact gunshot wound to the forehead. Scrawled in blood across two cabinet doors on the wall opposite the sink are five words: *MY WORK IS NEVER DONE.*

'You need any help, Dr Ferry?'

'What?' A film of sweat coats my skin.

'John Kaiser,' says the same voice.

I look over at a tall, lanky man of about fifty. He has a friendly face with hazel eyes that miss nothing. He's left off his title: Special Agent.

'You need help with your lights or anything?' he says.

Feeling oddly detached, I shake my head.

'He's getting more savage,' Kaiser observes. 'Losing control, maybe?'

I nod. The floor shudders as Sean sets my heavy dental case beside me.

Too late I tell myself to breathe. My throat is already closing. One step at a time . . . Shoot the evidence with the 105-millimetre quartz lens. Standard colour film first, then get out the filters and start on the UV. After that, take your alginate impressions . . . As I bend and flip the latches on my case, I feel a dozen pairs of eyes watching me.

'It's the same killer,' I say. 'He's got slightly pegged lateral incisors. I see it on the chest bites. That's not conclusive. Just my preliminary assessment.'

'Right. Of course. You sure you don't need some help?' asks Kaiser.

I'm opening the wrong case. I need my camera, not my impression kit. *Keep it together* . . . But I can't. As I bend further down a wave of dizziness nearly tips me onto the floor. I retrieve the camera, straighten up to switch it on, then realise I've forgotten to set up my tripod.

In three seconds I go from mild anxiety to hyperventilation, like an old lady about to faint in church. Which is unbelievable. I can breathe more efficiently than 99 per cent of the population. When I'm not working as an odontologist, I'm a free diver, a world-class competitor in a sport whose participants commonly dive to 300 feet using only the air trapped in their lungs. Yet now—standing at sea level in the kitchen of a ritzy town house— I can't even drink from the ocean of oxygen that surrounds me.

'Dr Ferry?' says Kaiser. 'Are you all right?'

Arthur LeGendre's corpse wavers in my vision, as though it's lying on the bottom of a shallow river. Don't let this happen, I beg silently. Please.

But no one hears my prayer. A train ploughs over me without pain or sound. And everything goes black.

A FEMALE MEDIC is kneeling beside me, reading from a blood-pressure cuff strapped to my arm. Sean Regan and Special Agent Kaiser are standing over us, looking worried.

'A little low,' she says. 'I think she fainted. Sugar's a little low, too, but she's not hypoglycaemic.' She notices that my eyes are open. 'When was the last time you ate, Dr Ferry?'

'I don't remember.'

'Anybody got a candy bar?' says Agent Kaiser.

A reluctant male voice says, 'I got a Snickers.'

And as I get to my feet, a paunchy detective steps forward and hands me the chocolate bar. I accept it, though I know I have no blood sugar problem. This charade is witnessed by a rapt audience that includes Captain Piazza.

'I'm sorry,' I say in her direction. 'I don't know what happened.'

'Same thing as last time, looks like,' Piazza observes.

'I guess so. I'm OK now, though. I'm ready.'

Captain Piazza leans towards me and speaks softly. 'Step out here with me for a moment, Dr Ferry. You, too, Detective Regan.'

Sean gives me a warning glance, then we follow her into a study off the central hall. Piazza leans against a desk and faces us, jaw set tight.

'I don't know what's going on between you two, and I don't want to know,' she says. 'What I do know is that it's jeopardising this investigation. So here's what we're going to do. Dr Ferry will go home. The FBI will handle the bite marks tonight. And unless the Bureau objects, I'm going to request that a new forensic odontologist be assigned to the task force.'

I want to argue, but Piazza has said nothing about my episode in the kitchen. She's talking about something for which I have no defence. Adulterers think they're discreet, but people always find out.

A patrolman steps into the study and sets my dental cases on the floor. After he leaves, Piazza says, 'Sean, walk Dr Ferry back to her car. Be back here in two minutes.'

Sean's eyes lock with his superior's. 'Yes, ma'am.'

Captain Piazza looks at me, her face not without compassion. 'Dr Ferry, you've done some remarkable work for us in the past. I hope you get to the bottom of this problem. I suggest you see a doctor, if you haven't already.'

She walks out, leaving me alone with my married lover and the latest mess I seem to have made of my life. Sean picks up my cases and starts for the front door. We can't risk talking here.

Warm water drips from the oak leaves as we walk to my car in silence. It rained while I was inside, a typical New Orleans shower that did nothing to cool or cleanse the city, only added more water vapour to the smothering humidity. In the darkness, though, the street has a deceptively romantic look.

'What happened in there?' Sean asks. 'Another panic attack?'

My hands are shaking, but whether from my episode inside, alcohol withdrawal or the confrontation with Piazza, I don't know. 'I guess.'

'Is it us, Cat?'

Of course it's us. 'I don't know.'

'I told you Karen and I are talking about seeing a lawyer now. It's just the kids, you know? We—'

'Don't start, OK? Not tonight.'

When we reach the Audi, Sean takes my keys, unlocks the door and loads my cases into the back seat. Then he turns to me. 'Tell me what's really going on. There's something you're not telling me.'

Yes. But I'm not going to play that particular scene here. Not now. Not like this. 'I can't do this,' I tell him. It's all I can manage.

His green eyes have a remarkable intensity sometimes. 'We have to talk, Cat. Tonight. I'll get away as soon as I can.'

'All right,' I say, knowing it's the only way to get out of here.

He squeezes my upper arms, then opens the door of the Audi and helps me inside. 'Be careful driving home.'

'Don't worry about me.'

Instead of leaving, he kneels beside the open door, clasps my left wrist and speaks with genuine urgency. 'I *am* worried about you. What is it? I know you, damn it. Tell me!'

I crank the engine and pull slowly away from the kerb, leaving Sean no choice but to let go of my wrist and close the door. I drive on, leaving him standing in the wet street, staring after my taillights.

'I'm pregnant,' I tell him, far too late.

TWO MILES from my house on Lake Pontchartrain, I realise I'm afraid to go there. If I do, I'll end up pacing the rooms like a madwoman until Sean arrives. Normally, after working a crime scene, I stop at a liquor store and buy a bottle of vodka. But the little agglomeration of cells growing inside me is the only pure thing in my life right now and I will not do it injury. Even if it means the screaming heebie-jeebies. My medical books told me that the first forty-eight hours of withdrawal would be the worst, so I've reluctantly self-prescribed enough Valium to blunt the symptoms for two days.

I wrench the car into a U-turn and stop at the base of the Interstate 10 on-ramp. Cars and trucks roar by, blasting their horns. An hour of driving west would put me in Baton Rouge. Highway 61 follows the Mississippi River north for ninety miles from there to Natchez, my childhood home . . . *Home. The place where, when you have to go there, they have to let you in.* I can't remember who said that, but it's always seemed apt to me. On the face of things, it shouldn't. My family has always begged me to visit. My mother actually wants me to move back. But I never could. You leave a place young and you don't know why, only that you have to get out. When I was sixteen, I left for college and never looked back. I returned for Christmases and Thanksgivings but little else, and this deeply wounded my family. Looking back across fifteen years, I think I fled because elsewhere—anywhere—Cat Ferry was only what I could make of her. In Natchez, she was heir to a suffocating matrix of expectations and obligations.

My cellphone rings out and lights up green on the passenger seat. The screen reads DET. SEAN REGAN. I switch the ringer to silent and turn over the phone so I won't have to see the glow. Then I drive up the ramp, joining the night traffic leaving the city.

IN THE SOUTH you are never far from the wild. In less than ten minutes, the highway leaps off terra firma and sweeps over a fetid marsh filled with alligators, pit vipers, wild hogs and panthers. All through the night they stalk and kill—predators and prey, an eternal dance. Which am I? Sean would say hunter, but he wouldn't be quite right. I've been prey all my life. I carry scars Sean has never seen.

For the past year, when anxiety or depression has become unbearable, I've run to Sean Regan. Tonight I'm running away from him. I'm running because I'm afraid. When he learns that I'm pregnant—and that I intend to keep the baby—he will either honour the promises he's made to me or betray them. And I'm terrified that he won't give up his family for me.

Sean has never hidden his doubts. He worries about my drinking, my depression, my occasional manic states. He worries that I can't be sexually faithful. And based on my history, these are legitimate concerns. But at some point, I believe, you just have to risk everything for the other person, regardless of your fears.

My hands are shaking on the wheel. I need another Valium, but I don't want to risk falling asleep on the interstate. As the landscape changes from wet bottomland to hilly forests of oak and pine, I sense the great river out to my left, rolling southwards as it has for millennia. The Mississippi River links the town of my birth to the city of my adulthood, a great winding artery connecting the two spiritual poles of my existence, infancy and independence. Yet how independent am I? Natchez, the upstream city, is the source of all that I am, whether I like it or not. And tonight, the prodigal daughter is returning home.

Hurtling round curves in the dark forest, I feel a sort of emotional gravity sucking at my bones. I'm not sure why—until the sign reading ANGOLA PENITENTIARY flashes out of the night. Then I know. Just to the south of the razor wire of the penitentiary, only a dozen miles to my left, a great island rises out of the river. Owned by my family since before the Civil War, it hovers like a dark mirage between the genteel cities of New Orleans and Natchez. I haven't set foot on DeSalle Island in more than ten years, but I sense it now the way you sense a dangerous animal stirring from sleep.

I step on the gas and put the place behind me, slipping into a driving trance that carries me the remainder of my journey. I slip out of it only on the high-banked curving drive that leads through a tunnel of oaks to my childhood home.

A high wrought-iron gate blocks the last fifty yards, but it's been unlocked for as long as I can remember. I stop and press a button on the gatepost. The iron bars retract as though pulled by unseen hands.

Why am I here? I ask myself.

You know why, replies a chiding voice. *You have nowhere else to go.*

After dry-swallowing a Valium, I drive slowly through the gate. The bars close behind me with a clang.

CHAPTER 2

I n a vast clearing ahead, moonlight washes over a sight that takes most people's breath away. A French palace rises like a spectre out of the mist, its limestone walls like pale skin, its windows like dark, glassy eyes. The scale of the place is heroic, projecting an impression of limitless wealth and power. In a Mississippi town of 20,000 souls, the mansion has a certain absurdity. Yet Natchez contains more than eighty ante-bellum homes, many of them mansions, and the provenance of this one perfectly suits the town, an anachronism of grand excess, much of it built by slaves.

My family arrived in America in 1820, when a Paris financier's youngest son, Henri Leclerc DeSalle, was sent to the wilds of Louisiana to make his fortune. He worked like a slave himself, surpassing all paternal expectations. By 1840 his cotton fields stretched for ten miles along the Mississippi. In that year he began building a regal mansion on the high bluff across the river, in the sparkling city called Natchez. It would be a perfect copy of Malmaison, the summer palace of Napoleon and Josephine, and was to become the centre of a cotton empire that survived the Civil War.

I pull around the 'big house' and park beside one of the two brick annexes behind it. The eastern slave quarters—a large two-storey edifice—was my home during most of my childhood. Our family's maid, Pearlie, lives in the western quarters, thirty yards across the rose garden. She helped rear my mother and aunt from infancy, then did the same with me. Well over seventy now, Pearlie drives a baby-blue Cadillac, the pride of her life, which sits gleaming in the darkness behind her house. She often stays up late watching television, but it's past midnight now, and her windows are dark.

My mother's car is nowhere in sight. She's probably in Biloxi, visiting her elder sister, who's embroiled in a bitter divorce. My grandfather's Lincoln is gone, too. At seventy-seven, Grandpapa Kirkland still possesses remarkable vitality, but a mild stroke a year ago ended his driving days. Undeterred, he hired a driver and resumed the exhausting pace he'd always kept up. Grandpapa could be anywhere tonight, but my guess is that he's on the island. He's an avid hunter.

When I get out of the Audi, the summer heat wraps round me like a thick jacket, and the whine of crickets and the bellow of frogs from the nearby bayou fill the night. As I glance towards the rear of the house, my eyes lock onto a gnarled dogwood tree at the edge of the rose garden that separates our house from Pearlie's. I can't look at it without remembering the night, twenty-three years ago, when my father perished under that tree, shot dead by an intruder he had confronted there.

I stopped speaking after my father was murdered. Literally. I didn't utter a word for over a year. But in my eight-year-old brain, I ceaselessly pondered what the intruder had come looking for that was worth my father's life. Cash? The family silver? Grandpapa's art or gun collections? All were possible targets, but no money or property was ever discovered missing.

I keep a picture of my father in my wallet. *Luke Ferry, 1969*. A dark, handsome man of medium height, smiling in his army uniform, somewhere in Vietnam. I like his eyes. Compassionate, human. It's how I like to remember him. A little girl's idea of a father.

I turn away from the rose garden and, with paranoia born from years of urban living, unload my dental cases from the back seat. Only when I'm halfway to the door of our slave quarters do I remember that in Natchez I could leave my cases in the unlocked car for a month and return to find them just as I'd left them.

The front door is locked. I have no key. Trudging round to the window of my old bedroom, I set down my cases and slide up the pane. The closed-in smell that wafts through the curtains hurls me back fifteen years. I lift the cases over the sill, then climb through and make my way in the dark to the light switch. It's easy, because my bedroom looks exactly as it did when I graduated high school. The walls are brown, the carpet navy-blue. Posters of rock stars adorn the walls, and photographs and swimming trophies line the shelves opposite my closet. The older photographs show my father standing next to a gangly little girl with long bones. As the girl's body begins to fill in, my father vanishes from the photos and an older man with silver hair, chiselled features and piercing eyes takes his place: my grandfather, Dr William Kirkland, who married into the family half a century ago.

It seems odd that my mother is in so few of the photos. But Mom took little interest in my swimming, an 'unsocial' activity, consuming vast amounts of time that could have been spent in more 'appropriate' pursuits.

Glancing into the closet, I see clothes I wore in high school hanging there and, beneath them, a wicker laundry basket filled with Louisiana Rice Creatures, the local precursors of the Beanie Babies that later became a national craze. There must be thirty of them in the basket, but the only one that really matters to me is missing. Lena the Leopardess. I loved Lena and carried her everywhere I went, including my father's funeral. It was in the visiting room prior to the service that I saw him lying in his coffin. He didn't look like my father any more. He looked older, and very alone. When I pointed this out, my grandfather suggested that Daddy might not feel so lonely if he had Lena for company while he slept. The idea of losing Lena *and* my father frightened me, but I comforted myself with the thought that Daddy would have a little piece of my heart to keep him company.

Standing in this bedroom is creeping me out, as it always does. Why does my mother preserve it this way? She's an interior designer, for God's sake, practically manic in her desire to transform every space over which she's given dominion. Is it a homage to my childhood? To a simpler past, before I 'veered off track'? In my grandfather's eyes, I didn't screw up until I was asked to leave medical school, which precluded my following in his footsteps and becoming a surgeon. But in my mother's eyes, my failure began during adolescence, since when a thousand small choices have taken me along a road that hasn't led within a stone's throw of a husband.

As I stare at a photograph of my father holding my hand high in triumph, a blessed calm comes over me. Because my father died when I was eight, it was he alone that I never disappointed. I like to think that, had he lived, he would be proud of what I've accomplished.

I take my cellphone from my pocket, and a pang of guilt hits me when I see thirteen missed calls. Checking my voicemail, I listen to the first message. In a reassuring voice, Sean tells me to stay calm, that Piazza is his problem not mine, and then he begs me to keep myself together until he gets there. 'There' being my house on the lake. I skip ahead several messages. The change in Sean's voice is astonishing.

'It's me again,' he says angrily. 'I'm still at your house, and I have no idea where you are. Please call me back, even if you don't want to see me. Have you stopped taking your meds? Something's wrong, Cat, I know it. Look . . .' There's a pause. 'Damn it, I love you. But this is why we're not together already, and—' There's a click, then nothing. The phone's memory is full.

I pull back the bedspread, slip off my jeans and lie down, drawing the covers up to my chest. I want to call Sean and tell him I'm all right, but the truth is, I'm not. And there's nothing he can do about that. As the cellphone drops from my hand, I feel the Valium course through my veins. 'Thank you,' I whisper, as sleep enfolds me and I swim down into the blue cathedral of the deep. My sanctuary from the world and from myself.

SUDDENLY, blue-white lightning is flashing above me, and a strange sound registers in my mind. Like the *snick* of a camera shutter. I smell acetone, too. Surfacing, blinking in confusion, I call out, 'Sean? Sean, is that you?'

A dark brown forehead and saucer eyes rise above the footboard of my bed. A nose and mouth follow, the mouth agape in wonder. I'm looking into the face of a black girl of about eight.

'Who are you?' I ask, half wondering if the girl is real.

'Natriece,' she says, her voice defiant. 'Natriece Washington.'

I glance around the room, but all that registers is the sunlight pouring through a crack in the curtains. 'What are you doing here?'

'I be here visiting my nanna. I didn't mean to make no mess.'

'Your nanna?' The smell of acetone is stronger now.

'Miss Pearlie.'

Suddenly it all comes rushing back. The phone call from Sean. The corpse in the house on Prytania Street. The zoned-out night drive to Natchez. 'What time is it?' I ask.

The child gives an exaggerated shrug. 'I don't know. Morning time.'

Pushing down the covers, I crawl to the foot of the bed. The contents of my forensic dental case are spread across the floor in disarray. Natriece is holding my camera; its flash must have caused the 'lightning' that woke me. Among the instruments on the floor lies a spray bottle of luminol, a toxic chemical used to detect latent bloodstains.

'Did you spray any of that, Natriece?'

She solemnly shakes her head.

I gently take the camera from her grasp. 'It's all right if you did. I just need to know.'

'I might've sprayed a little bit.'

I get out of bed and pull on my jeans. 'It's OK, but you need to leave the room while I clean it up. That's a dangerous chemical in that bottle.'

I walk to the door. Natriece lingers behind, staring into the dark room.

'What's that?' she asks. 'Did I do that?'

I look over the girl's head. On the floor, near the foot of my bed, a greenish-blue glow hovers. The luminol has reacted with something on the carpet.

'Freaky,' she says. 'That looks like *Ghostbusters* or something.'

Stepping round Natriece, I look down at the luminescence on the floor, and a numbness spreads through my body. I'm looking at a footprint.

I felt the same numbness twenty-three years ago, when my grandfather knelt before me, and said, 'Baby, your daddy's dead.'

'Natriece, stay back.'

'Yessum.'

Actually, it isn't a footprint but a boot print. And now another ghostlike image has taken shape beside it. The image of a bare foot. A child's foot.

With slow insistence, a percussive hiss intrudes into my concentration. Subtly at first, but growing steadily to a soft roar. It's the sound of rain drumming on a tin roof. Which makes no sense, because the slave quarters has a shingle roof—not tin—and I'm standing on the lower of two floors. But I've heard this sound before, and I know it for what it is. An auditory hallucination. I heard the same metallic patter a week ago, at the Nolan murder scene. Just before my panic attack. I was staring down at the retired accountant's naked corpse and—

A rapid beat of footsteps startles me. Natriece has bolted down the hall. Her scream cuts the air in the bedroom. *'Nanna! Nanna! Nanna!'*

Checking my watch, I wait for the glowing footprints to fade. False positives generally fade quickly, while the luminescence caused by the haemoglobin in blood lingers like an accusation.

Thirty seconds pass. The glow shows no sign of diminishing.

'Come on,' I whisper. 'Fade.'

My hands are trembling. I want to run for Pearlie, too. Could I be looking at the imprint of my own foot? Bloodstains can endure for decades on some surfaces.

'*Fade*,' I plead. But my plea does no good.

As I stare down at the two glowing footprints, half of me wants to run, the other half to lock the door. I want photographs of the prints, but to get them I'll have to act quickly. Once the chemical reaction that causes the blood hidden in the carpet to luminesce is complete, it can't be repeated.

I cross the bedroom and lock the door. Then I open my camera case, bring out my SLR, and fit a standard 35mm lens and cable release to it.

As I set up the tripod almost directly above the footprints, someone raps sharply on my bedroom door.

'Catherine Ferry?' calls a throaty voice as familiar to me as my mother's. 'You in there, girl?'

'I'm here, Pearlie. I'll be out in a few minutes, OK?'

'What you doing home?' Pearlie demands. 'Why didn't you call ahead? And why you in there? Did Natriece mess up something?'

'It's all right!' I snap. 'Just give me a minute.'

I hear the muted chatter of Pearlie interrogating the little girl.

As the glow begins to increase in intensity, I open the camera shutter with the cable release and look at my watch. To capture the faint glow of luminol, I need a sixty-second exposure. My hands are shaking with fear, but the cable release will keep the camera from vibrating.

When my watch hits the sixty-second mark, I close the shutter.

'*Catherine DeSalle Ferry! You open this door!*'

'I'm coming!' I call, going to the door.

As soon as I turn the knob, Pearlie pushes open the door and stands with her hands on her hips. She is tall, thin, with chocolate-brown skin and clear traces of Caucasian ancestry in her facial features. Her eyes flash still with intelligence and wit, and her bark—though intimidating to strangers—is considerably worse than her bite. Around my grandfather and my mother, Pearlie displays the quiet dignity of a servant, but she treats me like a daughter. She still wears a starched white uniform, and a shiny, reddish-brown wig to cover her grizzled white hair.

I've missed her more than I realised. And I see a mixture of pique and excitement in her eyes, as though she doesn't know whether to hug me or spank me. Were it not for Natriece's fear and the odd scene in the bedroom, Pearlie would undoubtedly crush me to her chest.

'Answer me this minute!' she demands. 'You ain't been home since your grandmother's funeral, and that's been a year now.'

'Fifteen months,' I correct, fighting a new wave of emotion that I can't afford to face right now. Last June, my grandmother drowned on DeSalle Island. Part of the sandbar she was standing on simply slid into the river. There was no warning. Four people saw it happen, yet no one could save her. Catherine Poitiers Kirkland was an excellent swimmer in her youth—she taught me to swim—but at seventy-five she'd been no match for the mighty Mississippi.

'Lord, Lord.' Pearlie sighs. 'Why didn't you call to say you was coming? I would have cooked for you.'

'It was an impulse,' I say.

'Ain't it always with you?' She gives me a knowing look, then pushes past me. 'What's going on in here? Natriece told me they's a ghost in here.'

I see the little girl standing just outside the door. 'There is, in a way. Go look at the carpet by the foot of the bed.'

Pearlie bends at the waist and examines the floor with the eagle eye of a woman who has spent decades eradicating the slightest specks of dirt from 'her' house. 'What's making that rug look like that?'

'Blood. Old bloodstains hidden in the carpet fibres. It's reacting with a chemical that Natriece sprayed on it by accident.'

'I don't see no blood. That the only thing makes that stuff glow?'

'No,' I concede. 'But I've seen lots of stains like this. Blood has a particular kind of glow with luminol. I'm ninety-five per cent sure it's blood.'

'Well, I don't hardly see nothing now.'

'It fades pretty quickly. That's why I took pictures of it.'

'Could be deer blood,' Pearlie suggests. 'Or armadillo. Dr Kirkland shoots them all the time. They always digging up the yard, nasty things.'

'There are tests that will tell me whether the blood's human. You know, it would take a lot of blood to make prints this well defined. There's a boot print, and also the print of a child's bare foot.'

Pearlie stares down with mute scepticism.

'Have there been any children around here since I left?' I ask. I'm an only child, and my aunt Ann, despite three marriages, has no children. 'Has Natriece been here much?'

Pearlie shakes her head. 'My kids live in Chicago and Los Angeles, you know that. And Natriece only been to this house two times before this.' She turns and glares at Natriece. 'You ever been in this room before, child?'

'No, ma'am.'

'Answer me straight, now.'

'I'm telling you true!'

As Natriece pooches out her lower lip, I glance down at the fading image of the bare foot. Pearlie's right: it's nearly vanished.

'Where's Mom, Pearlie?' I ask.

'Where you think? Gone to Biloxi again to see Aunt Ann. That sister of hers draws trouble like my Sheba draws tomcats. She'll be back later.'

'What about Grandpapa?'

'Dr Kirkland gone to Washington, DC. Supposed to get back later today.'

I want to ask more questions, but Natriece doesn't need to hear them. I cut my eyes towards the child. Pearlie gets the message.

'Run outside and play for a few minutes, Treecy.'

Natriece pooches out her lip again. 'You told me I could have a snow cone if I was good.'

I laugh. 'She promised me the same thing lots of times.'

'Did you get it?' Natriece asks with severity.

'If I was good, I did.'

'Which wasn't too often,' Pearlie snaps, taking a step towards Natriece.

'If you don't go play right this minute, you ain't getting *no* kind of cone. You'll be eating Brussels sprouts for supper.'

Natriece makes a face, then darts past Pearlie, just out of reach of the old woman's spanking hand. I close the door.

'Pearlie, I want to talk to you about the night Daddy died.'

I detect a deepening in her dark eyes. 'You done asked me about that a thousand times, baby,' she says. 'I told you what I saw that night.'

'When I was a child. But I'm asking you again. Tell me what you saw.'

'All right,' she says wearily. 'Maybe it'll finally settle you down.'

Pearlie sits on the edge of my old bed, her eyes clouding with remembrance. 'The truth is, I didn't see much. I was in the big house tending to your grandmother. She was having pains that turned out to be her gall bladder. Anyway, I heard a gunshot. About ten thirty, I guess. Your grandmother told me to call the police.'

'How long did it take them to get here?'

'Ten minutes. Maybe a little longer.'

'And you only went down to the garden after the police got here?'

She nods slowly. 'But I phoned down here to make sure you and your mama was OK. Dr Kirkland answered. He told me everything *wasn't* OK, but that I should stay with Mrs Kirkland. I panicked and made him tell me you was all right. That's when I figured out something had happened to Mr Luke. He was supposed to have left for the island about nine, but I just had a feeling. I ran out to the back gallery and looked down. When I saw Mr Luke lying under that tree, it broke my heart.'

I close my eyes. Blue police lights flash behind them, illuminating the great U created by the rear of Malmaison and the two slave quarters, painting the rain with a sapphire glow. Tall men wearing uniforms and caps stand talking to my grandfather amid the roses. I open my eyes before the memory can go any further.

'This is what I remember being told,' I murmur. 'Daddy and Grandpapa both heard someone prowling the grounds. Daddy was in here, Grandpapa in the main house. They met outside, talked a few seconds, then started checking the grounds separately. Both had guns, but Daddy was surprised by the prowler. They fought, and Daddy was shot with his own rifle.'

Pearlie nods sadly. 'That's what Dr Kirkland told me.'

'Is that what he told the police?'

'Course it is, child. Why you ask me that?'

Without realising it, I've already formulated an answer to her question.

'Because I think that footprint on the carpet is mine. And I think I put it there on that night.'

Pearlie shakes her head. 'That's nonsense, child. You ain't never got over losing your daddy, that's all. You been trying to make sense of it for twenty years, but there *ain't* no sense to things like that. Not unless you God hisself. Then you understand everything. But there ain't no sense for you and me.'

I ignore Pearlie's simplistic philosophy, however accurate it might be. 'Talking to Mom about that night was like pulling teeth. When she did talk, she told me conflicting stories. She heard the shot, she didn't hear it. She saw one thing, then she didn't see it. Why was that?'

Pearlie gives me a rare unguarded look. 'Your mama didn't see anything that night, baby. She was taking your father's sleeping pills back then. Or his pain pills. Whatever he took for his war wound and his nerves.'

'You're saying that was a habit?'

'Your mama swallowed most everything Mr Luke got from the doctor back then. She had nerve problems herself. Your daddy went to Dr Tom Cage back then, and I think Dr Cage prescribed enough for the both of them. Your mama wouldn't hardly go see a doctor.'

'So Mama was unconscious when Daddy was shot. And it was only when you came down to the garden that you saw me walk up to the body?'

'That's right.'

I close my eyes and try to recall something fresh from that night, but the impassable gate that guards that information from my conscious mind remains locked. 'Pearlie, who do you think that prowler was?'

Her dark eyes settle on mine. 'I think he was a friend of your daddy's.'

Pearlie's theory has my heart thumping. 'Why do you say that?'

'I think it would have had to be,' she says firmly. 'To get close enough to shoot your daddy with his own gun like that? Couldn't nobody slip up on Mr Luke without him knowing. No way, no how. I never seen a man so alert. I guess the war made him that way.'

'A friend,' I murmur. 'I don't remember Daddy having friends.'

Pearlie smiles with regret. 'They wasn't friends, really. Just boys like he was. Boys who'd been in Vietnam. A lot of them come back hooked on dope. Black and white the same. Anyway, them friends would've known your daddy had pills around. Plus, they probably figured Dr Kirkland kept drugs here. Not hard to figure the rest, is it?' Pearlie takes my hand. 'Baby girl, it don't do no good to dig up the past. Even simple folk know that. And you ain't simple.'

'I wish I were sometimes.'

Pearlie clucks softly. 'We can't change our natures. We come into the world with them, and they stay with us all the way through.'

I don't agree, but neither do I argue. Pearlie Washington has lived a lot longer than I have. We walk out into the sunlight of the rose garden.

'I have one more question,' I tell her. 'And I want you to tell me the truth.'

'I'll try, baby.'

'Do you think Daddy might have killed himself?'

She draws back. 'What you talking 'bout, girl?'

'I'm asking you if there was really a prowler that night, or whether everybody's been lying to me all these years to protect my feelings. Whether what Daddy went through was just too much for him. So bad that . . . even Mom and me weren't enough to keep him wanting to live.'

Pearlie lifts her fingers to my cheek and wipes away tears. 'Oh, baby, don't you ever think that. Mr Luke thought the sun rose and set in your eyes.'

I try to blink away my tears. 'Did he? I don't remember.'

She smiles. 'I know you don't. He got took from you too early. But Mr Luke loved you more than you'll ever know. So you get that foolishness right out of your mind. All right?'

'Yes, ma'am.' I'm surprised by the childlike sound of my own voice.

'I better find Natriece,' Pearlie says, squaring her shoulders and looking towards Malmaison. 'You holler if you need me.'

As Pearlie walks towards the rear of Malmaison, my cellphone starts ringing. It's Sean. 'Hey, I'm sorry about the missed calls,' I say.

'It's OK. I wouldn't have kept bugging you if it weren't important. But we've connected two of the NOMURS victims, Andrus Riviere and Arthur LeGendre. This morning we learned that Riviere's daughter and LeGendre's niece go to the same psychiatrist.'

My heart stutters. 'What's the shrink's name?'

'Nathan Malik.'

I run the name through my memory. 'Never heard of him.'

'I'm surprised. He's pretty well known, and fairly controversial. He's written a couple of books on repressed memories.'

'That's usually related to sexual abuse.'

'I know. Are you thinking what I am?'

'Revenge killings. Our victims are child abusers being killed to avenge their victims. From that angle, the sex and advanced age of the murder victims suddenly makes all the sense in the world.'

'That's what I thought,' says Sean. 'We're checking every relative of every victim for visits to Nathan Malik or any other therapist. It's not easy, though. The two women we've linked to Malik were hiding the fact they were seeing him. The only reason we figured it out is because they're both obsessive about keeping money records. Now, the FBI psychiatrist says there's a strong possibility that Dr Malik could be doing the murders himself. He says there's something called countertransference, where a shrink vicariously experiences the pain of his patients, and that could trigger Malik to commit revenge murder just as if he'd been abused himself.'

'Has anyone talked to Dr Malik yet?'

'No, but he's under surveillance. We want you to check his dental records. See if they match the bite marks on the bodies.'

'You already have them?'

'No. But we've got the name of Malik's dentist. And since you know damn near every dentist in the New Orleans area, we were hoping you could have an informal chat with this one. Maybe get a look at some faxed dental records. Just enough to tell if Malik is the killer or not.'

A red flag goes up in my mind. 'An "informal" chat? Are you out of your mind? There's no way a dentist is going to let me see his records without a court order. Not with all the new patient confidentiality regulations. If I break the law and that's brought out at trial, it could put the case in jeopardy.'

'OK, OK. But look . . . at least tell me if you know the dentist. His name is Shubb. Harold Shubb.'

I feel a quick rush of excitement. Harold Shubb once came to one of my seminars in forensic odontology, and he would love a call from me.

'I know him.'

'Is he an OK guy?'

'Yes. Get a court order, and Shubb will do you right.'

Sean sighs heavily. 'OK. But at least let me fax you what I have on Malik. You want to see that, right?'

'Send me what you've got. I'm at Malmaison at the moment.' I give him the number of my grandfather's fax machine.

There's a pause. Then he says, 'Are you coming back tonight?'

I actually hear loneliness in his voice. 'No.'

'Why not? You hardly ever go home, and when you do you don't like it.'

'Something's happened up here. I can't explain now. I have to go. If I notice anything interesting in the stuff you fax me, I'll call. Otherwise, it'll be tomorrow at least before you hear from me.'

Sean is silent. Then, after a few moments, he says, 'Goodbye, Cat.'

I hang up and suddenly, from the roiling mass of my thoughts, a clear image rises. I know where I need to go.

Breaking into a trot, I head into the trees on the east side of the vast lawn, and as I jog through them, I spy a dark figure standing in the shadows about forty yards ahead. A black man in work clothes. I bear left so that I won't pass him too closely, but as I near the figure I recognise Mose, the yardman who has worked at Malmaison since before I was born. Once a strapping giant who could carry railroad ties on his back, Mose now has a bent spine and white stubble. He lives alone in a small house at the back of the property, but once a week he commands an army of younger men, who groom the grounds like a crack army platoon. I wave as I pass to his left, then quicken my pace, towards a place I haven't visited in far too long.

CHAPTER 3

Brookwood is a residential area on the eastern border of Malmaison's grounds. I came here countless times during my youth, and always for the same reason. One of the homes belonged to the Hemmeters, an elderly couple who owned a swimming pool.

I came because my high school, St Stephens, had no swimming pool, and my grandfather, despite his enormous wealth and my fanatical dedication to swimming, refused to desecrate 'his' grounds by building me a practice pool. So I did my daily laps at the Hemmeters' place. The old couple became my biggest fans at local meets. Mr Hemmeter died a couple of years ago, but his widow kept the house.

Something about the place looks different as I approach, but at least the pool is being kept up. I jog round the house and check the garage. Empty.

Returning to the pool, I strip off my jeans and blouse and dive cleanly into the deep end. The dive carries me halfway to the far wall. I breaststroke to the shallows, then get out and search the flowerbed until I find a flat, heavy rock about the size of a serving platter. This I carry down the steps into the shallow end. After a period of pre-immersion meditation, during which my heart slows to around sixty beats per minute, I lie down on my back beneath the water and set the rock on my chest.

Free divers train by lying on the bottom of a swimming pool with a weight belt for over six minutes, a feat that would kill most people. Now, after three minutes, my chest spasms in its first 'physical scream' for oxygen. Free divers train themselves to ignore this reflex; after enduring a number of these spasms, humans can move into a more primitive mammalian state, one the body dimly remembers from its genetic heritage as an aquatic animal. Once in the dive state, my heartbeat decreases to fifteen beats per minute, my blood circulation alters to serve only my core organs, and blood plasma slowly fills my lungs to resist the increasing pressure of deep water.

I can feel the steady descent to a state of relaxation I find nowhere else in my life. Not in sleep, where nightmares trouble me. Not in the hunt for predators, where the triumph of trapping my quarry brings only transitory peace. Somehow, when I am submerged in water, the chaos that is my mind discharges itself. And now, with the pool water gently swaying my body, the crazed events of the past week begin to come clear.

Being pregnant doesn't seem as frightening down here. The child's conception is no mystery, after all. A simple combination of carelessness and lust. Sean's kids had gone to summer camp, his wife was visiting her mother in Florida . . . he stayed over at my house. I was taking an antibiotic that interfered with my birth-control pills, and that was that.

The mystery is why I haven't yet told Sean. I love him. He loves me. Up to now, we've shared every thought and feeling. My fear is that Sean will think I got pregnant on purpose. That I trapped him. And even if he believes the truth, will he leave his family to be with me?

As the level of oxygen in my tissues continues to fall, deeper questions bubble up from my subconscious. What's the significance of rain on a tin roof? Why am I hearing that? The only tin roof at Malmaison is on the barn my father used as a studio, and nothing about the barn elicits panic. And my nightmares? For years my sleep has been haunted by terrifying scenes of dark figures trying to kill me. I also have recurring dreams, as though my subconscious is trying to send me a message. Yet none of the therapists I have consulted has been able to decode the imagery.

The glowing footprint from my bedroom fills my darkening mind. If my eight-year-old foot left that track, whose blood was on it? My father's? I remember almost nothing from the night he died, nothing before I saw his body lying on the ground. Why? Where was I? Asleep? Or did I witness something? Something too terrible to recall? For the first time in my life, I have a witness to that night's events that cannot conceal or distort events: blood.

'Mayday!' cries a voice in my head. That voice is the product of five years of dive training. It tells me when I'm nearing crisis point. The level of oxygen in my tissues has fallen to a level at which most people would be unconscious.

My body tenses. Opening my eyes, I see a dark figure hovering above the water. Slowly, a golden spear separates from the figure and descends towards the surface, directly above me. I shove the rock off my chest and burst up into air and light, sputtering in terror. A tall man stands at the side of the pool, a ten-foot-long net in his hands. He looks more frightened than I am.

'I thought you'd drowned!' he cries. Then he blushes and turns away.

I cross my arms over my breasts, only now remembering that I went into the pool in my underwear. 'Where's Mrs Hemmeter?'

'Magnolia House. The assisted-living home. She sold the house to me. Do you want to put on some clothes?'

I kneel so that the water covers me to my neck. 'I'm decent now.'

The man turns round. He has sandy brown hair and blue eyes, and he's wearing khakis and a blue button-down Oxford shirt. He looks to be in his early thirties, and something about him is familiar.

'Do I know you?' I ask, studying his face.

He smiles. 'Do you? I'm Michael Wells.'

'Oh my God! Michael? I didn't—'

'Didn't recognise me, I know. I've lost eighty pounds in the last two years.'

I survey him from head to toe. 'My God, you look . . . well, *hot*.'

Michael's blush returns, redder than before. 'Thanks, Cat.'

He was three years ahead of me at St Stephen's, then at the University Medical Center in Jackson. 'Did you stick with paediatrics?' I ask.

He nods. 'I was practising in North Carolina, but then St Catherine's Hospital came up and recruited me.'

'Well, I'm glad you came back. You own this house now?'

'Yep.'

'I used to swim here all the time.'

He smiles. 'Mrs Hemmeter told me.'

'Did she? Well, do you like it? The house, I mean.'

'I do. It's no Malmaison, of course.'

'Be glad it's not. You don't want the upkeep on that place.'

'I can imagine. Did you ever live anywhere else in Natchez?'

'No. My dad came back from Vietnam with post-traumatic stress disorder. He couldn't hold a job, so my mom and he moved into one of the slave quarters. I was born four years later and we never left after that.'

'What did your father do before the war?'

'He was a welder.'

'Is that where his sculpting came from?'

'Yes.' I'm surprised Michael remembers that. After two years of wandering the woods and watching television, my dad fired up his welding equipment and began sculpting metal. In time, his work became quite popular.

'Is that a rock down there?' Michael asks, pointing into the water.

'Yes. Your rock. I used it to keep me submerged. I'm a free diver. That means I dive deep in the ocean using only the air in my lungs.'

Michael looks intrigued. 'How deep?'

'I've been to three hundred and fifty feet. It's pretty intense. As solitary as you can be on this planet, I think.'

He squats beside the pool, his eyes filled with curiosity. 'Do you like that? Solitude, I mean?'

'Sometimes. Other times I can't stand to be alone. Literally.'

'I learned to fly five years ago. I've got a little Cessna 210 out at the airport. That's where I get my solitude.'

'Well, there you go. Flying scares me to death, especially in small planes.' I look towards the trees that conceal Malmaison. 'You know I didn't finish med school, right?' I say cautiously.

'I heard.'

'What did you hear?'

He replies in a neutral tone, careful to keep any judgment out of his voice. 'Depression. Nervous breakdown. Oh, and something about an affair with a professor. He flipped out over you and lost his job, you got booted, something like that. I don't care much about gossip. Everybody's got a past.'

I smile. 'Do you?'

'Sure.' He chuckles softly. 'Maybe not as colourful as yours.'

We both laugh.

'I had a terrible crush on you in high school,' he says. 'I have to tell you that. I didn't have the nerve to back then.'

'And now I'm standing in your swimming pool in my underwear.'

'Yes, and you haven't changed at all,' Michael says.

'Now I know you're lying. You should have told me about the crush.'

He shakes his head. 'Nah. You only dated jocks or bad boys. And I was the chubby geek. You know that.'

I don't insult him by arguing. 'You seem to have reinvented yourself.'

He nods, his eyes reflective. 'Sometimes you have to.'

'You're married, of course.'

'Nope. One girlfriend all through med school, but we ended up splitting.'

'You must be the most eligible bachelor in Natchez.'

Michael expels a lungful of air with obvious frustration. 'The local divorcées certainly treat me that way. It's a new reality for me.'

My cellphone rings in my jeans pocket on the side of the pool. I slide over to it on my knees and check the screen. My mother is calling.

'Mom?'

'I've just got home, Cat, and Pearlie tells me you arrived from New Orleans last night. Where are you now?'

'Swimming at the Hemmeters' house. I just met Dr Wells.'

'Did you? Well, get home and tell me what's going on.'

I hang up and look at Michael. 'I need to get out.'

He grabs a towel from his back porch, hands it to me, then turns away. Walking quickly up the pool steps, I strip off my underwear, dry myself, then put on my outer clothes and wring out my underwear to carry home.

'All covered up again.'

Michael turns round. 'Please feel free to use the pool any time.'

'Thanks. I won't be in town long, though.'

'That's too bad. Do you . . .? Do you have someone in New Orleans?'

I start to lie, then decide honesty is best. 'I really don't know.'

He seems to mull this over, then nods with apparent contentment.

I turn to go, but something makes me turn back to him. 'Michael, do you ever have patients who just stop speaking?'

'Stop speaking altogether? Sure. But all my patients are kids.'

'That's why I asked. What causes a child to stop speaking?'

He bites his bottom lip. 'Sometimes they've been embarrassed by a parent. Other times it's anger. We call it voluntary mutism.'

'What about shock?'

'Shock? Sure. And trauma. That's not voluntary, strictly speaking.'

'After my father was shot, I stopped speaking for a year.'

He studies me in silence for several moments. There's a deep compassion in his eyes. 'Did you see anyone about it at the time?'

'No. My grandfather was a doctor, you know? He told Mom the problem would be self-limiting. Look, I need to run. I hope I see you again sometime.'

'I do, too.'

I walk backwards for a few steps, give Michael a last smile, then turn and sprint off through the woods.

MY MOTHER is waiting in the kitchen of the slave quarters, sitting at the breakfast table. She's dressed impeccably in a tailored trouser suit, but she has dark bags under her eyes, and she looks older than when I last saw her—a brief lunch in New Orleans four months ago. Still, Gwen Ferry looks closer to forty than fifty-two, her true age. Her elder sister, Ann, once had the same gift, but by fifty Ann's troubled life had stolen the lingering bloom of youth. At one time the two sisters were Natchez royalty, the beautiful teenage daughters of one of the richest men in town. Now only my mother carries what's left of that banner, occupying the social pinnacle of the town: president of the Garden Club.

My mother stands and gives me a hug, then says, 'What in the world is going on? I've always asked you to come home more often, and now you show up without even a phone call.'

'Glad to see you, too, Mom.'

Her face wrinkles in displeasure. 'Pearlie says you found bloody tracks in your bedroom.' She looks perplexed. 'But I went in there and didn't find a thing on the floor. Just a bad smell.'

The coffeemaker bubbles on the counter, and the aroma of coffee hits me.

'I'd appreciate you not going in there any more. Not until I'm finished testing the rest of the bedroom.'

Mom interlocks her fingers on the table, as though trying to keep from fidgeting. 'What are you talking about, Catherine?'

'I'm talking about the night Daddy died. I think those footprints were made that night.'

Two splotches of red appear high on her cheeks. 'That's just crazy.'

'Is it, Mom? How do you know? Weren't you knocked out from taking Daddy's pills?'

Her cheeks go pale. 'Who told you that? You've been talking to Pearlie, haven't you? I can't believe she'd say something so hurtful.'

'Does it matter who I've been talking to? We have to tell the truth around here sometime.'

Mom straightens up. 'You need to take some of your own advice, missy. There's no doubt about who's told the most lies in this house.'

I take a deep breath and slowly let it out. 'We got off on the wrong foot, Mom. How's Aunt Ann doing?'

'She's married another bastard. Third in a row. This one's hitting her.'

'Did she tell you that?'

'I have eyes. God, I don't want to talk about it. I need sleep.'

'Maybe you'd better skip that coffee, then.'

'If I don't drink this, I'll get a caffeine headache.' She takes a sip and makes a face. 'You ought to know about addictions.'

I fight the urge to snap back. 'I've got a fax waiting in Grandpapa's office,' I tell her. 'I'll see you in a few minutes.' I start to leave, then stop at the kitchen door and turn back. 'Mom, do you have anything personal left of Dad's? Like an old hairbrush.'

'What on earth for?' Her eyes widen. 'You want it for a DNA sample.'

'Yes. To compare to the blood on the floor of the bedroom.'

'I don't have anything like that.' She sighs wearily and takes another sip of coffee. 'For God's sake, Catherine, this is best forgotten.'

I leave and make my way across the garden to the rear of Malmaison's left wing. Entering the mansion, I walk past priceless antiques to the library, which functions as my grandfather's study. Patterned after Napoleon's library, it's a world of dark wooden columns and rich upholstery, with French windows that open onto the front gallery. On a long cypress table beside my grandfather's roll-top desk stand a computer, printer, copier and fax machine. The fax tray is empty. I take out my cellphone and speed-dial Sean.

'I'm standing by the fax machine,' I tell him. 'Nothing's come yet.'

'I'm sending it through now. There's a decent amount of public information on Malik, but it's mostly scholarly stuff. When you get right down to it, it's hard to get a feel for what makes this guy tick.'

'OK. I'll get back to you if I notice anything interesting.'

'Hey,' Sean says. 'Get back to me anyway. I miss you.'

I close my eyes as a wave of heat runs up my neck. 'OK.'

I hang up, then sit at my grandfather's desk and wait for the fax to come through. When I get tired of waiting, I pick up the phone, dial information and get the number of Dr Harold Shubb in New Orleans. What harm can it do just to talk to him? Before second thoughts can stop me, I let the number connect, then identify myself as a fellow dentist to Dr Shubb's receptionist.

'Just one moment, Doctor,' says the woman.

After a brief pause, a man who sounds excited to be taken away from his operatory chair comes on the line. 'Cat Ferry! What can I do for you?'

'Have you been following the recent murders in town?'

'Sure, yeah, of course.'

'Well, there's a bite mark angle to the case. The police are keeping it from the public. What I'm about to tell you, you can't mention to a soul.'

'Goes without saying, Cat.'

'We—that is, the task force working the case—we have a suspect. He's one of your patients, Harold.'

Stunned silence on Dr Shubb's end of the line. 'Are you kidding?' I hear his breathing, shallow and irregular. 'May I ask who it is?'

'Not yet. This is an informal call, Harold. The FBI is going to contact you today—officially—to get a look at any X-rays you have on this patient. The NOPD, however, wants you and me to have an informal conversation before that. Any specific discussion we have about X-rays or teeth could wreck the chance of a conviction, so what I was thinking was that we could have a general chat about this patient, but without getting into his mouth. Would you have a problem with that?'

'Fire away. I won't tell a soul.'

I pray this is true. 'The suspect's name is Nathan Malik. He's—'

'A shrink,' Shubb finishes. 'Holy *shit*. I've seen Malik quite a bit. Done two root canals on him so far this year. I just . . .' Harold Shubb falls silent. Then he whistles long and low, as if only now realising the implications.

I fight the urge to describe the bite marks, knowing that in less than a minute we could probably confirm or eliminate Nathan Malik as the killer. In a case this sensitive, procedure must be followed to the letter.

'What kind of guy is he, Harold?'

'An odd duck. Smart as hell. A little intimidating, if you want to know the truth. Knows something about everything. Even teeth.'

'Really?' It's rare for MDs to know much about dentition.

'I know you're going to think your call influenced me to say this, but the guy makes me a little uncomfortable. Not much for small talk. What he really gives off is intensity. You know the type?'

'I think so. Harold, do you know anything about Malik's modes of therapy? What he specialises in?'

'Repressed memories. We've had several conversations about it. He's an expert at helping people recover lost memories. Controversial stuff.'

'That's what I thought.'

'I'll tell you this. If Nathan Malik is your guy, I hope you have some rock-solid evidence on him. He won't be intimidated by the FBI or anyone else, and he'll go to jail before he'll tell you a damn thing. He's a fanatic about patient privacy.'

I jump as the fax machine beside me hums to life. 'That rock-solid evidence may be sitting in your X-ray files right now, Harold.'

He whistles again. 'I hope so, Cat. I mean—'

'*If* it's him.'

'Exactly.'

'Look, the FBI doesn't need to know about this conversation.'

'What conversation?'

'Thanks, Harold. See you at my next seminar.'

I ring off and watch a typed summary of information on Dr Nathan Malik spool out of the fax machine. As the second sheet emerges, I glance down, then grip the table to stay on my feet.

At the bottom of the page is a black and white photo of a bullet-headed, bald man with deep-set black eyes that silently order me back a step. What takes my breath away is that I first saw those eyes—this face—nearly a decade ago, at the University Medical Center in Jackson, Mississippi.

Grabbing the first page from the fax tray, I scan the psychiatrist's CV. Born 1951. Two years in the army, a tour of duty as a medical corpsman in Vietnam. Graduated Tulane Medical School in 1979. Several years of private practice followed, after which Nathan Malik took a position on the psychiatric faculty at the University of Mississippi Medical Center.

I feel my heart pounding. Malik *was* at UMC during the two years I was there. But something is wrong. I didn't know the man in this picture as Nathan Malik, but as Dr Jonathan Gentry. Higher up the page, I find what I'm looking for. Nathan Malik was born Jonathan Gentry and legally changed his name in 1994, one year after I was asked to leave medical school. I pick up my cellphone and speed-dial Sean.

'You got something?' Sean says without preamble.

'Sean, I know him! *Knew* him, I mean.'

'*What?*'

'Only his name wasn't Malik then. It was Gentry. He was on the faculty at UMC in Jackson when I was there. He had hair then, but it's the same guy. I couldn't forget those eyes. He knew that professor I had the affair with. He actually hit on me a few times. I mean—'

'OK, OK. You need to get here—'

'I know. I'll leave as soon as I can. I should be there in three hours.'

'Bye, babe. Hang tough. We'll get this straight.'

I put down the phone and gather the sheets from the fax tray. As I turn towards the study door, it suddenly opens, and towering in the doorway is my grandfather, Dr William Kirkland.

His pale blue eyes survey me from head to toe. 'Hello, Catherine,' he says, his voice deep and precisely measured. 'What are you doing in here?'

'I needed your fax machine, Grandpapa. I was just about to head back to New Orleans.'

He steps into the room and closes the door. 'I'm sure you don't want to leave before we've had a chance to talk.'

'It's pretty urgent. A murder case.'

He smiles knowingly. 'If it was that urgent, you wouldn't be in Natchez in the first place, would you?' He walks to the sideboard. 'What are you drinking, Catherine?' He pours himself a Scotch.

'Nothing.'

He raises a curious eyebrow.

'I really have to go.'

Grandpapa removes his white linen jacket, revealing a tailored dress shirt with rolled-up sleeves. Even at his advanced age, he has the corded forearms of a man who's worked all his life with his hands. 'Your mother told me you found some blood in your bedroom.'

'That's right. I found it by accident, but it's definitely blood.'

'You're assuming it's human?'

'Why do you say that? I never assume anything.'

'I say that because you look agitated.'

'It's not the blood. It's the murder case in New Orleans.'

'Are you being completely truthful about that? I just spoke to your mother. I know how much the loss of your father hurt you, how it's haunted you. Please sit down, Catherine. We should talk about your concerns.'

I look down at the pages in my hands. The hypnotic eyes of Nathan Malik are prodding me to leave for New Orleans, but then an image of glowing footprints comes into my mind—one tiny and bare, the other made by a boot.

I take a deep breath and force myself to sit.

My grandfather hangs his jacket on a rack in the corner and sits in a leather club chair. He's an imposing figure, and he knows it. William Kirkland looks the way people want their surgeons to look: confident, commanding, untroubled by doubt. Born into the Baptist farmland of east Texas, he survived a car crash that killed his parents while they were travelling to his baptism. Taken in by his widowed grandfather, he scored so highly in school that he attracted the attention of his principal. After receiving a full athletic scholarship to Texas A&M, he lied about his age and enlisted in the marines at seventeen. Twelve weeks later, Private Kirkland was on his way to the Pacific islands, where he won a Silver Star and two Purple Hearts as he fought his bloody way towards Japan. He used the GI

Bill to graduate from A&M, where he won a scholarship to Tulane Medical School in New Orleans. There, he met my grandmother.

A Presbyterian and a pauper, my grandfather was initially regarded with suspicion by the Catholic patriarch of the DeSalle family. But by sheer force of personality, he won over his future father-in-law and married Catherine Poitiers DeSalle without changing his religion. They had two daughters before he finished his medical training, yet still he managed to win top honours. In 1956 he moved his young family to his wife's home town—Natchez—and joined a local medical practice.

Then his wife's father died. As there was no male heir to take over the DeSalle family's extensive farming and business interests, my grandfather began to oversee those operations. He showed the same aptitude for business that he had for everything else, and before long he'd enlarged the family holdings by 30 per cent. Surgery soon became almost a hobby, and he began to move in more rarefied business circles. Now he runs the DeSalle empire— his family included—like a feudal lord. Without sons or grandsons to carry on his legacy, his frustrated dynastic ambitions have devolved onto me.

'Where have you been?' I ask.

'Washington,' he replies. 'Department of the Interior. Let me show you something, Catherine.'

He stands and goes to a large gun safe built into the wall, which he unlocks with precise twirls of the combination lock. Then, instead of the priceless antique musket I expect him to bring out of the gun safe, he produces a large architectural model. It looks like a hotel.

'What's that?' I ask, as he carries the model to a table in the corner.

'Maison DeSalle,' he says, sweeping his arm over the model like a railroad baron taking in a map of the continent. 'Sixteen months from now, this hotel and casino complex will be standing in downtown Natchez.'

I blink in disbelief. 'Why are you doing this? Where will the people come from? The nearest commercial airport is ninety miles away.'

'I'm buying the local airport.'

'*What?*'

He laughs. 'Privatising it, actually. I've already got a charter airline committed to coming here.'

'Why would the county let you do that?'

'I've promised to bring in ongoing commercial business.' He fixes me with a pragmatist's glare. 'People want glamour and stars, and I'll give them that. The high rollers will fly into the cotton capital of the Old South and live *Gone With the Wind* for three days at a time. But that's all window-dressing. What they really come for is the age-old dream of getting something for nothing. Of walking in paupers and walking out kings.'

'That's an empty dream. Because the house always wins in the end.'

Now his smile shows pure satisfaction. 'You're right. And this time *we're* the house, my dear. The cash flow from this operation could run to twenty million a month. And the profits will stay right here in Natchez. I'm going to rebuild the infrastructure of this town. Naturally, I'll receive fair compensation for spearheading the venture and laying out the initial capital.'

I see it now. My grandfather will be hailed as the saviour of Natchez. Yet despite the stated nobility of his goal, I feel uneasy.

'My Washington contacts tell me that I'll be hearing good news within seven days,' he concludes.

He takes a last look at his model, then carries it back to the gun safe. While his back is turned, I take a pill from my pocket and swallow it. I'd hoped to wean myself off the Valium today, but I'm going to need one for the drive to New Orleans.

'Tell me about the night my father died.'

My grandfather returns to his chair and his eyelids seem to grow heavy. 'I've told you that story at least a dozen times.'

'Humour me. Tell me once more.'

'You're thinking about that blood you found.' He lifts his Scotch and takes a swallow. 'It was late. I was reading here in the library. Your grandmother was upstairs with abdominal pain. Pearlie was with her. I heard a noise behind the house. A metallic sound. I went outside. I took a Smith and Wesson .38 with me. A metal drum had been knocked over on the patio, so at first I figured a deer had got spooked and knocked it down. Your father was standing outside your house. He'd heard something, too, and was holding the old Remington rifle he brought back from Vietnam. We separated. I went to check behind Pearlie's house, while Luke circled round yours. I was on the far side of Pearlie's house when I heard the shot. I raced round to the garden and found Luke lying dead. Shot in the chest.'

'Did you see the prowler?'

'You know I did.'

'Please just tell me what you saw.'

'A man running through the trees towards Brookwood.'

'Did you chase him?'

'No. I ran into your house to make sure you and Gwen were all right. I found your mother sleeping, but you weren't in your bed.' He closes his eyes in recollection. 'The telephone rang. It was Pearlie, calling from the main house. She'd already called the police and she and your grandmother were in a panic. She asked if you were all right. I said you were, but at that point I didn't know. I searched the house for you, but couldn't find you. I was worried, but I knew the man I saw running hadn't been carrying a child, so I wasn't panicked. I figured you were hiding somewhere.'

'Did you wake Mom up?'

'No, I knew Gwen would panic. But she soon woke up on her own anyway. She didn't believe Luke was dead, so I took her to his body.'

'Did she ask where I was?'

'The truth? Not at first. She wasn't in very good shape. She'd taken a sedative. I think she assumed you were asleep in your bed.'

'Was there a lot of blood around Daddy's body?'

Grandpapa tilts his head from side to side, as though filtering his memory of my father's corpse through decades of surgical experience. 'Enough for someone to track blood into your room, I suppose. The bullet had clipped the pulmonary artery, and there was a good-sized exit wound.' My grandfather's face gives away nothing.

'When did I turn up?'

'Right after the police arrived. I was telling them what happened when you walked up out of the dark. I remember the eastern slave quarters behind you, so I guess you'd come from there.'

'Was the prowler white or black?'

'Black.'

'Did you go into my room after the murder?'

'I did. To help your mother calm you down.'

'Was I upset?'

'Not that a stranger could tell. You didn't make a sound. But I could see it. Pearlie was the only one you'd let hold you. She had to rock you to sleep in the chair like she did when you were a baby.'

I remember that feeling, if not that specific night. Pearlie rocked me to sleep on many nights, and long after I was a baby.

'Well.' He takes a breath. 'Have I told you what you needed to know?'

I haven't begun to get the answers I want, but at this point I'm not sure what the right questions are. 'Pearlie thinks the prowler might have been a friend of Daddy's, looking for drugs.'

Grandpapa appears to debate whether to comment on this. Then he says,

'That's a fair assumption. Luke took a lot of prescription drugs. And I caught him growing marijuana down on the island once. I worried at times that he might be selling the stuff. When he was killed, I thought of telling the police to explore that avenue, but in the end I decided against it. What could it do but bring calumny on the family name?'

Of course. The family name matters even more than justice. I want to ask him the final question I put to Pearlie. But Grandpapa always saw my father as weak, and if he'd believed that fatal rifle shot had been self-inflicted, he wouldn't have concealed from anyone this vindication of his instincts. And yet . . . there could be factors I know nothing about.

'Did you really see a prowler that night, Grandpapa?'

His eyes widen, and for a moment I'm certain my blind shot has struck home. 'Exactly what are you asking me, Catherine?'

'Did Daddy shoot himself that night? Did he commit suicide?'

Grandpapa's eyes are unreadable, but I see a shadow of conflict in them. 'If you're asking me whether I think Luke was capable of suicide, my answer is yes. But that night . . . everything happened just as I said. He died trying to protect his family. I'll give the boy that.'

Only when I exhale do I realise I've been holding my breath. I feel such relief that it takes a supreme act of will not to get up and take a slug of vodka from the bottle on the sideboard. Instead, I stand and gather my fax pages. 'You really didn't like him, did you? Daddy, I mean. Tell the truth.'

Grandpapa's eyes don't waver. 'I don't think I made a secret of that. Perhaps I should have, but I'm no hypocrite.'

'Why didn't you like him? Was it just oil and water?'

'A lot of it was the war, Catherine. Luke's mental problems, I guess.'

'I heard some of the things you used to say to him. How Vietnam wasn't a real war. How it wasn't nearly as tough as Iwo or Guadalcanal.'

He stares curiously at me, as though wondering how I could remember something like that. 'I did say those things, Catherine. Because I saw things in the Pacific that were about as bad as a man can see, and I didn't let it paralyse me. A few men did and I guess maybe Luke was like them. Shell shock, the doctors called it then. I'm afraid we just called it, well—'

'Yellow!' I finish. My cheeks are burning. 'You called him yellow to his face. I heard you! I didn't know what you meant then, but I did later.'

Grandpapa fixes me with an unrepentant gaze. 'Listen to me, Catherine. Maybe I was too hard on your father. But at some point it doesn't matter *what* you've gone through. You have to pull up your bootstraps and get on with living. Because nobody else is going to do it for you. Your father's job was to provide for you and your mother, and he failed miserably. I gave him three different jobs, and he couldn't handle any of them.'

'How could he? You despised him! And didn't you just love being the big man, who paid for everybody's food and shelter, who controlled us all?'

He settles deeper into his chair, his chiselled features hard as the face of a mountain. 'You're distraught, my dear. We'll continue this at another time.'

'I have to get back to New Orleans. Please don't go into my old bedroom before I get back. You can't see anything without special chemicals. And please don't let anyone else go in there.'

'Don't worry, I'll keep the room secure. Test anything you like.'

I walk to the study door.

'You seeing anybody that looks like a potential husband?' Grandpapa asks suddenly. 'I'm wondering if I'm ever going to see some children around here before I die.'

If he knew I was pregnant now, he probably wouldn't even care that I'm not married. 'I wouldn't worry about that,' I say without turning. 'You're going to live for ever, aren't you?'

I'M TWENTY miles south of Natchez when the Valium starts to soothe my frayed nerves. Whatever the reality of the night my father died, I have to put it aside for now and think about my two years in medical school. They may soon be the subject of intense scrutiny by the FBI.

The facts are that I had an affair with a married professor and it got out of hand. After four months, I tried to end it. He wouldn't let me and, to emphasise his point, promptly attempted suicide. He didn't end his life, but he did end his teaching career, and also my days in medical school. Nathan Malik—or Jonathan Gentry, as I knew him then—was a friend of the guy I was having an affair with.

Halfway to Baton Rouge, my cellphone rings. It's Special Agent Kaiser. He asks me to summarise my time in medical school and my contact with Nathan Malik. I give him a concise account.

'Do you have any idea why he changed his name?' he asks.

'No. Where did he get the name Malik?'

'It was his mother's maiden name.' Kaiser pauses. 'So, basically, Nathan Malik—then called Gentry—was a friend of this doctor you were having an affair with. So it's the doctor I need to talk to. What's his name?'

'Christopher Omartian, MD. I think he practises in Alabama.'

Kaiser thanks me for my time, and signs off.

The road broadens to four lanes, and I open up the throttle and go flat out. I'm just passing the main exit to Baton Rouge when Sean calls.

'Where are you?' he asks.

'I'm at Baton Rouge, doing eighty-five,' I tell him.

'You can slow down, Cat. The FBI odontologist has checked Malik's dental records. His teeth don't match the bite marks on the victims.'

'Shit.'

'Looks like the Malik connection wasn't the break we thought it was.'

'Sean, there's no way Malik's connection to the victims could be coincidence. We just haven't figured it out yet.'

'You got any ideas?'

I think furiously. 'Does Malik have alibis for the murder nights?'

'Two out of four. He says he was with patients, but he won't tell us who.'

'Can he get away with that?'

'Not for long. But so far he's hanging tough. Why would an innocent man be so stubborn about hiding things? Especially with people's lives at stake?'

'We all have something to hide, Sean. You know that. He may feel that his patients' privacy outweighs the risk to their lives. Look, at this speed I'll be in New Orleans in an hour. Where should I go?'

'I don't know. The task force is sort of paralysed at the moment. You'd better go to your place first. I'll be there waiting for you.'

If we meet at my house, there will be no way to avoid the subject I've been keeping to myself for the past three days. 'God help me,' I whisper.

'You're breaking up,' Sean says. 'What did you say?'

'I said I'll see you in an hour.'

I PRESS my garage-door opener and anxiously watch the white panels rise. Sean's car is parked inside. A dark green Saab turbo, ten years old.

I walk into my house with my purse in one hand and a paper sack in the other. The sack holds a bottle of Grey Goose that I picked up at a liquor store. I pass through the kitchen and den, then climb the stairs to the living room, which looks out over Lake Pontchartrain.

Sean is on the sofa, watching a golf tournament on ESPN. He points at the paper bag. 'The news about Malik's teeth bum you out that bad?'

I set my purse on a glass-topped table in the corner. Then I take a high-ball glass from a shelf on the wall, pour two fingers of vodka into it, and take a bittersweet sip. 'I'm not thinking about Malik.'

'Hey.' Sean stands and comes to me. 'You need a hug.'

I do, but as his arms close round me, I feel his erection pressing into my abdomen and pull away.

'What's the matter?'

'I don't want that.'

His green eyes soften. 'It's OK. I can wait a while.'

'I don't want it later either.'

Sean leans back to study me, but keeps his arms round my waist. 'What's the matter, babe? What's happening? You and I have been through some serious shit together. Your mood swings, some bad arguments. I've spent the night here and done nothing but hold you when you were depressed. You *have* to tell me what's going on,' he says.

I want to. Yet I can't. I take another sip from my glass.

'Why did you stop drinking? I mean it's great that you did, but what prompted it? And why are you drinking again now?'

It would be so easy to tell him. But why do I have to? He's a detective, for God's sake. Why can't he figure it out?

'Cat,' he says softly. 'Please.'

'I'm pregnant,' I blurt, and tears fill my eyes.

Sean blinks. 'What? But . . . how? I mean, you're on the pill, right?'

'Yes. I was. But I took antibiotics for a bladder infection, and that interfered with my pills.'

'But you're a doctor. I mean, didn't you know—?'

My composure snaps like brittle glass. '*I didn't do it on purpose, OK?*'

Clearly unprepared for this level of anger, Sean takes two steps back. 'I know you didn't do it on purpose, Cat. It's just . . . a lot to get my mind around. How long have you known?'

'Three days, I think. My sense of time isn't working too well. I've been off my meds for three days. I know that for sure. But I couldn't tell you I was pregnant without a drink. Isn't that pathetic? I've been taking Valium, too, to keep from getting the DTs.'

'Jesus, Cat. Think about the baby, will you?'

My laughter rides an undercurrent of hysteria. 'Is that what you're thinking about? Or are you wondering whether you can still keep me a secret from your wife through all of this?'

He rubs his forehead with both hands. 'Look, I just need some time to absorb this. I'm not sure what to do right now.'

'Yeah, I got that.'

His look is pleading. 'Did you think I'd know in the first five minutes?'

'I hoped you would.'

He tries to come to me again, but I hold up my hands. 'Just go, OK? Leave me alone.' The next words spill out almost of their own accord. 'And leave your key here when you go.'

Sean stares at me in silence for nearly a minute. In his eyes I see a long history of hurt and confusion. He looks away, then pulls his key from his pocket and lays it on the glass table. 'I'm going to check on you tomorrow. Even if you don't want me to.' Then he goes downstairs.

When I hear his car start in the garage, I feel my chest caving in. But I have the antidote for that. Taking the Grey Goose bottle from the bag, I go down to my bedroom and lie on the duvet. With my free hand, I rub a little circle on my tummy. 'Just you and me now, kid,' I say in a desolate voice.

I sip from the bottle, savouring the anaesthetic bite as it spreads across my tongue. I hate myself for doing it, but I swallow anyway. Self-hatred is familiar to me, and familiarity brings comfort. As the chemical warmth diffuses through my veins, I hear the sound of rain again. The rain from my waking dreams. Not the soft hiss of drops falling on my shingles, but the hard percussive patter of rain hitting a tin roof. I hope oblivion comes soon.

I AWAKEN to the hiss of rain, but this time the sound is real. Sean Regan is leaning in through my bedroom window, his hair and shoulders soaking wet. I look at my alarm clock: 11.50 a.m. Sixteen hours have disappeared.

'You wouldn't answer your phone,' Sean says.

'I'm sorry about last night,' I reply, my throat dry and croaking. 'That's not how I wanted to handle it.'

'That's not why I'm here. Our boy hit again this morning.'

'No way.' I rub my eyes, not really believing it. 'Are you sure?'

'The victim was a fifty-six-year-old white male. We don't have a ballistics match yet, but we do have this.' Sean holds up a piece of paper and extends it towards the bed. It's a photograph. Even from this distance, I can see that it's of a window. On the glass above the sill, written in blood, are the words *MY WORK IS NEVER DONE.*

'We never released that to the media,' he says. 'So I'd say the ballistics match is pretty much a formality. Same for the bite marks.'

I wave Sean inside and push myself up to a sitting position. 'Where was Nathan Malik last night?'

'Home all night. Under surveillance.'

He climbs through the window and sits on the floor. From the shadowy circles under his eyes, I'd guess he's slept three consecutive hours since I last saw him. 'Do you want to talk about the baby?' he asks.

I close my eyes. 'Not right now. Not like this.'

Sean's green eyes focus intently on mine. 'Well, when you're ready to talk, I am, too.'

There's a hitch in my heartbeat. 'OK.'

CHAPTER 4

Sean and I sit at my kitchen table, case files and photographs spread out between us. Sean brewed coffee while I took a shower, and by the time I emerged, wearing scrub pants and a sweatshirt, a cup was waiting by my chair. This kind of courtesy grew rare after the first few months of our relationship, but the pregnancy is making him walk on eggshells.

Captain Piazza hasn't suspended Sean from the task force, but she did remove him as lead detective on the case. She toured him through the crime scene this morning only because his case clearance rate is so high. Joey Guercio, his partner, is shuttling between police headquarters and task force headquarters at the FBI building, keeping Sean informed of all new developments by phone. Ironically, the fortress-like new FBI field office is situated just five minutes up the shore of Lake Pontchartrain from my house.

'James Calhoun,' I read, naming the fifth victim. 'What makes him different from the others?'

'Nothing,' says Sean, leaning back in his chair. 'He was alone in the house. No sign of forced entry. One paralysing shot to the spine, then the bite marks, delivered ante mortem, and a *coup de grâce* to the head.'

'Trace evidence?'

'Aside from the note written in the victim's blood, nothing new.'

'This guy is too good,' I say with frustration. 'He must be wearing a space suit while he does this work of his. Time of death?'

'Probably about seven this morning.'

I feel a peculiar shock of surprise. 'So it happened in daylight.'

He nods. 'No witnesses yet. We're still trying to locate a couple of neighbours but, so far, nobody saw anything. Let's get off Calhoun for a minute.'

Sean taps a pen on some papers in front of him. 'The whole string—all five victims—what are you thinking? Just off the top of your head.'

'I think it's Malik. And if he didn't do Calhoun this morning, somebody's helping him.'

'That's who's leaving the bite marks? An accomplice?'

'Maybe, but not necessarily. That could still be Malik.'

Sean squints as though he doesn't understand.

'The killer could be using someone else's teeth.'

'Like dentures? But how?'

'When dentists make dentures,' I explain, 'they're attached to a hinged metal device called an articulator. It simulates the opening and closing of the jaw. Malik could make the marks with one of those.'

Sean looks intrigued. 'What about the saliva in the wounds?'

'That could be Malik's, or an accomplice's. Or he could even be swabbing in someone else's saliva. All we know so far is that the DNA in the saliva belongs to a Caucasian male.'

Sean mulls this over. 'I guess all Malik needs is some spit from a guy he knows we'd never check.' He takes a sip of coffee.

I look down at the photo of Colonel Frank Moreland's corpse. In some serial murder cases, close analysis of the first murder scene ultimately breaks open the case. Because serial killers get better with practice. They're frequently very anxious during their first murder and they make mistakes.

'First-victim angle led us nowhere,' I say, knowing Sean will understand my shorthand. 'What does that tell you?'

'Either he's killed before, or . . .'

'Or he knows a lot about murder,' I finish. 'A cop, for instance. Crime scene tech. Forensic tech. Pathologist. Or maybe a psychiatrist. Also, why was Colonel Moreland killed first? There's got to be a reason.'

'Kaiser's all over that kind of thing, Cat. The task force is taking apart every victim's family.'

'Just bear with me. Any likely suspects in Moreland's family?'

'He's got a daughter living here and a son in Biloxi. Daughter is Stacey Lorio, a registered nurse.' Sean shuffles through the papers on the table and comes up with a photo of a blonde woman with a hard-looking face. 'Thirty-six years old, divorced. Works two jobs. A private clinic and nights at Touro Infirmary. Alibis for the murders are rock solid.'

'The son?'

Sean finds another photo, this one of a good-looking man in uniform.

'Frank Moreland Junior. A major in the air force. His alibis are bulletproof.'

'Neither one has any connection to Malik?'

'Not that we can find.'

I shift in my chair. 'OK, forget that for now. Do you know yet if James Calhoun has any family members who've been treated by Malik?'

'Malik's still refusing to hand over that information. He's arguing doctor–patient privilege.'

'That won't hold up in a case like this, will it?'

Sean shakes his head. 'No. If we can show a judge a strong likelihood that the killer is choosing his victims from Malik's patient base, that creates a situation of imminent danger, which is a public-safety issue. It should override the privilege.'

I stand and begin to pace my kitchen. 'The real question is, why is Malik holding this stuff back?'

'Malik says some of his patients' lives could be at risk if it becomes known they're in therapy. He wouldn't say who they're at risk from.'

I stop pacing. 'What if he's not the killer, but he's *shielding* the killer? What if he's only told about the crime after the fact? Like a priest hearing it in confession?'

'Past conduct is protected under the privilege. If it weren't, nobody would ever disclose anything to their shrink. Or to their priest, or their lawyer. Exceptions are based on the risk of imminent harm.'

I feel a sudden rush of excitement. 'What if he's shielding the killer because he believes the murders are *justified*?'

'Like a twisted moral stand?'

'Maybe not so twisted. An abuse victim kills the man who's been raping her for years. In her mind, it's self-defence.'

'And to Malik, justifiable homicide,' Sean adds. 'But we have five victims. You think one of Malik's patients was abused by all five of these guys?'

'It's possible. If there was some kind of paedophile ring. How long—realistically—before you can force Malik to turn over his patients' names?'

'Kaiser thinks he can get a judge to order it this afternoon.'

'Good. Hey, has anyone been to the victims' families and asked point-blank if anyone is a patient of Malik's?'

'Yeah, but we're being cautious about that. Just in case Malik's right about his patients' lives being in danger. It wouldn't look good if we got one of them killed in some kind of domestic dispute.'

My mind drifts back to mid-July, after the second victim was killed.

Andrus Riviere, a retired pharmacist. I went with Sean to interview the Riviere family, and there I saw a strange sight. A granddaughter of Mr Riviere's, about seven years old, was running joyously through the house as though preparing for a birthday party rather than mourning her grandfather. Yet she didn't seem like an insensitive child. In fact, quite the opposite.

'How do you feel about a woman committing these crimes?' I ask.

Sean stands and goes to the refrigerator, but instead of opening it, he looks back at me. 'It's hard to see a woman doing what we've seen. The marksmanship and the torture weigh against it.'

'The bite marks are almost certainly made after the incapacitating gunshot,' I say. 'A woman would have to disable her victims before getting close enough to bite like that. But a sexually abused woman probably carries around a lot of repressed rage, Sean.'

'Yeah, but women turn rage inwards. They commit suicide, not homicide.'

'OK then, a *male* patient of Malik's. A large percentage of convicted serial killers were abused as young boys.'

'Now you're talking,' Sean says. 'The second we get that patient list, I'll work that angle.' His cellphone rings. 'It's Joey,' he says, glancing at the screen. 'Joey? What you got?'

The smile vanishes from Sean's face as he listens to his partner. 'Was Kaiser around when they found this? . . . OK. I'll talk to him later . . . Yeah. They checking all the other vics for the same thing? . . . OK. Call me with anything else they find.' He hangs up and looks at me. 'There's another connection between two of the victims. The first one and today's. Colonel Moreland and Calhoun both served in Vietnam. Colonel Moreland was in the army there from 1966 to 1969. James Calhoun was there as a civilian engineer on contract to the Department of Defense in '68 and '69.'

I find it difficult to believe that this connection is relevant to our case. 'Is there any evidence that the two men knew each other?'

'Not yet. The task force just found this out. But it's odd, don't you think?'

'Not really. Most of the victims are the right age for Vietnam.'

'Yes, but Nathan Malik did a tour in Nam, remember? Same time frame as Calhoun. What do you think about that?'

'It is sounding less like a coincidence.'

'We could be way off on motive, Cat. This directly links the victims themselves, not women who happen to be related to them.'

'But you're using Malik as part of that linkage. And we got to Malik through those female relatives.'

Sean nods. 'You're right. And if these murders have to do with Vietnam, why are we seeing sexual homicides?'

'Maybe we're not. Maybe that's just staging.'

As I search in vain for some new angle on the facts, Sean's cellphone rings again. He looks at the screen. 'It's John Kaiser.' Sean answers, listens for several moments. When he hangs up, the colour has left his face.

'What is it? What's happened?'

'Twenty minutes ago, Nathan Malik called the task force and said he wants to talk to you.'

My blood pressure drops twenty points. 'That's crazy.'

'You haven't heard anything yet. Kaiser's outside. He knew I was here.'

A hard knocking reverberates through the house. We both whirl towards the garage door and Sean looks at me in a dazed panic.

I shrug in resignation. 'I guess you'd better let the man in.'

SPECIAL AGENT John Kaiser is taller than Sean, and he fills the space in my kitchen in a different way. He seems denser somehow. But the friendly face from the LeGendre crime scene is gone, replaced by a piercing gaze.

'Dr Ferry,' he says, nodding curtly.

'Is this a joke?' I ask. 'Something you guys cooked up to scare me?'

'No joke. Nathan Malik has requested an interview with you.' Kaiser's eyes tell me he's not lying. 'Do you have any idea why he might do that?'

'No. I told you, I met Malik under another name over ten years ago, at med school. He hit on me a couple of times. I rejected him. That's it.'

'Do you want to talk to him?'

'Don't play games with me, Agent Kaiser. If I say I do, you'll suspect I was involved with him. If I say I don't, you'll think I'm hiding something.'

'I know this situation is difficult,' Kaiser says, 'but we've had two murders in three days. If the media find out Malik asked to talk to you, that's bad enough. If they find out about'—Kaiser indicates Sean and me with a nod of his head—'you can pretty much kiss your careers goodbye.'

'Why?' Sean asks, sounding defensive. 'So we're having an affair. That doesn't have anything to do with our work.'

Kaiser looks down at my table, which is covered with crime-scene photos and copies of police reports.

'Shit,' mutters Sean. I can tell from his face that he can't quite believe this is happening. He's thinking of his wife and kids. His retirement. I feel more alone and isolated than I did last night.

'I'm more sympathetic to you guys' situation than you might think,' Kaiser says. 'But right now, the thing to do is focus on this case.'

'How did you know I was here?' Sean asks.

Kaiser throws him a look that says, *Give me some credit*, then turns to me. 'If you're amenable, Dr Ferry, I'd like you to talk to Malik. The judge is almost certainly going to order his arrest today for contempt of court, as there's tremendous political pressure to force some kind of break in this case. But before we jail him I'd like to learn everything we can from him. Because he's asked to speak to you, we have a unique opportunity to do that.'

'But . . .?'

'A meeting like that is risky. Before we go ahead with it, I need to speak very frankly to you. No room for hurt feelings.'

'I understand,' I say. 'Ask away.'

'Your father served in Vietnam during 1969 and 1970, correct?'

'Yes.'

'And he was was murdered in 1981?'

'That's right. I was eight.'

'I tried to get a copy of your father's autopsy record, but the original appears to have been lost. Was there any aspect of your father's murder that could possibly relate to the murders here over the past month?'

'Nothing. Are you suggesting that he knew Nathan Malik in Vietnam?'

'It's possible. Maybe even before. Malik and your father were both born in Mississippi in 1951. Their paths might have crossed before Vietnam or after.'

Sean looks impatient. 'What do their army records say?'

'If only it were that simple,' says Kaiser. 'I've seen Malik's file, but Ferry's record is sealed by the Defense Department until 2015.'

I feel a sudden dislocation from the world around me.

'What the hell are we dealing with here, John?' Sean asks.

'No way to know yet.' Kaiser looks unhappy. 'But it's safe to say this case is a lot more complicated than I first imagined it was.' He turns to me. 'I know this is upsetting, but after you and I spoke yesterday I called Dr Christopher Omartian. To find out what he remembered about Malik.'

I close my eyes and steel myself. Chris Omartian tried to kill himself because of me. He probably had plenty to say, none of it good.

'Dr Omartian said some unkind things about you,' Kaiser confirms. 'And he suggested that you might be manic-depressive.'

'I'm not. But I have been diagnosed with cyclothymia, a mild form of bipolar disorder. I have symptoms of mania that fall below the cut-off for true mania. The episodes alternate with varying frequency. I can be suicidally depressed one week, then, a week later, flying. I take crazy risks. I do not-very-nice things sometimes. And *some*times—not very often—I don't remember those things.'

'Dr Ferry,' Kaiser says carefully, 'I'm trying to put together a picture. Is there any possibility that you've ever seen Dr Malik as a patient?'

'*What?* Malik and I don't fit into the same picture. I don't know the guy.'

'All right.' Kaiser steeples his fingers, his eyes uncertain. 'Do you feel that you're stable enough to handle a meeting like this?'

I start to answer, but he holds up a hand. 'I'm thinking of your panic attacks at the murder scenes. There's no telling what kind of head games Malik might try to run on you.'

'Where would this meeting happen?'

'Malik suggested his office. Just off Veterans Boulevard. He wants to talk to you face to face and alone, but you'd be wearing a wire, of course, and a SWAT team would be right outside.'

'No way,' snaps Sean. 'Malik could shoot her before your guys even made the door. I've seen it happen, John. So have you. Pick a neutral location. A place you can control.'

I lay a hand on his arm. 'Let it go, Sean. When are we talking about doing this?'

Kaiser stands and looks down at me. 'Malik's at his office now. I've got a wire team in the van outside. How soon can you get dressed?'

A thrill of anticipation shoots through me. Five men have been murdered, and I'm about to walk into a room with the man most likely to have committed the crimes. 'Give me ten minutes.'

'EVERYTHING OK?' Kaiser asks. He's standing beside me at the bottom of a metal staircase that leads up to Nathan Malik's office.

'I'm good,' I assure Kaiser, then I silently repeat the safety phrase that he gave me a few minutes ago. *Do you follow Saints football?* This mundane sentence—in theory, at least—will trigger an explosive entry by the NOPD SWAT team to pull me out.

The FBI agent pats me on the back, and I'm thankful for the touch.

I walk up the stairs and open the door at the top. I see a hallway with doors running down either side. Brown walls, threadbare green carpet.

'Hello?' calls a male voice. 'Is that you, Dr Ferry?'

'Yes,' I answer, embarrassed by the smallness of my voice.

'In here. End of the hall.'

The door at the end of the hall is partly open. I walk up to it, then pause.

'Come in. Nothing to be afraid of.'

Right, I say silently, and step through the door.

Nathan Malik sits at a large table facing the doorway. Despite the summer heat, he's wearing black slacks and a black turtleneck. There isn't a spare ounce of fat on his muscular frame, and his bald head seems posed upon his body like a carving. His skin is fair, a difficult feat to manage in the New Orleans summer, but the paleness dramatically sets off his eyes, which have irises so brown they look black.

In a single fluid movement, Malik stands and gestures at a black leather sofa opposite his desk. As I sit, I glance quickly around the office and register a few details. Soft white walls, teak shelves, a couple of Chinese paintings. To my left hangs a samurai sword, its truncated blade gleaming with threatening purpose. To my right, on a sideboard, sits a stone Buddha.

'Everyone likes the Buddha,' Malik says, taking his seat again. 'I brought it back from Cambodia. It's five hundred years old. I regretted taking it, but I'm glad I have it now.' A thin smile touches his lips. 'I'm curiously happy that you've come. I thought it would be you who showed up to take impressions of my teeth, but I got a rather ugly little FBI dentist instead.'

I'm confused. 'Did he take impressions of your teeth?'

'No. I assume that's because my X-rays were sufficient to rule me out as a suspect. He did swab my mouth for DNA.'

I decide to be direct. 'Why am I here, Doctor?'

He waves a hand as if dismissing a triviality. 'I was curious to see how you turned out. I mean, I've followed you in the newspapers, but stories like that never offer any meaningful detail. You're here because none of this is accidental. We knew each other years ago, seemingly in passing, and now we're brought together again. Synchronicity, Jung called it. A seemingly acausal linkage of events which has great meaning.'

'I call those coincidences. We didn't actually come together until you asked for this meeting. Why was that? Do you have a thing for me, Dr Malik?'

'A thing?' Feigned ignorance doesn't suit the psychiatrist well.

'Come on. An interest. A crush.'

'Do many men react that way to you?'

'Enough.'

He nods. 'I'll bet they do. You had them eating out of your hand at UMC. All those doctors salivating over you . . .'

'You were one of them, as I recall.'

'I noticed you, I'll admit that. You were beautiful, you could hold your own in conversation with people twenty years your senior. I was also bored.'

'Are you bored now?'

A thin smile. 'No.'

'If we're done strolling down memory lane, I have some questions.'

'Fire away. Only I hope they're *your* questions. I'd hate to think you volunteered to act as a mouthpiece for the FBI.'

'The questions are mine,' I confirm. 'Doctor Malik, do you treat only patients who have repressed memories?'

'No. I specialise in the recovery of lost memories, but I also treat patients for bipolar disorder and for post-traumatic stress disorder.'

'PTSD solely as it relates to sexual abuse?'

He hesitates. 'I also treat some combat veterans.'

I nod. 'I'm going to ask you this straight out. Why won't you reveal the names of your patients to the police?'

Whatever good humour was in the psychiatrist's face vanishes. 'Because I owe them my loyalty. I would never betray my patients in that way.'

'Would merely revealing their names constitute a betrayal?'

'Of course. Many of these patients are very fragile. They live in difficult family situations. For some, violence is a daily reality. I have no intention of putting them at risk to satisfy the whims of the state.'

'The "whims of the state"? The police are trying to stop a serial murderer.'

'None of my patients has died.'

'Their relatives have. Two that we know about. Maybe more.'

He looks at the ceiling in a way that's almost a roll of his eyes. 'Perhaps.'

Anger surges within me at his smugness. 'It's not *perhaps*, is it? You know who else is at risk, yet you refuse to tell the police.'

Malik simply stares at me, his dark eyes flat and steady.

'How many of the murder victims were related to people you treat?'

'Do you honestly think I'm going to answer that, Catherine?'

'Please call me Dr Ferry.'

A gleam of bemusement. 'Ahh. Are you in fact a doctor? You left medical school in the second year, I recall.' Malik is clearly enjoying himself.

'I'm a forensic odontologist. I hope you didn't bring me here to insult me, Doctor.'

'No. I merely want us to be clear about who we are. I'd like you to call me Nathan, and I'd prefer to call you Catherine.'

'How about I call you Jonathan? That's what you called yourself when I met you. Jonathan Gentry.'

The psychiatrist's eyes go flat again. 'That is no longer my name. You can call me what you like, Catherine. But before we go on, let's dispose of this issue of patient confidentiality. I tell you now, I'm quite prepared to spend a year in jail rather than betray my patients' privacy.' Malik turns his palms upwards. 'I spent six weeks as a prisoner of the Khmer Rouge. A year in an American jail can only be a vacation.'

Some of my confidence evaporates. There's more to Nathan Malik than I've been led to believe. As I try to decide how to proceed, the psychiatrist puts his elbows on his desk and folds his hands together. 'Listen to me, Catherine. You walked in here from the world of light. The world of malls and restaurants and Fourth of July fireworks. You see shadows at the edges of all that. You know that evil exists. You've worked a few murder cases. But mostly it's abstract.' Malik's pale cheeks colour with passion. 'But *here*, in this office, the shadows come out and play.' He sits back in his chair and speaks quietly. 'Here, Catherine, I deal with the worst thing in the world.'

'Don't you think you might be overdramatising a bit?'

'You think so?' A humourless chuckle escapes Malik's lips. 'What's the worst scourge of mankind? War?'

'I suppose so. War and the things that go with it.'

'I've seen war. I've seen hand-to-hand savagery and anonymous slaughter. I've killed. But what I've seen and heard inside this drab little office building is *far* worse. That's why I won't give you the names of my patients.'

I let the silence stretch out, hoping to dissipate some of Malik's intensity. Then, in a neutral voice, I say, 'My memory from med school is that therapists should maintain objectivity at all costs. You sound more like a patient advocate than a dispassionate clinician.'

'Should one be objective in the face of terror and torture? Any identity these children have is systematically destroyed. Hope isn't even a memory.'

'I'm a little confused,' I say softly. 'Are you treating children or adults?'

With an explosive movement Malik stands, as though the chair can no longer contain him. He's only about five nine, but he radiates power and projects a centredness I've seen only in devotees of the martial arts. 'A child's emotional development is typically frozen in whatever stage he or she was in at the time the abuse occurred. Sometimes I don't know whether I'm dealing with an adult or a child until the patient opens her mouth.'

'So what you're talking about now is repressed memories. Right?'

Malik hasn't moved towards me, but he suddenly seems much closer than he did before. And the SWAT team seems a lot further away than it did a minute ago. My eyes go to the samurai sword on the wall to my left.

'I think you know what I'm talking about,' Malik says. '*Doctor*.'

For the first time since entering the office, I am afraid. The man before me isn't the man I knew in medical school. Emotionally, he has evolved into something else. The psychiatrist I knew was an observer, essentially impotent. This man is as far from impotent as I can imagine, and his agenda remains a mystery to me. But I feel I can get him to reveal more.

'I suppose I'm a little suspicious of the theory that traumatic memories can be lost,' I say.

'Most people are. The word *repression* is freighted with Freudian overtones. We should drop it altogether. Memories are lost by a sophisticated neurological defence mechanism called dissociation. I'm sure you've driven your car while totally focused on something inside it. The CD player. A child. Your cellphone. Your body and brain perform the task of driving while your conscious mind is entirely occupied elsewhere. Well, when used as a coping mechanism against trauma, dissociation has far more profound effects. When human beings are placed under such severe stress that fight or flight are the only sane responses and yet neither response is possible, the brain—the mind, rather—will attempt to flee on its own. It may well watch the trauma occur, but it will not process it. Not conventionally, anyway. In extreme cases, these victims develop dissociative identity disorder. What we used to call multiple personality disorder. The mind becomes so adept at splitting off from reality that separate psyches come into being.'

'These traumatic memories,' I say, 'they remain intact? Even though the person isn't conscious of them? Intact and accessible at a later date?'

Malik nods. 'The memory is indelible. It's simply located in another part of the brain. If an adult woman finds herself in a situation similar to that in which the abuse took place, she may suddenly experience panic, pain, heart palpitations, anything. A smell can trigger the response. A hair cream the abuser wore, say. This phenomenon is called body memory. The sensory part of the brain recalls the trauma, but the conscious mind does not.'

'But how do you help patients access these lost memories?'

'Drugs, talk therapy, hypnosis—I could run clinical jargon past you for hours, precise but pointless. I find it useful to use symbolism when discussing my work. Mythology, most of all. Are you familiar with the concept of the underworld? The River Styx? Charon, the ferryman?'

'I know the basics.'

'If you want to understand my work, think of it this way. Victims of chronic sexual abuse aren't merely the walking wounded; they're the walking dead, trapped in the underworld. But though their souls have crossed the river of forgetfulness to the land of the dead, their bodies remain behind. My job is to journey to the underworld and bring back the souls of those poor children. I see myself as Charon, the ferryman. I guide travellers back and forth between this world and that.'

I think about the metaphor for a while. 'The main thing I remember about Charon is that he had to be *paid* to ferry the dead across the river.'

Malik smiles in appreciation. 'Yes, Charon had to be paid. With a coin in the mouth. But you misunderstand the metaphor. My fees don't pay the price of the patient's journey to the underworld. The patients have usually paid that price long before they see me. In tears and pain.'

To avoid Malik's challenging gaze, I look over at the Buddha. 'Repressed memory work is pretty controversial. Have you ever made a mistake? There are many documented cases of such memories being proven false. Recantations by patients. Right?'

The psychiatrist waves his hand. 'I'm not getting into that controversy with you. Recantations are a problem for therapists who are inexperienced, misguided or poorly trained.'

I understand why Harold Shubb warned me that the FBI had better have an ironclad case if they were going after Malik. The man never questions his own judgment. Maybe that's his weakness.

'You haven't asked me anything about the murders,' I say. 'I thought they would interest you from a psychiatric perspective.'

'I'm afraid sexual homicide is depressingly predictable, as a rule. I suppose trying to identify particular offenders offers a certain lurid excitement, but I have no interest in that.'

Malik's subtle cuts and insults remind me of my grandfather on a bad day. 'You don't see sexual homicide as an extreme form of sexual abuse?'

He shrugs. 'It's merely the poisoned chicken coming home to roost. Childhood sexual abuse is almost universal in serial murderers. Their turning that violence back on the world is as inevitable as the setting of the sun.'

I suddenly remember Kaiser and the others listening to the transmission from my hidden microphone. I have a unique opportunity to probe their most likely suspect, and I don't want to squander it.

'Do you have nightmares, Catherine? Recurring nightmares?'

Before I can dissemble, I see blue lights in the rain and my father lying dead. Hordes of faceless figures caper at the edges of the scene, the dark men of countless dreams. Then the image vanishes, and I find myself riding with my grandfather over a grassy pasture on DeSalle Island, in an old, round-nosed pick-up truck. We grind our way up a hill, towards the pond that lies on the other side. My grandfather is smiling, but the fear in my chest is like a wild animal trying to claw its way out. This dream began only two weeks ago. Yet each time it recurs, the truck moves further towards the crest—

'Why do you ask that?'

Malik is watching me with compassion in his face. 'I sense needs in certain people. I sense pain. It's an empathic ability I've always had. It's more a burden than a gift, really.'

'I don't remember you as particularly empathic. Or insightful, for that matter. Mostly I remember you as an arrogant smart-ass.'

An understanding smile from the doctor. 'You've obviously suffered severe trauma in your life, Catherine. You showed clear signs of PTSD when I knew you in Jackson. Similar to the Vietnam vets I was working with at the time. That's another reason I noticed you.'

I don't want to let Malik know how close to the bone he's come, but he's got me curious. 'What kind of trauma do you think I suffered?'

'The murder of your father, for a start.' He sighs. 'Perhaps we can go into more detail at another time. Would you consider coming to me as a patient?'

My scalp is tingling. 'This is a joke, right?'

'Are you over dating married men now, Catherine?'

'Go to hell. What is this?'

'Exchanging confidences is the basis of trust, Catherine.'

'All right, then. Let's do some sharing. Your spiel about being the ferryman to the underworld sounded a little shopworn to me. The other stuff was from the heart. You're not just a bystander to sexual abuse, are you? You speak from personal experience.'

'You're very perceptive.'

'You were sexually abused as a child?'

'Yes.'

I feel a strange quivering in my limbs, as though from a mild electric shock. This is the stuff Kaiser wants and needs. 'By whom?'

'By my father.'

'I'm sorry. Can you talk about it?'

Malik gives a dismissive wave of his hand. 'What's the point? It's not the crimes against no that make us unique, but our responses. How much do you remember about the night your father died, Catherine?'

'That's none of your business.'

'I'd like to make it my business. I think I could help you, if you'd—'

'I'm not here for therapy, Doctor. And now I want to know what I *am* doing here,' I say quietly.

The thinnest of smiles touches his lips, and then his eyes focus on mine at last. 'So do I, Catherine.'

'I'm here because I think you killed those five men.'

Malik's eyes flicker. 'Oh, Catherine. I expected so much more from you.'

His condescension is finally too much for me to bear. 'I think our murder victims are male relatives of your patients—sexual abusers—and that by killing them you see yourself as some kind of crusader against an evil you know only too well.'

The psychiatrist watches me in silence. 'What would you think of me if that were true? Abusers never stop, Catherine. They just move on to new victims. They cannot be rehabilitated.'

'Are you saying that murdering them is justified?'

'I'm saying that death or infirmity are the only things that will stop them.'

'Are you an expert shot, Doctor?'

'I can hit what I aim at.'

'Do you practise martial arts?'

He glances at the samurai sword on the wall. 'I could decapitate you with that before the SWAT team could get in here, if that's what you mean.'

A shudder goes through me. I've forgotten the safety phrase. Something about football—

I almost jump out of my chair when Malik stands, but he only folds his arms across his chest and looks at me with something like pity. 'I have things to do now. You can tell me your thoughts at our next meeting.'

'There won't be another meeting.'

Malik smiles. 'Of course there will. Much is going to come to you over the next few days. That's the way it works.' He leans across the table that serves as his desk and holds out his business card.

Out of curiosity, I stand and take it.

'Call me,' he says.

The meeting is over. I walk to the door, then turn back one last time. Malik looks odd standing there, clad in black from head to toe.

'Don't blame yourself,' he says.

CHAPTER 5

I'm sitting in the back seat of an FBI Crown Victoria, leaning against Sean as the car roars towards my house. John Kaiser sits up front with a Bureau driver, speaking on a large cellular phone that encrypts every word spoken over it.

'Get on the horn to the Department of Defense. I want to know about Malik's time in Cambodia. I didn't see it mentioned in his record. It's possible that he met one or more of the victims in a prison camp . . .'

I tune out Kaiser's voice and sit up straight. Throughout the meeting with Malik I held up fine, but once outside I began to shake.

'You'll be OK soon,' Sean assures me. 'You did great. I think Malik could be the guy.'

I squeeze his hand in gratitude.

Kaiser hangs up and turns in his seat to look at me. 'Do you mind answering a few questions before I drop you off?' he asks.

'No. Go ahead.'

'Was your father ever captured while overseas?'

'I don't think so. But I can't be sure. He wouldn't talk to us about what he went through. I mean, I was only eight when he died. But he never talked to my mother either. Or so she said.'

'Maybe she was just trying to protect you from things she didn't think you could handle.'

A week ago I would have argued, but after finding the bloodstains in my bedroom I'm not so sure. For all I know, my mother, my grandfather and Pearlie have been insulating me for years from realities I never suspected.

The driver turns right, and Lake Pontchartrain appears on our left, steely blue and rolling with whitecaps. Not many sails today.

'What's your gut feeling about Malik?' Kaiser asks. 'You looked him in the eyes; I didn't. Did he kill those men?'

A gull drops low over the road and dives towards the lake. 'If you're asking whether I think he *could* do it, my answer is yes. I think he could kill without blinking an eye. But if you're asking whether he did—I can't say. He seems above these murders somehow. What's *your* gut feeling?' I ask.

Kaiser looks thoughtful. 'I think that if Malik is killing these guys, it's because he thinks he's right. It's a crusade. They're child molesters, and he's decided that taking them out is the only meaningful response. And a lot of people would probably agree with him.' Kaiser sighs.

Before I can speak again, Kaiser's cellphone rings. He answers, his mind already back on logistical details.

The Crown Vic stops before my closed garage door, which has always shielded Sean's car from prying eyes. Not much point any more—everyone in the department will know about our affair by tonight. Sean reaches across me and opens my door. I wait to say goodbye to Kaiser, but his conversation shows no sign of ending, so I get out and start towards my front door. I'm nearly there when I hear a clatter of heels on the sidewalk.

'Dr Ferry!' It's Kaiser, trotting after me. 'I appreciate what you did today. I'd like you to come over to the field office later, when you're feeling up to it.'

I'm not really listening. 'Agent Kaiser, do you think I'm involved with these murders in any way? Or with Nathan Malik?'

Kaiser's face changes about as much as a rock when the wind blows across it. He's probably a hell of a poker player. 'I think you did everything you could today to help us solve this case.'

'Why do you think Malik said "Don't blame yourself" to me as I left?'

'I don't know.' Kaiser looks at the ground, then back at me. 'We'll just have to try to figure that out together.'

That's all I'm going to get. I offer him my hand, he shakes it, and then I walk inside my house without looking back.

IT'S EVENING, and I'm standing at my picture window, gazing out at the lake. My meeting with Malik profoundly disturbed me, and I'm not sure why. His cryptic comments about my father stirred up a stew of fragmentary memories, but none has told me anything useful. I'm not even sure the images in my mind are real, and not things I've pieced together from old photographs and stories. A few things I'm sure of—salvaged from nights I sat in the loft of the barn my father used as his studio, watching him work. The roar of the acetylene cutting torch, the hiss of steam as he dipped redhot metal into the cooling trough. The smell of acids he used for etching. For the last few years of his life, my father slept in that barn. It was only a couple of hundred yards from our quarters, but the separation was absolute. No one was allowed into it when he was working. No one, except me.

'What are you thinking?' Sean asks from behind me.

I don't turn. There aren't many boats out, but I need to watch them. A sail moving slowly across the horizon gives me something to focus on when my internal moorings start to come loose. 'About my dad,' I say softly.

Sean turns me round and steps close. I look into his eyes, trying to lose myself in them. I've done it before, lost myself in those green spheres like a little girl swimming in an emerald sea. Drifting and rolling—

I jerk backwards. Sean has kissed me, and the touch stunned me like an electric shock.

'Hey,' he says, worry in his face. 'What's going on?'

'I don't know.' I feel tears on my cheeks. 'I don't *know*. I have this feeling that everything's connected, but I can't see how. The murders, me, Malik. Kaiser thinks so, too. He just doesn't see any upside to telling me right now.'

'Come on, Cat. How could everything be connected?'

'How could it *not*? A month ago, these murders begin. Then I start having panic attacks at the crime scenes. The only connection between the victims is a psychiatrist I happened to know ten years ago. Then you make another connection between the victims: Vietnam. Who went to Vietnam? My father, Nathan Malik, and two of the victims. Maybe more of them. And they were there in the *same year*. What are the odds of that, Sean?'

'I'm no mathematician, but it's not impossible. Coincidences like that happen all the time.'

His attempt to minimise the significance of these facts infuriates me. 'My father was murdered, Sean. And I don't remember anything about that night before seeing his body in the garden. Yesterday I found blood in my old bedroom. And I'm having recurring dreams and hallucinations. I've always had them, but now they're getting worse.'

Sean is looking at me strangely. 'What are you talking about? You found blood where?'

I forgot he knows nothing about my visit to Natchez. 'In the bedroom I grew up in. Old blood. I think it dates from the night my father died. I only found it by accident. A little girl spilled some luminol in my room yesterday morning . . . For a while I was afraid my father had killed himself, but I don't think that any more. I think—'

Sean grips my shoulders. 'You've got to calm down. I want to hear this, but you're starting to fly. Can't you feel it? You're going too fast.'

He's right. My thoughts are racing, and I don't want them to slow down. I've experienced amazing epiphanies during manic episodes, when seemingly random details form themselves into coherent patterns. I'm almost certain that if my brain kicks up to the next plateau, the connections between myself, Malik, his patients and the dead men will leap into stark relief.

'After talking to Malik today, I'm thinking maybe I was so traumatised by what I saw the night my father was killed that I became dissociated. That's why I stopped speaking. And maybe the truth about his death is locked inside my head somewhere, but I can't reach it. I want to talk to Malik again. I think he knows something about me—'

'Jesus, Cat. What could he know? You told me your dad was killed by a prowler. And your nightmares about faceless men are consistent with that.'

I turn up my palms in frustration. 'I want to go to bed. I need to sleep. Right now.'

Sean gives me a long-suffering smile. 'OK. Let's get you tucked in.'

After managing a smile of gratitude, I walk past him and down the stairs to my bedroom. As I climb under the covers, Sean comes in and sits on the edge of the bed in the least threatening position possible.

'Go to sleep. I'll be out there watching TV,' he says.

'Wake me up if you have to leave. I don't want to wake up alone.'

'I will.'

He kisses my hair above the ear. As he leaves, I prop one pillow so that it blocks the light from the window, then turn to the wall and let my eyes lose their focus. As sleep draws its curtain over my fevered mind, I ask myself again if the adults in my life long ago decided to protect me from a reality they deemed too devastating for me to endure . . .

Where wakefulness becomes sleep I never know, because my dreams are as vivid as anything I experience while awake. This time I'm back on the island, in the ancient pick-up truck, riding through the pasture with my grandfather at the wheel. The truck's round hood is rusted orange and dented from a hundred impacts. The engine groans as Grandpapa forces the truck up the long slope towards the crest of the hill.

There's a pond on the other side of the hill, and I'm afraid. Something terrible is waiting over there. I want to warn my grandfather but my mouth is glued shut. I pray that God will spare us . . .

Suddenly there's a crash of thunder, and I wake to violence in the dark, thick arms flailing around me, fists cracking bone. I want to run, but I'm rooted to the bed. The combatants struggle over me in silent rage, their sole intent to kill. I've seen this battle before, but this time—unlike the other nights—I see the whites of two eyes flickering in the black mask of one face. As his face whips towards the bedroom window, I recognise my father. And I scream.

MY EYES open in the dark and I know the nightmares are over. My bedside clock reads 5.53 a.m. I've slept over twelve hours. Sean must be long gone. He promised to wake me if he had to leave, but it's morning, and here I lie alone. He is probably in bed with his wife right now.

Lying in the dark, I know one thing with absolute certainty. I must return to Malmaison. Today. I may believe that one of the bloody tracks on my bedroom floor was put there by my foot twenty-three years ago, but until that's a proven fact I can go no further. I have the tools and the knowledge to prove it, and I won't feel any peace until I do.

Walking down the hall to make coffee, I smell cigarette smoke. Then I hear a cough from the den. Sean quit smoking a year ago.

I creep to the end of the hall. The den is dark. As my eyes adjust to the gloom, I see a man sitting on the sofa.

I reach out and flip on the hall light.

Sean is wearing boxer shorts and his Oxford shirt, unbuttoned all the way down. His face is as haggard as I've ever seen it.

'Sean? What are you doing?'

He doesn't look in my direction. 'Thinking.'

I pad over to the sofa and look at him. A bottle of Bushmills stands on the coffee table, a saucer piled with crushed cigarette butts beside it.

'Are you all right?' I ask.

'No.' At last he looks up. His eyes are glazed. 'They know, Cat.'

'Know what? Who knows?'

'Everybody knows. About us. Somebody called Karen and told her.'

I've been expecting something like this for months. Now that it's finally happened, I feel a strange numbness in my chest. 'And?'

'Karen called about eight last night. She told me not to come home. I went to talk to her. She wouldn't let me in. And she's changed the locks.'

I look over at the picture window. A faint blue glow lightens the blackness on the left side of the lake. The sun is coming up. I need to move to avoid the Monday-morning traffic.

'Look, I know this is a bad time . . . but I have to go.'

He blinks in confusion. 'You're ready to talk to the FBI?'

'No. I'm going back to Natchez.'

He rubs his eyes. 'What are you talking about? You just came from there.'

'I have to know what happened in that room. The night my father died.'

'But you can't just *leave*. What about Malik?'

'Where is he now?'

'He's in the Orleans parish prison. He refused to obey the court order.'

This doesn't surprise me. 'I did what Kaiser wanted. That's all I can do right now. I'm done. I'm going home.'

Sean shakes his head as though trying to sober himself up. 'I've been thinking about the baby, too.'

I nod but say nothing.

'We can be together now. Right now. No waiting.'

I've dreamed of hearing him say this for more than a year, but now that he has, I feel only sadness. 'You didn't make that choice freely, Sean. You got caught. That's a different thing.'

He looks incredulous. 'Are you serious?'

'On top of that, you're drunk. For all I know, you'll be begging Karen's forgiveness tonight. I don't want to sound like a bitch, OK? I love you. But I have something important to do, and I can't put it off because you happened to get caught last night.'

'You do sound like a bitch.'

My laugh is a short, harsh bark that surprises even me. 'Thanks for making it easier.'

I PULL into the gravel lot behind Malmaison's two slave quarters and the rose garden. Mother's Maxima, Pearlie's blue Cadillac and my grandfather's Lincoln are in the lot. There's also an Acura I don't recognise. The Lincoln's engine is running and my grandfather's driver is behind the wheel.

Just as I get out of my car, Grandpapa marches through the trellised arch at the rear of the rose garden. He wears a dark, stylish suit that sets off his silver hair, and a white silk handkerchief sits prominently in his pocket.

'Catherine?' he calls when he sees me. 'Two visits in three days? What's going on?'

I'm not going to lie about my reason for being here, even though it might upset him. 'I came back to finish the work in my bedroom. I want to check the rest of the room for blood and other trace evidence.'

He glances at his watch. 'You're going to do this yourself?'

'I don't think so. I can't pretend to be objective about this and if something I discovered ultimately involved the courts, that could—'

'The courts?' He's giving me his full attention now. 'What could possibly involve the courts?'

Why is he forcing me to say it? 'Look, I know you told me that you and I probably tracked that blood into the bedroom from the garden that night, but . . . it was raining, Grandpapa. Hard. How could anybody track enough blood over thirty yards of wet grass to make those footprints?'

He smiles. 'You're as obsessive and tenacious as I am.'

'I know people who work at the state crime lab in Baton Rouge. They also testify in criminal trials. They could work up my bedroom in half a day and any evidence they discovered would be beyond reproach.'

'I understand.' He glances over at his driver, then back at me.

'Whose car is that?' I ask, pointing at the Acura.

'Ann's,' he replies, his eyes distant.

Aunt Ann rarely visits Malmaison. Her stormy personal life long ago alienated her from my grandparents. Diagnosed as bipolar in her mid-twenties, Ann became a cautionary tale in local society, an example of how great wealth doesn't necessarily confer happiness.

'Is she visiting Mom?' I ask.

'She's with Gwen now, but she actually drove up to see me.'

'What about?'

Grandpapa sighs wearily. 'What's it always about?'

Money. Mom told me that Aunt Ann long ago depleted the trust fund my grandfather set up for her. Yet she has no qualms about asking for money when she needs it. 'Mom said Ann's new husband is beating her,' I say.

Grandpapa's angular face tightens and I sense the slow-burning anger of a man who judges men by his own strict code. 'If she asks me for help with that problem, I'll intervene.' He looks at his watch again. 'Catherine, I have a meeting with a member of the Mississippi Gaming Commission about Maison DeSalle. I'd like you to postpone your plans until I get back.'

'Why?'

He reaches out and takes hold of my hand. 'It's a delicate matter. A personal matter. Personal for you.'

'For me? Then tell me now.'

'I can't now. I have the meeting. It won't take more than an hour or so.'

I shake my head in frustration. 'I'm tired of being in the dark, Grandpapa. Ever since I found that blood I've had the feeling you guys have been keeping something from me about that night. If you want me to hold off doing this, tell me whatever it is right now.'

Anger flashes briefly in his eyes, but instead of chastising me he walks slowly round the Audi and climbs into the passenger seat. His desire is clear. I get into the driver's seat beside him, but he's not looking at me. He's staring through the windshield with a faraway look in his eyes.

'We were foolish to think we could lie to you and get away with it for long.' His big chest falls with a deep sigh and then he faces me, his eyes solemn, the eyes of a doctor about to break bad news. 'Darling, your father didn't die where we told you he did. He died in your bedroom.'

My bedroom . . . A strange numbness seeps outwards from my heart. 'How did he die?' I force myself to turn, to focus on the lined patrician face.

'I was downstairs reading,' he begins softly. 'I heard a shot. It was muffled, but I knew what it was. I ran outside. I saw a man running from your house. I didn't chase him. I ran straight over to see whether anyone had been hurt.'

'Was the running man black, like you told me before?'

'Yes. When I got inside, I found your mother asleep in her bed. Then I checked your room. You were nowhere to be seen, but Luke was lying on the floor, bleeding from the chest. His rifle was beside him on the floor. He had been shot by the intruder. I examined the wound. It was mortal.'

I shut out the pain by focusing on details. 'Did you call the police?'

'Pearlie did. And the rest happened much the way I told you the other day. Your mother woke up. You walked into the bedroom moments later.'

'Where had I been? I mean . . . it happened in my bedroom.'

He takes a moment to consider this. 'Outside, I think.'

'Who moved Daddy's body into the rose garden?'

'I did. It was to protect you.' Grandpapa shifts on the seat, but his eyes remain on me. 'You were eight years old, Catherine. If the story had been printed in the *Examiner*, there would have been no end to the morbid speculation. I saw no reason to put you through that. Luke was dead. It made no difference where the police found his body. Pearlie helped me clean his blood off the bedroom floor before the police arrived. Not that it mattered. They never even checked the slave quarters.'

'Why not?'

'They believed what I told them. Luke was lying dead in the rose garden. I told them how it happened, and that was that.'

Of course. In the Natchez of twenty years ago, no local cop would question the word of Dr William Kirkland.

'Did they do any forensic investigation at all?'

'Yes, but as you pointed out, it was raining hard. They didn't put too much effort into it. It was a sad night. Everybody wanted it over.'

I gaze across the rose garden to the slave quarters that were my home for sixteen years. 'But Grandpapa . . . what if something *did* happen to me? Did you ever think about that?'

'Of course I considered the possibility, dear. I examined you myself, after the police had gone. But I saw no evidence of physical assault. Nothing happened to you.' He sighs. 'The psychological shock was clearly devastating, though. I suppose its possible you saw your father murdered.'

My grandfather grasps my quivering hands, stilling the tremors with the force of his grip. 'Do you have any memory of that night?' he asks.

'Not before I saw his body. I have nightmares, though . . . other things.'

He squeezes my hands harder. 'Those aren't nightmares, dear. Those are memories. I've said some bad things about Luke, I know. And God help me, I've lied to you as well. Hopefully for a good reason. But one thing I told you, you can take as Holy Writ. Your father died fighting to save your life.'

I close my eyes, but the tears come anyway. 'Who did it, Grandpapa? Who killed him? Did the police really look?'

'You'd better believe it. I rode them hard. But they couldn't come up with anything.'

'I can,' I say quietly. 'I can take apart that crime scene with tools that didn't even *exist* back then.'

Grandpapa is watching me with grief in his face. 'I'm sure you can, Catherine. But to what end? There were never any suspects. Are you going to take DNA samples from every black man in Natchez? And the killer could easily be dead now. He could have left town years ago.'

'Are you saying I shouldn't try to find out who murdered Daddy?'

'Catherine, you've spent your adult life focused on death. Now you're about to cross the line into full-blown obsession. I want my granddaughter to *live*. Not waste your time on some belated quest for justice with no chance of success. I want you to have a family, children . . .'

I'm shaking my head violently. 'It's not just justice I want.'

'What then?'

'The man who killed my father is the only person in the world who knows what happened to me in that room. *Something* happened. Something bad. And I have to know what it was.'

Grandpapa is saying something else but I can't make out the words. His voice seems to come from across a windy field. Pulling one hand loose, I yank open the door and try to climb out. He tries to hold me by my other hand, but I relax my fingers and the hand slips free. My feet hit the ground, and I start running down the hill towards the bayou, where the barn stands in the shadow of a wall of trees. I'll be safe there.

Voices cry out behind me, but I run on, like a panicked little girl.

I CAN'T get into the barn. For the first time in my life, my father's sanctuary is closed to me. The main entrance is padlocked, and the secret ones I used for years have been nailed shut. I wanted to look in the barn because I wanted to feel close to my father. Here, where his final sculptures are stored—unsold at my request—I feel a connection with him . . .

My cellphone beeps. It's Sean. My first instinct is to ignore the call, but something makes me answer. 'What is it?' I ask.

'Hold on to your socks,' Sean says, his voice raspy from a hangover. 'At eight o'clock this morning, Malik gave up the names of his patients.'

I can't believe it. 'Is he out of jail now?'

'Yep. And we were suspicious for the same reason you are. Why would Malik go to jail on principle then suddenly crack? It's almost like he did it for the publicity. Anyway, Kaiser realised that without Malik's medical records, we had no way to know whether the patient list was complete. So he got a court order authorising us to check Malik's computer records. Well, guess what? There *weren't* any. The hard drives were wiped clean.'

This I can believe. 'The data can still be retrieved. You just—'

'Cat, the data's *gone*. All of it. The FBI technicians said it would take somebody who really knew computers to pull that off . . . Hang on . . . I gotta run, Cat. Things are popping here. Miss you.'

He clicks off, and I turn reluctantly from the barn and walk up the hill towards the parking lot.

Something moves among the trees to my right, and it startles me. Then I recognise Mose, the yardman. He's setting mole traps in the scraggly grass beneath the trees. Looking at him bent over the ground, I recall Grandpapa's description of the prowler who ran away from the slave quarters on the night Daddy died. He was black. Could that have been Mose? He always drank quite a bit, and it strikes me now that he might have had some dealings with my father over drugs.

I veer towards the old man, but something makes me stop short of him. Is it possible that he tried to molest me? Could he have done something so traumatic that I blocked it out? Before talking to Nathan Malik, I wouldn't have considered this. But now, thinking of the nightmares that have troubled me for years, I wonder. Could Mose be the faceless man in my dreams?

Behind Malmaison, my mother walks out briskly to the parking lot with another woman, whom I recognise as Aunt Ann. They haven't seen me, and I can't face seeing my mother at the moment. My mind is in too much turmoil. Maybe I should go to Michael's house. He's bound to be at work, but I could still use his pool. Five or six minutes on the bottom might be just the thing to calm me down. Then the sound of an engine carries through the trees. Ann has climbed into the Acura and is backing up. I hear her shift gears, and then the car rolls slowly down the curving driveway towards the gate.

'Miss Catherine?' croaks a voice parched by thousands of cigarettes.

I whip my head round. Mose is standing erect, staring at me from behind his pile of mole traps.

'That you, Miss Catherine? My eyes ain't so good no more.'

'It's me, Mose,' I call, already walking back towards Malmaison. 'Don't work too hard in this heat.'

'Heat don't bother me none.' He laughs. 'I'll take it over the cold any day.'

I give him a wave, then race towards the house.

THE VIETNAM veterans' building, used by the vets for support group meetings, parties and as a place to hang out, is a small, one-storey building situated in the city's main public park. My dad did a sculpture for it, and I decide to drive over to take a look at it again.

I expected to find my father's sculpture inside the veterans' building—where I last saw it—but as I pull into the parking lot, I see the shining rotor blades that crown the piece jutting over the roof. I get out and walk around the corner of the building to have a look.

A house-size structure stands on the rear lawn, built of wooden poles hung with parachutes and camouflage netting. Inside the netting is a grass hut, and in front of the hut an army tent forms the centrepiece of a simulated military campsite. A steel beam rises out of the centre of this scene, and mounted atop it is my father's sculpture: a brushed-steel Huey helicopter with a wounded soldier suspended from its belly by a winch cable. It's one of the most realistic pieces my father ever did. Most of his work—especially the later stuff—was far more abstract.

'Can I help you, miss?' A heavyset man with a grizzled beard and a silver ponytail is walking towards me. He wears army fatigue pants, a black T-shirt and Harley-Davidson motorcycle boots, and looks to be in his late fifties.

'I hope so. My dad sculpted that helicopter up there. I came by to see it.'

A smile lights up the man's face. 'You're Luke Ferry's kid?'

'That's right. Did you know him?'

'Sure. Not real well, of course, but he came to a few meetings here. Kept to himself quite a bit. But he did this helicopter for us. I tell you, for anybody who served in Nam, the Huey medevac is a thing of beauty. Like a guardian angel coming to pull you out of hell.'

I nod. 'I thought you kept it inside the building.'

'We do, most of the year. But on July Fourth, the priest from St Mary's does the blessing of the fleet out at Lake St John. There's a boat parade out there, and man, people love to see that Huey as they come up the lake.'

I find myself smiling. 'Daddy would have liked that.'

The vet nods, sticks out his hand. 'Jim Burley, miss. Proud to know you.'

'Cat Ferry.'

'Well, what can I do for you, Cat?'

Tell me my father was a good man . . . 'Well, I was only eight when my dad died, so he never really told me about the war. Do you know much about what he did over there?'

Burley thinks for a bit, then scratches his thick beard. 'Why don't we sit down in the shade over here?'

I follow him to a picnic table beneath an oak tree and sit opposite him.

'Your dad was a quiet guy,' Burley begins. 'But a couple of the guys wangled a few facts out of him. The picture we got was this. Your daddy was a sniper in the Airborne. After a while he was taken into some kind of special unit. Sort of a raiding unit. They used to go into places like Laos and Cambodia, places we weren't supposed to be in.'

A shudder goes through me. I close my eyes and see Nathan Malik sitting before me, telling me about his stone Buddha. *I brought it back from Cambodia* . . .

'Anyway, there was some trouble about this unit he was in,' he continues. 'Accusations of atrocities, that kind of thing. The government got up an investigation, then they just dropped it all. Flushed the whole thing down the Pentagon toilet. I think Luke was dead by that time, though.'

'Look, Mr Burley, I want you to be straight with me. Do you think my dad was involved in war crimes?'

The vet thinks about this for a while. 'I tell you, Cat, looking back on it now, a lot of what I did over there seems like crimes to me. But I didn't think twice about it then. The rules of engagement didn't cover half the situations you ran into. It was survival. Bad stuff happened, I won't lie. But most guys just did the best they could to be honourable men.' Burley gives me a heavy-hearted smile. 'And whatever Luke did, you ain't gonna be able to understand by looking back from the USA thirty-five years later.'

'Is there anybody I could talk to who might know more? Somebody Daddy might have confided in?'

Burley shrugs. 'There was a black guy Luke was pretty tight with for a while. Jesse something. He was in the Airborne, too, I remember that. Different unit from your daddy's.'

'Was Jesse from here?'

'No, Louisiana. Down the river a bit. St Francisville, maybe.'

'You can't remember his last name?'

Burley squints. 'I know it . . . I just can't *get* it. Old-timer's disease, you know? Wait a second. Billings? No. Billups? *Billups*, that's it! Jesse Billups. Related to the housekeeper over at Malmaison. Second cousin, or nephew, something like that.'

My scalp and palms are tingling. 'To the housekeeper?' I stand so suddenly that I feel light-headed. 'I'm sorry, Mr Burley, I need to go. Thank you so much for your help.'

'No problem. Hey, listen,' Burley calls. 'Don't you worry about what your daddy done over there. He came back alive, that's the main thing. And he made us this Huey. Anybody makes something that pretty and gives it away, he's gotta be all right down deep.'

CHAPTER 6

Pearlie Washington is sitting on her porch reading the newspaper when I drive into the lot behind the slave quarters. My grandfather's Lincoln is back, but Aunt Ann's Acura hasn't returned.

'Where you been?' Pearlie asks, not looking up from her copy of the *Natchez Examiner*.

'Driving.'

'*Driving?* That sounds like what you used to tell me when you was a teenager out chasing boys.'

'I never chased boys. They chased me.' There are two rockers on Pearlie's porch. I sit in the empty one.

'Don't bother asking,' she says. 'I done told you all I know.'

'About what?'

'Whatever it is you gonna ask me about.'

I look over at the rosebushes. 'Pearlie, I think you could talk from now until next week and not finish telling me all you know about this family.'

'I ain't paid to talk. I'm paid to clean.' She licks her finger and turns a page.

'Pearlie, tell me about Jesse Billups.'

Pearlie goes still, like a deer sensing threat. Then she looks up from her newspaper. 'Who you been talking to?'

'A guy who served in Vietnam. Jesse Billups knew Daddy, Pearlie. I want you to tell me who and where he is.'

Pearlie closes her eyes as though in pain. 'Jesse is my sister's child. Half-sister, really. We had the same mama but different daddies.'

'Your sister from DeSalle Island?'

Pearlie nods. 'Ivy the only sister I had.'

'Where is she now?'

'She done passed, baby. Don't you remember? Almost four years now.'

I don't remember hearing that Ivy died, but I remember the woman well. She worked as my grandfather's assistant in the little building known on DeSalle Island as the clinic. Grandpapa maintains the clinic to treat the island's black population. At times, more than a hundred people lived and worked there, many of them using dangerous farm equipment daily. I saw Grandpapa stitch up so many lacerations that by twelve I could do it myself if the need arose. Ivy had no formal medical training, but Grandpapa taught her enough to do a good deal of 'doctoring' in his absence. Their most famous exploit was removing my aunt Ann's appendix by lantern light during a storm that cut off the island from the mainland in 1958.

'What about Jesse?' I ask. 'Is he still around?'

'Jesse's the caretaker on the island now. He runs the hunting camp.'

'If he was Ivy's son, why don't I remember him?'

Pearlie shrugs. 'He was gone a lot back in your day. Went off to the city with some big plan, but all he got was big trouble. Jesse's all right, I reckon. Some good boys went over to that war and came back different.'

'What happened to him in the war?'

'He never talked about it. Same as Mr Luke. They was thick as thieves for a while. Mr Luke spent a lot of time down on the island. Said he liked the quiet. Your daddy had a lot of pain from his wound . . . in his mind, too. I think he and Jesse smoked that weed together. No hard stuff, though.'

'When was the last time you saw Jesse?'

'Been a long time, now. He stay on the island, and I don't go down there. I don't like it. Don't like the peoples, and they don't like me.' She snorts. 'To them I'm a house nigger.'

'You're kidding me. That kind of stuff is ancient history.'

She peers at me over the rims of her reading glasses. 'Not on DeSalle Island it ain't. They never joined the modern world.'

'Well, I'm going down there. Today.'

Pearlie folds her newspaper and lays it beside her chair. 'You go poking a stick in a hole, you best be ready for a snake to crawl out of it.'

I'm about to ask her what she's afraid of when my cellphone rings. Pearlie gets up from her rocker and goes into the house. I flip open the phone.

It's Sean. 'The shit's hit the fan,' he says. 'A little after eleven, we got an anonymous call telling us to check an apartment in Kenner. The female caller said Malik rented it under an alias. We got a warrant, went there with some detectives and found a lot of video equipment. Pro quality stuff. We also found the murder weapon, Cat. Thirty-two-calibre Charter Arms revolver. The handgun that killed our five victims.'

My throat tightens. 'Did you arrest Malik for murder?'

'Yeah. He went like a lamb. They took him into the parish prison. The DA argued for no bail, but the judge set one anyway. A million bucks.'

'Can he pay that?'

'Probably. He's got a house he could put up as surety.'

The anonymous tip about the location of the murder weapon bothers me. It was too easy. 'Sean, do you really think Malik is the killer?'

'I'm more convinced than I was yesterday. I just found out that ten days after Malik got back from Vietnam his father was badly beaten. Spent two months in the hospital, and he never looked the same again.'

'Did Malik's father ID his assailant?'

'Said he didn't see anything. It was in his home, but nothing was stolen.'

'Did Malik have an alibi?'

'No one even asked him for one. He was a hero, home from the war.'

As I consider this, Billy Neal, my grandfather's driver, walks into my field of vision, just below Pearlie's porch. Thin-faced and muscular, Billy Neal reminds me of the men who relentlessly hit on me in bars. Quiet men who assume too much. 'Dr Kirkland wants to see you,' he says.

'Tell him I'll see him later. I have somewhere to go first.'

A strange smile distorts Billy Neal's mouth. 'The island, you mean?'

'Sean, let me call you back.' I put the phone in my pocket and address the driver. 'Have you been eavesdropping here?'

Neal ignores the question. 'He said I should bring you now. He doesn't like to wait.'

'Listen, you keep standing there, you'll be waiting all day.'

Billy Neal gives me his crooked smile. 'I wouldn't mind that. You ain't half bad to look at.'

The door behind me bangs open, and Pearlie walks out carrying an air rifle. Her eyes are squinted nearly shut and her jaw is set tight. 'Get away from here, trash,' she says in a menacing voice.

Billy Neal laughs, then walks slowly back towards Malmaison.

'Why did you do that?' I ask Pearlie. 'I can take care of myself.'

'He's a bad apple. I don't know why Dr Kirkland keeps him. You stay away from him, Miss Cat. Things have changed around here.'

'Have they?' I shake my head. 'I think things were always this way. I was just too young to see it.'

GRANDPAPA IS WAITING for me in his study in his leather chair, a glass of Scotch in his left hand. He's still wearing his suit, and his tanned skin and silver hair give him the appearance of a veteran Hollywood actor.

'I need to ask you a question, Catherine. Please sit down.'

Something makes me want to take the initiative away from him. 'Why do you keep that lowlife around?'

Grandpapa appears taken off guard. 'Who? Billy?'

'Yes. He doesn't belong here, and you know it.'

Grandpapa looks at the floor and purses his lips, then speaks in a tone of regret. 'The casino business isn't like our other family businesses, Catherine. Las Vegas wears a corporate image nowadays, but the old unsavoury practices are still around. The big Nevada boys don't like competition, and they have quite a stake in Mississippi. I need someone who knows that world. Billy worked in Las Vegas for twelve years, and he spent three working for a casino in New Mexico. I don't delve too deeply into the exact nature of his experience. Sometimes, to accomplish something good, you have to rub elbows with the devil. That's the nature of the gambling business.'

'It surprises me to hear you talk that way.'

He shrugs in the chair. 'This town is desperate. We can't afford our high ideals any longer. Please take a seat, dear.'

I sit in a club chair and face him.

'Have you shelved that plan to hire a forensic team to search your old bedroom, given what I told you this morning about Luke's death?'

'No.'

Grandpapa doesn't react at first. Then he raises his glass and takes a long drink of Scotch. After a moment, he says, 'I can't let you do that.'

'Why not?'

'Because I killed your father, Catherine. I shot Luke.'

The words don't really register at first. I mean, I *hear* them. But their actual significance doesn't really sink in.

'I know this is a shock to you,' Grandpapa goes on. 'I wish there were some other way, that you'd never have to know. But now you've found that blood, you won't stop until you know the truth. So, I'm giving it to you.'

'I thought you gave it to me this morning.'

He shifts in his chair. 'I lied to you before, darling, and you're probably wondering why you should believe me now. All I can tell you is this: when you hear what I'm about to tell you, you'll know in your bones it's true. And I wish to God it was a different truth.'

'What are you talking about? What is this?'

Grandpapa rubs his tanned face with his right hand. 'There was no prowler here on the night Luke died,' he says. 'I killed him.'

'But why? Did you argue with him? Was it an accident?'

'No.' He looks me in the eye. 'Two days ago you asked me why I didn't like Luke. I didn't tell you the whole truth. Yes, his reaction to his war service bothered me, and the fact that he couldn't provide for you and your mother. But from the very beginning, I had had a bad feeling about that boy.'

'I can't stand this. Please just tell me whatever it is.'

'Do you remember that when Luke was having his bad periods—his spells, Pearlie called them—you were the only person he'd let near him? The only one he'd let into the barn while he worked?'

'Of course.'

'He spent a lot of time with you, Catherine. You two had a very unusual relationship. And as time went on, I started to feel that it wasn't an appropriate relationship.'

A numbness spreads across my heart. 'How do you mean?'

'That night Luke died, I wasn't reading downstairs. I had turned off all the lights and pretended to go up to bed, but I didn't. I went out into the yard with a flashlight and sat on the grass.' Another swig of Scotch. 'I'd done this several nights in a row. After about an hour, I saw Luke come up the hill from the barn and go through the door of your house. I went to your window, saw a crack of light as he opened your door. I thought he might be checking on you . . . but he wasn't. The door opened and closed quickly, and I knew he'd gone into your room and stayed there.'

I'm dreaming. If I can wake myself up, I won't have to hear this.

'I slipped inside the house. Gwen's door was open, but she was sleeping. Then I opened your door and clicked on my flashlight.'

I'm shaking my head like a child trying to reverse time: to bring back a parent who was just lowered into the earth. But it does no good.

Grandpapa stands and looks at the French windows, his voice rising with emotion. 'Luke was in the bed with you, Catherine. He was molesting you. Before I could say anything, he jumped up and started trying to explain himself. But there was no denying it. I grabbed his arm and yanked him towards the door. He went crazy. He started hitting me.' Grandpapa turns to me, his eyes bright. 'Luke was so passive most of the time, it took me completely by surprise. I wanted to get you out of there, but he'd hit me several times and showed no sign of stopping. I remembered the rifle that hung over the fireplace in the den. I ran out and grabbed it, chambered a round, and went back in to get you.

'Luke was in the corner by the closet, down on his knees. Your bed was empty so I figured you'd escaped. I walked over to him with the rifle and told him to get the hell off my property and never come back.' Grandpapa's eyes are cloudy with memory. 'Maybe it was the sight of the gun that did it. Or maybe he couldn't deal with the idea that he was going to be exposed. But he attacked me again. He came up out of that corner like a wild animal. I pulled the trigger out of pure reflex. You know the rest.'

The silence in the study is absolute. Then, out of the vacuum that is me at this moment, a question rises. 'Did I see it happen?'

'I don't know, baby. You must have crawled through to your mother's bedroom and tried to wake her up. Do you remember any of this?'

'Maybe that,' I whisper. 'Trying to wake Mom up. But maybe it wasn't that night. I think that happened a lot back then.'

'But you remember nothing of the abuse?'

I shake my head with robotic precision.

'I thought not. But you've never recovered from it, just the same. It's haunted you your whole life. I've watched you all these years, wishing I could do something for you. But I didn't see how telling you about your father could help you. They say the truth shall set you free, but I'm not so sure. If you hadn't found that blood, I doubt I'd ever have told this thing.'

'Who else knows?' I whisper.

'No one . . . It might be helpful to speak to someone, Catherine. I can get you access to the top people in the country.'

'I have to go.'

'Why don't you stay here for a while? I'll have Pearlie fix a room upstairs. Take a few days and start trying to get your mind around this.'

'I have to go now, Grandpapa.'

I turn and walk quickly to the French windows that lead out onto the lawn. His footsteps follow me, then stop. In a moment I'm standing in bright sunlight on an endless plain of freshly mown grass.

And there the tears come. Great racking sobs as I fall to my knees. I am desolate. I want to crawl out of my own disgusting body.

'Catherine?' calls a frantic female voice. 'What's the matter? Did you hurt yourself?'

It's my mother. She's kneeling in the flowerbeds near the front entrance of Malmaison. The mere sight of her throws me into panic. When she gets to her feet, I stand and race for the far corner of the house. Rounding it, I sprint along the back wall of our slave quarters towards my car. My escape. I slide behind the wheel and slam the door. The revving motor is the first thing that slows the spinning panic in my chest.

Throwing the Audi into gear, I roar out of the parking lot, spraying gravel. Never have I wanted to leave a place so badly.

DESALLE ISLAND rises out of the Mississippi River like the back of a sleeping dog. Its long, low line of trees stretches four miles north to south, three miles east to west. The island is as much a part of me as Natchez and New Orleans, yet it stands apart from them. Apart from everything, really. Nominally part of Louisiana, it is in truth subject to no authority other than that of my family. It was created when the Mississippi River, having wound back upon itself like a writhing snake, finally cut off its own tortuous bend with a great rush of floodwater that shortened its course by more than five miles. Left in the wake of that cataclysm was a great island covered with timber, rich topsoil, wild game and the shacks of a dozen black families who worked for my ancestors for 150 years. The only whites who come here are members of my family, or business associates of my grandfather's invited here to hunt.

I'm parked where the narrowest part of the old river channel flows through a treacherous plain of mud. Here a dirt causeway stretches across to the island. Every spring it's washed away by overflow from the river, but every summer it's rebuilt again. The river is high for this time of year, and the backwater laps against the edges of the causeway with maybe an inch to spare. Looking up at a line of thunderclouds that has been blowing up from the south for the past hour, I try to decide whether it's safe to cross.

I drove here in a state of near hypnosis, my only goal to reach this place where my father spent so much time, to somehow solve the tragic mysteries of his life and mine. I was conscious enough to call Sean twice, but he didn't answer. Then, for some reason, I felt a compulsion to speak to Nathan Malik. I called his cellphone, and it kicked me over to his voicemail. I wanted to leave a message, but I didn't. If the psychiatrist is still in jail, his cellphone is probably sitting on the desk of some FBI agent, who is at this moment trying to trace the number of the person who called their main suspect.

When I couldn't reach Malik, I called directory assistance and got the number of Michael Wells's medical office. It took some convincing, but his receptionist finally put me through. I told Michael I'd really like to talk to him, if he had some time.

'I'm up to my ass in alligators right now,' he said, laughing. 'Sick two-year-olds, actually, but it amounts to the same thing. I'd love to see you later, though. Would you let me buy you dinner?'

I was silent for a moment—or maybe longer—because Michael said, 'Cat? Is something wrong?'

'Umm . . . yeah. That's what I wanted to talk to you about. Do you believe in repressed memories?'

'Related to what? That usually has to do with child abuse.'

'Yeah. Like that.'

He was silent for a bit. 'Is this a hypothetical question?'

I wasn't sure how to answer. 'Sort of.'

'Forget about dinner. Come to my office right now. I'm on Jeff Davis Boulevard. You remember where that is?'

'Sure, but it's OK. Forget I called. I'm not even in town right now. If I get back in time, I'll call you later, OK?'

'Cat—'

I hung up and put my ringer on silent. Why was I trying to involve a paediatrician who knew nothing about me and my problems? Because we'd known each other in school? Because he had a sympathetic face?

Across the channel, a green johnboat is plying the shore in the shadow of some cypress trees. I can make out the silhouette of a black teenager checking a line that has dozens of hooks hanging from it, baited with something stinky to attract the catfish. As the boy works his way along the line, I pick up my cellphone and speed-dial my therapist, Dr Hannah Goldman.

'Cat?' she says, apparently looking at a caller ID screen.

'Mm-hm,' I say in a tiny voice.

'Where are you? We have a bad connection.' Her statement is punctuated by a burst of static.

'Out of town.'

'What's going on?'

'I just found out that my grandfather killed my father.'

Not much throws Dr Goldman, but this does. After several seconds, she says, 'I thought your father was shot by an intruder.'

'I thought so, too. But my grandfather just told me a different story. It's complicated. I found some blood in my old bedroom. A latent bloodstain— I wasn't even looking for it. But it got me thinking about that night. I started asking questions. I was going to bring in a forensic team, so he decided to tell me the truth.'

'Was the shooting an accident?'

'No. He caught my father sexually abusing me. And he killed him.'

'I see,' Dr Goldman says in her most professional voice.

She says that to keep from saying *Dear God* or something similar. Hannah tries to be detached, but she's not. She is the middle ground between professional detachment and the activist commitment of Nathan Malik.

'Do you believe what your grandfather told you?'

'He's never lied to me before. Except about this—I mean, by omission. He said he kept the truth from me to protect me. And I always felt that something was wrong with the story they'd told me as a child.'

'Do you have any memory of the events he described?'

'No. But I've been thinking about repressed memories a lot lately, because of a murder case I'm working on. Do you believe in them, Hannah? I mean, can a person totally block something from their conscious mind?'

'Yes, I do. It's controversial, because very little is known about the neuromechanics of memory. But evidence indicates that some trauma victims dissociate during their experiences and suffer amnesia for those events. The strange thing about your case is that you've been handed corroboration of abuse before you even started to remember it. Considering the issues you and I have been dealing with for so long, this information could be the greatest gift you ever receive, though I know it's hard to see that now.'

'Uh-huh.'

'Listen to me, Cat. This is a dangerous time for you. I want to see you as soon as you can get to my office. After what you've been told today, there's simply no telling what might happen. Flashbacks, suicidal impulses . . . But there's a lot of work we can do. I know some very good people in this area.'

'Do you know Nathan Malik?'

'Why do you ask that?' Hannah's tone is suddenly guarded. 'Have you seen him as a patient?'

'No. Do you think he's good at what he does?'

'He's published some interesting articles. And he's had some surprising successes with recovered memories. But he uses radical techniques. They're unproven, maybe even dangerous. Cat, are you in a safe place?'

I look across at the island, forbidding beneath the grey clouds. 'Yeah.'

'Cat, the main thing is that what happened between you and your father is *not your fault*. You were a child. You—' Static blots out Hannah's voice.

'Thanks for answering,' I say into the static. 'Thanks for always—'

A blaring horn nearly knocks me out of my seat. I look in my rearview mirror and see a big white pick-up truck parked behind me.

'*Hannah?*'

The connection is gone.

The truck honks again. It's waiting to use the causeway. The driver behind me may trust the muddy span, but I don't. I want to back up and get out of his way, but I can't seem to move. The horn blares again.

Half a minute passes. Then a black man who looks like he weighs 300 pounds climbs out of the truck and walks towards my car. When he reaches it, I see he has a kind face. He looks about fifty years old and, though it seems unlikely, I wonder if fate has put me in the path of Jesse Billups.

I push the switch that rolls down my window.

'You look like you in the wrong place, lady,' he says in a deep voice.

'Are you Jesse Billups?'

The big man's mouth breaks into a broad smile. '*Hell* no. Jesse my cousin, though. You with them *Sports Illustrated* people who did that shoot here back in the spring?'

'No. I'm Catherine Ferry.'

A blank look, then a faint spark of recognition in his eyes.

'Catherine *DeSalle* Ferry,' I clarify.

The man straightens up. 'Sorry I didn't recognise you, ma'am. I'm Henry Washington. You want me to lead you over the bridge and find Jesse?'

'Is it safe to cross?'

Washington cocks his round head to one side. 'Well, that's a stretchy kind of word, *safe*. I been over this old thing many a time and it ain't caved in yet. Tell you what. Why don't you ride over with me? When you done talking to Jesse, he'll bring you back here to your car.'

'Sounds good to me.'

After backing the Audi under a pecan tree and locking it, I climb up into the passenger seat of Henry's truck.

'How come I ain't seen you down here before?' Henry asks, putting the truck in gear.

'It's been ten years since I visited, longer than that since I spent any real time here.'

'Well, it ain't changed much.'

We hit a muddy patch, and the tail of the truck slides almost out from under us. I clench every muscle, but Henry just laughs as we straighten up again. 'You think you scared?' he booms. 'My big ass goes into that water, it's all over but the crying, because I can't swim.'

As the wall of trees gets nearer, a few raindrops splash onto the windshield. I catch sight of a small shed near the water, and my heart pounds.

Parked beside it is the round-nosed pick-up truck from my dream.

THE MOMENT Henry Washington's truck rolls onto the gravel road that follows the eastern shore of the island, a strange thrumming starts in my body. DeSalle Island looks the same as it always did, the perimeter skirted with cypress trees, the interior forested with willows and giant cottonwoods. The cypresses are on my right now; we're driving north. I want to ask Henry about my grandfather's old truck, but the tightness in my chest stops me.

'Jesse's been on the north end chasing stray cows,' Henry says, shaking his head as though such labour requires a certain level of insanity. 'And he said something about doing some plumbing work at the hunting camp.'

I remember that the northern part of the island is pastureland dotted with cattle. At the centre is a horseshoe lake, and south of the lake lie the woods we're passing now. The cabins and utility buildings of the hunting camp are nestled among the trees at the lower edge of the woods.

Now the trees on my left thin to reveal the green lake and the cluster of shacks where the workers live. The sun has started to sink, and most of the porches have people on them, the old ones rocking slowly, the children scampering around in the dust with cats and dogs.

'Here we go,' Henry says, turning right onto a narrow gravel road.

Soon the cabins of the hunting camp appear ahead. Unlike the shacks of the workers, many of which are made of clapboard on brick stilts, the cabins are built of sturdy cypress, weathered grey and hard as steel. The roofs are corrugated tin that's rusted to dark orange.

'There Jesse,' says Henry.

I don't see a man, but I do see a brown horse tied to the porch rail of one of the cabins. Henry pulls up in front of the cabin and honks his horn.

A wiry black man wearing no shirt crawls from beneath the cabin, stands, and brushes himself off. At first he looks like a hundred other workmen I've seen. Then he turns, and I see the right side of his face. Blotches of bright pink skin stand out like splatters of paint from his right shoulder to his right temple, and his cheek is all scar tissue.

'He got burned over in Vietnam,' Henry says. 'It looks bad, but we used to it now.' He leans out of his window and shouts, 'Yo, Jesse! Got a lady in here wants to talk to you!'

Jesse walks over to the truck—my side, not Henry's—and looks me in the eye. Henry uses his switch to roll down my window.

'What you want with me?' Jesse Billups says in an insolent voice.

'I want to talk to you about my father. Luke Ferry.'

Jesse's eyes widen, and then he snorts like a horse. 'Goddamn. All this time, and now you come back? I met you when you was a little girl. I knew your mama pretty well. How'd you get down here?'

Henry says, 'Her car's parked on the other side of the bridge. I told her you'd take her back to it when she's ready. You got her OK?'

Jesse studies me for a bit. 'Yeah, I'll take her back.'

He opens my door and helps me down from the high cab. As Henry drives away, Jesse leads me onto the porch of one of the cabins. He sits against the cabin wall. I sit on the top step and brace my back against the rail.

Jesse takes a pack of Kool menthols from his back pocket and lights one. After a deep drag, he says, 'You here to ask about your daddy?'

'I was hoping you could tell me something about what happened to him in the war. Somebody told me he was part of a unit that was accused of war crimes. Do you know anything about that?'

Jesse snorts in derision. '*War crimes?* War *is* a crime, start to finish.'

I'm not sure how to continue. 'Well, there must have been some unusual events, at least, for the army to talk about prosecuting his unit.'

'*Unusual?*' Jesse barks a humourless laugh. 'Yeah. That's a good word. Luke was a country boy, see? He knew how to shoot. That's what got him in trouble. The army made him a sniper and took him into this special unit called the White Tigers. Supposed to be a volunteer thing, but the CO volunteered anybody he wanted into it. That's how old Lukie got stuck. The White Tigers was put together for what they call *incursion* into enemy territory.

Only this incursion wasn't exactly legal. The Tigers went into Cambodia to try to hit the Cong where they hid from our bombers. They went from village to village, looking for weapons, VC or VC sympathisers. They did some bad stuff. Punished anybody suspected of helping the VC or the Khmer Rouge. Questioned people vigorously.' He laughs bitterly. 'That means torture.'

'My father did some of this?'

He nods. 'That was the job, you know? But in the Tigers, the officers *instigated* this stuff. Shooting prisoners, cutting off heads and leaving them on sticks to scare the Khmer Rouge. Taking women from the villages and raping them . . . Luke did what he had to do and got the hell out.'

'What about the war crimes investigation? Who started that?'

Jesse takes a drag from his cigarette. 'All I know is, when the government questioned Luke, he didn't tell 'em a thing. They dropped the investigation.'

'Well, do you think—?'

'What you come down here for?' he growls with sudden intensity. 'You didn't come here to talk about no Vietnam. There's something else behind these questions . . . Hey, you look like you about to cry on me.'

I tilt back my head and blink away tears. 'You're right. I don't know what I came here for exactly. I was hoping for . . . something. I don't know what.'

'You looking for an explanation for the way Luke was? Hoping I'd tell you he was a saint or something, behind that closed-up face of his? He was just a dude, like me. We all got good and bad deep inside.' He points a finger at me. 'But I ain't telling you nothing you don't already know. I can see that in your eyes. You Luke Ferry's kid, I know you got both inside of you.'

Now the tears come, too many to blink away. 'Why did my daddy spend so much time down here, Jesse? What was it that drew him?'

The anger I sensed before seems to have leaked out of Jesse's pores. 'He walked around. Drew things in a notebook. Played a little music. Had him a guitar down here. He was all right, for a white boy. Had some blues in him.'

'Well, did he—?'

The ring of a cellphone stops me, but it's not mine. Jesse takes a Nokia from his pocket and answers. He listens for a bit, then says he'll get right on it and hangs up. 'I got to go,' he says. 'Gotta get some supplies from the mainland in case the water covers the bridge. We better get moving.'

'But I have some more questions.'

'We can talk on the way.' He walks over to his horse, unties him and leads him to where I'm standing. 'I'll get on, then pull you up behind me. Just stay clear of his hindquarters.' Jesse mounts the horse, and takes his foot out of the stirrup so I can get a foothold. Then he takes my left arm and pulls me effortlessly up behind his saddle. 'You can talk, but hang on while you do.' He puts the horse into a canter on the grassy shoulder of the gravel road.

'You work for my grandfather, right?' I ask.

'That's right.'

'What do you think of him? Do you like him?'

'Dr Kirkland pays my wages. "Like" got nothing to do with it.'

Before I can ask Jesse more, I see a woman riding towards us on a bicycle. The gravel road makes it difficult for her.

'Who's that?'

'Don't pay her no mind. She half crazy,' mutters Jesse.

The woman slows as she nears us, but Jesse spurs his horse as though he means to pass her without a word.

'Wait!' cries the woman, and when he doesn't stop she shouts, 'Goddamn you, Jesse Billups! Don't you run from me!'

I reach round Jesse and grab for the reins. 'Stop this horse!'

He curses, then stops the horse on a dime. 'You gonna wish we hadn't.'

From the woman's agitation, I expect her to start shouting accusations of battery or paternity at Jesse Billups. But now that the horse has stopped, she acts as if Jesse doesn't exist. She has eyes only for me.

'Are you Catherine Ferry?'

'That's right.'

'I'm Louise Butler. I want to talk to you. About your daddy.'

'Did you know him?'

'I surely did.'

Swinging my left leg over the horse's flanks, I drop to the gravel beside Louise Butler. She's about forty and very pretty, with the same milk-chocolate skin that Pearlie has.

'If you stay here and jaw,' says Jesse, 'you gonna have to get back to your car on your own. I got to go.'

'I know where my car is. I can get back to it.'

Jesse kicks his horse and leaves us in a small cloud of dust. I look at Louise, expecting an explanation. But she only stares at the sky.

'Gonna rain soon,' she comments. 'I got a place by the lake. We'd better start back that way.' Without waiting for an answer, she turns her bike round and starts pushing it down the road.

I fall in beside her, my feet scrunching the gravel as I walk. 'How did you know I was here?'

'Henry told me, Miss Catherine,' she says, not looking over at me.

'Please call me Cat.'

'Kitty Cat,' she says softly.

A chill goes through me. My father called me Kitty Cat when I was very small. He was the only one who did. 'So you did know my father.'

Now she turns to me. 'You might not like what I'm gonna say.'

'You can't make me feel any worse than I already do today.'

'Don't be so sure. Did Jesse tell you anything bad about Luke?'

'Not really. I thought they were friends, anyway.'

'They was for a while.'

'What happened?'

'Me.' She looks at me out of the corner of her eye. 'Darling, Luke was my man for seven years. From 1974 right up to the night he died. Jesse didn't like that. He'd always wanted me for himself.'

I stop in my tracks. This woman can't be more than ten years older than I. And she's telling me she was my father's lover?

Louise walks on, then realises I'm no longer beside her. She stops and turns back. 'I don't want to hurt your feelings. I just wanted to talk to you about him, see if I could see him in you.'

'Can you?'

She smiles sadly. 'He's looking out of your eyes at me right now. Every line of your face got a shadow of him in it.'

'Louise, what—?'

Before I can finish, the clouds open up and fat raindrops slap the cream-coloured dust on the shoulder of the road. Louise and I run like little girls, she pushing her bike at first, then jumping onto it and riding beside me.

'You're in good shape!' she cries as the shacks of the little village come into sight. 'My house ain't far, but it's past this bunch here.'

We race past the grey shacks, their porches empty now, and turn down a muddy path that parallels the lake.

'There it is!' Louise shouts.

In the distance I see a shack that's not grey like the others but bright blue. Now I know where I'm going, I sprint ahead. My feet have better purchase in the mud than her bicycle, and I beat Louise to her flimsy front door.

'Go on in,' she says, lifting her bike onto the narrow porch.

I walk through the door into a room that serves as kitchen, den and dining area. The moment I enter, two things strike me with startling intensity. First is the sound of the rain hitting the tin roof above me. It's my recurring dream made real. The second is the certainty that my father once lived here. On the mantle is a sculpture of an African woman: a blank oval face over a long neck and a trunk with graceful limbs. One glance tells me it's his work.

Suddenly I'm wavering on my feet. The heat in the house is stifling, and the rattle of the rain seems to grow louder by the second. As my knees go out from under me, Louise catches me under the arms and steers my falling body towards a sofa.

'DRINK THIS,' says Louise, holding a glass of iced tea under my chin. 'The heat got you, that's all. This place been shut up a couple of days, and it gets like an oven without the air conditioner going.'

'It's not the heat,' I tell her, taking a sip of syrupy tea. 'It's the rain.'

'The rain?' Louise looks confused.

'The sound of it hitting a tin roof. Lately I've been hearing that sound in my dreams, and even while I'm awake. I just couldn't take it.'

'Sometimes that's the way of it,' Louise says, walking to the sink. 'I got a lot of things inside me I don't understand.' She runs tap water into a carafe, switches on a coffeemaker, then comes and sits in a recliner on my left.

'Louise, what can you tell me about the pick-up truck by the bridge? I know it was my grandfather's. But did my father ever drive it?'

She closes her eyes. 'That old rusted wreck? Yeah, Luke drove it some, when the old man wasn't around. Dr Kirkland used to brag all the time about how long his old truck had been running. He said it had never quit on him and never would. Finally did, though. Why?'

'I think I saw something when I was in that truck. I have this dream where I'm riding in it with Grandpapa. We're on the north end of the island, riding up a hill in the cow pasture, towards the pond. We get closer and closer, but we never get over the hill. Lately, the closer we get, the more afraid I get. Do you know of anything that happened up there?'

She leans back in her chair and looks at the porch window. The storm clouds have brought a premature darkness, and the wind rattles the glass in its frame. 'Lots of bad things happened on this old island over the years. But the pond . . . you think you saw somebody get beaten? Killed, maybe?'

'I don't know.' A different thought strikes me. 'Did Daddy ever talk to you about the war?'

'Not with words. But he let me see the pain in different ways.'

'Did he talk to anybody about the war besides Jesse?'

'I think he talked to Dr Cage some, over in Natchez. That's who gave him his medication. Dr Cage is a good man. He likes to listen to people talk.'

I remember Pearlie mentioning Dr Cage.

'I've been told that his unit committed war crimes. That they tortured and raped. Do you think Daddy could have done anything like that?'

Louise stands suddenly and goes to a drawer, then takes out a pack of Salem cigarettes and lights one with a kitchen match. 'Luke had some problems, OK?' She exhales blue smoke. 'When he and I first got together, he couldn't make love. I knew something in the war had done that to him. Not his wound. Something in his head. It took more than a year to get him where he could be with me. I don't know why. I'm no doctor. But he may have done or seen things over there that made sex terrible to him.'

A blast of wind makes the windows shudder. 'How old were you then?'

'I was fourteen when I started following him around. I'd sit and listen while he talked. Which was funny, 'cause people who met him wondered if he could talk at all. But he could when he wanted to. He talked to me all the time. And we was just talking. We didn't do nothing till I turned sixteen.'

Sixteen . . . 'I can see you were in love with him.'

There's a faraway look in her eyes. 'You want to know if he was in love with me, don't you?'

'Yes.'

'He told me he was. I know that probably hurts you. But I'll tell you this, he wasn't ever gonna leave you to come to me. He hated that place, that Malmaison. Hated your grandfather, too.'

'And my mother?'

Louise gives me an intense look. 'He loved your mama, now. She just didn't understand him. But when I'd talk to him about leaving, he'd say, "I can't leave my Kitty Cat, Louise. Can't leave my baby in that house with those people." And he never did.'

'Did he say anything else about my mother?'

Louise hesitates. 'He said she had problems with sex. Even before he went to the war. At first he thought it was just shyness, but she never loosened up. I think she'd just been taught that sex was something to be ashamed of.'

'Thank you for being so honest, Louise.'

'I got no reason to lie, except to spare you pain. And you seem like you can handle it.'

'Did my grandfather know about you and my father?'

'He'd have to have been blind not to, and that's one thing Dr Kirkland ain't.'

'What do you think about my grandfather, Louise?'

She takes her time answering. 'Dr Kirkland's a hard man in some ways, soft in others. He's tough on dogs and horses. Good at taking care of people, though. He's saved a lot of lives here over the years. Saved my uncle after a chain-saw accident. The doctor's got a temper, now. If he gets mad, there's hell to pay. Luke's the only man I ever saw defy him and get away with it.'

A strange current of emotion wells up from my soul. 'Louise, what would you say if I told you Grandpapa killed Luke that night?'

She stares at me, then begins shaking her head like she's seen a ghost. 'Don't tell me nothing like that. I don't even want to *think* that.'

'If it scares you that much,' I say softly, 'you must think it could be true.'

'What are you saying, Cat?'

'Nothing. Crazy thoughts.' I want to tell her what I know, but something stops me. Louise has precious memories of my father. What good could it do for me to smudge them with accusations of child molestation?

'What do you do for a living, Louise, if you don't mind me asking?'

She looks at the floor. 'I got a man here takes care of me. I just keep up this house for . . . well, you know why.'

'Is the man Jesse Billups?'

Louise sighs. 'Not Jesse,' she says. 'Henry. The man who drove you onto the island. He ain't pretty like Luke, but he's got a good heart.'

'Are you married?'

'I ain't interested in getting married. The man I wanted to marry got killed.'

I reach out and take hold of her hand. I've never met this woman before, yet I feel more intimately bound to her than to people I've known my whole life. When I think about what Grandpapa told me about my father's death, it makes no sense. How could the man this woman loved commit unspeakable acts with a child? With his *own* child.

'Sounds like the rain's slacked up,' Louise says.

'You're right. I should go now, while I can. Do you have a car?'

She shakes her head. 'No, and Henry's gone to Lafayette to see his kids. They stay with his ex-wife. Jesse can take you.'

I shake my head. 'Jesse's gone to the mainland to get some supplies.'

Louise goes to the front window and looks out. 'You can use my bike. The rain won't be as bad if you cut through the woods. You'll be at the bridge in ten minutes. If you have a problem, call my cellphone, and I'll come get you.' She takes my cellphone from me and programs her number into its memory. 'If I need to, I can get there on my two feet in no time. And I'll call Jesse. If he gets back, I'll send him after you. He can drive you across.'

I move to the door, then turn back and hug Louise.

She squeezes me tightly. 'You going through some tough times, girl. But time will heal you. You come back and see me sometime.'

I promise that I will, then I walk onto the porch and carry her bicycle down to the path.

'Hey!' Louise calls through the rain. 'Wait!'

She disappears inside for a minute. I hope she's getting me a raincoat, but when she returns she's carrying what looks like a Ziploc sandwich bag.

'For your cellphone!' she says over the wind.

I slip my phone and car keys inside the bag, squeeze out the air and zip it shut. Then I stuff it into the front pocket of my jeans, and start pedalling towards the road that cuts through the woods to the hunting camp.

The wind slaps the rain against my right cheek, but soon I'm passing the shacks by the lake, their porches still empty. When I turn south on the camp road, the wind hits me full in the face. I lean low over the handlebars and bear down hard on the pedals. The shoulder is so muddy in places that I almost take a spill, but the further south I ride, the sandier the soil gets.

Beneath the black storm clouds, the world has gone grey. Everything ahead looks as flat as a black and white photograph. Then, out of the greyness, the old channel of the river appears, and relief washes through me.

A mile up the road is the bridge that leads to my car. I'm about to turn onto it when two bright beams of light swing across me from behind. I look back over my shoulder. Headlights. They look high enough to belong to a truck. Louise told me she would send Jesse after me if he got back in time.

I stop the bike at the turn and wait.

The driver of the pick-up flicks his lights to high beam. I raise my hand to wave, then freeze. The truck hasn't slowed at all. It's accelerating.

I dive into the ditch on the left side of the road. I regain my feet as the truck crushes Louise's bicycle beneath its bumper, then it bounces after me across the ditch. My only hope is the trees—but I can't outsprint a truck.

An unholy grinding of gears gives me hope. The bike must have been caught in the truck's chassis. As the driver tries to get his vehicle off the twisted wreckage, I reach the first giant willow and dart behind it.

Suddenly the truck's motor dies. The headlights remain on, though, and the interior light flicks on behind them. There's a figure inside the cab—a man—but his face is obscured by the rain. He leans forward. I'm squinting to try to see his face when a flash blooms in the dark and splinters pierce my left cheek. Only then does the crack of the rifle bullet reach me.

CHAPTER 7

Panic drives me through the trees without direction. A second gunshot quickly follows the first, and one look over my shoulder tells me that the shooter has followed me into the woods. Now and then he flicks on a flashlight to find his way through the trees. From his careful progress I know one thing: he's driving me south, and it's only a matter of time before he corners me on the tip of the island.

I need to find a way to slip round him, but on this ground that's almost impossible. The island here is like tropical jungle. The willow and cottonwood brakes give good cover, but there's too much underbrush on the ground to move quietly, even in the rain. There's one other chance.

I move to the right. On the west side of the island, facing the main channel of the river, there's a boat ramp where a fishing boat is kept tied up. If the shooter were further behind me, I might have time to launch the boat before he reached me. But he's not. I've got to slow him down. But how? I have no weapons. As I fight my way west through the underbrush, an image comes into my mind—*bull nettle*. It's a twisting green vine about four feet high, bristling with needles that inject a painful toxin into any creature that rubs against it. The southern tip of DeSalle Island is covered with bull nettle.

I veer south again. Tree branches whip my face and peppervine claws at the legs of my jeans. The sound of my pursuer crashing through the brush grows nearer. Sweat pours from my skin, and my heart thumps against my breastbone. Free diving keeps me in good physical shape, but terror steals my breath, and alcohol withdrawal probably isn't helping.

As I slow to get my bearings, the rifle cracks again. I duck down and scramble between two cottonwood trunks, then crab-crawl through the dark until my arms begin to itch like fire. *Bull nettle!* There's a thicket of the stuff all around me. I could never have imagined being glad to feel this pain, but at this moment I'm ecstatic.

Thirty yards into the thicket, I bear right, towards the boat ramp. Before I cover twenty yards, a scream of male rage echoes through the trees. I sprint across a level patch of sand, my heart lifting with hope until I spy a string stretched across my path at thigh level. It's an old line strung with rusty fish-hooks, and though I twist my body in an effort to avoid it, nothing can stop my headlong flight. The line rips free as I fall, but one of the treble hooks is well and truly buried in my right thigh. I swallow a scream.

The rifle booms again, its echo like cannon fire. My hunter heard my scream and got a new fix on my position. I'm almost certain that it's Jesse Billups behind me. Who else knew where I was?

The main channel of the Mississippi has appeared before me, its far shore a mile away, cloaked in rain and darkness. I race south along the bank, skirting cypress knees and driftwood. There's the boat ramp, forty yards along the shore. Its concrete slab runs down into the water at a steep angle and a small boat sits on a trailer about five feet above it.

I crouch near the river's edge, senses primed for the slightest sound. Something's not right. I don't hear my pursuer any more. The wind is louder on the exposed bank, but I should hear *something*. I need a weapon. A tree branch? A rock? Not much good against a rifle. What do I have with me . . .?

Cellphone. I take the Ziploc from my pocket, squeeze the phone through the plastic, and the light of the screen clicks on. My joy is short-lived.

The screen reads: NO SERVICE. I need to move to higher ground. I'm thinking of sprinting north along the shore, away from the boat ramp, when a flashlight beam shines out of the woods behind me and moves steadily along the bank. In seconds it will pick out my hunched body on the sand.

Without thinking, I shove the Ziploc back in my pocket, crawl to the river's edge and slip into the current. The water is cool but not cold, thank God, and it soothes the hives caused by the bull nettle. The waves are another matter. When I swam this river at sixteen, its surface was like glass. Now the whitecaps batter me, and soon the current pulls me out into the river.

I feel no bottom below me because there are no shallows here. This part of the island forms the outside of a river bend, so it takes the full brunt of the current. The cutting power of all that water is enormous. Wherever it hits a bank like this, the Mississippi gouges out a channel over a hundred feet deep.

I've got to get my shoes off. My jeans, too. I'm reaching down to pull off my left shoe when the flashlight pins me. I don't feel or see the impact of the bullet, but the whipcrack by my ear knocks my heart into my throat.

I yank off both shoes and dive, exhaling to bleed off buoyancy, extending my limbs to catch the current and drift more swiftly past the island. When I surface again, the flashlight is gone. Unsnapping my jeans, I try to peel myself out of them. My left leg comes loose, but the other won't. Kicking back to the surface, I see why. The fish-hook from the line has fastened the jeans to my thigh. Two prongs of the treble hook are buried deep in my flesh.

My fingers can't grip the free hook firmly enough to rip out the other two, but my watch has a steel band. Slipping the barb of the free hook into a crevice in the band, I turn my forearm so that I can jerk upwards with maximum force. Taking a deep breath, I curl into a foetal position, then explode out of it, yanking my right arm up and my right leg down. As a scream bursts from my throat, something tears free. I right myself in the water and look at my thigh. Where the hook was embedded is now only a ragged hole streaming blood. I carefully remove the freed jeans leg, making sure I don't let the jeans sink into the river, because they're going to save me.

Treading water, I tie knots in both legs, then take hold of each side of the waist, and whip the jeans back over my head in a wide arc, trapping enough air in the makeshift life vest to keep me afloat. Then I lay my chin in the inverted crotch of the jeans, with the knotted legs sticking upwards. I learned how to do this on the swim team, and it works surprisingly well.

I'm fifty yards from the island now. All I can see is a narrow strip of beach, but then that, too, disappears. *Fifty yards. Only fifteen hundred left to swim. Maybe seventeen hundred . . .* The safest thing to do would be to drift south along this bank for a mile or so, then climb ashore. The problem with that plan is that I'd be getting out of the river in an area of swamp uninhabited except by alligators and snakes. If I *cross* the river, I'll come ashore less than a mile from Louisiana Highway 1. There I can flag down a car, or walk to a place where I'll have cellular service.

Am I crazy to try it? Most people would say yes. But I swam this river fifteen years ago, and if I did it then, I can do it now. The trick is not to fight the current, but to float with it and gradually vector out towards the deepest part of the channel. Once you reach that, the river will do its best to deposit you on the opposite shore of the next bend. The biggest threat is logs, especially those half submerged in the muddy water.

Ten minutes of steady kicking moves me into the main body of the river, half a mile downstream.

The sound of an outboard motor penetrates the hissing rain, and chills my blood. It's probably the Evinrude on the old fishing boat I decided to leave on the island. Jesse has come looking for me.

Kicking up onto a wave crest, I see a flashlight bobbing up and down about thirty yards away. It's hard to believe my pursuer could get this close, but maybe he heard my scream. I try to calm myself with logic: the odds of his sighting me in this maelstrom are low, as long as I keep my head down.

Pulling the deflating legs of my jeans beneath my arms, I lie flat on the surface and stop kicking. The whine of the motor gets louder, then dies, only to return again not twenty yards from my right ear. Sucking in a lungful of air, I duck my head and drop three feet underwater, clinging only to the jeans pocket that holds my cellphone. I hear the prop spinning, a high-pitched whine. But the boat doesn't seem to be moving.

For two minutes I float like the foetus in my womb, listening to the spinning prop. He *must* have seen me. Why else would he remain in one place? Surfacing slowly, I raise my eyes above the water. This time a white shaft of light slices through the rain. It's coming from a spotlight mounted on the boat's hull. Whoever is piloting that boat either just remembered the spotlight or just discovered it. Maybe it *isn't* Jesse Billups. The island's caretaker would have switched on the spotlight as soon as he launched the boat.

The beam rakes over the frothing waves like a searchlight in a prison movie, first this way, then that. Once, when the light lingers upstream, I see the massive rootball of a tree floating in the glare. From the size of the twisted roots above the water, the tree itself must be eighty feet long.

The air in my jeans has gone now, adding to my weight. I need to reinflate them, but whipping them over my head would be like waving a flag. So I carefully remove the Ziploc containing my cellphone from the pocket, and let the jeans sink in the river. Then I kick towards the tree.

After thirty seconds underwater, I surface to check my progress. Miraculously, the tree arrives like a scheduled bus, and with my right hand I reach out and catch a trailing root. As the monster trunk drifts downstream, I climb onto the dry roots above the water line and suddenly I'm riding like Cleopatra on her royal barge, concealed by the tangle of roots and mud.

I can see much more from this vantage point. To my right, a haze of faint bluish light reflects off the clouds. That light is Louisiana Highway 1, and the river, true to its course, is driving the tree straight towards the far bank of the bend, beneath those lights. In about three minutes, I should be able to leap from these roots and swim no more than 300 yards to shore.

I open the Ziploc to check my cellphone and see its screen glowing green in the darkness. *I have service again.*

While deciding *whom* to call, I realise that my screen shows three missed calls. Paging through, I see that one was from Sean, one from Michael Wells and one from UNKNOWN CALLER. I check the battery to make sure I have adequate power, then listen to the messages.

Sean: *Hey, it's me, I'm sorry about not answering before. I was talking with Karen about the whole divorce thing, and about you. It's complicated . . .*

Look, there's something you need to know. Nathan Malik made his bail. A million bucks. The FBI had him under surveillance, but Malik drove out to Lakeside Mall and pulled some kind of switch in a store. They lost him. Anyway, you need to watch your back. Malik hasn't been declared a fugitive, but if he leaves the state, he will be. He's already the target of a statewide manhunt here. Don't come back to New Orleans, and—Karen's coming . . .

There's a click, and the message ends.

The next message says, *Cat, this is Michael Wells. I got your cell number from your mother. I'm done with work now, and I'd really like to talk to you. You didn't sound good on the phone earlier. You may be fine now, but I just want you to know I'm here for you. As a friend, a doctor, whatever you need. My home number is 445 8663. Call me, OK? No pressure.*

No pressure. God, how those words sound good to me.

The last message is only dead air, then static followed by a click. For a brief moment I wonder if that could have been Dr Malik, but the odds are against it. Probably just a wrong number.

After checking my orientation to the river bank—I have about a minute left before I swim—I dial Michael's number. He answers on the third ring.

'Dr Wells.'

'It's Cat Ferry, Michael.'

'Cat! Are you all right?'

'Yes and no. I'm in trouble, actually. I need a ride.'

'A ride? OK. I'll come get you. Where are you?'

I close my eyes in relief. 'I'm about seventy miles south of Natchez.'

There's a pause. 'That's fine. Just tell me where to go.'

God bless you . . . 'I'm going to be beside Highway 1 on the west-bank side of the Mississippi River. Somewhere near the Morganza Spillway. I can tell you exactly where I am when you get close.'

'I'm leaving now. Are you safe, Cat? Do we need police or anything?'

'Maybe a first-aid kit. I'm going to talk to the police myself. And there's no danger for you. I know this is a huge favour to ask, but—'

'Don't even think about it. I'm on my way.'

I'm less than a quarter of a mile from the bank now, but the tree is starting to slide left beneath me. The current is sucking us back out towards the centre of the river. 'I have to go, Michael. Thank you, thank you.'

'I'm on my way,' he repeats. 'Don't worry about anything.'

I hang up the phone, then replace it in the Ziploc.

Clenching the bag in my teeth, I climb down the ladder of roots until I'm half in the water. Then I push away and start swimming towards the bank. Fifteen minutes later I'm within twenty yards of it. My wind is still good, but my arms and legs are feeling like lead. The bank here is steep and there's nothing I can grab to pull me up, so I simply crawl snakelike onto the muddy slope, digging my fingernails into the earth for purchase.

I lie panting on the bank for several minutes. The rain still lashes my face but I hardly feel it now. The ground under me seems like the most solid thing in the world, and I don't want to get up.

My cellphone rings. Ripping open the Ziploc, I press SEND. 'Hello?'

'Cat? It's Sean. Where are you?'

'You wouldn't believe it if I told you. Where are you? Home with Karen?'

Silence, then: 'Actually, I am. Did you get my message about Malik making bail and evading surveillance?'

'Yes.' I'm still thinking about Sean being home with his wife.

'Have you heard anything from Malik?'

'No.'

'The FBI knows you tried to call him. It doesn't look good.'

'I don't care.'

'Do you care about staying alive?'

'Strangely enough, I do. I just found that out beyond any doubt.'

'What do you mean?'

I'm laughing softly. 'Somebody just tried to kill me.'

'*What?*'

'It doesn't have anything to do with Malik.'

'How do you know that?'

'It happened on the island. My family's island in the river. This is about something else. I'm not sure what, but it's not the murders. And, Sean?'

'Yeah?'

'I just found out that my father abused me. It explains a lot of the stuff I did. I think it's all to do with what happened to me when I was a kid.'

'Cat, you don't sound good. Let me . . .'

'What? Can you come get me right now?'

'I may be able to, yeah. Or I can send somebody.'

One more knife in the heart. 'Don't worry about it, Sean. Take care of your wife and kids. Goodbye.'

'Cat—'

I hang up before he can finish, and push myself to my feet. The glow of the highway is about a mile away. I start walking.

CHAPTER 8

I'm sitting against the cinder-block wall of an abandoned gas station on Highway 1, wearing only my underwear and waiting for Michael Wells to save me from the mosquitoes that are making a feast of my blood. A narrow overhang protects me from the rain, but I don't mind the rain tonight. It's the only thing relieving the stifling heat.

The moment I leaned against this wall, after I phoned Michael, a deep fatigue settled into my limbs. It wasn't exhaustion from swimming the river. There's a hollowness in my heart that must be the beginnings of grief. I've lost so much today. Sean—by my own choice if not by his. My father, who remained alive in my heart for all the years since his death, but who began to die this afternoon when Grandpapa told me what he'd done. My mother, who somehow could not protect me from my father's secret desires. Even Pearlie, who kept so much from me all these years.

And then there's me, the woman who isn't who I thought she was at all. The public persona—the superachiever who brooked no nonsense from anyone—was a professional doppelgänger who protected a little girl filled with self-doubt, who secretly drank vodka to numb a pain she didn't understand. Now the pain has a face—and that face belongs to my father.

My cellphone is ringing. The screen reads UNKNOWN CALLER.

I'm afraid to answer, as though by doing so I'll allow the caller to see where I am. But that's crazy. After a quick breath, I press SEND.

'Is this Catherine Ferry?' asks a precise voice.

My body goes rigid. 'Dr Malik?'

'Yes. I didn't want you to think I was ignoring you. We can't speak for long, I'm afraid, but we should get together soon. I'm sure you've had a difficult time since our last conversation.'

'I have,' I admit, my hands already shaking.

'That's only to be expected, Catherine.'

'I found out this morning that I was sexually abused as a child.'

'I suspected that when you were a medical student. Dr Omartian was twenty-five years your senior, after all. There were other signs, too.'

'You know the task force is hunting you?' I say. 'They think you killed the victims in New Orleans.'

'I know. Yesterday you thought that yourself. Do you still believe it?'

'I don't know. If the murders are true sexual homicides, I don't think you did it. But if they're something else . . . maybe you did.'

'What else would they be?'

'Punishment.'

A long pause. 'You're a perceptive woman, Catherine.'

'That hasn't helped me much. What was the video equipment for? The stuff the police found in your secret apartment?'

'Public education. I'll speak to you again soon. I have to move now.'

'Dr Malik?'

'Yes?'

'Do the murders in New Orleans have anything to do with me? With my life in Natchez?'

'Yes and no. I have to go now, dear. Be careful. Trust no one. Not even your family.' With one click he's gone.

I'm still holding the phone to my ear when a black Ford Expedition wheels into the parking lot and blinks its headlights three times. I stay where I am until Michael Wells climbs out.

'Cat?' he yells. 'It's Michael!'

'Over here.' Keeping my back against the wall, I push myself erect and walk towards the Expedition.

Michael looks worried as I approach, but then he smiles. 'Every time I see you, you're in your underwear.'

'Seems that way, doesn't it?'

He reaches into the vehicle and hands me a T-shirt, a pair of warm-up pants, and some slippers about five sizes too large for my feet.

'Thanks. Do you have a towel or something? I don't want to ruin the pants. I've got a lot of blood on my leg.'

He opens the passenger door and helps me up onto the seat. Then he bends over the ragged hole in my thigh. He cleans the wound with some antiseptic lotion and gauze he takes from a paper bag on the floor, then covers it with a large Band-Aid. 'I'll have to suture it when we get back,' he says. 'How about we get the hell out of here now?'

I nod gratefully.

Michael shuts me into the passenger seat and gets behind the wheel. As I pull the clothes over my underwear, he makes a three-point turn and skids back onto the highway, headed north.

I recline my seat and take a few deep breaths.

'I don't want to pry into your business,' Michael says, 'but what the hell happened to you today? You sounded bad when you called this afternoon.'

Suddenly, I don't see much point in holding back. 'Just before I called you, I found out that I was sexually abused as a child.'

He nods slowly. 'I thought it must be something like that, when you asked about repressed memories. I've been reading up on the subject today.'

'We can talk about it,' I murmur. 'I just need to rest my eyes a little.'

'CAT? WAKE UP!'

I blink awake and look around. I'm sitting in a brightly lit garage. 'Where are we?'

'My house,' Michael says. 'In Brookwood. I wasn't sure where you wanted to go. I tried to ask you, but you wouldn't wake up. I stopped by my office for some sutures, then brought you here. Let's get that cut stitched up. Then I'll take you to your grandfather's house.'

Nathan Malik's words come back to me like a brand burnt into my brain: *Trust no one. Not even your family.* 'I don't want to go there.'

'You don't have to. I'll take you wherever you want to go. Or you can stay here. I've got three extra bedrooms. It's up to you.'

I nod thanks but say nothing. I don't know what I want to do. I definitely want my leg stitched up. It hurts like hell, and stitching means local anaesthetic. At least I hope it does. 'Did you bring some lidocaine?'

Michael shakes his head. 'Nah. I figure anybody who can free dive to three hundred feet can handle a couple of stitches without breaking a sweat.' He looks serious, but after a few moments of eye contact he reaches into his pocket and brings out a vial of clear liquid.

'The magic elixir,' he says with a smile. 'Let's do it.'

We go into the house, and while Michael sutures the wound on my leg I sit on the cold granite of his kitchen island and look around. Michael's house was built in the 1970s, and until Mrs Hemmeter sold it the decor was all avocado green and heavy brown panelling. Michael has totally redone the place, and with surprisingly good taste for a bachelor.

'I like what you've done with this house,' I tell him.

'Do you? Your mom did most of it.'

'You're kidding.'

'No. When I first got to town, I was too busy to breathe, much less decorate a house. I stopped by Gwen's interior design store one afternoon and hired her to do the whole place.' He ties off the last stitch. 'You hungry?'

'Starving.'

'Steak and eggs?'

'Are you ordering out?'

'No.' He goes to the refrigerator and brings out a package of rib eyes. 'Go and sit down. You'll be digging into this in twenty minutes.'

I slide off the counter and sit down on a bar stool.

'You want to talk about today?' Michael asks, meeting my gaze long enough to let me know he's genuinely concerned.

'It isn't just today. It's the past month. It's my whole life, really.'

'Can you give me the gist in twenty minutes?'

I laugh. And then I start talking. I start with my panic attacks at the Nolan and LeGendre crime scenes. That leads me to Carmen Piazza removing me from the task force, and then to my trip back to Natchez and to finding the bloody footprints in my bedroom. I'm talking on autopilot, though, because what I'm really doing is watching Michael cook. He's good with his hands, and I can tell from the way he uses them that he's a good doctor. He asks questions during my pauses, and before long I'm telling him about the depression that began in high school, the mania that followed and my affairs with married men. He's a good listener, only I can't tell what he makes of all this. He looks as though he's hearing nothing out of the ordinary, but inside he may already regret rescuing this particular damsel in distress.

When the steaks and eggs are done, we move to a glass dining table, but I do as much talking as eating. I can't seem to stop. I tell him about my father, Grandpapa, Pearlie, my mother, Dr Goldman, Nathan Malik. The only thing I don't tell Michael about is being pregnant.

When at last my stream of words slows to a trickle, he sighs deeply and says, 'Want to watch a movie? I rented the new Adam Sandler.'

I'm not sure whether I'm offended or relieved. 'Are you kidding?'

He grins. 'Yes. You want to know what I really think?'

'I do.'

'I think you're under more stress right now than most people could stand. I think your life is probably in danger from whoever is behind these murders, not to mention the risk of dealing with your disease without adequate therapy or medication. I don't know much about the links between childhood sexual abuse and adult psychological problems, because I treat kids. But I do know about child abuse. As a paediatric resident, I've seen a lot of it.'

There's something in his eyes that reminds me of John Kaiser's eyes. Knowledge. Wisdom.

'I'll bet this isn't how you thought you'd be spending this evening,' I say.

Michael spears a piece of steak and chews it thoughtfully. 'No, but I'm OK with it. I was always curious about you. Why you picked the guys you did in high school. And those repeated relationships with married guys. That's not hard to figure out now, is it?'

'My therapist tells me I pick unavailable guys so I can't become too attached to a man. So the loss I experienced with my father can't be repeated.'

'Is it too late to get your money back?'

Michael's eyes silently apologise for joking about something so serious. But he's so honest that it's difficult to get angry.

'The good news,' he says, 'is that now you're aware of the abuse, this therapist—Dr Goldman?—should be able to make some real progress with you.'

'Maybe. But right now I just want to pretend it never happened. Even if it's the answer to everything, I don't want to think about it.'

'Who would? That's a normal response.' Michael gets up and starts clearing the table. 'I'm actually more concerned about this murder case you're working on. I mean, somebody tried to blow your brains out tonight.'

I carry the glasses to the sink, and he starts putting the plates into the dishwasher. 'I'm not sure that has to do with the murder case,' I tell him.

'What, then? These revelations of abuse? Your father's been dead for twenty years. I don't think that's it, Cat. I think the murders in New Orleans are somehow connected to your life here. To your past.'

It's oddly familiar, batting around theories about a murder case with a man. Only the man I'm doing it with is not familiar.

'Pearlie and Louise both told you that Tom Cage was your father's doctor here in town. He's been practising for more than forty years, and he's a great guy. You should talk to him about the Vietnam stuff. I'll be glad to call him for you, if you like. Set up a meeting.'

'Maybe tomorrow.'

Michael turns on the dishwasher, then takes a tub of ice cream from the freezer and starts scooping it into two bowls. 'I know you feel like this Dr Malik isn't the killer. But I think he's at the centre of this whole mess. He's the only known connection between you and the New Orleans murders. And he's already demonstrated that he's fixated on you. I think you should consider him the prime suspect.'

I hold some ice cream in my mouth, savouring the rich taste of vanilla. 'He couldn't have known I was on the island.'

'You don't know that. You do know he's going to call you back. Yet you haven't told the FBI that. I think you want to talk to Dr Malik without anyone listening in. You think he can figure out things about your life that other therapists never could.'

'Like . . .?'

'Like why this abuse happened to you. I read today that even when people find proof that their memories are real, they still doubt the truth of what comes back to them. Because accepting that the abuse really happened means accepting that the person who abused them never really loved them.'

'This is a depressing conversation.'

'You want to watch that movie now?'

'God, no. I want to sleep for thirty hours straight.'

Michael shrugs. 'Then that's what you should do. If you don't want to go home, the whole first floor is yours. You won't know I'm here unless you come downstairs and find me.'

'OK, deal. Show me the bedroom.'

'You can find it. Upstairs is all you need to know. Take your pick.'

The wide smile on my face surprises me. 'Thanks,' I tell him. 'I mean it.'

I climb the stairs and flick on the light in the first bedroom to my right. The walls are yellow, and the bed has a white quilt on it. I can sleep here.

The bathroom is stocked with towels and toiletries, even a new toothbrush. I strip off the warm-up pants and T-shirt Michael brought me. As I lean into the shower to turn on the taps, a familiar ringing fills the bathroom. I glance at the screen of my cellphone and my pulse accelerates. It's a New Orleans number I don't recognise. I press SEND, then hold the phone to my ear.

'Dr Ferry?' says a voice that sounds nothing like Dr Malik.

'Yes?' I say cautiously.

'This is John Kaiser. I need to talk to you about Nathan Malik. Did you speak to him earlier tonight?'

Sean's warning that Malik might be declared a fugitive from a murder charge comes back to me with all its implications. 'Yes,' I confess.

A brief pause. 'He called you from a payphone on the West Bank in New Orleans. By the time we got a car there, he was gone.'

'Is that right?' I stall, trying to gather my wits. One thing I realise: if Malik was on the West Bank when he called me, he could not have been shooting at me on the island.

'Dr Ferry,' Kaiser says in a softer voice. 'May I call you Cat?'

'Sure,' I say, pulling the T-shirt back on.

'A lot of people on the task force are very angry with you, Cat. I'm not one of them. I think you have some real insight into this case. Maybe insight you don't even realise you have. I also know that somebody tried to kill you tonight. Sean told me. Do you think that attempt on your life was connected to the murders in any way?'

'No. I'm looking into a separate matter up here. A personal matter. Look, if Malik called me from the West Bank of New Orleans this evening, he couldn't have shot at me on DeSalle Island thirty minutes before that. It's physically impossible.'

'I'm not sure what we're dealing with here,' Kaiser confesses. 'But I know Nathan Malik is involved. May I ask why you went to DeSalle Island?'

'I'm trying to find out something about my past.'

'About your father?'

'How did you know that?'

'I'm extrapolating from your conversation with Malik in his office. Did you learn anything important?'

'Nothing relating to your case.'

'Well, just be very careful if you speak to Malik. It's obvious the two of you feel an emotional connection—you could easily cross the line into aiding and abetting.'

I don't even respond to this.

'Cat, I'd like you to accept round-the-clock FBI protection. We're very good at this. *No one* would know we were guarding you.'

'Malik would know. I don't know how, but he would. And he wouldn't come near me.'

A long silence. 'Tell me why you want to talk to him.'

'I don't know why, to tell you the truth. He just knows something I need to know. I sense that.'

'Remember what curiosity did to the cat.'

I groan. 'Yeah, but cats have nine lives, remember?'

Kaiser delivers his retort like a valediction. 'From what I understand, you've used up most of yours.'

AS I STEP out of the shower, my cellphone rings again. I grab it and look at the screen. DET. SEAN REGAN. I don't really want to answer, but I do want to know if Sean is sleeping at home with his wife. I wrap a towel round me, press SEND and say, 'Don't say anything until you tell me where you are.'

'This isn't who you think it is,' says a precise voice.

My heart is pounding. 'Dr Malik?'

'None other. Are you alone, Catherine? I need to speak to you.'

A current of fear shoots through my veins, not for me but for Sean. 'How did you get Sean's cellphone?'

'I don't have his phone. I reprogrammed my phone to mimic Detective Regan's digital ID information. John Kaiser won't pay so much attention to this call if the electronic serial number belongs to your boyfriend.'

How the hell does he know all that? 'Go ahead, then.'

'I'm calling you because I need to leave something with you.'

'Why me? Why not a friend?'

'I don't have friends.' Malik laughs softly. 'I have only patients.'

'If you're trying to give me your patient records, I can't accept them. The FBI named those in a search warrant. They'd prosecute me if I withheld them.'

'It's not my records,' Malik says. 'It's a film. A film and the raw materials relating to it. DVD disks, audiotapes, stuff like that.'

'What kind of film?'

'I'm making a documentary about sexual abuse and repressed memory.'

This comes as such a surprise that I'm not sure how to respond.

'Nothing like it has ever been seen before,' he says with gravity. 'It shows women reliving abuse in a group setting. The women are part of an experimental group called Group X. I formed it after years of watching conventional therapy approaches fail. I chose patients who were at the stage where the eruption of delayed memories was beginning to destroy their lives, and we've done some ground-breaking things. If it reaches the screen, it will shake this country to its foundations.'

'Is that the extent of it? Women in group therapy?'

Malik makes a sound I can't interpret. 'You shouldn't denigrate what you've never experienced, Catherine. I can't discuss the specifics of the film with you. Right now I'm just concerned with keeping it safe. A lot of people would like this film to disappear. My film and all my records. These people are terrified of the truths I know.'

'If you're that worried, why not turn yourself in to the FBI?'

'The FBI wants to jail me for murder. I'll turn myself in when the time is right. For now, I need your help. Will you keep my film safe for me?'

'Look, I couldn't do it even if I wanted to. The FBI is probably following me. They may even be listening to this call.'

'By tomorrow maybe. We're safe for now. Do you have a pen?'

I glance around the bedroom, but there's nothing to write with. 'No, but I have a good memory.'

'Memorise this phone number. 504 802 9941. Do you have it?'

I repeat the number aloud and commit it to memory.

'If you need to speak to me after this,' Malik says, 'leave a message at that number.'

'I want to speak to you now, and not about your film.'

'Hurry.'

'Why did you tell me not to trust my family? Do you have information that you are keeping from me?'

'I'm not your therapist, Catherine.'

'I want you to be. I'll meet you somewhere for a session.'

'You want a session? Keep my film for me. You'd be doing yourself a favour, too.'

I'm tempted. I want to see what Malik really did behind the closed doors of his office. But the FBI could be listening to this call. 'I'd like to see it, but I can't promise I'll keep it for you.'

'Then we have no reason to meet.'

'Why the hell would you meet me anyway? I could bring the FBI with me. Why would you risk that?'

'There's no risk. I do know things about your father, Catherine. I know why he was murdered. And if you bring the FBI with you, I'll never tell.'

For once, I'm a step ahead of Malik. 'I know why my father was killed.'

'You don't. You don't know anything.'

My heart flutters like the wings of a panicked bird. 'Why are you playing games with me? I just want the truth.'

Malik's voice drops lower. 'The truth is written indelibly in the convolutions of your brain, Catherine. Just follow the memories where they lead.'

'I can't wait for that! Someone's trying to kill me.'

Malik sighs deeply. 'Who do you think tried to kill you today?'

'It might have been a black guy who knew my dad years ago. I don't know. Do you know?'

'No. But *you do*. If only you think about it in the right way.'

'You said the New Orleans murders both are and aren't connected to my personal life. What did you mean by that?'

'What do you think I meant?'

I close my eyes and try not to scream. Every question is answered by another question; everyone around me knows the truth about my life, but I can't see it. 'What are you trying to tell me? Everyone keeps asking me if I was ever your patient. Have you given them that idea?'

'We don't have time for this,' Malik says, his voice suddenly impatient. 'Not now. But I do want to talk to you. Then, when we're finished, you can take possession of my film. At that point, I'll turn myself over to the FBI. Now, I've been in one place for too long. Call that number I gave you tomorrow and leave a different number where I can reach you. Not your cellphone. And don't get too chummy with John Kaiser. He doesn't really care about either of us.'

The phone goes dead in my hand.

I know why my father was killed.

You don't. You don't know anything.

What I know, I can fight. What can be named, I can endure. But what lies in shadow, I can neither fight nor endure. My whole life seems a shadow now, a performance invented to fill the void of my true past. For every childhood memory I possess, a thousand have been lost. I've always known that. I reached back beyond a certain point in time, and found only a blank wall. And I never knew why.

This afternoon I thought I'd learned the answer. As terrible as it was, at least it put firm ground beneath my feet. But now that ground has shifted, a seismic change wrought by only a few words. *You don't know anything.*

I want the questions to stop. I want a drink. But I can't have one. And thinking of the reason why—the baby in my tummy—suddenly brings up my steak and eggs with a vengeance. I fall to my knees over the toilet, retching and shivering as I've done after the worst binges. I feel the substance of my body fading, as though I'm becoming transparent.

I lurch to my feet and splash cool water on my face from the bathroom sink. Then I climb into bed and pull the quilt up to my neck. The light is still on, and I'm not about to turn it off. I close my eyes, and pray for sleep.

On any other night I'd need a drink or a Valium to shut off the thoughts racing through my head, but tonight exhaustion does the job for me. As consciousness blurs, I pass through the last glimmering stratum of wakefulness into sleep. And dreams lie in wait, as they always have.

Tonight I'm back in the rusted orange truck. Back on the island. My grandfather is behind the wheel. We're rolling up the long sloping hill of the old pasture. On the other side lies the pond where the cows drink. The truck smells of stale motor oil. The sky is leaden. It's going to rain. We roll steadily up the shallow slope, making for the crest. Terror has closed my throat. I don't know what's on the other side of the hill, but I know it's bad. I've dreamed this dream so often that I know I'll wake up soon.

Only this time I don't.

This time Grandpapa downshifts and steps on the gas pedal, and the old pick-up trundles right over. The cows are waiting for us, staring with dumb indifference. Beyond them lies the pond, slate-grey and smooth as glass.

There's something in the pond. A man floating face down in the water, his arms outspread. I want to scream, but Grandpapa doesn't seem to see the man. Mute with fear, I point. Grandpapa squints and shakes his head. 'Goddamn rain,' he says. They can't work on the island when it rains.

Now the man is getting to his feet. He isn't *in* the pond, but *on* it. He's standing on its glassy surface as though on an ice rink. The man is my father. I pull at Grandpapa's shirtsleeve, but he won't look. Daddy is walking on water like Jesus in the Bible, but Grandpapa won't look!

'*Daddy!*' I shout.

Luke Ferry nods at me but says nothing. As he nears the edge of the pond, he pulls his shirt open. I want to shut my eyes, but I can't. On the right side of his chest is a bullet hole. As I stare in horror, Daddy puts two fingers into the hole and starts to pull the skin apart. He wants me to watch but I don't want to see. I cover my eyes with my hands, then peer between my fingers. Something is pouring out of the wound, only it's not blood. It's *grey*.

'*Look, Kitty Cat,*' he commands. '*I want you to look.*'

I shut my eyes and scream.

'WAKE UP! It's Michael! You're dreaming!'

Michael Wells is shaking my shoulders, his eyes frantic. 'Cat! It's just a nightmare!'

I blink myself back to reality and grab Michael's hands. He's wearing a T-shirt and plaid pyjama bottoms. 'I'm OK.'

He nods in relief, then stands and looks down at me. 'Is it one you've had before?' he asks.

'Yes. The truck, the island . . . my grandfather. Only this time we made it over the hill.'

'What did you see?'

I shake my head. 'It's too crazy. Did I scream out loud?'

He smiles. 'You screamed, but I wasn't sleeping. I've been thinking about what you told me. I've come up with a couple of ideas, if you're interested.'

I nod and prop myself against the headboard.

He sits on the end of the bed. 'Well, what I've been thinking is this,' he begins. 'You grew up with one version of your father's death. You got that from your grandfather. It's the same version he gave the police in 1981. Now, twenty-three years later, you discover some old blood in your childhood bedroom. You decide to investigate it, and you make no secret of the fact. What happens? Your grandfather revises his original story. By his own admission, he told you the new version—supposedly the truth—to stop you investigating the scene further. And you do stop investigating the bedroom. But you *don't* stop probing the events of that night. And when you decide to bring in professionals to search for more evidence, Dr Kirkland changes his story yet *again*, this time to a "truth" so horrifying that no one—not even you—would want to reveal it to anyone outside your family. In that version, he takes the blame for killing your father. But he also does something else, Cat. He lays the blame for your sexual abuse on your father.'

I feel a strange buzzing in my head.

'The only evidence you have that your father abused you is your grandfather's word. If you discount that, what evidence is there? Hearsay about some possible brutality in Vietnam.'

I swallow hard and wait for Michael to continue.

'So . . . I'm just asking, Cat, why should you believe that your grandfather's latest version of the "truth" is any more true than his first story?'

'Because it feels right,' I say softly. 'I wish it didn't. But it does. It's like I can almost see it in my mind. The two men fighting over my bed in the dark. I'm afraid that I *did* see that.'

'Maybe your grandfather did kill your father, as he said. But maybe not for the reason he gave you. I mean, why take his word for it that he caught your father abusing you? It could easily have been the other way round. Maybe your grandfather was the abuser.'

There's a hot tightness in my throat that won't let any more words pass.

'I've heard about him all my life,' Michael continues. 'And I can't say I like what I've heard. All the old docs around here say he did a lot of questionable procedures in his day. You know, too many appendixes removed that turned out to be normal. Exploratory surgery for belly pain. A ton of hysterectomies for fibroids. I spoke to Tom Cage last night, and he told me he stopped referring patients to Kirkland for exactly that reason.'

'Did Dr Cage say anything about my father?'

'Yes. Apparently Luke told him a lot about his war experiences. He wouldn't go into specifics with me. But he did say he thought your dad was a good soldier and a good man. And if Tom Cage thought your dad was a good guy, it's hard for me to picture him as a child molester. I'm not saying he couldn't have been. But I think you should hear what Tom has to say.'

'I want to. God, I have to know the truth.'

'You have no concrete memories of abuse?'

'I feel that the truth is buried in my mind, but it's too damned deep. It's like free diving to four hundred feet. I just can't hold my breath that long, can't swim that far down. I'm not strong enough to get there.'

'It's not a question of strength,' Michael says. 'When you first spoke to me about repressed memories, I didn't give much credence to the idea. But the more I've read, the more I believe it. There's a lot of evidence that, during severe trauma, information is encoded in an entirely different way than at other times. These memories make themselves known only when that person finds him- or herself in a similar situation to the one in which the trauma occurred. Those triggers bring back the emotions, but not necessarily the memories themselves. It's called body memory. Fascinating, really.'

My cellphone begins vibrating on the bedside table. Michael picks it up and shows me the screen. It's the same New Orleans number that called last night. I take the phone and press SEND.

'Agent Kaiser?'

'Yes. Hello, Cat. Sorry to bother you so early.'

Why is he calling me? He probably found out that it was Malik I was talking to last night, and not Sean. 'What is it now?'

'I have some information for you. A couple of things. First, we learned last night that Nathan Malik didn't pay all his own bail on the murder charge.'

'I don't understand.'

'A million-dollar bail meant that Malik had to come up with a hundred thousand in cash, and the rest in collateral. On paper he looked fairly wealthy, so when he put up his house across Lake Pontchartrain, we didn't look too closely at the cash. But it turns out that most of the hundred thousand was paid by someone else.'

'Who?'

'Your aunt. Ann Hilgard.'

I feel like I'm in a falling elevator, the basement rushing up beneath my legs. 'You have to be wrong,' I say.

'No mistake,' says Kaiser. 'Ann Hilgard, née Kirkland.'

My mouth is open, but I can't form words.

'I only learned that she was your aunt a few minutes ago, Cat. Is she also a patient of Dr Malik's?'

'If she is, I hadn't a clue until now.'

'She's definitely got the history for it. Confirmed bipolar disorder going back three decades. A string of bad marriages—'

'My God,' I breathe. 'No wonder Malik knows things about me.'

'We're trying to locate your aunt,' Kaiser says. 'Apparently she's involved in a bitter divorce and hasn't been home for a couple of weeks.'

'I saw her in Natchez yesterday. She was . . .' I trail off.

'What?' Kaiser asks. 'She was what?'

Borrowing money from my grandfather. Bail money, maybe? 'Talking to my mother about her marital problems. You said you had a couple of things to tell me. What else?'

'We just found one of Nathan Malik's patients in a coma on the floor of her apartment in Metairie. Margaret Lavigne. Twenty-seven years old. It was a suicide attempt. An overdose of insulin. We only found her because we'd got her name from the psychologist who referred her to Malik.'

'You mean she wasn't on the patient list Malik gave you?'

'Exactly. He never really obeyed the court order.'

'Did she leave a note?'

'She did. It reads, "May God forgive me. An innocent man is dead. Please tell Dr Malik to stop it." What do you make of that?'

Please tell Dr Malik to stop it. 'I'm trying to put it together. Is Margaret Lavigne related to any of our victims?'

'Not by blood. But I think you'll find this interesting. Ms Lavigne's biological father was arrested just before her suicide attempt and charged with multiple counts of sexually abusing children. Interesting timing, no?'

'I'm not sure I understand. Are you saying you think he's a potential target of our killer?'

Kaiser laughs drily. 'He may be *now*. But remember victim number three? Nolan, the accountant? Nolan was Margaret Lavigne's stepfather.'

'Holy God. Lavigne told someone her stepfather abused her, and that person murdered him?'

'Bingo,' says Kaiser. 'Then it turns out that her real father was the molester. I think Ms Lavigne repressed her memories of the abuse she suffered as a child. Dr Malik tried to help her recall those events, and she did. Only she made a mistake about who the molester was. I mean, wouldn't most kids prefer to think it was their stepfather rather than their father?'

All I can think about is Group X, and Malik's 'ground-breaking' treatment protocols. What the hell did Malik convince those women to do?

'Cat? Have you talked to Dr Malik since we last spoke?'

I want to tell Kaiser the truth—that I talked to Malik and that he denied committing the murders—but until I know exactly how Aunt Ann is involved with him, I'm not saying a word. 'Look, I can't talk to you any more right now. I've got to find my aunt. She could be in real danger.'

'Help us find her, Cat. We'll protect her.'

'If you need my help to find her, you can't protect her,' I say. 'But there is one thing. Those two patients of Malik's who were related to the victims . . . Riviere's daughter and LeGendre's niece?'

'What about them?'

'Ask them about something called Group X. It's a therapy group Malik ran. I think they might have been part of it. That's all I know that could help you right now. I'm sorry, John. I have to go.'

I click END and leap out of bed, startling Michael to his feet.

'What happened?' he asks.

'My aunt Ann paid Nathan Malik's bail. I saw her at Malmaison yesterday. She must have been borrowing the money from my grandfather. And she must be a patient of Malik's. *That's* how he knows so much about me and my family. May I use your phone? I don't want the FBI to hear this call.'

Michael looks at me. 'Are you calling Malik?'

'I'm going to leave him a message, yes. Are you OK with that?'

He goes out onto the landing and brings back a cordless phone. 'As long as you don't do anything to risk your life.'

Even as I nod, I decide to tell Michael nothing about Margaret Lavigne's suicide attempt or her note. When I dial the number Malik gave me last night, an automated voice instructs me to leave a message.

'This is Catherine Ferry. I've just learned that my aunt paid your bail. I'm assuming she's a patient of yours. You've been dishonest with me, Doctor. I'd like to talk to you as soon as possible. You can reach me at—' I look up at Michael. 'What's this number?'

Michael rattles off his number, and I repeat it into the machine. 'If you don't return my call within an hour, I'm telling the FBI everything you've told me to date. Goodbye.'

I hang up Michael's phone, pick up my cellphone, and scroll through the digital phone book. When I reach AUNT ANN, I press SEND.

Another recorded message. When the beep comes, I say, 'Ann, this is Cat. I know about you and Dr Malik. I've talked to him, and I know why you like him. I have no desire to hurt him, or to help anyone else hurt him. All I'm asking is for you to call me back. I'd like to talk to you about

Grandpapa. Also about Daddy. I'm trying to figure something out about my childhood, and I have a feeling you can help me. Thanks.'

Michael is staring at me like a doctor now, as though trying to decide whether I might be in a manic state. 'What can I do?' he asks.

'You already did it. You gave me a place to stay. Now I have to make some decisions.'

'What else did Kaiser tell you? Did they find another murder victim?'

Before I can answer, Michael's phone rings. The ID reads UNKNOWN CALLER. I show it to him. 'May I answer it?'

He nods.

'This is Dr Ferry.'

'Hello, Catherine.'

I nod at Michael and silently mouth, *Malik*. 'What kind of game have you been playing with me, Doctor? You've been acting like you have ESP, diagnosing my problems and hinting things about my family. The truth is, you had the facts all along from Ann. Didn't you?'

He takes his time before answering, 'Yes and no.'

'Oh, for God's sake! Where's my aunt, Doctor? Is she with you?'

'No.'

'Why did she pay your bail?'

'I asked her to. I was short of cash. I knew she could get the money.'

'You are one unethical son of a bitch. Why were you treating Ann?'

'You know that's confidential.'

'Bullshit! You break the rules when you want to and hide behind them when you don't!'

'We need to talk, Catherine. I don't have much time now. We need to meet face to face.'

I close my eyes. 'Tell me about Margaret Lavigne.'

'Margaret? But . . . What about her?'

'She tried to kill herself with a massive dose of insulin last night. She's in a coma now, probably will never recover consciousness, but she left a note implicating you in the murders.'

The silence on the line is absolute. 'You're lying.'

'You know I'm not.'

'What did the note say?'

'Something like, "God forgive me, an innocent man is dead. Please tell Dr Malik to stop it." '

'Oh my God.' His voice is a ragged whisper.

'Margaret's biological father has been arrested on child abuse charges. Stranger still, her stepfather was one of our five victims in New Orleans. Does any of this ring a bell?'

Malik's breathing is fast and shallow.

'Did you kill those men in New Orleans, Doctor?'

'No. I swear that to you.'

'But you know who did.'

'I can't tell you that. Not over the phone.'

'You expect me to meet you when you could be the killer?'

'You have nothing to fear from me, Catherine. You know that.'

For some reason, I believe him. But I'm not crazy. 'Will you turn yourself in if I meet you?'

'If you promise to keep my film safe for me, I will.'

'Where do you want to meet?'

'It has to be New Orleans, I'm afraid. Call the number I gave you when you're five miles outside the city. I'll tell you where to go.'

No matter what logic tells me, I can't refuse him. 'All right.'

'And, Cat? If you bring the FBI with you, you'll regret it. I don't want to threaten you, but I have to protect myself. I'm the only one who can tell you certain things about yourself. Goodbye.' The phone clicks. He's gone.

'You're not meeting that guy alone,' Michael says firmly. 'You should call the FBI right now and tell them everything. And I mean everything.'

'That's not an option. Not yet. Malik knows things I have to know, and if I bring in the FBI now, I never will. I'll be fucked up for the rest of my life.'

Michael reaches out and takes me by the shoulders. His eyes bore into mine with startling intensity. 'I want you alive, not dead.'

I nod slowly. 'I'll ask Sean Regan to come with me.'

Even as I make the promise, I know it's a lie. But I don't need Michael freaking out and calling the FBI about this meeting.

'Your married boyfriend?'

'Yes, but that has nothing to do with it. Sean is trained for this kind of thing. He can protect me, and I can trust him.'

Michael looks sad, but he says, 'You can borrow my Expedition. I can go to work on my motorcycle.'

'Thanks. I need to go to Malmaison before I leave for New Orleans.'

'What's at Malmaison?'

'I need some clothes.' Another lie. What I need from Malmaison is something that's always been there in abundance. A gun.

CHAPTER 9

Dawn is just breaking as I jog through the trees from Michael's house to Malmaison.

My Audi is parked beside Pearlie's Cadillac. Not far away stands a tall, white pick-up truck like the ones used on the island—the kind that tried to run me over. Someone on the island must have found my car and brought it back. But if that's the case, why doesn't Grandpapa have the police scouring the countryside for me? And why didn't someone call me?

After circling round to the front lawn, I stop and check my cellphone. The call log shows three missed calls from my grandfather's number. I must have slept through them. I listen to the messages.

'*Catherine, this is Grandpapa. Henry found your car across the channel from the island. There was no sign of you. Louise Butler says you set out on a bike for the bridge, but no one knows whether you made it or not. Please call me if you get this. I've got the sheriff's departments on both sides of the river combing the banks and roads for you, and Jesse's got a dozen men searching the island. If you've had an accident, help is coming.*'

His next message says, '*It's me again. If you're in any other kind of trouble—that is, if there are other people involved—then let them hear this message. This is Dr William Kirkland speaking. If you're from anywhere around the part of the country where you found my granddaughter, then you know my name. And you know you've made a mistake. If you hurt that girl . . . by God, you'd rather have the hounds of hell on your trail than me.*'

My skin is crawling. The voice addressed to my unknown abductors is that of an avenging angel, deathly cold and crackling with violence.

On his third call, my grandfather left no message at all.

Looking up at the floodlit face of Malmaison, I'm more sure than ever that I don't want to see anyone inside. Not Grandpapa. Not even Pearlie. That's why I came on foot. If I pulled up in Michael's Expedition, I'd be seen and questioned by everyone at home. My chances of discreetly getting a gun from my grandfather's safe would be greatly reduced. But this way . . .

I trot to the far end of the east wing. I've known since the eighth grade that the lock on one window here can be slipped with a credit card. Today I have no credit card—I left my purse in my car—but Michael lent me an expired driver's licence to do the job. I press the laminated card between the panels of the tall French windows. They part slightly, and the licence easily flips the lock. I climb through and move quickly to my grandfather's study.

The room is empty. I hurry over to the gun safe. The combination lock is easy to open using the date of my birthday. Four clicks left, eight clicks right, seventy-three left, then turn the handle. I freeze once as I turn the dial, sure that I heard footsteps in the hall, but no one appears.

When I turn the handle, the heavy steel door opens. The casino model Grandpapa showed me the other day is gone, but the guns are there. Five rifles, three shotguns and several handguns. The scent of gun oil is strong, but there's another smell, too. Burnt gunpowder.

One by one, I pull the rifles from their slots and sniff the barrels. The first two gleam in the light, their barrels clean. But the third has recently been fired. I turn it in my hands. A bolt-action Remington 700, scarred from use but well maintained. As I stare, my pulse begins to race.

Am I holding the rifle that killed my father? Would Grandpapa have kept it? More important, who fired it in the last couple of days?

I don't have time to speculate. Replacing the rifle, I grab an automatic pistol from the bottom of the safe: a Walther PPK we used for target practice on the island. I check that it's fully loaded, and close the door to the safe.

Back in the hall, something stops me. Faint voices floating on the air. Grandpapa first. Then Pearlie. Then a richer, warmer voice chimes in. It belongs to Henry, the black man who drove me across the bridge to the island yesterday. He's talking about finding my Audi this morning, and how it threw him into a panic. He found my spare keys in a magnetic case under the bumper. He's worried that I fell into the river and drowned like my grandmother. Grandpapa says I might die a lot of ways, but drowning won't be one of them. Then he thanks Henry for bringing back the car and bids him goodbye. A screen door slams.

'What do you think, Pearlie?' asks Grandpapa. 'Where is she?'

I move closer to the door, close enough to hear Pearlie sigh.

'I think somebody followed her after Louise put her on that bicycle. She never made it to that bridge.'

'Who would do that?' asks Grandpapa.

'Do you know where Billy Neal was yesterday evening?'

'Picking up some things for me in Baton Rouge.'

'That island ain't far off the highway to Baton Rouge.'

'What would Billy want with Catherine?'

'You'd know more about that than I would.' Pearlie's voice carries a sharp rebuke. 'What does any man want with any woman?'

Grandpapa makes a rumbling noise. 'I'll talk to him.'

The screen door bangs again.

I step into the kitchen.

Pearlie is standing at the sink, her back to me. She lifts an iron skillet and turns on the tap, then freezes. Slowly she turns, and her eyes go wide.

'Don't say anything,' I whisper. 'Not a word.'

She nods silently.

'I'm leaving town, Pearlie. Are my extra keys in here?'

She glances at the counter. The Audi key is lying on top of some mail. I grab it and return to the doorway.

'Where you going, girl?' Pearlie asks.

'I have to meet someone. I want you to tell me something first, though.'

'What?'

'Somebody did some bad things to me when I was a little girl. It was either Daddy or Grandpapa. And I don't see how you could have taken care of me for so long without knowing about that. I just don't.'

Pearlie glances at the outside door, and her face tightens in what looks like anger. 'Listen to me, child. What you doing running down to the island stirring things up? What good you think gonna come from all this?'

'I don't have any choice. I have to know how and why Daddy died? And why I'm the way I am. You don't understand that?'

She looks at the floor. 'The Lord works in mysterious ways. That's what I understand. There's a lot of pain in this world, but it ain't for us to question all that. Now, you gonna tell Dr Kirkland you all right or not?'

'You can tell him after I'm gone.' I'm about to turn and go, then I pause. 'I'm going to find out the truth about this family. And when I find it, I'll let you know. Then you can pretend you didn't know all along.'

Pearlie opens her mouth as if to speak, but no sound emerges.

I turn and run up the hallway.

I EXPECTED to find Billy Neal and my grandfather talking behind the house, but there's no sign of them. Glancing around the parking lot, I move quickly to the Audi, flicking the electric unlock button as I go.

As I grab the door handle, Billy Neal rises from behind Pearlie's Cadillac. His eyes are as dead as the snakes that adorn his cowboy boots, but they lock onto mine with mechanical precision.

'I'll be damned,' he says. 'A lot of people think you're dead.'

'Is that what you thought?'

A faint smile plays across his lips. 'I gave it even money.'

'Why do you hate me, Billy? You don't even know me.'

He walks up to the Audi and stares at me over the roof. 'Oh, I know you. Pampered princess, trust fund waiting, never had to worry a day in your damn life. You look in my direction and you don't even see me.'

'Exactly what do you do for my grandfather?'

'Things other people are squeamish about.' Billy lights a cigarette and blows smoke across the roof at me. 'I ain't squeamish.'

I'll bet. 'Have you fired the Remington 700 from the gun safe lately?'

A bemused smile. 'You're a sneaky little piece, aren't you?'

Suddenly I've had all I can take from this grease-slick urban cowboy. I open the Audi's door, climb in and drive off, spraying Billy with gravel as I peel away from the slave quarters I once called home.

MY DRIVE TO New Orleans is filled with thoughts of my aunt Ann. Though I've never spent much time with her, she has left a deep impression. I knew Ann as the life of every family gathering. Though four years older than my mother, she always seemed a decade younger. She could make off-the-rack clothes look like haute couture. She had the body of a *Sports Illustrated* swimsuit model. And she was something no one else in the DeSalle family ever quite managed to be—cool. She taught me how to dance, how to dress, how to wear make-up. She caught me smoking my first cigarette—stolen from her pack—and shared it with me. She told me how to get rid of guys whose attention I didn't want.

But coolness doesn't age well. As I got older, I overheard my mother getting calls at all hours of the night. Sometimes she'd drive hundreds of miles to rescue Ann, who by this time had been diagnosed with bipolar disorder.

What I remember most about Ann was her obsession with having a baby. At times this fixation seemed the root of her mental illness. Because I left home for college at sixteen, I missed many of the travails of her quest for infertility treatment. All I know is that nothing ever panned out.

What brought her to Nathan Malik's door? Was it bipolar disorder? Or emerging memories of sexual abuse?

I take the Audi off cruise control and accelerate to eighty-five. Soon, I'll be face to face with the man who can tell me about my troubled aunt and, probably, the identity of the man who molested me.

MALIK INSTRUCTED me to telephone him when I was five miles outside New Orleans, but I don't do it. Instead I pull off I-10 at Williams Boulevard, one of the first exists to Kenner, the westernmost suburb of New Orleans, and drive to a liquor store. I go inside but I don't buy anything. I stand staring at the bottles of Grey Goose, then I turn and hurry outside.

I walk to a payphone beside the store. With shaking hands I punch in the number Malik told me to call. It rings four times, but just as I think it's going to click over to voicemail, he answers.

'Catherine. Where are you?'

'I'm on Williams Boulevard.'

'Good. I'm in a motel a mile away from the airport. The Thibodeaux. It's a dump with an orange sign, about a mile past the airport turn, on the right. Room eighteen. Do you think you can find it?'

'I think I've seen it before. Should I just pull up to the room?'

'Yes. I'll be watching for you.'

I take a last look at the liquor store, then get back in my car and start the engine. Before I drive off, I open my purse, take out my bottle of Valium, and roll one yellow pill into my palm. With my left hand on my tummy, I whisper, 'Forgive me, baby. Just one more,' and dry-swallow the pill. Then I join the stream of traffic headed towards the airport.

MALIK WAS RIGHT. The Thibodeaux Motel is a dump. A low strip of rooms with a sagging roof and a row of bright orange doors. I park four doors down from room eighteen and get out. If I hold the Walther along my right leg, it's almost invisible.

I walk towards the door, and as I raise my hand to knock I hear the sound of rain. It can rain without a moment's notice in New Orleans, but today the asphalt is baking in bright sunlight. It's my hallucination again . . . The rattling is louder than the cars passing on the road thirty yards away.

I chamber a round in the Walther, then knock hard on the door. It moves inwards a few inches with the force of my blow.

'Dr Malik?'

No reply. Now I wish I'd called Sean. This is where pride gets you.

Bringing my gun to chest level, I kick open the door and rush into the room, checking the corners for threats.

Shoddy green carpet, two double beds, a TV on a stand. No Malik.

I cross the room and kick open the bathroom door, the Walther extended in front of me.

Malik is lying in the bathtub. He's fully clothed—all in black, of course—and the tiles above his head are spattered with blood. His once piercing eyes are as dead as those in a stuffed deer head.

My initial shock balloons into terror when I realise that the blood is running down the tiles. Whoever killed Malik could still be close by. As I whirl back towards the room, the gun in Malik's right hand registers in my mind.

Suicide? I can't believe that.

Then I see the skull in his lap. It's a human skull, entirely clean, like the skulls used to teach orthopaedics. Springs and screws connect the jaws.

As I stare, searching in vain for some explanation, Malik's chest heaves violently, and his head flies forwards as if pulled on a string.

The Walther jerks in my hand. The bathroom booms.

Everything goes white.

My head pounds. In the distance, someone calls my name. '*Dr Ferry . . .? Catherine!*' The voice is familiar, but I can't see anyone.

A flash of darkness spears through the white, and then dirty-yellow light frames a blurry face. 'Dr Ferry? It's John Kaiser.'

It is. His hazel eyes hover only inches over mine.

'What happened?' I ask.

'I don't know. We're hoping you can tell us.'

Blinking rapidly against the yellow light, I try to see who 'we' is, and where I am. I seem to be propped against a bathtub. There's a paramedic behind Kaiser, and behind him I see the dark face of Carmen Piazza, commander of the NOPD Homicide Division. She looks angry.

'Are you wounded?' Kaiser asks. 'They can't find any injuries, but you were unconscious.'

'My head hurts. How did you get here?'

'Don't worry about that. How did *you* get here?'

I turn to make sure Malik's corpse is still lying in the tub behind me. It is. 'Dr Malik wanted me to meet him here. I came.'

'Jesus,' mutters Captain Piazza, then she stomps away to speak to another NOPD officer.

'Did Malik try to kill you, Cat?' Kaiser asks.

No, I almost say aloud. But fortunately my common sense has survived. 'I want a lawyer.'

Kaiser looks disappointed. 'Do you *need* a lawyer?'

'I don't know.'

'Can you walk?' asks Kaiser.

'I think so.'

'Then walk with me.'

I get to my feet and follow Agent Kaiser out to the parking lot.

'Listen to me, Cat,' Kaiser says when we're about twenty yards away. 'I came to this scene directly from another one. Our guy hit his sixth victim.'

'Who was it?'

'You don't seem surprised.'

'We haven't caught our killer yet. Why should he stop?'

'You didn't think Malik was the killer?'

'I wouldn't have come here if I did.'

Kaiser studies me for some time. I glance back at the room and see Piazza talking to two detectives. She gestures at me, and the detectives both stare in my direction. They look like a pair of pit bulls.

'Same crime signature on victim six?' I ask.

'Yes. Two gunshots, bite marks, the same message on the wall. But while we were working the scene, task force headquarters got an anonymous call telling us Malik was hiding out here.'

'Your caller is your killer, John.'

Kaiser looks at me like a stern father. 'Tell me about Group X.'

'You didn't learn anything from the two patients you have?'

'We don't have them any more. Both women have disappeared. What I don't get is how they knew to run. I checked their phone records; no one suspicious called them.'

'Talk to *everyone* who called them,' I say, realising that Ann may now be the only other person who can tell us who the members of Group X are—unless Malik's documentary can be found.

'We're checking everybody,' Kaiser says. 'But you know more than you've told me. If you lawyer up because you're paranoid, we're going to lose time. If you have nothing to hide—nothing relevant to this case, anyway—then you don't have anything to lose by talking to me.'

I want to talk to him, but I know that an FBI agent, despite his best intentions, can't prevent the NOPD from arresting me for murder if they want.

'I came to find out what my aunt's connection to Malik was. And also some things about my past. Malik was dead when I got here.'

'Why were you unconscious?'

'My head feels like somebody hit me.'

'Your gun's been fired. The bullet went into Malik's chest.'

An icy spark shoots through me. Could I have killed Malik by accident? No . . . 'He was already dead. The autopsy should prove that. He had a nerve spasm, and it scared the shit out of me. I fired by accident.'

Kaiser takes my arm. 'If you had killed Nathan Malik, would you know it?'

'What do you mean?'

'I've been thinking a lot about you in the past few days. Your panic attacks at the crime scenes. Your psychiatric history—what I know of it, anyway. The crime signature, which primarily consists of bite marks that could be staged. And the fact that you were sexually abused—'

'Who told you that?' I cut in. 'Did Sean tell you that?'

'Yes. I'm sorry, Cat. But I think your past sexual abuse is what drew you to Malik, maybe as his patient, even without you knowing it.'

'Do you really believe I could be killing these men without *knowing* it?'

Kaiser shrugs. 'I've listened to the tapes of your meeting with Malik several times. He told you about dissociative identity disorder, and that's just multiple personality disorder under another name. Given the situation in which I just found you, it would be irresponsible of me not to suspect it.'

'John, I didn't kill Nathan Malik. Nor did I kill or help him kill any of the six victims in your case. Now, if I suffer from dissociative identity disorder, I grant you, I would not know I had done any of that. I'd believe I was innocent. But do you have any idea how rare that disorder is? There've been more cases of it in Hollywood movies in the past twenty years than in all of recorded human history.'

Kaiser is watching me. The slightest sign could tilt him either way.

'If you let them put me in jail,' I tell him, 'you'll be losing your best chance to solve the murders. I talked to Malik on the phone and he told me some things about the case. You arrest me, you'll never find out what they are.'

'What things?' he asks, his eyes narrowed.

'Did you find a box inside that motel room?'

'No. What was in the box?'

I shake my head.

Kaiser grabs my wrist. 'Come with me.'

As he pulls me towards the Crown Victoria I rode in the other day, I glance over my shoulder. Piazza and the two NOPD detectives are coming after me. Kaiser puts me in the back seat, closes the door and locks it. A heated discussion begins outside, but Kaiser moves the detectives away from the car, so I can't hear more than a few words. *Arrest. Conspiracy. Psycho.* After a couple of minutes, Kaiser returns to the car and gets inside.

'Are they going to arrest me?'

'They want to. Piazza thinks you've been lying to us from the start. That you've been feeding Malik information about the investigation. She's suspending Sean, and she wants your hide nailed to the barn wall. She wants to interrogate you herself. At this point, telling me what was in that box may be the only thing that can keep you out of jail.'

'A film.'

I see connections happening at light speed behind Kaiser's eyes. 'The video production equipment,' he says. 'The stuff we found at Malik's secret apartment. What kind of film is it?'

'Malik was making a documentary about an experimental therapy group he was working with. Group X. Female patients only. It was his life's work. No way would Malik have killed himself before he finished that film.'

Kaiser takes some time to process this. 'Did he tell you who any of the patients in Group X were?'

'No.'

'With Malik dead, we may never find out. Unless your aunt can tell us.'

That's not all we'll never know, I think with desolation.

'I guess Malik's killer took the film.' Kaiser glances back towards the NOPD detectives, who are still staring angrily at the car. 'Goddamn it. Tell me about that motel room, Cat.'

'I didn't know where Malik was until five minutes before I got here. He gave me a phone number to call. When I arrived, the door was open. I went in and found him in the bathroom. The blood on the wall was fresh. Then I saw the gun in his hand.'

'What if Malik was the killer and he offed himself because his "work" was done? After the sixth victim, I mean.'

'Malik's work was his film, not murder. Tell me about the sixth victim.'

'His name was Quentin Baptiste. At forty-one, the youngest victim yet. He was an NOPD homicide detective.'

'*What?*'

'Yep. It was probably Baptiste who was feeding information to the killer, knowingly or not. That's why Piazza wants to pin that on you.'

'What about Baptiste's female relatives? One of them could have been a patient of Malik's. I'd check daughters, stepdaughters and nieces.'

'I was starting that when we got the tip to come here.'

A revelation suddenly hits me. 'The skull. I need to see that skull.'

'Why?'

I try to rein in my excitement. 'The teeth in that skull made the bite marks on the victims. I'd bet anything on it.'

In a few minutes, summoned by Kaiser via radio, a female evidence technician walks out to our car carrying the skull in a large Ziploc bag. Kaiser rolls down his window, takes the skull and sets it in my lap.

'I need gloves,' I say.

'Give her your gloves,' Kaiser orders the tech.

My heart pounds as I struggle to put on the latex gloves. Even without opening the skull's mouth, I can see that its lateral incisors are slightly pegged, as were those that wounded the flesh of our victims. Once the gloves are on, I open the Ziploc and remove the skull.

The jaw opens easily on the springs screwed to the interior surfaces. Sometimes doing bite-mark comparisons can be long, painstaking work, but other times it's a no-brainer. This is one of those times. The maxillary arch of the bite marks at the murder scenes is engraved upon my mind, and the one in this skull matches it tooth for tooth.

'It's a perfect match,' I tell Kaiser.

As we zoom along the shore of Lake Pontchartrain towards the FBI field office, Kaiser speaks on the phone. When at last he hangs up, he turns to me. 'The chief of police is going ape because I wouldn't let Piazza arrest you. Now that I took you away from the scene, he's calling my boss.'

'Am I going to be arrested?'

'The field office is task force headquarters. If you'll remain there a while without making a fuss, that's your best bet for staying out of jail.'

'Look, the killer tipped you where to find the murder weapon and the video equipment, and the same person gave you the motel. He's trying to frame Malik. My showing up was just a bonus. If you figured out the suicide was staged, I was right there to blame for staging it. And with my experience, I'd know just how to do it.'

'It plays,' says Kaiser, 'but there's a scenario that plays equally well. The caller was female. The women in Group X know Malik is killing abusers, and that he killed an innocent man. One of them is having a crisis of conscience. Like the woman who tried to kill herself, Margaret Lavigne.'

'Lavigne's still in a coma?'

'Yes. I was actually thinking our caller might be your aunt.'

I turn towards the lake and watch the grey waves in silence. I suppose Aunt Ann could be making the calls. But I doubt it. If Ann paid Malik's bail, what would so quickly turn her against him? Finding out that an inno cent man had been murdered? Maybe. But I doubt it. 'These are personal attacks, John. And I've suspected from the start that the killer's a woman.'

Kaiser blows out a stream of air. 'That's a possibility, but a very remote one given the crime signature. There's no history of a woman ever committing sexual homicides like this. Not alone.'

'Five minutes ago you practically accused me of doing it!'

'You're a special case. Your past, your forensic training. And I suggested you were assisting Malik. A male-female team scenario.'

'Why not two women? Once we connected Malik to those first two female patients, the killer knew we were getting close, even if *we* didn't know it. So she planted the gun at Malik's apartment and gave it to us. We kept getting closer, so she gave us Malik and the skull wrapped up in a neat package. Our girl is probably feeling pretty safe right now.'

Kaiser is looking expectantly at me. Something is tugging at the back of my mind, but I can't quite make it out. 'Did you get anything at all on Quentin Baptiste's female relatives?'

'Hang on.' He calls Carmen Piazza. Their conversation is short and to the point. When he hangs up, he says, 'Detective Baptiste had six female relatives by blood. A wife, three nieces, two daughters.'

'How old are the daughters?'

'I don't have their ages, but one is a teacher. The other is a day-care worker. One of the nieces just graduated from police academy.'

'She'd know how to shoot,' I think aloud. 'So would the first victim's daughter, I'll bet. An army brat? Daughter of a colonel?'

'We've been all over the Moreland daughter, Cat. She's clean. But I'll get the task force on Baptiste's relatives right away.'

A tall white sail appears on the horizon. It soothes me to follow it with my eyes. As my eyelids grow heavy, I remember the Valium I popped before going to the motel.

'How's your head?' Kaiser asks.

'It hurts. Just take me to the field office. I need to lie down.'

I lean against the window and close my eyes, but my cellphone starts ringing. I reach into my pocket. It's empty.

'I've got it,' says Kaiser, holding my screen where I can see it. 'You know this number?'

'No, but that's a Gulf Coast area code. It might be Ann. I left a message for her to call me.'

Kaiser hands me the phone. 'Don't tell her Malik is dead.'

I nod and press SEND. 'Hello?'

'Hey, Cat Woman!'

It's Ann. I nod quickly to Kaiser, and he tenses on the seat.

'How you doing, baby girl?' Ann's voice has the brittle quality I've learned to associate with her manic episodes.

'Not so good right now, actually,' I say in a tired voice.

'You sound like you need a drink.'

'I wish. I'm on the wagon.'

'Ouch. Your message said you knew something about Dr Malik and me. What exactly do you know?'

'I know you paid his bail. The FBI knows, too.'

'That's not against the law, is it?'

Ricochet-quick response. Definitely manic. 'Dr Malik is mixed up in some murders, Ann.'

A pause. Then a craftier voice comes through the phone. 'Nathan couldn't do the things they think he did. He doesn't have that in him.'

'I've been talking to him quite a bit lately,' I tell her.

'Do you know where he is?' A hint of anxiety now.

'Yes.' I close my eyes. 'He's been arrested again.'

'Arrested?' The alarm in that one word is shocking. 'Where?'

'Here in New Orleans. I think you should drive over and see him. I'd like to talk to you, too. I just found out some things about my past that really messed me up, and I'd like to ask you some questions.'

'Oh, baby girl,' Ann says in a breathy voice, 'I've worried about you so much. But you should talk to Nathan about this, not me. I don't feel I can tell you everything at this point.'

Is she telling me she was abused? Why else would she worry about me?

'You're a lot like me, Cat,' she continues. 'Gwen told me they diagnosed cyclothymia, but that's just bipolarity by another name. We've got it in the blood. Nathan's the expert, though.'

'Dr Malik told me about Group X. He told me about the film, everything. Were you part of that?'

Ann starts to reply, then catches herself. In the hiss of the open line, I can feel her listening to me. Listening with the concentration of the manic mind in its focused state. It makes my skin crawl.

'Catherine?' she says, her voice imperious. 'What are you not telling me?'

Kaiser is watching me anxiously.

'What do you mean?'

'You know exactly what I mean, Cat. I hear your voice. You're afraid of something. Or someone.'

'No. You're reading things into this.'

A pause. 'I want to talk to Nathan.'

'Come to New Orleans. You can see him at the parish prison.'

'I can't come there until you tell me the truth, Cat.'

I grit my teeth and try to keep my voice even. 'I've told you what I know. I'm worried that you don't trust—'

The hissing line takes on a deadness like a blanket dropped over my heart.

'She hung up on me.'

THE FBI FIELD OFFICE is a four-storey brick fortress on the southern shore of Lake Pontchartrain. We stop at the heavy iron gate so Kaiser can show an armed guard his credentials. Once inside, we park and hurry through to the vestibule, where a woman waits behind bulletproof glass to handle the red tape. Afterwards, Kaiser ushers me through a metal detector, and we're on our way to the third floor, where the special agent in charge runs the field office and the 150 FBI agents spread across Louisiana.

When we get out of the elevator, Kaiser leads me down a hallway like those in every other corporate headquarters in America. He opens a door, glances inside, then enters and beckons me into an empty office with four narrow beds in it. Two are made up with sheets, blankets and pillows.

'Best I can do, I'm afraid.'

'It's better than a cell in the parish prison.'

Kaiser chuckles. 'I need to go straighten this mess out with the SAC.'

'Wait,' I tell him. 'I've been thinking about the saliva in the bite marks. If we put some of the fresh saliva from Baptiste's wounds in a petri dish, and see what grows out, maybe we'll get a strange germ that can tell us something. We might find our suspect suffers from a certain disease.'

'I'll tell the forensic team to do it.'

'May I have my cellphone back?'

'Cat, you've obstructed justice and maybe acted as an accessory to multiple murder. If I let you interfere in this case any more—which your cellphone would allow you to do—the SAC will throw you out and give you to the NOPD. And there won't be a thing I can do about it. OK?'

'Fair enough. But you'll tell me if Ann calls?'

'Absolutely. I'll bring your phone here and have you call her back.'

THE VALIUM carries me away from the waking world like a gentle river, and I slide down into my dream world without interference, till the myriad images of my subconscious surround me.

I am back in the loft of the barn. Watching my father while he sculpts with a cutting torch, bending the white-hot steel to his will. The roar of that torch fills my ears. When it dies, the silence in the barn is absolute. I hear the rain for the first time. I forgot it was raining. That's why he didn't hear me sneak in. The drops rattle against the tin roof like a barrage of hail.

Daddy is walking around, but I can't see him. Craning my neck, I find him squatting on the floor beneath the loft. He's beside one of the timbers that hold up the roof, working some kind of tool under a floorboard. After a moment, he looks around, then pulls the board up from the floor. Then another. And another. He pulls a bag from underneath the floor. It's dark green, like the Jeeps parked behind the National Guard armoury when I go to the flea market there. I've never seen the bag before.

He takes something out of the bag, but I can't see what . . .

The scene changes.

'Look, Cat,' says Grandpapa, pointing. 'Look at that fawn.'

I'm sitting in my grandfather's orange pick-up as it rumbles up the hill towards the pond. Fear is still stuffing my heart into my throat. It hasn't started to rain yet, but the sky is leaden.

We trundle over the crest of the hill. Ahead, the water of the pond lies smooth as glass, except where my father floats face down in it, his arms outspread. Mute with fear, I point with my finger.

Grandpapa squints at the clouds and shakes his head. 'Goddamn rain.'

As we roll down towards the pond, my father gets to his feet and starts walking across its surface. My heart pounds so loudly I can hear it above the sound of the truck. Daddy holds out his arms to me, then begins unbuttoning his shirt. He pulls his shirt open. On the right side of his chest is the bullet hole. He puts two fingers into the hole and pulls it open. I cover my eyes with my hands, then peer between my fingers. Something grey is pouring out of the wound. '*Look, Kitty Cat*,' he commands. '*I want you to look.*'

This time I obey.

The grey stuff isn't liquid. It's a bunch of plastic pellets, pouring out of my daddy's chest the way they poured out of my Louisiana Rice Creatures whenever I tore one open by accident.

Then Daddy reaches into his wound and pulls out Lena the Leopardess. My favourite Rice Creature. The one I put in Daddy's coffin.

I want to run to him and take Lena from his hands, but my door won't open. As Daddy nears the edge of the pond, his eyes are on mine as he digs his fingers into the leopardess, rips it apart.

I scream. Bright red blood pours out of Lena's chest. Somehow I know it's my daddy's blood. He turns pale as I stare, then his feet begin sinking. The water can't hold him up any more.

'*Daddy!*' I shriek. '*Wait! I'm coming! I can save you, Daddy!*'

I jerk on the truck's door handle, but it won't open. I bang my fists on the window, but it does no good. Then someone with soft hands takes my wrists.

'Catherine? Wake up, Cat. It's time to wake up.'

I open my eyes.

Hannah Goldman is leaning over my bed, holding me by the wrists. She is about fifty, with greying streaks in her hair and deep lines at the corners of her eyes. And she has the kindest eyes in the world.

'It's Hannah,' she says. 'Can you hear me, Cat?'

'Yes.' I smile for her, my best smile so she'll know I'm OK.

'Agent Kaiser asked me to come, to speak to you about something important,' she says. 'Cat, there's no easy way to tell you this.'

I smile encouragement and pat her hand. 'It's OK. I'm strong.'

'You are strong.' She smiles back. 'You may be my strongest patient. What I have to tell you is this. Your aunt Ann is dead.'

My smile broadens. 'No, she's not. I talked to her today.'

'I know you did, dear. But that was yesterday afternoon. You've been sleeping for quite a while. And last night, your aunt drove to DeSalle Island and killed herself by taking an overdose of morphine.'

AGENT KAISER was probably right to bring Dr Goldman here, but now that she's broken the news about Ann to me, I want Kaiser. Psychiatry isn't going to solve my current problems.

I sit up on my bed and set my feet on the floor. 'Hannah, I appreciate you coming here. But I need to ask Agent Kaiser some questions.'

'I'll get him for you,' she says. 'But I want you to promise me you'll talk to me alone afterwards. And I'll sit in while you talk to him.'

'All right.'

Left in the silence of the empty room, I enter a strange state where all the images in my mind spin wildly against each other. Until the sound of the door opening and John Kaiser's voice startle me.

'Cat, what can I do for you?'

I stand and face him squarely. 'I want the details of my aunt's suicide.'

'What do you want to know?'

'I want to know where Ann was found, who found her, how she did it, whether she left a note, everything. Forget I'm related to her, OK?'

Kaiser looks at Dr Goldman. When she nods, he leans against the closed door. 'A woman named Louise Butler found her in the clinic on DeSalle Island. Ms Butler was looking for you. Your grandfather's search for you had been called off, but she never got the word. She found your aunt instead.'

'Tell me how she looked when they found her.'

Kaiser glances at Dr Goldman again but answers anyway. 'She was naked, lying on the floor by an examining table.'

'Did she leave a note?'

'No note. But . . . she did leave something. Before she died, she drew two skulls and crossbones on her lower abdomen, about where her ovaries would be. There was a marker pen lying beside her body.'

For the first time, I feel the sting of tears.

'This means something to you?'

'Ann was obsessed with having a baby,' I say. 'But she never got pregnant, and she never got over the failure. My grandfather performed an emergency appendectomy on her in that clinic when she was ten years old. He always said the infection she had then was what made her infertile.' I turn to Hannah. 'I did wonder if that appendectomy might really have been an abortion.'

'I'm sure that ten is too young for pregnancy,' Hannah says.

'We need to be certain,' says Kaiser. 'I want an autopsy done as fast as we can. Would a botched abortion be detectable all these years later?'

'Possibly,' Hannah says. 'Depends on what kind of mistake was made.'

Something won't let me focus. It's not grief over Ann. I'm too numb to feel anything about that now. It's a sense of something missing.

'Have you told me everything about Ann's death?' I ask Kaiser. 'The scene? Did you leave anything out?'

His brows wrinkle. 'There *was* something. But I don't think it's important. There was a stuffed animal on the floor about three feet behind your aunt's head. I think it was . . . a turtle.'

'Thomas the Timid Turtle,' I sigh. 'Thomas was Ann's favourite toy.'

'Apparently there were several stuffed animals in the room. We figured they were for kids to hold while they got injections or something.'

'They were. But Thomas didn't live at the clinic. Ann brought him there. I'm surprised she wasn't holding him when she died.'

'The toy could have fallen to the floor after she lost consciousness.'

The tears run down my face.

'I think that's enough for now,' Hannah says gently.

'No,' I say. 'We have to keep going.'

'What does the turtle tell you?' asks Kaiser.

I quickly summarise my recurring dream about the pick-up truck, the pond, and my father pulling Lena the Leopardess out of his gunshot wound.

When I finish, Kaiser looks puzzled.

I take a step towards him. 'I have to get out of here. I want to see the stuffed animal I buried with my father. Give it every test known to forensic science. It was my grandfather who suggested that I put Lena into his coffin. To keep him from being lonely, he said. It's too much of a coincidence. And I want a new autopsy done on my father. You told me his original autopsy report was lost, right?'

'Yes,' says Kaiser. 'But I can't let you leave here. You know that.'

'Can you order the exhumation of my father's body for a new autopsy?'

'Expediting your aunt's autopsy is one thing, Cat. She died under suspicious circumstances. She's a material witness to Malik's activities at the very least, and at worst an accessory to murder. Your father, on the other hand, was murdered twenty-three years ago. And his death has no clear tie to this case. If I tell the SAC that my next big idea is exhuming Luke Ferry to look at a stuffed animal, I'm not going to get a lot of traction.'

I look to Hannah for help, but she's silent.

'If you want to analyse Lena the Leopardess, you're going to have to find a way to do it on your own. It's not that difficult for a family member to get a body exhumed. *After* you get out of here. OK?' Kaiser's tone sounds official, but something in his eyes is speaking to me in a different language.

'Right,' I say. 'OK.'

He moves to the door. 'If I hear anything I think you need to know, I'll come tell you. And I'm having some food sent up from the cafeteria. You must be starving.'

I'm not hungry, but I tell him thanks anyway.

And then he's gone.

Hannah takes my hand and pulls me down beside her on the bed. She puts an arm round me and hugs me like the sister I never had. 'That was tough,' she says. 'You're a tough cookie. But I think you're very close to cracking. I'm talking about total psychological collapse, Cat. Your aunt's illness was more extreme than yours, but in essence the same.'

I take her hand and squeeze it. 'Will you help me get out of here? I have to go back to Mississippi to exhume my father's body.'

Hannah looks at me seriously. 'You don't need my help. You're not under arrest. Even the FBI can't detain you without arresting you, unless it's on some trumped-up terrorism charge. Your problem is the NOPD.'

'I know. There are cameras all over the place, especially around the entrance. You'll have to help me. I need to use your cellphone.'

She takes a silver Motorola from her pocket and hands it to me. Before she can change her mind, I dial Michael Wells's cellphone.

'It's Cat,' I say when he picks up.

'Are you all right?'

'Yes and no. My aunt is dead, and things are very crazy right now. I'm in FBI headquarters on Lake Pontchartrain. I need to get back to Natchez. The police will be looking for me soon. Can I ask you for help again?'

'OK. If you can get to Lakefront Airport, I can fly down and get you.'

My pulse rate kicks up. 'Are you serious?'

'Sure. I've flown in there a dozen times. I'll have to arrange for cover, though. Call me in an hour. I should be airborne by then. We'll take it from there. If there's any problem with the phones, just get to Lakefront and start watching the planes come in. I'll be in a blue and white Cessna 210.'

BY THE TIME I walk into the hallway, Hannah Goldman has been gone for ten minutes. We agreed that she would say her goodbyes to Kaiser, then slowly make her way down to her car in the parking lot.

My job is to get to the FBI's motor pool without being seen by anyone who knows who I am. The motor pool has huge garage doors that open into the parking lot. I've been down there a couple of times before, when I worked with the FBI forensic team on the serial case where I first met Sean.

The elevator is only thirty feet down the hall, and I'm nearly to it when I hear John Kaiser's voice. 'Cat? Where are you going?'

I turn and give him a little wave. He's standing by the room I just left, looking more than anything like a concerned father.

'I feel sick. I need to get to the bathroom.'

'Down past the elevator, on the right. The nausea may be from the blow to your head.' He starts walking towards me. He's holding something in his hand. 'I was coming to show you the early results on those cultures you asked for. The saliva from the bite marks on Quentin Baptiste.'

Victim number six. 'Oh, right. What does it show?'

He hands me the lab report. 'You tell me.'

I glance over the letters and numbers, trying to pretend that my mind is on this piece of paper rather than on escaping. What I see is a microbiological snapshot of an average human mouth. Except for one thing. 'That's weird.'

'What?' asks Kaiser.

'Well, we ought to see some *Streptococcus mutans* growing after twelve hours. It produces the acid that causes cavities.'

'What would that mean?'

'That the saliva comes from someone taking a course of antibiotics. That would disturb the normal flora of the mouth. Or someone without teeth.'

'Somebody who wears dentures?'

'No. Dentures are ideal for bacterial colonisation, just like real teeth. You might look for somebody who needs dentures but can't afford them. Look, I really need to get to the bathroom.'

'Oh, yeah. Sorry.'

'May I keep this report?'

'Sure.'

I stuff it into my back pocket. 'Let's see what grows out after another six hours.' *When I'll be long gone.*

I walk quickly up the hall to the bathroom. As I push open the door, I cut my eyes right. He's no longer in the corridor. Back-pedalling fast, I dart to the elevator, step inside and press the button for the basement. In twenty seconds, the elevator opens to the concrete-floored motor pool.

About a dozen government sedans are parked diagonally against a wall on my left. To my right are two big black Suburbans, the SUVs used by the FBI forensic team.

I walk briskly towards the big electronic doors that can get me out of the building, and as I near them I see a large white button. I hit it, and an over-head chain drive lifts the big door in front of me. When it's four feet off the ground, I duck under it and walk quickly up the ramp to the parking lot.

Bearing right, towards the main entrance of the field office, I watch the lines of parked cars. Sure enough, Hannah's white BMW backs out of a space not far away, then pulls forward and stops beside me. I glance over the roofs of the parked cars, at the guardhouse by the main gate.

'Did you open your trunk?' I ask her through the car's open window.

'Yes, but I'm afraid you'll suffocate.'

I walk to the back of her car and lift the trunk lid as though retrieving something. Then I take a deep breath, climb into the small space, fold myself almost double, and close the trunk lid over my head. I have a few mental problems, but claustrophobia isn't one of them.

The BMW jerks forward. After a couple of bumps, we're rolling along at a good clip. Hannah is searching for a safe place to let me out.

At last the car stops. I hear her door open and close. Then the trunk lid pops open, and a backlit silhouette takes my hand and helps me out.

'You are really something,' Hannah says. 'I feel like Ingrid Bergman.'

I hug her hard, then pull away. 'Get out of here, Ingrid. You've done enough already.'

Hannah takes my right hand in both of hers and squeezes tight. 'You're close to finding out the truth, Cat. But don't expect a blinding flash of insight or instant peace. Getting the true facts is only the beginning.'

'I've been lost for a long time. A beginning sounds pretty good to me.'

She smiles sadly, then gets into her car and drives away. I look at my watch and wonder if Michael is airborne yet. I need to find a payphone.

CHAPTER 10

I'm 5,000 feet over the Mississippi River, flying north at 200 miles per hour. Michael Wells is beside me, piloting his Cessna as if he'd rather be doing this than anything else in the world. Natchez is thirty minutes ahead. Shock has pushed me to the point where flight in a small plane produces no airsickness at all.

'What are you going to do now?' Michael asks, when I've recounted the events and dreams of the past twenty-four hours.

'What I should have done in the beginning. Find out who killed my father. I'm going to exhume his body.'

Michael looks at me like I've taken leave of my senses. 'What will you learn from that?'

'For one thing, it will give me DNA to compare against any body fluids I find on my bedroom floor. I'm going to bring in a team to work the bedroom, no matter what my grandfather says. I'm also going into the barn to see if my father's green bag is still under the floor. The barn is padlocked, but I shouldn't have much trouble breaking in.'

'Do you think that green bag really exists?'

'Absolutely. May I use your cellphone?'

He unclips it from his belt and hands it to me. I punch in my mother's cellphone number. Just as I expect to be kicked over to voicemail, my mother answers in a sleepy voice that makes me think: *sedatives*.

'Dr Wells?' she says.

'No, it's Cat.'

A brief pause. 'I don't understand. Are you at Dr Wells's house?'

'No. Mom, listen, I know about Ann.'

'Well, I figured you must have heard by now.'

'How are you doing?'

'Fine, I suppose. I always knew this was a possibility with Ann, so I was prepared for it. I'm at work, and it's very busy. Which is good, I guess.'

'Mom, I need to talk to you. Will you be at home this afternoon?'

'I don't know. Look, I told you, I'm really busy today.'

'Please try to be home. This is no day to be worrying about work.'

'I don't mind talking to you,' she says, 'but I don't want you to start telling me how to feel about this. I deal with my own feelings in my own way.'

'Or you don't deal with them.'

Chilly silence. 'I may not wear my heart on my sleeve like some people, but I've managed fine so far, considering the obstacles life put in my way.'

'How is Pearlie taking it?'

'I don't know. She went to the island. Deserted me with barely a word.'

This throws me. 'The island? Pearlie hates the island.'

'Well, that's where she went, right after she heard the news about Ann. I've got to go, Cat. If I don't see you later, make sure you're at that funeral. Ann would want you there.'

Like I would miss my aunt's funeral? 'Mom, why did I go riding in the orange truck with Grandpapa on the island. I've been having this dream about it. It's always raining.'

'Ohhh,' she says, her voice suddenly musical. 'Daddy got so tense when it rained, because no work could be done. You were the only one who could calm him down. He'd ride round the island showing you the birds and cattle and deer, and when he got back he'd be tolerable to live with again. I just—'

'Mom,' I cut in, stopping what could become an endless flow. 'Try to come home this afternoon, OK?'

'Bye-bye, darling.'

I hang up and pass the phone back to Michael, more dazed than upset. Mom sounds distracted. *Sedated.* For some reason, I sense my grandfather's hand in this. How easy it would be for him to give her a shot and remove the inconvenience of her emotions from his life.

Michael touches my arm. 'Are you OK?' he asks.

'I don't think "OK" is something to be aspired to at a time like this. I just have to keep moving forward.'

He withdraws his hand and goes back to flying.

NATCHEZ AIRPORT is a tiny facility, two runways and a brick administration building. Michael makes a perfect three-point landing, then transfers me to his Expedition, and within fifteen minutes we're approaching Malmaison.

'You want me to drive up to the house?' he asks.

I wave him past the opening in the trees. 'Let's go to your house and walk through the woods to the barn. I'd rather have some privacy for this.'

Michael pulls into Brookwood and parks outside his house.

'Do you have bolt cutters or anything?'

'I may have a hacksaw.'

'That could work. What about an axe?'

'Yeah. We going to tear the place down?'

'Be prepared. Weren't you a Boy Scout?'

Three minutes later, we're jogging through the trees towards Malmaison. I'm carrying the hacksaw, Michael the axe. When I see the main house, I bear right, towards the low land bordering the bayou at the back of the property.

We approach the barn from the side, then circle round it, to be shielded from anyone glancing down from the parking lot behind the slave quarters. The wall boards are dry and weathered grey, but the door still resists a stout pull. Michael sets to work on the padlock with the hacksaw, the cords and muscles in his forearms bulging as he works.

'There,' he says, blowing metal shavings away. 'Give me the axe.'

I pass it to him. With the blunt side of the head, he bashes the lock off the heavy hasp. 'Open sesame,' he says. Then he pulls open the door.

My indrawn breath remains locked in my chest. Inside the barn there must be twenty Luke Ferry sculptures, most of them taller than my head, and some twenty feet high.

'Wow,' Michael whispers. 'It's like a museum.'

The sight of all that polished metal wrought into abstract yet beautiful forms by my father's hands is almost more than I can bear. When the smell hits me—the scent of hay that Daddy could never get out of the barn—my knees go weak.

'Cat? Are you OK?'

I clutch Michael's arm and take a step into the barn. 'I didn't know all this stuff was here. My grandfather must have lost his mind. He never liked my father's work. Now, it's like he's cornering the market.'

'Do you still want to look for the bag?'

'Hell, yes. That's why we're here.'

I take the axe from Michael and make my way to the foot of the timber post that my father walked to in my dream. It's uncanny how certain I feel that I'm standing in the right place. That the bag is beneath these boards . . .

With the head of the axe, I press down on one end of the first board I saw my father touch in my dream. When the other end lifts a little, my heartbeat stutters. I reach down and pull the raised end of the board out of the floor.

'Look at that,' Michael whispers.

My hand tingles as I slip it into the darkness beneath the floor. Then it closes round dry, rubbery fabric. The bag. As I pull on the neck of the bag, two more floorboards come up with it, exposing an olive-drab sack.

'I think we just proved that repressed memories exist,' I say.

Instead of poking blindly through the bag with my hand, I carefully shake out its contents. The first thing that falls out is a miniature photo album, then comes a small stack of envelopes held together with a yellow ribbon, followed by a sheaf of maps, some of them laminated. The top envelope in the stack of letters is addressed to Luke Ferry, and the return address is Malmaison. The cancelled stamp is dated 1969. The bag feels empty now, but when I shake it hard, some old prunes strung together on a wire fall out, and a shield-shaped patch showing an eagle's head with a scoped rifle above it, and the word SNIPER monogrammed in yellow thread above that.

'The 101st Airborne,' says Michael. 'They called them the Screaming Eagles. I saw that eagle emblem all the time on that HBO miniseries *Band of Brothers*. Was your dad in the Airborne?'

'Yeah. I just found out the other day.'

I glance at the maps. The top one shows the Vietnamese–Cambodian border west of Saigon. I go through the stack of letters. Most are from my mother to my father, some written from Natchez, but most from Mississippi University. My mother went to school there while my dad was in the army.

Tying the envelopes back together with the ribbon, I glance at the prunes. Desiccated, wrinkled and black, they look like something I might have brought home in my trick-or-treat bag in the days before Halloween candy was store-bought. I turn to the photo album.

'Come on, Cat,' says Michael. 'We can look at this stuff at my house.' He gathers up the bag and its contents, and leads me back through the sculptures.

I stop in my tracks and scream.

Hanging from a rafter above me is a sculpture I didn't see on my way in. It's a hanged man. Life-size, and ugly as death. The steel rope round his neck rises in a perfect line that terminates in a hook. At first I think of suicide, but something about the sculpture has a more official look. As if the man was just hanged for some offence.

'I've never seen that before. I thought I'd seen everything he ever did.'

'Cat?' says Michael. 'Come on. That scream was loud.'

He drags me towards the door.

As MICHAEL pulls me through the trees towards Brookwood, my legs feel full of sand and it's difficult to extract oxygen from the air in this humidity.

I stop walking. 'I need to talk to my mother,' I announce.

'Why?'

'She's my father's next of kin and I can't see getting any kind of exhumation permit without her support.'

Michael stares at me with eyes full of compassion. 'I think you should talk to Tom Cage before you do anything else. Remember what he told me? Your dad confided in him quite a bit about the war.'

I sag against the trunk of an oak tree. 'Can you bring the car?'

He studies me. 'Do you promise to stay here until I get back?'

'Of course.' I slide down the trunk onto the soft ground. 'Please, Michael.'

'I'll be back in two minutes.'

As soon as he disappears, I dump the contents of my father's bag on the ground in front of me. The maps, the letters, the prunes, the sniper patch, the album. I hold my breath as I open the album, with its photos tucked into plastic sleeves for posterity.

The first photograph shows a white-tailed deer in low light, a buck with ten antler points. Relief almost makes me exhale, but I don't. Every photo in this book is a potential horror. The next picture shows a black bear cub. The one after, a cottonmouth moccasin coiled round a cypress tree.

The next photo shows Louise Butler, thirty years younger. She's standing on the edge of the river at sunset, facing the camera. I flip the page. Louise again, at river's edge, this time sitting in profile against the sunset.

The next photo is of me, about two years old. I'm sitting on the floor of the barn with my legs crossed, my elbows on my knees, my chin in my hands. I'm staring into the lens with big round eyes that look exactly like my father's. I look more at peace in that picture than I've ever felt in my life.

What happened to me after that? What took away the peace in those eyes? *Who* took it away? The person who shot this picture?

I drop the album and it falls beside the prunes on the wire.

'Miss Catherine? That you over there?'

A black man in grease-stained khaki work clothes has appeared among the trees. It's Mose, the yardman. After so many years at Malmaison, he moves among these trees like a ghost.

'It's me, Mose.'

'You all right? You fall down or something?'

'I'm just resting.'

He moves closer, but his advance is solicitous. Mose can't be much younger than my grandfather, and time has worn him down to a bent nub, like a tree that finally gives way to decades of wind and rain.

'What you got there?' Mose asks, pointing at the prunes.

'Some kind of rotten food. I think it's prunes.'

Mose bends and picks up the string of blackened fruit. He studies one, pinches it between his fingers, then sniffs it.

'Mose, you're a braver man than I.'

He laughs. 'You ain't no man. You a girl. And these ain't prunes.' He places one of the blackened things between his front teeth and bites down, testing its texture. 'This here be hide. Some kind of animal skin.'

As he hands me the necklace, nausea rolls through my stomach. I stuff it quickly into the bag.

'Miss Catherine? You sure you all right?'

I nod and begin gathering the rest of my father's things. Far behind Mose, I see the Expedition negotiating its way through the trees.

'Do you know anything about DeSalle Island, Mose?'

'Well, I was born down there, wasn't I? I think everybody who ever worked up here for your family was born on the island. Dr Kirkland always saying people from the island still do a day's work for a day's pay.'

Poverty wages, probably. 'Do you like my grandfather, Mose?'

'Oh, yes, ma'am. Dr Kirkland been real good to me.'

'I think you know what I mean.'

Mose looks around as though someone might be eavesdropping. 'Your granddaddy, he a tough man, and he know how to squeeze a nickel till the buffalo shits—pardon my language.'

'What about my father? Mr Luke?'

He smiles broadly, revealing tobacco-stained teeth. 'Mr Luke always had a good word for me when he passed. I liked him, but I had to be careful around him. Dr Kirkland didn't like him none at all.'

Michael's Expedition is close now, threading its way through the trees like a tank. 'Did you like the island, Mose?'

He shrugs. 'Didn't know nothing else back then. I wouldn't go back now, though. I like my TV in the evenings. And I don't like that river. Too many people done died in that water.'

'Is there something bad on the island? Something you couldn't explain, but that you just feel? I used to feel something like that there.'

The yardman closes his eyes. After a moment, a little shudder goes through him. Then he looks at me like a small boy. 'When I was young, the old folks used to say killers from the prison roamed the roads at night. All that seems like a fairy story now, something they used to scare us. Still, a lot of kids wouldn't get near them roads anytime round dark. And, I'll tell you this . . . I got me a lot of kin down there, and I hardly been back there in forty years. And now that you ask me, I don't care if I never go back again.'

As Michael's Expedition rumbles up beside Mose, the yardman gives me a wave and vanishes through the trees.

Another ghost of Malmaison.

MICHAEL WELLS and I are sitting on a leather couch in the private office of Dr Tom Cage, a general practitioner in Natchez for more than forty years. Bookshelves line all four walls, stuffed with medical treatises.

'Hi, Michael. Sorry to keep you two waiting.' A white-haired man wearing a white lab coat marches into the room and pumps Michael's hand. Then he turns to me and smiles. 'So, you're Catherine Ferry?'

I stand and offer Dr Cage my hand. 'Please call me Cat.'

He squeezes it softly, then takes a seat behind his desk. 'And I'm Tom.' He fixes his eyes on me. 'Luke Ferry. What do you want to know?'

'I'm not sure.' I reach for my father's green bag, which rests between my feet, and rummage through it until I find the string of 'prunes'. Fighting my revulsion, I hold the string out to the doctor. 'Do you know what this is?'

Dr Cage takes the string and examines one of the blackened chunks with a magnifying glass from his pocket. 'Ears,' he says.

'What?' asks Michael.

Dr Cage looks up at us. 'It's an ear necklace. Where did you get it?'

'Daddy kept it hidden in a bag with some other things.'

'It's a war trophy. When some soldiers killed an enemy in Vietnam, they cut off one or both ears and strung them on a necklace. I've never seen one.'

'So, my father cut the ears off his victims?'

'It is difficult for me to imagine Luke Ferry stooping to mutilation,' Dr Cage says. 'After all, he risked his life to bring the men who'd done this kind of thing to justice. When he was with the White Tigers in Cambodia, he learned that if he failed to go along with the prevailing powers he'd wind up dead. But as soon as he got back to Vietnam, he went over his CO's head and reported what he'd seen. Higher authority did what they always do when someone ignores the chain of command. Within a week, Luke was back in action with the Tigers. That's when he was wounded—according to Luke, by his fellow soldiers. It's a miracle he got aboard a medevac chopper alive.'

'What happened to him after that?'

'He was never the same. The things he'd witnessed had pushed him beyond his limit. When he learned they were sending him back to the Tigers again, he lost it. He started yelling about everything he'd seen, and the next thing you know they were processing him out on a special discharge. Post-traumatic stress disorder kicked in even before he made it back to the States. But Luke was stubborn. He tried a couple of times after the war to get an investigation started, but it never came to anything.' Dr Cage gestures at the necklace on his desk. 'You don't know the circumstances by which Luke came to have this. It may have been sent to him as a threat.' He pauses. 'I sense there might be more to this than what you've told me.'

For some reason, I feel I can trust this man. 'If I asked you whether you think my father could have sexually abused me, what would you say?'

A deep sadness fills Tom Cage's eyes. 'I'd like to say no. But I'm too old to be offering certainty on a subject like that. The human sex drive is a powerful thing. It dictates to us more than the other way round. Luke was a good boy, but what he did in the dark of the night I don't pretend to know. Whatever he did probably had more to do with what was done to him as a child than anything else. And that I don't know about.'

When I don't speak, Dr Cage adds, 'You're looking down a deep, dark hole, Catherine. A lot darker than I first thought. But at least you've got a good man helping you do it.' He turns to Michael. 'You take care of this girl,' he says. 'She's tough, but not as tough as she thinks she is.'

'I will.'

We stand to leave, and Dr Cage shakes Michael's hand, then mine.

THE NATCHEZ CITY CEMETERY is one of the most beautiful in the world, but today it brings me no peace. I'm driving my mother's car down one of its narrow asphalt lanes, Mom in the seat beside me, looking as anxious as I've ever seen her. She has aged visibly since Ann's death.

I drive between mausoleums hidden among the trees, and pull the Maxima onto the grass beside a low brick wall. The DeSalle family plot lies just beyond it. No mausoleums for us, just fine Alabama marble behind wrought iron that dates to 1840. Grandpapa would have preferred that Luke Ferry be interred elsewhere, but my mother—to her credit—insisted that he be buried here. It may be the only time that she's stood up to her father and won.

I walk through the gate alone and stand before my father's simple black headstone. Before long, I hear the gate creak behind me, then a shadow falls across mine on the ground.

'Why are we here?' my mother asks softly.

I reach for her hand. 'Mom . . . somehow I've reached the age of thirty-one without you and me sharing much more than small talk. I blame myself as much as you. I want us to do better in the future. But you may never want to talk to me after today, because I want to exhume Daddy's body.'

Her indrawn breath might as well have been an explosion. I know the turmoil inside her is almost more than she can bear. But before she can scream or burst into tears, I push on.

'I need a sample of his DNA, but I also want another autopsy done. And I want Lena out of the coffin.'

'That raggedy old stuffed animal?'

'Yes.'

Her hand pulls out of mine. 'Catherine, are you out of your mind?'

'No. I think I'm close to *not* being out of my mind for the first time in my life. I'm asking you to help me, Mom.'

She's looking at the gravestone, not at me. 'But why?'

I turn and face her. 'Mom, I was sexually abused when I was a child.'

She blinks several times quickly.

'Ann may have been molested, too. I don't know. And I won't know until I see Daddy's body and get Lena out of that coffin.'

Mom has begun to shake. From her head to her toes, she's shivering as though stranded on an Arctic glacier. 'Oh, dear Lord,' she whimpers.

'Mom, there's so much to tell and not enough time to tell it. My whole life I've had problems with men, with alcohol . . . lots of things.'

She steps towards me, relief evident in her face. *Now I understand the problem*, she thinks. 'That's not your fault, honey. Anybody who lost their father the way you did was bound to have some problems.'

'No! It wasn't that. I always thought it was, but it wasn't.'

'Baby, of *course* that's it. You suffered so much pain—'

'Mom, please! There's so much you don't know. The night Daddy was shot, there was no intruder at Malmaison.'

'Of course there was. I told you—'

'No. You never saw one, and there never was one. Grandpapa made that up to keep from having to tell you what really happened. He said he caught Daddy molesting me in my bed that night. They fought, and Grandpapa shot him. I know that's a shock, but that's what he told me.'

The blood has drained from my mother's face. 'I don't believe you.'

I shrug. 'I'm telling you the truth. Only I'm not sure any more that Grandpapa was telling *me* the truth. There's a chance it could have happened the other way round—that Daddy caught Grandpapa abusing me. And that's what I'm trying to find out. Who molested me. If it was Grandpapa, he probably did the same to Ann.'

My mother has her hands over her ears, but I keep talking. 'Ann killed herself in the clinic with Thomas the Turtle beside her. Did you know that?'

'She did that because of her infertility,' Mom says almost defiantly. 'She blamed it on the appendectomy she had there. Daddy said as much several times. That the infection might have made her sterile.'

'Something very bad happened to Ann in that clinic. And deep inside, you know that.' As Mom stares at me in silence, I cross the final, unspeakable line. 'Mama . . . how could you not know? How could you not know that was happening to me? How could you let someone *do* that to me?'

Tears pool in the corners of her eyes, then slide down her face. 'You need help, baby. We'll find somebody, somebody really good.'

'No,' I say, my voice breaking. 'You can't fob me off any more. Nobody can help me through this except you. I'm *begging* you, Mom. I'm begging you to help me find the truth.'

WHEN I PULL INTO the parking lot behind Malmaison, I see my grandfather seated in a folding lawn chair by the entrance to the rose garden. When he sees me and my mother inside the car, he gets out of his chair, walks over and starts shouting at me. His face is red, his eyes blazing.

'What the *hell* do you think you're doing, Catherine?'

I stand my ground. 'What are you talking about?'

'You want to dig up your father's goddamn corpse?'

I can't believe it. Someone in the chancery judge's office must have leaked word to my grandfather. That has to be it. I called the judge's chambers during the ride from Dr Cage's office to collect my mother from her shop, so that I'd have some idea of a time frame on exhumation.

'Well?' he roars. 'What do you have to say for yourself?'

Remarkably, my mother interposes herself between Grandpapa and me. This may be a first. 'Don't shout at her, Daddy,' she pleads. 'Cat's not herself right now. She's dealing with some problems.'

He nods angrily. 'Oh, I know she's got problems. She's had problems her whole life, just like Ann. I've spent half my life cleaning up their problems, but today it stops. Today, I'm doing some bud-nipping, before she causes this whole town a problem it can't afford.'

'What are you talking about?' I ask.

'The casino, goddamn it! This city's salvation. We're one hair's-breadth from getting federal authorisation. But *you*'—he jabs a thick forefinger in my direction—'you could blow the whole thing right out of the water with your theories and questions. And now you want to dig up Luke Ferry's body for the whole town to read about in the newspaper? Well, I'm telling you right now, that's not going to happen. Unless it's part of an official criminal investigation, you need your mother's approval to dig that body up.'

Mom almost cowers when he glances at her, and I know she's not about to give me what I need. I take a step towards my grandfather.

'Then I guess I'm going to have to make this a criminal investigation. I didn't want to, but you're not leaving me any choice. I'll get the Natchez police out here, and the FBI, if that's what it takes to find out the truth.'

'The *truth*?' Grandpapa echoes. 'You think it's the truth you're after?'

'That's all I've ever been after! But every new story was just another lie to keep me from digging any deeper. What are you afraid of, Grandpapa? What can't you bear to have anyone find out about you?'

He glances at my mother again, then looks at the ground. When he finally raises his head, his eyes burn into mine. 'It's not myself I've been trying to protect. It's you. The bottom of this damn mystery you're so keen to solve is something I prayed you'd never have to know. But you'll tear down this house, this family, everything I've built to get what you want. So . . . you want the truth? You want to know who killed your father?'

There's no turning back now. 'I do.'

'You did.'

CHAPTER 11

I'm running. Harder and faster than I've ever run in my life. I want to turn back time. Push back the days to the point before I began asking questions—questions to which I thought I wanted answers.

Michael Wells's house appears between the trees, and the sight of it brings a strange feeling of hope. I sprint harder.

I skirt the pool and bang on the glass of the French windows at the back of the house. I see movement inside, and then Michael is hurrying to the door, his face all concern. Before he can speak, I throw my arms round his neck, stand on tiptoe, and hug him as tightly as I can.

'Hey, hey, what's the matter?' he asks. 'What happened?'

I want to answer, but my chest is heaving against him in great racking sobs that make my whole body shudder. *I killed my father!* I want to scream, but nothing comes from my throat.

'Calm down,' Michael says, stroking my hair. 'Whatever it is, we can deal with it.'

I shake my head violently, staring at him through a screen of tears.

Eventually, my mouth forms the words, but again no sound emerges. Then, like a distraught child, I manage to stammer out the truth.

Michael's eyes go wide for an instant, but then he pulls me tight against him. 'Your grandfather told you that?'

I nod into his chest.

'Did he give you any proof?'

I shake my head. 'But the minute he said it . . . I felt I'd finally heard the truth. Only . . . I was eight years old. Could I really have shot my father?'

Michael sighs. 'If you did, it was a clear act of self-preservation.'

I hear Michael's words but they have no effect. Words cannot penetrate the wounded region of my soul. He seems to sense this. Keeping one arm tight around me, he leads me to the master bedroom, then helps me take off my shoes and get into bed.

'Don't move from this spot. I'll be back in a minute.'

He vanishes, leaving me in the cool, dry darkness of his air-conditioned bedroom. I feel strangely at home here, in the room where Mr and Mrs Hemmeter slept for more than thirty years.

Michael reappears beside the bed, a glass of water in his hand. 'This is a Lorcet Plus. It'll take the edge off.'

I take the white pill from his hand and pop it into my mouth, but as the glass touches my lips I realise I'm making a terrible mistake. I spit out the pill and put it on the bedside table.

'What's the matter?' Michael asks.

'I can't take this.' I look up into his concerned eyes, wishing I didn't have to tell him the truth. But I can't lie to him any more. Not even by omission. 'I'm pregnant,' I say, my eyes never leaving his.

He doesn't flinch. But the warmth in his eyes slowly dissipates into a cool and wary look. 'Who's the father? The married detective?'

'Yes.'

He stares silently at me for a few moments. 'I'll make you some tea instead,' he says awkwardly and walks quickly to the door.

'Michael, wait!'

He turns and looks back, his face pale, his eyes confused.

'I didn't want this,' I tell him. 'It wasn't planned or anything. But I'm not going to terminate it. I should have told you before, but I didn't want you to think badly of me. But now . . . with everything else you know, it's absurd to hold anything back.' My next words take more courage than swimming into the middle of the Mississippi River. 'If you want me to go, I'll understand.'

He only stares at me, his eyes unreadable. 'I'll get the tea.'

EXHAUSTION overtook me before Michael returned.

When you dream the same dream over and over, you begin to wonder whether, like a Hindu who has lived an immoral life, your punishment is to be reincarnated again and again in the same body, unable to rise up the chain of being until you learn the elusive lesson of your sin.

I'm back inside the rusted pick-up truck, my grandfather behind the wheel. We're rolling up the sloping hill of the old pasture. Soon we will crest the hill—crest it and sight the pond on the other side.

I don't want to see my father walk across the water and pull open the bullet hole in his chest. I already know what he's trying to tell me. I already know that I killed him. Why won't he let me rest?

'Goddamn rain,' Grandpapa mutters.

He downshifts and steps on the gas, and we trundle over the hill. But today the pond is empty. My father isn't floating on its surface. The perfect mirror remains undisturbed.

Grandpapa brakes as we roll towards the pond, then stops twenty yards from the water's edge. I turn to him to ask a question, but I don't know what the question is. Fear is clawing in my chest like a trapped animal.

As I stare through the windshield, a curtain of rain sweeps across my field of vision, all the leaves trembling under its weight. In seconds the glassy surface of the pond is sizzling like water thrown into a hot skillet.

Grandpapa reaches across the seat, takes hold of my knees, and turns me sideways. When he moves towards me, I beseech him with my eyes. He hesitates, then reaches under the seat and pulls out Lena the Leopardess, and shoves her into my hands. As I shut my eyes and press her soft fur against my cheek, a warm feeling spreads through my body. The rain sweeps over the truck as Grandpapa pushes me back on the seat, and the hard, percussive patter of raindrops on a tin roof fills my ears. When his big hands unsnap my jeans, I don't feel them. Lena and I are a million miles away, padding through the jungle, listening to the endless music of the rain . . .

WHEN I WAKE to sunlight streaming through Michael's bedroom, I know. The scales have been stripped from my eyes. My recurring dream was no dream at all, but a memory trying to come back to me any way it could. The business of my father walking on water was something grafted onto it, a different message from my subconscious, pointing me towards something I've yet to learn. And today I will learn it.

I find a note on the pillow with a house key lying on top of it. The note reads, *Gone to work. You're welcome to stay as long as you need to. Call me at the office when you wake up. Michael.*

I take Michael's phone off the bedside table and dial Kaiser's number.

John Kaiser catches his breath when he hears my voice. 'Do you have something for me?' he asks.

'No. I need something from you.'

'That's not the answer I was looking for, Cat. The only reason you're not in jail is because I thought you could help me solve this case.'

'I can. But it's a quid pro quo situation. You help me with my problem, I'll help you with yours.'

'Christ. What do you want now?'

If I seem too anxious to get Ann's autopsy report, Kaiser might not give it to me. 'Tell me where you are with the murders first.'

Kaiser blows out a stream of air in frustration. 'Nothing more on the saliva cultures. We're checking all film-processing labs, in the hope that someone's done work for Malik. We need to get hold of that film. Unfortunately it was only video equipment we found in his apartment, but I'm hoping for a break. I've got the technical services guys trying to resurrect data off the drives we took from Malik's office computers, but they've got nothing so far.'

'I'm sorry I haven't been more help. I've had my hands full here.'

'You just get me the names of the women in Group X. Do that, and I'll keep you out of jail.'

'I'm trying, John. But I need your help, too. I need the autopsy report on my aunt. I'm looking for anything out of the ordinary relating to her reproductive system.'

Kaiser takes his time to answer. 'I shouldn't give you this. But didn't you tell me Ann was obsessed with having children?'

My throat tightens. 'Yes.'

'Well, that makes no sense at all, Cat. Because your aunt had been sterilised. And not by any normal procedure. Apparently, her tubes were cut just below something called the fimbria, and tied off with silk sutures. The pathologist said OBs haven't used silk for that procedure in decades. Nor would an OB cut off the fimbria. He thought it was damned odd.'

My hands are shaking, not from fear but from outrage. 'I have to go, John.'

'No!' he says quickly. 'You can't just go. I've given you a lot of rope to play with and I'm afraid you're going to hang us both. I've got superiors to answer to. And every hour you're on the street comes out of my credibility. I'm looking for some help here.'

Michael's clock reads 7.05 a.m. 'Give me eight hours, John. In that time I'll have something to give you, or I'll come back to New Orleans and let you throw me to the wolves.'

The silence seems interminable.

'Eight hours,' he says softly. 'Cat, if I haven't heard from you by five today, I'll have the Natchez police pick you up on suspicion of murder.'

'Thanks, John. Hey, could you fax me the autopsy report? I'm a member of her family, for God's sake. Please.'

'You're a pain in the ass is what you are. Do you want it sent to the same number where we sent you those files on Malik?'

'Perfect. I'll talk to you before five.'

I hang up. My father's body is coming out of the ground today, and nothing is going to stop that. If the judge needs an affidavit from my mother to issue a court order for exhumation, he'll get one.

MOM IS SITTING at her kitchen table, staring blankly into a mug of coffee.

'Has Grandpapa been here?' I ask.

She shrugs.

I've already slipped into my grandfather's office and retrieved the autopsy report that Kaiser faxed there. I was lucky Grandpapa wasn't in there when it arrived.

'I have some things to tell you, Mom. They won't be easy to hear, but you don't have a choice any more. You owe it to Ann.'

Her mind seems alert. Whatever drug she was on yesterday has been flushed from her system. So, in a soft but deliberate voice, I tell her what the pathologist discovered. That Ann was sterilised many years ago by an unorthodox procedure, probably during her 'emergency appendectomy' on the island. 'There's something else,' I add. 'I had a dream last night. A recurring one, about riding in the old pick-up truck with Grandpapa. Last night I saw the end of it. He parked by the pond, and then . . . Mom, he started touching me.'

Her eyes remain focused on the table.

'And right before that, he pulled Lena from under the seat and stuck her in my arms.'

A trembling has begun in my mother's hands.

'They found Ann with Timid Thomas beside her body,' I remind her.

She lifts her coffee cup to her lips, takes a sip, then sets it rattling on the saucer. *She knows*, I realise.

'Do you have any memories of Grandpapa touching you?'

She shakes her head. 'But one thing I do remember . . .' She crushes a paper towel into a wet ball and wipes her eyes. 'The way Ann looked at me. In the evenings, especially, when Mom was gone to play bridge. Ann would go into Daddy's study to keep him occupied. And I would stay in my room. I knew she hated going in there. I knew she was afraid of him. I was, too, down deep, though I wouldn't have admitted that to anyone. Not even to myself. How could I be afraid of my daddy? He loved me and took care of me. But whenever Ann left me to spend time with him, she looked at me the way you'd look at something you were trying to protect.' Mom's chin is quivering like a little girl's. 'And now,' she says, 'now I know that's exactly what she was doing. Protecting me from him. She was only four years older, but . . . dear God, I can't stand to think about it.'

She crumples over the table, sobbing. I lean down over her and hug her as tight as I can. 'I love you, Mom. I love you so much.'

'I don't know how . . . At least Ann tried to protect me. But I didn't protect you . . . my own baby.'

'You couldn't,' I whisper.

She sits up and grits her teeth, obviously furious at herself. She takes my hand in hers and squeezes it. 'What are you going to do, Cat?'

'I'm going to make him admit what he did.'

She shakes her head, her eyes filled with terror. 'He'll never do that!'

'He'll have no choice. I'm going to prove that he did it. And then I'm going to see him punished for it.'

'He'll kill you, Cat. He will.'

I start to deny it, but Mom is right. Grandpapa murdered my father to protect himself. He wouldn't hesitate to kill me for the same reason.

I hug her again in reassurance. 'I know you're afraid of him. But I'm not. The best protection we have is the truth. And the truth is in Daddy's coffin. In my dream, Daddy was trying to tell me something about Lena. I have to find out what it is.'

'Do you really believe that? That he was trying to reach you?'

'No. I think I saw something on the night Daddy died. Saw it and then blocked it out. But I won't know what it was until they open that coffin.' I take hold of her hand. 'Mom? Will you help me?'

When her eyes finally rise to meet mine, I see something I never saw in them as a child. Courage. 'Tell me what to do,' she says.

OUTSIDE McDonough's Funeral Home, cars are parked along the street for two blocks in all directions. It's a Natchez tradition: you see the parked cars along here and you know someone has died. Someone white. Blacks have their own funeral homes. Their own cemeteries, too. Some things take a long time to change.

My father's bronze casket lies on the floor of the prep room, waiting for the van from the Jackson medical examiner's office. As prescribed by custom in Mississippi, the funeral director is present as a witness. A kind and florid man of seventy, Mr McDonough has discouraged my intention to 'view the remains', as he put it. I tried to allay his anxieties by telling him I have considerable experience with dead bodies and autopsies, but he only sighed and said, 'No matter how much experience you have, when it's your own folks, it's different.'

I'll know soon. Mr McDonough has opened the coffin and taken a few discreet steps back.

I step over to it and look down.

My first reaction is disbelief. Except for the black suit, my father looks much as he did in life. But as I gaze at his face, I see that his cheeks have actually sunken in quite a bit—his eyes, too, despite the plastic caps they put beneath the lids. With a quick motion like a bird pecking at something, I bend and pluck Lena from Daddy's arms.

'You saw me remove this stuffed animal?' I say, in case I have to use this evidence in court.

'Yes, ma'am,' Mr McDonough confirms.

I open the box of forensic chemicals I brought with me and take out a bottle of orthotolidine, which is more sensitive than luminol. It will reveal any latent blood on Lena's coat, but also maintain the integrity of the genetic markers. Carefully parting the fur beneath Lena's jaw, I can see some stitching where Pearlie must have repaired her. I spray some orthotolidine on her fur, then I turn her and cover her other side with the chemical.

'What happens now?' asks Mr McDonough.

'We wait. If there's blood, it'll glow blue. May I turn off these lights?'

'Go ahead. How long does it take?'

'A minute or two.'

After two minutes pass, Lena's head begins to glow as though painted with blue-dyed phosphorus.

My heart is pounding. Grandpapa never mentioned Lena in any version of the story he told me of the night my father died. But he told me to put her into the coffin. And soon, I may know why.

I carefully turn Lena in my hands. Though smeared quite a bit—probably from cleaning by Pearlie—most of the blood seems to have been deposited on Lena's head, while very little touched her body. It's almost as though her head was stuffed into a wound to try to stanch severe bleeding.

You're looking right at the answer, says a voice in my head.

I study the stitches beneath her chin. Why was she torn there? The answer hits me like ice water thrown in my face.

On top of Lena's snout is a perfect arch of glowing blue, the size of the maxillary arch in an adult human being. And I know without checking that the arch on Lena's fur will exactly match Daddy's upper teeth.

For the first time, the reality of that night plays out in my mind's eye. Grandpapa shoved Lena into Daddy's mouth, possibly to muffle his screams of pain, but more probably to finish the job of murdering him. While Daddy lay bleeding on the floor, my grandfather shoved my favourite companion down his throat and held his nose to finish him off. To silence him for ever.

The lights are switched back on.

I can't begin to name the feelings swirling through me. It's a nauseating combination of excitement and dread. I've been hunting killers for a long time, but it strikes me that I've really been hunting only one killer all my life.

I'd like a few moments alone with my father, but if I'm alone with the body, that might cause legal problems later. So, in full view of the funeral director, I kneel beside the casket, lay my hand over my father's, and whisper softly, 'I love you, Daddy, I know you tried to save me. I'm going to save myself now. Mama, too, if I can.'

Tears are running down my face. The iron veneer of professionalism I've managed to maintain up to this point is cracking.

'Miss Ferry?' says McDonough. 'You all right?'

'No, I'm not all right.' I get to my feet and wipe my eyes. 'But I'm going to be. For the first time in my life I'm going to be all right.'

McDonough looks embarrassed. 'Can I close the casket now?'

'Yes. Thank you for everything.'

My knees barely carry me out of the prep room. As I enter the corridor, a thought strikes me. I turn around. 'Mr McDonough?'

'Yes, ma'am?'

'Have you spoken to my grandfather today?'

The funeral director looks quickly at the floor. That is my answer.

'Mr McDonough? You've just become involved in an FBI serial murder investigation. My grandfather is also part of that investigation, and not in a positive connection, if you get my meaning. If you interfere by communicating information on these matters to him, the FBI will be after you. Do I make myself clear?'

Mr McDonough looks as if he wishes he'd never set eyes on me. 'Ain't none of this my business,' he says. 'I won't be talking to nobody about it.'

'Good.'

When I step into the sun outside, I find myself facing several men wearing their Sunday best. They're pallbearers, I realise, and they've just carried the deceased from the funeral service that's just finished to a waiting hearse. Soon the family will emerge from the exit behind me.

I walk quickly down the side of the building, but I can't escape. A woman about my age rounds the corner with an infant in her arms.

'Cat?' she says. 'Cat Ferry?'

'Yes?'

'It's Donna. Donna Reynolds. Used to be Donna Dunaway,' she adds.
Recognition comes. I knew Donna in junior high school.

'Is this your baby?' I ask.

She nods happily. 'My third. Four months old.'

My eyes fix on the baby's round face as I search for something appropriate to say. 'What's his name, Donna?'

'Britney. She *is* wearing pink, you know.'

'Oh, God, I'm sorry.'

Donna is smiling. 'Are you here for the funeral? I didn't know you knew Uncle Joe.'

'I don't. I mean . . .' As my words fade into silence, my gaze settles on the baby's toothless smile. A long string of drool drops from Britney's mouth, and suddenly I know who killed the men in New Orleans.

'CAT? WHAT'S going on?'

I gasp in relief. I'm almost to Malmaison, and I've been trying to reach Sean since I left the funeral home. 'I know who the killer is, Sean.'

'Whoa, whoa, which killer are you talking about? Your family stuff, or the New Orleans case?'

'New Orleans!'

'How the hell could you know who the killer is?'

'How do I ever know? Something clicked in my head.'

'What clicked this time?'

If I tell him, there'll be no stopping the consequences. And right now I'm not at all sure I want the killer arrested. 'I can't tell you that, Sean. Not yet.'

'What are you up to, Cat?'

'I want you to meet me at my house. Are you still suspended?'

'Yeah.'

'Do you still have your badge and gun?'

'I've got a gun. And I have a badge that'll do in a pinch. What do you have in mind?'

'I want to talk to the killer before we do anything.'

'Talk to him. About what?'

'It's not a him, Sean. It's a her. I'll tell you when I see you.'

'Why did you call me?' Sean asks in a strange voice. 'Why not Kaiser?'

'Because I trust you.' I'm lying. I picked Sean because—to a certain extent—I can control him.

'OK. Call me thirty minutes before you get here.'

AS I SWING into the parking lot behind the slave quarters, I see Pearlie's blue Cadillac parked beside Grandpapa's Lincoln.

She doesn't answer my knock, so I walk quickly to her kitchen, where I find her sitting at her table, staring blankly ahead and smoking a cigarette. I haven't seen Pearlie smoke since I was a little girl. An ashtray full of butts is beside her, and a bottle of cheap whiskey stands beside her coffee cup.

'Pearlie?'

'I thought you was Billy Neal coming to get me,' she rasps.

'Why would he come get you?'

''Cause of what I know.'

'What do you know?'

A new alertness comes into her eyes. 'Don't play games with me, Miss Cat. Tell me what you come here for.'

'I'm about to confront Grandpapa. I wanted to talk to you first.'

She blinks once, slowly. 'How come?'

'Because you know things I need to know. And I want you to know what I've learned about him.'

'What you talking about?'

'Grandpapa murdered Daddy, Pearlie.'

'You just think that? Or you can prove it?'

'I can prove it. What I want to know is, did you know already?'

Pearlie exhales a long stream of smoke. 'Not to prove, I didn't. But I had thoughts that night. Later on, too. Wasn't nothing I could do about it.'

I knew it. 'You think Grandpapa's invulnerable, Pearlie. But he's not. I'm going to put him in jail. I've got evidence. Remember Lena the Leopardess?'

A glint of memory. 'The toy you buried with Mr Luke?'

'Yes. Grandpapa suggested I put her in the coffin. Do you know why?'

'I know there was blood on her. Dr Kirkland told me to throw that toy away. When I told him it was your favourite, he told me I could wash it off and sew the rip back together.'

'Do you know how Lena got torn?'

She shakes her head.

'Grandpapa stuffed her into Daddy's mouth so he would suffocate before you got downstairs. He wasn't dying quickly enough from the bullet.'

Pearlie winces. 'Lord Jesus. Don't tell me that.'

'That's not the worst of it. You remember the story about Grandpapa cutting out Ann's appendix by lantern light on the island? How he was the big hero for saving her life?'

'Sure I do. Him and Ivy both.'

'Well, he took out her appendix, all right. But he did a little something extra, too. He cut her Fallopian tubes, so she couldn't get pregnant.'

Pearlie bows her head and begins to pray softly.

'Why did you go to the island yesterday, Pearlie? You hate that place.'

'Don't want to talk about that.'

'You've got to start talking. You've been silent too long.'

She sips whiskey from her coffee cup, then lights another cigarette and takes a deep drag. 'I quit cigarettes twenty-three years ago,' she says, 'but when I heard Miss Ann was dead, I had to have me one. I ain't stopped since.'

I say nothing.

'I come to work here in 1948,' she says, almost to herself. 'I was seventeen. Miss Ann was born that year, but they was living in New Orleans then. Dr Kirkland was still training to be a doctor. He and Mrs Catherine didn't move to Natchez until 1956, and they didn't take over this place until sixty-four, when Mr DeSalle died.' She looks at me as though making sure I understand. 'That's why I missed it, you see? Miss Ann was sixteen when they moved in here. The damage was already done. But things still wasn't right. Not really. Any boy that come to call on Ann, Dr Kirkland frightened away. Even the nice ones. He was jealous of that girl. Mrs Catherine saw it, too, but she couldn't do nothing to change it.' Pearlie smiles sadly. 'Lord, how the boys liked her, though. Ann was the most popular girl in town. They couldn't see the pain hidden in her heart.'

'What about Mom?'

She takes another sip of whiskey and grimaces. 'Gwen was twelve when they moved in here. She didn't have the same problems Ann did. She could smile and laugh, and she seemed like a normal child. But she married young as she could to get away from this house. And then she didn't get away after all. The war brought her back. And the older she got, the more problems she had. Looking back, I think Dr Kirkland got to her, too. The damage was done when she was a baby, same as with Ann. Just not as bad.'

'I think Ann tried to protect her.'

Pearlie nods slowly. 'Ann tried to be everything to everybody. To save everybody. But she couldn't even save herself.'

'Did you ever see anything?'

She shakes her head. 'I think Dr Kirkland made sure I didn't. He'd walk this property all hours of the night, like your daddy. I think that's one reason he didn't like Mr Luke. He couldn't prowl around without being seen any more. The few times Dr Kirkland caught me out after nine, he warned me to stay indoors. Said he might shoot me by accident, thinking I was a burglar.'

In hindsight, it all seems so obvious. What's missing is the historical context. The idea that Dr William Kirkland, respected surgeon and paragon of virtue, could be tiptoeing around his ante-bellum mansion molesting his daughters was virtually unthinkable forty years ago.

'You never answered my question, Pearlie. Why did you go to the island yesterday?'

She turns her dark gaze onto me, and at last I feel the full power of her intelligence. All her life Pearlie has hidden her quick understanding, but the death of my aunt—one of 'her babies'—has caused a tectonic shift in the old woman's soul, and Pearlie Washington is never going to be the same.

'I don't think Mrs Catherine died by accident,' she whispers. 'I never did.'

This statement shocks me to the core. 'Are you saying Grandmama Catherine was murdered? But people saw her fall into the water.'

'Did they?' Pearlie's eyes glint in the dark. 'She was standing off by herself when she went in. But did that sandbar really cave in? Mrs Catherine practically grew up on DeSalle Island. You think she'd stand on a weak sandbar like some city fool and not know it? No, child. I think Mrs Catherine finally found out something so bad that she couldn't live with it . . . I think she just couldn't see what else to do but die. I think she drowned herself in that river, baby. The month before she died, Mrs Catherine wouldn't speak to nobody. Had a far-off look in her eyes. Hopeless.'

I get up and pull the curtains away from the kitchen window. Malmaison stands majestic and silent as a royal sepulchre. 'He's not going to hurt any more children,' I say softly. 'That stops today.'

'How you gonna stop him? Even the po-lice afraid of Dr Kirkland. Dr Kirkland got friends all the way up to Washington, DC.'

'Don't worry about it, Pearlie. Just promise me that, if you have to get up in front of a jury, you'll tell the truth about what you know.'

'Well, I'm too old to lie with my right hand on a Bible.' Pearlie stands unsteadily and walks to me, then hugs me the way she used to when I was a little girl. The way my mother never quite could. 'I'm just sorry I didn't do more, baby,' she says. 'Sorry I couldn't save you from all the pain you been through.' She pulls back and looks into my eyes. 'You're the strongest of all my girls. I'm just gonna pray for you, whatever prayers is worth. Maybe with the Lord's help, you can come through all right.'

I kiss her gently on the cheek, then walk out into the sunlight.

My grandfather's Lincoln is still parked beside Pearlie's Cadillac. As I stare at the two cars, I sense someone watching me. Turning to my right, I see Billy Neal staring down from the gallery of Malmaison. He's smiling.

I turn towards him and start walking, my strides long and resolute. As I get closer his smile fades. By the time I'm within speaking distance, he's scowling at me. Looking closer, I see the butt of an automatic pistol protruding from a shoulder holster beneath his jacket.

'You've hitched your wagon to a falling star,' I say in a flat voice. 'You should leave while you can.'

He laughs. 'What are you talking about?'

'Follow me and find out.'

CHAPTER 12

Grandpapa is talking on the telephone at his roll-top desk, his broad back clothed in a custom-tailored shirt of blue silk. His deep voice fills the room like a finely tuned bass viol.

'Hang up,' I say sharply.

He rotates his leather chair, and his eyes fix upon me. 'Just a minute,' he says into the phone. He presses the mouthpiece against his shirt. 'What is it, Catherine? I'm very busy right now.'

'I know you murdered my father.'

His only reaction is a slight narrowing of the eyes. 'I told you what happened that night, Catherine.'

'You told me four different times. A different story every time. But I know the truth now. You murdered him, and I can prove it.'

Grandpapa raises the phone to his lips. 'I'll have to call you back.'

'First you shot him. Then you shoved my favourite stuffed animal into his mouth to keep him quiet. Then I figure you held his nose shut with your fingers while he suffocated.'

In the time it takes Grandpapa to hang up the telephone, his eyes change from the benign blue of a loving grandfather to the cold slits of a wolf sensing threat. The transformation chills my blood. This is his *real* face.

He waves his hand at Billy Neal, who has appeared at the door.

The driver takes something from one of the shelves and walks towards me. It's a black metal wand like the ones they use in airports to check for concealed weapons. He sweeps it up and down my body. 'She's clean,' he says finally. He walks back to the door and stands beside it like a guard dog.

'All right. I told you I was busy. Is there anything else?'

I can't believe his arrogance. 'Didn't you hear me? I can prove that you murdered my father. I can also prove you sexually abused Ann. And worse.'

He dismisses this with another wave of his hand. 'That's ridiculous.'

'I have evidence.'

'Bloody footprints on a floor? I've already explained that.'

'I have a lot more than that,' I say. 'I'm remembering more every day. I know what you did to me.'

Grandpapa's eyes narrow again. 'Remembered evidence? Sounds like you've been taking your friend Dr Malik a little too seriously.'

What the hell is going on? I had no idea he even knew who Malik was.

'Catherine, so-called repressed memories count for nothing in court.'

'Ann's body will count,' I say evenly.

For the first time, I see a shadow of worry cross his face. 'What are you talking about?'

'How could you do that to her, Grandpapa? You cut her Fallopian tubes when she was ten years old. You're a monster. A *freak*. But you're going to pay for everything. For Ann, for Mom, for me.'

The jaw muscles flex in his impassive face. 'I'm not going to pay for anything,' he says. 'I have nothing to pay for.'

'Do you deny what you did? That's what child molesters do. They scream they're innocent all the way to the pen. But your kind doesn't fare too well in prison, Grandpapa.'

William Kirkland smiles coldly at me. 'I'm not going to prison. Your so-called evidence is worthless. A stuffed animal taken from a coffin that's been in the ground for twenty years? You can't connect me to that.'

'I can identify the maxillary arch of Daddy's teeth in the latent blood on Lena's coat.'

He purses his lips in thought. 'Luke must have grabbed Lena and bit down on her to fight against the pain after you shot him.'

'Don't even try that,' I snap, but I can see Grandpapa selling that story to a jury. 'Ann's body *proves* that you sterilised her,' I say softly. 'You should never have used silk sutures, Grandpapa.'

He rises calmly from his chair. 'Everyone knows Ann was obsessed with becoming pregnant. She went to all sorts of quacks for fertility treatments.

She even went to Mexico. God knows what procedures she had done, or what butchers performed them. You'll never prove I did anything more than remove her appendix.' His eyes brim with confidence. 'Catherine, you're obviously delusional. Have you been taking your medications? Maybe I should review your drug regimen with your psychiatrist.'

'I'm not the one you have to worry about,' I tell him. 'It's Dr Malik who's going to nail you.'

Grandpapa glances at Billy Neal. 'That would be quite a trick. Since the good doctor happens to be dead.'

A dry chuckle from Billy. I'm starting to wonder if it was Billy Neal who faked Malik's suicide in the Thibodeaux Motel.

'Dead or alive doesn't matter,' I say with a confidence I don't quite feel. 'He's going to speak from the grave. You're going to be revealed for what you are on TV screens from coast to coast.'

Neither Billy nor my grandfather is laughing now, and I thank God for it. If they were, I'd be pretty sure that Dr Malik's film had been destroyed. But it hasn't—not by them, anyway. They don't even know about it.

'I see you don't know about Dr Malik's documentary on sexual abuse.'

In seconds, the threatened wolf is back. He advances towards me, six feet six inches of rage, with blazing eyes and a voice like Moses' down from the mountaintop. 'Do you have any idea how much trouble you've caused me? I'm sweating blood trying to save this town, and you're working round the clock to sabotage everything I've achieved! The state gaming commission would *love* an excuse for a federal injunction to stop this project happening. I have money on the table, Catherine. Not other people's money. *Mine.* Your inheritance, if you give a goddamn—which you probably don't.'

'You're right,' I say quietly. 'I don't. All I care about is what you did to this family. That's all you should care about, too. But that was the problem all along, wasn't it? You didn't care.'

He takes another step towards me, squares his broad shoulders. 'I've watched you go from man to man . . . always searching . . . They're none of them man enough to handle you, are they?'

I want to interrupt, but my voice won't come.

'Everything you've said today is true. Great men have great appetites, darling. It's that simple. More hunger than one woman can satisfy. Your grandmother knew that. She didn't like it, but she understood.'

'Liar!' I shout, finding strength in my grief and outrage. 'Grandmama didn't *understand*. She did everything she could not to validate her fears.

But when she finally figured out what a monster she'd married, she drowned herself so she wouldn't have to live with what she'd let happen to us.'

Grandpapa's composure comes apart slowly, like mud cracking in the sun. 'You say she wasn't enough for you. Why didn't you take a mistress? Why come to *us*?'

He shakes his head. 'A mistress makes you vulnerable.' He reminds me of a maths teacher puzzled by kids who can't grasp the simplest concept. 'Your grandmother knew I needed more than she could give me, and she preferred that I get it at home rather than embarrass her in society.'

A coldness unlike any I've ever known envelops me. 'I don't believe you.'

Exasperation tightens his features. 'Damn it, girl, you act like I'm the first man who ever did this. The same thing happened to me when I was a boy. I'm not whining about it.' He stabs a forefinger at me. 'You came from my loins, Catherine. Your mother and Ann, too. You are the issue of *my blood*. You were *mine*. To do with as I saw fit.'

He walks to the gun safe, quickly spins the dial, and opens the heavy door. From it he takes a rifle, the Remington 700, which he calmly loads with a cartridge from a box on the shelf. As he walks towards me, he works the bolt and chambers the round. 'What if this gun were to go off?' He brings the barrel within a foot of my face.

'You'd be convicted of murder.'

He smiles. 'Would I? I think not. A woman with your psychiatric history? No. If I really considered you a threat, you wouldn't leave this room. But you're not a threat. Are you, Catherine? However if this Malik film you spoke of really exists, you'd do well to get it for me or destroy it. I'd hate to give you something to really be depressed about.'

'What are you talking about?'

'Life's little tragedies.' He smiles again. 'You hate me for being this way, but one day you'll thank God that you have my blood flowing through your veins. My genes determining your fate.'

When my voice finally emerges, it's utterly devoid of emotion. 'You're wrong. I wish I'd never been born. You don't know this . . . but I'm pregnant. And for the first time since I found out, I'm wondering whether I should bring that child into this world. I feel contaminated. Like I can never wash your poison out of me.'

He lowers the rifle and steps closer, his eyes glowing. 'You're pregnant?'

'Yes.'

He reaches for my arm. I jerk back.

'Take it easy, girl. Who's the father?'

'You'll never know.'

'Don't be that way. You'll come around. You've got more of me in you than you think.'

'What do you mean?'

A knowing smile now. A man hoarding a secret. 'I could be your father, Catherine. Do you realise that?'

With these words, what's left of my composure crumbles. My very being is unravelling into nothingness.

'Luke spent all his time on the island,' he says, 'chasing that nigger girl, Louise. And your mother just lay sleeping in her room here, half-looped on Luke's medicine.' He nods slowly. 'You see now?'

The savage joy I see in his eyes brings a horror I never thought imaginable. 'Is that true?' I ask in a small voice.

He shrugs. The triumph in his face is absolute. 'It's certainly something to think about while you're making plans to talk to the district attorney.'

I'm backing away from him, reaching blindly for the doorknob.

'And if you're thinking of Pearlie testifying to anything, forget it. She'll never say a word against me. Pearlie knows her place, Cat. You know your place, too, honey. Deep down, you do.'

I drop my shaking hand from the knob, then raise it and point a quivering finger at him. 'No. You were too strong for me when I was a baby. But not any more.' I pull open the door, stumble through it, then run down the hallway and out into the parking lot. I have to get away from this house.

'TELL ME AGAIN about the teeth,' says Sean.

We're sitting at the kitchen table of my house on Lake Pontchartrain, as we've done so many times before. Spread out on the table before us are eleven photographs of the women we believe most likely to constitute Group X. We culled these from the thirty-seven female relatives—ranging in age from two to seventy-eight—of the victims of the NOMURS killer. We chose them while talking on the phone during my drive from Natchez. In the middle of the row is the woman who I believe killed the six victims.

I turn from the table to the dark blue square of my picture window. Night is falling fast. 'We all have large numbers of bacteria in our mouths,' I murmur. The primary one is *Streptococcus mutans*.'

Sean taps a pen against the tabletop. 'And the culture of the saliva from the bite marks on Quentin Baptiste had none of this bacteria?'

'Right. At twenty-four hours, no growth. Very unusual. When Kaiser first showed me that lab report, a couple of possibilities hit me—like that would be the case if someone was on antibiotics—but I was distracted at the time. I'd just learned that my aunt had committed suicide, and I was trying to escape the FBI building. I knew that the saliva might have come from someone without teeth, but the possibility of it being a baby . . . I just automatically ruled it out. I mean, we're dealing with serial murders here. It took me seeing that drooling baby at the funeral home to put it together.'

'And this is what you came up with?' Sean taps the photo at the centre of the row, which shows a dark-haired girl of twenty-two. 'Evangeline Pitre?'

'It's her, Sean.' Evangeline Pitre is the daughter of Quentin Baptiste, the murdered homicide detective. 'Kaiser had told me one of Baptiste's daughters worked at a day-care centre. The only question was whether that centre handled any male children under six months old—the age when teeth erupt. I confirmed it by phone after I left the island, but I knew, Sean. I just knew.'

'You can't convince me this girl committed all six murders on her own.'

'Her father was a homicide cop,' I point out. 'There's no telling what kind of skills and knowledge she might have.'

'You think she's killing everyone's abusers for them? Punishing them?'

'Pitre could be killing them without anyone else in the group knowing what she's doing. But that's not what my gut tells me.'

Sean makes a wry face. 'My gut tells *me* that Nathan Malik developed the whole plan. Pitre may have got the saliva to put into the bite marks. She might even have pulled the trigger. But where did she get the idea to use a human skull to *make* the marks? No, this chick didn't come up with the crime signature we've been seeing. Hell, she didn't even finish high school.'

'I agree, OK? But that doesn't mean Malik was behind it. It could be any one of the other women in the group. One or all.'

'You're forgetting Margaret Lavigne's suicide note,' Sean reminds me. '"An innocent man is dead. Please tell Dr Malik to stop it." Malik was using those women's emotions to drive them.'

'He probably knew what was happening,' I concede. 'That doesn't mean he planned it or helped carry it out.'

Sean sighs. 'We can debate this all night. What are we going to *do*?'

'I told you. I want to talk to Pitre. Just you and me.'

'You want to go see this woman you think viciously murdered six men?'

'That's right. We won't be in any danger. She's only interested in killing child abusers, not cops.'

Sean nods. 'Yeah. And who killed Dr Malik? Who set that skull on his lap?'

'I'm hoping Evangeline Pitre can tell us that.'

'What do you have against bringing in the task force?' Sean asks. 'Do you have to be the one who personally breaks this case open?'

I look at him in disbelief. 'Can you say *projection*, Sean? Hell, I don't want this case to break open at all. I'm not sure the person behind these killings should go to prison. Not yet, anyway.'

His mouth drops open. 'You're kidding me.'

'I'm not. Child molesters aren't just committing rape, Sean. They're committing murder. The victims keep walking and talking, so we think they're still alive. But their souls are dead. It's the worst crime in the world. That's what Malik told me when I first met him, and now I know he's right. The victims are innocent children. Totally unable to protect themselves.'

Sean holds up the photo of Evangeline Pitre. 'This isn't a helpless child. She's twenty-two years old.'

'You have no idea what's going on behind that girl's eyes. For all you know, she may never have matured emotionally beyond the age of six.'

With a groan Sean gets up and takes a beer from my refrigerator. He takes a long swig. 'If we do this, and get caught, that's it for my career.'

'Sean I'm going to talk to Evangeline Pitre tonight, with or without you. But be warned. If you try to go round me on this—if you call the task force before I'm satisfied that I've got the truth from Pitre—then I'll go to your wife and tell her everything we ever did.'

He goes pale. 'You wouldn't do that.'

'Look at me, Sean. I will.'

He gazes at me as though seeing me for the first time.

'You have no idea of the intensity of emotions we're dealing with here,' I tell him. 'I know what an abused woman is capable of, OK? And before we throw Pitre to the wolves, I've got to understand what happened.'

He drains his beer, then tosses the bottle in the trash. 'No back-up,' he says. 'Dumb as it gets.'

A surge of relief goes through me. He's going to come.

Sean slips his jacket on over his shoulder holster. Then he bends, takes a small revolver from an ankle holster, and checks the cylinder.

'Pitre lives alone,' I tell him. 'It's a week night and she has to work tomorrow. She won't be expecting anything. We go in forcefully, scare her, then show her a way out.'

'And if someone else is there with her?'

'You take your Glock. I'll carry your throwdown in my purse.'

Sean shakes his head, but he passes me his throwdown gun, a Smith & Wesson featherweight .38. 'Could you use that on Pitre if you had to?' he asks.

I feel the cold weight in my hands. 'It's not going to come to that.'

EVANGELINE PITRE lives in a dilapidated white house in Gentilly, a tree-shaded working-class neighbourhood of one-storey clapboards. It's dark when Sean parks his Saab behind a beat-up Toyota Corolla at the kerb out front—a car that Sean's partner just confirmed belongs to our suspect. Sean hangs up his cellphone and surveys the house with a veteran cop's eye.

'Joey talked to the detectives who interviewed Pitre after her father's murder. They said they'd hardly asked anything when Kaiser showed up and took over the interview. If Kaiser already suspects Pitre, Cat, we could foul up this case.' He looks at me, his eyes sincere. 'You don't want to call him?'

I give Sean a hard look, then get out of the car and hurry up the sidewalk to the screened porch. He catches up with me as I knock on the door.

Quick footsteps sound inside. The curtain in the window to our left flips sideways, a dark silhouette peers out, then the curtain drops back into place.

'Who is it?' calls a muffled female voice.

'Police,' says Sean. 'Please open the door, ma'am. I've got identification.'

After a few moments, the doorknob clicks and the door opens to the length of a chain latch. Sean flips open his wallet and holds his badge up to the crack in the door.

'Detective Sergeant Sean Regan, ma'am. NOPD Homicide. Are you Evangeline Pitre?'

'Yes. What's this about?'

'Your father's murder.'

There's a pause. 'I already talked to the NOPD. The FBI, too.'

'I'm aware of that, ma'am. But we take the death of a fellow officer very seriously. We need to speak to you again.'

'Well . . .'

The door closes, but after a brief rattle it opens again, revealing the face from the photograph. Evangeline Pitre looks older and thinner than she did in the photo. Her dark hair hangs lankly, as if it hasn't been washed in days.

'Sorry,' she says. 'I've been paranoid ever since it happened.'

'Could we come inside?' Sean asks.

Pitre looks doubtfully behind her, as though unwilling for us to see the squalor in which she lives. 'OK,' she says finally. 'Come on in.'

She backs up, giving us room to enter.

The front door opens into a den, which is furnished with a flower-print sofa that looks like it was bought at a thrift store. In front of it is a rectangular coffee table. The sofa faces the left wall, where an old television shows the Home Shopping Network. Cigarette smoke hangs lazily in the air. I trace it to a cigarette burning in an ashtray on the floor beside a La-Z-Boy recliner facing the TV. Evangeline Pitre moves towards the sofa.

'Seat?' she offers.

'Thanks,' says Sean. He turns the La-Z-Boy round so that it faces the sofa and sits. I perch on the sofa, while Evangeline Pitre lights on its edge like a bird, as though she might take flight at any moment.

'Ms Pitre,' Sean begins, 'we'd like to—'

'Angie,' she cuts in. 'Call me Angie.'

Sean gives her his charming smile, but the official tone remains in his voice. 'All right, Angie. My colleague is a forensic expert we consult on cases like this. She wants to ask you some questions.'

I set my purse on the floor, and give Pitre my most confiding smile. 'Angie,' I say, 'I *am* a forensic expert, but I'm not here today to talk to you about forensics. I'm here to tell you what we know about these murders. I was a close friend of Dr Nathan Malik.'

Something has changed in her face. What? A tightening of the jaw? Whatever caused the change, it's so profound that I feel as though a second set of eyes has opened behind the ones I can see. Eyes glinting with a primitive survival instinct. I've never met Evangeline Pitre in my life, but I know her. I have that second set of eyes, too. The ones that watch in the quivering darkness, waiting for *him* to come—

'Angie, I know your father was a bad man.'

Her eyes have taken on a dull glaze.

'I know he came to your bed in the dark, Angie. He probably hurt other children, too. That's why he had to die, isn't it?'

For the briefest instant, her eyes dart towards the hall that leads to the bedrooms. Is she looking for escape? Or for help?

Sean stands quickly. 'Do you mind if I take a look around the house?'

I expect Angie to bound to her feet in protest, but instead she settles back against the couch. 'Sure,' she says. 'Whatever.'

Sean moves into the hallway, drawing his gun from beneath his jacket as he goes. To keep the girl from panicking, I ask, 'Were you one of the original members of Group X, Angie?'

A faint smile touches her lips.

'You're afraid to trust me, but you don't have to be. I know about Dr Malik's film. He wanted to give me the tapes for safekeeping, but I couldn't take them. The FBI was after me because they think I'm involved with the murders. I don't mind that. They don't have any real evidence.'

The hidden eyes probe me for deception, but they find none. 'I don't get it,' she says. 'You're with a cop.'

'Sean's not a regular cop. He's my boyfriend. I was molested, just like you, Angie. I know how that feels. I'm here to help.'

Her eyes narrow in suspicion.

'I know those six men were punished for what they did. But for me to help you, you're going to have to tell me how it all started. Did you ever meet a woman named Ann Hilgard?'

For the first time, I see fear in her eyes. Why?

'Angie, if you don't talk to me tonight, Sean is going to have to tell the task force what I figured out about these murders. About how you're involved. And I won't be able to help you after that.'

The fear ratchets up a notch. 'What are you talking about?'

Here goes . . . 'I know you're taking saliva from a baby at the day-care centre where you work and putting it into the bite marks on the dead men.'

Pitre's eyes widen, and her bottom lip quivers like a five-year-old's.

'What I need to know is, have you done all this on your own, or is somebody helping you? Was it Dr Malik? I know he knew about the killings. He told me that. Did he talk about them in the film?'

Angie's hands are shaking now, and her left leg is bouncing up and down. She's like a machine that has run reliably for twenty-two years, but is now about to vibrate to pieces. Sean was right: Angie Pitre couldn't have committed the murders alone.

She stands so suddenly that I jerk back in my chair.

'This isn't right!' she cries, jabbing her sinewy arm at me. 'You don't have proof of nothing!'

Sean races back into the den, gun in hand. 'What's the matter?'

'Nothing.' I motion for him to put the gun away. 'Angie was about to tell me who's helping her punish those men.'

'What will happen to me if I talk to you?' she asks Sean.

He gives me a pointed look that I have no trouble reading: *It's time to Mirandise this girl and put her in front of a video camera.* 'That depends on what you tell us,' he says.

'Angie,' I say softly, 'I know it's hard for you to trust people. But you need to listen to me now. Because I don't want to put you in jail. OK? I am the best friend you're ever going to have.'

The guarded look doesn't lessen, but there's confusion in her eyes. She sits back down on the sofa.

'Whose idea was it?' I ask. 'Who first said, "We can't just sit around and complain about this. We have to do something"?'

Her eyes flick back and forth, then she draws up her shoulders and hugs herself like a sullen child. 'It wasn't really like that. I mean, Dr Malik was always talking about how the men who do it never stop. You know? How none of the treatments work. He said only death or prison ever really stops them from doing it. And he didn't think any of the old ways worked for victims either. They didn't make you well. It was all a lot of feel-good talk, he said. It couldn't stop you from doing the bad things caused by what happened when you were a kid. You know? Numbing behaviour, he called it.'

I nod understanding. 'I've been an alcoholic since I was a teenager.'

'There you go. So, that's why Dr Malik started Group X. To try something new with delayed-memory cases like us. What was different was that Dr Malik did the work right there with all of us in the same room. And even though the bad stuff had happened to most of us years ago, in Group X it was like it was happening *right then*. All the terror and rage you couldn't express came blasting out of you like an explosion or something. And it made you *mad*. Even Dr Malik. You could see it in his face. But as intense as all that was, we got to be friends, see? All of us. We started meeting outside Dr Malik's office after group on Wednesdays. And it was then that we figured out the *really* scary thing: that the guys who had done this to us were probably still doing it.' She bites her bottom lip and nods as though talking silently to herself. 'Not to us, but to other kids. You know?'

'How many of you were there, Angie?'

'Six.'

'And now six men are dead.'

She nods again.

'So you're finished?'

'Yep.' She gives me a little smile. 'All done.'

Somehow, I knew this before I ever got here. That's why I didn't let Sean call in the task force. 'Who killed Dr Malik, Angie?'

Her smile vanishes, replaced by a profound fear. 'I don't know. Nobody knows what to do now.'

'Cat, it's time to make some calls,' Sean says quietly.

Maybe he's right. What guarantee do I have that one of these women won't decide tomorrow that someone else deserves a death sentence? Margaret Lavigne's stepfather already became an innocent victim.

'Cat? I have to—'

A muted thud cuts off Sean in midsentence.

When I turn, I see a blonde woman holding a green plastic barbell in one hand and a butcher's knife in the other. Half an hour ago, I was studying her picture on my kitchen table. She's Stacey Lorio, aged thirty-six, registered nurse and the daughter of Colonel Frank Moreland, our first victim. She's knocked Sean unconscious with the barbell. As I stare in shock, she kneels and yanks his Glock from his shoulder holster, then points it at my chest.

'I hid under the dirty clothes in the closet,' she says to Angie, panting from excitement. 'For a minute, I thought he saw me.'

'Why did you hit him?' I ask, glancing at my purse beside the sofa.

'Shut up!' Lorio snaps, straightening up. She's not much taller than Angie Pitre, but her rawboned body, in singlet and shorts, is mostly muscle.

'We didn't come here to arrest anybody, Stacey,' I say.

She laughs, then glances at Angie. 'I know better than that, you rich bitch.'

'Do you know me, Stacey?' I ask.

'What do you think? Your aunt screwed up my life.'

'What?'

'Yeah, she came along with her perfect teeth, her thousand-dollar shoes, her Southern belle voice, and he didn't know which way was up any more.'

Suddenly everything is clear. This woman was romantically involved with Nathan Malik until my aunt took him away from her.

'*You* killed Dr Malik,' I think aloud. 'You're the one who knocked me out in the motel.'

'He left me no choice,' she says. 'He was going to give us up to the police. He *wanted* us to go to trial. He wanted the world to see what sexual abuse had driven us to do.' She glances towards a small round table near the television. Underneath it is a cardboard box.

'Is that Dr Malik's box?' I ask. 'The one with the stuff for the film in it?'

'Yes,' Angie says, suddenly upset. 'I don't care who knows. We did what we had to do. God only knows how many kids we saved.'

Lorio looks at Angie like a protective older sister. 'That's right, Ange. But there's no need for you to waste your life in jail. The world's not going to understand what we did.'

'I think you're wrong, Stacey,' I say in the most submissive voice I can muster. 'I think a lot of people would understand.'

She laughs. 'That's easy to say. But I'm not spending my life in prison just to be the flavour of the week on *Oprah*. We accomplished what we set out to do. It's over now.' She looks down at Sean. 'And you two stuck your noses in where they didn't belong. I can't help that.'

Angie Pitre is wringing her hands. 'Stacey, this isn't what we said, you know? Nobody else would go along with this.'

Lorio looks sharply at Angie. 'Nobody else had the nerve to go through with any of it, did they? They sat back while we did their dirty work.'

Angie shakes her head. 'I know, I know, but still . . .'

Lorio's lips tighten into a white line. 'You just go in the kitchen, baby, while mama takes care of business.'

Stacey Lorio pulls a cushion off the sofa with her free hand, and I know then that I'm living the last moments of my life. My eyes go to my purse on the floor, but it might as well be a mile away. Lorio takes a step towards me, puts the gun behind the cushion, and fires.

Everything registers out of order. A horse kicks me in the belly. Tiny fragments of foam rubber fill the air, and a muffled boom sounds.

Then a woman screams. '*Stacey, no!*'

Lorio is following me, the barrel of Sean's Glock protruding through the foam padding of the cushion. She's two feet away when Angie Pitre jumps on her back, and they go down in a pile of flailing limbs.

I want to help Angie, but instead I sit down hard on the sofa. Blood is running down my front.

The gun explodes again, but the women keep fighting.

I can see my purse on the floor, but I can't bend to reach it.

Stacey Lorio is sitting on Angie's chest now, screaming at her to stop fighting, but Angie keeps flailing like a crazed little girl. With a loud curse, Lorio smacks Angie across the face with the butt of her gun.

Angie Pitre stops fighting.

Stacey is climbing off her when Sean's hand rises from the floor and grips her elbow. He must be only half conscious, because Lorio laughs and shakes off his grip as easily as the hand of a child. Then she lifts the other cushion off the couch and lays it over Sean's face.

I look down at my purse, willing myself to bend at the waist.

Stacey presses the barrel of Sean's gun over the cushion, right about where Sean's forehead would be, and fires.

As I scream in rage, a tiny hole appears in Stacey's chest. Within seconds she is sucking for air. Sean's Smith & Wesson is shaking in my hand.

Stacey's knees buckle, and she falls into a kneeling position beside Sean. She raises the gun over the cushion, then keeps raising it, trying to bring it to bear on me.

'*Don't*,' I whisper, but the gun keeps rising.

I shoot her again and, as she falls, all I can think of is the terrible irony that it was my grandfather who taught me how to shoot a handgun.

Then everything goes black.

CHAPTER 13

I spent much of the week after I was discharged from Tulane University Hospital going to funerals. Thanks to Stacey Lorio, I had to ride in a wheelchair to all of them. The bullet she fired from Sean's gun tore through my stomach and lodged in a muscle in my back. I lost a lot of blood and also my spleen. But I didn't lose my baby.

Sean's head had been turned sideways beneath the cushion when Lorio fired, so the bullet punched through his right cheek smashing five teeth and pulping part of his maxillary sinuses. Sean owes his life to Angie Pitre, who called 911 and stayed with us until paramedics and police arrived.

Stacey Lorio died instantly from my second bullet. I feel a deep sadness at the childhood trauma that created the hate-filled adult she had become, but I feel no guilt over killing her. She meant to murder both Sean and me in cold blood. Sean blamed himself for not cracking Lorio's 'rock solid' alibis for the murders.

Special Agent Kaiser spent a lot of time in my hospital room, trying to determine once and for all whether the six murders in New Orleans had any connection to the events in Natchez and on DeSalle Island. Given the link between Ann and Dr Malik—and, in a way, Malik and me—it seemed inconceivable that they weren't related. But it seemed they weren't.

Not even Dr Hannah Goldman could explain what it was about the murder scenes that had caused my panic attacks. What told me that I was looking at violence that was somehow related to sexual abuse similar to my own? In the end, I decided it was the smallest of clues. My first attack happened at the murder scene of the third victim. Eleven days before, at the home of the second victim—Andrus Riviere—I had seen a little girl who stuck in my mind. Her grandfather had just died violently, yet she was racing around the house as if her birthday party were about to start. And knowing what I know now, I believe that it was. Andrus Riviere's murder had released that little girl from a living hell. And something about her face—something in her too-wise eyes, I think now—sent me a message without my knowing it.

Kaiser stunned me by telling me that Dr Malik had willed all the video-tapes, patient records and other raw materials for his film project to me. As soon as they are released to me, I intend to begin working to finish Malik's film. I will do all I can to explain the motivation behind the murders.

The first funeral I attended was Nathan Malik's, a memorial service held in a New Orleans park. About fifty people attended, a Buddhist monk chanted and said some prayers, and everyone laid flowers by the urn.

The second funeral was Ann's, and it was held in Natchez. Michael Wells drove me out to the cemetery for the burial. While the minister gave a eulogy, I sat in the pews reserved for family and thought about how much Ann had suffered. For whatever reason, she had not dissociated during her abuse. And her primary concern had been protecting her younger sister—my mother. Though she failed in that goal, she had tried her best.

The third funeral—an unexpected one—was held today. I had Michael drive me out to the cemetery, and wheel me up to a vantage point where I could watch the burial service on the family plot without being bothered.

And here I sit.

The line of luxury cars behind the black hearse seems to go on for ever. I shouldn't be surprised. Dr William Kirkland was a wealthy, powerful and respected man, a pillar of the community. My mother tried to keep the funeral simple, but in the end she gave in to the friends who insisted on a large production, including a eulogy delivered by the governor of Mississippi.

Everyone seems content to pretend that my grandfather's death was an accident. That he drove off the edge of the bridge to DeSalle Island in bright sunlight seems to escape everyone's attention. A few people have men-tioned his 'recent' stroke, and recalled his doctor forbidding him to drive. His driver, Billy Neal, had disappeared, and that was why my grandfather had driven to the island alone to deal with some business matters.

The truth is much simpler. My grandfather killed himself. He knew that his life's foul secret was about to be exposed. That all of his power and money would be insufficient to stop one of his victims—me—from finally revealing his depravity to the world. And his pride could not abide that.

I'm here today because I need closure. When you've lived with a demon all your life, and you somehow escape him, it's important to see him buried.

The burial service is mercifully brief, as the sky is threatening rain. The mourners quickly return to their cars, and the long line begins to leave the cemetery. When all of them have gone, a solitary figure remains.

Pearlie Washington.

As Michael wheels me down the hill, Pearlie stands motionless, looking down at Grandpapa's grave. As we near her, a white Dodge Caravan appears in the lane and rolls slowly to a stop near a low wall. Two men in dark suits get out, walk to the back of the van and unload a bronze casket. They settle it onto a collapsible gurney, then work the gurney across the grass to the corner of the plot, where a green tarp is staked out over a hole in the ground. The headstone above the tarp reads LUKE FERRY, 1951–1981.

As Michael rolls me through the gate, Pearlie walks over to me and touches my hand. 'They doing what I think they're doing?'

'Yes.'

I see pain in her eyes. 'Why didn't you tell me? I loved that boy too.'

'I wanted to be alone with him. I'm sorry, Pearlie.'

'Where's your mama?' she asks.

'She said she couldn't stand to bury her husband a second time.'

Pearlie sighs heavily. 'She's probably right.'

Michael touches my elbow and leans down to my ear. 'I'm going to give you a few minutes.'

I take his hand and squeeze it. 'Thanks. I won't be long.'

Pearlie watches him leave. 'He seems like a good man,' she says.

'He is.'

'Does he know you carrying another man's child?'

I look up at the curious brown eyes. 'Yes.'

'And he still wants to see you?'

'Yes.'

She shakes her head. 'That's a man you need to stick with, right there.'

I feel my mouth smile. 'I think you're right.'

Pearlie takes my hand in hers. 'Lord, it's about time you settled down. We been needing some babies around that old place.'

I take a deep breath and look towards Grandpapa's grave. 'I think I was waiting for him to go first.'

Pearlie nods. 'Lord knows that's right.'

Daddy's casket lies beside the open grave now, the rain pattering against its burnished lid. Strangely, the sound doesn't bother me at all.

'Could you open it for me now, please?' I ask.

One of the men from the funeral home takes a key from his pocket and begins unsealing the casket.

'What?' Pearlie gasps, her eyes filled with horror. 'What you doing, girl? That's bad luck, doing something like that!'

I shake my head. 'No, it's not.'

As the man from the funeral home lifts the coffin lid, I reach beneath my wheelchair to the luggage pocket beneath. I feel soft fur in my palm. Using all my strength, I stand and walk slowly to the coffin. Gritting my teeth against pain, I bend at the waist and lay Lena the Leopardess in the crook of Daddy's elbow. Then I straighten up again. 'So you won't be lonely,' I say softly. 'Goodbye, Daddy. Thank you for trying.'

I turn from the casket and walk back to the wheelchair, signalling Michael as I go. He comes quickly.

'I want to see the river,' I tell him. 'Will you wheel me up to Jewish Hill?'

Towering 300 feet above the Mississippi, Jewish Hill offers the most commanding view of the river I've ever seen.

Michael can't hide his dismay. 'It's raining, Cat.'

'I know. I like it. Will you come with me, Pearlie?'

'All right, baby.'

'Can you make it?' Michael asks her.

Pearlie snorts indignantly. 'I may be over seventy years old, but I can still walk from Red Lick to Rodney and have strength left over for a day's work.'

Michael laughs, recognising the names of two tiny Mississippi towns over twenty miles apart. He pushes me up the hill at a steady pace, and before long we are at the top. As Pearlie and I stare over the mile-wide tide of river and the vast plains of the Louisiana delta, Michael wanders off a little way.

'That's too big to look at,' Pearlie says.

'I love it,' I say. 'I used to come here whenever I felt trapped in this town.'

'I think you always been trapped here, until your granddaddy died.' There's a long silence, then Pearlie asks, 'So what you gonna do now?'

'I don't know. Wait for my wound to heal, I guess. The bullet wound, I mean. The other could take my whole life.'

'I meant about the house. Malmaison. It's gonna be yours now.'

'What?'

'I thought you knew. Dr Kirkland always said Miss Gwen couldn't take care of her own self, much less the wealth she was born into. You gonna get just about everything.'

Her words take some time to register. I have no idea what might be included in my grandfather's estate, but it's bound to be enormous.

'That's why Billy Neal hated you so bad,' Pearlie adds.

'What do you mean?'

'He was the one called Jesse Billups away from the island the night you disappeared. Said it was real important, but never showed up. Must have been him who tried to kill you.' Pearlie is watching me closely, to see my reaction. 'Jesse told me something else: Dr Kirkland was Billy Neal's father.'

After all that's happened, the revelation doesn't have much effect. But I suddenly feel exhausted.

'So, what you gonna do? About Malmaison.'

'Sell it all,' I say.

Pearlie makes an uncertain sound. 'The island, too?'

'Why not? I don't ever want to see it again.'

'If you sell that island, the people down there won't have nowhere to go. You own it all, the houses and everything. They just rent.'

For a few moments, images of the island rush through my head. But the pain that comes with them is too much to bear. 'They can have it, Pearlie. The whole damn thing. It's theirs anyway. I'll have the lawyers draw up papers. You and Jesse work out fair shares for everybody. Except for Louise Butler. She gets the lodge.'

Pearlie shakes her head. 'I guess you know what you're doing.'

'For the first time, I think I do.' I wave Michael over. 'I'm ready to go.'

As Michael turns the wheelchair round, I catch a last glimpse of the river, vast and majestic under the shadows of the rain. The water down there will soon flow past DeSalle Island, Baton Rouge, New Orleans, and finally into the Gulf of Mexico. Where I'll be then, I don't know. But the chain of misery forged through the generations of my family has finally been broken. By me.

That's about as good a start as I can imagine.

As we move back down the lane, I lay one hand on my stomach and close my eyes. I don't need a drink now. I don't need anything. For the first time in my life, I feel truly free to choose what I want.

'It's going to be different for you,' I whisper, rubbing my tummy in a slow circle. 'Your mama knows what love is.'

GREG ILES

Born: Stuttgart, West Germany, 1961
Home: Natchez, Mississippi
Website: www.gregiles.com

Greg Iles was born and raised in Stuttgart, where his father was in charge of a medical clinic at the US Embassy. After getting an English degree at the University of Mississippi he spent several years working as a lab- and x-ray technician and playing in a rock band, Frankly Scarlet, before achieving success as a writer with his first novel, *Spandau Phoenix*, in 1993.

RD: If you hadn't become a writer, what would you like to have been?

GI: A film director. I have just broken into film, but the reality is that the writer has very little power to affect the film that is ultimately produced. In the film world, only the director has power analogous to that of the novelist.

RD: What sort of relationship do you have with your home town, Natchez?

GI: I love Natchez, despite its flaws. It's truly American and truly Southern, not a homogenised Spielberg town where everything has been sanitised. But the place is so small that its best and brightest kids have to move away to support themselves. I am lucky in that I've been able to stay.

RD: Where else in the world would you like to live?

GI: Maybe North Carolina or Virginia. Outside the US, I'd take Scotland. I like solitude. Of course, my wife would prefer the Cayman Islands!

RD: You were a musician for several years before you became a writer. Do you miss that life?

GI: I do miss parts of it, but it's a hard life. A lot of empty time on the road, the eternal struggle to find musicians who can help you get what you hear in your head onto tape or disc. As a writer I have absolute power to make anything I want to happen, happen.

RD: You do still occasionally play lead guitar for a band called Rock Bottom Remainders that also stars Stephen King (guitar), Scott Turow (backing vocals) and Amy Tan (vocals). That must be fun.

GI: It's unbelievable fun, and also done in a great cause, a children's literacy programme called America Scores. To hang out and play music with fellow authors and childhood idols like Roger McGuinn of The Byrds . . . it's one of the best times of each year.

RD: What would you say is your biggest weakness?

GI: The inability to organise and plan efficiently, relative to deadlines. I run purely on instinct, following whatever interests me that day or week.

RD: And your biggest indulgence?

GI: Weekly massages. I used to think they were a privilege of the spoilt rich; now I don't know how I lived without them.

RD: What would your family claim to be your most annoying habit?

GI: My tendency to seek solitude and exclude myself from normal life in order to think and work.

RD: Are there any subjects you'd like to tackle in future books?

GI: I'm currently looking into modern-day piracy, and I'm also working on a couple of things for kids. I need a little time away from the horrors of the world.

RD: Do you have any all-time favourite novels?

GI: *The Honourable Schoolboy* by John Le Carré. I re-read it once a year.

RD: And, finally, if you had to sum yourself up in a single word, what would it be?

GI: Obsessive.

A JEWEL OF THE AMERICAN SOUTH

Natchez, where Greg Iles lives and which provides the atmospheric setting for *Blood Memory*, is a delightful town perched 200 feet above the Mississippi River and named after the Indian tribe who first settled the area. It went through periods of French, British and Spanish rule before passing into American hands in 1798, when it became the first capital of the Mississippi Territory. Today, with its hundreds of fine mansions dating from the pre-Civil War cotton boom, it remains a fascinating place to visit.

MOSAIC
SOHEIR KHASHOGGI

When her husband suddenly leaves
home, taking eight-year-old twins
Suzanne and Ali to live with him in
his native Jordan, Dina Ahmad is
desperate to get the children back.

As far as the police are concerned, the
twins are with their father, who hasn't
broken the law in any way.

So, for Dina, desperate measures are
the only answer.

PROLOGUE

GONE.

The twins. Gone. Taken.

Dina couldn't grasp it, couldn't make it seem real, despite the dead silence of the town house, the clothes missing from the children's closets, despite even the note from her husband. It had to be his idea of a joke. A punishment. In the kitchen she glanced expectantly at the big refectory table, as if, this time, if she could only get it right, Suzanne and Ali would be in their chairs, eagerly awaiting the treats she had for them.

CHAPTER 1

It was a beautiful spring day in New York, the kind of day that made it possible to believe that the terrible events of 2001 would not hold the city forever in their grip.

Dina awoke early. She looked down on her sleeping husband, her body remembering their lovemaking the night before. It had been a long time since Karim had approached her with such passion, such hunger. She had responded in kind, and for a time all was as it had been during the early days of their marriage, when love was new and sex all-consuming. 'I love you, Dina,' he'd murmured over and over. 'Know that I love you, no matter what.'

How handsome he is, she thought, as she lightly stroked his face. His skin, under the morning bristle, was the colour of café au lait, his dark wavy hair was lightly silvered, his eyelashes were as thick as a movie star's. His mouth was generous, his cheekbones high and his patrician nose more Roman than Arab. He'd laughed when she told him that. 'For you, I'll be a Roman,' he said, 'or a Greek or whatever you want.' He was certainly joking, for during the years of their marriage, Karim had only become more and more Arab. More traditional. More—whatever she was not.

She slipped into her robe and slippers, made coffee and brought it to him in bed, something she hadn't done for a long time. He opened his eyes and gazed at her with such longing that she almost gave up the idea of going to work. Almost. But it was to be an important day at Mosaic, the floral design business she'd created and nurtured for so many years. There was an important order to fill and a meeting with the owner of a new hotel. Dina—and Mosaic—hadn't become regular items in *New York* magazine by taking days off. Not when there were so many others who would gladly take over what she had so painstakingly built for Mosaic: a reputation as Manhattan's premier floral design boutique.

After a shower, Dina dressed quickly but carefully in one of the designer suits that were her work uniform. Dina was a perfect size six, even after three children and twenty years of marriage; her luxuriant chestnut-brown hair was cut in a soft chin-length bob that framed her oval face. Her hazel eyes were clear and bright, her fair skin almost unlined.

By the time Dina went back downstairs, Fatma, the children's nanny, was bustling about in the kitchen. A spinster cousin of Karim's, Fatma was as punctual as an old-time railroader. According to the household's usual schedule, breakfast should already have been prepared for the eight-year-old Ahmad twins, Suzanne and Ali. Since Dina had not been present to do the cooking, Fatma had taken over, and the meal was now under way.

'Mommy, you're supposed to give us breakfast,' brown-eyed Suzy complained, 'but you were still sleeping.' And Ali, a carbon copy of his sister, but with shorter curly brown hair, agreed loudly.

'All right, all right,' Dina said, accepting the guilt that was constantly thrown her way, simply because she was trying, not always successfully, to be three people: wife, mother, career woman. 'Well, since I goofed on breakfast, how about lunch? What if I have Fatma bring you to meet me in the park? We'll have hot dogs and a nice visit. Would you like that?'

A loud 'yay' from the twins, and Dina thanked God that children were so quick to forgive and forget. Would that adults were so easy.

She glanced at Fatma and repeated her wish to have the children picked up from school and brought to the park. The older woman grunted an assent. Fatma had lived with the family for some fifteen years, yet Dina still hadn't figured out how to deal with her in a way that was mutually satisfactory. Dina always had the sense that Fatma disapproved of her; for her part, Dina found the woman dour and unlikeable. Ah, well, in spite of Fatma's difficult personality, those of Dina's acquaintances who were constantly hiring and firing nannies envied her a nanny who stayed—and stayed.

WHEN DINA arrived at work, her assistant, Eileen, was already looking frazzled. After a quick conversation, Dina understood why. Daniel Boulud, the famous chef, had asked for orchids in his restaurants' arrangements, but the morning delivery had brought no orchids. It would mean indignant phone calls to the supplier, who would insist the mistake had been Dina's, followed by phone calls to other shops begging for enough blooms to fill her order.

The morning brought other problems as well. The editor of a well-known home-design magazine wanted Dina to style the dinner setting on an antique table that was to be featured on an upcoming cover. Another coup for Mosaic—except that the job had to be done within three days.

She was tempted to call off the lunch with her children, but the prospect of an hour in the park, of putting all the pressures aside, had great appeal.

Dina arrived early. She staked out a bench and waited, closing her eyes for a moment and allowing the April sun to warm her face. When she opened her eyes, she saw them approaching: Fatma in her long dress and headscarf, and her two curly-haired angels, bounding towards her.

As she had promised, Dina bought hot dogs, which the children devoured enthusiastically. Fatma declined the treat, unwrapping the pitta sandwich she'd brought and consuming it slowly without any visible pleasure.

'This is so nice, Mommy. Can we do it again tomorrow? Can we, can we?' Suzy begged.

Again guilt tore at Dina. Such a small thing was being asked of her: just to give a bit more of herself to the children she loved. She ruffled Suzy's hair. 'Not tomorrow,' Dina said, 'but soon. I promise. Very soon.'

The children seemed content with that.

Fatma got up from her bench and prepared to take them back to school. 'Kiss Mother goodbye,' she instructed in her heavily accented English.

The twins kissed her, loudly and with gusto. Dina walked quickly back to work with the children's farewell tucked away in her heart.

The meeting with the hotelier went well. Contracts would be drawn up immediately, with the first arrangements to be delivered early next month.

Shortly after the meeting concluded, Dina's mother telephoned. Ever since Dina's father had undergone surgery for colon cancer, she had been on the alert for every bit of news her mother could give.

'Mom,' she said breathlessly. 'Is something wrong?'

'No, sweetheart, no, nothing's wrong. I just want to thank you for the thoughtful gift you and Karim sent over this morning.'

'Gift?'

'Yes, the dried fruit. Karim said he picked it up in Brooklyn—from one of the Arab shops on Atlantic Avenue. He said he knew how much your father loved the apricots and figs. He hoped they might restore his appetite.'

'Oh. Yes.' Why hadn't Karim mentioned such a lovely gesture? she wondered. The latest round of chemo had left Joseph Hilmi without much appetite. How sweet of Karim to try to help. She knew that he had been very busy, too, these past few weeks.

She dialled his office.

'Dina,' he said, 'what a surprise.' That was fair enough. She rarely called his office these days. When they were first married, they talked on the phone at least once a day.

'Thank you,' she said, 'for sending the fruit to my father.'

'It was nothing, Dina. You know I'm very fond of your father.'

'Thank you anyway. And Karim . . .'

'Yes?'

'Why don't I try to get away a little early today? Eileen can finish up. I could defrost those vine leaves I made—and I can pick up some fresh pitta and a dessert. We'll have a nice evening together,' she finished, thinking how good it would be to build on the warm feelings of last night and this morning.

'Ah, well, I—'

'What's wrong? Will you have to work late tonight?'

'No, Dina, I won't be working late tonight.'

'Great. I know I've been preoccupied with the business lately, but I really do want to spend more time with you and the children.'

There was a long silence, and for a moment Dina thought the connection had been broken. 'Karim?'

'Yes, Dina, I'm still here.'

'Well, then, I'll see you later. Bye now.'

'Goodbye, Dina.'

True to her word, Dina stepped up her pace to finish work that could not wait. Then she left instructions for Eileen on what remained to be done, and headed out of the door. She hurried to Grace's, picked up a pack of pitta, some yoghurt and cucumbers for a salad, and five pastries. She always bought enough for Fatma, though the older woman often refused the treats.

Fatma had been particularly sullen lately—not that she had ever been cheerful, at least not in the fifteen years since Karim had brought her over from his native Jordan. Possibly the woman was missing the old country, the old ways, Dina thought as she fumbled with the keys. Or maybe it had something to do with September 11th and its aftermath. Whatever it was, it made her presence an uncomfortable one.

Dina had debated speaking with Karim about it. But with the many points of dispute between them—mainly centred round the cultural differences that had grown over the years—she didn't want to raise another.

Dina called out as she entered the house. No answer. She shouted upstairs—there were three full floors and a basement, a vast space by New York standards. Nobody was home. Perhaps Fatma had taken the twins back to the park after school. If so, they would be back any minute.

The first hint of something wrong was the absence of a note. Fatma was meticulous in every duty that related to the children. She could not write in English herself, but always had one of them scribble a message as to their whereabouts and placed it under the wooden pepper mill on the kitchen table. Dina felt uneasy. She checked the answering machine. No messages.

Had Karim come home early and taken them all out somewhere? For ice cream, say? It seemed unlikely. After all, she'd made it clear that she was planning a special family dinner. She called his office.

'Mr Ahmad is unavailable,' the woman who answered informed her. Dina didn't recognise her voice. She certainly wasn't Karim's secretary, Helen.

'This is his wife. Do you know if he left for home?'

'He's not in the office. That's all I can tell you.' Coldly remote, as if Dina were some kind of crank.

'Is Helen there? May I speak with her?'

'Helen is not available.'

'What do you mean not available?'

'She's not here. Neither is Mr Ahmad. Do you wish to leave a message?'

'Have him call me. As soon as he can. It's . . . it's important.'

Surely there was a reasonable, ordinary explanation: some emergency meeting, something that required not only Karim's personal attention, but also Helen's. She told herself to be calm. Take a deep breath. Wait fifteen minutes. Then maybe check with neighbours. Andy, the newspaper vendor on the corner? He saw everything that happened on the block.

Dina went into the bedroom to change into her favourite sweats. It was as if their comfortable familiarity could restore routine, allay fear.

On the bed she saw the note—the letter, actually. *Dear Dina,* it began, and continued in what she recognised as Karim's formal mode:

I wish you to know that I have reached this decision only after long consideration. As you know, we have discussed, many times, my concerns about the influences to which Ali and Suzanne are subject . . .

Oh God, what was this about? Her heart began to hammer in her chest.

. . . and especially I am concerned for Ali, that he will not be influenced like his brother. But for Suzanne, too, I am concerned . . .

Dina read more words, words she'd heard before about the shortcomings of American society. But then:

For these reasons, and so that they know their other heritage, I have decided to take Ali and Suzanne with me, home, to my home, Jordan.

'No!' she sobbed. 'No! No!' The room began to tilt. She tried to breathe deeply, to steady herself so that she could finish reading.

There were some sentences about money. There were funds in the joint account, she would want for nothing. She hardly read them.

The children will be well; you should not fear for them. You know that my family, as well as I, will care for them. I have found work in Jordan also, an important job already arranged for . . .

A job? Karim had taken a job in Jordan? He had planned for God only knew how long to take her children? The same Karim who said he loved her? It didn't make sense.

By the time you read this, we will be on our way. I will call to let you know we've arrived safely, but please understand that you will not change my mind. This is my decision. It is not what I would have wished for, years ago, but I think it is the best for our children.

She set the letter on the comforter and stared, as if it had fallen from space. She couldn't believe it. It wasn't real.

Like a sleepwalker, she staggered into the children's room. Some clothes were gone. Favourite books and toys.

Fatma's room was cleared out. Of course she would have gone with them.

Years ago she had read a magazine article on foreign husbands who left their American wives and took the children back to Greece or Saudi Arabia or wherever. She had not imagined it might be relevant to her life. It was simply not something that could happen between Karim and her, no matter what their disagreements, their difficulties.

She had to do something. Call someone. Her mother? No, not yet. The news would crush her. And her father—in his fragile state, it might kill him.

Suddenly she thought of her older son. She was going to have to tell him about this. How would he handle it? Blame himself? She would have to protect him from such a feeling. But that would be hard, especially since her son—his name was Jordan, after his father's homeland—*was* clearly part of what had set Karim on this course. She could put off telling Jordy for a while—he was two hundred miles away. He didn't have to know that their family had been shattered, that just the two of them remained.

What to do *now?* That was the question.

She had friends. People from work. Couples with whom she and Karim socialised. But there were really only two people she could lean on in this greatest crisis of her life. She picked up the phone.

'IT WORKS, doesn't it?' said Emmeline LeBlanc, producer and star of the *Em—New York* lifestyle TV show—the poor, Creole Martha Stewart, as she jokingly called herself.

'Oh yeah,' Arnie Stern, the show's director, reassured her. 'It works.'

Tom Wu, the show's editor, nodded emphatically. The piece they were now viewing on his computer was about home security, and had been recorded that afternoon, with two guest experts. 'I'll just switch that spot where Mary Ann's looking at camera two,' he said.

To Tom, fresh out of NYU, Emmeline was a very exciting woman. The fact that she was a dozen years older than he was—and six inches taller— did not affect his fantasies. There were times when he had almost physically to restrain his hand from reaching out to touch her arm or cheek, just to see if her chocolate skin felt as soft as it looked.

Emmeline's assistant Celia poked her head in the door. 'Call for you, Em. Dina Ahmad. Says it's important.'

Emmeline went to her office to take the call. 'Hey, girl,' she said easily.

The ease quickly left her manner. 'What? Slow down. Tell me again. He what?' She listened intently. 'All right, you hang in there, kiddo. I'm on my way . . . Yes, I'll call her. Hang in there.'

She hung up and glared at the phone. 'That *couillon*!' she said. She had not used the word in a decade. In its fullest sense it referred to the trashiest kind of person or behaviour. She was applying it now to Karim Ahmad.

SARAH GELMAN heard the chirp of her pager but ignored it. At the moment a sick little girl named LaKwinta Thomas was more important than some pain-in-the-ass call from the office. She made a note on the chart to change the girl's medication and talked with the duty nurse to make sure the change was understood. Only then did she check the beeper.

To her surprise, the call was from Emmeline. What could that be about? Em knew that this was her day at Lenox Hill Hospital. Some kind of emergency? Nah. More likely an impromptu Girls' Night Out. It was overdue. It would be good to let her hair down, have a few drinks, gossip about acquaintances, co-workers and ghosts of husbands past (her own ex, Ari), present (Dina's Karim), and possibly future (Em's Sean, although in Sarah's book that one was beginning to look like a long shot).

She made a mental note not to mention the *get* this time. It was boring to everyone but her. No one else understood it, or considered it important.

She and Ari had divorced three years earlier, relatively amicably except for one thing: although they were divorced in the legal sense, Ari would not grant her a *get*, a divorce in the eyes of her Jewish religion. Why, she didn't know. Maybe because he knew it mattered to her. She wanted a fresh start, recognised by the State of New York and sanctified by her faith. If she were to meet someone, if it were to become serious . . . well, the chances of that were looking fairly slim, too. Seeing that she had no social life beyond the occasional Girls' Night Out and even-more-occasional dates with other doctors that invariably ended up with both of them playing beeper tag.

She walked to the doctors' break room, picked up a phone and called Em. Five minutes later she hung up in shock. What kind of *mishegoss* was this? Had Karim Ahmad gone completely crazy?

She dialled Dina's number. It rang several times before Sarah answered and said, 'I'll call you right back. I'm on the phone with the police.'

'Don't call back, I'm on my way,' Sarah told her, with no idea if Dina had waited long enough to hear her. The miracle of call waiting.

She slipped out of her whites and into street clothes. For half a second she thought of keeping the whites on for this crisis. She briefly envisioned herself striding into the airport control tower. *Stop that plane. I'm a doctor.*

That was the trouble with standing five two in heels and still wearing a size six: people didn't take you seriously. She noticed that Emmeline, at six one, got taken seriously just by walking into the room.

As her car cleared the hospital garage, Sarah was thinking that her immediate role in this crisis was going to be that of the voice of reason: to give whatever support was needed, to counsel a little calm.

CALLING THE POLICE had been a stupid idea. Dina understood that now, as she tried to make Officer Frances Malone understand what had happened.

'You say the children are with their father?' the officer repeated.

'Yes.'

'And you have no reason to believe they're in any danger?'

'No, but—'

'And their father is your husband, ma'am. You're not divorced? No custody judgment outstanding, anything like that?'

'No.'

'And there's been no violence? No threat, nothing of that kind?'

'No. He just took them out of their school. I called the principal before I called you. She said he and the nanny picked them up. And now he's on his way to Jordan. That's in the—'

'I know where that is,' Officer Malone said, a bit sharply.

'I'm sorry, but you don't seem to understand,' she said, desperation growing. 'He's taken my children. He doesn't intend to bring them back.'

The officer's tone softened. 'I do understand, Mrs Ahmad—we've had a couple of cases like yours—and I wish I could help, believe me, but this isn't a police matter. Your husband hasn't broken any laws.'

'But—'

'Mrs Ahmad, with all respect, ma'am, what you need is a lawyer.'

Dina stared at the telephone. Could a lawyer bring her children back? Karim used a lawyer for a few things. Should she call him? Some instinct told her not to. He was Karim's lawyer, not hers. But she had to do something. Hell must be like this: waiting, knowing nothing, fearing everything.

She poured herself a glass of water. She sat and reread Karim's letter, as if the words themselves might lead her to a solution. He didn't want the twins subjected to prejudice. Didn't she remember how they'd suffered after the World Trade Center tragedy? How they came home crying that they didn't want to have an Arab name because Arabs were bad? Surely she could see why he didn't want them growing up in New York?

But Dina couldn't see. Her own father had been born in Lebanon. Even though he'd emigrated to America when he was sixteen, he'd brought many of his customs—and his native cuisine—into his marriage to her Irish-American mother. In spite of their cultural differences—and on occasion because of them—Joseph and Charlotte Hilmi had built a strong marriage.

Dina, though she loved her Lebanese relatives, the country, the warmth and the food, had never thought of herself as anything but American. The Arab part of her was like a warm and loving aunt who lived far away, someone Dina could visit and embrace from time to time, basking in affection and memory—and then return home, to her American self.

Yes, Dina had felt terrible when the twins came home crying. She had explained to them that some people behaved badly when they were scared. She had promised the taunting would stop—and it had. After she'd spoken to the twins' teacher and their principal—and after the class (and later, the entire school) had been lectured on the subject of prejudice. Dina had taken action to protect her children; didn't that show she loved them as much as Karim did? More, really—for had he even asked himself how they were going to fit in Jordan? A culture that was, for the most part, foreign to them?

. . . *I am concerned for Ali, that he will not be influenced like his brother.*

That was the real reason that this had happened, she thought bitterly.

The doorbell sounded. Sarah's voice on the intercom.

Into each other's arms, a long hard hug. Then Sarah stepped back. Dina recognised the Dr Gelman look: What does this child have and what can I do about it? It was incredibly comforting.

Dina burst into tears.

AT 38,000 FEET there was still light in the sky, though the earth below was in darkness. Soon there would be a meal and a movie. Karim knew they were passing the eastern tip of Newfoundland; he had flown this route many times. But as familiar as it was, this flight was like none Karim had ever taken. For the past hour, with each mile further from New York, from America, he had felt tension draining from him. It was all right now, he told himself. By this time tomorrow they would be in Jordan.

With relief came weariness. He felt as if he had run a marathon.

He also felt like a thief.

He had expected this. Indeed he had experienced guilt almost from the moment he conceived his idea. He had concluded that it was an unavoidable side effect that he had to suffer in order to achieve the desired result.

He did not consider himself a paragon, but he did think that he was a man of honour and integrity. He would have preferred to talk it out with Dina and persuade her that his way was the best for them all. But that was impossible. Their world views had diverged too greatly and for too long. He still loved the young woman he'd married, but years had passed since they'd agreed on anything substantial. She would never have acceded to moving to Jordan. How many times in the heat of one argument or another—over proper discipline of the children for instance—had she insisted that they were Americans, not Jordanians? End of discussion. End of reasoning.

No. He had taken the only way open to him. But still . . .

Twenty years of his life were sliding away behind the aircraft in the growing night—a marriage, the dreams of a younger Karim Ahmad.

Of course he knew what he was doing to Dina. He had promised himself that he would never prevent her from seeing them. But still . . .

He had not the slightest doubt how he would feel if the situation were reversed. He would be prepared to . . . to what? Kill? Well, maybe not. But anything short of it. Dina would feel the same. She would hate him for ever.

It was the only way, he told himself for the thousandth time. Was it possible to do the right thing for wrong reasons? The wrong thing for right reasons?

'Do you have a headache, Daddy?' Suzanne looked up at him with concern in her eyes.

'No, darling girl,' he said. 'Just a little tired. But thank you for asking.'

She sat beside him, small in the outsized first-class seat. Directly behind them were Ali and Fatma. The children exchanged places from time to time.

'Will we be there soon?'

'Soon, precious. You'll go to sleep, and when you wake up we'll be there.' He hoped that the children would sleep shortly. And Fatma. He himself did not expect to rest well that night.

'And will Mommy be there too?'

'I told you, remember? Mommy won't be there right away. But when we get there you'll see your *Jiddo* and *Tayta*, grandfather and grandmother. And your Uncle Samir and Aunt Soraya. And your cousins, remember them?'

Surprisingly, given that she and Ali had only visited in Jordan once a year or so, they had vivid memories of their cousins, and for this Karim was glad. As long as there were amusing stories about Samir and Soraya's children, there would be no more questions about Mommy.

Dinner came as a further welcome distraction. Then there was a selection of movies on their personal TV screens. Karim chose the latest Harry Potter movie for the twins. Though they'd seen it, it kept them entertained. Afterwards, they held out against sleep for a while but eventually succumbed.

The last thing Suzanne said before closing her eyes was, 'I wish Mommy would be there when we wake up.'

'Later, darling girl. Soon. Sleep tight.'

Before long Karim heard Fatma's soft, weary snores as well.

Burning bridges, he thought. The words echoed from ancient military campaigns: an invading army would burn the bridges over which it had crossed so that there would be no temptation to retreat from the battles ahead. But Karim felt as if he *were* in retreat. Running from an enemy he could hardly define, burning bridges so the enemy could not pursue.

In the past few years he had begun to recognise the nature of the enemy, to understand that it was something in American culture itself, including parts of it that he himself had, as a younger man, enjoyed and praised. That, it seemed to him now, was precisely what made it so insidious: a certain maturity was required to see where freedom degenerated to licence and irresponsibility—and maturity was the last thing America valued.

It was hard to put it all in one piece, like a diagram, but certain images welled up. The teenage singers Suzanne worshipped: girls who seemed to compete for who could look the most like a prostitute. And the athletes Ali idolised: selfish young men with pierced ears and bleached hair and tattoos disfiguring their skin. In such a place, Ali would come to believe that the life his brother had chosen was normal, even commendable.

It was too late for Jordy, and Karim blamed himself, at least in part, for this failure. And it would soon have been too late for Ali and Suzanne. Another year or two, and they would have been caught up irrevocably in the moral relativism that was the result and reality of the 'American way'.

To top it all off, they would never be truly accepted in even this rootless society. He had learned that in the aftermath of September 11th, and it had been a hard lesson. Until then he'd enjoyed a certain prestige and autonomy in the investment bank where he'd worked for a dozen years. He was, unofficially, the 'Arab department', the one who handled deals with important companies and institutions in the Middle East. But after the attack on the World Trade Center, he found himself—and his clients—held to microscopic scrutiny, examined for possible ties to terrorist organisations. The atmosphere at the bank changed. He was not as trusted as he once had been.

And it was just as bad for the children: remarks from their classmates, things they saw on television.

No. America might corrupt them but it would never accept them. Better he should give them a new home, his own home, before it was too late. As for Dina, well, that would be worked out, in some way. Things did work out—eventually they did. He would see that they did.

EM PUT ON her sunglasses in the elevator—in case some autograph hound was lurking downstairs—and took a cab to Dina's Upper West Side address.

On her cellphone she called home. Sean answered. Though they didn't live together—Em was far from ready to go that route with Sean—these days he spent more time in her splendid loft than he did in his own tiny shared apartment. She explained Dina's situation briefly, promising to fill in the details later, maybe much later—no telling when she'd be home.

Sean said, 'No worries,' in a phoney Aussie accent that probably meant he'd had a couple of beers. He and some of the guys were going to the Rangers game. Michael had a party with some of his Stuyvesant High classmates. So no worries. But Em detected a faint undertone. They had been together for three years, and the first bloom was wearing off. Maybe it was Sean's acting career. It was tough to be thirty-seven and still waiting for that one big break. Perhaps that was all it was. She said goodbye with that small undefined something still hanging between them.

Maybe because she had just been talking about her own son, Michael, it was at this moment that the realisation fully struck her: Dina might not see Ali and Suzanne again for years.

She tried to imagine how she would have felt if Michael's father had spirited him away like that. She couldn't do it. Along with his faults, Gabriel LeBlanc had a fair assortment of good qualities, though a sense of responsibility was not among them. A few phone calls, some cheques, a few postcards, that was about his limit. Where could he go with Michael that she couldn't get at him? True, the zydeco that he'd played for a few dollars and free beer in every backroad dance joint in south Louisiana was now popular enough to get him gigs in Montreal or Paris—but he'd never live in those places. No, the furthest she'd ever have to go to find him would be to some trailer park or bar in Bayou Grosse Tête, Louisiana.

Em punched a number into her cellphone and spoke briefly with her lawyer, Manny Schoenfeld. She had just clicked off the phone when the cab pulled up in front of Dina's brownstone. Sarah's car was already there.

Em swept into Dina's kitchen like a troop of cavalry. Another big hug.

'Now look, darlin', I know you can't help but worry, but we're gonna get on this case. It's gonna work out. We're gonna *make* it work out all right.'

Sarah said, 'Read this,' and handed her the letter.

Em read it in one quick take and set it down. 'OK,' she said. 'The first thing we need is a lawyer. I've got Manny on it. He doesn't know jack about this kind of thing, but I've asked him to look for someone.'

'We definitely need a lawyer,' Sarah agreed. 'That's step one. But there are other things we may need to think about, too. Other avenues.'

'Like what?' asked Dina.

'Well, for instance,' Sarah said, 'I'm thinking State Department. Karim is connected back home, isn't he?'

Dina nodded. 'Yes, his family has some connections. And family is everything there. Certain people know each other . . .'

'Right,' said Sarah. 'So maybe that's a way to get at him. Back channels. And there's your dad, Dina.' Dina's father had been involved as a respected go-between, an honest broker, during the conflict in his native Lebanon.

'No,' said Dina. 'I don't want my father in this. He's not very strong yet.'

'OK,' said Em. 'What about your mom?'

'I haven't called her yet. She's got so much to deal with . . .'

'They're gonna have to know sooner or later.'

'Later, then. And maybe it will work out sooner.'

'What about Jordy?' asked Sarah. 'Have you told him?'

Dina shook her head.

'No point till we know a little more,' said Em. 'Karim says he'll call.'

Sarah nodded. 'What did the police say?' she asked Dina.

'They said "good luck",' Dina replied bitterly. She told them about her exchange with the policewoman. The conversation moved on from there.

By ten o'clock they had exhausted every possible idea. Dina looked from Em to Sarah and began to weep.

Sarah's arm went round her quickly, and she murmured, 'It's going to be all right, Dina. We'll figure out a way.' She might have been talking to one of her patients, reassuring even when she wasn't sure of the outcome.

A purring sound animated Em's bag. She pulled out the cellphone and said 'Uh-huh' three times while motioning for a paper and pencil. She scribbled down a couple of lines. 'He's *experienced*, right? A specialist?' She listened again. 'OK. Thanks, Manny. I mean it. Undying gratitude.' She clicked off the phone. 'Looks like we've got ourselves a lawyer.'

THE CALL came exactly at seven in the morning, as if Karim had been waiting for a decent hour to phone. His greeting was calm, perhaps a little wary.

'Dina.'

'Karim!' It was a cry from the heart more than a greeting. 'My God, what have you done?' she sobbed into the phone. 'How could you do this to me?'

A sigh on the other end. 'This isn't about you, Dina—or about me, for that matter. I did this for our children. I tried to explain—'

'How do you explain taking children from their mother?' she cried.

Another sigh. 'Dina, please . . . I can't discuss this with you now. I just wanted to assure you that the children are well, and that—'

'I want to talk to them,' she pleaded. 'I want—'

'Not now, Dina. They're tired and Fatma has put them to bed. I promise to call again soon. And then you can talk to them.'

'Karim, don't hang up' she pleaded. 'I've been going crazy with worry.'

'That's why I called,' he said. 'To assure you that Suzy and Ali are well.'

'You can't do this,' she sobbed. 'I won't let you, Karim. I won't—'

'Dina, please . . . it's done,' he said. And then: 'Goodbye.'

She held the phone in her hand for a long time, stared at the instrument as if it were a lifeline to her children. Which in a way it was. She dialled the number of her in-laws' home. But no one answered. She put her head down on her pillow, feeling the dampness of tears against her cheek.

CHAPTER 2

He looks like a nice man, was Dina's first thought, as David Kallas came out of his office to the tiny reception area. He was a slender man, conservatively dressed in a navy suit. The lines round his eyes suggested he was in his forties, but his manner was boyish.

'Mrs Ahmad?' he said in a soft voice, glancing at each of the three women.

'I'm Dina Ahmad. And these are my friends, Sarah Gelman and Emmeline LeBlanc.'

'Shall we go into my office?'

Sarah and Emmeline rose from their chairs, right along with Dina.

Kallas shot an enquiring glance at her.

Dina nodded. 'It's all right. I want them to hear whatever we discuss.'

He shrugged. 'If that's what you wish, welcome to my office. All of you.'

The office was scarcely bigger than the reception area, but it looked comfortable. The client chairs were thickly cushioned.

'Would you like something to drink? Coffee? Tea? Mineral water?'

They all asked for water. Kallas stepped into the reception area and returned with three bottles of Pellegrino on a small tray.

Emmeline spoke up. 'Manny says you know the Middle East pretty well.'

Kallas thought for a moment. 'I think it's fair to say that I have some understanding of the region. My parents were born in Syria. Like most of Syria's Jews, they emigrated about forty years ago. To Brooklyn. I speak Arabic, and I studied Middle Eastern affairs at Columbia.'

'And you're an expert on divorce law?' Emmeline pressed.

He shook his head. 'I don't call myself an expert on anything. But at least half of my practice relates to divorce.' He turned to Dina. 'Maybe it would be best if you just tell me what brings you here, Mrs Ahmad. Manny mentioned only that your husband had taken your children and gone to Jordan, without your knowledge. I'd like to hear the rest from you.'

Dina gulped some water, then took a deep breath. She told the story, stopping once or twice when she felt she might cry.

Kallas waited until she finished. When he spoke, his expression was solemn. 'I'm afraid I can't offer much encouragement, Mrs Ahmad. Since you and Mr Ahmad aren't divorced, there's no question of kidnapping here. Or of custody. If you were to press the matter in Jordan, I doubt you'd make much headway because there you would be a foreigner, and your husband would surely prevail. And if his family has powerful connections, then . . .' He spread out his hands as if to convey the futility of it all.

'Please,' Dina said. 'Isn't there anything you can do?'

He studied the three women for a moment. 'I'll talk to some people who have some experience with similar situations. Beyond that . . .'

Dina opened her bag and took out her cheque book. 'How much do I owe you?' she asked. 'Should I give you a retainer, or . . .?'

Kallas shook his head. 'Let's wait to see if I can do anything for you. Meanwhile, I've had the pleasure of the company of three lovely women. How often does that happen to an old bachelor like me?'

Dina was charmed by the gesture and the gallantry. 'What a nice man,' she said after they'd left the office.

'Hmph,' commented Emmeline, who was never one to make positive judgments in a hurry.

'Yes, he is,' Sarah agreed, smiling to herself. The phrase 'old bachelor' had triggered her mother's voice in her head. Try as she might, she couldn't seem to outrun Esther Perlstein's advice, admonitions and general instructions on how to live her life. Instructions that would certainly include what to do when you met a nice, single Jewish boy.

DINA ENTERED the ornate lobby of the building that had been home to her parents for almost fifty years. She couldn't put it off any longer. She would have to tell her mother that the twins were gone. Murmuring a greeting to the elderly doorman, she walked to the elevator, stepped into the gilded car and pressed 10. She had grown up in this building, and it usually warmed her to return to the scene of childhood memories: winter mornings snuggling under the quilts made by her Lebanese grandmother; family celebrations rich with good food and the booming laughter of relatives, both Irish-American and Lebanese. Today was different.

She reached the tenth floor, and rang the bell to 10A. A moment later, Charlotte Hilmi opened the door. Her smile, when she saw Dina, illuminated her face. At sixty-eight, Charlotte was still a beautiful woman, her green eyes clear and bright, her once-golden hair lightly streaked with silver.

'Mom.'

Charlotte enveloped her daughter in a warm hug, and Dina wished for a moment that she could stay there, protected and safe.

'Dina, sweetheart, it's good to see you.' Charlotte led her into an enormous living room furnished with overstuffed damask couches and tables inlaid with mother-of-pearl.

'What's wrong?' Charlotte asked as soon as they were seated.

Dina forced a smile. 'What makes you think something's wrong?'

'Dina.' The word was a reproach.

'Mom, promise me you won't say a word to Daddy about this.'

Charlotte's expression froze. 'Is it so bad?'

Dina nodded.

'The children? Has something happened to the children?'

'The children are fine, but . . . the twins are in Jordan. Karim has taken them and he's not coming back. He doesn't want Jordy,' she added bitterly.

Charlotte looked stunned. 'But how? What . . . ?'

Dina told her story, much as she had told it to David Kallas.

'I still don't understand,' Charlotte said. 'How could this happen? I didn't know you were having problems . . . not that kind.'

'I don't really understand either,' Dina said. 'Whatever problems we had never seemed so big to me.' She paused. 'But Karim seems to feel he's saving the children from getting corrupted. Like Jordy was.' A harsh laugh.

Charlotte was silent, as if trying to absorb what she had just heard.

Dina sighed. 'It's going to sound so simplistic, but for Karim, the problem seems to be the American way of life versus the Arab way of life.'

'Ah.'

'Ah—what? Does that actually make sense to you?'

'Not sense, necessarily. But it's something I might understand. Don't forget, your father and I have the same cultural mix as you and Karim.'

'But with you and Daddy the differences didn't seem to matter. To me, they seemed like a plus. I learned from you, Mom. That's why I was so confident that Karim and I would always be able to work things out.'

'And you imagined we never had any problems?'

'You argued sometimes, but your marriage always seemed . . . so right.'

Charlotte smiled. 'Adjustments have to be made in every marriage. And when they come from different cultures, the adjustments are even harder.'

'Yes, but Daddy's family is crazy about you.'

'Not in the beginning,' Charlotte said. 'When we got married, Joseph's sister made it clear I was . . . on probation, so to speak. Of course, that all changed over time, and now . . . well, now, we couldn't be closer.'

Dina couldn't imagine anyone not loving her mother. All she'd ever seen at home was love. Maybe that's why she expected it to last in her own marriage. The evening she'd first seen Karim at one of the Arab-American social events her parents attended, she had been attracted by his movie-star looks. The attraction was obviously mutual, for Karim made his way over to her like a homing pigeon. And after they had talked, she had been impressed by his intelligence. He could talk with such clarity about so many subjects.

'Do you remember when Karim and I first started seeing each other?' Dina asked. 'Remember how he used to say he was part of a new, forward-looking generation? How people like him would integrate the best that the West had to offer with traditional Arab values?'

'I remember,' Charlotte said. 'I think that's what impressed your father and me. Your father liked Karim's passion and sincerity, although . . .'

'Although what?'

'Well, your father felt that one of the reasons we were a good match was that he became an American: Arab in his roots and traditions, but a real melting-pot American. He felt that even if Karim lived here for the rest of his life, he might remain a Jordanian through and through.' She paused. 'Not that there's anything wrong with that,' she added. 'It's just that we weren't sure how that would match up with the way you'd been brought up.'

'But you never said anything.'

Charlotte smiled and squeezed her daughter's arm. 'But we did, sweetheart, don't you remember? I spoke to you about the freedom you'd been accustomed to all your life. The fact that you'd never been made to feel you were less important because you were a woman.'

Dina couldn't remember the conversation. 'What did I say?' she asked.

'You made a face. And you said that Karim was a modern man, just as you were a modern woman.'

Yes, Dina thought, she'd once believed that. But Karim seemed to have forgotten about 'integrating' the best of the West with his own traditions.

'But why are we talking about the past now?' Charlotte asked. 'We need to do something. Maybe your father—'

'No, Mom, I told you, we're not telling Daddy about this. As far as he's concerned, Karim has taken the kids to see his family.'

Charlotte nodded. 'I hate to lie to your father, but you're right. He tries to pretend he's fine, but he isn't.' She thought for a moment. 'How can I help?'

'I don't know, Mom. I've seen a lawyer. He isn't optimistic. I thought you might have the names of the State Department people who know Daddy.'

'That's a good idea. Most of your father's old friends are gone. But you can try Danielle Egan. She and your father spoke not long ago. She told him that America owed him a debt for all his good work during the trouble in Lebanon. He was so pleased to be remembered.'

'He should be remembered,' Dina said staunchly. Her father's family connections—prominent Lebanese Christians—had enabled him to undertake discreet behind-the-scenes assignments during the civil war that had all but destroyed his native country. And after the war had ended, her father had used his banking connections to steer investment money into rebuilding the hotels and tourist attractions that would bring Lebanon back to life.

Her father had done a great deal of good for a great many people. So perhaps someone would be willing to help her now.

'I'll get you Danielle Egan's number,' Charlotte said. She rose and headed towards the adjoining study, then paused. 'Do you want to spend the night here, Dina? I don't like the idea of you being alone.'

'Thanks, Mom, but if I do that Daddy is bound to ask questions. Besides, I want to be home in case Karim calls.'

KARIM did not phone again. Dina sat on her bed, waiting. Not reading. Not watching television. Just ruminating. Replaying scenes from the past. Perhaps she should have seen potential problems in her marriage from the start.

Karim was devoted to his family, and his family had not been welcoming to her. Her father-in-law, Hassan, a dignified paterfamilias, hadn't said much, but her mother-in-law, Maha, openly questioned the suitability of a Christian bride, the daughter of an American mother, for their Muslim son—the son of a prominent and well-to-do family, at that. Maha had gone so far as to suggest that she had several more suitable candidates in mind.

At first, Dina tried to take Maha's attitude in her stride; a woman in love overlooks so much. And Karim used to joke about it, saying that in his mother's eyes no woman would be good enough. Over time the jokes ended, and Dina found herself overlooking very little.

At first, she had tried to adopt her own mother's example in blending two cultures. She had faithfully prepared Middle Eastern dishes several times a week, had enthusiastically entertained Karim's visiting relatives, had respected his religion and made an effort to learn about it. To her children, she had spoken warmly of their Jordanian grandparents.

Still, although Jordan was one of the more progressive countries in the Arab world, elements of the culture remained unacceptable to her. Like the fact that arranged marriages were still common. Or the fact that while a man alone might dine anywhere he pleased, a woman alone could not. But most abhorrent to Dina were the so-called 'honour' killings, which constituted about a third of Jordan's homicides. These were perpetrated by fathers, husbands and brothers against women who supposedly had brought dishonour to a family, by actual sexual misconduct or by the appearance of it. Men who claimed they killed for honour received little punishment (a jail term of six months or so) or no punishment at all.

When Dina raised this issue once at her in-laws' home, her brother-in-law Samir had declared that if honour killings were not allowed, morals at home would become as loose as they were in America. Dina had looked around the room, waiting for someone to disagree, but Karim said nothing. Had she suspected then that her husband was not the man she'd fallen in love with?

She did remember that it was at that point that she began to question the frequent visits to Karim's family. Karim always seemed more Arab afterwards. He became more critical of some of her 'American' ways—her skirts that were too short, the fact that she was 'too friendly' with both men and women. Dina had no doubt that his intolerance was stoked by his brother, who bullied and dominated his own wife, Soraya, and who seemed to feel that Karim was not given the respect he was due at home.

When Dina gave birth to their first son, all that receded into the background. Karim was thrilled. His family sent good wishes and lavish gifts.

Yes, there had been arguments when she wanted to return to her floral design business a few months later. Karim had wanted her to sell Mosaic—or at least hire a manager to run it. They didn't need the money, so why couldn't Dina stay at home? She'd tried to explain that it wasn't simply about money; she needed to be something—something other than a housewife. Karim had not understood. And that was when they'd brought in Fatma.

Then, just months ago, came the trouble with Jordy.

It had started with a call from the counsellor at Jordy's school. Jordy had been caught 'engaging in a display of physical affection beyond what we consider appropriate' with another student. A male student. Both of them were being suspended for three days.

Dina's first impulse was to say that there must be a mistake. But she said nothing for a moment. Had she suspected? All the times she'd told herself that Jordy was a late bloomer, or more interested in his studies, or that nowadays teenage boys didn't moon over girls like they used to. She had said nothing to Karim. As it was, he blamed her for pampering the boy.

When she finally spoke to the counsellor, what she said surprised even herself. 'Do you suspend students for "displays of public affection" if they happen to be of the opposite sex?'

The counsellor managed to sound both sympathetic and primly correct. 'Ms Ahmad, I assure you we have a firm policy of non-discrimination. It's just that the . . . *level* of physical affection was beyond what we would allow for any student, regardless of orientation.'

'Orientation,' said Dina. It seemed the strangest word she'd ever spoken. She took a deep breath and somehow managed to end the conversation.

Oh God, she thought, could it really be true? Her beautiful, intelligent, sensitive boy. She left the office and went home. Jordy came in at his usual time. Dina wondered if he'd hoped to carry the suspension off without her and Karim knowing. But one look between them was enough.

'I guess the school called,' he said quietly. 'Mom, I . . . I just—'

'Just tell me what it's about, Jordy.'

He had seemed on the verge of tears. But now his face flushed with anger. 'What it's *about*, Mom? Tell you I'm a fag? A queer? A homo? Because that's what it's about!'

'Jordy, this is all . . . I mean, are you sure?'

'Give me a break, Mom. I've been sure since I was maybe eleven. Twelve. I just didn't . . . I couldn't . . . It's really hard to explain, you know? It's like, when did you know you liked guys? Well, I guess it's the same with me.' He gave a little laugh. The bitterness in it broke Dina's heart.

'OK.' It was all she could say.

'OK what?'

She swallowed hard. 'OK, we go from here. You think I'm going to stop loving my son because he's . . .'

'Gay, Mom. The word is "gay".'

'Jordy.' She went to her son and held him. He had been holding his backpack in one hand. Now he let it fall to the floor and put his arms round her. They held each other in silence. Dina willed herself not to cry.

'I'll bet you could use a drink, Mom.'

She smiled ruefully. 'You'd win that bet. What would you like?'

'Whatever you're having.'

Dina decided against the brandy she'd first thought of and made tea. They sat together in the living room as the city outside eased into twilight.

'I can't pretend I'm not upset,' she said slowly. 'It's just . . . it's just that I always wanted only the best for you, and—'

'And gay people can't have the "best"—is that it, Mom?'

'Jordy, sweetheart, I'm sorry if I'm saying the wrong thing. I just meant that life will be harder. And different.'

'Yeah,' Jordy said. 'Tell me about it. Different.'

'Look at me,' she said. She held his gaze. 'I love you. I'll love you until the day I die, no matter what you do. No matter who you love. Do you understand what I'm saying?'

'Yeah.' He attempted a smile. 'I guess we have to tell Dad.'

Dina had been wondering about that ever since the phone call from school. 'Maybe he doesn't have to know,' she said. 'Not right away.'

Jordy stared at her. 'I'm not going to be ashamed of who I am,' he said defiantly. 'Not any more.' He looked like the ten-year-old boy he'd once been.

'It's up to you, sweetheart,' she said quickly. 'I was just thinking out loud about what would be easier for you.'

'I know.' He forgave her with a smile. 'Poor Dad,' he said softly, and now he sounded like a mature man.

A short time later, as if on cue, there was the sound of keys in the door and Karim's voice, his typical greeting, 'Hello, the house.'

'We're in here,' Dina called.

He came in looking a little worn—a difficult day in the office, obviously. He seemed surprised to see them sitting so formally. 'What's wrong?'

'Something happened at school,' Dina said. And in a few words she told him what it was.

As she spoke, Karim's mouth slowly opened in astonishment. When she had finished, he looked at his son as if seeking confirmation of the obvious fact that Dina was talking nonsense.

'It's true, Dad,' Jordy said simply. 'I'm gay.'

Karim looked back and forth between them. 'This has to be a mistake.'

'No,' said Jordy.

'It's no mistake, Karim,' said Dina.

She watched the realisation dawn on her husband. His face crumpled, and at first it seemed he might cry, but then she saw the anger rising in him.

He turned on Jordy. 'If this is true, I do not want you in my house,' he said fiercely. 'This is against God. It's against nature. It's filth, do you hear me? I will not have it around me.' His voice had risen to a shout.

'Karim,' said Dina, pointing to the ceiling, 'the twins.'

He stared at her. 'Oh, yes, the twins. Do you think I want them exposed to this perversion?' He turned back to Jordy. 'I want you out of here. Now.'

Even in the worst of her imaginings, Dina hadn't foreseen this kind of primitive anger. This was their firstborn, the apple of his father's eye.

'He's not going anywhere, Karim. He's our son. And he's still a minor. You can't put him out, even if you want to act this way.'

He focused now on her. 'You! This is your fault. Didn't I warn you, all those years ago? But no, you just had to spoil him. Turn him into a woman!'

Jordy had stood. 'No, Dad. It's not Mom. It's not you. It's me.'

'You!' Karim moved towards him and drew back his fist as if to strike.

'Karim! No!' Dina shouted.

Jordy stood his ground, hands clenched at his sides.

Karim stopped, dropped his hand. 'The two of you disgust me,' he said. He turned towards the door. 'I'm going out. I can't stand to look at either of you.' He halted and turned back to Dina. 'I don't want to see him while I'm here. Morning or night. Let him eat in his room.'

'Karim, you—'

'Don't argue with me, damn you! Haven't you done enough already?'

With that he stalked from the room. They heard the front door slam.

Dina and Jordy looked at each other helplessly.

An exhausted sigh, almost a sob, escaped Jordy's lips. 'Well, I guess I know what my father thinks of me.'

Dina put her arms round him. 'He'll calm down,' she said. 'It'll just take a while, that's all.'

She had almost believed that. Dina knew that it would be hard for Karim to accept his son's homosexuality. In most cultures, there was some stigma; in some of the stricter Islamic cultures, it was punishable by death. But Karim was light years more enlightened than people in those societies, and eventually love would prevail—wouldn't it?

But Karim was adamant. Jordy was sent to prep school—Karim wanted the failure out of sight. And he continued to blame Dina: if she had raised the boy as a mother is supposed to do, if she hadn't been so intent on her career . . . et cetera, et cetera. She felt the injustice of his anger, but she understood his hurt. And still she loved him, still thought they could work things out, given time and effort. Only a month ago she had suggested that he go to counselling with her. He had said he would think about it.

And all along he had been planning this.

Now she realised that she had let her son down by not fighting harder for him—and all for nothing. She had let herself down, too, by allowing Karim to believe he could do anything he wished with regard to his family, and without consequence to himself.

THE FOLLOWING morning Dina made her call to the State Department. Danielle Egan was polite, even cordial when she heard Joseph Hilmi's name. But when Dina explained her problem, the woman's tone grew cautious, tentative. She made sympathetic noises but offered nothing.

'I was hoping you . . . the Department . . . could help me get my children back,' Dina finally said. 'Maybe someone could get in touch with my husband, put some pressure on him to bring the twins back.'

'It's not that simple, Mrs Ahmad. How would it look if the State Department attempted to interfere with a Jordanian national who hasn't broken any laws? Especially a Jordanian national with powerful connections?'

'So you're saying you won't help me?'

Egan's tone softened. 'Look, Mrs Ahmad, I have two children of my own. If something like this happened to me, maybe I'd be doing exactly what you're doing, trying to get help wherever I could. I'll make some enquiries. Unofficially, of course. Meanwhile, keep in touch.'

'Of course,' Dina said, wondering what the point would be.

ONCE AGAIN the telephone rang at seven in the morning. Dina picked it up.

'Dina . . .' Karim's voice was soft, almost tender.

'Karim!' was her anguished response. 'For God's sake, please bring my babies back! How could you take them from me?'

'Dina, Dina, the children are here because they'll have a better life in Jordan. They'll learn solid values, and grow up to be decent adults—'

'Not perverts like their brother, you mean,' she cut in bitterly.

Karim sighed. 'Dina, I blame myself, too, for this thing with . . .' Apparently he couldn't even bring himself to say his firstborn son's name. 'It wouldn't have happened if he'd been raised here, in the proper way. I won't let something like that happen to Ali. This isn't easy for me either, you know. But it's the only way.'

'The only way?' she repeated. 'To deprive my babies of their mother?'

'I'm not trying to do that, Dina. You can spend as much time with them as you want. But here—in Jordan.' He paused. 'Would you like to speak to Suzanne and Ali? They're eager to talk with you.'

'And what exactly did you tell them?' she asked coldly. 'That you've kidnapped them for their own good? To protect them from their mother? Because she refused to bring them up in the "right way"?'

'I haven't told them anything definitive yet. I just said that we were going to see their grandparents and cousins.'

'And what do you expect me to say when I speak to them? That I'm going along with this . . . his horror you've inflicted on me?'

'Dina . . . I leave it to you to say what you think best—for their sake.'

'You bastard,' she muttered. 'You know I won't say anything to hurt or frighten them. You're forcing me to be your accomplice.'

He sighed again. 'Let me put Suzanne on the phone. She's been very anxious to tell you all about her plane ride.'

'Mommy, Mommy,' Suzy shouted into the phone, 'wait till you see the pony *Jiddo* bought me!'

'Bought us!' Ali shouted in the background.

Suzy ignored her brother. 'It's fun here, Mommy. When are you coming?'

Dina felt her throat close up. Clearly her children were having too good a time to miss her yet. 'I'm glad you're having fun, Suze,' she choked.

'I am, I am. Aunt Soraya said I could help her make baklava today.'

Dina managed an appropriate response. She exchanged a few more heartbreaking words with Suzy, and then with Ali. As loath as she was to do it, Dina felt compelled to support Karim in the fiction that all was well and that they were still a family. By the time she hung up, she was almost choking with pain and rage. How she hated Karim! She hated his entire family. But stronger than hate was the longing to embrace her children.

She showered and dressed, prepared to go to work. But suddenly that prospect seemed absurd. Why had her career seemed so important? Yes, she got satisfaction from creating the floral sculptures that adorned tables in fine French restaurants, graced some of Manhattan's grandest homes. All right, maybe it was all a bit shallow, but was it so terrible? Clearly Karim thought their life together *was* terrible or he wouldn't have abandoned it.

Dina called her assistant, Eileen. 'I won't be coming in for a while,' she said. 'I'll keep in touch. Please contact that Barnard student who worked for us part-time last year. Ask her if she can give you a hand while I'm out.'

'Is something wrong?' Eileen asked.

'Family problems,' Dina replied tersely. Eileen got the message, and after a few questions about current clients, she hung up.

Dina couldn't help remembering the times Karim had asked her to take time off—and how important it had seemed not to. But why? She was not passionate about her work, though it gave her pleasure. If she'd been passionate about anything, it was the need not to be like the women in Karim's family: placid, boring, housebound. But now it was those women who had her children, and Dina thought she would gladly trade places with them.

CHAPTER 3

*A**hlan wa sahlan, ya Karim, ahlan wa sahlan,*' Karim's uncle, Farid, boomed as he entered the Ahmad home.

It was always like this when Karim came to Jordan. Friends and relatives streaming in and out of the big house, welcome upon welcome, hugs and kisses upon kisses and hugs. Ever since his arrival, Karim's mother had been running what amounted to a continuous open house, preparing one lavish meal after another for those who dropped in to see him and the children. Karim never tired of it; this was the way a family should be—close, strong and ever-present. Dina had sometimes complained of a lack of privacy when his family monopolised their time in Jordan. She hadn't understood that the concept of privacy was alien here.

'How long will you be in Jordan this time?' Farid asked.

'A while,' Karim replied, hoping that would satisfy his uncle. He was not ready to explain the full circumstances to one and all.

The old man sniffed the air, inhaling the fragrance of succulent lamb, butter-laden rice and other delectables.

Karim took the hint. 'We were just about to have lunch, Uncle. Let's see what my dear mother has for us today.' He led his uncle to the dining room.

Hassan, Karim's father, rose to embrace his younger brother, then pulled out a chair at the massive carved table. Farid sat down.

Samir's two children, Nasser and Lina, after a pointed look from their father, rose obediently, went to their great-uncle and kissed his hand. Farid patted the children, rewarded the gesture of respect with a blessing—and a few coins. Karim's children looked at their father and then followed suit. Karim smiled approvingly. Traditions like this were out of fashion in some households, but he wanted the twins to learn the old ways.

The formalities out of the way, eating resumed. The meal was a traditional one for festive occasions. Trays of meze—hummous, tabbouleh and *baba ghanoush,* with assorted cheeses and olives—preceded a main course of *mansaf,* the national dish: lamb cooked in a yoghurt sauce, piled atop a mountain of rice and flat bread, and enlivened with pine nuts. A soup of lentils, yoghurt and onions served as an accompaniment. Karim's mother and sister-in-law, with the assistance of Fatma and the family servant, had laboured for hours to put it all together.

For tradition's sake, the *mansaf* was being eaten in the old manner, by hand, each person reaching into the communal dish for the morsels he or she wanted. The technique of rolling the food into a ball and pushing it into one's mouth with the thumb proved especially difficult for Suzanne.

Her older cousin, Nasser, stepped in. 'Like this,' he said, adopting a grown-up tone. 'You have to hold the food firmly.'

Suzy tried, but the rice kept slipping through her fingers. Ali began to laugh. 'Suzy doesn't know how to eat,' he chanted, 'Suzy doesn't know how to eat.' Suzy's eyes began to fill with tears.

Her father came to her rescue. 'Of course Suzy knows how to eat, Ali. She just needs a bit of practice eating this way. Until she gets it down, I'm going to help. Come here, Princess,' he said, holding out his arms.

Suzy rushed to her father, who boosted her onto his lap and proceeded to feed her from his plate. She turned to her brother and smiled. Ali scowled. Although the twins shared a deep and abiding bond, they sometimes behaved as if they couldn't stand each other. Ali wasn't doing particularly well eating with his fingers either, but he would rather starve than admit he needed help. Soraya quietly brought Ali a plate and a fork.

Samir edged closer to Karim. 'Raised a couple of regular little Americans there, haven't you, brother?'

Karim laughed. 'Looks that way, doesn't it?'

'They'll get the hang of it, once they're here for a while.' Samir reached into the *mansaf* and expertly withdrew a healthy portion.

'*You've* got the hang of it at any rate, little brother,' Karim told him. It had become a running joke between them. His little brother was not so little any more, a middle-age belly bulging his shirt over the waist of his slacks.

'Ah, well, hazard of the business,' said Samir. It was his standard defence. Samir owned a travel agency, and maintained that heavy meals with clients were unavoidable. 'At least,' he added, 'I'm not some grey-headed old man still dreaming of winning the Olympics.'

This was a dig at both the silver that was creeping into Karim's black hair and his devotion to physical fitness; he had already found a Western-style health club in Amman, and went three times a week, just like in New York.

Before Karim could formulate a suitably withering reply, Soraya spoke to her husband. 'Do you think there's enough to eat?' she asked.

'It will have to do,' Samir answered gruffly. He could easily have said, Karim thought, that there was enough for an army and a navy besides.

Soraya turned to Karim. 'Have you told the children yet about Marwan?'

He looked at her blankly, having no idea what she meant.

Samir was waving a hand. 'I didn't tell him. Just slipped my mind. I talked to a young man about tutoring Ali and Suzanne,' he explained to Karim.

'Ah.' Karim had sought Samir and Soraya's help in finding someone to teach the children Arabic. It was something he had always wanted to do, but Dina had opposed it on the grounds that they were too young to spend long hours in extra study—though he had pointed out to her that childhood was precisely when it was easiest to learn another language. Now it was important, if the twins were to attend school and mix easily with their peers.

'Marwan Tawil,' Samir was saying. 'Son of a friend of mine. He's a good boy, smart, third year at the University. Speaks English better than you do. I'll arrange it, if you tell me what hours you want.'

'That's great,' said Karim. 'Let me talk with the children, come up with a schedule.' He saw his brother and sister-in-law exchange an amused glance. What was it about America, that adults let their children decide such things?

'He can teach more than just the language,' said Samir. 'For instance, he can give them a little religious instruction, if you're interested in that.'

It was another area that Karim had neglected. Dina had not opposed the children's learning *about* Islam, but it was her belief that children should not be indoctrinated in any religion, but be left to decide what they believed when they were older. In truth, until lately Karim had been only mildly observant himself. As a result, the twins had only a superficial awareness of Islam. As for Jordy, he had seemed interested in his father's faith—in his own actually, for according to Islamic law, if the father is a Muslim, so are his children. Karim recalled how he and Jordan had travelled to the mosque on 96th Street, how close he had felt to his son when they prayed together. He shook his head as if to shake away the pain of that memory.

'Sure,' he said to Samir. 'I wouldn't mind that. What's his orientation?'

Samir lifted an ironic eyebrow. 'His *orientation,* brother? Don't worry, he's not one of the fundamentalists. He's not related to any of the old Muslim Brotherhood, or the Taliban.'

Karim laughed. 'OK, OK. Have him call me at the office.' It would be something to do, he thought. He had been on the new job a week. It amounted to consultant work on aircraft procurement. But it also appeared to be about politics, office and otherwise. Until he learned exactly whose buttons to push when, he would not be doing much more than pushing papers.

'That's good.' Soraya brightened. 'Let me tell the twins. I'll make it sound like more fun than you two grim old soldiers will.' She was ten years younger than Samir, fifteen younger than Karim.

Karim gestured acquiescence, and Samir nodded with evident satisfaction at having resolved this difficulty for his naive, Americanised older brother.

'Dessert,' said Soraya. And she hurried off to help the other women set out plates of baklava and fruit.

After a time, Hassan rose from the table and nodded in a way that included all the men present. It was the signal to move into the smoking room, light the narghile, and talk of worldly matters while the women cleaned up.

The smoking room was furnished in the old style: walls lined with banquettes covered with hand-woven Berber fabric from Morocco. The house was a large one, as befitted the social standing of Hassan Ahmad. Set in one of the better northern suburbs of the capital, it sprawled round a large central courtyard, and combined Arab design elements with such modern comforts as a well-equipped kitchen and several lavish bathrooms.

Samir and his family lived in one wing; Karim and the children occupied a wing that had been reserved for guests, yet already he had begun looking at other properties. He had not mentioned this to his father.

The mouthpiece of the water pipe was passed to Karim. He realised that his father was addressing him.

'My grandson,' said Hassan. 'My oldest grandson, I mean. Jordan.' He spoke the name with a wry twist of the mouth, as if there were a private joke in it. 'If he were here, he would be old enough to share this pipe. Did you say when he would be coming, son?'

'No,' said Karim. 'I mean, it's not certain, *Abbi*. He's in school. Almost ready for university. It's important for him to finish his studies.'

Samir, who knew more of the truth, looked off into the middle distance.

Hassan merely nodded. 'Yes, of course. But I would like to see him all the same.' He smoked from the pipe and his face was sad. For the first time in his life, Karim thought of his father as an old man.

AN HOUR later, Karim and Samir walked together in the courtyard. They were alone for the moment. The party was winding down.

'I wonder,' said Samir, 'about Jordan. This episode you told me about—this kind of thing happens all the time. It doesn't necessarily mean anything. Remember the fuss that was made years ago with cousin Sharif, the same kind of thing? Well, now he's a married man with three sons. And no one cares what he did when he was a young boy.'

Karim said nothing.

'But you know,' his brother continued, 'I wonder about sending him off to that kind of school. It seems to me it might aggravate the problem. Why not bring him here? Is it Dina who stands in the way?'

It would have been easy to say yes. But Karim could not betray her in this small way. 'You don't understand,' he told Samir. 'America is . . . it's nothing like here. I can't do anything about Jordy. Take my word for it.'

'It's all right,' said Samir. 'We'll talk about it later.' And suddenly he gripped Karim by the back of his neck and kissed him on the forehead. 'My brother,' he said quietly, a world of meaning in two small words.

Karim nodded, brushed a tear from his eye, and knew he was home.

DINA KNEW the news would not be good. David Kallas had phoned and asked her to come to his office. It was like the calls doctors made after you had a test. If all went well, they'd tell you on the telephone that everything was fine. If they had bad news, they invited you to come in. Now she and her friends were once again seated in the small reception area. Once again waiting.

When David came out of his office, he smiled at the three women, but the smile didn't quite make it to his eyes. 'Good morning, Mrs Ahmad, Mrs Gelman, Ms LeBlanc.' He hesitated a moment. 'Mrs Ahmad, I know you said that you wanted your friends present at our discussions, but I'd like you to step into my office alone for just a moment.'

Dina looked at her friends. Emmeline shrugged. Sarah said, 'Go ahead, Dina, we'll wait right here.'

Dina followed Kallas into his office and sat down.

'I wish I had something positive to tell you,' the lawyer said gently. 'I've spoken to your husband's attorney in Amman. Mr Ahmad feels he's been generous as regards your finances. But as for custody of the twins'—here David sighed—'your husband's position is that they are to live with him in Jordan. And that you're free to visit them there at any time.'

Dina bit her lip to keep from crying out. She had expected something like this, yet she had hoped, prayed, for something better.

'We could, of course, sue for divorce,' David continued, 'and then for custody and a formal order for child support.'

'Yes,' she said eagerly, 'we could do that. Then the courts would force Karim to bring the twins back, wouldn't they?'

Kallas shook his head. 'Doubtful. I've done some research and found a number of cases like yours. One father snatched his children and took them to Uzbekistan. The American courts ruled for the mother, ordered him to return the kids. But the order was basically unenforceable.'

'Are you telling me that no mothers ever get their children back?'

'Well,' Kallas said, 'in one case, the children were returned to their mother after a large cash payment was made to the father. From what I can see here, that wouldn't work with your husband.'

'No,' Dina said. 'So there's no point in trying any kind of legal action?'

Kallas shook his head again. 'The only ones who would gain from that would be me and the attorney in Jordan.'

'Then there's nothing I can do?' Dina implored. 'Nothing? I want my children back. I would walk through hell if necessary to get them.'

David sighed again. And when he spoke, it was reluctantly. 'I know. That's why I asked you to come in here alone.'

Dina straightened up in her chair.

'You didn't hear this from me,' he said carefully. 'But there are ways outside the legal system.'

'What are you talking about?'

As David explained in purposely cloudy terms, she gradually understood. Stealing the children back. Kidnapping.

'There are experts in this kind of work,' he said. 'Professionals.'

'And you know some of these professionals?' she asked eagerly.

David nodded. 'I know of one. But I've heard that he's very expensive. That's understandable, since the work is dangerous. And illegal.'

Dangerous. Illegal. In normal times, such words would have frightened her off immediately. But these were not normal times.

'And that's why I'm not even suggesting such a step to you. In fact, if you were to ask, I'd advise against it.' David slid a business card across the desk. *Gregory Einhorn, Private Missions.* 'You didn't get this from me,' he said.

'I understand.' And she did.

'Good luck,' said David. 'I hope . . . well, I hope you get your children back, Mrs Ahmad.'

Dina believed him. She rose and offered her hand. He squeezed it lightly. As he walked her to the reception area, Sarah and Emmeline got up quickly.

Dina turned to David. 'Thank you,' she said softly.

'I didn't do anything,' he said quickly.

Sarah looked quickly from her friend to the lawyer, as if she sensed something hidden. Then she spoke. 'Mr Kallas . . . I wonder if I might come in to see you about a problem of mine.'

David looked startled, then pleased. He smiled at Sarah. 'Of course,' he said. 'Just give me a call and we'll set up an appointment.'

SARAH AND EM peppered Dina with questions. What was so hush-hush?

Dina wasn't ready to tell them about the possibility that David had raised. David had contacted Karim's lawyer in Jordan, she said, but nothing good had come of it. 'He told me I could file for divorce, but doesn't think that will help me get the children back.'

'And?' Em demanded.

'And . . . I don't know,' Dina said. 'Maybe I'll just go home and think for a while. Maybe there's something I haven't thought of . . .'

Em and Sarah looked at each other, then at Dina. 'Girl, are you sure that's all you talked about in there?' Em asked. 'You're acting kinda funny.'

Dina attempted a smile. 'I guess I am. Look, I'm sorry I dragged you here for nothing. But really, I think I'd better just get home.'

Reluctantly, her friends put Dina in a cab and went their separate ways.

Dina really did need to think. On her own. Should she even consider doing something that was not only illegal but terribly risky in other ways? If it failed, would she ever see the twins again? And if she did decide to go ahead, was it fair to involve Sarah and Em?

THE TREES were dappled with sunshine, the lawn was lush and green. But as Dina strolled round the Phillips Academy campus with her son, she was oblivious to the beauty of her surroundings. All she could think of was the task that lay ahead: telling Jordy that his father had taken the twins and intended never to return. Get it over with, she told herself. But how?

'We have a few hours before our dinner reservation, sweetheart,' she heard herself saying. 'Is there anything you'd like to do?'

'Well . . . I need to pick up some stuff at the bookstore. Do you want to walk over with me?'

Dina looped her arm through Jordy's, pulled him close. How she loved this beautiful boy with his thick dark hair, his smooth olive skin and his soulful dark eyes, so heart-breakingly like his father's.

The bookstore was located in a restored barn. Dina wandered aimlessly while Jordy looked for the texts he needed. Her eyes swam over titles, not lingering—then suddenly stopped, captured by words that pierced her apathy: *Prayers for Bobby: A Mother's Coming to Terms with the Suicide of her Gay Son.* Oh God, she thought, did you show me this as a reminder that there are worse things than having your children taken by their father? There were other, related books nearby. Her eyes moved quickly to *Sudden Strangers: The Story of a Gay Son and His Father.* It was as if the books were speaking to her, warning her to protect Jordy. She would buy them, she resolved. But not here. When she got home.

From the corner of her eye, she saw Jordy approaching. She moved towards him. 'Do you have what you need?' she asked brightly. Jordy said he did. She paid for his books and they walked out into the bright sunshine.

As they walked towards Chapel Avenue, she remembered the first time she and Karim had come to this campus. Without Jordy. 'My father made my decisions until I went away to college,' Karim said adamantly when Dina suggested that Jordy should have a say in which school he attended. 'And even then, he was always consulted on matters of importance.'

Dina had protested that America was not Jordan and that American children could not be expected to behave as he had. Karim had looked at her, almost pityingly, as if to say: Don't you understand—that's what I'm trying to change? She sighed now—and Jordy looked at her with those same dark eyes, but his were loving and tender.

'Something wrong, Mom?'

'No. I was just thinking what a beautiful campus this is.' Liar, said a voice in her head. Coward.

They arrived at the Addison Gallery of American Art, and Dina and Jordy spent a quiet hour admiring paintings by John Singer Sargent, Mary Cassatt, and the other artists that made up the permanent collection. Jordy was drawn to the section of the museum devoted to the photography of Margaret Bourke-White. He mentioned that he had been taking pictures of the many historic buildings on campus and in the town of Andover.

'Maybe you'd like a new camera,' Dina offered. 'If you're serious about this hobby, you could probably use—'

'Relax, Mom,' he cut in, with a knowing smile. 'My old Canon is fine. I'm not that good yet. And you don't have to buy me stuff to make things OK for me. I'm fine. Honest.'

Now, Dina thought, now is the time. She asked Jordy if he'd come back to the hotel with her for a while before dinner. They went up to her suite. She sat down beside him on the chintz-covered sofa.

'So,' she said, touching his arm, 'how are things at school? Really.'

'I told you the last time, Mom, it's fine, really.'

'And no one is . . . you know, bothering you about . . . being Arab?'

Jordy smiled. 'Not the way you mean, Mom. I mean, sometimes people say sh . . . stuff. And sometimes I feel I have to defend the whole Arab world when the only place I've ever seen is Jordan. But I'm handling it. In fact, I bet I get an A in History this term . . . I've had a lot to say in class.'

'You have? I mean what do you talk about?'

'About terrorism. About the Palestinian problem. The demonstrations in Jordan and Egypt and all the other Arab countries.'

Now it was Dina's turn to smile. In New York, Jordy had seemed not at all interested in politics, whether American or foreign. Odd, she thought. Given Karim's rejection, she might have expected him to turn completely away from anything Arab, but it seemed the opposite had happened.

'I've been in the middle of some pretty fierce arguments. And not always with the Jewish kids, which surprised me. But I've only had one real fight.'

'Oh, Jordy . . .'

'It's OK, Mom. I had to—or it would have been really bad for me. All I got was a bloody nose.' He added, 'I gave as good as I got.'

Dina was thinking of what to say next when Jordy asked, 'How's Rachel?'

Sarah's daughter? If Jordy hadn't been gay, she might have started thinking like a matchmaker. 'She's fine,' Dina said. 'Why do you ask?'

'We've been writing for a while,' Jordy said. He tried to joke. 'Two maladjusted kids who used to have fathers. We have a lot in common.'

The flippancy made her ache. She squeezed his hand. Then, panic. Had Rachel mentioned anything about Karim taking the twins? She couldn't have or Jordy wouldn't be so calm. So she had better do it herself, right now.

'Jordy, there's something I need to tell you.'

'I knew it,' he said. 'I knew there was something. You sounded so funny when we talked on the phone.'

Dina nodded. 'It's about your father . . .'

'What's he done now?' Jordy asked bitterly.

She told the story, simply and with as little emotion as she could manage.

'That bastard! That lousy bastard!'

She reached for him, held him close.

Suddenly he pulled away. 'It's my fault, isn't it? My fault he left you.'

'No, Jordy, no! It's not your fault.'

'Yeah, it is. Everything was fine before . . . before I told him I was gay. It's me he hates, not you. I bet he wishes I were dead instead of being gay.'

'Don't say that, sweetheart, don't even think it! It's not true.'

'I remember how he looked at me that day. He looked like he wanted to kill me. You acted like he was just, you know, being a dad. Like when a kid racks up the family car and the dad gets really mad. But this was worse, and you know it. And now he's gone.'

Dina sighed. She reached for her son again. 'It isn't that simple, Jordy. OK, your father went a little crazy that day. But things weren't all right before then. There were problems.'

He looked sceptical. 'Like what? What kind of problems?'

'There were differences. They didn't seem so bad . . . But your father seems to feel they were insurmountable.'

'Like what? You're not telling me anything.'

'Oh . . . like the fact that I wanted to work and your father wanted me to stay at home.'

'That's it? That's the big difference?'

'No. He wanted us to be more like his family at home, not so American.'

Jordy looked puzzled now. 'You mean he decided all of a sudden that he didn't like us because we were American?'

She shook her head. 'Not all of a sudden. I think this has been going on inside his head for a long time. I think September 11th brought it to a head. You know, his culture against the American culture. He chose his.'

'Christ,' Jordy muttered, 'that really sucks.'

She smiled in spite of herself. 'Yes,' she said, 'yes, it does.'

GREGORY EINHORN'S office was on Third Avenue, in a building occupied by a cross-section of typical Manhattan enterprises: accountants, talent agents, lawyers. He shared the thirtieth floor with a graphic design company and a travel agency. The sign on the door said simply EINHORN ASSOCIATES.

A fiftyish receptionist in a grey silk blouse took Dina's name and said that Mr Einhorn would be only a moment.

Einhorn himself came out to greet her. 'Mrs Ahmad?'

Dina wasn't sure what she had expected, but Gregory Einhorn wasn't it. Thirty-five or so, blond, crew-cut, square-jawed, he looked as if he had exchanged a Green Beret captain's uniform for an expensively tailored suit.

His office looked out towards the East River.

'Coffee? A cold drink? Something else?'

'No, thank you.'

Einhorn gestured towards a chair and she sat. He leaned comfortably against a dark cherrywood desk that had a look of extreme order, the few papers on it precisely aligned. A small black tape recorder. A laptop, closed, to one side. A high-tech-looking phone. On a wall a photo bore out Dina's impression about a military background: a very young Einhorn in uniform was shaking hands with the elder President Bush. The picture was surrounded by many smaller ones—they appeared to be family snapshots.

Einhorn opened a manila folder and inspected its contents briefly. She had stated the basics of her situation when making the appointment.

'So, Mrs Ahmad, your husband has taken your two children, twins, to Jordan. Eight years old.' He checked the folder again. 'Two weeks ago.'

'Yes. Two of our three children. I also have a teenage son.'

'Yes. Any new developments? Since you first contacted us?'

'He's called several times. Allowed me to speak to the children. But otherwise, no developments.'

'I'm going to record our conversation, if you don't mind.'

'No. I mean, fine.'

He turned on the recorder, spoke her name, the date and the time, and said, 'Tell me everything you can.'

She did. He listened intently, breaking in often with questions: Where precisely were Karim and the children? What kind of house? What kind of neighbourhood? Who else was in the house? When were the children separate from their father? Did they go to school, he to work?

To many of his questions Dina had to answer that she didn't know. 'I feel as if I haven't been much help,' she apologised.

He waved it off. 'No matter. We'll find out everything we need to know. Which brings me to the most important question.' He moved behind the desk and sat. 'In your opinion is there any chance of a resolution of this matter through normal channels? Any chance that you might reconcile?'

'I . . . I don't think so.' She was surprised she couldn't be more definite.

Einhorn studied her. 'It's early yet. I like my clients to be sure. It's for your peace of mind. And to save you some money. Quite a bit of money. But it's your call. We can carry out the mission regardless.'

The mission. 'Mr Einhorn, can you get my children back?'

'Yes.' Absolute confidence. Dina felt a surge of elation touched with fear. 'How would you do it?'

He shrugged. 'Depends on the specifics of the situation. Sometimes a well-placed bribe is all you need: a teacher takes her eyes off the school yard for a critical few minutes, for example. Or sometimes there's a resource on the other side: a girlfriend, say, who's found out that caring for someone else's kids isn't as rewarding as she expected.' He glanced at Dina. She'd already told him she didn't think there was another woman. Not yet, anyway.

'But sometimes there are no easy vulnerabilities,' Einhorn went on. 'In that case the best approach is usually the simplest: a quick removal by competent force, followed by a fast withdrawal.'

'What kind of force?' The word made Dina uncomfortable.

A quick smile. 'Don't worry. We're not going to war here. Our people are very, very good. The best. Nobody gets hurt. That's rule one.'

'Are two children a problem?' she asked. 'More difficult?'

'Not really. Multiples are fairly common. You can see several right here.' He gestured towards the photos on the wall. Dina looked more closely and saw that they *were* family pictures, but not of the kind she had imagined. They all showed a happy parent and child, sometimes two children.

One photo caught her eye. The woman in it and her kindergarten-age daughter both looked radiantly happy. 'Can you tell me about this one?'

'Belgium,' he said immediately. 'The father was a dual citizen. Divorced. Weekend custody, the usual kind of thing. An outing to McDonald's, then to the airport. Brussels. Weekdays the little girl was in the care of the grand-parents. A town house. Wealthy neighbourhood. There was a nice open park across the street. Our man—British—got in with some story about follow-ing the footsteps of his own dad back during the Second World War. We had two more men on the ground; he let them in. The granddad wanted to resist, actually grabbed the fireplace poker, but that was no problem. Nobody hurt. I told you we use only the best. Landed a chopper right in the park. An hour later they and the kid were in Germany, where Mom was waiting.'

The story disturbed Dina, as much as she'd like to have something simi-lar happen with the twins. It was the business about the grandfather. What if he'd had some other weapon? What if he had been younger, stronger? What if someone had alerted the police? 'Competent force'—it still sounded dan-gerous. With her children in the middle. Still . . .

'I suppose I need to know how much you charge.'

Einhorn leaned forward. 'Every job is different. Part of our service is a solid estimate up front. I'll have some basic research done, no charge, take just a couple of days.'

'What I need is a general idea of the cost. My resources aren't unlimited.'

'All right. Our minimum for a foreign mission is a hundred thousand. Beyond that it's a question of what needs to be done. As I said, we'll work up a firm estimate. But I think the max would be two hundred and fifty thousand. Unless there are very unusual expenses.'

The sum took Dina's breath away. Where could she possibly get that kind of money? But she said only, 'Do you need anything now? Any payment?'

'No. Half the minimum at the time you engage us for the mission.'

'Fifty thousand. Of course I'll need to think about this.'

'Of course.' There seemed little more to say. Dina rose.

'I know it's a difficult time for you,' Einhorn said. 'Remember what I said: it's early. Be sure. We'll be here whenever you need us. No rush.'

On the way back to her empty home, Dina considered that she didn't much like Gregory Einhorn. At the same time, she realised, she had not for a second doubted one thing: his ability to do exactly what he said he would do.

'A QUARTER of a million dollars!' Emmeline couldn't believe it. 'And you went to see that . . . that mercenary all alone?'

'He isn't a mercenary. Not exactly. He's a . . . kind of specialist. Very pro-fessional. And the quarter of a million . . . well, that's the maximum. Unless there are very unusual expenses. It might be less.'

'I wouldn't count on that,' said Sarah. 'I'd count on the unusual expenses.'

The three were meeting in a SoHo restaurant they remembered from the early days of their friendship. It had changed its name, ownership and decor, and seemed to attract a young crowd. As young as they had been then.

'Do you have it?' asked Emmeline.

'Not on hand. Just the deposit, the fifty thousand, would tap me out.'

'We could raise the money,' Sarah said.

Sarah could probably write a cheque for the balance. That was the last thing Dina wanted. 'I'm not dragging either of you into this,' she said.

'We *are* in it,' Emmeline said. 'And I have a fair amount vegetating in money market funds. Nice and liquid.'

Another last thing Dina wanted.

'Look,' she said, 'I know you're with me. I thank you. But I don't want you putting money into my problem. I can't have that—won't have it.'

'Can't. Won't. Tell me you wouldn't do the same if it was one of us.'

Dina felt tears in her eyes.

'We can get the money,' said Sarah flatly. 'That's not the issue—although we'll need to make sure it's well spent. The question is whether you think it's the best way to go.'

'Right now I . . . What other way is there?'

'Do you trust this Einhorn guy?' Emmeline wanted to know.

'Yes. He seems like he knows exactly what he's doing.'

'Then let's find out exactly what he has in mind and how much he wants for it,' said Sarah.

'Yeah,' said Em. 'And then let's do it.'

A NIGHT, a day, a night, a day, another night with no further word from Karim. Jordy's call of commiseration was a bitterly sarcastic diatribe against his father, which, though Dina agreed with much of it, provided little in the way of comfort. There were Em and Sarah, of course. Em was like a cheerleader. Sarah discussed finances. A bank loan made more sense than simply pooling their assets. Sarah could arrange for it and would be signatory.

All along, Dina's hopes hung on Gregory Einhorn. By the morning of their meeting she was bursting with a mixture of anxiety and anticipation. From the second he appeared in the reception area she knew that something was wrong. He ushered her into his office as before, made the same perfunctory offer of coffee or a cold drink, but something was different.

He came to the point as soon as she was seated. 'Mrs Ahmad, I've looked into your situation. And I'm afraid I'm going to have to pass on this one.'

'What are you talking about? Why? You said you'd do it.'

'I said I'd look into it. Mrs Ahmad, I'm not sure you were completely forthcoming with me. Your husband is part of a very important family with powerful connections. That changes things. Changes them very much.'

Dina was confused. 'But . . . I thought I'd explained that.'

The smile was very brief, patronising. 'In my business there's no substitute for accurate information. Believe me, my caution is for the benefit of my clients as much as myself.'

'So you're saying . . . you won't take this job? My children?'

'I'm afraid not. The risk factor is too great. For everyone.'

It was as if the floor were sliding away beneath her to reveal the thirty-storey drop. For three days she had thought of little except the tough, competent, experienced Gregory Einhorn commanding a 'mission' to bring back her children. And now he was turning her down flat.

'I can see that it might be more complicated than I thought.' She could hear desperation in her voice. 'I could pay more. Not much, but more.'

'Mrs Ahmad, I take chances for a living. But I'm not a gambler. The reward must be proportionate to the risk. Not only for me, but for my people. I couldn't take this case for less than two million dollars.'

'I can't pay that much.'

'I'm sorry. Truly very sorry. I can't do it.'

And that was that. She didn't let herself cry until she was in the elevator.

CHAPTER 4

I can't believe I'm doing this, Sarah thought as she checked her makeup in the compact mirror for the second time. I can't believe I actually asked the man for a date.

In truth she hadn't done all the asking and it wasn't exactly a date. But here she was, nevertheless, waiting for David Kallas to join her for dinner. All because she had called for an appointment and found he was booked during her few free hours. And because he had suggested an after-hours meeting. 'Perhaps a drink, if you like,' he'd added. 'Then we could talk without either one of us rushing off to the next appointment.'

'How about the Harvard Club,' she volunteered. 'It's near your office.'

'We could even have dinner,' he said, 'if you've time. We both have to eat.'

So actually he had made the dinner invitation. And now she was waiting nervously in the oak-panelled dining room. And David was coming towards her, smiling. She rose, said hello, extended her hand and smiled back.

'What a good idea this was,' he said. 'When I'm busy, I sometimes end up making do with a stale bagel or half of an old corned-beef sandwich.'

'And your Jewish mother allows that?' she teased.

He laughed. 'She wouldn't if she knew about it. I guess that's one of the reasons I moved out of the house as soon as I finished law school. Now at least once a week, I hear that my room, in my mother's splendid brownstone—so conveniently located near Ocean Parkway—is still there for me.'

'I know what you mean. I grew up in Brooklyn, too. Near Eastern Parkway. I had to get married to leave home. I just didn't see any other way.'

'That's terrible.'

'I'm joking. But just a little. And that's what I wanted to talk to you about. My marriage and my ex-husband.'

'So this meeting isn't about your friend, Dina? I thought you wanted to voice your concerns about some issue connected with her problem. Though you know I couldn't tell you anything about what we discussed privately.'

'No. Well, of course I'm very concerned about Dina. Em and I both are. But what I wanted to see you about was my divorce.'

'A divorce? I thought you just said "ex-husband".'

'I did. And he is. We were divorced three years ago. But he refused to give me a *get*. And he still refuses whenever I bring it up.'

'You want a *get*?' David was obviously surprised. Sarah understood his reaction. No doubt he was wondering why a modern woman like her wanted a religious divorce in addition to the civil one.

'I'm not sure I can explain,' she said slowly. 'I don't go to *schul* regularly. I do observe the Sabbath unless a patient really needs me. I observe the holy days, but I don't keep a kosher kitchen. I am a Jew in my heart and my soul even if I don't look the way some people think I should, or follow all the rules. But I believe marriage is one of the most important things we do. I want to end mine the right way. Does that make any sense to you?'

David thought for a moment. 'I suppose. My cousin Arlene paid her husband, Morris, a great deal of money to give her a *get*. I know that's not the spirit of the *get*—husband and wife are supposed to consent freely. But she wanted to marry again and have children, and without a *get*, any children from a second marriage would be illegitimate. So . . .' He shrugged. 'She gave him what he wanted. I'm sure you know that spouses sometimes withhold consent as a bargaining chip in the distribution of marital assets.'

'Ari doesn't need any more money. He has plenty for two lifetimes.'

'Then what? Why do you think he refuses you?'

'I'm not sure. I think it's about control.'

'Ah. Well, that makes a certain kind of perverse sense. Maybe he feels he can keep you from starting another family.'

'I'm not planning to have any more children.'

'But you haven't ruled out remarriage.'

'I haven't ruled it out.' She smiled ruefully. 'I just don't see it happening.'

'OK, so what is it that you'd like me to do for you, Mrs Gelman?'

'Sarah, please.'

'Sarah, then.'

'I'd like you to research ways of putting pressure on Ari.'

'Wouldn't that be better accomplished through a rabbinical court?'

'I've thought about that. But I just . . . well, I don't think I could prevail. Ari is a very good actor. I'm afraid that if we went before a court of rabbis, he'd come across as the good spouse, hoping against hope for a reconciliation. And I'd be the bad wife who doesn't even make *schul* regularly.'

'I see. But then why did you think I could help?'

'I'm not sure. You seemed like someone who cared about people. Not the kind of lawyer people make bad jokes about. I just hoped . . .'

A broad smile lit David's face. 'I believe that's the nicest thing anyone ever said to me.'

He's handsome when he smiles, Sarah thought, less intense. 'And my friend Dina said you seemed like a nice man,' she added.

The smile exploded into laughter. 'With a recommendation like that, I guess I have to try to come up with a solution to your problem.'

By the time their dinners arrived—lamb chops for Sarah and salmon for David—they were chatting comfortably about their respective Brooklyn childhoods, comparing the quirks of their families.

David was a good listener, an intelligent listener. I suppose good lawyers are like that, Sarah thought. It doesn't mean there's anything personal going on, she cautioned herself. After all, this isn't a date. Then she blurted out: 'You never married?' Because he'd referred to himself as an old bachelor.

'No.' He sighed. 'It wasn't for lack of trying, believe me. I just never met anyone I wanted to spend my entire life with.'

A brief conversational lull followed, but it wasn't uncomfortable. They ordered coffee and agreed to share a flourless chocolate cake for dessert.

'Your friend Dina's husband—what did you think of him, before this . . . this unfortunate business?'

Sarah paused. 'I don't think I ever liked him,' she said slowly. 'But maybe that was because I knew he didn't like me.'

'Why ever not?'

'I'm pretty sure it was because I was Jewish, though he never said anything. Neither did Dina. And, of course, Ari was from Israel. I don't think Karim liked Em, either. Not because she was black—I think that's a non-issue where he's from—but because she's so, you know, free: bigger than life, speaks her mind, never defers to men or women.' She paused. 'To be fair,' she added, 'Ari didn't much like my friendship with Dina. And that was definitely because Karim was an Arab.'

'But neither of you gave up your friends.'

'Hell, no!' she said emphatically.

'That's good. How was Mr Ahmad with the children?'

'Good,' she said grudgingly. 'Before the thing with Jordy, I'd have said you couldn't find a better father. He doted on those kids. Why do you ask?'

'Just to put my own mind at ease. Sometimes . . . well, sometimes parents take children just to cause pain to their spouses.'

'No,' she said, still grudgingly. 'I'm sure that's not Karim. He may be wrong-headed and a louse, but he took those kids because he wants them.'

The time seemed to go quickly, and when Sarah looked at her watch it was past ten. 'Oh, gosh,' she said, 'I'd better get going. Early day tomorrow.'

David insisted on paying, even though Sarah pointed out that it was her club and by rights she should take the bill.

'Next time,' he said. She was pleased by the remark, even while she told herself it was simply a polite rejoinder that meant nothing. She was even more pleased a few minutes later, when, as they walked out into the street, he said, 'This was fun, Sarah. I'd like to do it again. If you're interested.'

She agreed readily, noticing that he was but a few inches taller than she was. Why, she thought, we practically see eye-to-eye.

TWO DAYS passed with nothing very hopeful. And now, Saturday night, Dina was alone. She flipped aimlessly through TV channels but everything seemed totally vapid, even PBS.

The phone rang.

'Mrs Ahmad?' A man's voice, husky, unfamiliar.

'Yes.'

'My name is John Constantine. I sometimes work with Gregory Einhorn. He gave me your name. He tells me you have a case he can't take on.'

Dina was suspicious. 'He told you about me?'

'Only what I just said. And that I might want to take a look at the . . . problem. Assuming you're interested. Feel free to check this out with him.'

'You work for Gregory Einhorn?'

'*With* him. Sometimes.'

There was something in the voice besides the huskiness and a New York accent. A solidity. Dina took the leap. 'Yes, I'm interested in discussing it.'

'Sure. When's good for you?'

'Any time.'

'Well, if you mean that literally, we could meet in an hour. Tonight.'

Something in the voice. In for a penny, in for a pound, thought Dina. 'I'm free. Yes, let's meet.' She named a coffee shop three blocks away.

'I'll see you there in an hour,' he said.

For the first time in days Dina felt as if she were leaning on something solid. Forty-five minutes later she walked into the coffee shop, took a table and ordered coffee. Ordered a refill and checked her watch. An hour and fifteen minutes. Not a good sign. If the man couldn't even be on time, how was he going to manage something as difficult as getting her children back?

Finally a tall man with an olive complexion and craggy, faintly Mediterranean features, wearing a rumpled trench coat, came into the coffee shop. He glanced in her direction, then walked over to her. 'Mrs Ahmad?'

'Yes,' she said, trying to keep the annoyance out of her voice. He didn't look like a detective despite the trench coat. He didn't apologise for being late, which annoyed Dina even more. This wasn't a good beginning.

'Do you want something to eat?' he asked.

'No.'

'Well, I'm starved. Forgot to stop for lunch today.'

Oh great, she thought. He can't keep time and he forgets to eat.

After ordering a burger deluxe, Constantine went straight to the point. 'Einhorn didn't tell me much, but there are only two reasons he'd turn down a case: it's too dangerous or he priced himself too high. Or both. I figure both. They go together.'

'So what about you?' Dina asked. 'You're the second string? Cut-rate kidnapping?' She knew the questions were rude, but she had to get them out.

When it came to her children, she wasn't interested in anything second-rate.

Constantine smiled. It was an odd little smile. Just the corners of the mouth. 'We work differently. Maybe our priorities are different. I work small. I don't turn every job into D-Day. Do you want to tell me what the job is?'

She did. When she'd finished, he said simply, 'I get five hundred a day plus expenses. This case, if you hire me, the expenses will be mainly for travel.'

'And what do I get for that?'

'Your children back.'

Well. That took her breath away. But was it real or empty bravado? She should call Sarah and Emmeline. Or her mother. Or David Kallas. Or all of them. Yet what other choices were being offered?

And so she said, 'When can you start?'

DINA'S FIRST on-the-clock session with John Constantine took place at her home two mornings after their coffee-shop introduction. He was wearing a charcoal sports jacket over a black turtleneck and grey slacks. When she offered coffee he followed her into the kitchen.

'This is great,' he said, taking in the spacious room and easing into a chair at the refectory table. 'Like living in the country.' It was the only comment he made on the house.

While she brewed the coffee he brought out a reporter-style notebook and fiddled with a small tape recorder.

'Anything new from Karim?' he asked.

'Not since you and I talked.'

'Do you call him?'

'I've called several times trying to talk with Suzanne and Ali. But I always get some excuse. It's as if I'm only allowed to talk with my children when Karim makes the call.'

'Who answers the phone when you call?'

'Usually Soraya, my sister-in-law.' She poured the coffee.

Constantine had the notebook open; he wrote a few words in it. He turned on the recorder and said, 'OK. Tell me what happened the day Karim took the children. Then give me the background.'

She told him everything she could. He listened intently, saying nothing until she had finished. Then he asked to see the children's room. She showed him. He picked up a toy or two, opened the closet and glanced at the remaining clothes, but made no notes. They went back down to the kitchen.

'Twins,' he said. 'Is one of them the leader? The dominant one?'

'The dominant one?' Dina had never thought of it quite that way.

'I've never worked with twins before, but with all kids, brother and brother, brother and sister, sister and sister, one is the leader. I'm betting that's true even of twins. So I'm asking which one follows the other's lead.'

'Suzanne's a little more mature. Girls are at that age.'

'So her brother would probably go along with her in an unusual situation?'

'I think either one would go along with the other, if it seemed important.'

He nodded and slipped a new cassette in the recorder. 'All right, tell me all you can about the house where they are now. The people in it. Their lives. Their routine. Whatever you can.'

Now, while she talked, he broke in often with questions and took notes. He showed particular interest in Samir and Soraya. What did Dina think of them? What did they think of her? She told him that Samir disapproved of her, while Soraya seemed more sympathetic. Sometimes she felt as if she and Soraya had something in common. Maybe nothing more than that they were the wives of brothers, or women in a man's world. But something.

Dozens of questions. What was the neighbourhood like? Were there other children in the house? Servants? Where was grocery shopping done? When? By whom? Were the Ahmads strongly religious? What was the family's actual relationship with the power structure in Jordan?

She answered everything to which she had an answer. The family was religious, but not intensely so. They did know a great many important people, including the royal family. 'In case he didn't tell you, that's the part that seemed to throw your friend, Einhorn,' she said.

Constantine nodded, as if Karim's connections were of no great concern. Dina began to feel a little better about this man. He seemed to be even more thorough than Einhorn. Not to mention involved.

Finally he closed the notebook and clicked off the tape recorder.

'I'm going to do a little research here,' he said. 'Talk to some people, lay a little groundwork. A few days at most. Then I'm going to have to go over there, take a look for myself. I'm telling you because it's on your ticket.'

'I understand. All right.'

'Give me a week, maybe two, overall. Once I've seen the layout, done a few other things, we'll decide on a plan.'

'Any idea what . . . the nature of the plan will be?'

He shrugged. 'Not yet. Every job is different.' He was silent for a moment as if reflecting on missions past. 'The best job is the one that doesn't happen,' he told her. 'The one where the two parents work it out together.'

'That doesn't seem likely, I'm afraid.'

Again he shrugged. 'It happens sometimes.'

It occurred to her that she was putting her hopes in this man's hands, yet knew almost nothing about him. 'How did you get into this work?' she asked.

The corners-of-the-mouth smile. 'By accident. Someone had a problem, a friend of a friend. Asked me if I could do anything. I looked into it. Things worked out. Next thing I knew, someone else was asking me for the same kind of help. I found out that I was good at it and I liked it. Decided I might as well try to scratch out a living at it.'

'You were with the police?'

'At one time. You're asking about my qualifications.' The smile. 'When I was a kid I made the mistake of joining the Marines. Mainly to tweak my old man—I was going to Columbia at the time. Anyway, it was such a dumb decision that naturally I ended up in so-called Naval Intelligence. I re-upped a couple of times, might have been a lifer if I could stand the system. But I couldn't. Then I was with the NYPD a few years. Now and then I did something for the old outfit—on a freelance basis, you might say. They called me back for the Gulf War. Which is lucky for us.'

'You know Jordan?' Dina asked.

'Not really. But I happened to work with a couple of Jordanians. Very closely. Did a pretty big favour for one of them. So we won't be exactly alone on the ground over there.'

'That's good news.' It was. *Very* good, Dina thought. 'You like what you do now?' she asked.

'Yeah. I do. The jobs I take, they're—well, they're like yours. I feel like I'm on the right side, you know? Doing some good for someone. The kids.'

'Tell me about one of your jobs,' Dina said. 'I don't mean the confidential details. Just . . . what happened. How things turned out.' She remembered Einhorn's description of the dramatic helicopter rescue in Belgium.

Constantine thought it over. 'Mexico, last year. Guy out in Oregon, American, well off, cleaned out the accounts, took the kid—a boy, six years old—put him in the Mercedes and headed off for an early retirement in Margaritaville.' He took a sip of coffee. 'I had a couple of contacts down there. Found out this guy wasn't popular with the locals. Including the cops. He was a cheapskate, in a place where if you've got money you're supposed to spread it around a little. He never spread it around anywhere, except with some of the women. One of whom happened to be a big favourite of a police captain.' Constantine shook his head at the man's folly.

'So I went to this Mexican cop. What I paid him was probably just a fraction of what it would have taken if he hadn't had a personal grudge. I flew my client down from Portland, and that very night they busted the dad in his villa. Drug raid. They found enough cocaine that he'll probably be in a Mexican prison until the kid's grown. The mom was right there to take custody of the kid, all the papers ready and a good Mexican lawyer at her side.'

'The dad was a drug dealer?' Dina asked.

'I said they found it. I don't know how it got there.' He seemed to brood over this. 'I didn't like that part, but something along those lines was probably going to happen anyway.'

It was about as far from the grab-and-run helicopter escape as possible. Dina found herself oddly comforted by that fact.

'Don't count on your situation being that easy.' Constantine warned. 'It probably won't.' He rose, gathering his recorder and notebook, and softened this message with one last smile. 'Thanks for the coffee. Talk with you soon.'

And he was gone.

WHEN THE PHONE rang at seven in the morning, Dina knew it was Karim. He greeted her pleasantly and began to give her news of the twins. He had hired a tutor, he told her. 'They've really taken to the Arabic lessons,' he said enthusiastically. 'The tutor says he's never had such bright pupils.'

Silence. Did he have any idea what torture this was for her?

'They'll be starting school in a couple of months. I'm sure they'll keep up well.' Apparently he thought Dina would find this reassuring.

'The children belong with me,' she said stiffly, knowing it would do no good. 'Do you think I won't fight you on this?' Stupid, she thought. She wasn't supposed to let him know she was planning to fight in any way.

'I'm sorry, Dina,' he replied gently, sounding as if he meant it, 'but I've made up my mind. I'm doing what's best for them. You can fight all you want, but it won't change anything. Ask your lawyer. He'll tell you.'

And then he hung up.

Always after Karim's calls, there were tears. The difference this time was that she knew she had taken a step towards getting her children back.

DINA STOOD for a long moment gazing at the gold letters on the window: *Mosaic*. And in smaller letters: *Floral Designs by Dina*. The sight of her business usually gave her a small *frisson* of pride, but now she wondered if that pride had somehow cost too much.

Dina turned the key and went in. Mosaic was officially closed—today was Sunday—which gave her exactly what she wanted: a little time alone in the place where she had spent the hours away from her family.

Above Dina's desk was a photograph of her signature piece, the one that had been in such demand ever since she had made it for the awards banquet following the New York Marathon. She had taken her inspiration from the speech former mayor David Dinkins had made some years ago, when he'd described New York as a gorgeous mosaic. She had loved that sentiment, the concept of people of all races and nationalities bringing the richness of their diversity to this one place. Like her marriage, she'd once believed. She had fashioned a mosaic of flowers, bright blooms intricately woven together in a kaleidoscope of colours and complementary fragrances.

Once upon a time, Karim had appeared proud of her ability to design beautiful things. And yet . . . had their marriage really been a mosaic even then, with all the pieces fitting perfectly? How many times had he talked about how things were done 'back home'? And how many times had she reminded him that the children were only half Jordanian? She believed that she had tried to compromise, to blend—but had she really?

As always, the fragrance of flowers permeated the air of the small shop. She breathed deeply and willed herself to be strong. She wanted her children to feel her presence, to know she was thinking of them in between their brief moments on the telephone. Perhaps a letter . . . but could she be sure that it would reach the children? She had to try.

On impulse, she picked up her sketch pad and her coloured pencils. She drew a pair of conjoined hearts made of pink and blue flowers. Not original, perhaps even trite—but her audience wouldn't care. She wrote Ali's name, then Suzanne's within the hearts; below, she wrote: *I love you.* She put the sketch into a DHL envelope and wrote her in-laws' address on the air bill.

She spent the next two hours reviewing her books. Eileen was doing a good job running the business. Until she found a way to get her twins back, Dina could work mostly at home and fax her sketches to the shop, where an expert European florist would bring her designs to life. She wondered why she hadn't considered working like this before Karim left. Was it because that would have seemed a concession to him? Had they reached a stage where pleasing him would have seemed a kind of surrender?

She couldn't know. She locked up the shop, dropped the DHL envelope off at a box on the next corner, and took a taxi down to the Village, to her parents' apartment.

'YOUR FATHER'S much better today,' her mother said in response to Dina's question. Dina wanted to believe her.

Joseph Hilmi was stretched out on a lounge on the terrace. Though the day was warm, her mother had laid a light blanket over his legs, a reminder that he was fragile and not to be upset.

So when he asked, 'What's wrong, *elbe*?' the tenderness in his voice startled her. The endearment—'my heart'—she hadn't heard it for years.

'Nothing's wrong, Daddy. I'm fine.'

He shook his head impatiently. 'Why didn't you bring the children?'

It took all her self-control not to break. Gone were the days when she could throw herself into her father's arms and ask him to make everything right. 'Oh,' she said, striving for a casual tone, 'didn't Mom tell you? Karim took them to Jordan. Maha isn't well, and he thought a visit with the children might cheer her up.'

Her father's expression didn't change. 'Are things all right between you and Karim? Is he treating you the way he should? Because if he's not . . .'

Had her mother let something slip, she wondered, something to do with Karim? She thought for a minute, then decided a half-truth would be easier to sustain than a lie. 'We have our differences.'

'Of course. What couple doesn't?'

'Karim would like me to behave in more traditional ways. Stay home with the children. Dress more conservatively. You know.'

Joseph nodded. 'Yes, I see.'

'What do you see, Daddy? Please tell me.'

He reached over and squeezed her hand. He spoke slowly, as if choosing each word carefully. 'When Karim began courting you, he seemed a well-balanced fellow. Well educated, somewhat worldly, which I counted a good thing for a Muslim. Or a Christian, for that matter. In any event, I've seen Karim change over the years. Or perhaps the face he showed me was like a suit of clothes he'd acquired in the West and which no longer fitted him . . .'

Dina listened intently. 'But why didn't you say anything?'

'Say what? That your Jordanian husband is perhaps becoming more like his father?' Joseph shrugged, as if to say, What would have been the use of such a conversation?

So. Was it her fault after all for not seeing what others had seen? But what could she have done? Stolen the children away herself and run away? To where? She sighed. 'I don't want you to worry, Daddy. We'll work all this out, I promise.'

THE CALL she'd been waiting for finally came. John Constantine was using a phone card and a public telephone in the lobby of the Inter-Continental Jordan, in Amman. 'I'm here,' he said simply. 'I just wanted to let you know that I've made contact with the friend I mentioned to you. After I grab a few hours sleep, I'll meet him and we'll go from there.'

And that was all. She hated to hang up the phone, to break the connection between her and the man who was going to make her life whole.

'ALL RIGHT,' said Sarah, taking charge of a discussion that threatened to become a quarrel. 'You hired the man without discussing it with anyone?'

'Yes.' Dina glared at her friends across her kitchen table, daring them to give her grief at a time like this.

Em ignored the look. 'This guy sounds like a cowboy.'

Dina had recited the brief résumé that Constantine had given her.

'Maybe a cowboy is what I need,' she said.

'Have you talked with David about this?' Sarah asked.

'I haven't talked with anyone. You two are the first to know.'

'Hmmph,' said Em, miffed at being left out of the decision-making process.

'And he's in Jordan right now?' Sarah asked.

'Yes. He arrived earlier today. He's just checking things out.'

Sarah got up from the table. 'Be right back,' she said.

There was a long silence. 'Dina . . .' Em began tentatively, 'do you think it's a good idea for you to be sitting in this house all alone while . . . while all this is going on? I mean, maybe you need to get out more. Just—'

Dina shook her head. 'I feel like I should be here. For the phone calls . . . all of them. Karim's. Constantine's. Anything.'

'Well, how about I spend the night with you tonight? Michael can manage fine without me . . . I'll ask Sean to stay over, keep an eye on things.'

Dina started to protest that she didn't need a baby sitter, then stopped herself. Her days were bad enough, but the nights were even worse. 'I'd like that. If you're sure . . . '

'I'm sure. We'll have an old-fashioned girls' pyjama party. We'll eat junk food and popcorn and just hang out.'

'Who's eating junk food and popcorn?' Sarah asked as she came back into the room and resumed her seat at the table. 'What did I miss?'

'Nothing. I'm just spending the night with Dina, that's all. Maybe we'll have a pizza party. On second thoughts, maybe I'll make jambalaya.'

'Can I come, too?' Sarah asked, sounding like a kid.

'Nope. You can come over tomorrow. If Dina won't leave this damn house, then we'll just have to keep her company.'

'OK. Oh—I just called David. He says this Constantine is good. He said he would have recommended him in the first place, but he thought the guy worked for Greg Einhorn.'

'You told David?' Dina asked. 'You just called him up and discussed it?'

Sarah flushed. 'Well, he asked me to keep in touch.'

'When?' Em probed.

'Last night,' Sarah replied, poking at an imaginary crumb on the table.

'I see,' said Em, infusing the words with a rainbow of meaning.

'Oh, yes, I see, too,' Dina joined in, glad of the diversion, glad to escape for a moment into the teasing that was firmly rooted in affection.

Sarah's colour ripened into a deep pink. 'It was just dinner.'

'Just dinner, hmm,' Em went on. 'And how long has this been going on?'

'This is just a couple of dinners,' Sarah protested, but weakly.

'That's what you say today, sugar. But who knows where a couple of dinners might lead?'

'Nowhere,' said Sarah firmly. 'They're leading nowhere.'

LATER THAT NIGHT, after a splendid dinner of Em's jambalaya and a dessert of homemade bread pudding, the two women changed into soft, comfortable sweats and perched on Dina's king-size bed.

'Thanks,' Dina said.

'For what, cher?'

'For everything. For dinner. For being my friend.'

'You're welcome. Now tell me the truth. How are you holding up?'

Dina shrugged. 'I'm not going to lie and say I'm fine—but I'm not after a pity party either.' She thought for a moment. 'Let's talk about you. How's it going with Sean? You haven't said much about him lately?'

'There's not a lot to say. We have fun, but longer term . . . I don't know.'

'Is that because of what happened with Gabe? I mean, I never really understood what happened with Gabe. All you've ever said was that he was a musician. And that he left soon after you had Michael.'

Em smiled. 'He's doing OK now. Sends cards from different places. Sends a cheque now and then and asks me to buy something nice for Michael. Hasn't seen our son in I don't know how many years.'

Dina thought about that, about her own situation. 'But at least you have Michael. He's yours—and Gabe has never tried to take him from you.'

'Yeah. Guess I never appreciated Gabe's lack of interest in his son.' She looked at Dina's face. 'I'm sorry, cher, that wasn't funny.'

'Nothing is funny when marriages get broken, when kids are in the middle of the mess. At the beginning, you never believe your relationship can get so messy, so . . . cruel.'

Em closed her eyes; her face took on a dreamy expression. 'At the beginning, it was just pure magic with Gabe and me. The way it can only be when you're young. There I was, the best cook in Grosse Tête. Folks came from miles around for my sweet potato pie, my chicken and sausage gumbo. I didn't mind working hard then. Supporting Gabe. And then we got lucky. Or so we thought. Gabe's band made a record, and Lord, it was a hit. Played all over, not just Grosse Tête or New Orleans, but all over the south. It might have been just fine if we'd stayed where we were. But Gabe would go to New York. I told him New York was a different kind of place. But he would not listen. He acted like I was trying to cheat him of his big chance. So we came.' She sighed deeply. 'Only one good thing happened in New York. We made Michael.'

Dina smiled again. There was so much tenderness in her friend's voice when she spoke her son's name.

'The rest is . . . not so great. Well, Gabe was playing weddings and small clubs and he's barely making enough to pay the band's expenses. And his big-city success never came. Meanwhile, I was working like a dog, right up until the time I delivered Michael. It got worse after Michael was born. We never had enough of anything. Then one day Gabe just left. We didn't have a big fight or anything like that. He just left. Took eleven hundred dollars we had in the bank. And I didn't hear from him for almost a year. Then he sent back the money. No note. Just eleven hundred dollars.' Em paused. 'I guess he did me a favour, though I sure didn't see it that way then.'

Dina knew the next part of the story. Em had got a job in a popular Louisiana-style restaurant in Manhattan, started as a sous-chef, took over the kitchen when the chef left to open his own place. Food critics came, proclaimed her a rising star. Later, she opened a restaurant of her own. A recipe book followed. Em did it all: dabbled in interior design, in a casual, unstudied way. Then put it all together in what she modestly referred to as a 'little' cable show—though, in fact, the show had brilliant ratings. She sold the restaurant and then made some excellent investments. Now her agent was flogging her show for prime time.

'Did you ever see Gabe again after he left?' Dina asked now.

'Yes, once. When Michael was three, I took him back home to Grosse Tête, to see his grandparents. Well, you know how a small-town telegraph works . . . long story short, Gabe heard we were coming. And he just turned up one day, smiling that smile, asked if he could see his son.'

'What did you do?' Dina asked.

'Well, he promised to do better if I'd let him see Michael. So I did. Michael was shy at first, but he warmed up to Gabe. Most people do. Anyway, Gabe sort of kept his promise. He sends cheques for Michael— and postcards from the towns on the Texas–California zydeco circuit. I knew Gabe's career picked up after a while because the cards started coming from cities in Canada and France. Once in a while, he'll call . . . sometimes Michael will take the call, sometimes he won't.'

'What does Michael say about Gabe?'

Em shook her head. 'He's hurt and angry . . . I don't blame him. But I don't want him to poison himself with bad feelings. So I tell him: "I'm sorry you don't have the daddy you deserve, honey—because Lord knows you deserve the best. But Gabriel LeBlanc is what he is. I believe he loves you in his way, even if it isn't nearly enough. Best you make peace with what is—if you don't want to grow up to be an angry man."'

'And what does he say?' Dina asked.

'He says, "Humph",' Em replied with a smile, knowing how much her son sounded like her.

They talked a little longer, but eventually Dina drifted off to sleep, and Em followed soon after.

CONSTANTINE LOOKED tired. And, of course, he'd brought no children. But Dina had hurried to their meeting place, a classic Paris bistro transplanted to Greenwich Village. From the exchange of good-humoured insults between Constantine and the bartender, Dina gathered that they were old acquaintances. He ordered a substantial glass of 'the usual', which turned out to be Black Bush Irish whiskey. A glass of white wine for her. And then came the report. It was not encouraging.

'The kids are in the house almost all the time,' he said. 'I only saw them twice. Both times in cars. Once with their father and once with the sister-in-law and a woman about my age—probably the nanny.'

'Fatma.'

'Probably. I couldn't do my best street stake-out. I can pass for European in Amman, but not for a local. Most of the time I was using binoculars from a little hotel a quarter-mile up a hill. I didn't see any serious security. But the house is busy. People there, coming and going all the time.'

'Karim has lots of close relatives,' Dina said. 'It's a typical Arab family.'

Constantine nodded. 'That's a problem. The only good time to get the kids would be when they're outside the house. Without so many people around. From what I saw, that doesn't happen very often.'

Dina's shoulders slumped. 'So what can we do?'

'We need help from someone in the household—to learn the routine.'

'Who? Do you mean a family member?'

'Maybe your sister-in-law? You said she wasn't unfriendly towards you.' He paused. 'But actually I was thinking of you. You've got permission to visit the twins. Maybe we should use it.'

And that became the beginning of a plan. It was sketchy at first—and Constantine cautioned Dina that it might take more than one visit to get what they needed. On the other hand, opportunity could arise at any time. They would need to be prepared to move quickly.

'Your husband has resources that we don't,' he cautioned. 'And he'll use his connections. So you'll need to be careful. I bought you a secure cellphone to use when you get to Amman. You won't call me directly. We'll make contact through the friend I mentioned . . . we'll call him the Major. And if I need to, I can hire one or two good men I've worked with before.'

Could she do it? Dina wondered. Could she face Karim and pretend that she'd accepted what he'd done, that she would be content to be an occasional visitor in the twins' lives? Could she face her in-laws who had never been fond of her to begin with? And most important, would she be able to get whatever information Constantine needed to bring her children home?

'SO,' SAID SARAH, 'this is it. You're going through with this crazy scheme.'

'Yep,' said Dina. They were sitting in her kitchen sipping tea.

'I'll say it just once more,' Sarah said. 'I don't like it. I don't like it at all.'

'Of course you don't like it,' Em put in. 'You think Dina likes it? Nobody likes it. Liking it's not the point.'

'I'm open to a better plan if anyone has one,' Dina said, a little defensively. She had plenty of misgivings about the whole thing herself, but she felt that this was the time for support, not doubts, from her best friends.

'That's just it,' said Sarah. 'What plan? I mean, it sounds to me like you're both winging it, you and this detective or whatever he is.'

'Well, we can't make a plan until I get there and see the lay of the land.'

Sarah shook her head. 'Do you realise how dangerous this might be? David says'—Em and Dina exchanged a look—'that you could end up in a lot of trouble. Even in prison. I mean, we're talking about the Middle East here.'

'Oh, come on, Sarah. Jordan isn't Afghanistan or someplace like that.'

'Dina's from the Middle East,' Em pointed out. 'Her dad is, is what I mean,' she added quickly. 'And besides, she's been to Jordan before . . .'

'Yeah, with her husband,' Sarah pointed out.

Dina and Em both glared at her.

Sarah threw up her hands. 'OK, OK, you're gonna do it, I know. We know. I just wanted to . . . sound a little note of caution.'

'I appreciate that,' Dina said, meaning it. 'Look, I'm not some kid going off on a lark here. I'm a little scared, if you want to know the truth.' More than a little, she thought. Getting on that plane the day after tomorrow was going to be like stepping off a cliff in the dark.

'Scared is good,' said Sarah. 'Scared can stop you taking crazy chances.'

Now it was Em's turn to raise the caution flag. 'John Constantine doesn't sound like he's scared,' she said. 'I just hope he knows what he's doing.'

'He's a professional,' Dina said simply. 'I trust his judgment.'

'Well, OK, then,' said Sarah. 'So the main thing is what we can do.' Em leaned forward to show that she was with Sarah on this. 'Money, something. I mean, this is going to cost a bundle, and—'

'Let's just see how it goes,' Dina cut in. 'If it goes well, great. If not, I might need both of you more than any of us want to think about. If something goes wrong, I might need money. I might need someone like David. And if things go really wrong, I might need somebody to look out for Jordy.'

'Don't you dare talk like that,' Em said. 'Don't you dare. You know we'd do anything for you—or your kids. But I don't want any more of that "if anything happens to me" kind of talk, you hear?'

'I hear. Anyway,' Dina added breezily, 'you're both on standby. Remember the time difference when you get a call from me at three a.m.'

'No problem,' said Sarah. Em nodded.

Food was ordered, delivered and consumed, then Dina said it was time to call it a night. She had calls to make, to her parents and to Jordy.

'All right, guys,' she said, as she saw her friends to the door. 'This is it.'

Suddenly they were all hugging. There were tears. Last-minute warnings. Promises to take care. Then her friends were gone and Dina was alone.

Oh God, she wondered, what's going to happen to me? Am I really going to get my babies back?

THE FINAL meeting with Constantine, at the same bistro, was brief and to the point. 'I'll be flying out with you, but don't talk to me on the plane. Don't even look at me. When you arrive, remember you're playing a part. Your husband has the upper hand; he has your children. All you want is to spend some time with them. And to keep that possibility open in the future, you have to stay on good terms with him. Remember that when you're tempted to belt him one in the chops.'

Dina smiled. 'I'll try to remember.'

Constantine did not smile back. Dina supposed he was in his 'mission' mode now, totally focused on the work ahead. Good, she thought.

He passed her a piece of paper. 'This is the number of the contact we'll be using. As I told you before, we'll call him the Major. He's a good man and completely trustworthy. You'll call him if you need to communicate anything. And if there's any kind of opportunity where we can reasonably expect to take the children without any trouble, get in touch with him as soon as you can.' He passed her another piece of paper. 'This is the number of the pager I'll be using over there. For emergency use only.'

'I understand.'

'Good. Now, do you have any last-minute questions?'

She started to shake her head, then stopped. 'I just want to know . . . do you think we have a chance? A good chance?'

He reached over and squeezed her hand. 'If I didn't, we wouldn't be getting on that plane tomorrow.'

CHAPTER 5

As the jet descended from the northwest, Dina had a travelogue view of Amman. The white city, as it was called, for the white stone houses that sprawled over nineteen hills. When she'd seen it for the first time, on her way to her wedding, she'd felt as if she were flying into a fairy tale, a place where history reached back for centuries.

Karim and his parents had wanted the wedding to be held in Jordan, where their friends could easily attend. Dina had persuaded her parents it was what she wanted, too. Back then, she *had* wanted to make him happy, and in the end she had loved her wedding, which had been a spectacular affair. There had been parties for an entire week, and extravagant gifts of jewellery from Karim. The guest list for the reception included a troop of foreign diplomats and members of the Jordanian royal family.

The fairy tale continued in the weeks ahead. The lazy days and dreamy nights aboard Karim's yacht. The long drives to explore the country he loved so much. She'd had no sense of compromise then, no sense of 'giving in' by doing what made Karim happy. She had been happy, too. No one could have asked for a more romantic honeymoon.

Yet when things changed between them, he wanted things that did not make her happy. She'd noted every compromise she made, kept score. And now she understood that Karim had kept a scorecard of his own. She looked out of the window again. Somewhere down there were Suzanne and Ali.

Moments later the airliner landed at Queen Alia Airport. At the terminal, travellers in Western clothes mixed with robed Arabs from the Gulf and women wearing headscarfs and long dresses. Karim was waiting when she cleared Customs. He was alone. He had told her that he would not be bringing the children to the airport, but still it was a disappointment.

He looked no different. She wondered if she did. There was an awkward moment when it seemed as if he might want to embrace her in greeting, but if he did, he thought better of it. In the end they simply said hello.

She let him carry her two suitcases. Outside the sky was perfectly clear.

In the car, Karim asked, 'Where are you staying?'

'The Hyatt.'

He nodded. 'Downtown. I could have found you a place closer.'

Then why didn't you? she thought. But that wasn't fair. She hadn't asked for help or advice. She had chosen the hotel because Constantine had said that a large, anonymous, American-style place would be best. She wasn't here as a tourist. All she cared about was her children.

'I'll drop you there,' Karim was saying. 'You can rest awhile, freshen up, then I'll come and get you, bring you out to see the children.'

'I thought we'd go straight there.'

'You've got to be tired. And they're with their tutor until afternoon.'

All right. No need for a battle. She *was* tired.

They rode in silence, the city reaching out to meet them. Amman's ancient roots were visible through its modern façade. Roman ruins overlooked the bustling downtown; gleaming white contemporary buildings and smart new villas coexisted with turn-of-the-century stone houses; chic boutiques competed with old markets and souks. The city had grown since Dina had first come here. The last time she'd been here with Karim, he'd informed her proudly that the population was 1.5 million. It seemed to be still growing.

Karim tapped a finger nervously on the steering wheel. 'One thing I wanted to talk about, since we have this opportunity.'

Just one? Dina thought, but said nothing.

'I really haven't told my family the whole story,' Karim went on. 'About Jordy, for example. Or even about us. I told them we've separated, that we had some problems. I've come home with the twins. Nothing more definite than that, really.'

'You're saying they think we're trying to work things out?'

He shifted uneasily in his seat. 'Let's just say I've been a little vague. Purposely. I think it's best for everyone, including Ali and Suzanne.'

Dina fought back anger. 'So you want me to go along with this charade. Pretend everything's just fine, except that you took two of my children.'

'*Our* children, Dina. But that is not the point. I just think it's best for the kids not to think we're at each other's throats. And we're *not*.'

'If you're worried about the children, maybe you should have left them in their home. No, what you're worried about is what Daddy and Mommy and Little Brother might think, God forbid they should think their darling first-born son left his wife and kidnapped his own children.'

Karim's jaw tightened. 'Look, you're right to be angry. I wish things had worked out better too, but . . . I've done what I think is best for the children. I'm going to keep doing that. You see it your way. I understand that. But I won't have it spilling over in front of the kids. My family has nothing to do with it. They would support me no matter what.'

Dina made no answer.

'All I'm asking is that we don't go into all the unpleasant details. Don't you agree that's best? Because if you don't . . .' He sighed. 'Then I'd really rather you didn't see the children. Even now.'

She knew that he meant what he said. Nothing she could say or do would change his mind. And he held the two trump cards. For now, at least.

'Don't worry,' she told him grimly. 'I'll be the perfect little separated Stepford Wife. Just tell me when I can see the twins.'

Relief showed in his face. 'Sure. You can come for dinner if you like. Or after. Either one would be fine.'

'After, I guess.' She felt uncomfortable at the thought of sitting round the dinner table with all the Ahmads eyeing her.

'Fine.'

The Hyatt could have been in Los Angeles, palm trees and all. Karim tipped the porter who took her bags, and they said goodbye at the door.

The lobby was a vast expense of marble and steel. If the clerk had any doubts about registering a woman travelling alone, she didn't detect them. This is Jordan, she reminded herself. Women have rights here: they run businesses; they even hold political office.

The window of her room overlooked the hotel's swimming pool and beyond that a sweeping view of the city. In the near distance a blue dome marked the King Abdullah Mosque, completed a dozen or so years ago—Dina could remember seeing it under construction.

She glanced at the phone. The message light was dark. She doubted that Constantine would leave a message here. So it was up to her to make contact with the man he'd called the Major. And then . . . and then, what?

Suddenly it all seemed absurd and impossible, like being trapped in some bad television show. She was too weary, too angry, too lost to cry. She lay on the bed and closed her eyes.

AT THE SIGHT of her children, Dina felt as if her heart would burst. 'Mommy, Mommy!' the twins shouted in unison, throwing their arms round her. How beautiful they were, Dina thought. Their chubby faces were lightly tanned, their dark eyes glowing with health and energy.

'Come see the jungle gym,' Ali insisted, fairly dragging her to the garden.

'Daddy and Uncle Samir just finished putting it up,' Suzy said proudly. 'Daddy hurt his finger and said bad words and *Jiddo* heard and yelled at him!'

Dina smiled in spite of herself, and hugged Suzy again. But she hated the new installation; it spoke to her of permanence.

Soraya brought her a cool and welcome lemonade. Dina smiled tentatively at her sister-in-law, offered her hand. Soraya took it, then moved in for a hug. 'Welcome, Dina.' The gesture warmed her. Maybe this wouldn't be so difficult. Her other in-laws greeted her stiffly, but correctly.

Karim was the soul of graciousness, polite to a fault. Showing her what a reasonable man he was, no doubt. But as the evening progressed, Dina saw something beyond the show, something real. Karim was happy here, she realised. And to her great dismay, so, too, were her children. They'd missed her, of course, but it was clear that they had a full and fun-filled life here: picnics in the gardens surrounding the home, pony rides, cousins to play with, a big, extended family—and more attention than they'd ever had.

As she watched them climb the jungle gym, she felt off balance, a little disorientated. She had come to slay dragons, but there didn't seem to be any dragons here. What she saw was the kind of life Karim had always wanted: there was always time for children and family, for a visit with neighbours, for news and gossip over the never-ending cup of dark, sweet coffee. For a fleeting and painful moment, she thought: Maybe I'm the one who has been wrong all along. No, she told herself, I can't afford to think like that.

'It's better here than it is in New York, Mommy,' Ali declared. 'Are you going to stay with us now?'

'For a while,' she replied evasively, watching Maha's lips tighten. What else could she say, surrounded by Karim's family? And what answer would make sense to the twins? She smiled noncommittally and held her babies.

When she glanced up, Karim was smiling too, his expression tender and loving. 'It's a beautiful picture, Dina . . . you and our children. It's the way things should be,' he said softly. 'It's the way I always hoped we would be.'

She wanted to be angry. But when she attempted an icy stare, she saw not the monster who stole her children but the man she had fallen in love with a long time ago. His smile was warm and genuine and a little sad.

And now it was time to say good night to her children, to leave them and return to her cool, impersonal hotel room. She kissed her twins, hugged them hard. And then there were tears in her eyes.

Karim guided her to his Mercedes. She closed her eyes and pressed her head back against the headrest, uncomfortable with the silence, yet too weary to make conversation.

'Dina . . .'

'Yes?'

'I know this is difficult for you, but wouldn't you rather spend all your time here with the children, rather than travelling back and forth?'

'What are you saying?' she asked, knowing the answer.

'I'm saying that it would make sense for you to stay at the house. There's plenty of room.'

Stay under the same roof with the enemy Fatma and the in-laws who probably couldn't wait until Karim got himself a new wife? And yet . . . what better way to look for opportunities? It might be difficult to communicate with Constantine's friend, the Major, without being overheard, but she could always step out into the garden and pretend to be calling New York.

'Yes,' she said, after an appropriate pause to show her reluctance. 'Yes,' she repeated. 'I don't want to waste precious time away from my children. Thank you, Karim,' she forced out. 'That's a very considerate offer.'

THE MAJOR was not what she expected. With his silver hair and matching handlebar moustache, he looked like someone's jolly old uncle—or even grandfather—not someone who had ever been in Constantine's line of work, whatever that had been. Yet Constantine had hinted that they had, over the course of years, exchanged favours. And now, after a few cryptic phone calls, here was the Major, seated across the table from her, at a tiny café about a mile from the hotel.

'Be sure to walk,' he had instructed. 'If you see anyone who appears to be following you, return to the hotel. I'll call to make another appointment.'

Dina had done what she'd been told. And she had not been followed, she was reasonably sure of that. There were no introductions. When he spotted Dina, the Major stood up and held a chair for her.

When she was seated, he said, 'So—you are the brave lady who has been separated from her children.'

Startled to hear herself described as brave, Dina blushed. 'I . . . I suppose that would be me.'

The Major smiled broadly. 'And modest, as well. I can see why our friend admires you.'

Another surprise. Constantine admired her? But why?

'So—tell me what has happened since you arrived.'

'I've been to the house. To see the children. My . . . the children's father invited me to stay at the house. So I could have more time with them.'

'And you accepted?'

'Yes.'

'*Brava*. That was excellent. Now you will be able to give our friend the information he needs. But,' he added quickly, 'you must be careful. If you arouse suspicion, that will make his task more difficult.'

'I understand.'

'Is there anything I can do for you, dear lady? Anything that will help?'

She thought for a long moment. 'Pray for me,' she said simply. 'Pray that I will somehow get my children back.'

He smiled tenderly. 'That I will do, dear lady, and with all my heart.'

DINA CLOSED her eyes and let the stillness settle over her. The cool breeze from the garden carried the scent of jacaranda and night-blooming jasmine. The quiet eased her tension, and she had just begun to drift, remembering when she had slept in this house, in this very room with Karim, when she heard a tapping at her door. She got up, walked barefoot.

It was Karim. 'What is it?' she asked. 'Is something wrong? The twins?'

He shook his head. 'No,' he said quietly. 'I just wanted to talk. Alone. With your permission.'

'Yes . . . yes, of course,' she agreed.

He moved towards her and she stepped back hastily. Did Karim imagine that he could pretend they were still man and wife after what he'd done? But he sat down on the room's single chair and gave her the sad smile she had seen more than once since she'd arrived. She sat down on the bed.

He sighed deeply. 'Dina,' he said, 'is there no hope for us?'

Was he mad? she thought. 'How can you talk about hope for us when you took my children like a thief in the night? I believed we were going to counselling. But all along, you were plotting, laughing behind my back—'

'I was never laughing, Dina,' he cut in. 'It broke my heart to leave you. And as for your counselling, it's a joke. Half the people in New York are in counselling—and most of them get divorced. I knew you wouldn't listen if I told you the truth. I want our children to grow up to be decent adults with good family values. Not . . .' He trailed off, unwilling to speak Jordan's name.

Dina sighed. What was the point in trying to reason with Karim? 'I'd really like to get some sleep. I want to make the most of my time with the children,' she added, more sharply than she'd intended.

He got the point, flushed beneath his deep tan. 'Of course,' he said a little stiffly. 'I didn't mean to . . . to interfere with your rest.'

But after he left she felt as if sleep would be a long time coming. Karim's plaintive plea, his hangdog demeanour, his . . . sincerity. She could believe he did still care for her. But that made matters even worse. Because if he did indeed care, and he was still capable of this, then there was no hope for anything. Except John Constantine.

IF HER first day under her in-laws' roof had been difficult, Dina's next morning was near impossible. The breakfast table was certainly inviting, laden with fresh pitta bread, cheese and olives, as well as pastries from one of Amman's Western bakeries.

But the atmosphere was far from inviting. After a cursory 'Good morning', Samir ignored her. 'I hear great things about you, brother,' he said to Karim. 'I hear that you have a great future at the ministry.'

Karim shrugged. 'I'm simply doing the job I was brought here to do.'

'You're being too modest,' Samir persisted. '*W'Allah*, I know your children will be very proud of you. As they should be.'

'Yes, indeed,' Maha chimed in. 'Anyone with any sense would know what a fine, upstanding man our Karim is. And would respect him accordingly.'

Dina flushed.

Soraya leaned towards her. 'Dina, would you like to try one of these excellent croissants? They're very good with my homemade jam.'

Soraya earned herself a stern look from Samir and a jab in the side from Maha. Now it was her turn to flush, and she fell silent.

'No. No, thank you,' Dina said softly.

As Fatma shuffled in from the kitchen, bringing fresh coffee, she looked at Dina as she had never dared when she worked in New York: with contempt. Dina couldn't help but return the look.

As soon as she could do so without making a scene, Dina left the table and busied herself with her children. Only they made it possible for her to stay here. They were eager to tell her tales of adventures with their cousins, to describe places and wonders they'd seen.

More than once her fortitude wavered. What did she have to offer that could compete with this idyllic childhood?

It was Suzanne who, innocently enough, gave Dina her answer. She turned serious eyes on her mother and asked, 'Mommy, why did you let Jordan be unnatural?'

Before Dina could even think of an answer, Ali declared fervently that he would rather die than be like his older brother.

No, Dina thought, a place where they will learn to hate and despise their own brother is not a place for my children. An inner voice demanded: But is it better that they grow up in a country that hates and despises their father? Dina's response was quick: Maybe not, but at least they will be with me.

THE PEONIES arrived at five o'clock. Em was having a cup of tea and waiting to hear from Sean, who was having a breakfast interview with a prospective agent, a young woman Em had met during a media event. When Em told her about a talented young actor, she had said she was interested.

And now here were these beautiful flowers. Maybe Michael had reminded Sean that it was her birthday? And had she mentioned that peonies were her favourite flower? The bouquet was huge and clearly expensive. She was touched because she knew Sean couldn't afford such a lavish gift—and because there was no card, an omission that seemed somehow romantic.

He called an hour later. The agent had agreed to take him on. 'Thanks for the introduction, Em,' he added. 'I think this one's going to work out.'

'You're welcome. And Sean—the flowers are beautiful, and I thank you for them. You remembered my birthday!'

There was a long silence. 'I didn't send any flowers, Em. I wish I had. And I wish I'd remembered it was your birthday. But I know now. I'm going to take you out tonight—someplace really nice. I'll pick you up at seven.'

When he hung up, Em contemplated her flowers again. Had Michael sent them? But when he came home from school, he, too, declined to take credit for the peonies. He did give her a beautiful antique perfume bottle. And teased her about a secret admirer. 'Bet old Sean's going to be jealous.'

To Em's annoyance, however, Sean wasn't jealous. If he really cared, he would be a little jealous, she thought. Or at least curious. Em was as curious as hell. The mysterious flowers insinuated themselves into the dinner—a special one, as Sean had promised, at Le Cirque.

The following morning, Em called Dina's assistant, Eileen. 'I'm sorry to bother you, honey, I know you've got your hands full with Dina gone. But I got some flowers without a card yesterday, and I'm dying to find out where they came from. They came through the FTD network. If I give you the name of the local florist, do you think you could find out who sent them?'

Eileen could. She called back an hour later. 'The flowers came from a Mr Gabriel LeBlanc. The order was phoned in from Texas, Houston.'

So he remembered, Em thought. After all this time, he remembered.

WHEN DINA and Suzanne entered the kitchen, Soraya and Karim's mother, Maha, were there, along with a rich aroma of stewing chicken. Maha gave Dina a hard look, stood, and left without another word. Soraya seemed disconcerted by her mother-in-law's rudeness.

'Can I get you something, Dina? Coffee?'

'A glass of water, thanks. And Suzanne was hoping for a snack.'

'Can I have a Pop-Tart?' Suzanne elaborated.

'Why not?' Soraya rummaged in the pantry for the desired treat.

'And one for Lina too?' Suzanne pressed.

Soraya smiled and put two Pop-Tarts into the toaster.

Dina was surprised to see Pop-Tarts in Jordan. 'I passed a supermarket a mile or so away when I was coming in. Do you shop there?'

'Sometimes. In America I think you call them Safeway.'

'See you later!' bubbled Suzanne, taking her prizes with her.

There was an awkward moment. 'They seem to get along well,' Dina said to break the silence.

'Suzanne and Lina? Oh, yes. The boys, too.'

'Well, that's good.' Dina didn't know what else to say. It *was* good that the children got along with their cousins. But in her heart, Dina had hoped that they would be desperately unhappy, begging her to take them home. Instead the only question they had asked was whether *she* would be living here with them. She had told them that, no, this wasn't going to happen.

'Does that mean we'll be going on airplanes a lot?' Ali had asked.

'We haven't got everything worked out. Right now, I'm visiting you *here.*' To her dismay, that had seemed enough for Ali.

'You're here for a few more days?' Soraya asked now.

'Well, another week at least.'

'Ah.' Soraya opened a large pot on the stove and stirred. 'The children have been begging me to take them to the zoo,' she said. 'Since you are here for such a short time, maybe we could go together, before you leave.'

'Sure,' Dina answered quickly. It had suddenly hit her: a place away from the house, away from Karim and the other men. Just her and the children and Soraya. Wouldn't that be the kind of situation Constantine wanted? 'I didn't know Amman had a zoo,' she said to cover her eagerness.

Soraya turned from the stove. 'It's new. It's supposed to be quite nice.'

'Well, thanks,' she said casually. 'I'd like that. Just let me know when.'

'Sunday, I suppose, when there's no school and the twins don't have their tutor. But maybe you'd rather be alone with them, have them to yourself.'

'No, the zoo sounds like fun.'

Soraya gave her a cool, evaluating look. 'I remember when I first met you,' she said. 'I liked you. I admired you. I thought I would like to be like you someday. Can you tell me what happened?'

'With what? Me and Karim?'

'Yes. Or actually no, not unless you want to. I understand you've had trouble between you. What I can't understand is how you—how any woman—could give up her children so easily. Is this something American?'

Dina was stunned. She wanted to shout that she wasn't giving them up, easily or in any other way. Instead she said lamely, 'It's not like that. I'm hoping . . . hoping for the best, I guess.'

'You want to, how do you put it, fix things up?'

'I don't see how that can happen,' Dina said. This was dangerous territory. 'I really can't explain it. Karim and I grew apart, I guess that's the phrase. Only I didn't realise how much. And he wanted to come back here . . . for a while. And bring the twins. It . . . it came as a shock to me.'

Soraya said nothing.

'About that zoo trip,' Dina said, 'I really would like to go. Just let me know.' She stopped herself from adding *as soon as you can.* After all, she was supposed to be the woman without an agenda.

As soon as she could, she would find a way to be alone and she would call the Major. Then she would wait for his instructions.

A FEW tinny bars of Bach sounded in the middle of breakfast. It was Dina's cellphone. She excused herself and took the phone into the next room.

'Hello?'

'Dina Ahmad?' It was the Major. 'Pretend you are talking with one of your friends in New York.'

'Oh, Em! You don't sound like yourself. Must be the connection.'

'Good. Go grocery shopping today. The Safeway supermarket at the Seventh Circle. You know where it is?'

'Yes!'

'Tell me if you can do this today, any time after noon.'

'Yes. We're just eating breakfast. My God, what time is it there?'

'Someone will contact you and give you something. If you are accompanied, try to be alone for a minute. It won't take longer. Can you do this?'

'Oh, yes. I'm having a wonderful time, really. The twins are fine.'

'Our friend's plan is simple. When you are at the zoo, your sister-in-law will have a fainting spell. You will cry for help. During the confusion you will slip away with the twins. Our friend will be there to help. What you will be given at the supermarket today is what will cause your sister-in-law to faint. It's very safe. She won't really faint, only become very sleepy, then sleep. You must make it look as if she has fainted. You understand?'

'Sure. I think so.' Dina was trying to process it all.

'You will be eating at the zoo, yes? Put it in whatever she is drinking. This is important. She will be the only one there who could raise the alarm.'

Dina could see into the dining room, where Karim was looking at her with irritation or suspicion—or both. 'I miss you, too, kiddo.'

'There will be a private plane waiting. There will be no difficulty boarding it. No delay. By the time your sister-in-law awakes, you will be gone.'

'Yes, I'll bring something back for you. If I have time.'

'Clear the callback feature on the cellphone. And the log. Unobtrusively.'

'Sure. But I'll see you soon.'

'Be at the supermarket if you possibly can. The person who gives you the package will also give you a phone number to be used in an emergency. Memorise it and use it only if absolutely necessary. Goodbye, Mrs Ahmad.'

The connection ended. She pretended to be mystified by the phone. As she returned to the table, she pressed buttons that seemed to remove any record of the call she had just received. 'Damn. We must have got cut off.'

'Who was that?' Karim asked.

'Em. Emmeline.'

'What did she want?'

'Oh, she and Sean were out celebrating. He got a commercial.'

Karim sighed. 'I suppose a commercial is cause for celebration in some circles.' He rose and actually smiled. 'I have to get to the office. I hope you all enjoy yourselves while I'm working for the greater benefit of our country.'

'How lucky we women are,' said Soraya, 'that we never have to work.' She looked at Dina and winked.

DINA WAITED till one o'clock before mentioning casually that she wanted to go to the Safeway.

'What for?' Soraya asked. 'We have enough for an army here already.'

'Just some American junk-food type stuff for the kids, for when I'm gone.' Dina felt deeply ashamed about lying to Soraya, not to mention about what she was planning to do the next day, but she saw no way round it. 'And a couple of little things for the picnic at the zoo,' she added brightly.

'How will you get there? I have to go out, I told you.'

Soraya had indeed mentioned that she had a meeting of one of her charity groups at two. That was why Dina had waited this long.

'Oh, I'll just call a cab.'

'Don't be silly. Samir will drive you. Won't you, Samir?'

Samir grunted an assent. He had been hanging about unhappily all day. There was some story about him not being needed at work, but Dina suspected he'd been assigned to keep an eye on her.

There was no way out of it. 'Thank you,' she said.

A half-hour later they pulled into the Safeway lot in Samir's Land Rover.

'I'll only be a few minutes,' Dina told Samir.

'I'll come with you. Help you carry.'

'There won't be much. Nothing I can't handle.'

'I come with you,' he insisted.

She thought fast. 'Maybe you're right. I want to get some Maxi-Pads, and the box is bulky. You can help with that?'

'Maxi-Pads? This is what?'

'You know. For women. For their time of the month.'

Samir paled. 'If you say it's easy, OK,' he said hastily, 'I wait here.'

'No problem.' Dina smiled sweetly.

Inside, she put M&Ms, Froot Loops and several packets of Kool-Aid in her basket. No one appeared even to notice her. She took her time selecting apples for the picnic. She became aware of a man in a business suit who was squeezing avocados for ripeness. He was in his forties, and was studying her more than the avocados. She paused, waiting. He smiled at her but did not approach. She moved out of the produce section, expecting him to follow.

He did, casually and at a distance. Was he the contact, or just some horny local? Damn. Almost forgot the Maxi-Pads. She roamed until she found the aisle. The man was still trailing her, half the length of the aisle away. If he was going to pass her some mysterious package, he needed to get on with it.

'You. Tell me this.'

Dina stepped back, startled. She was confronted by a late-middle-aged woman in very conservative dress and a headscarf. She was brandishing a box of Pampers. 'You. Tell me. Is this the thing they use now for babies? My granddaughter asks me to buy this for my great-grandson.'

'Yes,' Dina stammered. 'Yes, they're for babies.'

'Unh.' The woman stared disapprovingly past Dina down the aisle. Dina turned in time to see the man in the suit beat a retreat.

'I'm Alia,' the woman whispered. 'I am here because a man asks me. If another man asks, I say no, let Americans take care of Americans.'

Dina stared. This was her contact, then?

The woman grasped her hand and, in a normal voice, said, 'Thank you, daughter, for your help.' Dina felt a small, hard object pressed into her palm. Alia's voice dropped again. 'Don't look. Put it away. Now look at this.'

She held up the Pampers. Stuck to the package was a small Post-it note with what appeared to be a phone number written on it.

'Memorise it—now,' said the woman who called herself Alia. 'Call it only in the last circumstance. If you cannot do the thing you wish to do.'

Dina tried to engrave the number on her mind. 'I understand,' she said.

Alia looked at her as if true understanding was quite beyond the capacities of such a neophyte, and an American to boot. 'You have the number?'

'I think so. Yes.'

Alia wadded the Post-it into a tiny ball. 'Use all of the medicine. It is strong, but harmless. It will cause sleep in five minutes. No more than ten.'

'It's safe?'

'Do you listen at all? One more thing: wear sunglasses. The person you are meeting will wear them as well. If either of you suspect something is wrong, you will push the glasses up on your head. That will cancel the action.'

Alia touched her lips, and Dina realised that she had eaten the Post-it. 'Thank you, daughter, once again. May God give you great-grandchildren as well.' With that, she turned and was gone.

Dina checked to see that no one was watching, then put the thing she had been given under the waistband of her skirt. As she did so, she saw that it was a small glass vial of clear liquid. She paid for her purchases and went back outside. But when she reached the Land Rover, it was empty. Oh, God, where was Samir? Had he followed her after all? Had he seen her with Alia?

The door was unlocked, so she put her packages into the vehicle and climbed in. She tried to compose herself. Should she call the Major? Then she saw Samir coming towards her, carrying an ice-cream sandwich.

She forced a smile onto her face and said brightly, 'All ready to go?'

He grunted and stared at her, taking a bite of his ice cream.

'Did you get that from the supermarket?' she asked. 'I didn't see you there.'

He stared a moment longer, then started the car. They rode back to the house in silence.

As soon as she could arrange a moment of privacy, Dina called the Major and quickly told him what had happened.

'I will contact our friend,' he said. 'When he decides what he will do, I will call you back.'

The call came just as the family was sitting down to dinner. When Dina's phone began to chirp, all eyes turned towards her.

'I'm terribly sorry,' she said, getting up to leave the table. 'I have to take this.' She hurried to the garden, pressed the green button and said, 'Hello?'

'Our friend says he will proceed as planned,' the Major said. 'He will be cautious and so should you be. You will both use the sunglasses if necessary.'

'He's sure?'

'He said, dear lady, that he did not wish to waste this opportunity and that there would be no risk to you or the children.'

No risk to us, she thought as she ended the call. But what about him?

When she returned to the table, all eyes were once again directed at her.

'We do not use the telephone during meals,' Hassan declared.

'I know,' she said, 'and I'm so sorry. But this *was* important. Jordy had the flu when I left. Sarah just called to let me know he was recovered.'

'*Nushkorallah*, thanks be to God,' Hassan said fervently. He loved Jordy almost as much as Karim had once done. 'I hope he will come to see us as soon as he finishes with school.'

Dina looked at Karim, who had gone strangely still.

'If that's what Karim wishes,' she said sweetly, 'I'm sure it can be arranged.'

'Excellent, excellent.'

Karim had little else to say during the meal, and for the bit of discomfort she had caused him, she was glad.

CHAPTER 6

Sunday morning dawned clear and bright. After breakfast, Dina and Soraya prepared a picnic lunch. They made peanut butter and jelly sandwiches and packed fruit, cookies and drinks. The children were fairly bursting with excitement as they all piled into the Land Rover.

The zoo in East Amman was partly under construction, but what had been completed was first-rate. The star animals appeared to be the big cats, especially lions and tigers. But as they passed among the well-designed habitats, Dina looked more at the streams of human beings than at the animals. She saw no sign of Constantine. She was nervous. No, she was terrified. Maybe there was a better way to do this. A less dangerous way.

She fought to calm herself. If she truly couldn't cope, she could always abort the action simply by putting her sunglasses atop her head.

They had seen the oryxes, gazelles, other indigenous and exotic animals— less interesting to the twins and Nasser and Lina than the fiercer species. The day was warming towards noon. Soraya suggested that it was time for their picnic. The children chorused enthusiastic assent.

They made their way to the zoo's little park playground. There were slides and other children's rides. Green grass and picnic tables. Men and women with their children.

Soraya spread a cloth on a tree-shaded table. The children ran to play on a small roundabout. Dina opened the picnic basket. She barely trusted herself to set out the plates. The pleasant little park felt like a battleground to her. She felt to make sure the vial was still in her pocket.

She looked once more for Constantine, didn't see him. Then she did. She realised that he must have been there for some minutes, but she hadn't noticed him. Or hadn't recognised him.

It wasn't that he was disguised, exactly, unless you counted the designer sunglasses, but he *did* seem different—his dark hair sleeked back, a light-weight silk sports jacket, the collar of an expensive shirt open to reveal gold jewellery on his chest, a compact, high-tech-looking video camera in one hand. The first impression was of a successful Mediterranean businessman whose enterprises might be less than perfectly licit. But what had caused Dina to overlook him was the boy who was with him. Twelve or thirteen, in an Oakland Raiders jacket and Nike shoes, he looked enough like Constantine to be his son. And that was how Dina had seen them, if she had seen them at all—as just another father and son on an outing to the zoo. She wondered who the boy was. A relative of the Major's? Some street kid?

She was so caught up in the surprise—and in a surge of admiration for Constantine's resourcefulness—that it took another moment for the realisation to hit her: this was it. The thing they had planned for.

Her hands were ice and she felt light-headed. Oh, God, don't faint, Dina. Breathe slow and deep. She looked to Constantine for—what? Guidance? A signal? He was talking with the boy, not even looking in her direction.

His sunglasses were in place. It was a go.

Dina drew the little vial from her pocket. 'Would you like a drink, Soraya?' she heard herself ask.

Soraya was opening food containers. 'Yes, I'm dying of thirst. A Coke.'

'Sure.' The drinks were in a small cooler pack. Dina set it on the bench to open it. The move concealed her hands. She would pop the cap first, she decided, then quickly open the vial and pour it into the Coke.

She looked for a last time. Constantine was showing the boy something about the camera. The boy looked in the viewfinder and panned round the playground. Constantine followed the direction of the lens as if to see what the boy was seeing. Then he laughed and clapped the boy on the shoulder. He took back the camera and adjusted something on it, pushing his sun-glasses up onto his forehead to see the controls better. Then he said some-thing to the boy and they both turned and casually walked away.

It didn't register with Dina for a moment. She had the vial in one hand and Soraya's Coke in the other. Constantine appeared to be abandoning her at the crucial moment. Was it a ploy? Did he mean for her to go forward?

The sunglasses! The signal! Something had gone wrong. What?

She forced herself to be casual. To look around as if savouring the balmy day. She turned in the direction the boy had aimed the camera. Fifty yards away she saw a man. He was wearing sunglasses himself but she could tell he was watching her. A few yards beyond him stood another man, looking in the direction Constantine and the boy had taken. Both men seemed familiar.

'Where are you, Dina?' said Soraya, waving her hand as if to interrupt a trance. 'Don't tell me an American doesn't know what to do with a Coke.'

Dina smiled and handed her sister-in-law the can. She should empty the vial onto the ground, she thought. The words *chemical traces* came into her mind. But there was no alternative. She started to unscrew the top.

She would have recognised the cry anywhere in the world: Ali! She spun and saw him, howling, fallen beside the roundabout, clutching his arm. She rushed to him. Suzanne was wailing too, not hurt herself, merely in empathy with her twin. There was a nasty scrape on Ali's hand. Blood oozed.

Christ! Now the first man was coming this way. He must have seen what she was doing. She pushed her own sunglasses to the top of her head, even though she knew it was pointless; Constantine was no longer watching.

The vial was still in her hand. She didn't dare put it in her pocket with the two men walking straight for her.

Soraya was right behind her. 'Is this bad?' she asked.

'No. No, just a scrape, I think.' Dina was holding Ali's arm with her free hand and cuddling Suzanne with the hand that held the vial. A gaggle of children and parents had gathered, their attention focused on Ali's injury. They formed a screen that would last only for a few more seconds.

With a quick flick of her wrist behind Suzanne's back, Dina tossed the vial under the roundabout.

'He's all right, Mrs Ahmad?' someone said in Arabic. It was the first man. He addressed Soraya but he was staring at Dina. The second man was close behind him. She moved her newly empty hand into plain view.

'Yes, it looks all right,' Soraya said, then focused on the man. 'What are you doing here, Khalid?'

Khalid shuffled his feet and looked into the distance before answering. 'Mr Ahmad—Mr Karim asked us to see if you needed anything.'

Soraya snorted and gave Dina a quick, pained look. 'What we need right now is a bandage and some antibiotic ointment for Ali's scrape. But I don't suppose you have anything like that, do you? So I think we'll go back to the house. Your services won't be needed, thank merciful God.'

Khalid stared at Dina a moment longer, then shrugged. 'Whatever you say, Mrs Ahmad. We only do what Mr Ahmad asks.' He and the other man exchanged a glance. Then they turned and walked away together.

'Who are those guys?' Dina asked innocently.

'They work for the family sometimes. Security. But why were they asked to follow us here?' Soraya looked Dina in the eye. 'Do you know why?'

Dina held her gaze. 'I don't know,' she said. 'I think it's crazy.' It was, it occurred to her, a perfectly honest answer.

Soraya shrugged and stood up. 'Let's get this little man home.'

Dina washed Ali's scrape with water from the cooler and wrapped his hand in a napkin. Then, gathering what was left of the picnic, the six of them beat a slow retreat from the playground. Just before they reached the Land Rover, Dina thought she caught a glimpse of an Oakland Raiders jacket turning a corner in the distance. But she couldn't be sure. All she was sure of was that there would be no plane bound for New York with her and her children on it. Not today. Maybe not ever.

WHEN THEY returned to the house, the children were tired and cranky. Dina tended to Ali's scrape and coaxed them both into taking a nap, promising them a treat later. She tried to think of when she could safely call the Major.

She walked through the garden and towards the kitchen, where she thought Soraya might be. Instead she found Samir, blocking her way.

'You have to leave the house today, Dina,' he said, his tone and expression reflecting his pleasure. 'Pack your things and I will call you a taxi.'

'But why?' she demanded. 'Karim invited me to stay. He—'

'I've spoken already to Karim. He wishes you to go.'

She knew it would be no use arguing further. Now, it was really over.

AT THE HOTEL, Dina called the Major. She recited the morning's events as best she could remember them. 'What do we do now?' she said finally.

'That is not for me to say. I will tell our friend what you have told me. It's possible that he will want to meet with you.'

After the Major hung up, Dina waited in her room. She felt like a prisoner under luxurious house arrest, chained to the telephone. She expected to hear from either the Major or Constantine any minute. Two hours passed. Three. Four. Her despair was turning steadily to anger. Didn't Constantine realise how much she needed to talk with him?

She had been trying to work up her courage to call the house. Now her anger pushed her to do it. Fatma answered.

'Put Ali or Suzanne on, please.'

There was an interruption on the other end, hurried mumbles.

'You don't call here.' It was Maha. 'You are not good for Karim and not good for children. You go to New York and stay with all the bad people.'

'What? Listen, old woman—' But Maha had hung up.

Dina slammed down the phone. 'Damn, damn, damn!' They were going to stonewall her.

She wanted desperately to hear a friendly voice. Em or Sarah. Or both. She reached for the phone again, then remembered the time difference.

Instead, she ran a hot bath, poured herself a brandy from the minibar and let the water and the alcohol soak away her disappointment, her defeat.

She must have dozed in the tub, because at some point she realised the water was tepid. The brandy glass was empty. She dried herself and slipped into the soft terry robe the hotel provided.

It was dusk outside, the lights of the city coming on like evening stars.

She gasped and backed towards the door. A man was sitting on the couch, silhouetted against the window.

He stood quickly. Light from the bathroom fell on his face.

'Son of a bitch,' Dina said. 'You scared me to death.'

'Sorry,' said John Constantine.

Dina flicked on the lights. She had never been so happy to see someone in her life. And so furious at the same time.

'What are you doing here? How did you get in?'

'Old Indian trick,' he said vaguely. He looked tired. 'You were dozing. Had to be a tough day. So I waited. Must've dozed off myself.'

Dina felt herself blushing. If he had seen her 'dozing'—well, she was damned if she was going to acknowledge it. 'You know, the phones work in this country,' she said.

'Yeah. Maybe they work too well. Maybe that phone I got you isn't as secure as my source told me it would be.'

'God. That would mean we never had a chance.'

Constantine shrugged. 'It could have been the guy in the market. Samir. Whatever. But Karim's spooked. He's got two men sitting in a car in front of the house. Same two I saw at the zoo. One of them looks like he's carrying.'

'You mean a gun?'

Constantine nodded. 'As far as I can see, his security effort is defensive. I don't think he's got anybody on you now. I watched the street for an hour and the lobby for another hour. *Nada*. The room's not bugged. I checked.'

'So what do we do now?' she asked.

He sat wearily on the couch. 'Nothing. Call it off. We didn't plan for this and we don't have the resources to handle it.'

'Just give up, then?' Her own words seemed distant to her, as if someone else were speaking them. *Just give up my children* was what they meant.

'Not give up. Go home and . . . regroup. Come up with a better plan. You'll visit again. He's angry now, but when he cools down he'll figure out a way to let the kids see you—and guard them from anything you might try. Maybe in a few months we'll get our chance. Or maybe it'll work out some other way . . .' His voice trailed off. He looked beaten. Dina hadn't realised until now how much this mission had meant to John Constantine.

She wanted to comfort him. She moved across the room and put her hand on his shoulder. 'It's all right,' she said.

'Nah,' he said. 'It's not all right. It sucks.' He gave her hand a quick squeeze. That was all. His hand completely covered hers. Then it was at his side.

'So what do we do?' she repeated. 'While we're still here, I mean.'

'You try to see the kids. If you back off now, that would just confirm his suspicions. I'll stick around till Saturday, make sure you get your flight OK.'

'No need for that. Go tomorrow if you want.' She didn't mean it.

'Might as well stick around,' Constantine said. 'See the sights, have a drink by the pool. But it's on my dime from now on, not yours.'

'I wonder,' she said, relieved that he would be nearby, 'if he'll even let me see Suzy and Ali again.' She told him about her call to the house.

'He'll let you see them, at least to say goodbye,' he said with certainty. 'I should go,' he added. 'I think it's OK, but no sense in taking chances.'

He stood and so did she. Suddenly she didn't want him to leave. The night ahead seemed to stretch into endless empty darkness. But more than that, she realised now how much she needed and trusted John Constantine.

'Don't leave just yet,' she said softly.

He looked at her enquiringly.

'Hold me for a second,' she said. 'Just for a second. I . . . just—'

He didn't wait for her to finish. His strong arms went round her, drew her close. His hand went to her hair, her cheek. His touch felt so good, so right, she felt weak at the knees. Stay, she thought, for more than a second.

He pulled back to look at her. There was sadness in his dark eyes. And longing. He wanted her, she knew. But did she want him? Here? Now?

The phone rang.

It was the front desk. 'You have a visitor, Mrs Ahmad. A Mrs Soraya Ahmad. Shall I send her up?'

'Soraya? Well . . . yes, of course, send her up.'

Constantine raised a questioning eyebrow.

'My sister-in-law. I have no idea what she's doing here.'

He nodded, and moved quickly to the door. 'I'll be in touch one way or another.' And he was gone.

A minute later Dina opened the door to Soraya's knock.

Before coming in, the younger woman looked down the hall both ways, as if fearful of being observed. 'I was just on my way home,' she said, eyes darting around the room, 'from a charity meeting.'

'Come in, sit down. It's a pleasant surprise.'

Soraya sat but didn't remove her light coat. 'I can't stay but a minute. I just wanted to say . . . I'm sorry about this morning. About how Samir spoke to you. I don't know what happened. Men, you know.'

'Yes. I know. It's OK. Listen, I don't want to cause trouble for you. But I need to see my children.'

'I understand. It's only . . . well . . .'

Dina decided to take a chance. 'Soraya, if I tell you something, will you promise not to say anything? Not to Samir, especially not to Maha or Hassan.'

Soraya hesitated. She had already taken a chance by coming here.

'It's nothing bad,' Dina assured her. 'It's just that Karim doesn't want me to tell his family . . .'

'What?' Soraya asked. Curiosity had apparently won over caution.

'Soraya, I never gave up my children. Karim took them away while I was at work. I came home and all I found was a note saying that he had the children and wasn't going to give them back. Ever.' She paused.

Soraya looked stunned. 'My God, what a thing to happen.'

'I need to see my children,' Dina said, pressing now. 'Do you think I can drop by tomorrow? I called this afternoon and Maha gave me a hard time.'

Soraya grimaced. 'That woman.' She appeared to gather some resolve: 'Come anyway. I'll let you in.'

'I don't want to cause you trouble,' Dina said again.

'Well . . . maybe you should call Karim. At work, you know? He won't keep you away. It would make him look bad.'

'That's an idea.'

Soraya stood abruptly. 'Maha will begin to wonder if I stay out too long. And then she'll say something to Samir.' She walked to the door, then stopped. 'So perhaps I'll see you tomorrow.'

'I hope so.'

'It's a shame about this morning. The children, mine and yours, get along so well.' She put her hand on the doorknob, then stopped again. 'There's something I want you to know.'

'What?'

'If Karim will allow it, there's a chance you might see the children tomorrow. But on Friday Karim is taking them to Aqaba. He has a boat there. At the Royal Palms Marina. The twins are very excited.'

'They went on the boat once, when they were small. A few years ago.'

Soraya gave her a searching look. 'Do you see what I am telling you?'

'That I won't be able to see the children after Friday?'

'No. Not just that. They will go Friday and stay at a hotel and take the boat out on Saturday. They will come back Sunday. It will be just the three of them. Or maybe just one other man, to help with the boat. No one else.'

Then Dina *did* understand. She saw her understanding register on Soraya, who nodded as if confirming an idea she had held all along.

Soraya turned the doorknob and spoke more to it than to Dina. 'I don't know why I'm telling you this. It's just . . . the children, you know.'

She was gone before Dina could find words to thank her.

CONSTANTINE called back two minutes after Dina rang his pager. 'Something?'

'Yes, something. Maybe. We need to talk.'

'Not on the phone. Can it wait till morning?'

Why was he being so casual? Had she done something wrong? Maybe he was just tired—he sounded exhausted.

'It can't wait long. Not long at all.'

'First thing tomorrow. Why don't you take a nice morning walk?'

'Anywhere in particular?'

'Just a walk. See you tomorrow.'

To her surprise, the night was not the misery she had feared only an hour ago. She ordered a room-service meal and found herself drifting pleasantly towards drowsiness. The sleepy thought came to her that now there was one last chance. And in the warm darkness cradling her to dreams came a final conscious image: John Constantine's soulful dark eyes looking into hers.

EMMELINE donned her new Nikes and headed downtown at a brisk, if not exactly Olympic, pace. It had been a good day, spent booking and prepping prospective guests. But somewhere she had come up with a nagging headache. She'd take a couple of aspirin when she got home.

A Pakistani—or maybe he was Indian—was lowering the steel shutter of a small electronics shop. He wore a white skullcap. It looked like an Islamic kind of thing, and that made Em think of Dina. In truth Dina had been in the back of her thoughts, and often in the front of them, ever since she had gone to Jordan. What was happening over there? Not a word of news. And Dina was supposed to be returning home in a few days. Em said a silent prayer for her friend and the twins. To have them all back safely.

Turning into her street she bumped into a neighbour, and they chatted briefly. Then, hurrying a little to her appointment with a couple of aspirins, she almost failed to notice the man crossing the street towards her. She registered only that someone was intruding on her projected path. New York instinct clicked on: she avoided eye contact and firmed up her stride.

'Em? Emmeline?'

A fan? But that voice. She stopped and faced him. Oh sweet Jesus and Mary! Surprise of surprises. 'Gabe?'

He laughed. The old Gabriel laugh. The melt-your-insides laugh. 'Yeah, me. And you're you, I see.'

'What . . . what are you doing here?'

'Oh, I'm in town for a couple of days. I just, you know, thought I'd drop by and say hello.' He actually shrugged.

'Uh-huh.' She was recovering from the shock. 'You get this craving, what, every fifteen years? Like clockwork?'

'I know, I know.' He looked down and then away, a six-foot-two, thirty-seven-year-old little boy caught with his hand in the cookie jar.

'And you were just going to knock on the door? Not even a phone call?'

He raised his hands. 'I was in the neighbourhood, you know?'

She stared at him. He looked good. She remembered him as a tall, rail-thin young man with features so perfect they bordered on pretty, rather than handsome. He had filled out now, broadening in the chest and shoulders. His jawline was stronger, and the two little dimples she had once loved had deepened. She realised that she had known him as a boy; now he was a man.

'So this is where you live, huh?' He nodded towards the limestone building.

Obviously he knew where she lived or he wouldn't be here. 'Not the whole building,' she said sardonically. 'Just an apartment. A loft, actually.'

'So I guess you're not going to invite me in,' he said after a moment.

'No, I'm not,' she said. She wasn't about to spring Michael's father on him in this manner—or on Sean, either, if he was here.

He nodded resignedly. 'Didn't figure.'

'I hope you didn't figure, Gabe. I hope you didn't figure you could just waltz out of my life for fifteen years and then just waltz back into it. You want to talk to me, you want to talk to your son, you get on the phone. Write a letter. Send a goddamn email.'

He traced a pattern on the sidewalk with his toe. Nice new Italian loafers. She had a flash of him making the same nervous gesture with his old running shoe on a gravel parking lot in Grosse Tête.

'You know,' he said quietly, 'I don't think there's been a day that passed, not a one, without I thought about you one way or another.'

She didn't want to hear it. Or maybe, deep down, she did. But so what. It was history. She crossed her arms.

'Don't take me wrong,' said Gabriel. 'You know, I just—'

'What gives you the crazy idea that I'd take you wrong, just because you show up on my doorstep after fifteen years? Fifteen years, Gabriel. That's how long ago you dropped the ball. And guess what, baby? The game's over.'

'I know that,' he said softly. 'I just . . .' He trailed off. He'd never been very good with words, she remembered, unless he was singing them.

She waited. Finally he said, 'Well, it's good to see you, Em. You look great.'

'Thanks. Nice to see you too, Gabe. You look like you're doing OK yourself. Let's do it again in another fifteen years.' Christ, what a bitch, she thought even as she spoke. But wasn't she entitled? She turned towards her door.

'Em, wait.'

She stopped.

'Look, cher, coming here was dumb, I see that, me, yeah. But I didn't . . . just drop by. I been walking up and down this street, two hours, maybe more. Every time I get to one end, I say, "Forget it. Go home. You got no business here." But then I think I'll do one more time, up and down. Maybe you'll come out your house, or to the window. Or maybe the boy will.'

She said nothing.

'I wanted to see you, cher. I wanted to ask . . .' He looked at her searchingly, then averted his eyes again. 'People do change. Time changes 'em, if nothing else does. What you say is true. I dropped the ball and that game is over for me. But Michael, he's got his own game, and it's just starting.'

Em listened. It was the longest speech she'd ever heard him make without a few beers in him.

'I know I can't be a father, not like a real one, to the boy. I dropped that ball too, me. But what I want . . . what I'm hoping, is maybe I can be something for him. What you think, cher? You think it's too late for that, too?'

'I don't know,' Em said. 'You'd have to talk with Michael about that.'

He brightened so obviously it almost hurt to watch. 'You think I could? Talk with him. I don't mean now. I know you're busy. But sometime?'

Suddenly Em was crying. 'God damn you, Gabriel, what are you doing here? Why are you pulling this . . . this number?'

He looked as if he wasn't really sure himself. 'I don't know, cher. Maybe just, for once, you know, I'm trying to do the right thing.'

'Great. Doing the right thing. I don't need this shit, Gabriel. Why don't you . . . just go? Go back to Grosse Tête or wherever.'

'I'm sorry, Em,' he said simply. He still didn't move.

She turned away, fumbling wlth her keys. Oh, damn it to hell. She turned back to him. 'All right,' she said, 'I'll think about this. No promises.'

'That's all I'm asking . . . thanks.'

'Don't thank me. I haven't done anything and I might not do anything.'

'I leave it up to you. Whatever you think is best.'

'No. Whatever Michael and I think is best. Assuming I decide to tell him.'

'Right. You want me to call? Tomorrow, maybe?'

'No. Where are you staying? I'll call you.'

'Just up at the Holiday Inn. I'm in and out, some appointments, but you can get me there in the evening. I appreciate it, Em, I really do.'

'I'm not making any guarantees. And whatever happens, Michael is not going to get hurt any more than he has been already. You understand?'

'I understand.' Gabe smiled. 'Thanks, cher. I mean it.'

He watched until she got the door open and went inside.

The apartment was empty. A note from Michael: studying at his pal Brendan's. Sure. Nothing from Sean. She needed a glass of wine. No, a real drink. There was something she was forgetting. What was it? Oh, aspirin.

But for some reason her headache was gone.

I CAN'T believe I'm doing this, Sarah thought—and then smiled as she realised she'd had this same thought any number of times since she'd started seeing David. Sure, she was halfway to crazy about him. But there was no reason to be meeting his relatives, was there?

They were at the house of one of David's cousins, Simon the Designer. It was a bold modern statement in gleaming white and glass. Perched on a gentle slope overlooking the ocean, it offered sweeping vistas to forever.

Cousin Simon was about David's age—and perhaps even more boyish. He was dressed in a white silk T-shirt and a pair of immaculate white linen shorts. As he was showing Sarah around, his mother, Effie, arrived from Brooklyn, complaining loudly and passionately—about traffic, about the doubtful quality of the bread she had picked up from Shlomo the baker, as well as the cheese, the filo dough, and just about everything else. In short, she was absolutely certain her dinner would be a disaster.

Eventually she turned her attention to Sarah. 'So, sweetheart, you like our David?'

Well, that was right to the point. Sarah nodded. 'David's terrific,' she said.

'Of course,' Effie said, as if Sarah was being slow. 'And you, sweetheart, are you SY? I don't know your family, do I?'

Sarah looked baffled. David intervened. 'No, Aunt Effie, Sarah's Jewish, but not SY—that means Syrian, in case you didn't guess. Her family lived near Eastern Parkway.'

'Ah,' Effie intoned, infusing the single word with layers of meaning. 'Well,' she perked up a moment later, 'at least she's Jewish.'

Sarah might have taken offence from someone else, but Effie was a force of Nature. She began unwrapping food. Boxes and plastic containers disgorged their contents, until every available kitchen surface was covered.

'She carried all that from Brooklyn?' Sarah asked in a whisper.

'Aunt Effie brings Brooklyn with her, whenever she travels.'

Effie's dinner was nothing short of spectacular. And it was clearly appreciated by the throng of assorted relatives and friends who showed up to partake of the hummous and tabbouleh, the baked squash and meat pies, the broiled fish and the chicken with lemon and olives.

Sarah liked the food as much as she liked this loud and boisterous family, their easy laughter and the pleasure they took in Effie's dinner. Now she thought she could see why David was such a sweet and caring man.

After dinner they sat on the back patio. A sliver of moon hung over the cobalt ocean, laying a silver sheen over the water. Sarah sighed contentedly.

David took her hand. 'I've made some enquiries about your *get*,' he said, 'and I think we should do a little investigation in Israel. My cousin, Abe the Rabbi, has connections there. He said he'd make enquiries on your behalf.'

Sarah looked doubtful.

'You said Ari does a fair amount of business in Israel. Abe and I thought we might find someone there who would have some influence on Ari.'

'Do you think that will do some good?' Sarah's expression brightened.

'I think it's our best chance. I'll do everything I can, Sarah, I promise.'

He drew her close and kissed her. Sarah kissed him back.

THE SUN was well up when Dina woke. She nearly panicked at the thought that she might have overslept whatever contact Constantine had in mind. She threw on her jogging clothes, the big sunglasses, and her Mets cap.

It was a beautiful day, crystal-clear and cool. She went down the long crescent drive of the hotel and out along the avenue at a good power-walking pace. Three blocks later she became aware that a car was prowling along behind her. She turned.

'You the American lady?' said the cabbie. It wasn't really a question. 'The Major sent me. Please to get in.'

'The Major?'

'Yes.' He was a handsome, smiling young man. Dina hesitated. Should she trust him? She decided she couldn't afford to be paranoid.

'We don't go far,' he said when she was ensconced in the back seat. Indeed, in just a few minutes he had pulled up at the Roman amphitheatre.

'Busy today,' he observed. Tourists were already swarming the site. 'Up above there is a nice overlook. You enjoy the view. I wait.'

She got out and climbed through the amphitheatre. On the heights, there was a little overlook with coin-operated telescopes. A man was looking through one of them. Constantine. She edged up beside him.

'Need change for the machine?' he asked. He fed a couple of coins into the slot. 'Take a look, and tell me what's up.'

She looked through the telescope and told him what Soraya had said. He was unenthusiastic. 'A boat,' he said. Then came the questions: How big a boat? Twenty-eight feet, she told him. Was Karim an experienced sailor? Capable, but no America's Cupper. Who was this other man who might help? She didn't know. Did Karim keep any weapons on board? She didn't think so.

'What the hell, it doesn't matter, if this guy's a bodyguard, they might bring a piece or two along for this trip. Let's walk.'

They strolled through the amphitheatre site, to all appearances just a couple of Western tourists enjoying the brush with a civilisation far more ancient than their own. Constantine had even brought a camera.

'Maybe I'm just dreaming,' Dina said. 'Maybe this is crazy.' The questions about weapons had reminded her that there was very real danger—with Ali and Suzanne in the middle of it. How had she managed to forget that?

Constantine said nothing. He had a glowering look. 'I can picture ways of doing it,' he said at last. 'I'm not wild about it, and I need to think it through. I also need to get down to Aqaba and take a look at this marina. Meanwhile, you should go see the kids. Act normal, like nothing's happened. Deny that you've done anything. Learn whatever you can, but for God's sake, don't ask any questions. Nothing, you understand?'

'I'm not even sure they'll let me in the house.'

'Find a way. Don't make a scene, but do it.'

'OK. Whatever happens, I don't want Ali and Suzanne in any danger.'

'Dina,' he said softly, 'that's been understood from day one, hasn't it? Look, I'm gonna check this thing out to the best of my ability, then I'll give you my evaluation. Whatever I come up with will be minimal risk. And it's your call anyway. Or'—he paused—'we can forget it right now. Go home and regroup, like I said. Just tell me what you want.'

It couldn't hurt to have more information, Dina decided. 'Go to Aqaba.'

'OK. Good. I'll see you tomorrow.'

On the ride back to the hotel, the cabbie smiled in the mirror and handed her a card. 'My name is Nouri. My numbers. Bottom is the pager.'

'All right.' Dina had to wonder what kind of other jobs the Major and Nouri worked on together.

'I like your cap!' Nouri added.

She took it off. 'It's yours.'

'You kidding!'

He was still thanking her for the cap when he pulled up at the hotel. 'Call any time,' he said. 'The Major says take care of you, I take care of you.'

THE APARTMENT was quiet. It was Sean's acting-class night, and he'd be out late with his classmates afterwards. There was the usual note on the fridge from Michael: he was at Brendan's. Of course. Em wondered if she needed to talk with him again about his father's reappearance. It was strange how Michael had taken the news that his father was back. After digesting Em's account, he had asked simply, 'Do you want me to see him, Mom?' When she told him it was his decision, he said he'd think about it. That was all. Until he asked for Gabe's phone number. And then closed the door to his room while he made a call. Em hadn't asked how it went, and Michael had volunteered just one bit of information—that he'd agreed to meet his father.

Now she took a bag of homemade marinara sauce out of the freezer. Some mushrooms and pasta would make a cozy little feast. She would prop her feet up and watch TV, maybe read a book, try not to worry about Dina.

She was putting water on to boil when the phone rang.

It was Sean. 'Hello, beauty. Feel like a night on the town?'

'What happened to your class?'

'I decided to blow it off. I have something to tell you. Thought we might go to the Orchid.' A little Italian restaurant on the Lower East Side, the Orchid had been their special place when they first knew each other.

'I don't know. It's been a long day. I just want to chill.'

'Come on. I'll pick you up. Twenty minutes?'

Out of curiosity more than anything else, she gave in. Had he finally landed the big part he was forever expecting? That would be nice.

In the cab he still wouldn't tell her the big secret. He was at his most charming, but she detected little lines of anxiety in his professional actor's smile.

The Orchid was the same place it had been since about 1970: candles, checked tablecloths, a faded mural of Venice on the wall. Sean ordered a scotch and soda for himself and a white wine for Em.

'So what's the news?' she asked when the waiter had brought the drinks.

'A toast,' Sean said. 'To us.'

Em took a sip of wine. 'I like a drawn-out story as much as anybody, Sean, but this is getting silly.'

He laughed. The little lines were still there. 'OK. So here it is. You know how we've been talking about me moving in . . . you know, the two of us living together?'

Actually, no, she knew nothing of the kind. The only times the subject had arisen, she had gently dismissed it.

'Let's do it,' Sean went on, sincere and serious now. 'It's time for that commitment, don't you think? I do.'

'That's it?' Em said. 'That's what you wanted to tell me?'

Sean's face fell, but he recovered quickly. 'Well, it's pretty big, isn't it? I thought it's something you wanted, too. It seems like the logical next step.'

It was pleasant to have Sean's company a few days a week, but it was clear to her in that moment—if it hadn't been for months—that he wasn't the man she wanted in her life for ever. She couldn't tell him that, though. Not in so many words. His expectancy and anxiety were so obvious.

But then something else clicked.

'Sean, this isn't about the lease, is it?' For weeks Sean had been complaining that his lease was coming up for renewal and the landlord was bumping the rent to the max. Sean and his roommate Dean, another struggling actor, could handle it, but it was the principle of the thing.

'The lease? Hell no. I hadn't even thought about it. But since you mention it, it would be logical. Otherwise I'm locked in for another two years.'

So it was about the lease—at least partly. Em was beginning to get angry.

'Sean! Hey, dog, what's happening?'

It was a friend of Sean's, yet another actor. He was with a pretty blonde.

'Brad, what brings you here, my man?'

'Well, it's a restaurant. Got to eat, no? Hey, how about our boy Deno?'

'Yeah. So how's it going? Introduce us to this beautiful lady.'

Em realised that Sean was trying to change the subject.

'Deno?' she said to Brad. 'Dean? What about him?'

'Our boy here didn't tell you? Deno hit the jackpot—they cast him for the FBI agent in Ron Howard's next movie. Off to La-La Land.'

'Dean's going to LA?'

'Gone already, right, Sean? Who wouldn't?'

'Who indeed?' said Em. So that was the whole story.

She waited until Brad and his date had left them before she picked up her bag. 'This is for the wine. And don't bother coming round tomorrow.'

'Come on, Em. You've got this wrong. I was going to tell you about Dean, but it's no big deal. I mean, it doesn't affect me. I can handle the rent myself.'

He couldn't even have handled the old rent without a roommate.

'Don't call either. You've got some stuff in my closet. I'll have one of the guys from the studio bring it to you. Goodbye, Sean.'

She walked out. He didn't follow her. Providentially, a cab appeared; they were rare in this neighbourhood. She didn't cry until she was home.

'THE CHILDREN are not here. They have a class.' Fatma was lying. Dina was sure she had heard Ali's voice in the background.

'When will they be back?'

'I don't know. Much later. Late.'

Bitch, Dina thought, and hung up.

All right, she thought, enough was enough. She'd endured enough lies and evasions over the past two days. She found Karim's office number in her address book. A secretary asked who was calling Mr Ahmad.

'Mrs Ahmad.'

'Hold on, please.' A full minute passed. 'Mr Ahmad is out of the office. May I take a message.'

'Mr Ahmad is new there, isn't he? Why don't you ask him the company policy on employees' wives who come to the office and raise holy hell? Because that's exactly what I'll do if you don't put him on this phone.'

There was a longer hold this time.

'Dina,' her husband said coldly, 'this is totally uncalled for.'

'Don't give me "uncalled for", Karim. I came all the way to Jordan to visit my children, and I'm damned if I'm going to spend my time watching television in the Hyatt. You call the house right now and tell whoever is guarding the door that I'm coming over and the door had better open, unless you want to continue this conversation right there in your office.'

She could almost hear him wondering if she were bluffing. 'All right,' he said. 'I'll accommodate your wishes once again. But the children are not to leave the house with you. Or anyone else. I'll go this far. No further.'

'All right. Thank you,' Dina said formally. There was no sense in pushing harder. She had what she wanted.

She went to the house after lunch. The two men from the zoo were parked out front. They watched her as she alighted from Nouri's cab.

She spent the afternoon just being with her children. Touching them. Talking. Listening. Watching them play with their cousins. Loving them.

'We're going on Daddy's boat,' Suzanne said at one point. 'Saturday. Can you come too?'

'I can't, Suze. I'm going back to New York on Saturday—remember?'

Suzanne pulled a face. 'I wish you weren't going. When will you be back?'

'I don't know. But soon. I promise.'

The afternoon went too quickly. Dina had just called Nouri when Karim came in. It was early for him to be home.

'Oh, Dina,' he said. 'I'm glad I caught you. Can we talk a minute?'

'Why not?'

He drew her into the living room. 'I'm taking the children on a holiday.'

'Suzy told me. Saturday. The boat.'

'Yes.' He seemed taken aback for a moment. Had he really expected that the children wouldn't mention such a thing?

'So I can't expect to say goodbye to them at the airport.'

'Well, actually, we'll leave on Friday. So tomorrow is the last day that you'll see them. I'm sorry, but this is the only time I can take off.'

'I don't believe you. You're doing it on purpose.'

'Believe as you wish. But let's not make this more unpleasant than it has to be. Come tomorrow. Then we'll have dinner together, just the four of us.'

Dina pretended to consider it. He had said 'just the four of us', so perhaps it would be manageable. 'You don't give me much choice,' she said.

He smiled. 'Tomorrow, then. I look forward to it.' He looked out of the window. 'Your cab is here.'

The two men in the car were still watching as she left.

BACK AT the hotel, Dina had never felt so alone. She thought of calling Sarah or Em, but both would be at work. In the end she called her mother. Of course, Charlotte knew only that Dina was here to see the children, nothing more. So it was understandable that she might still hold out hope for a meeting of the minds, perhaps even a reconciliation.

'Remember, Dina, remember what I told you: things weren't always perfect between your father and me. Maybe Karim will come to his senses . . .'

Dina asked about her father.

'The same,' Charlotte said quietly. 'He asked about you today.'

'Give him my love,' Dina said.

She tried the television, watched the king greet some visiting foreign dignitaries, gave it up. She read a couple of chapters of a not-very-suspenseful suspense novel she'd bought in the airport in New York, then took a pill for sleep. Tomorrow was going to be a very long day.

'GOOD NEWS, Sarah. I have some good news for you.'

'What? What are you talking about?' At a little past seven on her day off, Sarah was still groggy from sleep. She pushed herself up on her pillow.

'My cousin Abe the Rabbi found some information that could help you.'

Now she was fully awake. 'Help me how? What information?'

'Information about Ari's . . . activities in Israel.'

'Activities? Illegal activities?'

'No, no, nothing like that. Look, let's meet for breakfast and I'll tell you in person. Then you can decide how you want to proceed.'

Sarah agreed, and an hour later, she and David were seated at a booth in the Greek diner that delivered so many of her meals-on-the-run.

'May I say that you look beautiful this morning,' he said with a smile.

'No, you may not. You don't get me out of bed on my day off to pay me compliments. Just tell,' she demanded. 'Tell me everything.'

'Well,' he said, 'it turns out that Ari has been leading a kind of double life. It seems he's engaged—not formally—but the woman in question believes it is. She's very well connected politically and socially and she's been a great help to Ari in his business dealings.'

Sarah shook her head. Just the kind of woman he had always wanted.

'She wants to get married.'

'And?'

'From what we could find out from friends of hers, Ari told her he was having difficulties getting a divorce. A difficult wife who wouldn't let go . . .'

Sarah began to laugh. 'He's kept me tied up all this time—and he tells some other woman that I've been hanging on to him, is that it?'

David nodded. 'That's it.'

She leaned over the table and kissed David soundly on the mouth. 'I love you, I love your cousin Abe the Rabbi, and I love the woman in Israel, whoever she is. Now let's figure out how we're going to tell Ari he isn't going to screw around with me any more.'

David smiled. 'I thought you'd never ask.'

CHAPTER 7

Dina didn't intend to go to the house until after lunch on Thursday, since it was clear that her presence was not welcome. That left the rest of the morning empty. She didn't feel like bringing anyone a remembrance of this trip, but she decided to do it anyway. Nouri took her to places that he swore offered the best bargains in Amman.

In the end nothing appealed to her. Everything seemed either too tacky or too expensive or impossible to fit into her luggage. She finally bought a few scarves, more to satisfy Nouri than anything else.

She suddenly realised that Constantine might be calling her from Aqaba. She could almost hear the phone ringing back in her room. She asked Nouri to take her back to the hotel, and arranged for him to pick her up in two hours.

In the room the message light was dark. Nor did the phone ring during the next two hours. She didn't know why she hadn't gone to the house earlier. This might be her last day with the twins until . . . well, maybe until sometime next week in New York. Or maybe, if something went wrong . . . she would not think about that.

It had been hot outside when she came in. She would like to have dressed in the lightest of clothes. A sundress. But if Maha should be home, her lip would curl in a sneer that said 'loose woman'. Dina chose a short-sleeved green linen blouse, a matching skirt, and sensible shoes.

Nouri was waiting for her, his Mets cap turned stylishly backwards.

'They have moved,' he said as they pulled up in front of the house. 'Those two men who were here yesterday. Now they are further down the street. You should not look.'

But she already had looked. The car was perhaps a hundred yards away, the figures in it little more than indistinct shapes.

'You have good eyes,' she said.

'Yes, always. What time you want I pick you up?'

'I don't know.'

He lifted his cellphone from the seat. 'Any time. You call.'

Soraya opened the door, looking both uncomfortable and relieved. 'I'm glad you're here,' she said.

'Is something wrong?'

'No. Not really. Just that Suzanne and Ali have been . . . at odds.'

'Over what?'

'Who knows? The heat. Excitement about the boat.' She paused for an instant and added, 'Maybe you leaving.'

'Oh.'

Suzanne was at the kitchen table, staring gloomily at a book. Harry Potter, Dina noticed. She looked up and brightened as if someone had flipped a switch. 'Mommy!' She flew to Dina and they hugged fiercely.

'Sweetheart. Where's your brother?'

The switch was flipped off. 'I don't know.'

Through the kitchen window Dina could see Ali in the garden. He was alone, lying on a bench, and looking as down in the mouth as Suzanne had.

She knocked on the glass. His reaction was decidedly different from Suzanne's: he frowned, then reluctantly undraped himself from the bench and lounged into the house with an elaborate lack of enthusiasm.

'What's up, tiger?'

'Nothing.'

'I hear you two aren't getting along. What's the trouble?'

'Nothing,' they said together.

'Well, then. Tell me what's happened since yesterday.'

Apparently nothing had happened—nothing they wanted to mention, at least—so she told them a funny story, with her as the bumbling tourist, of her haggling with a shopkeeper over the price of scarves. Suzanne laughed. Ali still was out of sorts but took enough interest to offer advice.

'You have to act mad when they tell you how much it costs. Aunt Soraya does it really well.'

'Do you, Soraya? Show us. Show me, I mean.'

Soraya did, with Ali playing the shopkeeper and Suzanne correcting his errors in the role, and the ice was broken. The rest of the afternoon was not much different from old times back in New York. Something still hung in the air between the twins, but they obviously had made a tacit truce.

At one point Hassan came in from his study and joined the talk, telling a story about a hunting trip he'd once taken with the old king. It was not of great interest to the women—although Ali ate it up—but Dina could have kissed the old man for simply acting like a grandfather.

Maha did not appear. Fatma did. Ignoring Dina completely, she set to work preparing the table for the evening meal. Soraya joined her. The cousins bounced in, raising the energy level by half.

Late-afternoon shadows had covered the garden when Karim arrived, bluff, smiling, hugs to the twins, compliments to Dina and Soraya.

The dinner, of course, did not turn out to be 'just the four of them'—that was impossible in an extended-family household, and Dina couldn't understand how she had ever imagined otherwise. Everyone was there except Maha, who was 'not feeling well', and Samir, who was 'working late'.

It was all so warm and homey, Dina thought, that no one would ever have guessed the true situation hidden beneath the smiles and laughter.

It started to fall apart with Hassan's little speech. It was just a few words about how good it was to have seen Dina again, and how he hoped it would not be much longer before she would be able to rejoin her family. Could the old man really be that clueless? Dina wondered. Had no one filled him in on what was truly going on? Or was this some pro forma exercise in courtesy? But Soraya and Karim, and even the cousins, were nodding as if Hassan were expressing not only their fondest wishes, but an imminent reality.

Not Suzanne. She was staring straight ahead, looking so miserable that Dina leaned over and whispered to her, 'Something wrong, Suze?' The child shook her head.

Karim noticed and tried to smooth it over. 'I know you're already missing Mommy, precious, but she'll be back soon. And meanwhile, we're going to Aqaba tomorrow.'

That was when it happened. Suzanne slammed her small hands on the table so hard that her dish rattled. 'No! I don't want to go to stupid Aqaba! I don't want to go on some sucky boat! I want to go home!'

She had started with a shout and ended with a wail, tears rolling down her cheeks. For a moment everyone sat frozen in surprise. This was not a country where children spoke in this fashion to their elders.

Karim flushed with embarrassment and anger. 'Be ashamed! Be ashamed, Suzanne! Go to your room this instant!'

Dina turned on him. 'No! You heard her!' She looked fiercely around the table. 'You all heard her!'

'She's upset because of you. God knows what you've been telling her.'

'I haven't told her anything. I haven't told her how you took her and Ali without a word to me! I haven't told—'

'Shut up, Dina! Just shut up! You're a guest here.'

'A guest? You jerk, I'm her mother!'

'A mother talks like this in front of her children? You're a—'

'Enough!' Hassan's voice was like thunder. 'We do not do this at table!'

Even though his glare was directly on his son, Dina felt like a scolded child herself. The old patriarch had the power of unquestioned authority.

'We eat in peace,' he declared with finality, and went back to his food.

No one else seemed hungry. Karim took a bite or two as if to placate his father. The cousins picked at what was in front of them. Suzanne sat with her hands in her lap. Ali pushed a piece of eggplant round his plate.

Dina was seething. The veil of pretence had fallen for a moment, and the moment had felt good. But she forced herself to stay silent. Two more days, she reminded herself. She mustn't do anything that might cause Karim to cancel his planned outing.

'We have ices!' Soraya said too brightly, trying to salvage the occasion.

She met with silence. Hassan pushed his plate away and stood. The meal was over. Karim followed him from the room without a word. The cousins melted away. To Dina's surprise, Ali went with them. Soraya mechanically began to clear the table. Dina just as mechanically helped. Suzanne, as if making a decision, pitched in as well.

Dina set down a stack of plates and hugged her daughter. 'It's OK, Suze. You'll be home someday soon. I promise.'

Suzanne hugged her back. 'I know, Mommy.' She managed a smile. 'But do you know when? Daddy won't tell me . . .'

Just then Karim came back in. Either the storm had passed or he was making a heroic effort to ignore it; only the smallest cloud still hung in his dark eyes. 'I'm sorry for the . . . scene, Dina. I wanted this to be different.'

She shrugged. 'It's a difficult situation.'

'Yes, well . . . It's getting late. Almost the children's bedtime.'

'Oh, please,' Suzanne began.

'No,' Karim said, raising his hands placatingly, 'I'm not saying you have to go to sleep just yet. But get ready for bed. Your mother and I need to talk. Then she can come and tell you good night.'

'Go ahead, Suze,' said Dina. 'I won't be long.'

'Aauugh,' Suzanne groaned. But she went.

'Tell your brother,' Karim called after her. Then he turned to Dina. 'In the garden? It's a beautiful night.'

'All right.'

He was right: it was a beautiful night—balmy, almost cool, with a silver moon skimming the tree tops. Dina was struck by the unreality of it all. How had she ended up in this place, walking in this garden with this man who was still her husband. Waiting to tell her children goodbye. Wondering what another man was planning in order to steal those children back.

'What are you doing here?' Karim asked abruptly. 'I mean, what are you *really* doing here?'

It was a little scary, as if he had read her mind. 'I don't understand. I'm visiting the children. Our children. And talking with you.'

He shook his head. 'Don't lie, Dina. You're here to take the children.'

'What are you talking about?'

'You know what I'm talking about.'

'I know that your imagination is running wild. What, you think I'm going to grab the kids and make a run for the border?'

'Actually, I do think something like that.'

'If I *was* planning "something like that", do you think I'd tell you, Karim? So why bother with this . . . this cross-examination? And even if I was planning to take the children, isn't that exactly what you did?'

'No, damn it, it isn't exactly what I did. Do you think I *wanted* to do this?'

'If you didn't want to do it, who forced you?'

'You'd know more about that than I, Dina. You—' He stopped. 'My God,' he said. He seemed genuinely contrite. 'Is this what we've come to, Dina: fighting like two hyenas on this beautiful night?'

His words staunched the rush of anger. For just a moment, she felt like reaching out to touch him. Just his cheek. A moment, only that. An impulse, not of love—that was gone for her—but of tenderness.

'Of all the gin joints in all the towns in all the world,' she said.

Karim actually laughed. It had been their favourite movie. 'I've only done what I thought was best,' he said softly. 'For Ali, most of all.'

She said nothing. She didn't want to begin the argument again.

The silence stretched between them. When Karim finally spoke it was quietly. 'I've been thinking: what if we were to compromise? For now, anyway. What if you were to take Suzanne back to New York?'

She could not believe what she was hearing. 'And leave Ali here?'

'I think it will be better for him to be with me. I think it might be better for Suzy to be with you.'

Was this some kind of trick? A trap? 'You want to split them, the children, the twins? Divide them up, here's your share, here's mine?'

'I don't think of it that way. I'm trying to reach a solution that's best for everyone.' He turned to face her and his voice became harder. 'You should think about it too. Whatever ideas you might have about taking them both aren't going to work. I won't let you, and this is my country.'

'Don't threaten me, Karim. You're just . . . springing all this on me.'

'I know it seems sudden.' He had softened again. 'Look, I don't want us to be like those people who poison their children with their hatred of each other. I don't hate you. I hope you don't hate me. I'll make it easier for you to visit Ali. Maybe we could meet in Lebanon, with your father's people.'

'You're serious, Karim? You want me to take Suzanne home?'

He sighed. 'She's not happy here. At first she seemed to be adjusting beautifully. But she misses you, Dina. You saw that for yourself.'

'What about Ali?'

'He has no problems; he likes it here. You can ask him yourself. I think he and Suzanne argue about it. More since you're here.'

So that was the conflict between them, Dina thought.

'Do you want to do this, Dina? Take Suzanne with you?'

Of course she did. But it wasn't that simple. They were twins, for God's sake. Inseparable. If that were not enough, there was her secret knowledge that, two days hence, she might have them both together. 'I can't decide now,' she told Karim. 'Not this . . . spur of the moment.'

'I need to know soon. I've promised the kids this boat trip. I don't want to call it off. Can you tell me by tomorrow morning?'

'What happens if I say yes? Do you and Ali still go off sailing?'

'I don't know.' He seemed genuinely unsure. 'He might not want to go.'

'I'll say good night to them,' Dina told him. 'I'll call in the morning, one way or another.'

'Thank you,' he said simply.

In the house she called Nouri, then went to Suzanne's room. She was reading the Harry Potter again. She put the book down and Dina held her close.

'I've got to go now, sweetheart. I love you.'

'I love you, Mommy.'

'Listen. I meant what I said about you going home. But what would you think—I'm not saying it's going to happen—if you came home and Ali stayed here? For a while, anyway. Would you still want to go?'

Suzanne's eyes were very dark and deep. 'Yes,' she said.

In his room Ali had dozed off. Dina woke him with a hug. 'Night, Mommy,' he said sleepily.

'Ali, tell me one thing: do you want to go home? To New York?'

He rubbed his eyes irritably. 'Sure,' he said, then added, 'someday.'

'Not soon?'

'Not really.' He tried to explain. 'I mean, I missed you, Mom, when you weren't here. But I like being with Daddy, too.'

It wasn't surprising. He was at the prime age for a boy's hero worship of his father. A father who could show him jet fighter planes, who could take him sailing. It wasn't surprising at all. But it broke her heart.

'Good night, sweetie,' she said.

IN THE CAB her mind was racing. She could not bear the thought of separating Suzanne and Ali, even for a while. But a small voice was saying, *At least you'd have your daughter.* And what about those visits with Ali? In Lebanon? Who could say what might happen under those circumstances? And there was still the boat trip—the rescue plan. What to do about that?

She barely heard Nouri until he repeated a question: 'This is all right?'

'What's all right?'

'That we see this friend John of yours. At my place. He waits there.'

'John? Well . . . yes. Yes.'

Nouri lived in a low-rise apartment building that managed to look both new and rather worn-out at the same time. The elevator wasn't working, so they climbed five flights of stairs. Nouri knocked an obviously agreed-upon sequence on his own door and John Constantine opened it.

He was deeply tanned—obviously he had got more sun in Aqaba. His linen shirt was open at the neck, revealing a whitened scar she had not noticed before. He looked, she thought, like a movie pirate.

Nouri bustled about making coffee for them, then excused himself. 'You will want to talk. I have something I forget in the cab. I will go check.'

They sat at a coffee table in the little living room.

'So,' they both said at once, as soon as Nouri had left.

'Go ahead,' Constantine said.

'Karim offered to give me Suzy.'

'What?'

'He said I could take Suzy home. Ali stays with him.'

Constantine frowned. 'And this is OK with you?'

'No, dammit, it's not OK!' she exploded. 'But I don't know what to do.'

He reached out, took her hand. 'I can't make this decision for you,' he said gently. 'All I can do is try to give you what you want.'

Dina bit her lip, nodded. 'What were you going to tell me?'

'OK. Well, the set-up for a rescue looks pretty good. Eilat, in Israel, is a few miles across the Gulf of Aqaba, nothing in a fast boat.' He sipped his coffee. 'There are a couple of ways to go about it. One: sabotage Karim's yacht—get aboard it in the marina the night before, fix it so the steering breaks a few miles out, mess up the radio. I've got a man for the job. A real pro. He's a diver, among other things.' He waited for a comment, but Dina had none. 'So the boat's dead in the water, but here's a nice fella right there to offer a tow: me. And my friend. We grab the kids, head for Eilat.'

Finally Dina spoke. 'And where would I be?'

'On a plane for New York. If you agreed to the deal Karim offered, you'd have Suzy with you. We'd want everything to look normal to Karim.'

'What was the other way? You said there were a couple.'

Constantine frowned. 'The other way would be to have my man do his frogman thing and get aboard before daylight. He'd take control.'

'What does that mean?'

'It means he uses the threat of force. That's going to have to happen sooner or later either way. This way is just a little surer.'

Dina was silent. Then she said, 'Do you think it would work? Either way?'

He hesitated. 'On paper it should be a piece of cake.'

'But it's not on paper. And you don't seem enthusiastic.'

Constantine stood up and walked to the window. 'When things go wrong at sea, they could go wrong in a big way. And there's a lot I don't know. Like are there any weapons aboard? Anyone who'll use them?'

Now the silence was long. Then: 'Don't do it,' Dina said suddenly.

Constantine turned and stared at her. 'You mean not the second way?'

'No. Not *any* way. Let's forget it.'

He sat down again. 'It's your call,' he said quietly. 'You're the boss.'

'I'm going to do it, John. I'm going to take Suzanne.'

'Well . . .' He seemed at a loss for words. 'It's a move. It's *something*.'

'I didn't decide until this minute. When you talked about using the threat of force. It only just hit me what it could mean.'

He nodded. 'If I were in your place, I might make the same decision.'

'Another thing. If we took the twins—or either one of them—by force, they'd be cut off from their father. I don't think he'd even come to visit them after that. But this way they still have him. All our options are still open.'

Constantine looked closely at her. 'So you're sure about this, then?'

'Yes.' She saw the concern in his eyes. 'If we did go ahead and someone —anyone—got hurt, I don't think I could live with myself.'

Constantine nodded, smiled at her. 'OK,' he said finally, 'peace is always better than war. In my book, anyway.'

'I think I've disappointed you.'

'No,' he said softly, 'you haven't disappointed me. I just wanted to get you what we came for. Suzanne *and* Ali.' He looked down at his hands, clenched and unclenched them. 'OK,' he said, 'you'll take Suzy—and maybe we'll find another way to get Ali.'

The coded tap sounded at the door, and Nouri entered. 'All is well?' he asked. 'I can do more things if you like.'

'Everything's fine,' said Dina, 'but I need to make a phone call.'

'There is my phone,' Nouri said.

'I've got to call Karim,' Dina said to Constantine. 'If I'm going to do this, I want my daughter out of there tomorrow.' Now that she had made her decision, she wanted desperately to affirm it, make it solid.

She called the house. Karim answered. He must have been waiting.

'My answer is yes,' she said. 'I think you're right. I'll pick Suzanne up in the morning.'

Even now she half expected him to back out. Instead he merely sounded relieved. 'It's the best thing, Dina. You'll see.'

There was a pause. 'So that's that, then,' Dina finally said.

'Yes. Look, Dina, I want you to know . . . I want you to know I wish things had worked out differently. Better. But—'

'I know. In case I don't see you tomorrow, goodbye, Karim.'

'Goodbye, Dina.'

She hung up. All the rescue plans, the hope of having both her children back, had come down to that: the final click of the receiver into its slot.

WHEN DINA arrived at her in-laws' home, Maha was nowhere in sight. There were just the four of them now, seated side by side in the spacious living room. The family they had once been. Suzy was dressed in a pretty yellow sundress. To Dina, this was the most beautiful sight in the world: her little girl, all suppressed energy and smiles now, eager to begin her adventure with Mommy. She doesn't really understand what it's going to mean, Dina thought. But she will soon enough. Dina looked at Ali, solemn as a grown-up, sitting close to his father, holding his hand, needing reassurance.

Karim cleared his throat. 'Perhaps you'd like me to step outside for a moment,' he said, 'while you say good— I mean, while you speak to Ali?'

Dina shook her head. She wouldn't make Ali any more miserable by forcing him to leave his father's side. She put her arms round her little boy and kissed him. 'I love you, sweetheart, and I'll miss you very much.'

He pulled away. 'Then why are you going?' he demanded, furrowing his brow. 'And why are you taking Suzy?'

She and Karim had both tried to explain the arrangement they had agreed on, but now he was asking the same questions he had asked before. Dina sighed and said simply: 'This is what Daddy and I decided to do, sweetheart. I'll see you soon, Ali, I promise. And you'll see Suzy, too.'

He was unmoved, and when she pulled him closer for a final hug, he was stiff and unyielding in her arms. My poor baby boy, she thought.

She turned to Suzy, whose ebullience had started to fade. Karim put his arms out and Suzy ran into them. 'My princess,' he said softly. 'You're going to have another plane ride now, and you're going to see another film, and soon . . .' Here his voice broke. 'Soon you'll be back in New York.'

DINA REFUSED Karim's offer of a ride to the airport the next morning. Was she afraid he would change his mind and take Suzy back? Perhaps, for all during the cab ride, she kept glancing behind, searching the road for any sign of one of the family vehicles.

The plane ride was painful: Suzy kept talking about the trip they had made with their father. How she and her brother had passed the long hours they were airborne. Her narratives were punctuated with bouts of tears.

This is impossible, Dina thought. She had made the decision, but how could she live with it? To have Ali snatched from her was one thing, but to leave him behind was agony. She would have to think of something. Maybe John could help her. Yes, she thought, maybe John would help.

THEY ARRIVED home midafternoon. Dina saw that the place was cleaner and neater than when she had left it. And there were vases of fresh flowers in the hall and in the kitchen. Bless her friends, she thought. Yet the house felt somehow wrong. Something had happened to the family that had lived here, and now the house, like the family, was different.

Suzy was tired and cranky. Dina took her upstairs to bed, where there were more tears and more questions about Ali. What was he doing now? Was he playing outside? Was Daddy tucking him into bed? Dina sat with her until she drifted off, then went to check the mail and the answering machine.

The red light was blinking. Dina smiled. No doubt her friends had left messages to welcome her back. She punched the play button.

'Damn you, Dina. Damn you for your lies and your tricks!' Karim's voice, hoarse and angry. 'I tried to be fair with you, but that didn't mean anything, did it? You won't get away with this, I swear! I swear I'll get him back!'

What on earth was he talking about? Another message followed. Anger and fear in Karim's voice. 'I heard you telling Ali you'd have him soon. I should have stopped you then and there. But I didn't think you'd take him.'

Puzzlement yielded to alarm. If he thought she had Ali, then Ali was missing. Oh God! Ali was missing!

With trembling fingers, she dialled the number of her in-laws' home.

Karim answered. 'You must be very pleased with yourself,' he began, 'outsmarting the stupid man who trusted you. You—'

'Karim, stop. I didn't take Ali. I don't have him.'

'You're lying. He's—'

'Karim, don't. I swear on Suzy's life, I don't have him.'

Silence.

'My God, are you telling me he's disappeared?'

'I thought . . . I was sure you had him.'

'I'm coming back to look for him. I'll get someone to watch Suzy and—'

'No. Stay with Suzy,' he said. 'There's nothing you can do here. I'll contact the police—and we'll start looking, too, Samir and I.'

For a desperate moment, it occurred to her that Constantine might have carried out a rescue without her permission. But surely he would have let her know if he'd taken Ali. He'd realise she'd be out of her mind with worry.

She thought of the Major. Of Nouri. She would contact Constantine, ask him to get in touch with them. Perhaps they could help in the search.

She agreed to stay in New York after Karim promised to call her the minute he had any news.

Dina's friends arrived an hour later. They had expected a woman who was not exactly happy, but one who had her daughter back.

Her face told a different story.

'What?' Sarah asked. 'What's wrong?'

She told them. For once, no one had an answer.

KARIM and Samir had been cruising the streets for hours, Samir at the wheel. At first, every time Karim saw a boy in the distance, his heart lifted with hope. But a hundred disappointments drained him of that feeling. They had questioned everyone they saw, showing a snapshot of Ali. But in Amman there were thousands of boys who resembled Ali and wore American-style clothes. Everyone had seen one—or several.

'Do you think anyone in this neighbourhood speaks English?' Karim asked his brother, as they drove through one of the poorer quarters.

'Of course,' Samir assured him. 'A little anyway. Some of them.'

Karim grunted. All day he had been agonising over the fact that his son as yet knew only a few words of Arabic.

Samir pulled over. 'Coffee,' he said. 'You want something to eat?'

'No. But coffee is good.'

While he waited, Karim called home. Hassan answered.

'Anything?' Karim asked.

'No. But they're putting his picture on the news this evening.'

The whole family had mobilised for the search. Soraya and Maha were on their cellphones, calling the hospitals, as well as nearby sweet shops, coffee houses, any place a tired and hungry child might go for refuge. A half-dozen cousins and a dozen hired searchers were patrolling the streets. It had been hard to persuade Hassan to remain home and man the phone. Karim had accomplished it by referring to the house as 'the command centre'.

Of course the police were on full alert. Karim had gone straight to the top to see that this was the case. Surely it wouldn't be long. Any minute.

Samir returned with the coffee.

'He can't just have disappeared,' Karim said.

And yet that was exactly what seemed to have happened.

DID THEY have sex offenders in Jordan? Had someone taken her baby for ransom? Was his disappearance the act of someone with a grudge against Karim's family? Dina could not bear the thought of her little boy being scared or in pain, and the fear that he was tormented her.

Em and Sarah tried to reassure her: Ali would be found, nothing bad would happen to him. But words gave Dina no solace.

'I shouldn't have done it,' she sobbed. 'I shouldn't have agreed to separate the twins. It was wrong to leave Ali without his sister, just wrong—'

'Oh, honey,' Em said, 'how could you not take Suzy when Karim offered? It's all his fault.'

Dina shook her head. It was no comfort to blame Karim. None. She knew he'd be going crazy, too. But that was no comfort either. She was alone in this misery and it would not end until Ali was found.

Please God, she prayed, let him be all right. I'll do anything if he's all right. I'll even leave the twins with their father, if that's Your will.

FIVE THOUSAND miles away, Karim stared into the darkness of Ali's bedroom. He touched the pillow on his son's bed, the computer game Ali loved, the pyjamas he had worn before he'd vanished.

How he wished now that Dina had taken Ali with her. At least he would be safe. Was this a kind of retribution for what he'd set in motion? But how could he know that things would turn out this way? He had wanted only good for his children—and yet it had all come to this. His darling daughter gone from him. His precious son—no, he wouldn't even think about that.

Samir came up behind him, placed his hand on Karim's shoulder. 'Get some rest, brother. Get an hour's sleep, and we'll go out again.'

Karim nodded, but there would be no sleep until Ali was found.

IT WAS two hours past midnight prayer when Samir finally persuaded Karim to give up the search till morning. 'He's indoors somewhere, brother. We'll never find him, driving around like this.'

Karim shook his head, but not very vehemently. Samir was right. There was hardly anyone out now, and certainly no children.

'Someone has taken him in,' Samir said. 'We'll find him in the morning, *insh'Allah.*'

God willing, Karim repeated to himself. But he could not see God anywhere in Ali's disappearance. He told himself that some ordinary, caring man or woman could have taken in a lost child, but he could not keep darker possibilities from his thoughts. Ali would need only to speak a few words to be recognised as an American, and many in Jordan had no love for Americans. There was also the chance that this was a kidnapping. The police didn't seem to think so, and no ransom demand had come, but it was early yet.

Still, driving around the empty city streets would not help.

'All right,' he told Samir. 'Home.'

At home, Hassan was dozing in his chair by the phone. A police officer drowsily manned a telephone line that had been set up in case of a ransom call. Karim talked with him for a while.

The policeman was full of official-sounding reassurances, ending with,

'Best get some sleep, sir. Don't worry, I'll wake you if anything happens.'

But before Karim could rest, he had to do one more thing. He called Dina, tried to make his lack of progress sound as benign as possible. Ali had wandered off somehow. It appeared that he had got lost. Everyone was searching and he was certain to be found any minute now.

'My God, Karim, he's a little boy! How did this happen? He just left?'

'Yes. Little boys do these things, and in a strange city it's easy to get lost.' Karim tried to give her comfort. 'I did it once myself, in Aqaba,' he said. 'I was lost for hours. When they found me, my father didn't know whether to beat me or kiss me. In the end, he did both. Don't worry, Dina, Amman isn't New York. We'll find him. Nothing will happen to him, I promise.'

But the words sounded hollow even to his own ears. How could he promise anything when he had no idea where Ali might be?

DINA PACED in the kitchen, feeling she would go mad if she didn't do *something*. She tried Constantine—office, home, cellphone—and got his voice message on all three. She asked him to call her right away. She had no idea where he was. Could he still be in Jordan? Once again, she wondered if he had Ali. No, that couldn't be. Then where in the name of God was her son?

She did the only thing she could think to do. She dialled the code for Amman and then the number she had memorised in the supermarket.

It rang several times before there was an answer; it was the middle of the night in Amman.

'Yes?'

'Alia?'

'You have the wrong number.'

But Dina had recognised the voice. 'Wait! Please don't hang up. It's . . . it's the woman you met in the supermarket.'

'No. Wrong number.'

'Please!' she begged. 'My boy is missing. My son. In Amman. Could you please ask . . . the man you work with . . . if he can help find him?'

A silence. Then: 'I know nothing of this.'

'Just tell him. And ask him.'

'Yes. Goodbye.' And Alia hung up.

When she put down the phone, Dina saw Suzanne standing in the doorway, her dark eyes fearful. 'Mommy, what's wrong with Ali?'

Dina sat down and tried to tell her that everything would be all right, that Ali had just gotten lost and Daddy was looking for him.

KARIM was as exhausted as he had ever been in his life, but sleep wouldn't come. The thought that had tormented him throughout this nightmare could not be kept at bay: this was his fault, his doing. He had been a fool. And his foolishness might have cost his son's life.

The first grey light was breaking when he finally closed his eyes and sank into a dream-tormented sleep. Long before then, he had promised himself that if Ali were to be found alive and well, he would be reunited with his sister and mother in New York. Anything else would be a new mistake piled upon all those Karim had already made.

IN AMMAN, the man known as the Major was fast asleep when the phone rang. Not his ordinary phone, but the unlisted one.

He listened to what Alia had to say.

He had seen the story about Ali Ahmad on the television news. He had assumed that Constantine was somehow behind this, in which case it would be known soon enough. If that was not the case and the boy had simply run away, he would no doubt be quickly found by the police.

Yet there were people in many walks of life in Jordan who would never deal with the police if they could avoid it. Some of these people dealt with the Major on a regular basis; they tended to be highly observant individuals in possession of all kinds of information. With three or four calls, he could initiate a chain of contacts that would alert all of these people to the importance of finding a lost American boy. Though he was not overly fond of Americans—John Constantine was one exception—Dina Ahmad's situation had touched him. He leaned over his bed and picked up the phone.

IT WAS well past ten when Karim woke. To his horror, he appeared to be the last of the family out of bed. From time to time the phone rang and Hassan answered. His body language, a slight slump of the shoulders, told them that it was just another well-wisher. Hassan always thanked the caller courteously but briefly and explained that they wished to keep the line open.

The phone rang again and Hassan irritably snatched it up. By now none of them paid much attention to the instrument, so a moment passed before anyone realised that something was different in the old man's voice—and that his shoulders hadn't slumped. 'Yes?' he said. 'Yes? Who? . . . Yes, of course. And you're sure of this?' He was motioning urgently for Karim.

Even as he put the receiver to his ear Karim heard his father say something to the others that was greeted with shouts of 'Thank God!' He found himself speaking with a man who introduced himself as an officer in military intelligence. He wondered what military intelligence had to do with the search for his son, but the man's next words banished such concerns.

'We have him,' the man said. 'He's fine. A little tired, that's all.'

Karim was light-headed with relief. 'Where is he?'

'I'm bringing him to you myself. Would you like to speak with him?'

'Yes. Please.'

An instant later, Karim heard Ali's voice. 'Daddy? It's me. I . . . I got lost.'

'You're all right, Ali?'

'Yeah, I'm OK. But I'm really hungry.'

Karim felt as if he'd burst with happiness. 'You won't be hungry long once you get here. Or maybe we'll let you go hungry a bit longer, while you think about all the worry you've given us all.'

'I won't do it again. Daddy,' Ali said fervently. 'I promise.'

The officer came on again. 'A man, a labourer, found your son late yesterday, and he and his wife kept him overnight. We'll talk with him, of course, but I don't think there's any question of anything untoward. I believe this fellow was simply concerned about a lost child on his own.'

'Thank God,' Karim said. 'And thank you, sir. Thank you very much.'

'You are most welcome. We will see you shortly.'

'Wait. The man who found Ali. You said he's a labourer. Is he poor?'

'Poor as dust. He doesn't have a television set, or he'd have known who he had under his roof. We found him through one of his neighbours.'

'If you'll give me his name and address, he won't be poor after today.'

'Then there will be two happy families in Amman.'

Karim hung up and was engulfed by the arms of his family. Hot tears coursed down his cheeks.

ANY THOUGHT of punishment vanished when Ali was returned to his family. Maha spirited the boy into the kitchen and began to put out all the 'foreign' foods she usually scorned: breakfast cereal, candy bars and sweet drinks.

'No, *Tayta*,' he said, 'I want some of *your* food.'

'Anything for you, Ali,' she said. Quickly she prepared a plate of *kefta* and potatoes—and then watched him devour every last morsel.

Outside, Karim was escorting the officer to his waiting car. He had realised some time ago that he knew the man, at least by reputation.

'Not to pry,' he said carefully, 'but I can't help wondering how you . . . your division . . . became involved in the search for my little boy.'

The man smiled benevolently. 'Oh, I didn't mention that? I saw the story on television. I thought it couldn't hurt to put some of our people on it.'

'Well, I'm very grateful.'

They had reached the car. The officer hesitated before getting in. 'Forgive me, Mr Ahmad,' he said, 'it's certainly nothing that concerns me. But when we found your son, he asked if we were taking him home. I told him we were. He said, "Home to New York?" Do you know what he meant?'

Karim nodded, said nothing. In the joy of recovering Ali, he had forgotten his pre-dawn promise to himself. Now, it was as if this distinguished man had reached into his conscience to remind him of it.

'It was an honour to meet you all and to be of service to your family,' the officer said. 'God be with you and yours.'

'And with you,' Karim said. Before he reached the door of the house, he knew what he had to do.

ALI LAY quietly in his bed, too tired to stay awake, yet too anxious to sleep. He had expected to be punished, but instead he'd been smothered with kisses and hugs, fed until he could eat no more. He didn't understand this, any more than he understood why his sister had been taken away from him.

No one here seemed to think it was wrong that Suzy was gone. That's why he had known it was up to him to find her. It didn't matter what he had told Mom. Sometimes he couldn't stand being Suzy's twin, but without her he didn't want to be here any more. A boat trip would be no fun without her.

He had thought about the airport. Suzy had gone there, with Mom. They got on a plane and went home. That was what people did at airports. There was some matter of tickets, but that seemed to happen automatically.

He'd crept out of bed and dressed quietly. In the kitchen, he put a couple of leftover pittas and a handful of Froot Loops in the pocket of his windcheater. He thought about writing a note and putting it on the refrigerator door but there wasn't anything to write on or with. It wasn't like at home.

He went out of the front door, closing it softly. The car with the two men in it wasn't there. The street was so dark and quiet it was scary.

Ali had an idea of which way the airport was. It hadn't seemed very far when they came in from it. He started walking.

He was still walking hours after the bread and Froot Loops were gone. He'd been sure the airport would be easy to find, but he must have taken the wrong street. Still, the airport was huge, and if he kept walking in its general direction, surely he would find it. Soon, however, he had lost any sense of general direction. Then some older boys had bothered him. When they learned he couldn't talk with them, they'd punched him and wrestled his windcheater off him. His nose had bled for a while.

His mother had warned him not to speak with strangers, but once or twice he asked people where the airport was. Their replies were incomprehensible. He thought of giving them his father's name. Or his grandfather's. Everyone knew his grandfather, he was sure. But then he would have to go back to the house, and he would be in trouble, and Suzy wouldn't be there.

He walked until he couldn't walk any more. He sat with his back against a building. The wall was warm from the sun, but the sun was setting now. Ali started to cry.

Two men came down the street. Ali felt them standing over him. One man spoke to him. Ali couldn't understand a word, but clearly the man was asking what was wrong. Ali told him. The man shrugged and spoke with his friend. The friend tried saying something to Ali. He couldn't understand that either. The first man motioned for him to stand, and when Ali was slow to do it the man lifted him by his arm.

If he wasn't supposed to talk with strangers, he definitely wasn't supposed to go anywhere with them. But the man held his arm and he was too tired to run. They walked down a narrow street. At a corner the second man said a few words to the first, clasped his hand, and went away down the side street. The first man towed Ali a few houses down the street and through a door. They went up some stairs and into a small, dark room. It took Ali's eyes a few seconds to adjust. Then he saw that there were other children there, two boys older than him and a younger girl. There was a woman and the smell of cooking. He realised that this was the man's home. A radio played Jordanian music. There was no TV.

The woman asked questions and the man answered gruffly. The woman put out food: bread, beans and olive oil. Ali ate it hungrily. The older of the two boys spoke to him. He didn't understand. Then the boy said, '*Eengleesi*?' Yes, Ali told him. The boy turned to his father and said, '*Eengleesi*.'

Bed was only a worn rug on the floor, with the two sons beside him. He was asleep almost before he put his head down.

When he awoke, it was day again. He was lonely. He missed his sister, his mother, his father—everyone who loved and cared for him. Though his father had told him a man should be brave, he began to cry.

Ali didn't like to remember the crying. But remembering what came later was good. There had been shouting from the street, people at the door.

One of them Ali recognised from the night before. The other was an older man, who was much better dressed than anyone Ali had seen since he'd got lost. After that, everything had happened quickly. The well-dressed man had taken charge of Ali; there had been a ride in a car. And then he was here, safe and comfortable. But still there was no Suzy. And though he told himself he should be brave, once again he began to cry.

TWO DAYS later, Karim stood outside the door of the place that had been his home for twenty years, holding his son's hand. Was he doing the right thing? he wondered for the hundredth time. He had made a promise, but what of Ali? What about his identity? Would he be ashamed of his name and heritage? He sighed deeply. He would drive himself mad with these thoughts. He rang the bell, just as if he were a stranger.

Dina pulled open the door, cried out when she saw her son. She grabbed Ali and held him close, covering his face with kisses. Karim cleared his throat. Dina looked at him. 'Karim. Thank you.'

He nodded. He couldn't bring himself to say 'You're welcome.' This was his son, his hope for the future. He did not want to give him up, yet this seemed to be the right thing to do. For now.

They stood there for a long awkward moment. 'Suzy's not here,' Dina said finally. 'I wasn't sure when you'd arrive, so I let her go to school.'

Karim nodded. 'Well, in that case, I guess I'll be going . . .' He reached once again for Ali, took him into his arms, felt his throat clog with tears. He couldn't linger; the pain he felt was too intense to prolong and he would not break in front of Dina. He kissed his son on both cheeks. 'Be good,' he said, his voice husky, 'and write to me. I'll call you every week. And I'll see you soon,' he promised, though he did not know when that would be.

THERE WAS a loud and enthusiastic reunion when Suzy came home from school. She showed Ali a picture of him that she had drawn and hung above her bed. 'I missed you,' she said. 'I wanted you to come home.'

'I wanted to come home,' Ali said, not quite ready to admit out loud that he'd missed his sister. 'I didn't want to leave Dad, but—'

'I know,' Suzy said. 'Me, too.'

Two hours later, by the time Dina was preparing dinner, she heard the familiar sounds of bickering coming from the second floor. She smiled and heaved a great sigh of relief. Normal, she thought. Maybe, one day, things will be normal again, whatever that was.

CHAPTER 8

'Sweetheart!' Dina flung her arms round her firstborn son, hugging him so hard that he called out, 'Hey, Mom, take it easy.'

'Sorry.' When she pulled away, her eyes were shiny with unshed tears. 'I'm so glad you're home, Jordy, I'm just so glad.'

'Yeah. Me too.'

She pulled him inside, then tugged at his suitcase, which felt as if it were filled with bricks.

'Jeez, Mom, don't. I'll get it.' And he did, with only a moderate effort. He seems stronger now, she thought, and not just physically.

A moment later, the twins came hurtling down the stairs. Dina had told them Jordy was coming home, had warned them not to repeat anything they'd heard about him at their grandparents' home. But now she held her breath.

'Jordy!' Suzy cried out, flinging herself into her brother's arms.

He picked her up, swung her around and hugged her close. 'It's good to see you, peanut. I missed you.'

'I missed you, too, Jordy. Are you really going to stay home now? And go to school here?'

'Yup. You'll be stuck with me until I go to college.'

'Yay!' She clapped her hands, turned to Ali, perhaps thinking he would second her delight.

Ali was silent, staring hard at his older brother. Was he trying to see what was 'unnatural' about him? Dina wondered. Her eyes sought Jordy's, willing him not to be hurt by this latest manifestation of his father's rejection.

He smiled, sadly, she thought, then ruffled Ali's hair. 'Good to see you, champ,' he said, then followed Dina into the kitchen.

'I'm sorry about that,' she said softly, after the twins had gone back upstairs to their games. 'I—'

'It's OK, Mom. I can only imagine the brainwashing they got while they were with . . . him.'

'I don't believe it was like that,' Dina said. 'Look, your father did a really awful thing, but I don't think he tried to "brainwash" the twins. He probably talked to his brother or his father, and the twins just overheard them.'

'Yeah, sure. Whatever.'

'Jordy,' she pressed, 'your father is wrong about you. That's his problem. Maybe *he* was brainwashed—by the culture he grew up in.'

Jordy frowned. 'Mom, do you mind if we don't do this right now?'

'Of course, sweetheart. You must be tired. And hungry. Let me fix you something. Anything you want, just name it.'

'Umm,' he considered. 'How about scrambled eggs, sausage and toast?'

She watched her son eat—ravenously, as if he hadn't enjoyed a good meal in days. As she studied him, she reflected once again that he seemed different, changed during this past year.

'What?' he asked. 'Why are you staring at me?'

'I'm not staring. I'm . . . drinking you in. I'm so happy to have you here.'

When he made no reply to that, she asked: 'Jordy, when your father sent you away to school, did you . . . did you think I wanted you to go?'

He looked up from his food. 'I wasn't sure. I knew it was Dad's idea—I mean, he was pretty clear about what he felt. With you, it was different. You said all the right things, but you never asked me how I felt about going to Andover. How I felt about leaving my friends, so I thought, well . . .'

'Jordy, I'm so sorry.' She reached over and took his hand. 'Please forgive me. I should have fought your father if you didn't want to go.'

'Forget it, Mom. It's over now. Maybe it was a good thing for me to go away—no, let me finish—because I didn't have anything to live down in a new place. I didn't have anything to prove.' He paused. 'And there was a counsellor at school, a really good guy. I felt like I could talk to him.'

Dina felt the pain of her son's loneliness, his need for someone to talk to. She understood that there would be no Band-Aids for whatever hurts Jordy was feeling. As for Suzy and Ali, Dina knew that they needed her more than ever. And that it would be a long time before the family felt whole. She made her decision at that moment: she would continue to work from home, and if her business suffered while her family healed, so be it.

EM AND SARAH wanted to give a party to celebrate Dina's reunion with her children. But Dina refused. Perhaps she was being superstitious, but she felt as if her newly regained family was still too fragile to celebrate. Maybe in a few months, she told her friends. Instead she suggested dinner at her house.

The meal was simple: grilled tenderloin and steamed asparagus, with a tomato, basil and mozzarella salad to start, and chocolate cake baked from scratch for dessert. After coffee had been served and the children retired to their rooms, Dina told the full story of Ali's disappearance and recovery.

Em and Sarah listened in uncharacteristic silence. They had lived the story on Dina's side, had witnessed her terror and her pain. As she looked at them now, she thought, This is the truly gorgeous mosaic: the friendship of three women, all different, each unique in her personality, yet enriching one another's lives with their love and loyalty.

'Well, at least he finally did the right thing,' Sarah said of Karim.

Dina nodded. And yet, with the nightmare behind her, she could easily imagine how bereft Karim must be, and how lonely. No matter what misery he had caused her, she had never doubted for a minute his love for Suzy and Ali. Knowing that made her sad, so she turned to Em and said brightly, 'Tell me what's been happening with you. I'm so out of touch.'

'Well . . .' Em hesitated.

'Nothing bad, I hope,' Dina said, her body suddenly tense.

'No, no, cher, nothing bad. What's new is that Mr Gabriel LeBlanc himself turned up while you were away. Like the proverbial bad penny.'

'Really?' Dina studied her friend. 'And what does Sean say about this?'

'Sean's no longer in the picture.'

Strange, Dina thought. From Em's expression, it seemed he was not missed.

'And how does Michael feel about his father's being around?'

Em smiled. 'He's more mature about it than I am. He says "We'll see." He's been out with Gabe a couple of times. It's one day at a time with him.'

'He's wise,' Dina said. Turning to Sarah, she asked, 'And you? What have you been up to while I was away?'

Sarah's smile was part Mona Lisa, part mischievous elf. 'Well, David and I are, you know, seeing each other, and—'

'"Seeing each other"!' Em laughed. 'So that's what you call it! Don't listen to her, Dina; this girl is having an honest-to-goodness romance.'

'That's wonderful, Sarah,' Dina said. 'But . . . is Ari still giving you grief about the *get*?'

Em laughed again. 'You tell her, Sarah, tell her what David did.'

'Well,' Sarah began, the elf smile reappearing, 'It turns out that Ari has a fiancée in Israel. The poor woman thinks the only thing standing between her and a wedding ring is me. According to Ari, I'm a clinging, neurotic wife who refuses to give him a divorce so he can marry his true love.'

'Oh, that's rich,' Dina said, laughing. 'But how—?'

'Let me finish,' Sarah said. 'This woman is very well connected—I don't know why Ari isn't anxious to marry her. Anyway, once we found this out, David's cousin, Abe the Rabbi, asked Ari to give me a *get*. Ari, of course, said no. So Cousin Abe told him that maybe his fiancée might like to know that he's been free of his terrible wife for a long time. And free to marry.'

Dina clapped vigorously. 'That's wonderful, Sarah! And did he cave?'

'He caved,' Sarah said with evident satisfaction. 'So we'll be doing the *get* next week. It only takes about two hours, you know. After waiting for years, my marriage will be officially over in just a couple of hours.'

'Now exactly how does that work, Sar?' Em asked.

'We go to the rabbi's office. We each say we understand what we're doing and that we're acting freely without coercion.'

Em laughed aloud.

'What I did wasn't coercion,' Sarah protested, 'just effective persuasion.'

JOSEPH HILMI died later that day, just one week after Ali had returned home. The funeral was held at St Joseph's on lower Sixth Avenue, the church that he and Charlotte had attended for half a century. When Dina got up to speak, she talked of her father's great love for his family and his two countries— the one he had adopted and the one he had left behind.

Afterwards, Charlotte served a buffet lunch that featured her husband's favourite Lebanese dishes. Dina had no appetite for the food or the drink. When she noticed that her mother was not in sight, she went into her parents' bedroom. Charlotte was there, staring out of the window.

'Oh, Dina,' she said when she saw her daughter. 'What are we going to do without him?' She began to cry, and Dina wept with her, cradling her mother's head on her shoulder.

CHRISTMAS SEASON in New York. Snow and biting cold. Dina had spent every Christmas for twenty years with Karim. Though it was 'her' holiday and not his, Karim had always been respectful of her wish to give the children a traditional Christmas. His absence made her realise how accustomed she had become to the seasonal routine into which they had fallen. Now it all felt pleasantly free-form. She decided to give a Christmas Eve dinner party. It was important, she felt, to make the holiday as festive as she could, different from the way it had been with Karim, but good all the same.

The guest list was short: Sarah and David, Em and Gabe (who was back in Em's life in some not-yet-defined way), one or two other couples, her manager, Eileen, and a few other singles. And John Constantine.

He filled the door with his broad shoulders, his arms loaded with presents. 'Merry Christmas, Dina. It's good to see you.'

'You too, John.' It was.

He passed her the gifts. 'Suzanne, Ali, Jordy. And you.' The children's packages were professionally wrapped. Hers looked decidedly amateurish.

'Let me put them under the tree,' she said. 'Say hello to everybody.'

She was still arranging the packages under the tree when he rejoined her. She pointed to a shinily wrapped gift. 'That one's for you.' Having no better idea, she had bought a bottle of his favoured Black Bush.

He eyed the package. 'I have my suspicions about its contents.'

'Well, you're a professional investigator, after all.'

'Yeah, I am.' The corner-of-the-mouth smile she had come to like. 'Are we going to open the presents tonight?'

'No. You can open yours if you want. We open presents Christmas morning. Anyway, there's something similar to yours in the liquor cabinet.'

He seemed in no hurry, taking in the room, the tree, and her. 'This is nice, Dina. It's been a while since I did Christmas.'

'It *is* nice, isn't it?' And I am lucky, she thought. To have my family, my friends. 'I feel bad about our dinner out,' she said. The hecticness of the holiday preparations had caused her to cancel their regular monthly 'date'.

'No problem,' he said quickly, then more slowly: 'We could make up for it on New Year's. Dinner. Bubbly. Watch the ball come down.'

'I don't know,' she said. It was true. She didn't know if she was ready for New Year's Eve with John Constantine. 'I'll probably be asleep by ten.'

He thought it over. 'OK. I'll give you a call between now and then. It's not like I've made other plans,' he added meaningfully.

Just then Sarah bubbled up to say that they were putting the food on the table. It was, from Dina's point of view, good timing.

CONSTANTINE was among the last to leave. It was the first moment he and Dina had been alone together since their conversation early in the evening. He stood in the doorway, cradling the gift-wrapped Black Bush.

'I really enjoyed tonight, Dina. I mean it.'

'So did I. I'm glad you could come,' she said. 'There's . . . there's something I should have told you before.'

'What's that?'

'Just thanks. For everything you did.'

He shook his head. 'Hey, you thanked me. And paid me. Even though I didn't really accomplish anything.'

'No, that's just it. It wouldn't have happened without you. None of it.

Getting Suzanne back. Finding Ali—then getting him back too. I just want you to know how grateful I am.'

He made a think-nothing-of-it gesture. 'Nah. It was you. You made it happen. You just don't know how special you are.' He turned up the collar of his overcoat. 'I better go. Hope you like your present.' He grinned mischievously. 'They say it's always a mistake for a guy to buy a woman a hat, but hey, I think I know your taste.'

'A hat?'

'Night, Dina.' He leaned down, kissed her lightly, then whispered in her ear. 'Merry Christmas.' And with another grin, he was gone.

An hour later, with all the guests vanished and the children asleep, she sat with a last glass of wine before turning out the lights. A hat. What could the man have been thinking? The package sat under the tree. She wasn't about to spend half the night wondering about it. She opened it.

A New York Mets cap.

The note said, *Don't give this one to a man in Amman. Merry Christmas.*

In the soft, multicoloured glow of the Christmas lights, she smiled.

DINA ENDURED serious telephone cross-examinations from both Sarah and Em the next day, but she declined to categorise John as her 'new boyfriend'. Romance could wait until she was certain her family was whole again.

She spent a great deal of time with Suzanne and Ali. For a time after the Jordanian episode, they had seemed to regress to being much younger children: bad dreams, small problems at school, insecurities surfacing every time Dina had to go out.

The family counselling helped a little. The therapist, a Dr Hollister, saw Dina and the children once a week as a family; she saw Dina and Jordy on their own as needed. Dr Hollister assured Dina that the twins' behaviour was normal; they would have to learn to trust that Dina would always return. She would have to prove it over a long period. The same was true of her relationship with Jordy. It was not enough to say she was sorry for not having the courage to stand up for him; she would have to show him in a hundred and one ways how much she loved and accepted him.

When she had told the twins that she and their father soon would no longer be married, they absorbed the news sadly but calmly. Clearly they had already considered this possibility together.

In fact the divorce proceedings were moving forward rapidly. Karim was not contesting the divorce itself, and under the circumstances, it was certain that Dina would be awarded custody of the children. Money was not an issue either. Karim had offered an alimony and child-support package that Dina considered more than adequate. Karim's attorney was requesting visitation rights, details to be worked out, whenever Karim was in New York.

One morning the phone rang. It was Karim.

They had spoken briefly whenever he called from Amman to talk with the children. Coolly, not cordially, but not angrily either. It was as if their mutual fear over Ali had made blame and recrimination seem a little silly.

'I tried the shop,' he said. He always referred to her business as 'the shop', as if it were some storefront florist. 'They told me you were here.'

'I work at home a lot these days. I was just checking the payables and receivables. Is something wrong?'

'Wrong? Nothing,' he said. 'I'm in New York.'

She digested this information in silence.

'I wanted to let you know,' Karim said. 'And see if I could stop by sometime. I'm here for a few days.'

'Stop by?' She felt a little stunned.

'To see the children. And you. Talk. You know.'

'No. I don't think that's a good idea.'

'Why not?' He sounded genuinely mystified. Then injured: 'I mean, you don't intend to keep me from seeing my—our—children, do you?'

'My lawyer tells me that there should be no visits until visitation rights are settled.' She was lying. They had not discussed this. But it sounded good.

'Well, I . . .' There was indignation in his voice. Then Dina heard a defeated sigh. 'All right. I guess that's the way it has to be. Lawyers. God.'

'I'm sorry,' Dina said, surprised that she actually was. But she wasn't ready to take any chances. Not yet.

'Well, what if I come by to see *you*, then?' he said. 'Just to talk.'

She thought it over. 'All right,' she said. 'Say two o'clock.' She would make arrangements for the children.

'Well. Yes. Two o'clock. Yes, I can do that. See you then.' He hung up.

THE DOORBELL rang at exactly two. Karim had always been punctual.

'Hello, Dina.'

'Hello.' A pause. 'Come in.' There was an awkwardness to it, being invited into the house they had shared for so long.

He followed her to the living room. 'You look good, Dina.' He meant it. She wasn't the girl he had married. Or she was, but she was also better.

'Thanks.'

'You said you're working at home a lot now?'

'Quite a bit. But I have to go in sometimes, and there are meetings, like this morning with a prospective account.'

'It went well?'

'Yes. I think I got the account.'

'Ah. Well, good.'

Karim had the strangest feeling of experiencing the past in the present. There was something about Dina that reminded him of the first time he had seen her. It struck him that this was an aura of unattainability. He had been smitten the moment he laid eyes on her, but he had laughed at himself for dreaming an impossible dream. She was too beautiful, too much her own creature, even for a man like him. But he felt the same desire, then as now.

Don't be an idiot, he told himself. You've lost her. He cleared his throat. 'It seems that I'll be in New York fairly often.' He waved vaguely. 'War on terror, politics . . . all that has affected aircraft procurement. I'll need to be here and in Washington. So—I'm looking for an apartment.'

'Really. *How* often?'

'Maybe once a month. For a week or so. And once we work out the details of the children—I mean, we *will* work out something, of course— then it seems good for me to have a place, a settled place, not some hotel or something, where they can spend their time with me when I'm here.'

'Well, yes. That makes sense.'

'Good. We agree on this, then.'

'Sure.'

Feelings were tumbling over Karim. He felt as if he were in an aircraft whose controls were not functioning properly. He had made a mistake, he knew, although he had done what he thought was best. But it had turned out differently than he had expected. Now the controls snapped completely. 'I wonder, Dina, if we could see each other sometime. I mean, not just when I see the children. I'm not talking about, you know . . .' He was babbling, he realised. 'Just have dinner together or something. Talk. Maybe everything isn't . . .' He had started to say *hopeless* but caught himself in time. 'I mean, so many things now . . . your working at home, all that, this is what I . . .' He caught himself again. He had almost said *wanted all along.*

'No, Karim,' Dina said quietly.

He stared at her. He knew her now. Knew her better than he had ever known her before. Knew that he had lost.

'Well,' he finally said. 'I should be going. I only wanted to tell you . . . you know, about my plans.'

'Well, thanks. That's good.' She stood. He did too.

'I'll let you know about the apartment. Address. Phone number. All that.'

'Good. I'll tell the kids you came by. That you'll see them soon.'

'Oh, yes, good. Dina, I—'

There was the sound of the front door opening and clumping shut. They both recognised the footsteps before they heard the voice.

'Hey, Mom. It's me.' Jordy.

And then he was standing before them, his expression first surprised, then quickly blank. 'Oh,' he said. Nothing more.

Karim regarded his son. It had been nine or ten months since he had last seen him. The boy was taller than Karim now. A strong-looking young man. Hard to believe that . . . Karim forced the thought from his mind. He knew that he had been right, morally right, but was it so important to be right? At this moment Jordan had his mother's expression—cool, unreachable. And yet he looked so much like Karim. People had always commented on it, and now it was almost like looking at a picture of himself as a teenager.

Dina said, 'Your father was just—'

'I just dropped by to say that I would be in New York more often,' said Karim. 'I . . .' He couldn't formulate his thoughts. There were things he wanted to say, but the words weren't there. 'I know that . . .' There was so much he had lost. He didn't want to lose this one more thing, although it might be lost already. 'Look, Jordy, things . . . went wrong. A lot of things. Maybe someday, if we could . . . if you and I . . .'

Karim felt tears welling. Where were the words to tell his son what he was feeling? He swallowed hard and held out his hand.

Jordy looked directly into Karim's eyes. Man to man. He straightened up, losing the schoolboy slouch. Then he reached out, took his father's hand and shook it, his grip strong and sure.

Thank God, Karim thought, thank God for this.

SOHEIR KHASHOGGI

Born: Alexandria, Egypt
Home: New York
Website: www.soheirkhashoggi.com

'My books are banned in Saudi Arabia,' says Soheir Khashoggi. 'Because I'm an Arab woman, I'm not supposed to talk about culture, not supposed to talk about love.' Having spent a large part of her adult life in the United States, where she now lives, Khashoggi has been able to break free of that taboo and write three novels about the pressures on women who are caught between Western and Islamic societies.

Soheir Khashoggi's father, a noted Saudi Arabian doctor, sent his six children back to live in Egypt with their mother so that they would get an English education. Soheir flourished at school, and during her teens won many prizes for art and writing. After a stint at an American college, she was forced by her father into an arranged marriage at the age of twenty-four. 'It's hard for a woman from my part of the world to do whatever she wants—women have to obey,' she explains.

She went to live in Saudi with her husband but found life there was stifling. With the help of her elder brother Adnan (the billionaire businessman), she left her husband and fled to London with her baby daughter. She eventually married again, this time for love, and had three more daughters. The marriage failed after ten years, however, and she had to bring up her children alone. 'It was tough, but I'm strong and I did a good job,' she recalls proudly.

Khashoggi started writing after her second divorce and discovered it was something she loved. Her first book, *Mirage*, was published in 1996, and was followed in 1999 by *Nadia's Song*. Written in the aftermath of the September 11 terrorist attacks, *Mosaic* is dedicated to a friend who died on one of the hijacked planes. Khashoggi's life has had more than its share of tragedy: both her mother and her sister died relatively young and her much-loved nephew, Dodi al Fayed, was killed in a car crash in Paris along with Princess Diana.

Although Khashoggi hasn't lived the life of a traditional Muslim woman her religion is very important to her. 'I love many of the traditions of my culture,' she says. 'I may be against some of the teachings, but I can't change what's in my heart.'

THE BROKER © 2005 by Belfry Holdings, Inc.
Published by Random House

SOLO © Pen Hadow, 2004
Published by Penguin

BLOOD MEMORY © 2005 by Greg Iles
Published by Hodder & Stoughton

MOSAIC © Soheir Khashoggi 2003
Published by Transworld

The right to be identified as authors has been asserted by the following in accordance with
sections 77 and 78 of the Copyright, Designs and Patents Act, 1988: John Grisham, Pen
Hadow, Greg Iles, Soheir Khashoggi.

Illustrations and Photos:
Page 4, and on back jacket: authors (top): © Sam Abell; (bottom) © Fadil Berisha; page 5:
© Martin Hartley; (bottom) *The Times*.
The Broker: 6–8: illlustrator: Curtis Phillips-Cozier; images: ImageBank and Taxi (Getty
Images); 4, 151 © Sam Abell.
Solo: 152–3: background map and progress chart: © John Plumer; Pen Hadow/clothes ©
Martin Hartley; 154: © Martin Hartley; 282: photographs 1 to 6 Pen Hadow; 7: Chris
Chapman Photography; 283: photographs 8 to 11 and author © Martin Hartley.
Blood Memory: 284–6 Images: Stone (Getty Images); 455 © Lee Foster/Lonely Planet
Images.
Mosaic: 456–7: Images: Stone and Taxi (Getty Images); 575 © Fadil Berisha.
Dustjacket spine: Stone (Getty Images).

Reader's Digest, The Digest and the Pegasus logo are registered trademarks of
The Reader's Digest Association, Inc.

Printed and bound by GGP Media GmbH, Pössneck, Germany

236/05